THE DISSERTATION

THE DISSERTATION
R. M. KOSTER

THE OVERLOOK PRESS
NEW YORK, N. Y.

This edition first published in the United States in 2013 by
The Overlook Press, Peter Mayer Publishers, Inc.

141 Wooster Street
New York, NY 10012
www.overlookpress.com
For bulk and special sales, please contact sales@overlookny.com,
or write us at the above address

Library of Congress Cataloging-in-Publication Data

Koster, R. M., 1934-
    The dissertation : Tinieblas book two / R.M. Koster.
        pages cm. — (Tinieblas ; book two)
    Summary: "The second book in R.M. Koster's highly acclaimed Tinieblas trilogy (following *The Prince*), *The Dissertation* is the story of—and a story by—Camilo Fuertes. To fulfill his Ph.D. requirement, Fuertes decides to write about his father, the martyred president of Tinieblas, a country in Latin America. We follow Leon as he winds his twisted path through delinquency, learning, bravery, and incest to the presidency. At once a powerful vision of Latin American history and a brilliant parody of the academic form—complete with endnotes!—*The Dissertation* is an essential postmodern novel in the tradition of Vonnegut, Barth and Nabokov, ready to be embraced by a new generation of readers"— Provided by publisher.

1. Politics and government—Fiction. 2. Latin America—Fiction. 3. Political fiction. I. Title.
        PS3561.O84D5 2013   813'.54—dc23   2013029478

Book design and typeformatting by Bernard Schleifer
Manufactured in the United States of America
ISBN: 978-1-4683-0118-2
1 3 5 7 9 10 8 6 4 2

For H. K. and L. S. K.

PREFACE

This is the second of three books in which I invent the Republic of Tinieblas—its history, geography, politics, and "atmosphere," as well as a number of its inhabitants. The books are related in theme as well as in setting. Certain actors appear in all three, now as principals, now as supporting players, now as extras. And there are interlacings done for my private amusement. Each book, though, can stand on its own and bear separate viewing, so that while *The Dissertation* (1975) was done after *The Prince* (1972) and before *Mandragon* (1979), I think of it less as tome two of a trilogy than as the central panel of a triptych.

Its structure is, for better or worse, unique. No one else has ever written a novel in the form of a Ph.D. thesis, and no one else is likely to write one now. *Pale Fire* (in the form of a poem and commentary) provided a measure of precedent I gratefully acknowledge this and other debts to the master. The chief inspiration or irritant (See Note 12) was furnished, however, by an academic colleague. We both were in our mid-thirties. Neither of us had the Ph.D. He, though, was working en his and urged me to do likewise. I told him I couldn't be bothered: if I was going to spend two or so years writing something no one would ever read, I preferred to go first class and write a novel. (I was then the author of six unpublished ones.)

"Why not admit it?" he sneered. "You couldn't do a dissertation, you haven't the grit."

The remark rankled. It lodged, in fact, like a splinter in my mind's paw. A few years later, when I was finishing *The Prince*, I resolved to teach the fellow a lesson: I'd do a dissertation and a novel at once, and (in passing) a send-up of Ph.D.s and their foolishness. Many hundreds of times during the next four years I regretted that resolution, but true grit (or blind pigheadedness) saw me through.

What I had, then, when I started this book was the form. I decided to locate the action inTinieblas, but not because I intended to do a triptych. That came later. I'd invented large tracts of Tinieblas writing *The Prince* and was in the position of a film producer with a spacious, costly set all carpentered together standing idle. The thrifty thing to do was use it again, expanding and refurbishing as necessary. But I hadn't any story, any "content"; I had the form first.

I consider this a very good procedure, though I confess I haven't followed it since. The form gave me the makings of one chief character, Camilo Fuertes: dissertations, after all, are written by scholars. It suggested a style—long, balanced, periodic sentences, and a possible leitmotif of historical allusion. It was time I got some practical benefit out of all the dabbling I'd done in history books. It allowed me to use the method of counterpoint: one story in the Text, one in the Notes. (I have favored contrapuntal storytelling, both as addict and pusher, since the summer of 1943, when a lucky sniffle plucked me from the beach at Neponsit, Long Island, and deposited me in Edgar Rice Burroughs' Africa.) Finally, the dissertation form compelled me to an invention that brought me infinite delight and agony, and besides, pleased some readers: the afterlife according to Camilo. Dissertations must be documented. Camilo's researches groped back more than a century into Tinieblan history. I found it tiresome to invent imaginary texts and hit on the idea of making him a spirit medium so that he could cull his data from imaginary "dead" people. All sorts of wonderful things ensued.

There is something more. Anthony Burgess has written somewhere—and unlike Camilo (see pages XVIII-XIX) I have searched and searched for the reference—that the adoption of odd forms is useful both in revivifying the genre of the novel and in stimulating the novelist. I don't know anything about revivification, but as to stimulation I can say this: the form's outlandishness and intricacy, the number of balls (plates, indian clubs) it obliged me to keep in air at once, the difficulty of packing story into a box designed to carry scholarship imposed mind-breaking tensions that goosed me to the very top of my game.

The Dissertation is my favorite book, the unrivaled love of my literary life. Like all great loves it caused me torment, but it always made everything up to me sooner or later. As for its reception, the reviewers applauded and fans wrote from distant lands. Bantam, Morrow, and Norton did paperback editions. Now Overlook has brought it back for another encore.

Many good things happen if you live long enough.

—R. M. K.
Panama, August 2013

NOTE

I hold with León Fuertes (see Chapter 17): "A careful fake is better than the truth." Hence, I write fiction.

This book is fiction. I made it up.

I began inventing the Republic of Tinieblas a few years ago in another work of fiction. I have invented more of it here. I have also invented a "next world," an "afterlife." It and Tinieblas have the same kind of reality.

If the reader of this note is interested exclusively in the so-called "real world", I advise him not to spend time or money on *The Dissertation* but to invest instead in a ride on the New York Rapid Transit System or some similar experience. The "real world" is a sloppy actuality. *The Dissertation* is a careful fake.

—*R. M. K.*

SUNBURST UNIVERSITY

THE LIFE AND TIMES OF LEÓN FUERTES

FORTY-THIRD PRESIDENT

OF THE REPUBLIC OF TINIEBLAS

BY

CAMILO FUERTES, M.A.

A Dissertation submitted to the
Department of History
in partial fulfillment of the requirements
for the degree of Doctor of Philosophy

Approved:

_____

Constance S. Lilywhite, Ph.D.
Professor and Chairman of History

_____

Dustin Grimes, Ph.D.
Professor of History and Dean of Graduate Studies

THE FUERTES GENEALOGY

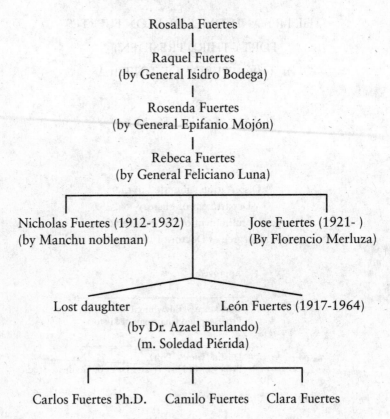

Rosalba Fuertes

Raquel Fuertes
(by General Isidro Bodega)

Rosenda Fuertes
(by General Epifanio Mojón)

Rebeca Fuertes
(by General Feliciano Luna)

Nicholas Fuertes (1912-1932)   Jose Fuertes (1921-)
(by Manchu nobleman)   (By Florencio Merluza)

Lost daughter   León Fuertes (1917-1964)
(by Dr. Azael Burlando)
(m. Soledad Piérida)

Carlos Fuertes Ph.D.   Camilo Fuertes   Clara Fuertes

CONTENTS

PART FOUR
His Maturity, His Ministry, His Martyrdom
(1946-1964)

FOREWORD

Little is known in the United States about the Republic of Tinieblas. One sympathizes with the confusions of the unlettered, the inquisitive cabby, say, who upon extracting a disclosure of his passenger's nationality can squint into his mirror and remark: "Tinieblan, huh? Ya don't look like a African." Tinieblas is neither large nor much endowed with resources. It has refrained entirely from international barbarism. Why should the "man in the street" know anything about it?

The strident ignorance one finds in academe is another story. The inevitable mention of bananas, as though their cultivation were our only national pursuit; the ubiquitous delusion that the Reservation-a tract adjacent to Ciudad Tinieblas which the U.S. *leases* as a military base-is a U.S. territorial possession; the crass quip by one tenured ichthyosaur that "Tinieblans clock their history in revolutions per minute"; the conviction of a former classmate (who proved his solidarity with the masses by defecating in the dean's filing cabinet) that since my father and uncle were both Presidents of Tinieblas, I belong to an exploiting class—all this has been a bottomless font of pain.

Nor are Tinieblans themselves very much better informed. Political rapists have made our history their slavey, have bent her to grotesque, degrading postures to serve their powerlust. Those of our intellectuals who have not pimped in these abuses have committed others on their own, distorting our heritage in undocumented screeds. The world perceives Tinieblas through the glazed eyes of wire service stringers and nomadic hacks from Time. Tinieblans know their country through the lies of demagogues, or through the half truths of lazy poseurs. There is, then, a clear need for authoritative investigations by qualified scholars into aspects of Tinieblan history and culture. This dissertation is such a work.

The Text presents the life and times of my father, León Fuertes—street-urchin, vagabond, self-made degenerate, lecher, and main-chance legal trickster; also athlete, artist, scholar, soldier, preserver of the nation, and forty-third President of the Republic. The span is from the discernible origins of our family in 1840 to León Fuertes' assassination in 1964. The setting is mainly Tinieblas, but extends to North America, Europe, and Africa. The scope is epic, the events enthralling, the prose at all times vivid and delightful.

The Notes document the Text, but because of the original research technique I have developed and perfected (see note 4), also provide extensive information about the next world, our life after so-called "death." No writer since Dante Alighieri has addressed this subject in comparable depth. My treatment is less panoramic than Dante's, but a good deal more accurate.

Either Text or Notes alone would amply satisfy that doctoral requirement which the Regents of Sunburst University term "an achievement in research constituting a significant contribution to knowledge." But I am no skinflint, dear Drs. Grimes and Lilywhite. I give you both.

I trust, besides, that this dissertation will do more than merely meet requirements. It is not often that an act of historical inquiry is also one of filial piety and civic duty; or that the grist of scholarship is also that of national epic and universal cosmology; or that the material of a Ph.D. thesis is the stuff of pity and terror. But here's a hero blown to tartar steak at the height of his powers; and here's a once fortunate land cruelly oppressed; and here's a scholar mining the next world for veins of truth. I shall fulfill the requirements. Fear not, Professor Lilywhite; doubt not, Professor Grimes. But at that stroke I'll ease an honored ghost, unmask a tyrant, and describe the universe—, and all the while amuse my gentle gringo readers.

My subject is my father, my country, and (to a certain, unavoidable extent) my special gift. I care about my subject passionately. Much is made, nowadays, of the value of scholarly objectivity, as though the less one cared about his subject the better he would treat it. This attitude, which is characteristic of graduate schools and the dissertations they produce, corresponds to the alienation of assembly-line workers, business executives, and other slaves. But Ortega y Gasset has commented wisely (somewhere in *Estudios sobre el amor,* and don't expect me, pig-headed examiners, to interrupt the crafting of this Foreword to track down and snare page references for you) on obsession as the mark of both love and genius. The lover is obsessed with his beloved; the artist is obsessed with his art. So it is with the true scholar and his subject. An idea disturbs him. He cannot dismiss it. It lies reeking on the pavement of his mind like a blasted chunk of human flesh. It magnetizes his attention day and night, waking and sleeping. It gives him no peace. It haunts him and hunts him until he makes it mean something. Meanwhile his associates snicker and tap their foreheads; his wife whines that she's neglected; quacks and deans combine against him to condemn and punish his deviation from respectable mediocrity. He accepts it all, the inner torment, the outer hostility. For he serves truth and knows that anything less than an obsession engenders only doodling, or the pack-ratting of random scraps.

I had once thought to preface this dissertation with a few pages of backhanded tribute to the numerous morons, academic, psychosnoopic, and otherwise, who in attempting to thwart me, unwittingly spurred me on. Naming them, however, would be an act of resentment and revenge, very stupid pursuits (it strikes me now) for a man of talent. I do wish, though, while leaving them anonymous, to thank those who furnished me suffering. Without them I should never have achieved mastery. I owe as well a great debt to my wife, Elizabeth Cleaver Fuertes, who besides sometimes wandering into the group mentioned above, preserved the manuscript of this dissertation during some very dark hours; to the spirits of several close relations, who sustained, encouraged, and aided me; and to all those in this world and the next who helped me in my research. Should this work contain any inaccuracies—something which, by the way, I very strongly doubt—, the blame is, of course, my own.

It is an abomination on one's reader to make him yo-yo down and up the page between text and notes. I have marshaled my Text in the van, my Notes in the rear. This dissertation may be approached in that order. Yet should you prefer, revered examiners, accomplished Professor Lilywhite and gifted Professor Crimes, to swing your attention leisurely back and forth, like fortunate spectators of an entrancing Tilden-Budge rally, that is perfectly Jake with me. By all means please yourselves! Your lives are, I know, in the main dull and tedious, but you are now about to be enlightened, uplifted, and entertained. Sit back. Be at your case. Enjoy the slices I shall serve you "Of what is past, or passing, or to come."

CAMILO FUERTES
May, 1975

PART ONE
HIS ORIGINS (1840-1917)

1. Three Señoritas Fuertes

GENERAL ISIDRO BODEGA (1780-1848, President and Dictator of Tinieblas 1830-1848) was the first and longest-lived of our uniformed gorillocrats. Like many despots, he despised his fellow countrymen and surrounded himself with foreigners. Among the several Europeans whom he advanced out of all proportion to their merit was a French adventurer, Jean-Luc Bout de Souffle, who stole enough during three years as Minister of Culture to finance his repatriation, his retirement, and his reminiscences. These contain the earliest Fuertes reference, enveloped in some Gallic commentary en Tinieblan women.

To illustrate his thesis that "Tinieblan women display a uterine arrogance Mme. Merteuil might envy," Bout de Souffle tells of one Rosalba Fuertes, *"vierge rustique et belle"* who presented herself at the Presidential Palace in the spring of 1840, "her ample charms imperfectly concealed by the thin native costume," and requested an audience with General Bodega. Those charms must have worked some magic on the guards (who could not have been much more courteous than the orangutans commanded by our current simianisimo),[1] for she was admitted; whereupon she astounded all present by informing General Bodega that she had come to the capital for the purpose of conceiving a son by him. General Bodega examined her gravely for some moments; then, announcing that he had never received a challenge he could so willingly accept or a petition he would so earnestly strive to fulfill, he ordered the salon cleared.

Bout de Souffle goes on to say that while Señorita Fuertes left the capital the next day and never again sought contact with General Bodega, the General was unable to forget her. He inquired after her and learned that she was, in fact, enceinte. The following year he sent a courier to her with his offer to recognize her son. She replied that her son was a daughter, could never hope to be President of the Republic, and might just as well keep the name Fuertes. General Bodega then sent his personal aide-de-camp to bring her to Ciudad Tinieblas, where she would have every luxury and he the leisure to give her not only a president but an archbishop and a banker as well, but she answered that, while she appreciated General Bodega's hard work and good intentions, she would never live with a military man who couldn't hit the target with his first shot. *Bravisima! Bravisima,* Great-Great-Great-Grandmother Rosalba!

General Epifanio Mojón (1801-1860, President and Dictator of Tinieblas 1853-1860) was an authentic hero of Hispano-American independence, cited by Bolívar himself for valor in the field at Ayacucho. He later ripened into one of the cruelest tyrants of a continent particularly rich in such, and as his hell is a burcaucracy,[2] presently sits buttock-to-buttock with Tughlak and Caligula on an executive committee for the dissemination of terror and despair. General Mojón was sufficiently concerned about his place in history to keep a record of his principal victims, the citizens he fed to sharks and the virgins he deflowered. Here we pick up the Fuertes trace. The *Gaceta Oficial* for 23rd August, 1860, which records state events for the week before General Mojón was deposed and crucified on one of the posts he had set up in the bay as racks for human shark biscuits, lists one Raquel Fuertes, natural daughter of Rosalba Fuertes of Belém, La Merced Province, among the presidential bonbons.

This is the entire written record, but Theopompos Canelopulos, General Mojón's procurer,[3] remembers Raquel Fuertes perfectly. Of the more than five hundred girls Canelopulos furnished General Mojón during six years of service, she alone volunteered.

In the last century—in fact, until the third decade of our own— Ciudad Tinieblas was effectively cut off from the interior of the republic by mountains and jungles through which one moved only on foot or horseback, and since General Mojón did not want his virgins worn out by walking or, worse, defoliated by riding, Canelopulos's procedure[4] when farming the province of La Merced was to go by sloop to the port of Mituco de Tierra Firme, pick up a string of mules and a covered wagon, make a circuit of the chief towns—San Carlos, La Merced, Belém—and then reembark with his livestock. He entered

Belém, then, late in the evening of 29th July, 1860, in a steady down-pour, the mean between our spring showers and the torrents of Novem-ber, and lodged with the military chief of the plaza, a sergeant. The six girls he had rounded up en route spent the night fettered in the wagon. They were inferior both in number and in quality to General Mojón's expectations. The news of Canelopulos's presence in the province had traveled faster than his mules, and the parents of Belém had taken steps to hide their nubile daughters or disfigure them. He was due back in the capital by 1st August, and Mituco was by pres-idential decree exempt from his depredations. All this caused him a certain malaise: it had cost him his testicles to enter General Mojón's service and would cost him his life to fail in it. Then, as he was curs-ing the climate in Spanish and the general in demotic Greek, a young woman entered the sergeant's house, identified herself as Raquel Fuertes, asked Canelopulos if he was the President's pimp, and when he said yes, told him to take her with him.

Now, Canelopulos had been ordered to examine all candidates carefully, for an old Negro woman who read the future in chicken entrails had warned General Mojón that a virgin would be his down-fall—a prediction which proved true, though the girl was not Raquel. And while it was strange that any girl would willingly go to General Mojón, who was physically repulsive arid mentally deranged, and who, besides, followed the practice of giving the girls to his soldiers once he was through with them, it was more than strange in the case of Raquel, who was so lovely—small but well made with firm haunches and calves; clean-featured and proud, with soft olive skin and flashing black eyes—that Canelopulos ground his teeth in grief for his lopped ballocks. So he told her his consignment was filled, and when she persisted, said she was crazy and ineligible en that ac-count. Only when she declared that she would go to the President on her own power if he would not take her did he agree to give her a place in the wagon, and then only if she could explain to his satisfac-tion why she wished to go. She answered readily that she had prom-ised her mother on her deathbed that only a President of the Republic would have her virginity. She had planned to wait for General Mojón's successor, but General Mojón had been in power for seven years, and the last military dictator had stayed in power for eighteen years, and she was nineteen already and could wait no longer.

With that the sergeant, who had been drinking white rum, stood up and said he was as much a man as any president, past, present, or future, and as far as he was concerned she needn't wait another minute, much less the three days it would take her to reach the capital and the God-knows-how-long which would pass before General Mojón got around to her, and when Canelopulos warned him that she was now state property, he said that didn't matter a donkey's prick to him and General Mojón could feed him to sharks if he cared to, but the Señorita would not be kept waiting. He made it so clear he was not joking that Canelopulos had to knock him senseless with the butt of his mule whip. He and his wagon left the same night for Mituco and sailed for the capital the next day.

Thus my Great-Great-Grandmother Raquel. If she had waited another month, we would have got the stolid bourgeois genes of Alcibiades Oruga (who revived the Constitution and founded the Liberal Party and stepped down graciously when his term was up), not General Mojón's. But then my father, León Fuertes, might have lacked some of his greatness and I my demonic drive to fabricate the past. Well done, Doña Raquel! You waited just long enough.

General Feliciano Luna (1851-1893, President of Tinieblas 1883-1893) was a ranch hand who turned guerrillero in 1878 when Lázaro Torcido overthrew the constitutional President of the Republic, Saturnino Aguila. By 1883, when Torcido died, Luna had collected several hundred hard riders behind him. He proclaimed himself President on 7th March, 1883, in the plaza at La Merced and was recognized by the governors of La Merced, Salinas, and Otán Provinces. He carried his capital in his saddlebags during a decade of civil war and was on his way to being considered immortal when he was lured to Ciudad Tinieblas and hanged by Monseñor Jesús Llorente (1837-1916, President of Tinieblas [by vote of the Ciudad Tinieblas Municipal Council 1883-1893).

General Luna was a decidedly cinematographic *guerrillero,* tall and heavily built, with huge, drooping moustaches. Strong lacings of Indian blood showed in his fiat face and violent moods. He shot his friend and lieutenant, Nicademo Lágrimas, in a quarrel over a horse, then wept like a maid at the funeral. At times insanely suspicious, he went naively to his death when Monseñor Llorente sent him a safe-conduct endorsed by the U.S. Ambassador. Though innocent of letters, he was a genius at cavalry tactics; it is doubtful that his century produced a more gifted leader of five hundred or a thousand men. He rode like a centaur and was the strongest man and surest shot in his army, an insatiable eater, drinker, and womanizer. He had fifty sons by fifty different women, all of which progeny he recognized in law, except the last, who was born posthumously. Since he did not recognize his daughters, their exact number and identity is difficult to establish, but his secretary and minister, Pantuflo Saenz, kept a log of the women he consorted with following his autoinauguration. This record states that a Señorita Rosenda Fuertes spent part of the night of 31st July-1st August, 1883, with General Luna in the Town Hall at San Francisco de Otán.

According to her own account, Rosenda Fuertes grew up in Ciudad Tinieblas, where her mother, Raquel, remained after her brief but fruitful connection with General Epifanio Mojón. Like her mother and grandmother before. her, Rosenda vowed to have herself a President of the Republic, but as Saturnino Aguila was impotent and Lázaro Torcido a pederast, she was still virginal when the latter died and Monseñor Llorente and General Luna simultaneously advanced their claims. Llorente was widely rumored to take his vows of chastity to heart, so Rosenda had no choice but to join the Governors of La Merced, Salinas, and Otán in recognizing Luna. She went after him.[5]

Rosenda Fuertes arrived at the town of La Merced at the same time as the column of regular troops Monseñor Llorente had dispatched to capture General Luna. Luna had left thirty-six hours earlier (though the soldiers took the precaution of cannonading the defenseless town all day before entering it). Rosenda set out after her prey the same night and remained a day or twos journey behind him all through his masterly retreat along the western rim of Salinas Province and into Otán. (General Luna never, of course, allowed himself to be brought to battle but tormented the column at a hundred ambushes until its effectives were decimated, its morale dissolved, and its ordnance embedded in the mud of our summer. The opposing commander finally abandoned pursuit, satisfied his military honor by massacring a number of peasants, left a garrison at Córdoba [which Luna butchered at leisure later on in the year], and slunk back to Ciudad Tinieblas with a marvelously inventive report of the number of guerrillero bodies he had counted.) By the end of July, Luna was able to rest at San Francisco and Rosenda to catch up with him.

Their union was consummated on a thinly upholstered bench in what was normally the mayor's office and for that month the President of the Republic's. In regard for Rosenda's virginity, General Luna removed his silverspurred boots and black sombrero. She bore his weight as willingly as any mare in his corral, smiling up over his shoulder at the gas-lit ceiling fresco, which depicted Simón Mocoso, first President of Tinieblas, accepting the sash of office from the Speaker of the Constituent Assembly. She was certain, after all, that she was realizing the dream of her mother and grandmother: gets a son by a president, who would be president in his turn.

(In fact, she gave birth on 6th June, 1884, to a daughter, whom she named Rebeca. And it was Rebeca who, without the help of any president, military or civilian, constitutional or no, gave birth to not one but two presidents, León and José Fuertes. Chromosomologists will, nonetheless, take note of these recurring conjunctions of Mars and Venus and not be disturbed, when studying our family, by the genetic fallout from three presidents, all of them soldiers of sorts, and three very headstrong women.)

General Feliciano Luna spasmed, stilled, snorted, hefted his bulk off Great-Grandmother Rosenda, stepped back into his boots, put on his black sombrero, repantsed, and, buttoning, returned to the council of war which was proceeding in the outer office. Great-Grandmother Rosenda took a final smile at the fresco of Simón Mocoso, sat up, dabbed the blood from her thighs, with a corner of her skirt, and, since she had got a good, steady look at the Tinieblan Civil War while stalking General Luna, left to have the son she was convinced she carried in the one peaceful spot in the country. This was Mituco, a large island and, opposite it, a small port (mentioned above in connection with the wanderings of Theopompos Canelopulos), Hong Kongishly arranged on the Pacific coast of Tinieblas about a hundred miles northwest of the capital.

Mituco Island was not inhabited in pre-Columbian times but was consecrated as a place of ritual magic. So, at least, hints that most articulate of *adelantados*, Diego Masa de Vizcocho, who discovered the place in 1524 and described it in his *Víajes*. After prosing lyrically on Mituco's "*brisas fragrantes*" and "*la musica que nos serpeaba sobre sus aguas,*" Masa de Vizcocho complains that the island, though "naked of men" was "infested from end to end with the ghosts of sacrificial victims and the demons raised by indian mages in the practice of their abominable heresies." This blurb was, no doubt, the reason why the Spanish never colonized the island.

Sir Francis Drake passed within sight of Mituco in March, 1579, some two weeks after his celebrated fight with the treasure galleon *Nuestra Señora de la Concepción* or "*Cacafuego*". Thirty years and three months later, a former boatswain of the *Golden Hind* was drinking dry sack in a London tavern at the expense of a balding gentleman in black velvet.[6] Or rather, lest I give a social cast to what was actually a business meeting, the old sailor was peddling his past, for the gentleman in black was a dealer in dreams and nightmares who (above what he simply lifted from dead authors) was wont to buy up odd tales and mixed exotica at a pint of wine the gross and then retail the best of them, refurbished, rearranged, and buffed, in his playhouse. The man was as efficient as any Chicago sausage works—a chance glimpse at a passing blackamoor had netted him the hero of one tragedy, the villain of another, and a simile for the heroine of a third—and he pumped the sailor mercilessly. The latter had already forked up a raid on Panama, the defeat of the Invincible Armada, and great chunks of the circumnavigation of the globe, when he remembered Mituco, verdant and inviting on the brass horizon of the Southern Sea. He had never set foot on the island, of course, but be had had a long, yearning gaze at it and had, besides, had Masa de Vizcocho's book read to him by a creole woman in Hispaniola when, in 1586, Drake and General Carlile seized the town of Santo Domingo, sacked it, and held it for a month. So, as he was still thirsty, he began yarning about Mituco. The dream-factor's interest perked. His eyes, which resembled nothing so much as shafts into so immensely deep and empty mine, glowed with dull light. He pulled the small gold ring in his left earlobe. "Magic?" he asked. "Did you say witches? Sweet air, and music that crept to you on the waters? A wooded isle possessed by salvage sprites? By heaven, the very spot for Prosper! though I'll move it to Bermudas. A boatswain, were you? I'll put you in it too then. But tell me more. Come, Francis Francis! Draw our brave mariner another pint!"

When God feels conscientious, He imitates good writers. Mituco, accordingly, became populated by wild men, escaped slaves who found the island a haven against recapture and who, in fact, being both numerous and determined, so roundly thrashed a series of punitive expeditions that the Spanish Governor of Tinieblas granted them autonomy. They were then tamed by a shipwrecked intellectual, a defrocked Jesuit named Cortada, who was expelled from Manila and washed up on Mituco when an Acapulco galleon, driven far off course, foundered on the Tinieblan coast. The Island of Mituco is exceedingly rich in aromatic woods, as well as mahogany, teak, and balsa, which grow in great stands, and Cortada turned the ex-slaves to commerce. Ships came from all parts of the world to load Mituco wood, and since the forests grew back as fast as they were harvested, Mituco was, by the time of independence (7th June, 1821), the most prosperous region of Tinieblas.

There were, of course, greedy men in the capital who sought to appropriate Mituco's wealth, but the *mituqueños* defended themselves through a policy of bribery and menace. (The last depended en Mituco women's expertise in pronouncing curses. General Isidro Bodega's Dutch Finance Minister, who would have confiscated the island for his personal estate, was, for example, visited with the Curse of the Tides, and his belly alternately swelled zeppelinically and shriveled to his spine—the tides run twenty feet in Mituco Bay—until he gave the project up,) So while Mituco recognized the government in Ciudad Tinieblas and paid such taxes as the Chamber of Deputies could not be bribed to rescind, the island, with its mainland port, remained a privileged sanctuary even in the worst days of General Epifanio Mojón's tyranny and during the Civil War of 1883-1893.

Meanwhile the *mituqueños* used their good fortune wisely. Cortada had arranged for the island and its sylvan wealth to be incorporated as a joint-stock company, each head of family receiving one share. (Cortada himself broke his crucifix, cast his prayer book into the sea, and founded three families of his own.) Everyone was soon living off his dividends, while the company (Compañía Mituqueña de Progreso Infinito) provided enlightened public services. The streets of Mituco Marítimo, the town which grew up on the northeast corner of the island, were carpeted in wood; not precious local wood, of course, but hard pine imported from Oregon. There was a medical clinic, free to stockholders and their dependents, an excellent primary school, and a *liceo* staffed with teachers hired in Europe.[7] The company maintained a large foodstore-haberdashery-pharmacy and generally supplied the needs of the community. Residence on the island was restricted to stockholders, most of whom passed their lives in leisurely enjoyment of their polyglot educations, a few of whom practiced professions or held executive positions with the company.

Menial employees lived in the mainland port, Mituco de Tierra Firme. It was here that Rosenda Fuertes came to have her son; here that she had, instead, her daughter Rebeca; and here she remained, her heart gnawed out with bitterness over General Luna's poor aim, sewing dresses for the aristocratic ladies of Mituco Marítimo. Near the end of the century she entered a common-law union with a lumber gang foreman who gave her a strong, chocolate-skinned son every year for seven years. None of these ever came to anything. It was Rebeca who bore the Fuertes name and the Fuertes demon and the Fuertes future.

2. Rebeca[8]

THE DECISIVE MOMENT in my grandmother Rebeca's life came on the rainwashed afternoon of her tenth birthday (6th June, 1894), when Don Patricio Garza bought her from her mother for ten gold sovereigns. Mituco de Tierra Firme was then a pie-cut of high ground shambled with board huts and wedged into a wilderness of tidal quicksands, where staggering mangroves braced themselves with roots dropped from their branches, and fat singleclawed crabs scuttled drunkenly across the heaving ground, and armadas of mosquitoes mustered each night to strafe the helpless town. In the mud alleys that spidered off the one board street (which began at the company pier and ended at the highroad to Belém) schoolless children bathed in alternate cascades of rain and sunlight, and here Rebeca was carried in love and born in hope and nursed in anger and swaddled in resentment, and here she grew, wild and canny as an otter, but showing such promise of loveliness that Don Patricio chose her at first glimpse for his Galatea.

I can recall a few early scenes from a hallucinovision documentary

on Grandma Rebeca which I viewed three years ago. In one Rosenda
sits before the unscreened and open-shuttered window of the family
hovel, stitching at a piece of organdy. To the right an iron frame bed
with sheetless tick mattress kneels beneath last year's Palm Sunday
cross of jaundiced frond; to the left the door is held open by a pillar
of sunlight in which galaxies of dust specks gyre calmly. Flies buzz
on the sound track, and a vendor calls, "*Mangos, papayas, melons.*"
Six-year-old Rebeca felines in to rub herself against her mother's
shoulder. Rosenda fends her with an absent-minded elbow, mumbles,
"Go play," but is sufficiently distracted by the show of affection not
to notice as Rebeca unpins from mama's waist the handkerchief in
whose free end the petty cash is knotted. Exit Rebeca on bare and
dusty feet. Rosenda sews on. Fade out on Rebeca seen through the
window, sinking bright teeth into a plump mango and then aiming
us a grin from whose corners sweet juice drips.

In another Rosenda has borrowed a neighbor's razor strop to discipline her daughter—not, we may assume, for the offense filmed
above, for the palm cross has been replaced by a greener one and the
girl is somewhat larger. She stands cornered on the bed. Rosenda,
her hair unbound by the chase, grunts "*Bandida!*" and swings her
arm. The strop hisses through the air, bites the side of Rebeca's left
calf and the back of her right, and snakes against her shin.

Thwap!

"It didn't hurt."

"You should have been a man."

The strop recoils, stiffens in air, and bites again.

Thwap!

"It didn't hurt."

"You should have been a man."

The scene fades, leaving this triologue repeating itself like an object
placed between two mirrors.

And, finally, ten-year-old Rebeca, Ondined in summer rain at the sea
end of the company pier, still barefoot, still dirty, still uncombed, sleep-
walks through a rabble of drenched urchins, her face and palms uplifted
to the liquid sky, while an elegant gentleman with waxed moustache
and seal-black silk umbrella descends the gangway of the Colombian-
flag paddle-wheel steamer warped alongside, blinks toward Rebeca,
halts transfixed, and has to be prodded by the passenger behind him.

Don Patricio Garza Cortada was the last heir of Mituco's incorporator, one of the richest men in Tinieblas, and by far the most cultivated. He was forty years old on the day he saw Rebeca and had lived the last twenty of them in Paris, friend to Gauguin and L'Isle-Adam, companion to the gaudy Prince of Wales, sharer (along with Maitre Saint-Saëns) of the Comtesse de Pourtalès' box at the Opéra, guest at cozy little dinners *chez* la Marquise de Saint-Paul, Bois de Boulogne paint pal (she did the flowers, he did her) to Madeleine Lemaire and (he followed Dumas, fils) her lover, conversational umpire to Wilde and Whistler, voice of encouragement to the young Valéry.[9] He had exquisite taste—Octave Mirbeau both prized and pirated his opinions—but rode and fenced too well to be labeled an esthete. In his first years in Paris, when the term was still in vogue, he was approvingly called "dandy," but he was too passionate at heart to fit Baudelaire's definition. He was a great lover of women and had had many lovely friends, but they all betrayed him, not because he was crass or ugly or cowardly or dull—for he was none of these—, but because he had an honest heart and a faithful nature and was, thus, bound to be betrayed. Still, he blamed his companions' vices, not his own virtues, for his misfortunes in love, and that summer (1894), as he sailed home to Mituco to claim an inheritance, began to dream of finding a strong but malleable girl and crafting her into the perfect mistress. He saw Rebeca, and the dream dug its steel talons in his brain.

He did not send his Portuguese valet but went himself, brushing among the penny-pleading children, and took her arm in his gloved hand and had her lead him to her mother. He wished, he said, to make the girl his ward. He proffered gold to prove his good intent. Rosenda accepted. As far as she was concerned, she was selling her daughter for more than she was worth to a rich lecher with a yen for prepubescents. Rebeca thought much the same and expected to be raped that very evening, an idea that disturbed her less than the fact that Rosenda, not she, was being paid for it. As it was, she was merely bathed and put to bed in vast and canopied four-poster two stout doors from Don Patricio in his teak and cedar mansion on Mituco Island. She was neither old nor refined enough for his tastes. He had resolved not to touch her until her fifteenth birthday—the traditional moment of female maturity in Latin America—, by which time she would be schooled in all the arts and bound in loyalty to him. More, he decided not to return to Europe until Rebeca was fit for publication.

Rebeca had the private attentions of the best teachers from the Liceo, who taught her French and English and history and math, voice by the solfeggio of Lablache and ballet in the Cecchetti method. She had Don Patricio for a special master, honing her mind and polishing her accents, teaching her to draw in ink and paint in aquarelles, to play chess and compose verses, to jump the Peruvian mare he bought her for her twelfth birthday, to hold his foil and shoot his pistol. She had Paris frocks and Seville mantillas and a pink silk parasol to hold above her head when she drove about the town in Don Patricio's lacquered phaeton. She had a maid to hang her dresses and a groom to hold her horse and the Bishop of Mituco to hear her brief confessions. She lacked only for physical affection, for in the five years she spent on Mituco Don Patricio never so much as took her arm to help her to the carriage, much less caressed her, for fear of losing his artistic objectivity. He wove grand polychromic visions of their future, threading the bright strands of her youth into his sombre heart. He conjured up their life in Europe, unraveling his dream on afternoons when they sat on the gabled porch, he holding a firm profile, she sketching his portrait. His voice would take her, gowned and ermined, to hear Melba sing at Covent Garden or into Paris salons glittering with jewels and intellect. But watch: He ends his phrase; she gasps, "*Qué bello!*" throws her pencil down, and rushes to him; he draws his head away, raises his arm, and fends her back.

Rebeca's fifteenth birthday party was the grandest ever given in Tinieblas before or since, grander than Alejandro Sancudo's last inaugural party, which featured the Spirochetes, flown in from London with their electronic twangs and howls, grander even than the party given by General Manduco on the third anniversary of his so-called revolution.[10] Don Patricio began making preparations a full year before, ordering three hundred cases of champagne from France and a ton of ice from Canada, contracting a string ensemble from New Orleans and another one, just to be safe, from Lima. He hired forty cooks and a chef from Paris to supervise them and a Sorbonne licentiate from Ciudad Tinieblas to be the chef's interpreter. And since there was no ballroom on Mituco big enough to hold all the guests he wanted to invite, he had two acres of land cleared at his own expense and built a pavilion which, after the party, would go over to the shareholders of the Compañía Mituqueña de Progreso Infinito for any use they or their heirs might give it. And after all this, which he considered a bare minimum, he cast about for some special entertainment—a good tenor, or perhaps a group of players—and, at length, wrote to the impresario of a Belgian ballet company which was on tour in the United States and which was scheduled to return to Europe via San Francisco and the railroad at Panama. He offered expenses and a thousand pounds for a performance of *Swan Lake* to be held in the theater at Mituco Marítimo, with the condition that his ward, Rebeca, have a variation in the third-act pas de six. The final plan, then, called for a reception at Don Patricio's home for two hundred special guests (including the President of the Republic and the ambassadors of the more important nations); the ballet, where these and three hundred more would witness Rebeca's artistic debut; and a grand ball in the new pavilion, to which all the shareholders of the Mituco Company and their families, three thousand souls, would be invited. And when the last guest had departed and the musicians were loosening the strings of their instruments and putting them to rest in their velvet-lined cases, Don Patricio would take Rebeca to his bedroom (rosed—so he imagined—with the first rays of dawn that glanced across Mituco Bay from the dark brow of the cordillera) and lead her into womanhood.

For which Rebeca was altogether ready. There never was a *jeune fille* so stridently *en fleur*. She had her father's height and the Fuertes women's brilliant eyes. She was strong and slender from hours at the barre. In body she was, at fourteen, fully womaned, as is common in the tropics, and her mind throbbed with fantasies of love and art and glamour. At night she squirmed in moist longing for caresses, and, if Don Patricio had not shown her a thousand times he would not give her any, no door could have kept her from his bed. Her ballet teacher, the only other male she was alone with, might have had her any afternoon, but his embraces were reserved for sailors. There was nothing morbid in the ready flush that appled in her breasts at the first chords of the nocturne that her teacher played for her pliés, at the sight of Don Patricio, scarleted like an English squire, returning at a canter from his morning ride, at the scent of wild jasmine that gorged her room on sultry evenings, at the very thought of man. She was simply well-hormoned and famished for affection.

As a man of the world, Don Patricio was aware of Rebeca's condition; as an artist he was too immersed in the creative trance to pay it much attention. He was engaged in shaping a perfect woman and preoccupied with problems of form. His sense of structure demanded that Rebeca's debut in love be preceded by her debuts in art and in society. That made for a crescendo of tension and an elegant progression of scenes. Any other arrangement would be clumsy, would flaw Rebeca's development. Ballet, ball, then bedroom, and his dream, gestating now five years, would be fleshed out. And so he bent in patience to the labor of creation, never imagining that his nearly finished work might be vulnerable to a plagiarist.

The tide was full on the morning of Rebeca's birthday, and S.S. *Pluto* (Pacific Steam Navigation Company) was able to dock at Mituco Marítimo long enough for the Ballet Concert d'Anvers to disembark. Most of the town was on the quay to greet them, and they made a passable entrance, led by the impresario (the only Belgian in the lot), a red-faced gentleman with a spade beard and a prosperous expanse of waistcoat, who puffed down the gangway clutching the guardrail in one hand and a carpetbag full of the prima's tutus in the other. This lady followed on the arm of the first dancer. She was Italian, spare and nervous as a race mare, bonneted, parasoled, and ruffled in grey silk.

"*Sommes-nous en Afrique?*" she asked loudly and languidly, turning her huge brown eyes (made up as for a performance) toward the thicket of mahogany faces below her.

"*Pas l'Affique, ma chére Carla,*" replied her French partner, his pale brow pearled with sweat. "*L'enfer.*"

Next came the soloists: in front a German girl, a little plump, perhaps, for modern tastes but perfect for her time, light-stepping with laughing eyes and bobbing breasts. Her best role was Giselle, the peasant pas de deux, where she was fetching with her blond braids twined about her head and her bust cross-strapped in velvet. Her partner, a beautiful young Dane, his eyes as vacant with seasickness as Nijinsky's were to be with madness, walked beside her. There was a Russian girl, as haughty as a borzoi, whose modish hat (gift of a gentleman from San Francisco) bore a stuffed partridge, and a pretty

Swiss, all muslin frills and ruches, still pouting that her spot in the pas de six that night was going to Rebeca. Behind her stalked a tall and moustached Serb, a strong dancer, immensely vain of his jumps and vainer still of the opal-headed walking stick (pinched from a shop in Boston) which he carried on his shoulder like a mace. With him was his protégé, a slim Pole. Next came a Hungarian couple, the czardas partners, the girl's gold ringlets flowing to her shoulders, the fellow's jacket swaggered on one shoulder like a hussar's cape. They smiled glowingly at the onlookers while hissing back and forth in bitter Magyar. And finally, the object of their quarrel, a gorgeous animal from Odessa, Rumanian-Russian-Gypsy-Jew, flash of dark eyes beneath a lilac bonnet, hint of musk in the salt air, enough temperament to outfit twenty primas but far more skill in bed than on the boards.

After them trooped the corps de ballet: French girls, Dutch girls, Austrian girls; four prancing Czechs soon to be magicked into linked cygnets, a pair of twins from Naples, a trio of blond Letts. They spilled down the gangway from their week at sea and foamed about the impresario, who watched, squealing in rage and terror, as a cargo net bulging with boxes yawed wildly toward the bay and then swung back, spilling out an ancient trunk, which floated down into a space miraculously opened in the crowd and exploded on the quay, shrapneling out pink tights and white tulle dresses, kid boots and ballet shoes, the prince's crossbow, his mother's paste tiara, the swan queen's feathered headdress, and Von Rothbart's hawky mask.

This cued the entrance of a final member, the ballet master and character dancer Vyacheslav Sukasin. He was of middle height (he wore a pompadour and special shoes), athletically slim (he used a French corset), and youthful (he dyed his hair and touched his cheeks with rouge). Under his arm he carried a flaked morocco case stuffed with old programs, announcements of performances—the kind that hang in bunches in theater lobbies and that departing audiences strip off, glance at, and then drop in the street—, newspaper ads for companies he'd danced with, photos of girls he'd partnered, of composers and conductors, of choreographers and impresarios (a few of them inscribed), and many of himself, and yellowing reviews in all the languages of Europe, the passages that named him scored in violet ink. This case never left him, and he was never slow to open it—at restau-

rants, on trains, in hotel lobbies, or backstage before performances—
to show the pressed mementos of his art. He had been famous—well,
at least well-known. He'd partnered all the greatest primas and
soloed with several companies. He'd danced before the Tsar, and,
see, that night in Zagreb he'd taken seven calls in *La Sylphide*.

Sukasin had a clean line and a grasp of miming, a knack for cam-
ouflaging his mistakes, and the ability to seem restrained when he
was actually out of training, but his true talent was for ballet politics.
He could set a troupe of dancers so at odds that only he seemed
tractable. He knew how to skewer an established rival with slander
and maim a potential one with quick wounds to the sex. And he was
agile on both sides of the lust ladder. But he loathed practice, and
his intrigues always came unsewn sooner or later, so he never danced
as well as he might have nor lasted long with any company. Now, in
his mid-forties, he found himself dancing character parts—Casse-
Noisette, Dr. Coppelius, and Von Rothbart, the evil magician in
Swan Lake—and serving as ballet master with what he knew was
not a first-rate group. Worse, he was about to lose even this. As he
had once used sex to advance himself professionally—he won his
first solo in Tchaikovsky's bed—now he used his profession to advance
himself in sex. Or, more accurately, he practiced the kind of *Macht-
politik* noted in baboon tribes, with the difference that your baboon
is usually satisfied with symbolic presentation. Sukasin had had every
member of the company, males and females. He was sensitive enough
to the weaknesses of others to capture the unwary by stealth; for the
rest, surrendering him an orifice or two became the only way to keep
a part or get a better one, to avoid being insulted at rehearsal or having
a costume disappear at curtain time, to insure against last-minute
changes in choreography or wanderings of the spotlight during a solo.
And since he had a gift for making the act of love at once extremely
pleasant and degrading, he caused such discord, bitterness, and rage,
so many tantrums, jealousies, and botched performances, that the
impresario had told him he could seek another place once they were
back in Europe.

But none of this showed in Sukasin's placid smile, in the jaunty
gait with which he descended the gangway—almost unnoticed, for
the crowd was oohing the smashed trunk and ogling the dancers—,
or in the charming grin he flashed when the first mituqueño he ap-

proached knew enough French to aim him toward the theater. Surely
Rebeca thought him decent enough when he arrived to inspect her
variation and rehearse her with the other dancers in the intrada and
coda to the pas de six. She was a bit ashamed of the way Don Patricio had bought her a solo, yet the ballet master was neither harsh
nor patronizing. He nodded with reserved approval at her variation
and then spent twenty minutes polishing it while her five partners
lounged in the second row of the orchestra and stagehands unrolled
backdrop curtains and began tying them to lowered booms. He
would throw both palms in air and call "*Arrêtez!*" and stride across
the bridge laid over the orchestra pit and then, gently and paternally,
correct her, bending to take her calf in both his hands and turn it to
a better line or marking the steps himself while counting out the
measures.

"What's happened to the monster?" the Polish boy whispered to
his friend. "He seems almost human."

"Ha!" snorted the Serb. "He smells fresh meat!"

He smelled talent also, and with it presence, that indefinable power
through which a very few performers can magnetize an audience
whether they're talented or not. Besides, Rebeca was young and vulnerable—a property, in short, which he might steal, build up, and
live off.

He stopped her as she stood on point, arms bowed above her head,
and molded her position. A not-so-accidental hand pressed her upper
thigh. Rebeca blushed and shuddered.

"*Voilà, donc!*" sneered the Serb. "*De la bonne viande à point!*"

Sukasin turns and with a lift of palms summons the other dancers
to the stage. He waves them to their places, tells Rebeca to watch
him, calls "*Numéro dix-neuf*" to the pianist in the pit, claps his
hands twice. First notes of the intrada (*moderato assai*). Enter the
dancers, marking, with Sukasin in Rebeca's spot. The stagehands,
who have already raised the palace garden and the lake with ruined
château and who are about to start hauling at the backdrop for Act
Three, pause for a peek, but there is nothing particularly exciting
about six foreigners shuffling about in street clothes. They turn back
to their ropes. The wall, window, and stairway of the palace hall rise
slowly, and as our camera follows them aloft, the lights dim up and
strings and woodwinds infiltrate the soundtrack. The camera trun-

dles back, widening the shot, and we discover the performance in full progress. The darkened house is packed with fan-flapping doñas and dusky dons in ice-cream flannel suits. Onstage, drenched in bright amber, the grand betrothal ball proceeds, guests crescented from wing to wing and, at the footlights, three couples: the Serb and the Russian girl, the German and her Dane, the Polish boy and— there she is—Rebeca.

The dream Europe Don Patricio had built for her had suddenly materialized on Mituco. Within this dream was another, where swans turned out to be enchanted maidens, where chaste Odette merged into lewd Odile, where love and death were rounded into music. And Rebeca was part of a divertissement within the inner dream. She forgot her birthday, the French chef, and the pavilion, the three hundred cases of champagne and the President of the Republic. She forgot Don Patricio, the five years she had spent in his house, and the life they were to lead together. She forgot the theater and the audience and danced in the great hall while Odile vamped the prince and the young girls mourned not to be chosen for his bride and the queen smiled puzzledly and Von Rothbart brooded in his inky cape. In another life his hand had pressed her thigh, awakening wild longings, and her young thoughts were mingled up in moonlight off a sylvan lake where sad-eyed maidens fluttered to their beaked and feathered master.

In my country the sweet fruit does not wither on the bough. When it is ripe it falls, and the first crow pecks it. After the intrada, when Dane and German had begun their variation, Sukasin slipped into the wings, took Rebeca's elbow, and pushed her to the room he used for changing. He touched her carefully, peeled down her tights, and bent her back into a nest of curtains. The room was hot, thick with the smell of sweat and grease paint, swollen with music. When she looked up, he had pulled off his boots and tights, put on his mask and bird wings. He knelt before her and spread her thighs with his plumed forearms. She was already in climax when he entered her.

Sukasin restrained his own pleasure—it was in his interest not to make her pregnant—and took her *andante con moto* with the first variation, *modorato* with the second, *allegro* with the third. There were multiple ovations. Harp arpeggios were already cuing Rebeca when he uncoupled, pulled her to her feet, drew up her tights, and thrust her, wobbling, out the door into the wings.

"*Danse, fille!*" he hissed, and she fled onstage.

Maria Taglioni was in retirement when Don Patricio arrived in Europe; Pavlova had not début'd when he left. But he had seen every important ballerina between these two, and he decided, with the objectivity he had at such cost managed to retain, that Rebeca was as good as any of them. It was, in fact, almost impossible to see in her the girl he'd tutored these five years. The wild looks she blended to the eerie music[11] of her variation, the frenzy she projected in the coda, were new to him. He marveled to see her so transfigured and congratulated himself on having arranged the performance and thus brought out these hidden traits, At the entr'acte he went backstage with the President of the Republic to pay her his respects, but the ballet master, M. Sukasin, told him she had gone home to rest and dress for the ball. After the performance the whole audience came to compliment him. By the time he left the theater the sets had all been struck and the dancers, still in costume, had gathered on the quay for the lighter which would take them and their baggage out to the *Pluto*. His carriage took him the few yards to his home. He hurried to Rebeca's room and found it empty. He went to his own and saw a letter on the chiffonier. He had time, while reading it, to admire the elegance of her hand and the correctness of her French grammar; he thought the style a little florid. She was, she wrote, at once possessed by shame and joy. She had given her heart and body to a stranger, lost her honor and found her happiness. Since she could neither face her friend nor leave her lover, she was fleeing Mituco forever. She thanked him for his kindness and regretted she had been unworthy of it. She would never forget him.

"Very well," be said aloud. "I found her in the streets. No doubt she belongs there."

He folded the letter, replaced it in its scented envelope, and laid it where he'd found it. He opened the top drawer and took out his pistol. From the balcony he could see both the harbor, with the steamship swinging at anchor and the lighter putting out to it, and the pavilion, where his guests were gathering. He stood there for a moment. Then he pressed the pistol muzzle against his right eye, the one, he calculated, which had seen Rebeca first, and blew his brains out.

3. Rebeca's Odyssey

MY GRANDMOTHER Rebeca Fuertes returned to Mituco fifteen years to the day after her departure. She arrived on the *Ceres* from Shanghai with a Chinese wardrobe and a Chinese maid and a Chinese child who she said was the maid's but who was really my uncle Nicolas. She took a suite at the company Guest House on the Plaza Cortada, the main square of Mituco Marítimo, and could be seen each morning mincing along the board sidewalk in her tightly-twisted, high-slit Chinese dress, first to the Church of San Roque for mass, then to the theater, where she would sit in meditation for a quarter of an hour. In fact, she was soon the chief attraction of the town, not just because she was a gorgeous woman, but because she had long since been enshrined in the mythology of Mituco as Rebeca *la fatal,* so that as soon as her identity and schedule were known, men took to congregating in the square, sitting on the wooden benches beneath the almond trees or lounging against the pedestal of the statue of Javier Cortada, to observe her comings and goings.

It was Don Onofre Salvatierra who spoke to her first, tipping his straw fedora to her as she sallied from the theater and inquiring after her health, which, she replied, was excellent. His wife scolded him so cruelly for this boldness that he never spoke to Rebeca again, but the next day Don Policarpo Madera, who managed the Mituco Company Food Commissary, sent her a Fortnum & Mason assortment of fine teas, and that afternoon she permitted him a cup of Ceylon with her on the screened terrace of the Guest House.

Within the hour all Mituco knew that she was lately widowed of a wealthy merchant of the French concession and was taking a last look at the scenes of her youth before proceeding to the splendors of Paris.

The facts were that she had never been a wife, much less a widow, that she had not the fare to Panama, much less Paris, and that had she somehow managed to arrive at the City of Light, she could have expected no more splendor than the lampglow on a corner in Clichy. She'd ditched the easy life for good fifteen years earlier, along with her Peruvian mare and her pink parasol and her doting Don Patricio.

Some are expelled from Eden, others desert; none return, except in dreams.

The morning after the Pluto cleared Mituco harbor, Sukasin had Rebeca up on deck learning a version of Salome's dance in which she finale'd barebreasted and G-stringed with a papier-mâché head of John the Baptist nuzzled between her thighs. He sold this act to a cabaret in Panama while they were waiting for a ship to Europe, and kept her working from then on. She went to Covent Garden right enough, but never to a box in the grand tier. She joined the opera company and soon became a soloist, but Sukasin enraged the director, jewed him to raise her salary, sought leverage by seducing his first dancer. The director fired Rebeca, vowing that though she danced like an angel, she would dance no more in England while she was managed by "that Russian pimp." She visited the Paris salons— or such of them whose hostesses might, as a special treat, hire a young *danseuse* to interpret M. Ravel's *Pavane* or Maître Saint-Saëns's Cygne—and showed herself off well enough to win a place in a French troupe. They lived well for a while—or Sukasin did, patronizing the best tailors and playing high-stake baccarat—, but in the end it was the same: he ran up debts, dunned the impresario for money, tried blackmail, and, his bluff called, kept Rebeca from a performance for which she'd been announced. So she was sacked again, and they fled France and a leash of yelping creditors. It was the same, too, in Bavaria, though here the end came when Rebeca was at the point of being chosen prima, and when it came Sukasin pawned everything, even a gold medal Prince Rupprecht had had struck for her, and left the bundle on the tables at Baden-Baden. So they were brought to dancing adagios around the cabarets of Middle Europe, Sukasin puffing like a tugboat but upstaging her every four measures and peacocking obscenely at the calls, and, of course, playing their pay away at gambling tables when he didn't waft it up the bums of hotel boys. And withal, Rebeca stayed with him, though she might have soloed with any company in Europe, and/or been kept in stylish ease by Graf von This or Generaldirektor That; out of stubbornness, for she had left Don Patricio for him and had to justify the choice; and as self-punishment, since she had learned of Don Patricio's suicide while yet in England; and through gratitude, since Sukasin had been an earnest, if self-interested, instructor; and from pity, for though he beat her like a dray horse when he drank, he could, hang-over mornings, weep pitchers of repentant tears and whine and grovel marvelously; and by addiction, since he was always able, with a few caresses, to wilt her to a whimpering heap of mingled shame and pleasure: in short, from all the frayed and greasy motives which serve to bind worthy and worthless people.[12] She was sustained by the radiant toughness gened to her by her forebears, the knowledge (Don Patricio's gift) of her own metal, which base earth could not tarnish, and by her art, which opened little forest glades of order in the wilderness of passion where she lived. Then one night in Vienna Sukasin dropped her off a lift and smashed her talent.

There's solace in the thought that God was punishing Rebeca for her disloyalty or making an example of her for other girls, but the likelier hypothesis is that He has a vulgar streak. So much of His work is, after all, suitable only for serialization on daytime TV. Hence the next few months, which Rebeca spent in the dingiest of Bahnhofplatz hotels, naked (since Sukasin sold her clothes) save for her cast and a blue peignoir, anticipating Adolf by aquarelling little Tyrolean views for selling to the tourists. Sukasin would sneer at these in contempt, then snatch them up and disappear for days, leav-ing her without food or attention, and on returning, whine and beg forgiveness, then scold her for a meager earner, then ask her pardon once again and tempt her with his leechy love and, once he had her wiggling, plaster-bandaged leg and all, spattle her over like a flapjack and pretend she was one of the poofs he had no money left to buy or charm to con. Then, sated, he would towel off with his second shirt, step back well out of fingernail range, and remind her how he meant, soon as her bones were knit, to bring her sufficient gentlemen in rut to give him a good living. So it went until Rebeca's cast was chipped away and God, weary at last of putting out the sort of nat-uralistic drivel any hack[13] can write, regained his sometimes wander-ing sense of humor and the marvelous. As Rebeca Fuertes awoke the next morning from troubled dreams, she found herself transformed in her bed into a man.

She, or rather he—since such a metamorphosis extends even to one's pronoun—was lying on his night side and, rolling onto his stomach, stubbed a fine, early-morning hard-on against the thin and lumpy mattress. Sharp, unfamiliar pain brought him awake. Or half awake, since at once he found that by hunching his hip and realigning he could melt the ache to pleasure. He began to rock gently. The silk peignoir purveyed a pleasant friction, which would have soon brought *frisson,* had not the strangeness of it pierced his drowsy mind and sent him scuttling around, bedclothes flying, into a cross-legged sit. He yanked up the peignoir and found not petals but a sprouting stalk. The grossly-lidded, polyphemic eye winked at him gravely.

The room remained unchanged. There was the sway-backed table with oxidizing apple core and set of paints. There, leaned against the wall, was last night's work: a short-pants'd yodeler and his flax-braided liebchen framed between two point-peaked, piny Alps. There was the soot-streaked window with its smattered pane and frayed chintz curtains, and beside it the familiar jaundiced stain shaped like a map of France with Alsace triumphantly reannexed. There was Sukasin's much-soiled second shirt balled in a corner; there was the pewter basin at which he had sprinkled himself briefly the night before. Why not goes back to sleep and forget this foolishness? But it couldn't be done, for now Rebeca felt a painful heaviness in his bladder. Everything seemed about to gush out of the strange spigot stuck on in front of him. Ah, well, he thought, I'll just have to let it be my master. Thank God Sukasin isn't here. He'd want to look at it and do heaven knows what else, and I'd never make it to the chamber pot in time.

He got to the floor, his new parts swinging awkwardly like spread wings on a grounded albatross. Turning, he caught his reflection in the mirror on the door of the wardrobe. The peignoir, tented at his loins, hung loosely above, Oh, God, my lovely breasts! Sliced away clean, oh, God! He clapped hands to his cheeks and felt the prickle of new beard. Oh, God!

Some six or seven hundred yards away, sheltered by mounds of longhand notes and stacks of open volumes, Dr. Sigmund Freud sat spasmed in conception. Tumescent pride throbbed in his mind's cervix and planted an idea which seemed to organize the hysterical confessions that echoed from the walls of his consulting room. He swept the litter from the center of his desk, took up his pen, and on a virgin sheet of foolscap scribed a phrase' destined to gestate more than thirty years before it was delivered to the World: "In woman, *penis envy*[14]—*a* positive aspiration to possess a masculine genital organ." He put the pen down and reached absently toward his crotch. Humming softly, he read what he had written. *Penis envy.* He squeezed reassuringly. Yes. Yes. It needed thought, of course, more checking with the data, but surely that was what was wrong with them. Poor things, how could one blame them? They each one craved a *Schwanz!*

Rebeca would have argued. Rebeca might even have induced the great man to wastebasket his page and thereby deny the world one of his most charming fantasies. Quite true, Rebeca had from time to time wished for the sort of organ Dr. Freud was just then clutching fondly, *but only as owned and operated by someone else.* He was acutely distressed to find one grafted on him. In the first place, he had no notion how to use it, Witness his pitiful attempts to aim it (rigid as it was) at the chamber pot. Observe him (after some painful efforts to depress its elevation below the horizontal) kneeling before the pot, wetting his belly with ricocheting spray. Then, too, it was dangerous to have such stuff bangling there unprotected. Watch him flop to the wooden chair, jouncing his ballocks against the edge, mashing them between his left thigh and the seat. And worst of all, the new equipment seemed inadequate replacement for the old, with which he had always been perfectly content and even, oftentimes, deliriously happy. His was not a morning of gratifled envy. Given the chance, he would have changed right back.

But it could not be done, and so he made the best of things. He examined his new body—hard and haired—in the mirror and decided that were he still a woman, he might have looked with favor at such a stranger. He auditioned his new voice—dropped a full octave— and discovered a timbre of command in it. He practiced walking with his new parts, even tried strutting as he had seen the young men do on Paris boulevards and on the malls of German spas, and began to siphon pride from the bunched vulnerability beneath him. And late that afternoon he used his broadened fists and newly muscled shoulders to give Vyacheslav Sukasin the beating of his life. He dealt less enthusiastically but just as efficiently with the young Englishman who showed up afterward with a photo of arabesquing Rebeca in his jacket and some very lewd imaginings in his mind. The two were of about the same height, weight, age, strength, and agility, but the tourist never got his guard up, being altogether thunder-struck at finding not the pliant ballerina who'd been touted to him but a long-haired chap in a blue nightgown who hit like a mule's hoof. The rendezvous cost him a tooth, a suit of clothes, and forty pounds in cash, but returned him the best wogs-begin-at-Calais story of the London season. An hour later Rebeca, dressed now from Savile Row and smartly shorn by the Bahnhof barber, decamped Vienna on the Orient Express.

My grandmother Rebeca Fuertes was a man for five years. He went out to the Far East as a journalist, "the only profession [this is Bismarck's phrase] for which no training is required." He took part (since after 14th May, 1904, neither he nor his dispatches could get out) in the defense of Port Arthur, was cited by the Russian staff for valor and captured by the Japanese. He escaped—disguised as a woman, logically enough—and wandered into China, where he stayed in a succession of capacities, first tutor to the children of a Tsingtao merchant, last confidential secretary to the Imperial Viceroy at Chengchow. Throughout he pressed his sexual reeducation, beginning the first evening of his manhood in the Wagon-Lit outside Budapest. A demimondaine, a resident of transcontinental trains— she later switched to trans-Atlantic steamers and went down on the Titanic—reviewed his application in the dining car, accepted him (fees and tuition waived), found him a zealous student, renewed his scholarship for the duration of the trip, and contrived to ground him firmly in the basics before they gasped into Constantinople. He took his doctorate five years later in Honan with the Viceroy's favorite concubine. The girl was cultivated, prized, and just fifteen; despite the risk, he fled with her downriver. Till then the taste of love had been less savory than what he'd known while still a woman, but now refracted echoes of his former life stirred him to ecstasy. Unable to keep lips or fingers from the girl, he took her from the steamer at Kaifeng. That night as she mewed and gibbered beneath him (even as he had done beneath Sukasin), his mind stepped from his body into hers. He felt her pleasure and shaped his movements to it—one body that was hers, one mind that was his. Later, after the girl had fixed his pipe and come to lie exhausted and sweat-glazed beside him, he gazed into the darkness billowing above their bed and said aloud, "Mother was right; I was meant to be a man." He woke next morning to hoarse shouts and hammering on the door and found himself changed back into a woman. The Viceroy's torturer, sent out to eunuchize the trespasser, saw that Rebeca had been miracled beyond his razor's reach and sold her across the province boundary to a brothel in the Treaty Port Tsinan.

Rebeca's memory of the next few years is hazed in opium fumes. The functionary's after-pleasure pipe became the whore's addiction. Her life was drawn in constant foreground on a scroll of dreams; it flowed like the great slow ocher river, which rose in an unseen distant hinterland and emptied into an unseen distant sea. Men drifted in the current. Rebeca says she fished them easily and pierced their souls with pleasure, that she was from the first not just that house's prize attraction but the best whore in north China, if not the world. I have no cause to doubt this estimate. She had lived five years in a man's body, after all, and knew the frets and flutings of that instrument and how to play fine tunes on it. She chose to see herself—and here the opium may have helped—not as a slave or worker but as an artist. She approached what may be called fier public with the artist's blend of solicitude and scorn, interpenetrating feelings which imply an eagerness to please and a refusal to be influenced. Thus while she touched her lovers deeply and enjoyed their applause, she took no inspiration from them. Her heart and womb were sealed by a strong membrane of contempt. Her lovers were chiefly European—merchants and soldiers, no doubt a diplomat or two, from the concession—and as she was too profitable to be for sale, it oftentimes amused her to suggest one buy her for himself. "*Amène-moi en Europe je te ferai heureux.*" She would smile softly as he bit his cheek in longing, smile as he slunk away, smile now and melt the hours in her pipe until the next man drifted by. Two years wisped toward her lacquered ceiling, while out beyond her window an empire was stumbling toward nightmare.

I say two years because the clearest explanation for her exit from the brothel is that the Hankow rising (10th November, 1911) convinced the keeper to liquidate his assets. All Rebeca knows is that one day she dreamed of being rocked in a sedan chair through choked and squeaking streets, and next of kneeling over a parchmented old man who giggled as she mouthed his flaccid flesh. The latter dream became recurrent. She had been purchased by a Manchu

nobleman, in whose own poppied fantasies there was a role for foreign devil, female.

   She lived then in a pleasure garden in the hills above the city, where
miniature grottoed mountains recalled the scenes of Chinese paintings. Dwarf cypresses and willows moaned beside a pool of carp
born in the time of the Ming emperors and so wise with their age
they could relate the antique stories of Stone Monkey and the Flaming Dragon. And there were gilded butterflies with ruby eyes who
fluttered their bright wings, and onyx tulips whose jade petals spread
and folded with the light, and a shamefaced gelded tiger which the
old man led about on a silken leash. It pleased him sometimes to
have Rebeca stripped and spraddled and splashed with cream, to
watch her writhe as the beast laved her with his rough tongue. And
sometimes it was not the tiger but ten or twenty famished Siamese
cats, and a servant poured cream on her from a great bowl, and the
tongues lapped at her crepitating flesh until her mind capsized in a
typhoon of pleasure. There was, besides, a Japanese tattooist who
illuminated her in obscure, painful sites, and a succession of coolies,
culled from the alleys of the city, bathed and perfumes, primed with
spice, and put to mount, according to the old man's orders and
before his avid eyes, upon Rebeca. Then, on a day when he had
heard his ancient carp tell stories and mused upon his gilded butterflies and walked his tiger on its silken leash, when he had marveled
how the Japanese tattooist's art took life when Rebeca's body quiv-
ered under feline tongues and observed the energetic stabbings of a
coolie boy who'd never till that moment had a woman, the old man
felt his potency restored. He had his servants drag the coolie off and
mounted in his place. Giggling, he spiked long, poppy-yellow nails
into Rebeca's back. Blood bubbled to his knuckles, and when his
eyes rolled upward and his loins burst, Rebeca felt her contempt dissolve into self-hatred. Her womb, which had repelled the seed of near
a thousand men, accepted his.

   Then he was no more at the villa. One may surmise—since my
uncle Nicolas was born on 12th November, 1912—that Rebeca's
owner had learned of the Empress Regent's abdication (12th February, 1912) and, like most of the Manchus, fled north whence they
had come three centuries before. At Tsinan the young servants pulled
up the onyx tulips and broke away their jade petals and caught the

gilded butterflies and took them off to sell. The old ones and Rebeca stayed. The silver carp were netted up and fried; the cats were skinned for the stew pot. They were dining off the tiger when a company of Kuomintang soldiers found them some months later.

No doubt their captain had stern orders to respect all foreign devils, for Rebeca came to herself in a Christian mission in the city. Racked with pain, for she had no choice but to withdraw from opium. That was well for my uncle Nicolas—it was enough to bear a dynasty of suppurating chromosomes without also being born an addict—, but it almost killed Rebeca. In pain she painted background back into her life. In pain she recomposed her shattered sense of self. And in pain she bore her first son. Pain cleansed her mind and soul.

On the night after my uncle Nicolas was born, Rebeca dreamed she slept in Don Patricio's mansion on Mituco. Unlike so many dreams, it was not a translation into childhood. She was her full age; Don Patricio was dead. She dreamed that she slept dreamlessly. On waking from her dream, she found it good. She had had art and passion, a medal from Prince Rupprecht and a citation from the Russian staff, a viceroy's concubine and near a thousand lovers, and a full season in the garden of despair. Now it seemed good to sleep dreamlessly in a familiar house. And so she found a Chinese girl to pose as her child's mother, and took them both to Shanghai, where she taught language in a private school for girls,[15] and earned the money for a wardrobe and their passage to Tinieblas. She planned to find a man to buy that house for her, but all those years had not been molding her for dreamless sleep. In seeking that she found something quite different, her true destiny, which was to bear a hero.

4. The Conception, Gestation, and Birth of León Fuertes

TWO MORNINGS AFTER her tea with Policarpo Madera, Rebeca received magnificent arrangement of chrysanthemums and dahlias, an inlaid rosewood box of native candies, and a letter, which esteemed her in salutation, kissed her feet in *envoi*, and begged her company in between. The sender was Dr. Azael Burlando[16] who possessed the largest private bloc of Mituco Company shares and the most controversial reputation on the island.

Dr. Burlando, who was then in his early forties, was like Rebeca a native of Mituco de Tierra Firme. Like her he was a bastard. Like her he had left home on his tenth birthday. Thirty years later—in other words, about two years before Rebeca's return—he appeared on the island with a wife whom he kept veiled, engaged the very suite in which Rebeca was now installed, and gave out that he would buy Mituco shares at any reasonable value. His first client was young Balbino Olmos, who was engrossed in dissipating a considerable inheritance. An offer of ten shares at five hundred inchados[17] the share was accepted without haggling. Dr. Burlando inspected the certificates, unlocked an ironwood coffer that stood beside his bed, removed one of seven casaba-sized bags, and weighed out the price in gold nuggets. By the month's end he had acquired one hundred shares, the maximum allowed a single owner under the statutes of the company.

As a shareholder, Dr. Burlando was now entitled to reside on the island. He bought—still with gold nuggets—a roomy if inelegant house from the heirs of Don Augusto Roble, repaired it, saw to the furnishings himself, and moved in with his wife and his coffer. The woman, who had never stepped outside the Guest House, never stepped outside her new home. Nor did anyone except Dr. Burlando and the servants ever enter it. He frequented the Café Progreso, standing his round of drinks, playing chess and dominoes, participating in political discussion, and partaking of the unshelled shrimp and crayfish which the manager set out in saucers on the bar each afternoon at six. He attended shareholders' meetings. He subscribed an aisle seat at the theater and went to every show. But he accepted no invitations nor offered any of his own.

Dr. Burlando seemed rather fat to some men, to other men quite skinny. Acquaintances would sometimes be surprised to find him taller than he'd appeared at their last meeting. Sometimes he looked caucasian, sometimes negroid, sometimes mestizo. Or two friends, observing him from the café bar, looking across their drinks to where he sat immobile at the chessboard, watching now as his hand flashed like a lizard's tongue to snatch a piece, would disagree as to his size or shape or color. Similarly, there was no getting his past straight.

The doctor storied freely and amusingly about his thirty years of absence from Mituco, but the stories varied. He was doctor of medicine from Leipzig, or of philosophy from Coimbra, or of canon law from Rome. He had panned his gold from rivers in the Yukon, amassed it in South Africa purveying guns and bullets to the Boers, traded for it in Makassar and Celebes, along whose coasts he'd piloted a brig, or mined it in the *sertão of* Brazil. And since each tale was nuggeted with detail, each sounded true while it was being told, yet when they were compared none sounded truer than the others. Mituco was disturbed by the good doctor, angered and fascinated. Men craved his company and resented his tricks. And by the time of his meeting with Rebeca—that is, by June, 1914—the common view was that he was not doctor of anything and that he'd got his gold by selling his soul to the devil.

Like many common views, this was correct in drift but formulated inexactly. All the claimed doctorates were self-conferred, yet there was no question but that Burlando qualified for a doctorate in imposture. Just as he was unwilling to confine himself to one physical aspect, he refused to make do with one personality or profession, and from the age of ten had buffeted about the world inventing Burlandos as the pleasure struck him—this partly from a heightened sensitivity to the possibilities of life and partly from a taste for mocking the rest of mankind, who set such store by unity. And if each of his several lived ended in failure, it was not because he lacked ability or boldness but because he would lose interest in an identity once he had mastered it and would destroy it so that onlookers might see it for the fabrication that it was and realize what fools they'd been for believing in it. Thus Reverendo Padre Azael Burlando, S.J., whose gravity and erudition, casuistry and talent for intrigue commended him to the Bishop of Salamanca and gained him a secretaryship, whose beaked nose, humped back and withered leg seemed excellent (if superfluous) guarantees of his chastity, seduced the bishop's niece in the cathedral during Good Friday mass, was discovered, and narrowly escaped the fate of Peter Abelard. Thus Azael Burlando, M.D., who had impressed the senior surgeons of Melbourne General Hospital not only with his skill in lopping limbs and excavating entrails but with his dedication to the healing art, began one morning following an amputation to saw away at the patient's good leg, gleefully quipping to his horrified assistants, the nurses, the gallery of students gaping down in anguish ("Let's take this one for symmetry; I've never done a left leg and can use the practice; for two he gets a discount on the fee . . ."), until he was dragged, still chattering, out of the operating theater. Thus Burlando El Magnífico, Tamer of Wild Beasts, whose steamer trunks were plastered with bright posters of him romping tigerback and prying at a lion's jaws, who proved his disdain for death and danger by leaping from the promenade deck of the Titanic into an icy sea to save a lady's lap dog, who, on the night of terror, as the first boats were weighed away, stood calmly at the high-side rail puffing a cheroot and keeping time with an index finger to the forlorn, brave playing of the ship's orchestra, emerged two hours later from the fur wrap and silken veils of a demimondaine (she was never found), shameless beneath the gunwale of a lifeboat. Dr. Burlando even failed as an actor—on the face of it the perfect profession for him—simply because he would not stick to a role even for a short run and mocked his public with happy Hamlets and limp-wristed Don Juans. As for his gold, the seven casaba-sized sacks of nuggets, the doctor had in fact traded his status in the next world for it. The transaction[18] was not a sale, however, but an enlistment, while the enlister was not the devil, who, as commonly conceived, does not exist.

Dr. Burlando did no more to dispel the rumors of fake doctorates and dealings with the devil than he did to stabilize his physical appearance or suppress the contradictions in his autobiographical yarns. Puzzling his neighbors was the great pleasure of his life. When Rebeca reappeared, he resolved to make her his mistress; what better way to mock and shock Mituco? Rebeca *la fatal* kept by a parvenu! Rebeca, as we know, was fishing for a rich protector, so in effect they were made for each other. But since both were canny bargainers and altogether free of romantic illusions, they did not come so easily to terms.

The courtship of my paternal grandparents, like the mobile phase of Europe's *Totentanz,* began with Sarajevo and ended with the Battle of the Marne. On 28th June, 1914, Dr. Azael Burlando paid Rebeca Fuertes a state visit. He paraded his best clothes and offered her his heart. (His hand, alas, was unavailable; he had the misfortune to be married.) Rebeca feigned high outrage, spurned his offer, and riddled his vanity with scorn. There followed diplomatic fencing, mutual mobilization, his declaration that he meant to have her whether she willed or no, and her demand that he restore her the lost paradise of Don Patricio's mansion. He pressed his advances; she withdrew. The town took sides, some hoping a comeuppance for Rebeca, some longing to see the doctor put in his place, most more or less convinced that he was strong enough to force capitulation. The crisis came on 5th September, when Dr. Burlando bribed a passkey from the Guest House manager and non-interference from the staff and reached Rebeca's bed. The subsequent engagement, joined after weeks of vigorous maneuver and pressed at closest quarter, exhausted both to stalemate. Forcible rape was the one sexual experience Rebeca had so far not encountered, and Dr. Burlando's ever-changing aspect made him the most intriguing of all her lovers. Rebeca, for her part, commanded charms such as the doctor had never believed possible. After a night made two weeks long by the heavy curtains of Rebeca's bedroom, the following equilibrium was reached: Dr. Burlando agreed to buy Don Patricio's house and keep Rebeca there, but refused to give her any stock or title to the building; Rebeca agreed to receive Dr. Burlando three nights a week, but refused to let him see her naked or to have his child. Then they settled down to bombard each other with demands for what each had refused, neither one able to advance, neither one willing to retreat, both in their hearts as interested in inflicting damage as in securing gains. In other words (lack of anointed vows notwithstanding), they found themselves in the trenches of marriage.[19]

"If you want a son so badly," Rebeca might say as they lay in the oleaginous, postcoital stifle of a dry season night; "if you must have a son," smiling felinely with her voice, since her face was obscured by the darkness in which she habitually received the doctor; "if your vanity demands a reproduction of yourself, please try your wife. There are sufficient bastards in this world already."

"She's sterile," the doctor would reply, puffing his cheroot violently, then holding the dim beacon of its tip over her belly in empty hope of glimpsing her bare flesh. "Sterile," not adding that her sterility was well-contrived by him, that it was Rebeca's son he wanted, partly because she was the first furrow he'd deemed worthy of his precious seed, partly because she steadfastly refused to cultivate it.

"If," the doctor might say of a wet-season morning as they sat beneath the streaming gables of the porch, he in his undershorts and slippers stirring coffee, Rebeca in her lobstered kimono sipping tea; "if you truly crave the right to live here"—nonshareholding Rebeca stayed on Mituco as the doctor's ward—"and if you can't buy stock because your fabulous late husband's fabulous Strasbourg mine and all your fabulous wealth—observe the twin significance that word may bear—is now in German hands, then why not simply marry one of the moist-eyed, wag-tailed tongue-droopers who're always sniffing after you? I won't stand in your way. I've had you, which is all I ever wanted, especially as you're not woman enough to breed—though a suspicious man might wonder at the love show that little Mongol of your maid's. I can find you a husband at my café by lunchtime. Just say the word."

"My dear Dr. Burlando," Rebeca would reply, "you will never comprehend it, I know, but I have too much shame to offer myself to a decent man now that I've been soiled by you," not mentioning that it was shares from Dr. Burlando that she wanted, first because he refused to give her any but also and importantly because she did not care to take another man until she had driven the doctor gaga as she had all her other lovers.

Rebeca did not have the dreamless sleep she'd hoped for. She lay awake brooding about Mituco Company shares, or when she did sleep, dreamed about them, clouds of certificates fluttering like albino bats across her mind. The doctor lost rather than gained in notoriety. Mituco was not mocked or shocked for long, since quite soon after he took up with Rebeca he began to age markedly and, stranger still, varied ever less in his appearance, while the townspeople grew ever less disturbed and puzzled by him, concluding that he was no different than so many men of middle years who, trying to keep a younger woman, become incapable of controlling her. Men laughed behind his back and whispered that Rebeca must be leading him a terrible dance. He even became something of a figure for pity, another victim of Rebeca *la fatal*. This mutual frustration led, finally, to a realignment of positions, Dr. Burlando declared that he would give no less than twenty shares to any child of his Rebeca bore, Rebeca, naturally, to hold the shares in trust. He even signed an affidavit to this effect and had it notarized before the Comptroller of the Compañía de Progreso Infinito—an event which caused the town to suppose Rebeca already pregnant and notably redeemed the doctor's reputation. Rebeca, for her part, set about to conceive.

First she tried to conceive some respect for Dr. Burlando, and with it the desire to give him heirs. Failing of this, she searched for some maternal yearnings, but the creative urge in her had been turned away from breeding and aimed at art. Then she went over to Mituco de Tierra Firme and consulted Señora Perfecta, a midwife and a witch, but Señora Perfecta refused to sell her a fertility charm, having read in Rebeca's face (and confirmed the reading by inspection of her coffee grounds) that all her offspring would either be cripples or come to violent ends. Meanwhile Dr. Burlando toiled away like a field hand, night after night, glazed in sweat and rage, trying to trowel a child into her stony womb.

When, in February, 1917, she told him he had failed again—it was two months since he'd sworn out the affidavit—he drew up a new instrument (and had it duly notarized and filed with the Town Clerk), deeding the house to Rebeca in the event she bore a son. He brought the copy to her and slammed it down on the bureau where, eighteen years before, she'd left the note for Don Patricio, and said, "I give you one more month. One month and then the deal's off and I'm leaving. While I still can. Before you squeeze me dry."

Rebeca told Dr. Burlando not to come again until she sent for him, and she retired to her bedroom and let the rolls of woven bamboo fibers down over the windows and lay down on her bed to concentrate on the stock and the deed. She told her Chinese maid to bring her a plate of rice and beans each evening, and when the food remained untouched for three days to call Dr. Burlando. Then she beamed her mind on the deed and the stock until all the rest of life was but a vague penumbra.

The maid summoned Dr. Burlando on the night of 12th March, 1917. Rebeca was unconscious of his arrival. She lay tranced and naked in the darkened room, and Dr. Azael Burlando entered and undressed and climbed on board like a galley slave. Rebeca lay corpselike, thinking of shares and deed, aware of Dr. Burlando only as a half-sleeping neurasthenic might become aware of another patient[20] pounding his head slowly and despairingly against the wall four or five rooms away along the clinic corridor. Then, at the moment of his discharge—perceived like yelpings muffled by a practiced hand as three attendants drag the madman to his bed to strap him in—Rebeca realized she was finally a whore. Not in the Tsinan brothel nor in the Manchu's villa had she achieved true whoredom, first since she'd chosen neither and second since in one she'd been an artist of a sort and in the other a mere plaything. But now she'd put herself to rent exclusively for gain. Self-hatred flooded into her, and she conceived.

My grandmother Rebeca Fuertes stayed in her bed from March to November, 1917, rising only to perform natural functions. From the instant she conceived she suffered headaches, nausea, and weird cravings—customary symptoms of gestation, but in her case abnormally acute and prolonged until the hour she delivered. She was, as well, subject to seizures of hysteria and suicidal urges, fits of mania and depression, which she had never known, not even in the darkest hours of her life. She was obsessed by the vision of her own hand driving sometimes a knife, sometimes a pair of scissors, into her belly, and ordered her maid to collect every sharp instrument in the house and bury them under the flagstones of the patio. Through it all she stubbornly refused to be examined by a doctor, and when, during a week of violent nausea, which saw her unable to keep a grain of rice on her stomach, Dr. Burlando presumed to bring a Spanish surgeon—the Director of the Mituco Clinic and an extremely well-trained man—to her house, she howled them off with curses such as the Spaniard, who had served in Morocco against the Riff, had never heard, even from wounded legionnaires.

Dr. Burlando visited her each afternoon at five to feed her teaspoonfuls of *blanc de blanc* (he bought ten bottles at an absurd price from the cellar of the Hotel Colón in Ciudad Tinieblas) and slivers of *foie gras truffé* (he had to send to Boston for it) on Jacob's biscuits (he got four tins from Kingston); to hear her whine for Vienna sausage and Munich bock (as if the British blockade were his fault); to bear her curses and complaints. She carped at his neglect when he came late, at his intrusion when he showed up early, at his machine-like lack of feeling when he was on time. On sunny days she groused about the heat, and when it stormed complained of chills and ague. She screeched her maid to tears and little Nicolas to terror. She cursed Burlando for making her pregnant and herself for letting him and God for having dreamed up pregnancy in the first place. Most of all she cursed her belly and the bastard child inside it, both of which grew prodigiously as though fed by her curses, and as Rebeca swelled, Burlando aged and wasted. His hair turned white, then fell. His flesh dissolved until his wrist and check bones seemed about to pierce the skin. He grew all bent and bowed, took up the use of a Malacca walking stick, and had to pause to rest a dozen times along the doddering two hundred meters from Rebeca's house to the Café Progreso. There he no longer played at chess or dominoes, having so waned in skill and concentration that the rankest chump could drub him, nor took part in discussions, nor offered up new chapters to his autobiography, but huddled in a corner sipping medicinal infusions and when he spoke at all, spoke only of his child, the way it kicked under Rebeca's nightgown, how full of life it was, a son for sure. The others would nod absently and when he'd left, sometimes before the strings of beads that hung across the doorway had swung behind him, would break into rude laughter, exclaiming that one could make a better bargain with the devil than with Rebeca Fuertes, referring to the doctor as "the old fool" or "the poor pubic hair." Meanwhile Mituco bore the oddest weather in memory, unseasonable weeks of burning drought broken by thunderstorms and tempests grown more violent each succeeding month; earth tremors; a tidal wave which spared the island only because the bishop, having remarked the draining of the bay, ordered the effigy of San Roque carried to a sea-ward beach, the statue, its bearers, and the bishop (in full vestments, carrying his crook) arriving just before a bulwark of black water, which parted marvelously north and south and spent its force upon the mainland. The islanders, especially good matrons of the town, re-lated these phenomena to Rebeca's pregnancy, declaring her a witch and whispering it was the devil, not the doctor, who had sired what-ever beast there was inside her and saying that as she had destroyed Don Patricio and was destroying Dr. Azael, so she would finish by destroying all Mituco.

Rebeca Fuertes entered labor on the night of 12th November, 1917, exactly eight months after she conceived. Dr. Burlando hap-pened to be in her house, restrained by a tremendous downpour. He had fed her the last of the pâté, had endured five hours of her petu-lant abuse, and, leaving her at last in a light sleep, had descended to the *sala* for a cup of manzanilla tea. At her first scream he dropped his cup, which shattered on the tiles. He dragged himself upstairs, his steps punctuated by staccato squealing. He found Rebeca lying as if pinned beneath her bulging belly, a tuft of her own hair in either fist. He shouted for the maid and ordered her, rain or no rain, to run to the clinic for the ambulance.

Rebeca shook her head. "Send for Señora Perfecta."

"Look, woman," said Dr. Azael Burlando. "I've stood your whims eight months, but now it's finished. With luck you'll die tonight and I'll piss on your grave, but first you'll bear my son." He poked the maid with his stick. "I said run!"

Rebeca sat up screaming and raked her nails across the doctor's check. Then she fainted.

Though small, the Mituco Company Clinic was the most modern medical facility in the Republic of Tinieblas. Rebeca was admitted there at 11:12 p.m., again in faint, having come to in the clinic's Studebaker ambulance, mauled Dr. Burlando's other check, and bitten the attendant's forearm to the bone. The Spanish surgeon ordered her anesthetized and prepared for Caesarean delivery. Then he went to treat the wounded. He had bandaged the attendant's arm and was swabbing Dr. Burlando's face with alcohol when a squeak of horror from the duty nurse brought both men to Rebeca's bedside. In the course of undressing and disinfecting Rebeca's body the nurse had found the artwork of the Manehu's Japanese tattooist, the reason for Rebeca's stout refusal to let Dr. Burlando see her naked or to be examined by a physician. Tiny blue toads and lizards romped out of her armpits down along her flanks; two triple-file processions of green centipedes marched up her inner thighs; an orange caterpillar oozed out of her navel; and a red-and-yellow speckled snake twined round her spine and disappeared into the crevice of her buttocks. The nurse took these in stride, but was unable to contain her fright when the shaving of Rebeca's pubis revealed a baseball-sized, purple tarantula. Dr. Burlando caught one glimpse of this over the surgeon's shoulder, clapped both hands to his crotch, and fell twitching to the floor in obvious and massive apoplexy.

The Spaniard saw at once his case was fatal, did what he could to case Dr. Burlando's final hour, then operated on Rebeca. The wisdom of this decision was soon vindicated, for there were two children, not one, both of them, though one month premature, too large-headed to have passed Rebeca's pelvic bone. My father, León Fuertes,[21] was extracted into this world by Caesarean section at midnight 12th November , 1917, his first wail chiming with the Administration Building clock and rattling with the death throes of his father. A sister followed him by some few seconds.

PART TWO
HIS EARLY LIFE (1917-1936)

5. The Flight from Mituco

IT IS TEMPTING to speculate how León Fuertes might have developed had he received his birthright: the twenty shares of Mituco Company stock and the income of their dividends; the Garza family mansion with its spacious rooms and seignorial appointments; access to the fine schools of Mituco Marítimo; and membership in a directing class. Tempting but idle. He was programmed genetically for excellence, and noblesse oblige serves just as well as poverty for a whetstone to ambition. More important, I think, than the fact of his disinheriting was the process by which it was accomplished. The town combined against him and his mother; he began his life not just unlegacied but outcast and reviled. This no doubt exacerbated the strange duality[22] in his character: an intense yearning for respectability alternating with (linked to, balanced by) a total unconcern (if not contempt) for what others might think.

Before León Fuertes had spent eight hours in this world, all Mituco knew the details of his coming into it, down to the last hair on the eighth leg of the tarantula inscribed on his mother's mons and the synchronizing of his father's death with his first cry. As I have noted, gossips had long suspected Rebeca of malevolent powers and intentions. By the morning of 13th November, 1917, many *mituqueños* were ready to accept (and none was willing to dispute in public) the thesis of Señorita Zoreida Bocanegra (who had preserved her virginity[23] for Don Patricio Garza during the twenty years he lived in Paris, only to discover that neither he nor anyone else wanted it) that Rebeca Fuertes was a witch, that she had bewitched first Don Patricio then Dr. Azael Burlando, that she had engendered little León and his sister in connection with Beelzebub, and that she had murdered Dr. Burlando by enchantment.

That diabolical agencies were operating on Mituco became even plainer at Dr. Burlando's wake, which was attended by a great number of *mituqueños*, despite the fact that few of them had cared much for him in his life and none had ever spoken to his widow. A tempest such as had not struck the island since the shipwreck of Javier Cortada or been associated with it since 1610 raged all that night, and at the stroke of midnight wind burst the shutters and blew out all the candles in the house. When, after much confusion, light was restored, mourners discovered the image of the horned god blazoned on the coffin and a large crucifix hanging inverted in its niche beside the *sala* door. Then, at dawn, when the pallbearers (five of them directors of the Mituco Company, the sixth Don Pedro Caoba, who claimed the right by virtue of having lost more games at chess to Dr. Burlando than any other habitué of the Café Progreso) tried to lift the coffin, they could not budge it. It took twelve men to lug it from the bier out to the glass-walled, horse-drawn hearse. Then one man stumbled, another lost his grip, and the coffin fell and splintered on the ground. There was no corpse; the casket was filled with rocks. The obvious conclusion was that Dr. Azael Burlando had, in fact, a contract with the devil, and that it covered his body as well as his soul.

Despite these strange events and the great volume of accusatory gossip they engendered, no official action was taken against Rebeca for a time. A small mob collected about the clinic on the evening of 14th November and set up quite a noise of shouting for Rebeca to leave the island, but though the constable on duty at the door made no move to disperse them, they were finally shoo'd off by the Spanish surgeon. When Rebeca went home on the 16th, she found the façade of the mansion scarred with obscene slogans and warnings to get out or else, and heard from her maid and little Nicolas, both badly frighted, of shots fired in the night and shouts of "Burn the witch-bitch!" When she reported these depredations to the chief of police, he joined her in deploring them, adding, however, that given his small force and the general mood of the community, he could not guarantee that they would not recur. It was not until the 18th, after Rebeca had presented herself at the offices of the Mituco Company and requested that twenty shares of stock and the deed to the mansion be made over to her, that Mituco acted officially. That afternoon Licentiate Jacobo Mangle, the Public Prosecutor (and also Counsel General to the Mituco Company) filed charges against Rebeca Fuertes for the crime of witchcraft, citing a statute drafted in the 17th Century by the Holy Inquisition.

Crime was so rare in Mituco Marítimo that the island had no jail. A small room on the top floor of the Administration Building was fitted hurriedly with bars, and Rebeca was confined there *incomunicada*, for the statute specified that an accused witch be permitted contact only with her confessor, while Rebeca felt she had enough to bear without suffering the intrusions of a priest.[24] Fatigued as she was, solitude was solace. Her great distress was that León was kept from her. Rebeca had, at the moment she emerged from anesthesia, conceived an almost superhuman love for her second son. This was a new emotion for her, since the love for my uncle Nicolas which Dr. Burlando had supposed he'd noticed wasn't love at all, but rather a clever counterfeit which Rebeca, appalled that her first-born meant no more to her than any other infant, had crafted in hope that Nicolas might take it for *bona fide* and so be spared the resentment of a loveless childhood. As for her daughter, Rebeca was hard put not to hate her outright, for the little girl seemed proof that Dr. Burlando had unfairly won his bargain, getting two children when he only paid for one. But (perhaps in compensation for the hatred she had felt for him while he was in her womb) Rebeca's love for León was spontaneous and true, and from the moment she was shut away she screamed so stridently for him that Licentiate Mangle, who had offices below her cell and, with the din, was quite unable to prepare his case, after a day or two relented and had León brought. León Fuertes was, thus, nursed in prison—albeit a clean one with walls of wood, not stone—a circumstance in which he took rather more pride than shame during his later life.

As far as I can ascertain, Rebeca Fuertes was the last person to be tried for witchcraft in the Western world. Because of the great interest in the case, the process was conducted not in the courtroom of the *Alcaldía* (which, since Mituco Marítimo saw mainly civil actions, was quite small) but in the Municipal Theater, the venue of Rebeca's initiation to both art and love. Subscribers to the regular dramatic season were allowed to buy their customary places at a mark-up; other seats sold briskly; and when the court convened at 9 A.M. on 1st December, 1917, the house was packed. Care was exercised, however, to preserve the solemnity of the proceedings. A backdrop originally painted for the third act of *Man and Superman*, and which the artist, eschewing Shaw's stage directions, had amply strewn with hungry tongues of flame, hung from the second lift. Dr. Emilio Cedra, the Magistrate of Mituco (and Chairman of the Board of the Mituco Company), presided from a dais draped in black velvet, and there were costly tables of mahogany for Licentiate Mangle and Dr. Everardo Palo de Bamboa (a Director of the Mituco Company), appointed by the court for the defense. There was an elevated witness stand and a sumptuously carved enclosure for the seven jurymen (who were all Directors of the Mituco Company and whose foreman was Don Arnulfo Bocanegra, Señorita Zoreida's brother). The Bishop of Mituco was present as amicus curiae and was seated beside Dr. Cedra on a ceremonial throne brought over from the Church of San Roque. Spotlights illuminated the central dais, the prosecution and defense tables, the witness stand, and the jury box, while from above the stage, red and amber lights played on the backdrop. Spectators were forbidden to enter while the trial was in session, and the refreshments on sale in the outer lobby were limited to nonalcoholic beverages.

The charges against Rebeca Fuertes[25] were substantially those gossiped up by Zoreida Bocanegra. They were read off by the clerk as soon as the jury had been impaneled. Rebeca smiled calmly throughout this reading. She had chosen, over her counsel's mild protest, to wear a dress of yellow silk brocade, a relic of the Chinese wardrobe she had brought to Mituco three years before, and her refusal to wear mourning had the effect of confirming all present in the prejudices they had carried with them into the theater: the vocal many were more than ever certain of her guilt; the silent few were convinced that she was being tried unjustly. All were forced to admire her composure, but it was evident that childbirth and imprisonment had wreaked a toll. Her face was haggard, her complexion ashen. And though none present realized it, she achieved serenity only by blacking out events about her and casting her mind across the plaza up to the room where her maid minded little León. She had ceased, in fact, to think about herself at all and existed only as a mother.

The case for the prosecution consumed three days. Licentiate Jacobo Mangle established that Don Patricio Garza had been known

both in Mituco and in Europe for his great culture and mature judgment and that nonetheless he had taken the defendant, then an un-
washed urchin, into his home and lavished luxuries upon her. Don
Patricio's former valet testified that he had on numerous occasions
observed the defendant whispering to her Peruvian mare, and the
Bishop of Mituco was then called upon to read into the record and
clarify in layman's terms a great volume of material from the science
of demonology, explaining how witches operate with the aid of familiar spirits who take the form of animals. Mangle then summoned a
cloud of witnesses to testify how Don Patricio had doted on Rebeca,
exceeding the boundaries of good taste and stretching the limits of
imagination in preparing entertainments for her fifteenth birthday.
He established that Don Patricio's suicide was a direct result of Rebeca's
desertion. He then called Señorita Zoreida Bocanegra, who describes
herself as Don Patricio's childhood playmate, sometime fiancée, and
lifelong friend, and who stated under oath and in the strongest terms
that the only explanation for Don Patricio's comportment vis-à-
vis the defendant was that he had been bewitched. Through all this
testimony Rebeca's counsel sat gazing up at the fresco of nymphs
and cupids which adorned the theater ceiling and made no move to
cross-examine.

Dr. Palo de Bamboa was similarly silent while the prosecution built
a case for the enchantment of Dr. Burlando and for Rebeca's copu-
lation with the devil. He waived cross-examination even when Tim-
oteo Ramos, a noted guzzler of *flor de sueño* tea, testified that when
Dr. Azael Burlando informed the chess and domino players of the
Café Progreso that Rebeca was pregnant, forty-two demons issued
from his mouth, led forth by Asmodeus, Astaroth, and Belberith and
followed in descending line of rank to lowly Urobach, who slunk
out last. Dr. Palo said nothing when Rebeca's tattoos (described by
the nurse) were confirmed by the bishop as Devil's Marks, insignia
fixed on the bodies of women who have intercourse with Satan. His
only intervention came after Licentiate Mangle had called the Spanish surgeon to establish the time and manner of Dr. Burlando's death.
In cross-examination of the surgeon, Dr. Palo made it clear that at
the moment of Dr. Burlando's seizure, as at the moment of his death,
Rebeca had been unconscious under heavy anesthetic.

When it came time for the defense to make its case, Dr. Palo refused to take the line Rebeca urged on him: that the case against her had been fabricated by the Directorate of the Mituco Company to confiscate her mansion and little León's stock, and that the company, not content to rely on gossip and coincidence, had exacerbated superstitions by contriving to steal Dr. Burlando's body and fill his coffin with rocks. He refused as well to put Rebeca on the stand. He called one witness, Señora Perfecta, whom he had subpoena'd from Mituco de Tierra Firme. He introduced her as a witch of thirty years' active practice and asked the court to consider her testimony expert. Here Licentiate Jacobo Mangle objected and with great histrionics demanded to know what evidence the defense could show that the witness was anything more than a busybody and a fake. The public applauded vigorously, and while judge Cedra was hammering for order, the witness beckoned Dr. Palo with a forefinger and whispered something in his ear. When the theater was quiet and after judge Cedra had instructed the bailiffs to remove any person whose conduct interfered with the calm tenor of the trial, Dr. Palo asked if the honorable and valiant counsel for the prosecution wished the witness to prove her expertise by cursing him. Mangle blanched and, to the great amusement of all present, hastily withdrew his objection. Judge Cedra concealed his smile behind a handkerchief, cleared his nostrils into it, rapped twice, and ruled that in the absence of current protest from the prosecution, the witness's testimony would be considered expert. Señora Perfecta was then sworn and asked to tell the court, in her own words, about witches.

Señora Perfecta was, by her own claim, forty-seven years of age and looked no older. Her skin had the sheen and color of a telephone, but she was straight-nosed and high-foreheaded. Grand matriarchal bosoms swelled beneath the bodice of her dress, and when she gestured, folds of flesh flapped from her upper arms with elephantine dignity. Her voice was clear, her gaze firm even in the spotlight. Neither Judge Cedra nor the Bishop of Mituco commanded more authority.

Señora Perfecta said, first of all, that local witches got their powers not from Satan but from the spirits of Mituco, who had sojourned on the island in vast numbers during pre-Columbian times and who, though now diminished, still visited there more frequently than in any other region of America. A Mituco witch could use her powers only to do good for Mituco and the mituqueños, as when, almost a hundred years before, Doña Filomena de Balsa had hit General Isidro Bodega's Dutch Finance Minister with the Curse of the Tides. As for powers, the powers were three, the Powers of Love, of Death, and of Eternity. And the Powers of Love were three, and they were love potions, aphrodisiacs, and fertility charms. And the Powers of Death were three, and they were the Curses, the Curse of the Tides, and the Curse of the Winds, where the accursed dried up and shriveled and blew away, and the Curse of the Rocks, where the accursed solidified. And the Powers of Eternity were also three, but they could not be revealed.

When Señora Perfecta concluded her discourse on witchery, the theater was silent, except for a heavy gasping from Licentiate Jacobo Mangle, who was probably wondering which of the three Curses Señora Perfecta had meant to aim at him. Then Dr. Everardo Palo de Bamboa thanked the witness for her deposition and asked if, in her expert opinion, the defendant, Rebeca Fuertes, was a witch.

"Ha!" said Señora Perfecta, smiling contemptuously in the direction of the defendant. Rebeca Fuertes was no witch at all. She commanded no magic, either for good or evil. She had no powers other than those a clever and good-looking woman might be expected to enjoy in a community where men were pigs. Señora Perfecta declared that she had known the defendant as a child, when all she did was eat mangoes and make mischief, whereas a witch was serious from birth and began her apprenticeship at seven years. Señora Perfecta related how Rebeca had consulted her, then asked rhetorically if any witch, much less a witch with all the powers Licentiate Mangle had attributed to Rebeca, would go all the way to Mituco de Tierra Firme or offer good money for a fertility charm. Certainly not! A witch would make her own and be done with it. She Señora Perfecta, had been brewing up love potions and fertility charms since she was twelve and selling them (with precious few complaints) since she was seventeen. "Rebeca Fuertes a witch? Ha!"

Dr. Palo then released the witness for cross-examination, and Licentiate Mangle asked if Rebeca might not have acquired witchly powers in some foreign country, China, for example. Señora Perfecta replied that such powers would be invalid in the Mituco area. Licentiate Mangle then asked if that might not explain why Rebeca

consulted her. In other words: some of Rebeca's powers—those for
fertility charms, for example—might be invalid on Mituco, whereas
others . . . In the expert opinion of the witness, then, was it not possible that a witch coveted in foreign parts might retain her evil powers on Mituco, her powers, say, for bewitching men, even for casting
death spells on them, while losing her benevolent powers, her powers, say, for fertility charms?

For the first time Señora Perfecta seemed to be uncertain of herself. She hesitated, looked long toward Rebeca, then set her chin
and said no.

But could the witness be sure?

Completely.

Might not the witness be influenced by considerations of personal
pride and professional jealousy?

Dr. Everardo Palo de Bamboa leaped to his feet and objected to
this unethical attempt to discredit and intimidate an expert witness.
Señora Perfecta fixed her gaze on Licentiate Jacobo Mangle and
began muttering under her breath. The prosecutor felt his thumb tips
go hard as stone and withdrew his question before Judge Cedra had
had time to rule.

"No further questions," he mumbled, and walked shakily back to
his table.

"The defense rests," said Dr. Palo de Bamboa.

That night the air above Mituco Marítimo was thick with spirits.
Clouds of them obscured the moon and hissed at those few passers-
by unwise enough to leave their homes. The greatest concentration
was in the Plaza Cortada. The constable on duty in the square huddled beneath the statue of Javier Cortada and counted more than a
thousand between midnight and twelve-thirty. They streamed in
from the wooded southern portions of the island toward the upper
storey of the Guest House, where Señora Perfecta was lodged at
court expense. All the milk in the town curdled. All the cream
turned sour. And Licentiate Jacobo Mangle woke to find his two
big toes calcified to granite. They broke off cleanly when he tried to
put on his shoes, and from that day on he walked flatfooted, like a
duck. These happenings, which were the common knowledge of
everyone in town before the trial reconvened to hear charges to the
jury, were variously interpreted: loudly as signs of Rebeca's guilt;

silently as proof of her innocence. She alone took no notice of them, having slept quite soundly all night long with little León nestled to her breast.

In his charge to the jury Licentiate Jacobo Mangle reiterated all the testimony he had introduced to substantiate the charges against Rebeca. He was particularly graphic about the nature and placement of her tattoos, and his description of how the tarantula's "foul and hairy members gripped even to the core of that fragrant fruit with which this modern Eve poisoned her poor Adam" drew titters and applause from the public. When it came time for him to refute the testimony of the defense's single witness, he remembered his vanished toes and took valor from his anger and denounced Señora Perfecta's denial of Rebeca's witchhood, pointing resolutely at the witness, who sat in the first row, and declaring that she had allowed jealousy, or perhaps even a bribe from the defense, to lead her from the truth. Here the little fingers of both his hands solidified and broke away and fell to the board floor of the stage with slight, dry thumps, and Mangle, his fury throttling his fear, ground them both to dust with the heel of his right shoe and screamed that Rebeca had cursed him and called upon the jury to convict her and judge Cedra to impose the harshest penalty provided by the law.

The applause to this was such that Licentiate Mangle permitted himself half a dozen bows before waddling back to his table. In fact, most of those present were agreed that the Municipal Theater of Mituco had heard no such ovation since Rebeca's *Swan Lake* variation eighteen years before. Judge Emilio Cedra pounded for three solid minutes before the theater grew quiet enough for his voice to be heard threatening to clear the courtroom if the public would not keep order. Then Dr. Palo de Bamboa rose and called meekly for acquittal. The jury ought well to disregard the ranting of the prosecutor and the wholly circumstantial evidence he had introduced and attend instead to the testimony of the one witness (with all respect to Monseñor Ramillo, who knew much more about divine than witchly matters) qualified to pronounce on who might or might not be a witch: Señora Perfecta. The calm examination of her testimony by reasonable men could only, Dr. Palo said, result in an acquittal for his client. He called again for such a verdict, then resumed his seat and his inspection of the ceiling frescoes.

Judge Emilio Cedra admonished the jury to consider the evidence with care and dismissed them to the main dressing room behind the stage. They were back within five minutes. Rebeca Fuertes was guilty, Foreman Arnulfo Bocanegra said, on four counts of witchcraft, that is, of all the charges brought aganist her save that of having caused Dr. Burlando's death.

Rebeca took this news with no show of emotion. She was thinking that it was close to little León's feeding time and scarcely heard the verdict or the applause which followed it. Judge Cedra thanked the jury and advised the Clerk of the Court (who was also the Chief Clerk of the Mituco Company) to proceed forthwith with the sequestering of any and all property obtained by the defendant from the late Dr. Azael Burlando. Such goods had been extracted by enchantment, and under law a felon might not benefit from his crime. He then ordered the court adjourned until nine next morning, when he would pass sentence.

This sentencing aroused some speculation. The penalty for witchcraft, established in the 17th Century and unchanged since that time, was death by fire. On the other hand, the Republic of Tinieblas had abolished the death penalty by constitutional amendment in 1912. Would judge Cedra cite Mituco's quasi-independent status and order Rebeca burned? Or would he impose some lesser penalty not mentioned in the statute? Discussion of this problem waxed virulent in the Café Progreso, where the lists were drawn between those who liked to consider Mituco the most advanced and civilized area of the republic and those who, masking their excitement behind an outraged moral sense, longed privately to witness so unique a public entertainment as a burning at the stake. And in every other corner of the island people were wondering about the sentence, or commenting on the verdict, or rehashing the highlights of the trial. In fact, the only person on Mituco whose mind was not totally occupied by Rebeca Fuertes, her trial, or her forthcoming sentence was Rebeca herself.

Rebeca neither wondered about her punishment, nor minded that she stood condemned and destitute, nor suffered that her child was branded as the devil's spawn. She had descended into apathy deeper than ever she had known during the opium'd twilights in the brothel at Tsinan. She lay wide-eyed yet unthinking, while her cell filled up with darkness, while, below her window, the board streets of Mituco emptied, while the human noises of the town dissolved into mosquito hum and cricket chirp. And it seemed that little León had sucked this same dullness from her breast, for he lay awake yet silent beside her and neither wailed nor whimpered as his feeding hours passed. Then, at midnight, the spirit of Rosalba Fuertes entered Rebeca's cell.

Rosalba called to her great-granddaughter in the same resolute tones with which she bad propositioned General Isidro Bodega, and told her to rouse herself. And when Rebeca hesitated, Rosalba told how she had journeyed all the way to Ciudad Tinieblas in a vain effort to conceive a President of the Republic. Was Rebeca so slothful and despairing as not to do as much to save a future president already born? And so Rebeca rose and found the door to her cell standing open and her guard sleeping as though dead beside the threshold, and she took up her son León and carried him out into the passageway and let her great-grandmother's spirit lead her down the darkened stairways of the *Alcaldía* out into the Plaza Cortada. And there Rebeca waited, still dazed, until the spirit of her grandmother, Raquel Fuertes, appeared before her and showed her the constable sleeping as though dead beside the statue of Javier Cortada. And when Rebeca hesitated, Raquel Fuertes told how she had fought her way into the bed of the tyrant General Epifanio Mojón in hope of conceiving a President of the Republic, and asked how Rebeca, with a future president already in her arms, could waver undecided. And so Rebeca let the spirit of her grandmother lead her across the square and down the board street to the quay where, eighteen years before, she had taken the lighter out to S.S. *Pluto*. And Rebeca waited at the head of the quay until the spirit of her mother, Rosenda Fuertes, appeared to her and pointed out a sloop warped at the far end of the quay with its sails flapping in the offshore breeze. And when Rebeca hesitated, Rosenda scolded her and told how she had journeyed all through the violent summer of 1883, from Ciudad Tinieblas to La Merced, from La Merced across Salinas Province to Otán, and how she had given up her virginity to General Feliciano Luna on a hard bench in the mayor's office, all in unrealized hope of conceiving a President of the Republic, and now Rebeca, ungrateful as always, had conceived and born and suckled a future president, the greatest of all the Presidents of Tinieblas, yet stood like an idiot not knowing what to do. And so Rebeca let her mother's spirit lead her out along the quay to where the sloop was waiting. And its crew was General Feliciano Luna and General Epifanio Mojón and General Isidro Bodega. And there Rebeca hesitated for the final time, asking if they could take her other children and her maid,[26] who had gone over to Mituco de Tierra Firme when the court bailiffs evicted them from Don Patricio's mansion. But the three generals said there wasn't time, and when Rebeca stepped over the gunwale with León in her arms, General Isidro Bodega slipped the bow line and General Epifanio Mojón hauled at the mainsheet and General Feliciano Luna swung the tiller, and the sails filled with a sound like cannon fire, and the sloop swept out into the bay. And when the sun came up five hours later over Ciudad Tinieblas, Rebeca Fuertes was standing on the sea wall near the public market with her baby in her arms.

6. The Reservation

IN APRIL-MAY, 1898, Tinieblas and the United States collaborated (as victim and thug, respectively) in a particularly blatant extortion caper.[27] Tinieblas was exhausted by ten years of civil war and five more of uncivil corruption. The U.S. was the very picture of robust cupidity. For years Captain Mahan had been nattering the American people about sea power and the joys of owning bases; within months Mr. Kipling would exhort them to "Take up the White Man's burden"; the *Maine* was nestled on the bottom of Havana harbor; William Randolph Hearst was supplying war with Spain. At this uneasy juncture Wilhelm II, Emperor of the Germans, decided to annex the Republic of Tinieblas for debt.

At once the undersea cables were athrob with invocations of the Monroe Doctrine as Uncle Sam reminded Kraut and Greaser that he was bully of the Western Hemispheric beach. Cruisers steamed south from Newport and Seattle; Marines honed bayonets and oiled their yummy dumdums. But all stopped short of violence. The bald eagle paid the double eagle, exacting reimbursement from the alligator.

Dr. Ildefonso Cornudo (1852-1919, President of Tinieblas 1898) was a Spanish veterinary who immigrated to Tinieblas in the 1880s but never bothered to take up citizenship. He restored the potency of a seed bull belonging to Hildebrando Ladilla (1847-1908, President of Tinieblas 1896-97), and Ladilla appointed him Minister of Health and instructed him to steal his fee from public funds. Ladilla set a high example for his ministers: in December, 1897, he appropriated the entire treasury and fled to Lisbon. This, coming with Tinieblas a decade in arrears on its debt to Germany, led to Wilhelm's annexation bluff.

As the crisis deepened, Tinieblans who might be held responsible began bailing out of office. President Ernesto Chinche (formerly Ladilla's Vicepresident) resigned on 14th April, with the arrival of a German cruiser off the breakwater at Bastidas. Succession then passed through the cabinet like castor oil. Minister after minister received the presidential sash, took one gander at the situation, and resigned. On 22nd April, when two U.S. ships of war arrived, one at Bastidas, one at Ciudad Tinieblas, Ildefonso Cornudo, who was last in line, found himself President of the Republic.

He too would have resigned, but there was no one to accept his resignation. The Assembly was adjourned, the Supreme Court in recess. The Commandant of the Civil Guard refused to go to the Palace or admit Cornudo to the barracks. Cornudo called on the Archbishop and tried to file his resignation with the Holy Trinity. On being turned away, he offered the presidency to several passers-by. None would accept. For the final time in Tinieblan history, no one wanted to be president

That afternoon the Ambassador of the United States went unsummoned to the palace, escorted by a body of Marines. Cornudo at once offered him his resignation and was again refused. The ambassador proposed instead a trip to Washington on board the Atlantic Fleet cruiser. Assuming himself kidnapped, Cornudo left at once for Bastidas, whence he embarked on April 24th. To his unspeakable surprise, he was accorded full honors and given the captain's stateroom. Five days later the U.S. Secretary of State met him at Annapolis and showed him a treaty written in English, a language he was innocent of, and a draft on the Guaranty Trust Company for two hundred fifty thousand dollars. Cornudo's crisis of conscience lasted some ninety seconds, until the secretary explained that he need not return to Tinieblas. He signed the treaty, snatched the draft, trained to New York, and sailed to Paris, where his heirs as yet reside.

Under the terms of the Day-Cornudo Treaty (which is still in force), the United States assumed the Tinieblan debt to Germany and Tinieblas granted the United States a nine-hundred-ninety-nine-year lease on a large tract hard by the capital. On 7th May, 1898, the Tinieblan National Assembly ratified the instruments at six-inch gunpoint.

> So twice ten miles of swampy ground
> With cyclone fence were girdled round,
> And here were coastal guns to sweep the seas,
> And men-at-arms, and fearsome men-of-war,
> And men of science battling disease-
> Short-arm inspections Saturdays at four.

As this bit of parody[28] suggests, the enclave, called the Reservation, acquired as the years went by all that a Mahan might yearn for in a base: a coaling station (transformed into a tank farm when the fleet converted to oil burners); a dry dock, and a row of wet ones; a battery of shore artillery, whose twelve-inch rifles tumesced from the flank of Dewey Hill; a detachment of Marines adept at charging down to the Presidential Palace to defend the stooge of the moment from the patriotism of his countrymen; an Army camp with barracks for a battalion (later a regiment, then a brigade); a many-officed headquarters (basemented soon after World War II with an H-bomb-proof war room-communications center a hundred feet below it); a weapons range with bull's-eyes and bobbing silhouettes and dummy tanks, all suitable for boisterous blasting at with small arms, machine guns, rifle grenades, bazookas, recoilless rifles, and field pieces—, missiles from which have an uneasy way of wandering past the fence into some peasant's hut or yucca plot or of being found, still fizzing, by inquisitive small children; an airdrome, whose clipped grass hardened to concrete and whose complement of planes increased and mutated like bugs in frequent generations; a swelling cluster of screened bungalows for pallid-wived, profusely-infanted journeyman loafers imported from the States; a labor office, which recruited Tinieblans to do the actual work and set two wage scales so as not to spoil the natives; a legal office, whose code generously embraced Tinieblans caught inside the fences; a military police station, a courthouse, and a penitentiary, whose facilities were open to all, regardless of race, color, creed, or national origin, Tinieblans nonetheless receiving preference; a school system; a hospital; a cemetery; a commissary store, where U.S. citizens might purchase, duty-free, every imaginable necessity, accessory, and luxury; a porticoed and columned Reservation Club ("Dogs and Tinieblans Not Admitted") with sturdy wicker armchairs and dollar-sound mahogany tables and slow-whirring ceiling fans and yowsuhing Barbadian waiters; churches or meeting halls for Baptists, Methodists, Episcopalians, Lutherans, Calvinists, Presbyterians, Congregationalists, Quakers, Mennonites, Moravians, Nazarenes, Christian Scientists, Unitarians, Jehovah's Witnesses, Seventh-Day Adventists, Mormons, and Holy Rollers; local branches, chapters, or affiliates of the Boy Scouts, the Girl Scouts, the Cub Scouts, the Young Men's Christian Association, the Salvation Army, the Woman's Christian Temperance Union, the American Society for the Prevention of Cruelty to Animals, the American Federation of State, County and Municipal Employees, the Metal Trades Council (AFL-CIO), the United States Army Association, the Navy League, the Benevolent and Protective Order of Elks, the Ancient Order of the Mystic Shrine, the Masons, the Rosicrucians, the Knights of Columbus, the Daughters of the American Revolution, the American Legion, the Veterans of Foreign Wars, the National Rifle Association, and the Ku Klux Klan; twelve bowling alleys, eleven children's playgrounds, ten tennis courts, nine holes for golf, eight basketball courts, seven baseball diamonds, six soda fountains, five swimming pools, four movie theaters, three trapshoot ranges, two roller rinks, and a partridge in a pear tree; and in all official buildings twin sets of public excretoriums marked "U.S." and "Non-U.S." Scrub and jungle were morphed as by enchantment into lawn and asphalt. Ravines filled up, hills flattened, rivers left their beds. And such familiar landmarks as endured were rebaptized from the hagiography of U.S. history. Meanwhile the capital crept up beside this alien growth as more and more Tinieblans occupied themselves in making life less dreary for their uninvited guests. On the afternoon of her arrival from Mituco, Rebeca Fuertes joined this number.

I do not mean she joined the rum- and bum-vendors in the warren of cantinas, burdels, and impromptu assignation burrows on the Tinieblan side of Avenida Jorge Washington. Tinieblas had become an exporter of alcoholic glee and sexual euphoria, a transit zone for *Pediculus pubis,* an importer of human semen, but Rebeca did not involve herself in this sector of the national economy. She found work as a servant in the household of an American major, her excellent command of English overweighing her encumbrance with a nursing child.

It might be supposed that a woman of gentle breeding if not birth, one who had charmed the most discriminating audiences of Europe, enjoyed the affections of a German prince, and shared in the governance of a Manchu province, would make an inferior domestic chattel. Much the reverse in Rebeca's case. Her whole energy was focused now on providing for her son; work in the Reservation seemed the best way to ensure his welfare; and so for three years she became the perfect servant, much as years before she had become, for three hours on a stage in Munich, the perfect Giselle. She cooked,[21] sewed, washed, ironed, cleaned the house, made the beds, scrubbed the floors, did the market, taught the major Tinieblan history, soothed his wife when he was grumpy, helped his daughter with her homework, served his colleagues coffee at all hours, and, withal, worked such prodigies of loyalty, abnegation, and good cheer that she was looked upon by Reservation wives as something strange and marvelous, a djinn out of a bottle, say, and touted east and west around the enclave as an example to no-more-than-human servant girls. But the major could not possess so rich an ornament in his house without exciting the envy of the powerful. Not many months passed before Rebeca found herself transferred into the service of the chief of staff and promoted to the rank of housekeeper.

Brigadier General Harmon Goody occupied a mansion on the metaphorical seventh tier of Roosevelt Hill on Fort Shafter—that is, immediately below the palm-graced earthly paradise where the commanding admiral resided. Here Rebeca's room and salary were twice what the major had afforded: space for two beds and fifteen dollars monthly. General Goody, whose conversation with female servants had, hitherto, been limited to pinches, pats, and prods, liked to stop in the pantry to chat with her about China and the gay times he'd had pummeling the Boxers with the old "Can Do" 15th Infantry. Mrs. Goody deferred to Rebeca's taste in every particular and soon was incapable of choosing so much as a face towel without Rebeca's advice and consent. Rebeca had a cook, a houseboy, and a maid under her orders and exercised rather more authority than the general over the soul and body of his orderly, Sergeant Ned Cod. This thick-forearmed, hammer-headed, cleft-chinned down-easter had joined the cavalry at age sixteen to put as much firm ground as possible between himself and the Grand Banks, had soldiered in Cuba and on the Mexican border and in France, had won his stripes grenading machine gunners of the Prussian Guard and his cushy job with General Goody by showing great powers of persuasion over the girls of Reims and Mézlères, but now he found himself more off his balance than on any swell-tossed Kennebunkport trawler. Now his disposition altered with Rebeca's smile or frown, while his health, so firm before that fever germs and mustard gas bounced off it, swung delicately with the tone of Rebeca's voice. He robbed time from his duties to help Rebeca inventory sheets and china, to fetch food parcels from the commissary, to polish silver; he spent his leisure carving toys for León, telling him war stories, carrying him on his back—all this without one leer in Rebeca's direction, much less a proposition, for he had made his stolid mind up long ago that he would never fall in love with a foreign woman and hence had no idea of the nature of his bondage. Not since the days of Eleanor of Aquitaine was female so respectfully attended, and Rebeca had a day off every week and time to spend with León in the evenings and, for him, safe home and wholesome food, clean air to romp in and a surrogate father who would never shout at him or claim conjugal rights.[30] And, more, she had the promise that when General Goody would receive his second star and relieve the admiral, she and her son would rise up with him to Commander's House, the highest point in all the Reservation, whence, in due time, to be assumed in flesh and bone into the heaven of the U.S.A.

Some time after Rebeca was installed in the Reservation, she had tried discreetly to make contact with her former maid, with Nicolas and León's twin sister, only to learn that they had disappeared from the Mituco region. Now she forgot them and forgot as well the prophecies of León's future and her covenant with fate. Wandering the goods-crammed labyrinth of commissary aisles, she dreamed of gringohood like any servile peasant. She laughed as León mixed his Spanish with gleanings from Ned Cod's quick-baa'd New Englandese, and when he strutted with his wooden gun she saw him happily an officer of the same empire that occupied her country. She could gaze through the pantry window to where he played in diapers and see the incarnation of Lieutenant Pinkerton, clothed all in white, collecting broken hearts to the strains of a Puccini aria, or a trim cavalry major in gleaming boots and Sam Browne belt, jumping a hunter at the London trials while all the ladies sighed. There'd be no more wars, after all, only dress uniforms and diplomatic missions and a cozy cottage for his mother, aging so gracefully, in a clean northern town. Off below the general's spacious screened veranda, the rusting roofs of Ciudad Tinieblas seemed every day more distant and unreal, the strife of freedom each day more noisome and unnecessary. And so it fell to León to take a hand in the accomplishment of his destiny and lead them from the fleshpots of the Reservation.

It came to pass, then, that on the morning before his third birthday, while the world was still minutely organized and sprucely groomed and bounded by the fences of Fort Shafter, little León erred from its center, which was his and his mother's room in General Goody's house on Roosevelt Hill, into a grove of khaki mannequins on the parade field. These grew thickly but at even space out of the spongy ground and, rooted at shoe soles and rifle butts, stood in botanic stoicism while insects buzzed their napes and roosted on their ear lobes and while, from time to time, one or another of them, chopped at the knee by an invisible machete, rolled his eyes up under his domed campaign hat and timbered sideways to the sod. Barefoot, bagged in a pair of mud-splotched skivvies, León toddled among them, looking for Ned Cod.

He was a hundred meters off, crouched under the reviewing stand. The post afforded shade, immunity from being sent by General Goody on some fool detail or another, and, now that the spectators had risen, a bonus peek up the silk frock of Hermelinda Ladilla, daughter of the President of Tinieblas. She and her mother stood two rows above and back from where Don Heriberto, white panama clasped to the left lapel of his white linen suit, white head well bowed, white eyebrows deeply furrowed, mourned all the millions of his allies fallen in the war to end all war. His minute of silence had to be particularly reverent since Tinieblas, though formally a belligerent for as long as the United States, had sacrificed no blood or treasure. Beside him Vice-Admiral Dewey Keyle, the Reservation commandant, scarcely dipped his brow. On Ladilla's left was his Vice-President, Felipe Gusano; on Keyle's right General Goody. Behind them were

Ladilla's cabinet, Keyle's aides and staff, and a small host of faintly perspired ladies and high-collared officers. Beside them stood the twenty-two-piece band of USS *Tallahassee,* horns gleaming, nautical bell-bottoms clasped in white puttees. Before them lay the parade ground, unnaturally green after an all-night rain and heavy drenchings of bright sunlight, with four officers standing to attention in the center, their eight-inch shadows telling the eleventh hour. Beyond these were arrayed the colors (Old Glory and Keyle's pennant, not, you can be sure, our infinitely more picturesque Tinieblan emblem), borne by two Marines and guarded by two others, and the three companies—three royal-blue guidons drooping in the soggy air, five hundred forty men (less those who'd fainted) with Springfields ordered next to their right legs—of 3rd Battalion U.S. 19th Infantry.

Now, while this grand *tableau vivant* shows forth the panoply of empire, off to the left, under the thirty-foot-wide garrison flag that hangs at half-staff by the headquarters, a cannon booms. Three of the officers at center field make their about-face, strut off to their companies. The fourth, their colonel, salutes the commandant, then turns to face his troops.

"*But-tal-yuuuun . . .*"

Guidons stab up; the captains echo, "Compny!" "Compny!" "Compny!"

"*Paaaass . . . in r'view!*"

The guidons drop, then rise again as captains yell, "Right face!" Metallic, six-eight stirrings, clash of cymbals; the band takes up "Washington Post." The color guard wheels right and steps away. G Company jaunts off, and then the rest.

Admiring murmur from Admiral Keyle to General Goody; nod of acknowledgment from General Goody to Admiral Keyle. "*Magnífico!*" exclaims President Ladilla, whose election, one of the more mendacious frauds in a rich history of disappearing ballot boxes, might have been protested but for these soldiers' presence. Officers smile; some ladies clap their hands, but look: yes, over there, a small and nearly naked infant scurries from the ranks of I Company, stands for an instant in bewilderment, then, grinning happily, trots to the colors, which have already wheeled left and now are waving up toward the reviewing stand.

During war service (1941-1945), León Fuertes was commissioned

in the field by General Alphonse Juin and decorated for valor by the
French Republic. Later, while head of the Tinieblan state, he was
hailed with cannon at some twelve or fourteen foreign ceremonies.
His first martial honor came, however, on 11th November, 1920,
when, while marching beside the colors at the head of a United States
review, he took the salutes of an American admiral, a Tinieblan president, and numerous other officers and officials.

   The honor had not been granted formally. That he was out of uniform and under age was universally remarked. In all, his participation lent the day an air of levity which, however welcome to some
spectators and opportune for him—in the resulting uproar Sergeant
Cod managed to spirit him back home—was not appreciated by Admiral Keyle. In fact, as soon as the Yankee proconsul had gained the
relative privacy of General Goody's house, where he was taking
lunch, he gave way to a fit of rage nearly equal in severity to the
apoplexy that killed him fifteen months later when the United States
government agreed (at the Washington Conference, 21st November,
1921-6th February, 1922) not to build any capital ships for ten years.
The battalion commander and the captain of the *Tallahassee* com-
miserated. General Goody, who was so taken with young León and
his mother that he planned to limit his reprisals to a mighty chewing-
out of poor Ned Cod, feigned outrage and, of course, gave no indi-
cation that he was harboring the offender in his home. But when
Keyle railed in a fine quarterdeck bellow about the "filthy little hea-
then nigger whore's melt" who'd botched up his parade, all chance
was lost for a calm ending to the incident. Out in the pantry Rebeca
Fuertes experienced what Saint Paul called "conversion" and Dr. I.
P. Pavlov the "ultra-paradoxical phase." In the space of a few seconds and without resort to conscious thought, all her beliefs about
the United States of America were revised, all her responses reversed.
Great plans were scrapped. Dreams were folded down like the tents
of a carnival raided by the vice squad. And action was initiated to express these mental transformations. Scarcely had the admiral crossed
the *t* in "whore's melt" when Rebeca swept into the living room,
threw a dish towel in his face, and cursed him and the whole race of
gringos so forthrightly (in English, Spanish, French, and Mandarin)
that no man in the room could speak coherently for a full five minutes. Then she went to her room to pack.

Ned Cod chose this moment to realize that he loved her. He went to her all trembling, hung by the door[31] awhile, and finally, as she was stuffing clothing into paper bags, gasped out his wish to marry her, adopt her son, and—greatest proof of love he could advance—make them both U.S. citizens. His last phrase made her remember insults she hadn't used on the admiral, and her rejection drained all the confidence he'd gathered in a hardy youth and twenty-three rough years of army service. He never fully raised his head again and grew so listless, slovenly, and disrespectful that before the year was out he had been broken back to private and booted down the hill to a line outfit. Ned Cod gave León Fuertes his first model of manhood (one which stood him in good stead, I think, two decades later on the crests of Belvedere) and his swing-armed upright bear's walk (a learned trait learned in turn by León's second son), but Rebeca Fuertes ruined him as surely as she did every other man who got too close to her.

Rebeca never set foot in the Reservation after that day, nor looked across the fence except by accident. She never again spoke or read a word of the English language, or acknowledged understanding of it, or knowingly bought or used a product made in the U.S.A. Nor did these sentiments die with her death. León was her favorite, of course, the only child she truly loved, while José, perhaps because of his deformity, received a certain measure of her affection, more, surely, than she ever gave to Nicolas. But in one respect she preferred her first-born, whose career as a Sandino soldier-executioner she learned of only in the next world. When I interviewed her in research for this history, hardly a session passed without her stating firmly that of her three sons, only Nicolas knew bow to deal with gringos.

7. The Urchinhood of León Fuertes[32]

BY CHRISTMAS, 1920, Rebeca Fuertes was established in free union with one Florencio Merluza, off-and-on welder at the Reservation docks, who bad been circling her for years, floating in wait for her in shallow pools of lamplight on her evenings off, gaping hungrily week after week, almost getting his gills pinned back on one occasion by Ned Cod. Merluza was a short, thick, slurvoiced man with skin the hue and texture of a chestnut. His heavy-lidded eyes

and lazy movements made him look drugged, though in fact he neither smoked *canyac* nor even drank but was quite simply so afflicted
with the Latin plight *machismo* that all his energy of mind and body
went to the service of his reproductive organs. He earned fair money
when he worked, and when he didn't, sold contraband cigarettes
cantina to cantina, and on this income he maintained three common-
law wives and near a dozen children, three households where bed,
board, respect, and pliant flesh at all times awaited his unannounced
arrival. He was, besides, ever alert to targets of opportunity: cantina
barmaids unattended on the nights before an Army payday, lurable
servant girls, the odd Reservation wife disposed to play a matinee
while her husband worked, such whores as might take busman's holidays, and on one marvelous occasion, an elegant young matron of
the best breeding in Tinieblas who'd warned her husband if he
walked his mistress out in public one more time she'd horn him[33]
with the lewdest drifter in the city. It was a rare moment when sub-
stantive sensation crept above Merluza's pelvis, much less to his
brain, but then he'd ponder vainly to comprehend the mystery[34] of
his letch for Rebeca, the city being gorged with younger, better-look-
ing, and more willing women. Still, not a Thursday evening passed
without his putting himself in her path one way or another, and when
she and León left the Reservation and sought refuge in a bare room
above a billiard parlor in an obscure alley off Plaza Bolívar, his dong
led him to her like a dowsing rod. All was made clear to him the
morning she allowed him to possess her (in a bowed fiber hammock
slung across a corner of the room). When Rebeca sloughed her dress
to the splintered floorboards, he felt the insects tattooed on her body
swarming in his blood and guessed he'd smelled them on her years
before when he first saw her. Within the hour (and until he died) she
had him mooning like a cunt-struck adolescent. He got his job back,
peddled his contraband more eagerly than ever, left his three wives,
forgot all other women, installed Rebeca and León in two rooms beside the dockyard fence in the La Cuenca quarter, kept them as best
he could, and hammocked with such frequency and energy that inside the year Rebeca bore his son.

Perhaps because this son, José,[35] was born club-footed and dark-
skinned, Merluza never cared much for him. He beamed paternal affection on young León and took an interest in his education to the

extent of including him on his commercial forays through the nether regions of the capital. These usually began late in the afternoon with visits to certain barmaids who could be counted on to wheedle cigarettes from their commissary-carded gringo lovers: to Mariluz for Luckies, to Marisol for Camels, to Mariquita for Old Golds and Chesterfields, to Maribel for Raleighs, to Mari Carmen, Mari Pilar, Mari Lourdes, since some might be out of stock, or have locked doors and squeaking bedsprings. Merluza bought at five centavos the pack—all profit to the girls—and sold at ten out of a. paper sack on street corners, at stand-up eateries along Bolivar Avenue, in cantinas and poolrooms, beside hag-tended pans of lard-fried *patacones* and braziers where men broiled goat cutlets and chunks of skewered beef, in the vestibules of walk-up three-whore brothels, along the row of lottery vendors who parked their trays of hope before the statue of the Liberator in the center of Bolivar Plaza, outside the entrance of Hotel Excelsior, and, when the doormen weren't looking, in the nightclubs down the block. León made rounds with him and learned the business, took part, in fact, contributed to its growth, for Merluza found that profits could be upped by bribing those nightclub doormen to let León sell inside. Let a whore fondle him or a soused swabby muss his hair, and León could move two packs at twenty-five centavos each and pick up a tip besides. So from the age of five or thereabouts León was trudging through the Black Jack (which showed a framed oil portrait of old Pershing over the bar and catered to the army), the Happy Time (a navy haunt), the Jacaranda, and the Gay Paree, inching his barefoot way among our Prohibition-parched Good Neighbors and the "hostesses" who helped them spend their pay, while horns blared dixieland and rumbas, and striptease dancers flounced their feathered merkins.

None of this sat well with Rebeca, but Rebeca was not herself. At first there were belt-thrashings and tongue-lashings for León and his stepfather when they came home, but soon she lost energy for this. Rebeca was born an artist, not a breeder; each pregnancy disturbed her more severely, and from the moment she conceived my uncle Pepe she fell into a depression, which deepened through a decade. She had hallucinations and obsessions. The ghost of Dr. Azael Burlando lurked in the plumbing of the tenement's one toilet, and for years she never ventured to that corner of the hall but used a chamber pot, that León had to empty. She dreamed her skin turned black like Señora Perfecta's and after that would not go in the sun or let one ray glance on her through the window. She grew fat and petulant, given to tears and screaming. She would lie fitfully for weeks on end, neither awake nor sleeping. And her memory became so vagrant that León, who'd got the gift of lying from his father, could claim, on creeping in two hours after midnight, he'd been in bed all evening and had merely slipped out now to use the toilet. Rebeca kept the pale ghost of a grip on him by whining out the catalog of sacrifices she'd made. He did the market and helped care for his brother. But mostly he was on his own, living in the streets and rounding with Merluza, wise and wary, sharp and tough, a veteran of the struggle for existence and an expert in the sociology of squalor and the economics of despair.

Which was just as well, for Merluza too went in decline, beginning with his union with Rebeca. First of all, he became a figure of contempt among his co-workers and nightgown *compadres* the instant that Rebeca transformed him, without the benefit of clergy or of law, into a husband. He husbanded his pay check and husbanded his seed and in return was nagged and scolded mercilessly. Worse, once she turned pregnant, Rebeca never let him in her bed again and made no bones at telling half the quarter of his exile. And when, after some months, he went in fear and trembling to seek release and self-esteem in the place where hitherto he'd always found them, that well was dried up too: he was impotent as an ox. He continued to fawn on Rebeca in hope she would relent, and in the meanwhile took to drink. Before long he had lost his Reservation job and grown quite useless as a peddler. Then León led him around or, like as not, would park him in a cheap *bodega*, a half-inchado piece clutched in his quivering hand, and go to buy the goods and vend them on his own. (Merluza lingered in a semistupor until the night of 29th-30th November, 1930, when, in the course of disturbances attendant on Alejandro Sancudo's first leap onto the Tinieblan body politic, one of the coffee peons whom Sancudo had infiltrated into the capital swung his machete at a stevedore (who favored the constitutional President) and, missing, split poor Merluza's head like a dry melon.) By age nine León was head of the household and sole source of its support.

I shall now show some slides procured at great trouble from diverse sources:[36]

The first offers a barman's view of the Happy Time cabaret on a payday evening in 1927. In the background (hazed by smoke and/or imperfect depth of focus), three jazzmen formed of melting Hershey bars aim clarinet, cornet, and trombone at the ceiling while, below them, a mob mills on the dance floor. Our interest is, of course, the foreground group of three: a U.S. Navy chief, a B-girl, and young León. You will observe that despite his ragged shirt and grimy neck, my father makes an excellent impression. His curly hair and clear complexion are aesthetically appealing, while at nine he already shows the broad forehead, firm jaw, and wide-set eyes which, three decades later, proclaimed sincerity, integrity, and trust from all his public portraits. He holds up a pack of Camels, which the chief declines, and is just managing, in a most manly way, to hide his disappointment. The chief, whose weather-beaten face is youthed by whiskey, appreciates this stoicism, smiles as he shakes his head, and shoves a nickel toward him along the bar. Meanwhile, on the right, the girl, a beige mestiza whose flimsy, cheap red satin flapper shift suits her spare body, takes advantage of the diversion to pluck a dollar off the mound of bills stacked on the bar before our nautical booby.

This companion shot, next, shows the very scene again, except that now the girl has tucked her loot away and gropes her hand down in the sailor's crotch. He, understandably, has turned to face her. And León, his noble stare dissolved in twinkles, scoops a buck for himself while winking at the camera.

Now, here we have the port of Ciudad Tinieblas on a dry-season day (the sky is cloudless) sometime before 29th November, 1930 (the north side of the Presidential Palace, just visible there at the extreme left, is not yet pockmarked from Sancudo's coup d'état), and after 7th August, 1929 (when that Costaguanan schooner—a close look at her stern will show the legend "LOLA, MICHAGRANDE"—anchored at middle distance was impounded by Tinieblas on a smuggling charge). The grey cranes on the right belong to the U.S. Naval Dockyard in the Reservation. The destroyer beneath them, her stern (and hence her flag) obscured by the pier shed, is (if *Jane's* silhouettes can be trusted) French, perhaps on a good-will visit. The U.S.-flag freighter warped against Tinieblas's one cluttered pier is not, as you undoubtedly assume, a banana boat—Tinieblan bananas were (and still are) shipped from

Bastidas, on the Caribbean—but probably on charter to the Copperhead Mine Company: she will have debarked a cargo of mixed goods and be preparing to sail empty to Puerto Ospino in Otán Province, there to load ore. The yellow blur in the foreground is the bent-back tree of the child's wagon in which León Fuertes pulled his crippled younger half brother, Pepe (our photographer), around the town. And the white blur just below and to the right of the crosstree on *Lola's* mainmast, there, is León himself, bare as a plucked gamecock. He has swum out to the deserted vessel, climbed her anchor chain and then her spar, and dived off. Now he plummets like Icarus down toward the oil-streaked water, while Pepe and those three less venturesome ragamuffins grouped beside the little pile of León's clothes look on in (we may assume) respect and envy.

Next, yes, is an unnamed alley behind the Plaza Cervantes filmed through the bleary lenses of Florencio Merluza two or three hours after midnight in November, 1930. The scene is lit from the back doorway of a cantina called Viva Mi Desgracia, through which Merluza has recently staggered, led by León, after a night spent, respectively, in guzzling and hard work. León, as you observe, lies in a scatter of garbage in the posture of the Dying Gaul. He has just regained consciousness and is trying (fortunately without success) to rise. The nasty gash on his left cheek comes from a ring (we'll see it later) on the right middle finger of the thug in the left center of our picture. This specimen (note his moronic grin and his skullcap made from a woman's stocking) has pushed Merluza to the ground (hardly a problem with the load of booze he carries), has knocked young León down four times and robbed him, and now stuffs a fat fist of coins into his jeans while grinding an unsold pack of cigarettes with his right instep. The dark mass at the top center of the picture is part of the tower of the Cathedral of Ciudad Tinieblas, a fine example of Spanish Colonial church architecture, completed in 1664 and extensively restored in the 1880s.

Now, this next shot may at first glance seem somewhat gross, but I include it in the belief that scholars will not be so distracted by its lewder elements as to miss the deep insight it offers into the character of León Fuertes. It shows a room in one of the cut-rate stews I mentioned earlier and was, in fact, taken by an employee who came up the stairs with an impatient customer, noticed the door ajar, assumed the premises vacant, and stuck in her head. The gentleman there supine on the bed may be identified by his moronic grin (equally brainless in lust as in cupidity) and by his skullcap made from a woman's stocking. Close examination of his right hand, drooped almost to the floor, will reveal a cobra ring, the tail and body writhed about his middle finger, the hooded head raised to make the knuckle-duster. I suggest that you tear your eyes away from the naked, kneeling girl who is performing on him what is called an "unnatural act" and direct them to the lower foreground, where León Fuertes is also kneeling. The golf ball-sized object which he has tweezed up from the small box near his knee and now so carefully inserts into the discarded sneaker of our ecstatic fellatee is a plump Tinieblan scorpion, whose legs (but not whose sting) have been snipped off. From the condition of the star-shaped scar on León's left check we can date this incident as having taken place some four or five months after that depicted in the previous slide. Revenge is a dish that is best eaten cold.

Next, a final slide. No grossness here; this is a rite of passage. The nude youth candidly captured in the manly act is León Fuertes. The nude girl whose slim legs twine his waist and who stares at us over what seems to be his left but is, in fact, his right shoulder is Maribel Canoa, one of his cigarette sources and our photographer—she snapped the shot in the tilted mirror above her chiffonier. The newspaper on the table beneath the open window beside the bed is the *Correo Matinal* for 2nd May, 1931 (the date can be mirror-read with a good glass); it establishes León's age at a precocious thirteen years, five months, and twenty days. The blood-red sun there in the upper left-hand corner of the window is about to fall fizzing into the Pacific, establishing the time at 2354 hours, GMT. Maribel met León about ten days before through a fellow barmaid at the Cantina Trópico. Though only seventeen herself, she was wise enough to recognize him as more of a man than anyone else she knew. He maintained a strictly professional attitude in their business dealings, but when, on the afternoon of the incident depicted in the slide, she mentioned that the sergeant who was paying her rent that spring was on guard duty, and offered to throw in a kiss with the four packages of Lucky Strike she had for sale, León required no further encouragement.

Now, if you can bear the scene a little longer, I am going to ask you to clamp your mind's eye shut, to tune your mind's ear to the jolly

squeak of bedsprings, to nuzzle your mind's nose into the hollow of
Maribel's neck, to accustom your mind's back and waist to the eager
clutch of young and ardent flesh, to dip your mind's member in the
warm pouring of requited love, and so to know in your mind's gonads the joys of manhood, achieved at age thirteen and at another
man's expense. Have you got it? Another moment? Very well: the
sun won't set, the girl won't age, the ardor will not cool until I flip
the switch. All right, folks? Thank you, folks. Lights, please.

8. Learning[37]

THE DECISIVE MOMENT[38] in my father León Fuertes' life came
on the starstreaked early morning of his fourteenth birthday, when
Dr. Escolástico Grillo became his mentor. León had then already
formed the best part of a world view. He had decided, for example
(he would have said he *knew*), that life is a serious business—just to
stay in it asked his constant vigilance and effort; that despite the
risks, it was worth staying in—the payoffs were so tasty; and that
success in it was much superior to failure[39]—nobody soothed him
when he failed. On the other hand, he was a virtual illiterate, a street
beast whose horizon reached no farther than the gutter, a night-
prowling, tart-doweling petty hustler, addicted to tobacco and
afflicted with the clap, with, to the common view, no higher
prospects in this life than crime and vice. Dr. Grillo divined potential
in him, took him in hand, and led him to that discipline of mind and
formal culture essential to fulfillment of his destiny.

Escolástico Grillo was the most learned man who ever lived in
Tinieblas. His doctorate was in philology from Salamanca, but it in no
way fixed the limits of his lore. A member of the same large and
wealthy Grillo family which gave Tinieblas one president and countless unsuccessful candidates, he renounced the family occupations of
commerce, law, and politics and gave himself to study. He mapped
and crossed field after field, he mastered subject after subject, until he
thought no more of fields or subjects, only of knowledge. He produced
nothing. "I am a drone," he proclaimed proudly to his brother Ernesto
when the latter, who was Minister of Justice under Heriberto Ladilla,

asked him to do an essay for the centennial volume put out in 1921.
"A drone does not produce; he fertilizes." Accordingly, Dr. Grillo
wrote to Einstein and Ortega, to Jung and Schweitzer, to Toynbee and
Karl Barth, parceling off now this insight, now that line of thought,
and his remarks, had they been taken seriously, would have embarked
these gentlemen on important work or saved them years of misdirected
research. But the idea of a selfless scholar, one willing to be published
by others, is evidently so foreign to our age that minds that could grasp
curved space or contemplate a historical Jesus could not see the au-
thenticity of Dr. Grillo. At first he felt some pain at never being answered, at never seeing his comments reflected in his correspondents'
work. Before long, though, neglect ceased to distress him. He continued to write whenever he had something cogent to convey ("Dear Dr.
Whitehead: I think that you and Mr. Russell ought to consider . . ."),
rather as meticulous and pious Hebrews set an extra place at their
Passover for the prophet Elijah. But no one even nibbled. Dr. Grillo
never fertilized another mind until he met my father.

Around the turn of the century, Dr. Grillo inherited a twelve-room
house in the Calle Danton del Valle and a good income. He sold all
the furniture except a bed, the dining table, and its fourteen chairs.
Then he bought similar tables for the other rooms and had the walls
shelved floor to ceiling. The shelves filled up with books, the tables
with his notes. He had an illiterate mestiza to sweep the floors, cook
rice, and do his laundry. For about twenty years he kept an illiterate
indian woman, whom he visited three nights a week at midnight.
One night he knocked and got no answer, went home, slept soundly,
and never felt a sexual urge[40] again. He saw his mother for an hour
every Sunday. Sometimes he ran into a brother or a stray niece or
cousin. That was the total of his contact with the human species. His
only true communication was with himself.

Dr. Grillo rose each day at six, took coffee, worked till noon, ate and
siesta'd, rose and worked till six, ate and worked till close to midnight.
Work meant reading and note-taking; or sitting in thought, his long,
transparent fingers pressed against closed eyelids, his elbows wading in
his notes, or wandering from room to room, from shelf to shelf, from
worktable to worktable, letting past or projected studies play in the
front of his mind while, in the back, his current thoughts combined
and recombined in varying order. Sometimes he'd turn up a decaying

sheet of paper, scan it, and smile bow clever and absurd he'd been to glimpse an insight which now, after thirty years' more reading, he knew had been captured and tamed long centuries before by other men on distant continents. Sometimes a thought would seize his interest, and he'd sit down and work a month or two there at that table. He always had a line of study going; his mind was always open to divergent possibilities. October torrents beat upon his roof and splashed the tiles below his open windows; dry-season breezes rearranged his notes and turned the vellum pages of his dictionaries. On the morning of 6th September, 1905, as he was trying to decide what Dante meant by *"sacra fame" (Purgatory,* XXII: 40), U.S. Marines entered the city to depose President Amado del Busto and, getting some sniper fire from del Busto's brother, who lived next door, sent a trigger-happy hail of rifle bullets through the doctor's window, past his head, and on into the ceiling. Dr. Grillo pushed his notes away and considered for a moment the relative expediency of continuing his work versus taking shelter beneath the table. But the philological problem so insisted itself that, in a matter of seconds, he lost interest in the fusillade outside, forgot the danger to his person, composed his notes, and wrote: "Surely Dante could not deem the hunger for gold sacred. Perhaps he used 'sacra' here as we so often use 'sagrado' and the French their 'sacre,' ironically, so that it makes a synonym for 'damned.' That was as close as he ever came to letting his work be interrupted by current events.

Although he lived almost entirely in his mind, Dr. Grillo conciliated his body with a two-kilometer walk each night before he went to bed. Like Kant's through Königsberg, his itinerary never varied. In the three decades that he made these walks, however, some items changed. He aged, for one thing. One of his favorite streets became a slum. A world depression reached Tinieblas, putting men out of work and into crime. Just after midnight, then, on 12th November, 1931, as he was striding toward Bolivar Plaza in his white linen suit (yellowed at the lapels and with jacket pockets stuffed with notes), Panama hat (brim turned down all the way around), and patent leather shoes (worn sockless in a losing fight against toe fungus), directing with his right hand an imaginary chamber orchestra in a rehearsal of a Vivaldi flute concerto and tugging with his left now at his moustache, now at his white beard, two hoodlums dragged him to an alley, knocked him senseless with a piece of pipe, and stole the two inchados seventeen centavos he had on him. He came to forty minutes later face up in the dirt and since it was a clear night with the heavens bulged with stars and meteors, was at once reminded of a problem in astrophysics he had been pondering some years before and had abandoned still unsettled. Now, amazingly, the solution[41] seemed almost within his grasp, and as the night was warm, his head unbloodied if a little sore, and his position not uncomfortable, he lay there revolving equations in his mind. He was still there two hours later when León Fuertes pranced into the alley en route to the back window of a girl he knew.

"Time to go home, grandfather," said León, who was willing to postpone pleasure for the reward he could expect for getting this upper-class drunk to bed. He bent to grab an arm.

"I've got it!" Dr. Grillo wrenched his arm away.

"I've got it too; no matter. The whores say if you give it to a virgin it'll go away." He bent for the other arm.

"No." Dr. Grillo shook his head absently. "I'll have to work it out on paper. "

"Good for you, if you can do it. But come on. You can't sleep here. Someone'll rob you."

"Someone already has," said Dr. Grillo, getting to his feet, and here the course of history and heaven knows how many lives, my own included, hung in the balance, for León was not so philanthropic as to assist the penniless, nor Dr. Grillo so insightful as to discover León's worth without the help of science. But Dr. Grillo didn't have his balance and, seeking it, placed a thin palm on León's head, thereby reactivating an interest in the science of phrenology, which had absorbed him for the best part of the year 1908. Amazing! Here was a mirror wherein shone all Spurzheim's theories of the signs of genius!

"Quit groping my head, old fag!"

"Be still, young fool!" It was one thing for Dr. Grillo when Max Planck ignored his commentaries, another to be insulted by a guttersnipe, and since the doctor rarely spoke to anyone except himself, even more rarely used the imperative mode, and hadn't raised his voice in forty years, his tone carried authority. León stood still while Dr. Grillo palped his cranium, then while the doctor stepped back to regard him, while both were, in their turn, regarded by the stars.

"Have you parents?"

"My mother."

"Is she at home?"

"You think she's some kind of streetwalker?"

"At present I am not thinking. I am ascertaining points of fact. Is she at home?"

León nodded.

"Are you ambitious? That is, do you want to improve yourself?"

"I want more."

"More of what?"

"More."

It was Dr. Grillo's turn to nod "Take me to your mother."

When my grandmother Rebeca Fuertes heard the door snap shut behind León and Dr. Grillo, she woke not just from sleep but from her decade-long depressive trance. For the first time in ten years she felt a pressure in her bladder without fearing the malevolence of Dr. Azael Burlando's ghost and gazed out at the heavens without fearing that the dawn would turn her black, but since, in this life, no problem melts without another swelling up to take its place, she remembered her transgressed duties to my father's destiny and found her soul encased in the loose flab of guilt. She might, in fact, have asked León his pardon when he came in to say they had a visitor, except that in my family—and in Tinieblas generally—we don't ask pardon because we don't forgive. She did resolve to make up for her neglect, not realizing how soon her chance would come.

"What can I offer you?" She asked Dr. Escolástico Grillo when she came out from the bedroom wrapped in the same lobstered silk kimono she 'd bought in Shanghai seventeen years before.

Dr. Grillo raised himself two inches off the straight-backed wooden chair and hung there until Rebeca had sat down opposite him across the oilclothed wooden table. During the interview that followed he continued to furl and unfurl his pliant white sombrero while León leaned against the sink, examining the new person his mother had become.

"Your son," said Dr. Grillo.

"I suppose you mean to pay me ten gold sovereigns? Or has the price gone down?"

Dr. Grillo sighed. "It is obvious, señora . . ."

"Senorita. Señorita Rebeca Fuertes."

"It is obvious, señorita, that you misconstrue my aims. I do not care to buy your son, even if that were possible."

"I don't know, señor . . ."

"Doctor. Doctor Escolástico Grillo. At your orders," he added, already exhausted by so much conversation.

"Doctor, then. I don't know what world you live in . . ."

"I live as far as possible in the world of ideal forms."

"That explains it. In this world"—Rebeca's glance took in the squalid room, the cracks between the warped boards of the walls, the damp wash drooping from a wire strung across a corner, the squad of glossy roaches mustered beneath the stove in the oil lamp's penumbra—"people are bought and sold each day."

"I have studied sociology. It does not particularly interest me at present. A little while ago I had occasion—accidental, may I add, to make a very cursory examination of your son's cranium. I found configurations that, according to the science of phrenology, show strength of concentration and diverse other talents. I should like to conduct experiments to substantiate or refute these indications. Since this requires a controlled environment, I will give him board and lodging. I will pay him five inchados weekly for his time. Should my experiments tend to substantiate the indications . . ."

"They will."

". . . then I might undertake to educate him."

"You are a teacher?"

"I have never taught anyone except myself. On the other hand, I am the most learned man on this continent. I would continue to give board and lodging. I would pay nothing, but neither would I charge a fee. All this, of course, is contingent upon the results of the experiments and your son's complete cooperation. I think he has the makings of a scholar."

"He is going to be President of the Republic."

"I shall not be able to teach him how to lie."

"He knows already. León, do you accept?"

León fished up a pack of Camels, shook one out, lit up, blew smoke, and nodded slowly. "Put Pepe to work. Or go yourself. I need a vacation."

My father's "vacation" lasted four years, eleven months, and seven days. It was a term of fierce and unremitting mental effort, but first to last and, later on, in retrospect, he saw it as a holiday: not simply as a furlough from the struggle for existence but as a time when he owed service only to his talents. When he arrived at Dr. Grillo's house, he got a washtub full of water and some soap. Later he got a medical examination and the first treatment of an irrigation cure for gonorrhea. He got a meal, a hammock, and ten minutes of hypnosis, which established him on a diurnal schedule. The next morning he got the first in a series of tests which continued seven hours a day, seven days a week, for seven weeks, until the Feast of the Epiphany: Dr. Grillo dealt out ten playing cards face up at poker speed, then bunched and turned them and asked León to recite the order; León did so without an error rather more briskly than they had been dealt. Dr. Grillo noted the results, shuffled, and dealt out half the pack. Such tests of visual memory crescendo'd in difficulty through several days until Dr. Grillo presented León with a full-sized reproduction of the center panel of Bosch's *Garden of Earthly Delights*, permitted him to study it for three minutes, then took the work to a far corner of the room. (They were in what once bad been an upstairs sitting room, a small but well-lit room, which gave on the patio and from whose worktable Dr. Grillo had removed all former notes.) He asked León to describe it in detail; León's reply consumed two hours. He blocked out the picture like a chessboard and told off the contents of each quadrant, h8 to a1, rattling on without a pause, though Dr. Grillo began to moan "Enough!" when he was five-eighths done.

León was similarly impressive in the tests of aural memory that followed. He sang back Puccini's aria *"Che gelida manina"* (which Dr. Grillo played him twice in a Caruso disc) with perfect pitch and diction, though he confessed that while the language sounded like Castilian, he couldn't understand it. He performed other feats (which, incidentally, showed a massive gift for music), such as recording, separating, and then humming back all the orchestral voices of R. Wagner's Tristan chord, until at length, seeking a limit to his memory, Dr. Grillo read him the first chapter of the Book of Genesis in Hebrew and received, to mingled joy and terror, a faultless playback.

Using both hands, Dr. Grillo poured out a dram of Cardenal Mendoza brandy from the decanter that he now kept on a corner of the table. He drank it off, shook himself like a doused dog, then glanced across to León. "Can you recall," he asked in an offhand way, "the ten cards I dealt you on our first day three weeks ago?"

León shot him a grin like that captured in the barman's photo. "Old fox!"

"You can't remember!"

"Hold on. I've got them. I've just got to go get them."

And while the doctor rummaged for his first notebook, León threw his hands over his face and pressed his brow and squeezed out the first card and then the second and then all the rest, the last ones fluttering forth quite easily.

"You keep it all, then? The Bosch picture and the Puccini aria, and the passage from the Costaguanan penal code? You keep whatever goes in?"

"I guess so," said León. "I don't think about it. But I can get it if I need it."

"I think," said Dr. Grillo, groping for the decanter, "we'd best wait until tomorrow before going on."

They moved to problems in logical deduction.

"Quesada, Quemada, and Quebrada," Dr. Grillo might say, "are a physicist, a physician, and a philosopher, though not necessarily in that order. Quemada earns more than Quesada. Quesada has never heard of Quemada. The physicist earns more than the philosopher. The philosopher tried to get the physician to treat charity patients, but he refused because he was engaged in research with the physicist. Who is who?"

And León would relax and close his eyes and let the bits of information fall in place and, outwardly calm, work it out—without pencil and paper, of course, because he couldn't write—and give the answer.

When Dr. Grillo had exhausted his invention constructing problems that León never failed to solve, he passed to uttering Delphic solutions for which León then provided problems. Through all this period of trial, which saw Dr. Grillo greatly expand his intake of Cardenal Mendoza brandy and sometimes even lose his temper, León cooperated with immense good cheer, out of delight in exercising new-found talents and from an urge to please, astound, and captivate his audience. On 6th January, 1932, having determined Spurzheim's theories proved as far as any single case could prove them and León's gifts worthy of any teacher, Dr. Grillo declared the experiment complete and began formal instruction.

The curriculum of my father's education was in the main conventional. He learned to read with ease and penetration, to write with clarity and grace. He learned French and Italian, since Dr. Grillo kept a monopoly on Greek and Latin, while Rebeca vetoed any study of English. He studied chemistry and physics, mathematics through the calculus, literature from Homer to Proust, social thought from Plato to Ortega. More original was Dr. Grillo's use of history to neutralize the centrifugal pull of disciplines. He built my father's course like an orchestral score, the strings of poetry, the horns of science, the tympani of war sounding their interacting blended themes along the staves of time. This laudable approach made León see things whole, although his native urge was to simplify by separating. In recitation, in argument, and in the papers that he wrote, León forever strove to sever science from religion, math from music, polities from poetry and, generally, to unweave Dr. Grillo's integrated tapestry into its separate threads, just as, in later life, he chose to be a number of separate men, each with a separate worldview, style, career, persona, and collection of accomplices, each fully formed and native to a special habitat, each different and distinct from all the rest, rather than be a single, integrated human.

Besides this act of rebellion, which scarcely disturbed Dr. Grillo since everyone worth teaching rebels against his teachers one way or another, León disappointed Dr. Grillo in one respect: learning was not the be-all or the end-all of his life. He could lose himself in study for a time, seal himself up hermetically in books or composition. He learned voraciously. Knowledge and competence were part of the "more" he wanted. They were certainly important means to get more of that "more." But he did not revere learning for its own sake or find more than a fleeting satisfaction in it. It was the same for him later on with music, sport, and the celebrity these brought him, with comradeship in war and polities, with respectability, with wealth, with power, with the planetary system of disciples, sycophants, girl friends, and relatives (adoring wife and kids of course included) that revolved about him in firmly programmed orbits bound by his gravity and magnetism with life itself. He found no moments of fulfillment, but rather interruptions of his hunger.

Dr. Grillo included in his course of instruction one peculiar, nonacademic element: from the onset he nurtured León in techniques of auto-hypnosis and yoga so that he gained phenomenal control over his mind and body. It was not just that León soon rid himself forever of dependence on tobacco or that, three decades later, during his state visit to Canada, he could win a wager and impress a crowd by ordering a hole sawed in the ice of Lac Saint Charles, stripping to briefs, and splashing merrily for some three minutes. Wounded by mortar fragments during the assault on Pico, in the last phase of the Battle of Cassino, León stanched the flow of an internal hemorrhage by mental force alone, a trick few fakirs have in their repertoires. Similarly, he was able to block his mind into compartments and thereby keep his several lives and persons separate. More, he was proof against the seductions of appetite and attraction—or, put another way, he lacked the average fellow's grand excuse that such and such an urge was irresistible. My father never fell; rather he dived.

In recompense for all this education León taught Dr. Grillo how to love. He did so by never feeling or evincing the slightest gratitude for Dr. Grillo's labors, by treating everything that Dr. Grillo gave him—bed, board, clotting, applause, encouragement, a strong mind against which to hone his own, opportunity for extracurricular development, and, of course, a quality of personal instruction surpassing that of any school or tutor—as entirely his just due. He did his part: he studied. Dr. Grillo's was to contribute in every possible way to the education of León Fuertes. One would have inferred from León's behavior that Dr. Grillo had no other purpose on this earth. He gave no thanks when Dr. Grillo spent long nights preparing classes or large sums procuring books for him. He was never really rude, but he showed no special respect either. Dr. Grillo was a "sly dog" if he caught León in a paradox, a "bluffer" if his argument wasn't airtight, a "dirty old man" if he asked León what he'd been up to staying out all hours. And León was capable of chiding him if the doctor got distracted with some research of his own, or showed up late for class, or tired early, or took too long to read a León theme. And so Dr. Grillo was quite soon confronted with a choice: either fling León back to La Cuenca or accept León's view of their relationship. Or rather years later Dr. Grillo realized he had had a choice, for at the start he was so enthralled by León's gifts he excused León's comportment as an unwanted legacy of the slums which he'd give up in time, and then tried to write it off against his good points—the boy studied, after all—until he had gone on so long and far allowing León to set the tone of their relationship that he was past the point of choice. He had, without realizing exactly when, accepted León's clear if unspoken thesis: Escolástico Grillo's one purpose on earth was to educate León Fuertes. The only possible justification for this was love.

Having taught Dr. Grillo how to love, León permitted him to love fully by restraining as far as possible his own expressions of affection and by accepting Dr. Grillo's sacrifices without reluctance. Dr. Grillo began contributing to the maintenance of Rebeca and my uncle Pepe. By 1935 he had entirely abandoned his own investigations to concentrate on León's education. In 1936 he wrote a will leaving his library, his income, and his house to León, a will which the Grillo family later had overruled but to which León made neither objection nor excessive show of gratitude. The same year León left him and Tinieblas. Dr. Grillo went in precipitous decline, gave up his walks, read nothing but *Père Goriot*, and took to keeping his mestiza housemaid from her work with reminiscences of when León was there. His last words in this world were of León.

My father allowed Dr. Grillo a monopoly on love to go with his monopoly on Creek and Latin. Dr. Grillo responded by loving without stint. It was a pattern for many succeeding relationships.

9. Music

IN THIS and the next chapter I shall introduce two young men: two because as soon as he was furloughed from the struggle for existence, León began to take after his father—with the difference that the innumerable Azael Burlandos were patchy, cheap bamboozlements flung together with a minimum of care and designed, like cars and wash machines, to fall apart after a certain time, while each León Fuertes was a finely crafted figure built to last; young men because despite their age (fourteen-eighteen) we cannot call them adolescents, what with the unappealing connotations of pustulant self-doubt which drip from that poor term. It would be fun to split my screen and bring them on together like the famous pair of scalpeled Siamese twins conceived by Dumas père, and played by Fairbanks fils: two chaps identical in physiognomy yet, since they live in different worlds, different in manner, gesture, attitude, etc. But one of the problems of a verbal-linear confection like history is that it can present only one thing at a time, so I shall show the artist first and then the athlete, trusting my examiners to remember that they co-existed.

Quite soon after he took León as a pupil, Dr. Grillo found a music master for him. This was Sofonias de Bisagra, who is remembered now for his long reign as queen mother of Tinieblan faggotdom and for his numerous successful efforts to scandalize the country. Two years before his death, for example, having won a large sum in the lottery, he staged his funeral, partly to hear Fauré's Requiem properly sung and partly to settle scores. He rehearsed a choir and the Orquesta Nacional in Fauré's work, supposedly for a concert, and meanwhile secretly arranged for von Karajan (whom he knew from his conservatory days) to bring Fischer-Dieskau and Victoria de los Angeles to Tinieblas on an appointed day. He then gave out that he had cancer and published a will leaving bequests to the Tinieblan Church and all his nephews. He summoned Padre Benjamin Lechuzo, who was notorious for dining out on the secrets of the confessional, and whispered up four hours of fabrications and exaggerations implicating all his many enemies in a miasma of sodomic vice. Then his confederate, the painter Orlando Lagarto, announced that he had given up the ghost. The three famous musicians were even then on their way to Tinieblas, well paid, of course, though no one knew it, but according to Lagarto, moved in their grief to pay a last farewell to a beloved colleague. The archbishop was quick to authorize use of the cathedral for a requiem mass. Bisagra passed the most ecstatic night of his life lying in a richly-chased, well-perforated coffin while half the town and a consistory of clerics moped about murmuring unfelt encomiums. The next morning he heard the cherished requiem performed as he had always felt it should be, to the smell of incense and the splash of crocodile tears, and at the final note sprang from his coffin to applaud.

But when Dr. Grillo sent León to him, Bisagra was a shy young man recently returned from European studies. He had a Swiss cellist wife with whom he played duets. He had a symphony-in-progress, the first movement of which had drawn encouraging harumphs from his conservatory teachers. He had a decent salary as Director of the Escuela Nacional de Musica, a house, and a good name. He had, in short, some prospect of a reasonable life. Then finkish fate surprised him with a *wunderkind*.

From the first post-siesta hour when León sat down before Bisagra's termite-nibbled Baldwin, his talent gorged Bisagra's house. It pressed against the mold-stained walls and bulged the rusty floor-to-ceiling screens and swelled into the crucifix-hung sala where Bisagra's widowed mother, all swaddled up in shawls despite the heat, worked at her needlepoint, and throbbed into the bedroom where Bisagra's wife sat fanning herself with her book, wilting like an edelweiss remorselessly transplanted to our tropics. León's talent raised a framed daguerreotype of Monseñor Jesús Llorente (in whose cabinet Bisagra's grandfather had served) off the mantel and kept it suspended in midair for several minutes. It started the pendulum of a long-unwound grandfather clock (the bulk of Frau Bisagra's dowry) swinging like a metronome, and caused a miniature reproduction of Bernini's statue of Santa Teresa de Avila to flutter its eyelids coquettishly. It set the floor tiles rippling rhythmically and made the roof beams bend and squeak. At once Bisagra craved to share this energy—for talent is, quite simply, the orderly expression of personal energy—to have it about him as much as possible, and generous León accommodated him. León allowed Bisagra to teach him piano and harmonics and, chiefly, to train his voice, all without pay; to give him classes in the history of music at hours of León's convenience; to neglect his wife, his job, even his symphony in León's favor; to covet León's company to the point of self-debasement; to dine him out, to buy him clothes, to give him a phonograph and shower him with discs; to take him to parties in the homes of the ruling class; to cluck over him like a brood *poulet* among the artists and intellectuals who met at the Café Bahia; to flit and flutter in his presence; to fawn on him in public and to plead in private for forgiveness for imaginary wrongs; to install him in the center of the universe; in other words to love—at first platonically, then to the suffocation of his manhood. And at the same time, León took pains to lavish demands upon Bisagra, to treat Bisagra harshly on occasion, to make him now and then the butt of jokes, and to withhold all but the merest signal of appreciation, so that Bisagra might enjoy the sense of sacrifice which the activity of love requires.

Not many months went by before it was sniggered round that Bisagra had become young León's bride. This scandalmongering[42] which
is normal in Tinieblas, which is, in fact, our chief art form (since the
inventive minds here are too lazy to proceed from gossip into literature), waxed prolific after Bisagra's wife ran off with a Dutch sailor.
One version held that as Bisagra had taken a husband, he wasn't much
of one to her. An alternate line went that León had seduced her (a)
with Bisagra's blessing or (b) despite his pleas, excited her to prodigies
of appetite, and then abandoned her in such a state of heat that she
snatched up the first hardy fellow who came by. Inevitably a synthesis
was produced in which León studded for both, was forced to state his
preference, and gave the palm to Sofonias—at which poor Hilde fled
in shame. These tales, instant best sellers, never went out of circulation.
Twenty-five years later, León's political opponents had no trouble
moving new editions of them, though it appears they did no damage
to his career. All versions agree, after all, that whoever were connected,
León was penetrator, and in this country (and in the rest of Latin
America too, for that matter) a *macho* is a macho so long as he pene-
trates, who, what, or how remaining, generally, inconsequential.

In actuality, however, the sexual relationship between León Fuertes
and Sofonias de Bisagra was limited to fantasy on Bisagra's part, fantasy which fueled a lot of solo fiddling but which only began to be
acted out after León left Tinieblas in 1936, and then, of course, with
surrogates. As for Hilde, neighbors do recall her heartless screech-
ings, her less than philharmonic scoldings of Bisagra for "consorting
with that incubus," her tears of jealousy, which argue that she oozed
for León too, but while I am unable to prove he never tossed her a
hump in compassion, or suaged her passion in some other fashion, I
tend to doubt it, there being metal more attractive strewn all about
our happy little land, then as now. Certainly gossip, like its refined
kid sister, literature, must tell the truth if it's to last beyond the blush
of publication, and as I've said, the tales survived a quarter of a century, far longer than those of your ordinary, talk-show-blabbing
scribbler, but literary truth comes riddled. León had the Bisagras, all
right, along with heaven knows how many others, but he had them
metaphorically, without undoing a single literal fly button.

The first attribute of León, artist's magnetism was his exceptional
good looks. I have mentioned his broad forehead and firm jaw, his

wide-set eyes which, like his mother's, were particularly brilliant. Besides this his skin was clear, his body well formed. By fifteen he had his full height, a little under five feet, nine inches, which is average in Tinieblas. He shared these basic physical characteristics with all the other Leóns, but as artist he wore them with the pampered nonchalance of an aristocrat. On close inspection, nonetheless, his face revealed the hardness of the gutter fighter, the fellow who would rather use his feet[43] than his hands. This León was chary of his smiles. When he released one, it was cold enough to be alarming in one so young, dripping with catnip for any masochists in the vicinity. In 1936 Lagarto painted him as Perseus, posing him as in Cellini's statue and using for Medusa's the head of Doña Rosa Aguijón de Alacrán, who had banned both him and León from her home. León seems altogether proper in the role of destroyer.

There was, besides, his voice, which was tenor, its range a little greater than the average, its tone clear, its pitch perfect. His voice possessed great sweetness and great power, hence the argument as to whether his tenor was "lyric" or "robust." Bisagra claims for it both qualities and is convinced that had León continued to train seriously, he would have been the tenor of his age. An adoring discoverer and master is not, of course, the model of impartial judgment, but this opinion is borne out at least in part by León's posthumous career, during which he has excelled in many of the most demanding operatic roles, proving himself equally at home in the passion of Canio's lament in *Pagliacci* and the tranquil charm of the dungeon duct in the last act of *Aida*. In any case, his was the most remarkable vocal talent ever produced in our continent, one that seemed sure to place him soon in the first rank of the world's singers, and there is no gift so universally charming as the gift of song.

In complement León devised a personality evocative of Rimbaud and Rasputin. This León took the position that he was unique and wonderful, and made the world accept him on those terms. Of afternoons he might be spotted lounging at the Café Bahia, his jacket caped over his shoulders, his cream silk shirt unbuttoned to the navel, his gaze flung languidly out at the sun-gulesed sky, sipping a glass of chicha (which doting Bisagra would ensure was always fresh and full) while men twice or more his age aimed their remarks at him and allowed him to determine by a smile or sneer if they were clever or banal. Of evenings he frequented the houses of the ruling class, with Bisagra fetching him drinks, serving him from the buffet, accompanying him at the piano when he let himself be honey'd into song. Here he provoked the most amazing reactions. People who were appalled to see Bisagra, a cultured man of thirty, one of their class, nose-led by this mongrel puppy, found themselves kowtowing too or paying León the unconscious respect of behaving like savages. Doña Beatrix Anguila de Sancudo, daughter of a Knight of the Holy Sepulcher, sister of one President of the Republic and wife of another, one of the most strait-laced women in the hemisphere, suffered León's bawdy comments with meek little smirks, while Don Plineo Hormiga, who had been to Cambridge and, styling himself a kind of tropical Lord Balfour,[44] cultivated un-Latin casualness and an immense aplomb, took a machete to the strings of his piano to forestall a musicale, planned by his wife, at which León was to be the star attraction. Later on, León might show up at one of the very nightclubs where before he'd peddled smokes, accompanied by half a dozen dissolute young bucks (Don Plineo's son Nacho, for example) and two or three of the journeyman guitar strummers who used to hang about cantinas in pre-jukebox days. While his entourage commandeered the best table and prepared to receive the assault of waiters and whores, León would mount the stage, dispatch performers to their dressing rooms, push the microphone aside, and bring up his musicians. Then he would sing *rancheros* and boleros till the dawn.

On such nights the word that Fuertes was singing at this club or that would flash through all the center of the city. Cantinas and other clubs would empty out, patrons flinging down their cash, bartenders balling their aprons into dusty comers, owners scooping out their tills and locking up, all scurrying cross the street or round the block to hear the music. Cabbies would drop their passengers and park and push inside. Men sound asleep would wake and grab their shirts and trousers. One night the driver of a tram abandoned his contraption before the Happy Time and rushed inside, and when two *guardias* came in to arrest him for obstructing traffic, León's singing so enthralled them that they forgot the charge and stayed to listen. Another night the commanding general of the Tinieblan Salvation Army, an immensely dignified Barbadian Negro named Disraeli Brathwaite, who from time to time would tour the night spots in full uniform, taking collection and preaching against Demon Rum, found himself in the Gay Paree when León started singing, and such was the effect on him that he emptied out his pockets on the bar and bought a round of drinks for all the house.

Those who knew León only in his avatar of artist maintained that he was human only when he sang. Then his cruelty[45] and conceit dissolved in music, and a great warmth spread from him, bathing every hearer in well-being. He seemed to grow while he was singing, in age as well as size, so that people who might have been his grandparents took confidence as though from a paternal blessing People laughed and wept at once, hearing pain's gaiety and joy's lament, and León would chide them gently between songs for taking it so to heart. Then he would laugh and toss his head and shout, "You think that was good? Listen to this!"

Every nightclub and theater owner in the country and many from abroad offered him engagements at the sum he liked, but he never gave formal concerts or accepted money, and he took care to make his visits in rotation so that no club was favored more than any other. He battened on applause and often sang with greatest joy and power after he'd been on stage for hours. People who heard him felt as though they were plugged into an inexhaustible dynamo, and certainly he poured out his art with boundless generosity, as though repaying some great debt. But when a session ended he shrank alarmingly, appeared wan and decrepit, drained unto death, his face twisted and hateful,[46] and once Nacho heard him snarl under his breath, "I hope that satisfies the donkeys!" It is perhaps correct that León, artist, achieved humanity and full life only while performing.

This León accorded himself all an artist's rights and obligations. He had an artist's humility, which was never displayed toward anyone around him but was reserved for great composers and performers. Even while he formed a personal style, he strove to make his voice a faithful instrument for transmitting each composer's personal vision, and he listened to Caruso's records with the respect a coyote shows for places where a wolf has raised his leg. He had an artist's warmth and generosity, the solicitude of a lover or a parent for people he was entertaining while he was entertaining them. But he had as well an artist's arrogance, a glazed irreverence for wealth, for title, for social position, even for the common humanity of a fellow being;

for everything, in fact, save first-rate talent. Once when a hostess delayed serving dinner because the President of the Republic was expected, León informed her and everyone in hearing that he was a citizen of the Republic of Music and would wait only for Mozart; then be sent Bisagra out to the kitchen for a plate of food. And in 1935, at the party Doña Blanca Cisterna de Marmol gave for the Czech tenor Soyka, who though past his prime and bothered by our climate had sung that night with reasonable credit at the Teatro Municipal, León dragged Bisagra to the piano and repeated with improvement every number on poor Soyka's program. Then, in encore, he challenged Soyka to recommend him for the Conservatoire de Paris, and the Czech, dumbfounded by such talent and such gall, smiling, disarmed, at once raped and seduced, agreed.

This, then, was the figure León Fuertes fashioned to bear his musical talent. Many believed it to be the only or the principal León. It was, in fact, only one member of a strolling company, others of whom we shall encounter as we go along.

10. Sport

DR. ESCOLÁSTICO GRILLO never played any sport himself, but he recognized the value of athletics in a young man's development. He had, besides, made an extensive study of games, concluding that they are artificial substitutes for combat and that of all games involving physical movement the most artificial, the most elaborately structured, the most removed from reality, and hence the most human, is baseball.[47] Accordingly, as soon as the term of experimental tests was finished—the dry season being well begun by then, he sent León out to the Alameda to play in the pick-up games there, hoping merely that he might learn teamwork and get some exercise and domesticate a portion of his aggressive urges. The result was the creation of an entire and distinct León, a stellar member of the troupe and a most durable performer who strutted his last hour on the stage as late as January, 1964. Then León Fuertes, forty-six years old and President of the Republic, came up as a surprise pinch hitter for the Cerveza Cortes Teutones of the Tinieblan Winter League and, with one down and men on first and second, singled to right field off Clyde Hyde (the future Cy Young Award contender of the Cubs), driving the tying run across and advancing what proved to be the winning run to third.

How different was this León from the artist! He hung around the Alameda for two weeks before he even tried to get in a game, watching the others play, chasing the ball[48] when it went foul. Then he had to wait another week until a scarcity of players gave him his chance. Picked last, sneered at by the team captain, exiled to right field and told to stay out of the way, placed ninth in the line-up[49], and studiously ignored, he served meekly for the first two and a half innings. One imagines him scuffing his street shoes in the sun-parched, stunted grass, thumping his borrowed mitt, holding his position brave- and uselessly outside the shade of the brown palms that marched along the sidewalk foul line out to the tiny, kid-propelled carrousel. Undoubtedly he watched the play while he was in the field, but when his side came to bat, perhaps his glance wandered across the street to the red-tile-roofed bungalow that he bought for his mother two decades later. Perhaps he mentally installed her in a rocker on that porch and himself in the dugout at Forbes Field, but the several Leóns were, generally, much too adept at realizing their dreams to waste a lot of time composing them. When he got his licks he stepped in calmly, neither twitched the bat nor tapped the plate, and socked the first pitch over the left fielder's head, beyond the junglegym, past the three backless granite benches near the statue of his grandfather General Feliciano Luna, and out (on two hops) into the Via Venezuela. Rounding the bases, he denied himself even the merest particle of a gloat.

From then on, at the others' urging, he was a team captain. Acknowledged the best player on the field, he displayed a humility worthy of the mature Gotama. He did not presume to set positions. He hit fourth only at his teammates' insistence. If another kid wanted to bunt, to bring the infield in or move the outfielders around, he didn't carp, though any such attempt was likely met with protest and an appeal to León to decide. No amount of adulation could swell his head, and when, late in February, a man who had, been browsing the park for several days offered him five inchados per game to play for a semi-pro team sponsored by Cigarillos Amapola, he first suggested that the fellow draft some older, more experienced kid and accepted only after much persuasion.

León had eyes so sharp that he could watch the ball and bat make contact—something he at first assumed all hitters did but which is rare even in the majors—a strong, unerring arm, speed in the field and on the baselines, quick, steady hands which made him a faultless fielder even on the unkempt, pitted diamonds where he played. He brought to baseball all the jungle cunning and ferocity of the La Cuenca alleys but masked his lust to win behind an earnest, doing-the-best-I-can grimace and allowed his talents to reveal themselves discreetly, in the context of the play. Pitchers scowled down at his unprepossessing figure from the eminence of the mound, then discovered there was no safe pitch to throw him. Batters stopped running out ground balls hit to his section of the infield, and third-base coaches learned that if he was handling a relay it was unwise to send the runner in. His peg was going to come fizzing in, fiat and heavy, smack on the catcher's mitt. The spectators—sweatsmeared, crotch-gouging loafers who sprawled in little clots about the all-but-empty grandstands of the Estadio Nacional or the Campo Hernán Ladilla, pausing betwcen hitters to screw beaded quart bottles of Cortes Beer into their cocoa-colored faces—adopted him as their favorite, predicting an illustrious career for him with Los Bravos de Boston or Los Tigres de Detroit or Los Gigantes de Nueva York. This opinion was shared by a scout employed by Los Cardenales de San Luis, who saw León at the Central American Games in 1934 and reported that he was ready for the big leagues at sixteen, that he had everything but home-run power and would develop that if he stayed in the game[50] and put on weight. Only León seemed unconvinced of León's excellence. Others made fearsome gestures upon stepping in, waved their bats menacingly, pulled their cap brims in defiance, glared at the pitcher. Others touted themselves, leaned insolently out to glove a throw, gave the ball a contemptuous little flip to the mound on making a third out. León, on the other hand, approached the plate with diffidence, as though banking on luck to put him on, eschewed autoadvertisement, and no matter what feats he performed, allowed himself no more than a shy grin or deprecative shrug—as though all his game-winning hits; all his miraculous backhanded, hit depriving grabs; all his immaculately-timed fall-away slides were merely happy accidents. Fans howled their praise; teammates engulfed him in ebullient, moist embraces; but his modesty never flagged, not even when he became a national hero.

This came on New Year's Day in 1934. The admiral commanding in the Reservation had noted that the benighted greaseballs of Tinieblas showed some interest in the U.S. National Pastime, and he deemed it in keeping with the Good Neighbor Policy to invite them over and give them a sound thrashing. He offered a silver cup to be presented to the winners of an all-star game between Tinieblas and the United States command; then he set about assembling a congregation of ringers who would insure the cup stayed in the glass case in his office. He got a pitcher transferred to him from Fort Dix, a young member of the Dodgers' regular rotation who had enlisted in the army while drunk. He knew that U.S.S. *Des Moines* had a gunnery mate who'd caught two seasons for the Phillies, so he arranged for the cruiser to make a good-will visit. He got the All-Armed Service infield shipped down to him on temporary duty from Fort Ord and Fort Devens and Norfolk and Lejeune, and he sent all the way to Subic Bay in the Philippines for a clean-up hitter, Ensign Dan Hardcock, who'd captained the Annapolis nine and who had standing offers from half the teams in the big leagues to play pro ball when his tour of duty expired. He picked the umpires with equal care: two Marine sergeants and a Navy petty officer, men of probity, well versed in baseball and endowed with twenty-twenty vision, but first and foremost patriots. Like his friend Doug MacArthur, the admiral knew "There is no substitute for victory." Meantime Tinieblas gathered up the gauntlet he had thrown. Tryouts were held and a national selection chosen, among them León Fuertes, who was placed at second base. And the First Lady of the land, Doña Eneida de Tábano, designed their uniforms: yellow flannels with purple pin stripe and toothy green alligator gamboling across the chest.

I shall forgo description of the pre-game ceremonies, the command chaplain's invocation, the admiral's speech of welcome, which extolled fraternal competition as the key to hemispheric bliss, President Juan de Austria Tábano's unintelligible remarks in what he thought was English, the playing of the two national anthems ("Star-Spangled Banner" first, of course), and the tossing out of the first ball by Marine Lieutenant Victor Steel, who had recently received the Congressional Medal of Honor in regard for the record number of Nicaraguan insurgents he'd exterminated. I shall, in fact, vault past the first seventeen-eighteenths of the game to land in the last half of the ninth inning. The Tinieblans, who had scored three times in the first inning due to U.S. overconfidence, clutched to a one-run lead. The admiral was becoming a bit testy in his pidgin small-talk with President Juan Tábano. The admiral's wife was grinning in repressed fury as Doña Eneida for the ninth time drew attention to the Tinieblan uniforms and recounted the problems of their design. The Americans in the stands were clapping for a rally. The few Tinieblans—all prominent people, present by invitation—were experiencing mingled embarrassment and fear: Tinieblas was not supposed to beat the United States in anything, certainly not baseball, and while it was legitimate for their team to make a decent showing, they were carrying things too far in menacing so earnestly to win. And the umpires were imagining how little their lives would be worth should the home team, despite all the admiral's work, end up defeated.

That the first two batters made out was entirely their own fault. Had they but left their bats on their shoulders, they would certainly have walked, no matter where the pitches went, but the fools, caught up in the excitement of the game, insisted on swinging. One dribbled meekly to the box; the other raised a flaccid pop-up to third base. That left it up to Dan Hardcock, who had so far passed a frustrating afternoon. True, he had accounted for both U.S. runs with a colossal homer which cleared not only the left-field fence but the roof of the headquarters building beyond it, yet apart from that he was all goose eggs. In the fourth inning, with two out and a man on third, he drove a shot between the pitcher's legs that damn near gelded him—a sure hit if he ever saw one—but the sour-faced runt at second base went out behind the bag into short center field, snatched the ball with his bare hand, and threw him out. Then, in the sixth, with only one out and the bases loaded, he punched a sinking curve ball toward right field, only to see the same sawed-off, chili-eating greaser launch himself up and out to spear the liner in the webbing of his glove and turn a single with two R.B.I.s into a double play. And as if that wasn't enough, the punk had made a jackass of him in the seventh. The sneaky spic had singled over the first baseman's head and making his turn had pulled up lame (or so it looked) and fallen. But when All-American Dan Hardcock took the bait and threw on in to first to pick him off, he bounced up and scooted down to second. Stung by these torments, Hardcock pawed the earth of the batter's box and snorted fire.

He took two high and tight and then, deciding that he wasn't going to get a home-run ball, slashed the next pitch up the alley in left center field. A double, maybe more, but as it came off the first hop, the left fielder got a bit of glove on it and ticked it—*coño!*—to the center fielder. Who, in his dazzlement, let it run up his arm like a pet mouse, then found it near his chin, and pegged it—the best throw of his life, he said for years—in to León. One hundred ninety pounds of Hardcock plunged down the line, but the throw was on the bag ahead of him.

Dan Hardcock had spent forty minutes that morning honing his spikes on an emory wheel and than anointing them with lime from the little threewheeled cart with which the umpires marked the foul lines. He left his feet and stabbed them at León. León put the ball on Hardcock's right ankle and held it as the spikes went in his legs and he went down, half under Hardcock, both of them on the bag. The umpire squinted closely, remembered the Alamo, the Maine, and the admiral, and hollered, "Safe!"

Play was suspended for a quarter of an hour while the call was (unsuccessfully) protested and León's wounds attended. Dr. Alonso Gusano Bosquez, who as Minister of Public Health had appointed himself team physician, at first refused to let León continue. Both his legs were badly lacerated and his left shin bone exposed in two spots. Gusano doused the cuts with denatured alcohol and decreed that León be removed to a hospital at once for stitching. León said nothing, knit his brow in meditation, then pointed to his legs. All bleeding ceased and the wounds closed up like tulip folds at sunset. Dr. Gusano rubbed his eyes with the backs of his fingers and relented, insisting, however, that León's legs be wound with gauze from knee to ankle. Then León pulled up his tattered stockings and limped to his position. A polite ripple of applause spread from the stands. The plate umpire bawled, "Batter up!" The game resumed.[51]

On the next play León Fuertes was charged with the only error of his baseball career, though considering the outcome, that scoring may be questioned. The hitter bunted down the first-base line—clearly a move called in the *yanqui* dugout to capitalize on León's injuries. The first baseman dashed in to field the ball, and León hobbled to his left to cover first. He arrived there just before the runner, took the throw, glanced toward third base, where Hardcock was sliding in, stepped on the bag, noticed the ump begin to make another swindling safe sign, *and dropped the ball,* kicking it toward the Tinieblan dugout!

Let us now watch the action in slow motion: Hardcock, who has, popped up from his slide and heard the coach's shout of "Score!" churns dreamlike down the line from third, head dropped, knees lifted. The first baseman, in an effort to recover from his follow-through and so pursue the ball, has tripped on his own feet and floats horizontally to the ground, his right arm and forefinger extended in the attitude of God the Father in Michelangelo's Sistine fresco "The Creation of Adam." And León, like Zeno's Achilles, strides toward the dugout behind the tortoise ball. Observe that he shows no sign of hurt, no limp or stumble. See how he plucks the ball with all five fingers from the lip of the dugout, lifts it, pushing back with his right foot then pivoting on his left, holds it a long instant over his right shoulder, and then wings it—his blurred arm makes one think the film is running at full speed—not to the catcher (who crouches, mask off, straddling the plate) but five yards up the third-base line. Note (from the bow-stringed tendons of his neck) that he has put a pint of mustard on the throw.

The ball bit Hardcock square in the left car. He continued running for a step or so, but he was out cold as a cucumber. He fell head forward, slithered in the dust, and ended with his nose furrowed in the foul line and his left index finger (limp as Adam's in the fresco mentioned above) three inches from home plate. The ball caromed back toward León, who picked it up and trotted to the plate. There he halted, turned, held the ball out respectfully toward the box where President Juan Tábano was standing, then bent and touched it gently to the back of Hardcocks neck.

That night, at a reception at the Presidential Palace, León Fuertes received the Order of Palmiro Inchado in the degree of Grand Cross and several ladlefuls of presidential praise. Juan de Austria Tábano was not a particularly effective polemicist—he lacked the magnetic lunacy of an Alejandro Sancudo and the cold irony of a Eudemio Lobo—but he was the finest occasional orator to occupy the Tinieblan presidency during this century. His presentation speech assembled in León's honor an all-time, all-global squad of monstercides. He spoke of Theseus and Beowulf, of dragon-whackers Siegfried and Saint George, of little Juan Belmonte, who'd confronted and destroyed so many great horned beasts, and of young David, who was himself a part-time musician and whose elegant dispatch of hulking Goliath seemed but a first draft of León's humbling of the gringo bully. León bore it like a scolded child, head bowed, face flushed, feet shuffling. Then he presented Tábano with the ball which made the final out,[52] phrasing his brief remarks so modestly one might have thought he'd spent the whole game on the bench. It was the first time the worlds of León, athlete, and León, artist, overlapped, and guests who heretofore had known him only in the latter incarnation were hard put to reconcile the two. Don Plineo Hormiga refused outright to make the connection and taking León aside, urged him to drag his scandalous twin brother to the playing fields and teach him some gentlemanly virtues. León nodded respectfully and backed away. That night León told President Juan Tábano he was unworthy of such honor, yet only four nights later he made his impudent remark and refused the same President the courtesy of waiting dinner for him. He had by then put on another role.

Small-minded frumps who had occasion to observe León Fuertes in more than one manifestation were wont to snort, "Hypocrisy!" and, exhausted by their effort, to smile complacently, believing everything explained. I myself was trapped on the flypaper of oversimplification at the unwary age of eight: Well aware that my father doted on my mother to the point of idiocy, granting her most outlandish whims even as she uttered them and spiking all the canons of good manners by virtually ignoring other women in her presence, and also cognizant (as who was not?) of his almost suicidal loyalty to his friends, I happened by his law office one noon when all the staff were out, entered his private sanctum without knocking, and surprised him in *flagrante* with the beautiful, long-limbed Irene Hormiga, wife of his old-time buddy Nacho. Years passed before I realized that what I took for an archhypocrite's double treason was the blameless pleasure of a total stranger to my mother and Don Nacho. One León Fuertes was a faithful husband and a loyal friend, a serious man, in short. Another was a casual rounder who saw the female sex as bonbons offered for his spare-time munching and who cared no more for marriage vows—his own or anybody else's—than migrant fowl do for the frontiers they sail across. The two chanced to share a body along with many other Leóns, but each was different, each had his own world, and each was true to himself.

Why did he never forge what the psychoanilinguists call an "integrated personality"? He wanted more. He realized that an identity is limiting, while the possibilities of life are infinite. He chose not to deprive himself and had the energy and courage of his choice. Rather than stuff a wardrobe of different attitudes, each suited to a different life, into one groaning personality—which personality gets bulged all out of shape while loose ends dangle messily (an artist's ego, say, fouling the mesh of teamwork on a ballfield)—he contrived a different personality for each different life and kept each separate. (Cf. Zeus Gynomachos, who chose a feathered tenderness for Leda and for Europa lusty taurine thrusts.) He constructed a number of worlds within this world, and denizens of one learned that they blundered to another only at their peril. Or, if you like, he had no personality, was by nature protean and undefined, felt himself liable to slip from avatar to avatar without control, and hence invented characters (attending to the details of each one so that they would not merge) and played them out, taking what care he could not to get publics and supporting casts mixed up, nor to be caught uncostumed in the dressing room.

11. Love

IN AUGUST, 1936, there washed up on the Caribbean littoral of Tinieblas the wreckage of a Spanish operetta company, a restless, zestless group who traipsed the provinces of Spain and the less cultured regions of America giving zarzuelas and Castilian versions of *The Merry Widow* and *The Count of Luxembourg*. The impresario, a certain Lépido Perron,[53] who besides handling business matters sang bass baritone and managed things backstage, possessed great gifts of stubbornness and self-deception. He thought his shows surpassed the most entrancing spectacles of Paris or New York, and he argued with such pitiless insistence that he was able to extract more than his company was worth from theater owners. The ladies of the company used as much make up off the stage as on, showed a great deal of leg and bosom, distilled a pungent promise of sophisticated sin. They drew the burghers and sometimes furnished the more generous of them horizontal as well as vertical diversions. The men wore permanent sneers, tight-fitting double-breasted suits, and high-heeled pointytoed elastic-sided ankle boots; their hands were dazzled with cheap rings, their hair was slicked down to a carbon-paper gloss. They were as adept at casual theft as at extorting from the ladies (either by pain or pleasure) a portion of the burghers' generosity. In short, the troupe survived, or did until General Francisco Franco raised the Morocco *Tercio* and sent the Spanish people tripping out to civil war.

The company was in Honduras at the time, in San Pedro Sula to be exact, banana country. The tenor had sung so many heroic roles that he had come to think himself a man of courage. He embarked at once for Spain to fight for the republic, taking his leading lady, the baritone's wife, along. The baritone drank himself out of voice, and the company's repertoire was thus reduced to a zarzuela called *La Gran Via,* in which Perron could sing the lead. As a firm capitalist (if more in aspiration than reality) he sided with General Franco and quarreled with the mezzo, a spirited *catalana* whose brothers were anarcho-syndicalists. On stage one night they took to hissing insults at each other until his face came so to infuriate her that she slapped it violently three times and then exited in tears through an archway painted on the backdrop, taking the set with her. The audience demanded its money; the theater owner sued for his receipts and huge imaginary damages; Perron found his properties attached and his company enmired in a swamp of writs. Idleness wreaked further injury. The most accomplished dancer accepted an offer of concubinage from the manager of a fruit plantation. Some members of the chorus became involved in a café discussion, voiced insufficient joy over the communist coup in Barcelona, and were set upon by banana workers and badly beaten. As a result of this incident all members of the company were hailed into police headquarters and interrogated as possible extremist agitators. A routine search of their hotel rooms revealed among the second lead's belongings a quantity of silverware from the home of the Spanish Vice-Consul, their only friend in town. Thus dispatched of costumes, properties, and his best artists, bayed at by lawyers and policemen, robbed of all hope of comfort from his consulate, Perron gathered a remnant of his company about him and decamped in secret to Puerto Cortés, where they took deck passage on the first ship that was sailing. After two days and nights of rain and seasickness, they landed at Bastidas.

There the disintegration of the company continued. Two of the men found and snatched a chance to work their way to Argentina on a Swedish tramp. A third established himself as business manager for two of the ladies, who, as the most sprightly pair of mounts along that coast, raised their passage back to Europe in a few months. Meantime Perron and the two remaining ladies made their way over to Ciudad Tinieblas, where they were engaged for a pittance at the Jacaranda.

Lépido Perron was a year or two under fifty, short-legged, thick-jowled, and barrel-chested. His eyebrows bushed temple to temple without a break; his hair shagged dankly to his collar; his ears and nostrils were luxuriantly tufted. He had tiny, narrow-set black eyes and a very few ideas, all of them false, which he held with unshakable conviction. He believed, for example, that he was, an artistic and commercial genius, that Stalin was a Jew and Christ a Spaniard, and that women ought best be classed among the animals because they lacked immortal souls. He was vain, truculent, and boastful, at best a minus seven on the Fuertes Scale (see note 12).

The women he appeared with at the Jacaranda—and he appeared excessively, belching his numbers earnestly while strutting back and forth about the stage—were, in order of seniority, his mistress and his wife. The former, a *sevillana* possibly part gypsy who called herself Natalia de Triana, was about ten years younger than Perron, short and heavy-breasted. In the right lighting she achieved a kind of whorish elegance which she considered beauty. Her voice was alto and (to middle-aged provincials well along in drink) seductive. It seemed to promise—and the promise was fulfilled to those with coin to test it—an appetite for vice. She had been with Perron for twenty years, was In all ways his temperamental equal, and loathed him as intensely as he detested her, although (perhaps because) each was incurably dependent on the other for the indulgence of certain particularly swinish habits.

Perron's wife, Rosario, was something else entirely: she was lovely, honest, and eighteen. Her loveliness was head-turning, breath-taking, traffic-stopping—heart-breaking ultimately, for she seemed to every man who saw her the incarnation of his private dream of woman. Her legs were long and graceful, her body slim and voluptuous. Her dark hair tumbled softly past her shoulders; her brilliant eyes laughed easily; her warm mouth asked no rouge. Her walk broadcast such sensuality that café mashers, louts who pissed their days away leering at every nubile female who went by and hissing out degrading invitations, gaped hang-jawed and mute until she passed, while their unguided robot hands continued to spoon sugar into gummy cups or pour wine into overflowing glasses. Ice-hearted womanizers blew all self-control over Rosario and often finished permanently maimed. Don Horacio Ladilla, for example, was the acknowledged master cocksman of Tinieblas, a man who boasted with conviction that he consumed more women than he did cigars and who, more or less as a hobby, built and stocked the richest brothel in the continent and kept it closed on Tuesdays for his private delectation. He offered Rosario de Perron two thousand inchados, an unheard-of sum, for one hour of her charms, and when she told him she did not make love for money, cried like a punished child. She took pity on him and went the next afternoon to the suite he kept at the Hotel Excelsior, but the sight of her naked struck him impotent, an affliction he had never known before and which she treated with such tenderness and gaiety that from then on he was capable of manhood only by casting her image on the screen of his closed eyelids and calling all his paramours Rosario.

Unlike so many truly striking women, Rosario neither feared her power over men nor let it turn her cruel or conceited, and yet a different class of men from Don Horacio, wiser men, better bred, romantics, if you like, who kept a chivalrous regard for womankind, found in her their *princesse lointaine* and, although much allured by her and certainly not frightened of her husband, revered her spiritually and were content to take a passive pleasure in her freshness and her love of life. Dr. Alonso Gusano, whom Rosario consulted on her first day in Ciudad Tinieblas, went every evening to the Jacaranda and entertained her with great opulence between her numbers, but when a waggish friend asked if he'd not been putting his examination table to a double use, Gusano, who besides being a respected surgeon was a fairly decent amateur violinist, replied frankly and a little sadly that, professional ethics aside, he had no more right to make love to Rosario than he did to play Auer's Stradivarius. She marked men deeply, and they wondered what she was doing married to Perron, where he had found her, how he'd captured her, and why she stayed with him.

Perron had bought her outright for a hundred Ticamalan pesos when she was ten years old. This was in November, 1927, during his company's first tour of Central America. There was a piece then in their repertoire with a child's part, and Perron would cast it locally. He would announce an opportunity for a gifted little girl to perform on the same stage with internationally acclaimed artists. Then he'd hold an audition, choose a kid, and pay her parents with a pair of tickets. And since families tend to be large and loyal in our part of the world, he'd like as not sell a good dozen more to relatives. The system had drawbacks, though. The brats were trouble to rehearse since he could neither beat nor curse them, and it was a rare one who could last her quarter hour on the stage without bumbling a line or stumbling against the set or fumbling in her nose while someone was singing. So when the theater porter in Puerto Guineo offered him Rosario, whom he would have in his control and who was so talented that he expected he would make his fortune on her, Perron decided to give up renting kids and buy instead.

She wasn't the porter's child; she didn't even know her parents. She'd had a foster mother who one afternoon left her at the theater for a silent-movie matinee and never came back. In continuing along the street, the woman had the misfortune to pass a cantina at the precise moment when two citizens, the best of buddies actually, who had been drinking rum together all day long, tried to annihilate each other with their pistols and succeeded only in making Rosario an orphan for the second time. The porter's wife took her in, and after two years of watching films and vaudeville every day Rosario could mimic Clara Bow and Chaplin, sing all the hit boleros from Havana, tell risqué stories, juggle fruit, and do flamenco heel-stomp. Perron caught her act—done in the alleyway beside the theater for an audience of urchins—and was impressed. The porter was tired of feeding an extra mouth, and when the company left town, Rosario went with it.

She took to the roving life with ease, became the mascot of the company, but never made Perron rich. There was a kind of casualness in her that stepped between her talent and its commercial exploitation. It was not that she lacked energy. She made their travels bright with wisecracks, pranks, and ad-lib entertainments, aped members of the troupe, burlesqued this one's delivery of a song and that one's style of dancing, put out hilarious, mock-innocent commentary on their ever-shifting amorous entanglements, but no matter how Perron might howl at her, she loafed during rehearsals and often gave only the minimum on stage. She preferred life to art and refused to act like a professional—a refusal that, in due course, she extended to her love life.

Perron initiated her himself when she was fourteen, responding to the only moral imperative he recognized—i.e., he might as well, since if he didn't someone else would. Rosario experienced no trauma. Much the reverse; she was pleased by the sensation and by the docility that overcame Perron, temporarily, to be sure, but regularly whenever the operation was repeated. She soon learned it could be even more fun with other men, but unlike the other ladies of the company, she neither asked nor accepted payment. When, on her return from her first assignation, Perron, in the tradition of the troupe, slapped her about and then demanded his cut, she explained as to an infant that since she'd picked the man herself and enjoyed him thoroughly, money hadn't figured in the episode. When Perron realized at last that she was telling him the truth, he concluded she was feebleminded and undertook to prostitute her himself. Rosario not only balked but threatened so vehemently to set the law on him that he took the precaution of marrying her, a step that infuriated la Triana and with which Rosario went along out of good nature. It cost her nothing and calmed the impresario. In the same spirit she went to bed with him from time to time and permitted him illusions of possession. That is, she lied whenever she made love with someone else, cooking up the most blasphemous protestations of chastity and smiling sweetly while he gulped them like communion wafers. There was no dishonesty in this. The lies she put out to excuse her absences were too outrageous to constitute deception. Like all good women, Rosario tried to please men where she could, and so she furnished Perron the necessary equipment to deceive himself. Meantime she stayed with the company because staying was as easy as leaving, did at all times exactly as she pleased, had many lovers, both platonic and otherwise, to whom she gave affection, tenderness, and joy, but never chanced to fall in love[54] herself. In fact, except for what she'd seen in others, she knew no more of love than León Fuertes did. Then, five or six nights after she and la Triana and Perron began performing at the Jacaranda, León came in to sing.

Since love is nowhere studied systematically—and it's the only universal human pastime that is not—no data are available on the incidence of mutual true first love at first sight. One feels, however, such occurrences are rare. Love is a common enough form of monomania—an intense and narrow enfocation of the mind upon a particular object, usually human, and the consequent formation of a psychological (and, sometimes, physical) dependence which binds one to the object forcefully and leads one to invest the object with a great importance, even more importance than one gives oneself. But since one can (and often does) contract love repeatedly, first love (the primary affliction) is less common. As love often develops gradually—e.g., a benign growth of gratitude metastasizes from the pelvis to the brain and runs malignant—love at first sight, where one is seized with the condition instantaneously upon eye contact with the object, figures to be of a higher order of improbability. True love is the disease in its acute form. Here the obsession is profound, pronounced, and (relatively) proof against the eroding effects of space and time and the distractions[55] posed by other potential objects. All the pathologists of love concur in true love's rarity. Finally, mutual love involves two individuals in a reflected and reverberating dymania, the object of an obsession being simultaneously possessed of a more or less equally severe obsession for the subject of the first. It is a very unicorn in the bestiary of emotions. Nonetheless, as soon as León shooed Perron down from the stage and mounted there himself with his musicians, he saw Rosario, who sat ringside with Dr. Gusano, and she saw him, and each felt instantly, acutely, for the first time, and relative to the other that absurd confusion of joy and sorrow, peace and longing, languor and excitement, possessiveness and generosity, liberty and bondage which the English language eloquently links with loss of balance: they fell in love. And since both León and Rosario were willful, brave, proud, confident, and free, they at once abandoned themselves to their love, so that from the onset there was no arresting its course or alleviating its symptoms.

Parapsychology is now a recognized science, but it as yet provides no firm statistics on the incidence of two-way extrasensory perception. Here again, however, we may assume improbability, for such perception is not truly extra sensory at all but rather hangs upon a sense all humans have but which few own to or employ. Reading another's thoughts is seen as freakish; ergo, it must be rare. For two people to read each other's must be rarer. Nonetheless, the moment their eyes met—eyes singularly alike in color, depth, and brilliance—Rosario and León, neither of whom had ever telepathed before, knew one another's thoughts, not as vague hints but as if each were whispering his mind into the other's ear. León was, for example, specifically aware that the unknown, delicious female at his feet wanted to suck his lip almost until it bled, whereas Rosario realized that Le6n, whose name Dr. Gusano had just told her, craved to repay that favor in more meridional regions. A microsecond later each knew the other knew, both blushed, yet neither looked away. Instead each offered free and full assurance that he would that same night and for all nights to come be at the other's disposition for the calming of all wants and cravings. Then, happy to have this problem solved so speedily and simply, they smiled.

With that Rosario became aware that León wished to sing a song for her, and León was at once in mind of a popular paso doble whose lyric he had never really known until that moment, so he held up his hands to the audience, which was growing impatient as well as larger, with people beating on their tables and others hurrying in off the street, and spoke over his shoulder to his musicians, who strummed up an introduction, and began to sing, first to the audience in general and then directly to Rosario. During the verse, which told in superdramatic Spanish fashion of a bullfighter who sees a lady in the crowd and straight off offers her his cape, his heart, et cetera, he received from Rosario, who was watching him with great pride and tenderness, a number of messages: the suggestion that he try an Andalusian accent (lisped z's and c's, slurred d's, dropped s's), the news that she would like to share the stage with him (he wished he'd thought of that himself), and the plan for a joint number. He agreed to all, of course, sang the chorus as if she were the only person in the room, and in the four-measure break before the second verse, bowed to her and helped her to the stage with an exaggerated gallantry which they both laughed at inwardly while holding very stern Iberian frowns. Then Rosario danced, body and face immobile, heels and castanets aclatter, and León sang, posturing like a bullfighter and drawing her past him back and forth with his spread hand, until the song closed with her whirling at the far end of the stage, her long dress flowered out above her knees, and him half turned toward her, back arched, chin lifted, hand above his head. The audience suffered hysterics of applause.

God, that was corny! thought León happily as they both bowed.

Don't be a snob. They loved it; so did you. How you milked the applause!

And you? Showing off your legs!

Ha! The great macho! *One more chorus and you'd think you were doing a real bullfight.*

There's going to be a real enough goring for somebody later on tonight

Oh, darling, I can hardly wait!

Me either.

They waited for more than an hour, though, playing with their talents and with the marvelous commeddling of their minds, which was so natural they scarcely were surprised at it, singing song after song as though they'd been rehearsing all their lives, while the public beat their palms raw with applauding, and Perron alternately ground his teeth at being so upstaged or licked his chops at all the money he would make presenting the show[56] in Europe, and Dr. Alonso Gusano decided be had never seen so perfectly matched a couple—they even looked alike—or so touching a tableau of young romance. Then León bent down to a ringside table and got the key to his friend Gustavo Oruga's *garçonnière*, and stood up and shouted that in honor of Doña Rosario's art, his friend Juanchi Tábano, son of the most excellent former President of the Republic, was buying drinks for all the house, and in the resulting uproar he and Rosario slipped out the performers' door into the salt-breezed night. Their hearts and minds were joined; it remained only to connect their bodies.

The flat Gustavo Oruga kept as a trysting place was on the top of a slim concrete cube his father, Don Constantino Oruga, bad put up in 1934 and given to him for his twenty-first birthday. This was an admirable location, for as a noted gynecologist had his consulting rooms on the third floor, a lady could afford to be seen entering or leaving the building. (It's hard to say, in fact, who benefited more from the arrangement, Gustavo, who had a grand time horning all his married friends, or the doctor, whose practice waxed impressively.) Besides, since there was no taller structure at that time within five hundred miles, one could make love alfresco on the terrace without fear of being seen, except by passing birds. The penthouse was comfortably furnished, stocked with food and drink, and cared for by a stone-blind chola woman. León and Rosario remained there twenty-seven days and nights, naked from the time they entered till the time they left, unheedful of the knocks of lovelorn matrons.

They made love in every room of the apartment: in the bedroom, naturally, and in the dining room and *sala,* and in Oruga's office, Rosario sitting, heels spread, among the rent receipts inside the roll-top desk while León stood before her, and in the kitchen, and back in the blind chola woman's room while she was doing market. They made love in the twin Otán armchairs, whose uncured cowhide backs were seared with the double-O brand of Oruga's uncle's ranch, and on the dining table (made in Bengal and sold by Casa Singh on Avenida Jorge Washington), from beneath whose plate-glass top carved Hindu deities observed them, and in the white-fringed Venezuelan hammock that hung across a corner of the *sala.* They made love on the terrace, reclining on the wheeled rattan chaise longue, or nested in a mound of sofa pillows, or perched like sparrows on the four-foot-high, two-foot-wide parapet whose outer edge dropped seven storeys sheer down to the street, or standing so that each enjoyed a panoramic view over the other's shoulder of the sea or jungled hills, or kneeling among the fronds and blossoms of Oruga's roof garden while warm rain beat on León's bobbing bum and lightening flashed about them. They made love in all the ways dreamed up or stumbled into since the dawn of man and, at length, devised a new way to make love wherein they lay apart, eyes closed and voices mute, exchanging telepathic fantasied caresses, until their bodies melted and their blended minds flowed up among the stars.

Their first embrace stopped every timepiece in the building, then set them running backward, with the result that since the event took place at midnight, tenants could read the time correctly using mirrors. At the same hour the checkgirl at the Jacaranda noticed a wisp of smoke curl up from Lépido Perron's cordovan briefcase, and when (thirty-six hours later at Civil Guard Headquarters) he drew from this same case the scrolled certificate (issued by the Republic of Costaguana) which proved his marriage to Rosario, he found it baked to an illegible, dun-colored ash, which crumbled in the ceiling fan's slow breath and blew away. Some few days later, at Perron's cabled supplication, a clerk in Chuchaganga went to the register for 1933 to make a copy: the pertinent page was charred away to dust; Rosario's marriage was, effectively, annulled.

Throughout the quarter during that whole month people experienced a randiness uncommon even in Tinieblas. Men who kept youthful and demanding mistresses found themselves, late at night, embracing their own wives with ardor. Board-breasted ancient spinsters, lace-shawled for mass, made eyes at passing workmen. Wasted ex-libertines arose from decades of lank detumescence and leaped their servant girls. Marriages glaciered in scorn for years thawed and blossomed. Since upper-class parents were too busy swiving to surveil their daughters properly, an entire generation of the Tinieblan ruling class was married hastily, and in July, 1937, the obstetricians of the city worked night and day delivering what everybody claimed were seven-month babies.

Oruga's roof plants, gorged with the echoed energy of love, flourished prodigiously and thrust thick, leafy stalks against the penthouse. By month's end, Rosario and León could no longer see out through the windows, and when they left, Oruga had to bring a peon from his uncle's ranch to hack the vegetation down with his machete. More and most marvelous, Rosario and León began receiving sense impressions from each other's bodies, until each felt that he was now outfitted with a twin set of procreative organs. For them the gulf between the sexes, the abyss which Rebeca twice had leaped, closed up. Each became male and female equally and, therefore, whole.

The wholeness conferred by love endowed León with new traits of character. Rosario noted in him, for example, a womanly (though not effeminate) softness of heart which no one, he included, had observed before. All month long their thoughts flowed on a single circuit, so that when León recalled his childhood, Rosario trudged the alleys of La Cuenca with him, and she was touched by his maternal tenderness for little Pepe, for Rebeca, for Florencio Merluza—a feeling foreign to the street beast who provided for himself and his de-

pendents only by never showing anyone a shred of pity. If it was in
him then, he squelched it; more likely, it was engendered by his love
and felt retroactively. Similarly, Rosario found in León a compassion
for Dr. Grillo and Bisagra, which those two gentlemen would certainly have been amazed at. Often she woke long after midnight,
when the heat had lifted and the moist breath of sea and of savannas
hung about the room, and held his sleeping head and shared his
dream, and in such dreams his benefactors might emerge and he return their love. León himself was startled by these sentiments. Perhaps he was a little scared of them, as though, while they were safe
to savor in Rosario's arms, they were a dangerous indulgence in the
world beyond. Nonetheless, through the remainder of his life he
showed from time to time a female nature strange (if not outlandish)
in a Latin man of action. He was a stern father when the occasion
asked it, but suffered, I think, more than we children did when he
punished us. He led the coup, which drove Alejandro Sancudo, a
despot and a maniac to boot, from the presidency in 1952, but spoke
out alone for leniency at the dictator's trial. In war he killed, but he
pitied also. His love for Rosario furnished a balancing dimension.

This wholeness ... Who has not known[57] that glimpse of déjà vu
wherein a person or a place, though newly-met, appears familiar?—
although instead of learning from such flashbacks to a previous existence (or such flash-forwards to a future one) most people sweep
them under the carpet of coincidence. From their first moment in
each other's arms Rosario and León felt they'd been joined before,
felt that they were, in fact, the severed halves of one sole life, separate
for years, now reunited. Yet while they judged this insight honest,
they did not query it for further news. They were too busy living as
whole human beings to wonder how or why they managed it, or to
ask questions, or to probe the past, or to seek out a meaning.

Perron, meantime, enjoyed no similar peace but rather scrambled
about like a roach in a paper bag, seeking to square Rosario's elope-
ment with his marvelous opinion of himself. By midday after she cut
out with León, all Ciudad Tinieblas was blabbing cheerfully about
them, and that night a group of León's pals greeted Perron's first
song with chorused yelps of "Cuckold!" until his head bowed helplessly under the weight of his enormous antlers. Even his great powers of self-deception were for the moment inadequate to soothe this

bruise to his vanity, so, after the charming Spanish fashion, he arrogated to himself the right to do Rosario (and León too, provided that he caught him with his back turned) frightful injury. At the same time his greed remained tickled by the thought of León and Rosario's packing the Paris music halls while he raked in the cash, and so he seized on the idea of forcing them to sign a long-term—no, a lifetime contract to him. Thus haunted by mixed visions of revenge and riches, he went to the police, took from his case the bill of sale for Rosario which he'd had the Puerto Guineo theater porter put his "x" on almost nine years before, and demanded that his chattel be returned and the thief punished. The duty officer informed him that the Republic of Tinieblas was a civilized country and did not recognize the institution of human slavery. But, Perron said, Rosario was his wife—and an attendant sergeant, who was a fan of León's and a patriot as well, snickered something about Tinieblan sausage being tastier than the Spanish brands. Perron thereupon plucked out a small and rather fragile Toledo-work snap-knife (a gift from la Triana, who'd fished it from the unoccupied trousers of a gentleman friend) and waving it in large and frenzied arcs, stomped toward the door, where he was subdued and disarmed. Then, gathering his dignity, he asked to know what was Tinieblas's claim to being civilized when its public force scoffed at the sanctity of the home and then denied a husband lawful right to butcher his adulterous wife and geld her lover. Touched by the justice of this view, the duty officer, who was a family man himself, chastised the sergeant and advised Perron that if he would swear out complaints against Rosario (for adultery) and León (for alienation of affection, not for theft), the Civil Guard would apprehend them and place them at the instruction of the public prosecutor. Would the señor please have the kindness to show his certificate of marriage . . .

Fifteen days later Perron was back, handcuffed, gripped by two *guardias* (who dodged to stay out of range of foam-flecked canines), and charged in such a manner that the duty officer pondered whether to send him to prison, which was at hand and nearly empty, or to the overcrowded lunatic asylum in Otán. The disappearance of the official record of his marriage, coming on top of the desintegration of his own certificate, had provoked in him a Copernican effort of creative imagination, and he had—at 4:16 A.M. on

17th October—realized that a rival impresario, a man of immense wealth and powerful connections whose shrewd familiars scouted all the nightclubs of the world for unknown talent, had, through his agents here and down in Costaguana, kidnapped Rosario and expunged all record of her marriage and now held her captive until such a time as he could book her along with León (who, no doubt, had long been in his pay) in London or New York. Perron, then, like King Richard Lionheart's loyal minstrel, had begun erring round the town in the dead hours after midnight, crooning a song he and Rosario had sung in an old show. She would, he was convinced, once she had heard him, sing her part back, and when he knew her whereabouts, he'd rescue her. After three nights of being pelted with old shoes and rotten fruit, he was admonished by a *guardia* on duty near the home of Colonel Genaro Culata to stop his drunken howling, and sore offended by this insult to his art, he cursed then kicked then clawed then bit the copper. That he was neither crippled on the spot nor beaten cockeyed after his arrest—which would be getting off lightly these days for such comportment—shows something of how much the Guardia Civil has since changed. In the end it was decided to deport him, and he was put aboard a ship bound through the Panama for Cádiz. There seemed, therefore, no obstacle at all to León's and Rosario's love when, after four weeks of unaccustomed abstinence, Gustavo Oruga went to plead for the return of his love nest.

León and Rosario were about ready to emerge—it was not that their ardor had cooled—not hardly!—but that León wished to solemnize their love with Rebeca's blessing. But, as in the case of Héloïse and Abélard, a yearning after sacraments undid them. When Rebeca looked up from her mending and saw Rosario, wan from four weeks of love and smiling shyly, her blood froze and she drove her needle through her palm and never felt it. Before she fainted, Rebeca thought she had been snatched through space and time and stood again before a mirror in a Vienna Bahnhofplatz hotel in 1904: Rosario was the image of the young Rebeca.

When they had lifted Rebeca to her bed and laved her face with tepid water, after Rosario bid loosed her bodice and León had crushed a vial of spirits of ammonia near her nose, then came the questions León hadn't asked during his four-week idyll and, when,

some answers had been driven out, solutions to such diverse mysteries as Rosario's uncanny likeness to the young Rebeca, the wanderings of a Chinese servant girl and certain missing children, and the
presentiment León and Rosario shared that they'd been joined before. These revelations, coming four weeks too late, had the depressing savor of a good-news bad-news joke. In fact, not even in the
works of Aeschylus could one find a more pathetic recognition scene
or a less joyful family reunion than was played in Rebeca's room that
day. There were roars, of course, moanings and self-assaults. Rosario
raked her lovely cheeks all bloody with her nails. León knocked his
forehead on the iron bedpost. Rebeca beat her breast. We Fuertes
are a histrionic breed.

Had León and Rosario not loved each other truly, the denouement
might have turned out less tragic. But they did love and, therefore,
acted in what each thought was the other's interest. That night León
stepped off a chair in Dr. Grillo's attic with a noose around his neck,
but the inch-thick Manila hemp parted as though axed, and he suffered no more than a turned ankle. He then tried to blow his brains
out with a Colt revolver he had taken from Nacho Hormiga one
night when the latter was drunk and liable to commit some folly, but
all six chambers misfired. Next he took poison but couldn't keep it
on his stomach long enough. He was on his way to Oruga's penthouse to jump off when an acquaintance stopped him and announced that Rosario, my aunt Rosario,[58] had gone to the back row
of the Teatro Trópico, drunk off a bottle of insecticide, and died con-
vulsing. With this León realized that he was not destined to know the
felicity of suicide. The next day he left Tinieblas.

PART THREE
HIS YEARS IN THE WILDERNESS
(1936-1945)

12. Some Modes of Autodegradation

MY FATHER, León Fuertes, was gone from home ten years, first wandering, then at war. During his errantry and vagabondage he learned their cognate woes, error and vagueness; for having missed on three clean shots at what he thought would be oblivion, he set about to thanatize himself in messy increments of degradation. This failed, as had rope, ratsbane, and revolver, and yet it served for a preparatory trial. It left his personality dismantled, hence ready to be reassembled more in concert with his fate.

Exile was a strong opening move; it forced the sacrifice of precious figures. There was no place for León, scholar, León, artist, León, athlete, in the dank fo'c's'le of the Galactic Line fruit boat which he boarded at Bastidas, and since León, lover, had perished with Rosario, he started out peeled of identity. He took the clothes he wore and, for spiritual baggage, two equal weights of grief and incest guilt wrapped in self-hatred, sewn with shame, embroidered with his mother's curse.

Move two: he ceased to bathe, to shave or groom himself,[59] to wash his clothes. The deck plates glowed and buckled under the Carib sun like a biscuit tin forgotten in an oven, and all hands toiled the days out hoisting banana bunches from the hold and heaving them overboard (to keep the New York market firm, you know), so that what with his natural sweat, smear of banana oil, meal stains and galley sloppings, coal soot, salt grime, and brassy tarnish, León was soon a salient spectacle of filth, a fount of stench even to those misbegotten anthropoids his shipmates. From them and, through

them, from the women, sodomites, and beasts they coupled with in
mixed-blood, vermin-ridden ports of call, he recruited three separate
regiments of lice, which quartered on his head and chest and pubis.
He suffered these to bivouac in his beard, to march and countermarch along his eyebrows, to trench his groin, to forage in his navel,
to invest his armpits, to cache their stores of eggs in every follicle of
his body, and so to reinforce their numbers that in sleep his whole
crown writhed with their maneuvers, until the man who bunked
above him—a syphilitic Berber from Oran who liked, for his diversion while on shore, to bugger drakes and then feed off them
roasted—gagged at the sight. He likewise let himself be occupied by
several armies of bacteria, for whom he was content to furnish transport, via his fingernails, to all the orifices of his body and to every
scratch break in his skin, till he was studded all about with sores and
ulcers, buboes and carbuncles, verdigris abscesses and azure boils,
cankers, swellings, cysts, festering impostumes, and creeping rot. By
the time his ship had rounded Sandy Hook and run past Bedloe's to
the Battery, he felt himself a fellow to the foulest plagues on board,
kin to the grey-backed bilge rats, sibling of roaches, heir to fleas and
maggots. He'd sunk, in fact, to such a depth of rankness that his
shipmates, not a fastidious bunch, refused out of disgust to sail with
him. They attacked warily, all twelve of them at once, until they saw
he'd offer no resistance. Then they dragged him down the gangway
to the pier and flung him down against the clapboard shack that
served for a longshoremen's union hall and kicked him unconscious,
stole his pay, cursed him and spat on him, pissed in his bleeding face,
and left. An early gloom crept in to nuzzle his cringed neck. The wind
flailed freezing rain across The Narrows, dampening his cotton shirt,
goading him back to consciousness and pain, to exile and the smell
of his own filth. Then León felt he was beginning to approach a level
of debasement proper to him.

  Next he became a beggar. Work, after all, always confers some dignity no matter what the task. Granted, during those years thousands
of more enterprising men than León panhandled too, but León neither looked for work nor would have taken it if it were offered. He
didn't even work at begging, which, as a performing art, might have
enjoined his talents. He did not, for example, wait by the traffic light
in Union Square or trudge the inching lines of cars on Second Avenue

to wipe the sleet from windshields—a performance which dirties the glass but makes the driver feel both warm and prosperous. He lacked the English for sad tales of woe, but it is clear he'd not have told them if he could have, since he neglected to put on such mimings-out of loneliness and famine as might have touched a tender-hearted housewife. Nor did he wield his ugliness to give the squeamish chills, to fright a coin from that paunched, velvet-collared advocate by conjuring forth the fellow's dread of revolution, to nauseate (by an adroit manipulation of his stink) a bill from one of those two window-shopping dowagers, short-sellers' widows, maybe, in their Persian lamb coats, their snug fur hats and muffs, or the beneficiaries of a pair of broking partners, richly-insured reliable bread-winners who, having tossed their own and all their customers' money in the bear market's maw, had tossed themselves off the Singer Building five years back. León would play no roles—and not because of pride either. He simply didn't give himself the trouble. He shambled the avenues and sat in vacant doorways with a meek cupped palm, and if a nickel dropped, he clutched.

He was dependent, therefore, on such poorly compensated patrons[60] as could make their own diversions from him: on Mrs. Esther Tunafish of 219 Amboy Street, Brooklyn, who was about to treat her son Larry, aged eight years, to a movie at the Roxy when the latter commented on how "dat bum deah" wore the *Daily Forward* as a muffler and who, mistaking León for a fellow yid, dropped him a dime; on Finnegan, the novelist and storywright, gloomed at that time in the dead waste and middle of his soul's dark night, who was writing little and selling less, suffering much and drinking more, who was just back from his disastrous trip to Norway and about to leave on his disastrous pilgrimage to Hollywood, and who, as he emerged from luncheon at the Plaza (supported by his publisher, Mr. George Jaggers, and by his literary agent, a Mr. Cannon), spied León slumped against the famous fountain—famed in good part by one of Finnegan's own legendary revels—and, feeling much better at the sight of one worse off than he, crossed the square under his own power, split a crisp five from the hundred dollars Jaggers had just loaned him, and pressed it in León's paw; on the Honourable Miss Diana-Anne Withers and Mr. Richard Abrhams-Hoof, both British subjects (she was on tour with Mother, he enrolled at Berkeley), both nineteen years old, both terribly in love (Richard with Anne and with his own emotions, Anne with her own emotions, with her fiancé in England, and with Richard too), who had met first in San Francisco, then shortly afterward in Sacramento (Richard had glimpsed a page of Lady Withers's Thomas Cook itinerary), then in Los Angeles (Anne had let drop the name of their hotel), and, finally, here in New York (with unsuspecting Lady Withers embarked for home on the *Queen Mary* and Anne permitted to stay on a week "alone"), who, being booked (in separate bedrooms) at the Dorset, had semiconsummated their romance in an Eden of dry humping, and who, both sad yet both a bit relieved to have come through unscathed, spent their last twilight in a stroll along Central Park South, until, breaking from an embrace, they were confronted by a ragged, pestilential beggarman shuffling sideways with his left palm cupped, his right arm drooped, his rheumed eyes pulled to slits, and thereby blessed with such a firm presentiment of death, and decay that they at once dumped to him all their change and then dashed back to their hotel, stripped themselves naked, and made forthright, procreative love all the night long; on Beulah Jane Nell Dosby, chocolate-skinned granddaughter of household slaves, who had lost her (common-law) husband to the First World War and her baby to the 1919 influenza epidemic, who since then had earned her keep mothering other people's children, and who, when her Tuesday-night-off companion Jimmy Blue kicked León savagely out of the servants' entrance of the town house where Beulah worked, hollering, "Get out my way, white trash!" felt her forever-close-to-hand maternal instinct roused, cussed Jimmy for a "mean nigger if there ever was one," and gave León a quarter; on Mr. Barney Ross, Welter Weight Boxing Champion of the World, who was helping a brace of Harlow-style platinum blondes out of a cab in front of the Stork Club when he saw León stumble by, received a futuregram, wordless but woeful clear, to the effect that he, B. Ross, would soon be on the skids himself, and ordered his manager, who was paying the taxi tab, to "Give the bum a buck"; and, of course, on many others.

Then he gave up begging, which, after all, brought in some little money no matter how desultorily he practiced it. He ceased to venture from the Bowery—trash-heap of garbaged lives on which the after-images of used-up men scuttle like phantom rodents. No beg-

ging there—well, no professional begging. A passer-by might sometimes spare a dime, but passers-by were few while bums abounded,
and León never saw another fin again to buy him a full month of
sheltered flop. He slept outdoors, in pawnshop entrance ways, under
the dinged marquees of closed-down burlesque theaters, against tenement walls, beside crate fires built in empty lots. He wore newsprint
underwear beneath his now-disintegrating clothes and over them a
1918 U.S. Army blanket which he'd peeled from a dead bum. He
groped his grub out of the offal pails of unswept hash houses and
was, both to himself and to any observer, just another lump of refuse,
a well-squeezed orange rind in which the counterman has ground
his cigarette, or the end product of a Bleeker Street abortion swaddled up oozy in the *Evening Sun* and tucked in someone's ashcan.

Though cold and inanition numbed his brain, here and there—beneath the spark-fretted firmament of the Third Avenue el, in the vast
antres under Brooklyn Bridge—he yet recalled a León who had bat-
tled hostile circumstance and won, provided for himself, protected
others; as well as other Leóns later on who'd been lauded and loved.
But those identities seemed giant's robes for such a dwarf as he was
in his spirit. León, garbage, fitted much better. Despite his compost
of encrusted filth, the wheeze of phlegm-choked lungs, the feeble,
agued twitch of his bent shoulders, now and then—as, for example,
when a burly bum elbowed him cringing from a spot beside a fire, or
the night when he lay too weak to move under the pelting of a pitiless
storm—he could remember when his body bad been healthy, clean,
and strong. But since his soul was sick, wasted and soiled, pest-
ridden, vermin-swarmed, infected, illness and frozen slime became
him more. As death would perfectly. Death by starvation. Death by
cold. Death by disease. Or death by violence—yes! Killed for his
greasy blanket. Stuffed down a manhole, Drowned in a sewer.

He would have died, no doubt, except he had an accident. One
midnight he lurched off the Bowery sidewalk after what looked to
him like a stray dime (and was in fact a lamp-gleamed gob of spittle),
into a passing car. Now, it happened that this car—a twin-six
Packard limousine with swooping swan radiator cap and fender-
mounted spare wheels—was piloted by one Seamus Grodiham, pre-
Great War racing colleague of E. Rickenbacker's, Western Front
ambulance driver, now private chauffeur, who knew the perils of the

Bowery route to the Manhattan Bridge and was proceeding with great caution, and who had the wit and self-control not to stomp on the brake when he saw León lunge out toward the slushy street but rather nudged the Packard's flank against the forged steel stanchion of the elevated railway, doing a frightful deal of noisy scraping to the car but cutting its speed. This car, furthermore, chanced to be owned and occupied by Dr. Felix Heilanstalt [61] one of the great surgeons of his time and the most arrogant, a man who believed in neither God nor Satan, who, acknowledging no agency higher than his own skill, could never be resigned to losing patients no matter what smashed-up, run-down, or otherwise unhappy shape he found them in, and who, besides his wealth and culture, had enough New York savvy to have made many unbilled attentions to the police. Thus the impact and injury to León were less violent than they might have been. Thus, scarcely had he cannoned through the air, bounced on the pavement, slid, and come to rest against the curb, when he was in the care of a brilliant practitioner, who not only ministered first aid and diagnosed a wealth of trouble beyond shock and broken bones and a concussion, but who actually looked forward with great joy not to saving a clearly worthless life but, as a point of pride, to curing a tough case. And thus, also, León was not afflicted with the kind of bureaucratic bumf that has killed healthier victims of less serious accidents, for when a cop who'd heard the noise steamed up, looked from the Packard to its grubby victim, decided (rightly, but for wrong reasons) it was the dumb bum's fault, touched his cap to minked and sobbing Mrs. Heilanstalt, growled at the clutch of derelicts bunched in the headlamps' stare, mushed to where Dr. Heilanstalt knelt tuxedo-trousered in the gutter bandaging León's head with his silk scarf, tapped him upon the shoulder, and reached ponderously for pencil and notebook, the doctor had but to flash his wallet with the miniature gold badges—gifts of commissioners and precinct captains—pinned inside, and all red tape was sliced.

The cop chugged for his corner call box. The doctor asked his wife to move up front. He and his chauffeur bundled León in the velvet car robe and bore him gingerly into the Packard's stern. Doors slammed. The V-12 engine roared. From off away on Centre Street came the siren wail of the police motorcycle escort which was to meet the doctor on Manhattan Bridge. The Packard churned ahead, its fantail slewing, its right rear wheel flinging a curtain of grey glop on an abandoned pair of fur-lined pigskin gloves, toward which the derelicts converged in feeble scrum and which, after much vapor-panted cursing and some swaying motions more like dance than battle, emerged divorced and departed, one uptown, its ex west along Prince Street, on the hands of different bums.

Five months later León Fuertes emerged from Dr. Heilanstalt's deluxe private hospital, cured in body and convinced in mind that passive modes of self-degradation were inadequate. From then on no sloth attended his career in defilement and dishonor. By dint of will he drove himself ever lower.

During his sojourn in the hospital León was sullen. His body was reluctant to respond. Though first and last a surgeon, Dr. Heilanstalt had enough interest in mental influences upon disease to have named one of his sons after S. Freud, and he remarked León's thanatotic urge and welcomed it as yet another challenging complication. More, he liked his charity cases to provide some entertainment or instruction, so as soon as he had dragged León off the critical list, he saved some time each evening to drop by and try (in French, their only common tongue) to draw him into conversation, thereby to learn who León was, what made him tick, how he'd descended to skid row, and why he seemed unwilling to be cured. Failing in this—for León at the best answered in grudging monosyllables and wouldn't say a word about his past—the doctor set about cajoling him toward a desire to live, said he was young and tough, bright too, as far as one could see, promised to put him on his feet once he was cured, give him some cash, find him a job, arrange his passage home, told him that he, Dr. F. Heilanstalt, had known hard times himself, had started out with nothing but his brain, his steady nerves, and his ambition. Then, when he realized León's problem wasn't lack of cash or lack of work or homesickness or dejection at being down and out, that León simply didn't enjoy living, Dr. Heilanstalt offered to send him off to Spain, where there was a cracking good war in progress and a demand for corpses *in potentia*. This was a particularly exciting subject for the doctor, who had a strong if secret urge to join that war. He'd never been to war, having arrived in France with the old AEF at the very hour of the Armistice. He'd never have gone into surgery,

he knew, but that he had a taste for blood and chopping up live bodies, and while surgery, like war, offered a means to slake this taste
with honor, war, unlike surgery, gave one a chance to risk one's own
life, not just someone else's. Sometimes he wondered if he wasn't just
a mite afraid to lose his marvelous life, which was filled up with honors and affection and respect, with money and the love of women,
with fame and the grand kick of saving otherwise doomed people.
The possibility that he might have some fear only intensified his urge
to go to war, to risk his life and therein test himself, and he controlled
this urge only with difficulty by thinking of his wife and family, his
hospital and patients. In the end he lost control of it. He joined the
U.S. Army on the morning following Pearl Harbor and three years
later found his ordeal and his Valhalla when, as a brigadier of Medical Corps, he went forward to inspect field hospitals and was engulfed into the Battle of the Bulge. But at the time of León's injury
Spain had the only decent war-in-progress, and, yes, León should go
off to Spain and fight. For either side; the doctor didn't care. He was
partial to the Loyalists but, in the end, it was the war that mattered,
not its occasion or who won or lost. There León might discover joy
of life—or, if he didn't, fling his life away in a more picturesque and
thrilling manner than he could do down on the Bowery. León listened
to all this with a great, sullen weariness, an attitude that to an eaves-
dropper might have suggested that he was a psychoanalyst engaged
in therapizing Dr. Heilanstalt. Meanwhile he went about his business
of autodestruction by making himself a morphine addict.

In his first weeks at the hospital León received morphine regularly
against the pain of broken bones. He found it the best surrogate for
death he'd come upon so far, and he appreciated its potential as a
means to self-debasement, so when the dosages began to be diminished, he exaggerated his pain—not by gross screams or wailing but
by using all his histrionic talent to portray a man racked by great
agony who tries his best to bear it but cannot. There was a nurse assigned to midnight shifts, not a young woman but a greying Irish
spinster, whom his performances moved with peculiar force. She had
great soccer-ballish bosoms on which a silver crucifix jello'd benignly, a round red face puffed to enforced good cheer, and not a
few taut lines about her eyes and mouth which, to a careful judge, argued some secret sadness and much tension. León discovered that if

before she made her rounds, he gouged his nails deep in his palms or, better yet, gobbled a fold of cheek between his molars and chewed it so bloody that her tongue depressor would emerge all gulesed, this woman, Nurse Edna Scallop, would, despite the language barrier, appreciate his torment and slip him a fix. And since Dr. Heilanstalt had put him in a private room, he could by gesture get her to stay on a bit, say a "Pater noster" with him or an "Ave Maria." And of course she would, at his dumbshow request, massage his chest and neck to ease the discomfort of lying pinned in traction all day long. And then one night, as she massaged him so, he put his own hand to her meaty nape, raising a startled yelp, a stare of disbelief, and a hiss of indignation reflexed across the decades from the memory of adolescent pawings that Edna Scallop hadn't stood for, but then, since he persisted and they were alone, she smiled and closed her eyes and let him touch her for a moment before brushing his hand back with a feigned roughness and saying, "No more of that, my lad." But of course, the next night there was more. Nothing remotely sexual: he kneaded the tense flesh above her clavicles and palped her nape with the same blend of clinical solicitude and sister-of-mercy charity that she showed him. By the third night she was prepared to give herself up to this kindness for a few minutes. Before long his attentions had traversed her pachydermic back and reached her hips, and she would leave his room at once eased and excited. Then—But there is no need in a work like this to stendhal out a step-by-step account. Let it suffice to say that by the time León had been six weeks in Dr. Heilanstalt's hospital, the character of his paddlings of Nurse Scallop had entirely changed, and that he had (at two-fifteen of a still Sunday morning, while a shuttered night light jaundiced half his sickroom floor and his freshly-emptied bedpan tottered frenetically atop the pushed-back bed table to the bump of Edna's butt) manually proportioned to her the first orgasm of her life. From then on morphine was no problem. She was as badly hooked as he. One solace well deserved another. She might as well be damned for a thief as for a lecher. And what could she deny to the dear boy who gave her such joy and peace? León took with him from the hospital a morphine habit the size of Yankee Stadium.

There is a dignity to certain lives of vice. One may feel awe before the priestly dedication of the man who gives his life to booze, or heroin, or gambling. Strange gods, and yet some people live as truly for them as some others live for science, or for Christ, or for their countries. But León Fuertes never worshiped morphine. He sought his purpose in himself, not in external absolutes or causes, nor (saving his lunar month with Rosario) in other people, nor (much less) in groups or institutions. He was a man self-fixated. During the period I am describing his passion was self-hatred, and he strove to sink as single-mindedly as during other times he strove to soar. Morphine was but a means to his defilement. It fouled his brain, warped his metabolism out of balance, and robbed him of control over his life. And of course, it demanded daily propitiation whether one believed in it or not, thereby presenting him with further opportunities for degradation. I suppose León felt properly debased dipping his fingers in the cotton drawers of a kindhearted yet most bloat, repulsive woman, but once he left the hospital he found an even more disgusting way to procure morphine: he became a catamite.

M. Braquemard Fauconnier, the fifty-year-old Belgian who became León's protector, believed he'd made the conquest of a lifetime. He was a tall, pale fellow with a slightly bulbous lower lip and milky blue eyes in which, if one looked closely, one could see an asthmatic eight-year-old who cannot get to sleep until *maman* brings him a good-night kiss. His schooling and some early lovers had endowed him with a wide though superficial culture. His Parisian tailor composed his flabby body into the counterfeit presentment of good health. His large inheritance permitted him indulgence, of his hobbies, which were art criticism and travel, and his vocation, which was sodomy. Although he hunted ceaselessly for fresh meat, he bore himself with great restraint and circumspection, exhaling but the faintest fragrance of effeminacy in his way of brushing his clear-lacquered fingernails across his lips while yawning or his tendency to speak a trifle quickly when a potential *cher ami* was within hearing. He was vain of his exquisite taste, his delicate, impeccably refined sensibilities, but he didn't really like himself at all, and thus he marveled at what he thought was his seduction of a perfectly beautiful, ostensibly hetero, anally-virginal young man. In fact he was seduced by León.

Having decided to become a whore, León might certainly have looked to women. He had his youth, his education, his good looks.

Dr. Heilanstalt had given him some cash and a good suit of clothes; five months abed had furnished that ethereal pallor which your money-eyed dame often finds fetching. His experience with Edna Scallop must have shown him gigoloing is revolting. Perhaps he considered it and then rejected it as foul but not quite foul enough. In any case, he took the doctor's gifts and Edna's parting thank you of six flasks of morphine and went trolling for a wealthy invert. He fished M. Fauconnier so skillfully that Fauconnier believed himself the predator.

One may imagine[62] León perched at the bar of the St. Regis, nursing a goblet of vermouth and soda, ostensibly immured in his own thoughts but keeping the room cased by discreet spyings in the mirror. Fauconnier glances in, sees something interesting, strolls up and takes a stool one stool away from León's, shoots his cuffs, spikes elbows on the bar, orders Pernod, and passes some remarks in French to the jowled barman. León retains eyes front but smiles effusively at the first clever mot. Fauconnier looks over suavely, hesitates, receives no answering look, continues chatting—in a most animated manner, strewing out pearls of wit. In due course León smiles again—as to himself, you understand; as one who does not seek but cannot help to overhear; as one who knows the language, appreciates good talk, admires the speaker's brilliant sense of humor, and, perforce, smiles. Fauconnier takes the bait:

"*Vous parlez français, par hasard, jeune homme?*"

They chat—or rather Fauconnier displays his cleverness and culture like a peacock's plumage; León admires. The cocktail-hour tide seeps in, filling the tables, bubbling about the bar, and M. Fauconnier moves from his stool to stand at León's side. They switch, at Fauconnier's invitation, to something stronger—"*Un whisky maintenant, par exemple? Bien? Formidable!*"—and go on chatting. Yes, agrees León as Fauconnier drains his second whisky, it grows stifling in here. Yes, in point of fact, he's free for dinner.

One may imagine them sconced in a fashionable corner at the Chambord, sucking braised capon. Fauconnier discourses with sibilant respect of Proust and Gide—of their literary genius, not their love life. It's a bit early for the latter, but then he can't resist and works it in discreetly, praising "pauvre *Marcel*" on the skill with which he fashioned blossoming young girls from his male playmates. And the delicious boy takes it in stride, shows no repugnance, even remarks that (he supposes) love remains love no matter whom it's felt for or how it's expressed.

One may imagine their handshake upon parting: León presses virilely before retreating to the Y. to plot campaign; Fauconnier lays his left hand over León's right, breathes "*Cher jeune homme,*" then taxis off to an androgynous bordello on West Fourth Street to 'suage his thirsty letch. One may imagine their next day's rendezvous at the Met Museum, their evening at the theater, their afternoon with Rubinstein and Chopin at Carnegie Hall. One may perfectly well imagine both their lunch at Rumpelmayer's (where Fauconnier, after checking slyly to make sure that the two silver-fox-draped Jewesses at the next table, who might know French, were too engrossed in their own gossip to eavesdrop, delivered—just in passing, you understand, just to make conversation—his famous Bumberry Prize lecture, "Great Faggots of Art and Letters,"[63] in which he proved by unassailable logic that since the golden days when Socrates cornholed Alcibiades, everyone with any taste or talent was queer) and their dinner at Delmonico's (where León told with poignant entirely fabricated innocence how through his orphaned youth he'd yearned, to have a father and then looked up, moist-eyed and reverent, toward the slavering Fauconnier). While one is at it, one may also imagine their late evening conversation in Fauconnier's suite, during which León reeled the fat cod in. León reclines like Mme Recamier on a silk-upholstered, blue-and-beige-striped chaise longue. Fauconnier, bleary with lust, has dragged a scrollarmed desk chair to within half a meter of León's crotch, has clasped his hands firmly together to impede their premature activity, and has invited León to move in with him and to travel with him to Europe as soon as passages can be procured. León temporizes by declaring that he has no passport. Fauconnier lets his hands fly ceilingward, assures his dear fellow that such things can be remedied, what is money for? León looks down demurely and pleads that he feels so strongly drawn to M. Fauconnier that were they to live in close proximity, he might begin to feel, to do . . . Fauconnier grinds his teeth, manages to smile, to shrug avuncularly, and to whisper that there is nothing to fear in friendship, in the true friendship of men. Then León topples into sobs and confesses that he has already betrayed their friendship, and Fauconnier shudders, conjuring up the image of a youthful rival to whose muscular embraces

León repairs each night. León confesses there is something terribly wrong with him, and Fauconnier glances mentally into a glossy tome filled with illustrations of scabrous maladies. Then, finally, León blurts out that he's a morphine addict, and Fauconnier, unspeakably relieved—no, not just relieved, exultant, since he will have the wretched boy entirely in his power—reaches a trembling hand to León's knee, calls him his dear, dear boy, grants him full absolution— "*Ça! Ça n'est rien entre deux hommes du monde*"—feels his hand tentatively touched in gratitude, in love, reaches it higher, transfers his buttocks to the chaise, leans forward, and flops, gasping and gaffed, in León's net.

But if one is going to imagine all that, one is then obliged to imagine, one is forced to imagine, one is remorselessly compelled to imagine what follows in suite. An implacable and iron hand seizes one's poor imagination and stuffs it down into the mess that follows next. One cannot help imagining a supine and unbuttoned León allowing those clear-lacquered fingers to roach over his flesh, letting that flabby body leach against his, permitting that bulbous lip to snail across his abdomen and clam his manhood. One is unable to avoid imagining León twitching his loins in uncontrolled, unfakable pleasure as several million of his potential sons and daughters spurt hotly onto Braquemard Fauconnier's gold inlays. And one is powerless to blot out the image of León Fuertes kneeling before the chaise, resting his naked belly on the silk, submitting peacefully while the old pervert trowels cold cream onto his (León's!) pouting bung, anoints his own puffy lob, and slides it in.

My father, León Fuertes, was a kept boy for three years—a Ganymede, a pederast, a gonzel. He delivered himself entirely to this profession, leaping with abandon to gross couplings, till Fauconnier wondered if he was truly a fresh convert and not a refugee from some Calcutta burdel who'd been at them from childhood. The acts, in themselves, would not have been degrading, but that they were inauthentic and done as self-punishment. León wasn't gay, he wasn't bi. He didn't crave to have sex with men, he didn't enjoy it. He flogged himself to it, against disgust, and later indulged in feasts of self-pity. He put on all the trappings: the twittered moues and languid mincings and simpering smirks, warping his mind so that his body altered. His voice mounted an octave, his hips rounded, his legs slimmed. He might have vaulted the sex barrier as cleanly as Rebeca had, but that he kept the organs he was born with. With Rebeca, the change occurred, and she adapted. León forced the change to procure defilement.

He went with Fauconnier to Europe on a fake passport with a phony name and a false nationality, luckily enough, or else the evil reputation that he won there might have blocked a return to himself and smashed his life. Nowhere on that decaying continent, not in Capri or fuming Venice, was there a more flagrant and disgusting swish. He mastered all the repertoire of vice, adding refinements of his own which would have shocked Gomorrah, and played on Fauconnier, wasting his body and reducing him into an idiocy of sexual dependence wherein León was able to extort large sums for this or that caress and get away with any infidelity or insult. His public behavior was a perambulating scandal up and down the Côte d'Azur. He referred to himself loudly in the feminine gender, flirted in blatant glee with handsome waiters, squealed sluttish epithets in packed cafés, and boasted of his loves, some real, some fancied, with a shamelessness and wealth of filthy detail that embarrassed even other perverts. At Cannes he rose from a winning hand at baccarat to embrace the croupier, kiss him on the lips, run mousy fingers down his shirt front and inside his pants, so that the poor man had convulsions, and the cards and chips went flying, and the game broke up, and León was whisked rudely from the building and warned on pain of jail never to step inside again. In Nice he put on drag and captivated a thirty-nine-year-old Wyoming cattleman, a dead ringer for Gary Cooper and as straight a man as ever pulled on boots. He'd heard about those Frenchy wimmin and their wiles, but he'd never bought much of it till he met the real McCoy, and León led him a terrific chase: check-to-cheek dancing under smoldering stars while saxophones moaned passion and the sea lapped softly at the smooth stones of the *plage;* hand-holding midnight strolls along the Promenade des Anglais; slow horsecab rides to nowhere punctuated by deep endless kisses; and at length, an intimate rendezvous, at which León (Léona to the gringo), pleading virginity and fear of pregnancy, stayed fully clothed but made him profusely happy with a triad of concatenated blow jobs. That night the man proposed. The next day León met him for lunch on the well-frequented Negresco terrace and (between the pâté and the sole amandine) pitched him to gibbering, foam-flecked lunacy by removing first earrings, then silky lashes, then lip rouge, then auburn wig, and then frock, so that before the maître d'hôte hustled him off, León stood a moment in male bathing costume, thrusting the pouched proof of his virility into the gringo's face. And in Villefranche one night he took on the entire starboard watch of a Greek frigate. He delighted in seducing married men, in splitting pairs of homosexual lovers, in debauching schoolboys, and he vaunted his conquests proudly, as though there were no finer thing in all the world than to have been reamed by every dingus in the south of France.

Actually, he stewed in self-loathing. His pose of shamelessness drenched him with shame, in which he soaked as punishment for shameful actions. Hence be was drawn to that particular class of thug (homos themselves, if often latent ones) who like abusing queers. He would pursue them—pimps, degenerates, the rankest sewer flotsam—and beg for love, or attempt fondling, till, whining and blubbering, he got his longed-for beating. And so, as yet another step in his descent, he put himself in bondage to such a type, a certain minor gangster of Toulon called Dédé-le-julot. He fell in love with Dédé, that kind of love whose gratification is injury and humiliation, a coprophagous love engendered by its object's foulness. He left Fauconnier and became one of Dédé's cocaine pushers.

This move paid him abundant dividends of squalor. Dédé abused him with satisfying regularity and cruelty. Dédé reviled him. When one of Dédé's streetwalkers fished a particularly kinky client, Dédé made León accommodate the fellow. And when Dédé staged exhibitions in the shuttered barroom of a *hôtel de passe,* León's was the main act in the repertory. Sconced on a mattress ringed by sweating men and prospecting harlots, he played Desdemona to a Mauritanian longshoreman, a marvelously well-equipped performer whose sole thespian defect was that he tended to become personally involved in the drama and to jam prologue, rising action, and catastrophe into three frenzied minutes. Thus León clawed himself down into the slough of degradation. Thus he indulged himself, for self-hatred is a mark of pride, and León surely cared about himself immensely to take such pains in his defilement. He did everything, absolutely everything, to lower himself.

At length he reached bottom.[64] One night as he lay whimpering in his room—a cubicle in a weary old fornicatorium beside the harbor in Toulon—his grandmother Rosenda and his great-grandmother Raquel and his great-great-grandmother Rosalba came to him, although he saw them not, and brought him a kind of clearness. He remembered his bright promise and reviewed his terrible descent, his headlong fall which was no accident of chance but freely sought. He looked at himself with the eyes of that young León who had seen the bums and perverts of La Cuenca, his drunken stepfather, Florencio Merluza, for example, or the abject sweeper of the cheap cantina where Merluza drank. And these seemed decent men worthy to wear God's image beside the 1940 model León Fuertes.

Then León wished himself a dung beetle or a toad or any crawling thing to which such baseness might be native, but there was nothing lower than himself and nowhere lower to descend to. And so he got up from his bed and went past the window—which let in the warm breeze of the May night and the immemorial raucous bruit of harbor revelry—and took his razor from the shelf above the washstand and cut his throat. He looked in the stained mirror, smiled sickly at himself, and cut his throat. He laid the edge of his razor against his flesh above the bridge of his clavicle and cut his throat. But no blood flowed. He pried the gash apart with his fingers and stared into it and rubbed it with his knuckles, but his veins refused to bleed.

Then León thought that he was dead and gone to hell. He had died the same night as Rosario and had been in hell ever since. One of his suicide attempts had worked, and he had dropped into a proper Christian hell where incest was punished with imaginative rigor for eternity. His damnation would drag on across the eons, on and on without release.

While he was thinking this, he watched the deep slash in his throat pucker and heal, and this recalled the way his wounds had healed years before on the Fort Shafter ball field. Then León suddenly decided he had gone to hell alive, not dead, that he had written his own ticket for the trip, but that something inside him had remained unsoiled and uncorrupted. Next he decided he had indulged himself enough in that kind of tourism, that it was time to search for a route back. He looked at himself in the mirror and laughed, half bitterly but half in cheer as well, and decided that he had seen some things of interest but that wherever he went from now on, he would not pass this way again. Then he bathed himself as thoroughly as he could and left that place and his morphine and his syringe and his life of shame. A few hours later the Wehrmacht smashed into France and furnished him a path to reclamation.

13. Journey

IT IS NOT KNOWN if Churchill, when he offered the British blood, sweat, and tears, considered these detergents. We are accustomed to regard them soiling agents, and so they are in all too many cases. But they can cleanse as well. Some stains can be expunged only in blood. Sweat works for others. Tears are fine solvents too, if they be tears of grief and not self-pity. Besides these, many heinous blots are washed away in the adrenaline of fury. León Fuertes bathed in these hot fluids for five years and emerged clean.

War is an evil, or is thought so now. Love is a good, or so it's held to be. But nothing in this world is pure or simple, nothing is absolute, no general truth obtains in every case. Love has ruined millions— war, which is mostly waste, sometimes preserves. Such was the case with León.

In late June, 1940, when he'd recovered from the torments of morphine withdrawal, my father, León Fuertes, lay, feeble and penniless, in a flophouse in Marseilles, more or less in the same moral condition as the French Republic: after years of self-indulgence and excess he was defeated and dishonored. Then his three military ancestors[65] came to him in a dream. General Feliciano Luna wore the stylized vaquero outfit with twin six-guns in which he had been decked with a bogus presidential sash in La Merced in 1883. General Epifanio Mojón wore the blue uniform of a subaltern in Simon Bolivar's army. General Isidro Bodega, who had never seen a battle, not even from a distance, was the most resplendent of the three, festooned with glittering stars and decorations and dangles of gold braid. He stayed in the background and said nothing. The others talked of war.

War, said General Epifanio Mojón, appeared a monstrous evil to all men of worth—that is, men who had work to do and loved ones to care for. It came to the worthless, though, wearing the mantle of a savior. In war, the general said, worth didn't matter. One man was as good as the next for filling up a rank and stopping bullets, and if it came to close quarters, the worst men were the best. And there was plenty of fresh death about to cure all past remorse. War was a resurrection.

War, said General Feliciano Luna—why, if it hadn't been for war, he would have pissed his life out nameless in Salinas. War had made him a national hero, with all Tinieblas fiesta'd on the anniversary of his hanging, and schoolboys parading in their Sunday suits. León couldn't see his own good fortune. He, General Luna, had had to make his own war, while León had a full-scale conflagration raging on his doorstep. León should get off his back and go to war!

León woke resolved to follow in war's train, and with this very resolution his hormones began to flow correctly once again, and his beard grew, and his voice dropped, and his body regained male contours.

León Fuertes took part in the Second World War on the side of the Allies. One would prefer to say he joined them for the justice of their cause, but that would be dishonest. He knew nothing of politics in those days and had lived the four preceding years in utter disregard of world affairs. He viewed the war not as a struggle between good and evil but as a personal opportunity, and since it seemed the Axis had it all but won, there was a better chance for death or glory with the Allies. England's pigheaded resistance appealed to him, but the English still had their island and the empire and their pride. As a loser, he identified with the French. They had nothing but ignominy, a brigadier general invented by Cervantes, and a military unit designed expressly for men like himself. So he sold his beautifully faked passport to a refugee Czech Jew and got a piece of paper from the Tinieblan Consul attesting his true name and nationality and took himself over to Sidi-bel-Abbès to join the Foreign Legion.

The Legion wouldn't have him. The Vichy government was holding back recruitment. The Legion leadership adored Pétain, despised de Gaulle, and were in such a state of moral paralysis that they scarcely had will enough to keep the Nazi Armistice Commission from pirating legionnaires into the Wehrmacht or the concentration camps, much less make room for men who wished to fight. It was a bad blow to León's fragile self-esteem to be turned off by a formation famous for its hospitality to the worst scum of Europe, but in his dreams General Feliciano Luna growled for him to go somewhere and fight, so he decided to cross North Africa and join the British Army on the Nile. Then, when he was in Constantine, he heard the most amazing tale from Central Africa: a French nobleman who, wounded, had survived the May debacle and escaped through Spain, who, feeling France's shame in his own person, had taken a *nom de guerre* and joined de Gaulle, who had appeared as by enchantment in the Cameroons, embarked a handful of adherents in native dugouts, gone to Douala, seized full power, and declared the colony for Free France, was now at Fort-Lamy, where, with a little ragtag army, he was going to command operations in the Sahara. It was the sort of thing León had read of in old poets but didn't think occurred in the "real" world. Here was this disinherited knight knocking about Africa with visor down and no device upon his shield except the Cross, the Cross of Lorraine, looking for a fight. León thought of great blundering British divisions with their Sandhurst officers and the stiff-collared sergeants major; then be thought of operations in the Sahara and thought no more. He hadn't really thought at all, in the sense of weighing alternatives and making what is called a mature decision. General Luna was sympathetic. The fellow was a cavalryman. His "operations" sounded like mobile raiding on an open flank, out of a base too poor and too remote for anyone to threaten, over country too tough for a regular army's taste: in short, the kind of war he knew about and savored. León had made his mind up anyway. For the first time in years he had a clear sense of purpose. He headed for the Chad and Jacques Leclerc.

Had León Fuertes never reached the war, his journey toward it would have served to purge the shame of his preceding years. Fort-Lamy is a good twenty-eight hundred kilometers from Constantine as the crow—or more usually the buzzard-flies, and León did no flying. He rode a bus[66] to Biskra and an oil truck from Biskra to Touggourt. He rode a mule from there past Fort Lallemand. He rode a stretcher for a while after that, and later on a series of bad camels. Often he walked,[67] leading a beast sometimes or packing all his water and belongings. He covered over four thousand kilometers, more than twenty-five hundred miles, a lot of it on foot, *across the Sahara Desert*. It took him the best part of a year. It taught him an abiding respect for the value of water, so that years afterward and in a country where it rains daily, often in torrents, from May to December, he couldn't bear to see it wasted and would come in the bathroom while my sister, Clara, or my brother, Carlos, or I was washing up and close the tap down to a trickle. But mainly it gave him hardship, the sovereign remedy against the moral ravages of self-indulgence.

At Fort Lallemand he was arrested by Vichy police and questioned. He showed them his piece of paper with its rampant alligator stamp, and they checked and learned that the Tinieblan government was stridently pro-Axis and released him. But he suspected that the man in charge had doubts about his reasons for being in southern Algeria, and so he set out at once across the Grand Erg Oriental: on muleback: with a pocket compass and a map torn from an atlas.

It was a stern welcome to the desert: dunes, building as he progressed until they rose two and three hundred feet above him; airless ravines between them through which he had to tack; stifling oven heat which killed his mule; loose, sliding sand that seized his feet with every toiling step and scorched his ankles. His luck was that he didn't know *erg* means death, and that he was delirious after two days and scarcely suffered. A Legion patrol, a group of anti-Nazi Germans sent south to escape an Armistice Commission visit, found him stumbling in circles on a stretch of packed-sand *reg*, raving with thirst and heatstroke, less than a day from death. They carried him down to Fort Flatters.

He came to a week later but could think only of the time he'd lost and the two hundred-odd kilometers now added to his journey. He set out again as soon as he could stand, crossing the Erg Edeyen to Fort Polignac with a Legion column and the Tassili-n-Ajjer alone on camelback. Northwest of Ghat he blundered within range of his camel's teeth and nearly died of blood poisoning. He lay in that filthy crossroads village for a month, stewed in fever, writhed in a monster-thronged delirium which faded only into the greater horror of a traveler from Tombouctou who claimed to be a doctor and who proposed to lop his arm off at the shoulder. He had long staring sessions with Death, who bore a great resemblance to an ebony carving from somewhere in black Africa that his half-Arab-half-Italian host left in his room. Death was about half a meter tall, thin, hard, and shiny black. He stared at León for hours on end, ready to collect him the moment his concentration waned and he turned his eyes away. Sometimes Death swelled gigantically until he filled the room and his face was but a millimeter from León's. Mostly he simply waited, and León would bite his lip and stare back at him, till he shrank smaller and smaller and then looked away. At length Death grew familiar and no longer frightening and would look away almost at once. León learned that Death's rumored implacability is vastly overrated and that there is no call to fear him. When he saw Death again in Italy three years later, it was like meeting an old acquaintance, one he knew for a dull companion, and he told Death to go away and come back later.

The desert was a harsher master. It tested León cruelly. There was the endless weariness of day on day with the sun drumming on him, while some nights chilled his bones so that he felt he might as well be bedding on an ice floe. He was always thirsty, usually hungry, often famished. He ate things out of Arab pots that would have turned his stomach when he was scavenging on the Bowery, ate them and licked his chops. He was chafed raw when he rode and blistered when he walked. He was bitten by flies and stung by wind-blown sand. Once he woke to find himself infested with huge ants which swarmed inside his clothes and gnawed such chunks out of his thighs he couldn't sit his camel and went for days at a kind of searing waddle. He lost his way time and again and had to backtrack. He knew that any day might bring one of a large variety of deaths, all disagreeable, and that if he survived, he had nothing to look forward to except another day of painful journey. He pushed on till he forgot who he was, why he'd come, where he was headed, until he moved out of a kind of mindless habit, like an ox who trudges round and round, pushing a mill wheel, and the desert glittered at him, winking from a million separate pinpoints, striking him like a tremendous noise out of an endless blue-white sky.

There was the hardship, too, of isolation. Once or twice, early on, he came upon some Berber nomads, but he kept his distance, taking what companionship he could from the flare of far-off campfires. Along one stretch he moved with a caravan, but he felt far from welcome and came, rightly or no, to suspect that every whisper touched on him with murderous intent. Between Ghat and Marzúq, a trek of near five hundred kilometers, he straggled in the wake of some

Senussi pilgrims bound for the oasis of Al Jaghbúb and the tomb of Sayed Mohammed bu 'Ali, the founder of their sect. He felt an instinctive fraternity with these Arabs, who had fought the Italians for nineteen years, who thought war the only occupation that befitted a free man, who lived in the most pure austerity, bound by a rigid code for which they were at all times ready to lay down their lives, but though he picked up something of their language, he could hardly converse with them; and besides, he had, as usual, been tricked when he bought his camel, and it soon grew too weak to bear him, and by the time he'd staggered in along their tracks each night to the Senussis' camp, he was too weary to do more than gulp some food and drop in sleep. And for weeks at a time he did not so much as glimpse another human.

At first this isolation was a tonic. The desert, unsullied by the touch of man, threw up a barrier of purity between him and his years of degradation. But later his solitude grew oppressive.[68] It struck him that his death out there would mean no more than the shriveling of a desert nettle or the expiration of a lizard torn by a bird of prey. He took to singing entire operas out loud, just to hear a human voice. Asleep at midday in some wadi, his blanket staked above him for a shade, he dreamed long conversations with Rosario wherein they played at being married and spoke of homes and children, and though on waking he felt guilty at these dreams, he fled into them eagerly at each lying down. On march he imagined dialogues with Dr. Grillo, inventing the doctor's speeches and replying to them, and then for days on end it seemed that Dr. Grillo walked beside him, flapping his white-linen-jacketed arms, pulling his panama down over his brow, interspersing philosophical remarks with comments on the desert, drawing in references to the *Pharsalia and Travels in Arabia Deserta* and Burton's memoir of his journey to Medina, books León had never read and couldn't recall Dr. Grillo's ever having mentioned back in Tinieblas. Quite often he was accompanied by his grandfather General Feliciano Luna, who rode a large bay gelding and wore silver spurs, who related his own hardships as a *guerrillero* and reminded León that swamps can be as difficult to cross as burning rock. These conversations made León's isolation bearable, but when they faded he was buffeted by fears for his sanity, for he thought his visitors hallucinations.

Still, León's journey was a beneficent ordeal. Austerity fed his spirit; hardship strengthened it; the desert sun tempered it and burned it pure. Enduring, he forged himself new and found a strange and telling joy of life. He would come to himself sometimes on waking, or after a day-long trance of march, and define the torments of his body: everlasting rasping thirst; hunger; sun headache, which made him feel like carving a wedge out of his cranium to let the pressure down; cramps of dysentery from bad water; saddle chafe; the sting of open sores and burst blisters; the itch of insect bites and filthy clothes; the anguish of stiff joints; the rebellious twitch of overloaded muscles; the general hubbub of complaint screamed out or whined from every segment of his organism at having been goaded so long across a hostile habitat. And having made this inventory, he'd likely think: *Isn't this fine! I'm still alive! I'm crossing the Sahara, and I'm still alive! This is the sort of thing you read about, and I'm doing it, on my own too! Why, I'm a better man than I thought I was!*

No matter what happened to him—even when his camel took to lying down two hundred miles south of the Bi'r al Wa'r oasis, and after he'd got her going several times by lighting his Sterno under her, gave an evil smirk and died, and he had to walk two hundred miles to Bilma; even when he was caught in a sandstorm and lay three days, his face[69] wrapped in his blanket, chewing sand—there was always a part of him which was taking joy in life. Such feelings coexisted even with fear and the conviction that he wasn't going to make it.

He found his lost taste for life out there, found it redoubled, so that years later, he could smile kindly when he answered a despaired "I can't" from his children or his associates with "You'd be surprised what you can do, truly surprised." Through every moment of his journey he was sure that he was doing the right thing: in other words, he was happy.

He came down from Agadem oasis across the Tin Toumma Steppe out of the desert to Nguigmi. He crossed Lake Chad by boat and went up the Chari River to Fort-Lamy. He walked into French military headquarters in rags and tatters, and when a Senegalese sergeant tried to shoo him out, stood his ground, making a racket, until a captain—St. Cyr, from the look of him: crisp manners and a strong air of disdain—came out and asked his business.

Was the war still on? asked León in return.

Ah, yes, assuredly it was, and who was he to ask?

Was Commandant Leclerc still in the field?

General Leclerc had taken Kufra in the Soudan, had put his headquarters north on the border and was raiding into Libya, but what was that to León?

"I've come to fight," said León. "Germans if possible; Italians, *faute de mieux*; if need be, Vichy Frenchmen."

"Who the devil are you?"

"I'm nobody really, from a place you've likely never heard of, but I've come across the desert from Algeria, and I'd like to fight."

An hour later he was a private in the Army of Free France.

14. Soldier

IT IS SUPPOSED by some historians that the hod carriers of Chartres considered themselves with pride cathedral builders, that though they did menial work, they felt part of an exalted company. War brought this sense of unity to my father, León Fuertes, but not at once. For a long time war for him consisted in nursing an elderly Ford two-and-a-half-tonner back and forth between Fort-Lamy and towns like Faya, Zouar, Fada: ports on the shore of the vast sea of sand across which Leclerc's captains cruised and raided. He baked through the long passages with a black soldier-stevedore beside him and a load of food or fuel or ammunition stacked behind, hung in a sort of limbo between sloth and action, trying to feel himself as part of something grand but not succeeding. He couldn't see the liberation of mankind in the steam of an overheated radiator, or hear the flash of arms in a snapped piston, and though he wore a uniform and was carried on the roll of Leclerc's force, he felt more isolated than when he was crossing the Sahara.

It was no help at all that General Feliciano Luna was accustomed to drop in from time to time during his dreams and tell how León's "comrades" were stinging the enemy on his southern flank. Oh, they were marvelous lads, rode their tanks and armored cars like ponies and could operate a thousand kilometers from their bases. There wasn't an oasis up in Libya that was safe from them, and if the Germans mounted anything too strong, why, they would disappear into the desert like scorpions. And their commanders—that Massu, for instance: he was a man after General Luna's heart, hard as a stone, a killer to the core and terrible for discipline. And their columns were small, and self-contained, and on their own. It was a first-rate war out there, wonderful fighting. Why wasn't León in it? León would wake with the question in his ears and go pester his CO about a transfer. The man would reply, at first in sympathy, later in outright rage, that everyone wanted to be out there, that it couldn't work that way, that he should do his job.

Twenty years later León Fuertes was to express a gratitude at having been denied the taste of General Luna's kind of war. This was in May, 1962, a few weeks before his inauguration as President of Tinieblas. He was filling appointments to his government, and Aquilino Piojo came to him at his beach house at Playa Medusa on behalf of César Enrique Sancudo, asking why Sancudo had been offered the embassy at Madrid—a kind of exile instead of a decent post at home. President-elect Fuertes received him on the terrace overlooking the Pacific (out of the view but not the hearing of his nosy younger son, who pressed his naked back against the cool of the cement wall below them and squidged his toes in the sand), and let Piojo speak his piece about Sancudo's energy and promise and his services in the campaign.

Then he said, "Kiki's a man on horseback. The same as his father, Alejo, and it won't do. I know the mounted man's perspective—not firsthand: I used to see them when they were going out or coming back. It's the same, you know, basically, whether one has a charger or a tank, a lance or a cannon. They're up out of the dirt, you see, with plenty of momentum, and a little separated from the mess one's weapon makes. It gives them a sense of privilege to ride over people. It has a way of making violence seem romantic. I wanted to be a cavalryman myself, but luckily enough I missed the chance. Kiki was born to it, and trained to it by example. Father and son, both men on horseback. But I'm going to run an infantryman's administration, so I can't have him around."

At the time, though, León felt anything but lucky. He felt, in fact, more or less as he had on childhood Christmas mornings: the other boys had toys to play with and he didn't.

Then, in late fall of 1942, as Montgomery drove west across Cyre-
naica from El Alamein, Leclerc grouped all his force into a mobile
column and flung it north out of the Chad into Fezzan. They
smashed the German flank guards and took Sebha and Marzúq and
dashed on into Tripolitania, and León, still in his truck but now
within the sound of cannon and enemy aircraft, began to feel a part
of what Montgomery's staff were calling "L Force" and looking to
link up with. At the end of February, 1943, Leclerc took a position
called Ksar-Rhilane out on the *erg* west of Matmata, and Montgomery radioed him to hold it and cover the approach of the New
Zealanders of the Eighth Army's left wing. And so the mobile column
was transformed, like it or not, into a blocking force, and on 10th
March they were attacked by elements of the 21st Panzer Group and
bombed by Stukas. They held in the desert, and their transport convoys went out to resupply them, and one moment León was leaning
forward, peering through a windshield caked with sand thrown by
the truck in front, and then he heard aircraft engines, and then he
woke up in a hospital. An English nurse smiled at him and told him
in halting French that he was in Tripoli, that he'd been in coma for
two months, that Afrika Korps had surrendered and the campaign
was over.

He hadn't a nick on him. A bomb he never heard had blown him
from his truck and sent his conscious mind on nine weeks furlough.
He was watched for another month, found fit for duty, and sent to
a big depot in Algeria—back where he'd started almost three years
before but without much feeling that he'd served with Jacques
Leclerc or taken part in operations in the Sahara. He felt mightily
sick of truck driving, though, and not a little angry at the Germans
for having tried to kill him. He asked to be sent to some formation
where he'd have a weapon, and since the French command was for
the moment undecided whether to disband L Force or build it to a
division, he was assigned as a replacement rifleman to the 3rd Algerian infantry Division, refitting at Kléber in Oranie.

León was now among the regulars, the hard-ranked big battalions
of the French African Army.[70] It was an army laden with tradition,
sodden with glory, weighed with the valor of *chasseurs* cut down at
Balaklava and Moroccan infantry pounded to morsels in the trenches
at Verdun. It was charged, too, with shame: from the moment, eight

months before, when it had turned to face the Germans it had fought bravely, but its Tunisian combats were too brief to atone fully for its years of idleness and indecision, and it yearned to its lowest private to prove itself an equal to its allies. Its ranks, once starved by Vichy policy, were now engorged with escapees from France, with Muslim volunteers, with mobilized *pieds-noirs*. Its formations were being thoroughly reequipped with U.S. weapons and materiel. León felt as if he had been dropped into a huge and pulsing mass which was about to rumble forward with invincible power. He sought eagerly to graft himself to it.

As mentor he had his great-great-grandfather General Isidro Bodega.[71] It is true General Bodega never saw a battle, never took part even in the briefest skirmish, never so much as heard a cannon except on ceremonial occasions; that at the first gesture of Tinieblan independence he surrendered the plaza at Otán without a shot and went over to the insurgents; that he lived by guile, not violence, and died, boots off, of gastroenteritis—but it is just as true that in his youth he was the finest drillmaster in all the Spanish Empire. He came at night to León and drenched his dreams in discipline and in *esprit de corps*. For six months León trained day and night, and his flesh-and-bone officers and noncoms were like gentle nannies beside General Bodega. Each night General Bodega marched León to an astral barrack ground, barked him through squad, drill and the manual of arms, set him the rule of military bearing, taught him to love his weapons as himself and his unit above himself. General Bodega put León to riflery until his concentration never strayed from sights and target, drilled him at bayonet until his hand was sure as any surgeon's, read him the principles of tactics until he could have led a regiment in combat. Most tellingly, he molded León to group thought and action, so that in his battalion exercises at Kléber, in mountain training in the Saharan Atlas, in divisional maneuvers, León grew able to anticipate commands and sense the movements of men out of his vision.

Under this tutelage León learned to modulate his heartbeats to the cadence of a marching column, to make himself a single and dependent cell in the great body of his regiment. When on the dusty route marches across the bled the first sergeant would sing out "*Auprès de ma blonde,*" León would join and feel that in some past existence he had marched in Holland with the army of King Louis. On parade, with the division ranged in heavy regimental squares before a huge and floating *tricouleur*, with massed bands blaring out *"La Marseillaise,"* he felt one with the army of Bonaparte. By late December, when his division boarded ship for Italy, he had been merged into the army and transformed into a regular and rewarded in this metamorphosis by promotion. And now, a soldier, he was to take part in a great battle.

Naples did not put on its chrome and azure for the men of the Three Crescent Division. The sky was grey. A cold wind blew in tempest. North, the old villages crouched in a sea of mud, a strange mud, imprecise of color, liquid as milk, which splashed above house windows from the heavy wheels of the division's columns. Above San Vittore they went into the Fifth Army line, forcing themselves up paths glutant with mud and snow, struggling along ridges swept by gases and thunderclouds behind the mules that bore their rations and ammunition. Sometimes a mule would lose its footing in the frost and tumble, dragging the whole string into a ravine, and they would clamber down and shift the loads onto their backs and clamber back, while gaunt and hard-eyed muleteers went about cursing, blasting injured beasts with pistols, lashing the sound ones up along the slopes. Some sections of their route were under observation of the enemy, and here they went by night, bent double under loads, groping their way. In this manner they relieved the U.S. 45th Division and took their place between the 4th Moroccan and the U.S. 34th. On 12th January, 1944, they went to the attack. In the pitch dark of 5 A.M., cannon spoke out behind them and were answered from the heights across the valley, and at dawn the 7th and 3rd Algerians went down through the barrage and up Monna Casale to meet the Panzer Grenadiers. They fought four days and nights. A Moroccan regiment joined on the right, then a battalion of another. The 1st Battalion 4th Tunisians was committed, but León's stayed in reserve. Its only wound was to its pride and came when the fight was over. At noon on the 16th as they moved up behind the newly-won positions, a *goumier* of the Tabor Palange came by them on a stretcher, waving a German ear in his filthed hand and repeating an old saying of the bled: "Tunisians are women, Algerians are men, Moroccans are lions!" For a week they waited opposite the Gustav Line while both armies took their breath under cold rain and hawk sweeps of Messerschmitts and Mustangs. On the night of the 20th they heard cannon south, and then word filtered to them that the Texas Division was getting minced on the Rapido River. Two days later the sounds of battle moved closer, and they were ordered to relocate south and to prepare for action. None of them knew because a soldier never learns such things till later, but the Battle of Cassino[72] had begun.

Montecassino and its adjacent heights form the strongest natural defensive position in Europe: an abrupt mountain wall, pitted with deep ravines, glacis'd with rugged ridges, barbed with jagged crests. This serried pile of rock beneath which Hannibal and Belisarius had marched, which had been stormed by Saracen and Goth, was for five months in 1944 the point of contact for two mighty armies. Both disposed of the most modern weapons of an advanced technology and hurled upon each other an immense weight of steel and high explosive, yet much of the battle was fought hand to band in the hardest possible circumstances of terrain and weather. The positions round Cassino were held by Germans and Austrians and were successively assaulted by Americans, by Frenchmen and North Africans, by Rajputs, Gurkhas, and Punjabis, by white New Zealanders and Maoris, by English, Welsh, and Scots, by Canadians, and by Poles. They fought, it turned out, solely for the suffering and joy, the pride, the exercise of their humanity in the profoundly human enterprise called war, because the battle was entirely needless and indecisive. It need never have been fought: when the Allies had collected enough men, they flanked Cassino to the south and the Germans simply abandoned the positions they had held against bombardment and assault. And since Kesselring's army got away intact, Cassino accomplished nothing—save to provide action for its participants (along with great expense of blood and goods), spectacle for onlookers, study themes for students, and a delineation of the shame and glory of the human species for anyone who cares about such things. Thus Cassino possessed all the chief attributes of a great work of art: it was grand in theme, apt in setting, of good duration, and intense; it was at once contemporary and traditional; it transcended race and nationality; it depended on nothing outside itself; it served no useful purpose. Cassino was *bellum gratia belli*.

North of Cassino, overlooking it, though overlooked itself by

higher peaks, there is a hill called Belvedere, a naked rock that rises
nine hundred meters from the valley of Atina. In January, 1944, this
hill was separated from the Allied line by two fresh torrents and a
line of blockhouses, and it was strongly fortified and held by German
mountain troops. On 23rd January General Mark Clark, Commander, U.S. Fifth Army, asked General Alphonse Juin, Commander,
French Expeditionary Corps, to take Belvedere, and Juin assigned
the task to Major General Aimé de Goislard de Monsabert, Commander, 3rd Algerian Infantry Division; and Monsabert gave the assault to Colonel Roux, Commander, 4th Tunisian Tirailleurs; and
Roux picked his 2nd and 3rd Battalions (Commandants Berne and
Gandoët), which had not yet seen action in the campaign. Plans were
made and routes mapped and coordinates worked out, and at dusk
on 24th January Sublieutenant Bouakkaz assembled his section of
11th Company, 3rd Battalion, and told them they were going to earn
their pay at last and justify their training and their weapons. He
pointed out the crests of Belvedere, just visible in the darkening sky
five miles away across the valley, and told them that by this time tomorrow they would be there or in Paradise. *La Allah il Allah! Vive
la France!* Then Sergeant Mohammed Ben Abdelkadar told the section to stand fast and said that every man would clean his weapons
and check his equipment and fill his canteen and make up his bedroll
with his extra shirt and socks inside and bend the roll for slinging
and take his knapsack to the supply tent to be packed and be ready
for inspection at midnight, for they would move at two A,M., and
any man who was not ready would surely wish his she-camel mother
had never dropped him, and when they moved they would move
silently with no talk or any clatter of equipment, and they must
surely now be grateful for this chance to meet their enemies and
prove that they had something more between their legs than what a
woman has there, and while he knew to his despair how lazy and
stupid they all were, he prayed that tomorrow they might not disgrace France and Tunisia and the regiment and him dismissed!

Then Corporal León Fuertes went to his sangar,[73] a four-foot-high,
six-foots square, three-sided, poncho-roofed fort of piled-up rocks—
the kind of shelter built by all the men who fought around Cassino,
for the ground there was too stony to dig holes in—which he shared
with his squad leader, Sergeant Jabara, and got out a stub of candle

and lit it and glued it with hot wax to a projecting ledge and disassembled his U.S.-issue, 1903 model Springfield rifle down to the firing pin and cleaned each part slowly and carefully and then wiped all the oil away so that nothing would freeze. Then he replaced his cleaning rod and brush and little oilcan and wad of patches in the well in the butt and put the rifle back together and dry-fired it and put the piece on safety and loaded it, thumbing one round into the chamber and stripping a clip of five down onto the spring follower and closing the bolt. Then he dug into the pocket of his olive green woolen shirt and got out the condom which a soldier of the 45th Division bad tossed him three weeks before, shouting to his buddies that the Frogs would sooner fuck the Krauts than fight them, and peeled the foil and rolled the rubber down on his rifle's muzzle so that no dirt could enter and laid the piece carefully, bolt up, beside the sangar wall.

Next he drew out his fourteen-inch World War I model bayonet and tested its edge and found it sharp enough to shave with, but nonetheless he moistened it with saliva and stropped it on his shoe, and then wiped it and eased it in its sheath and clipped the sheath to his cartridge belt. He got out his clean shirt and a clean pair of socks and rolled them in his blanket and rolled the blanket in his poncho and tied the two ends of the roll together so it would sling over his shoulder, and while he was doing this Sergeant Jabara crawled in and began to make his own equipment ready, but León exchanged no words with him, nor did he think of anything except what he was doing. Once or twice, since his actions were all rote, thoughts did begin to infiltrate his mind, but he pinched them out instantly.

León left the sangar then and went two hundred meters back to the open latrine and let down first his U.S.-Issue field pants and then his khaki drab woolen trousers and squatted in the freezing drizzle and emptied himself as completely as he could. Then he went to the back of the officers' mess tent and took off his steel helmet and got it two-thirds full of fairly clean hot water and walked back to his sangar, holding the helmet cupped in his two palms, enjoying its warmth and hunching over it to keep the rain out. He sat down cross-legged and set the helmet between his thighs and got out a cake of soap and his shave brush and the razor he had tried to kill himself with three and a half years before and lathered up and stropped the razor on his shoe and shaved slowly, carefully, and well, by touch. He set the helmet in a corner of the sangar and took off his shoes and socks and washed his feet, dipping them in the deliciously warm water, and rubbed them dry and put on his last pair of socks and his shoes and his World War I style leggings, fitting the straps under his arches and drawing the laces tight enough to hold his field pants bloused but not so tight as to cut off circulation. All this time he thought only of what he was doing.

Then he leaned out of the sangar and emptied his helmet and put it on over his knit wool, cap and took his empty knapsack and went out. He went first to the wheeled water tank and filled his canteen, then to the supply tent, where he packed his knapsack with rations and hand grenades under the eye of the First Sergeant, Le Grevez, and filled the empty pouches in his cartridge belt with rifle clips, and hung three more grenades on his field jacket. Then he went to see the other soldiers of his squad.

Dax and Barelli had their gear in shape, and Barelli asked permission to visit Pére Bérenguer, the Catholic Chaplain, saying Dax would get his knapsack packed for him, and León thought first of sending him to Jabara but then gave him permission himself, wondering for an instant whether he ought go as well and deciding that since the Fuertes family never gave pardon, no member had a right to ask any, even from God if he happened to exist, and then he pinched that kind of thought out of his mind. Reveil crawled out to León when León looked in on him and his sangar-mate, Djemal, because Djemal, whose Browning Automatic Rifle was propped against his leg, had his phylactery wrapped round his arm and rocked in prayer. Reveil held out a grooved copper telephone *jeton*, which was the only thing besides his clothes he had brought out of France when he escaped, and asked León to take it in safekeeping, and León first thought of asking why Reveil thought it might be safe with him, but then took it and put it in his shirt pocket under his field jacket. Sergeant Jabara was in with Privates Boulala and El Haoui, honing his bayonet on Boulala's tiny whetstone. He looked up at León with his soft brown gazelle's eyes and smiled and said they would kill many infidels—Germans, he meant—the next day. León nodded at him in agreement. Then he went back to his sangar and set down his knapsack and took off his cartridge belt with its

pendent bayonet and aid kit and canteen and lay down in the dark
to think.

He did not simply relax and let thoughts swim haphazard to his
consciousness. He took grip on his mind and beamed it down across
the Rapido River into the German line. First he searched out the sentry posts, sweeping his mind left and right across the far bank of the
river until he found first one guard, then another, hunched over rifle
and field telephone, slapping their palms against their arms from
cold, peering into the darkness. He focused his mind so that he had
clear image of these men as they shivered out their hours of guard,
straining to catch some warning sound over the monotone low rush-
ing of the river, feeling the wind (dry now of rain) bite cold into their
checks, clenching their jaws to hold their teeth from chattering. Then
he swung his mind up and back into the sangars, some with riflemen
and some with Spandau teams, where some men watched and worried and some others slept, chins tucked to knees and hands between
their thighs. León reached his mind down through the filth-encrusted
blankets into these men's dreams and found them filled with warmth
and calm and safety—shimmer of sunlight on a Baltic plain, heavy
caress of *Vatti's* work-roughed hand, food smell and muslin rub of
Mutti's apron—but monstered at their borders with ice fangs and
shapes of terror. Then he aimed his mind into the deep concrete
blockhouses and candlelit cellars of L'Olivella. Here men were playing skat, slapping bent, sweaty cards onto scarred tables, or reading
letters. The readers would run their eyes down the thin paper and
purse their lips and shake their heads and rub their brows, reading
that Hansi was dead and cousin Paula's husband missing or that the
British bombed each night and people went to bed at six to get some
sleep beforehand, or that the cold was terrible in Russia and one was
lucky to be down in Italy. Then León's mind found other men who
lay sleepless, thinking of their children howling in bomb-quaked
shelters or of their mothers racked by fear and worry or of their
wives spraddled in frenzy under schnapps-breathed, sweat-rank men.
Still others thought of themselves blasted to mangles by a bomb, or
blinded by rock fragments, or pounded crazy by artillery, or gelded
by mortar shrapnel, or pierced by a bayonet—pierced through the
belly wriggling helplessly, pierced through the throat, pierced through
the groin and anus, pierced and pierced again, pierced through the

chest and hearing the bone grate, pierced through the temple feeling
the bone crumble, pierced through the back and nailed, pierced
through the spine and paralyzed, pierced through the lips and
tongue, biting on steel—, or buried alive under the crumbled roofing
of a bunker, or skewered by tracer bullets, or torn apart by grenades,
or killed, maimed, broken, crushed, wiped out, destroyed in still another fashion too hideous to imagine yet quite real. Others talked
softly to each other of better times, and others touched themselves in
the dark and thought of women, and others listened to the sounds of
battle to the south and wondered If attack would come that night or
in the morning, some fearfully and some in the wild, joyful hope of
seeing men cut down in sweeps of fire. León's mind reached out over
the valley and down across the Rapido and through the minefields
and the bunkers of the Gustav Line and on across the Riosecco and
up the cliffs behind onto the slopes of Colle Belvedere, even to the
crests, groping among the men in *Feldgrau* whom in the morning he
would try to kill and who would try to kill him, until he could smell
the wine and bad tobacco on their breaths and feel the stubble on
their faces and hear their talk and read their thoughts and know their
hopes and terrors. And when he had built this vision of his enemies
and stretched it even to include the gunners far off among the heavy
batteries, men who would never see his face though they might kill
him, León brought his mind back and gauged, himself.

He was a soldier and, as such, a follower of the best way of life.
He was precisely located within an ordered segment of an otherwise
chaotic world: corporal, 3rd Squad, 4th Section, 11th Company, 3rd
Battalion, 4th Tunisian Tirailleurs. He was placed on a clearly marked
pathway to the highest virtues: loyalty, courage, and self-sacrifice.
He was lodged in an endless, vital moment with his bungled yester-
days all cut away and his tomorrows taken care of. He would probably be killed before the war in Europe ended, perhaps in a few
hours, and if not, there was a war in the Far East and would be other
wars in other places: soldiering would go on. The men about him
were his brothers, his officers father surrogates. He was bound to
them all in love, and bound as well to the great company of men
now dead who'd served under the colors of his regiment, and to that
other company, still children or as yet unborn, who'd serve in years
to come. And he was kin to men in all the other armies, all those

who had embraced his calling round the globe and since the time of Troy and on till doomsday. He was about to go armed in company to meet another company likewise in arms, and they were going to kill each other over a piece of ground: a fundamental human activity which had engaged much of the energies of Homo sapiens since its emergence as a species. His ties to the members of his company were strong and satisfying, while the mere existence of a force[74] in opposition filled him with equally strong and satisfying sentiments of enmity, so he would go freely with enthusiasm. He possessed weapons that he cherished and respected; he had good knowledge of their use. He was encumbered by no obligations to absent people who depended on him or for whom he cared. He was conscious of having used his life fully if not particularly well. It would end someday, and since he was among comrades in a custom-hallowed calling, tomorrow was as good a day as any. His mind was calm yet wonderfully alert and most obedient to his will. His body was strong and fit. His senses were sharp, somewhat in fear, more in anticipation. He was ready for battle.

15. Warrior

IN THE CHILL black of early morning, 25th January, 1944, 2nd and 3rd Battalions, 4th Tunisian Tirailleurs went down from their bivouac along paths marked in their minefields, soundlessly down across the rocks and shingle to the Rapido River. A lead group forded without loads or rifles, stretching lines over and then stealing up to kill the German sentinels and cut the wires of the field telephones. Then the two battalions entered the river, which flowed colder than death about their thighs and waists, which rushed about their chests and pulled their feet from under them as they clung to the lines. They forded all in silence and went up out of the river into the colder air and set themselves along the farther bank to wait, shivering, for dawn and their assault. My father, León Fuertes, was with them.

All night his great-great-grandfather General Isidro Bodega had been beside him, watching him ready his equipment, reading his thoughts and feelings, and when he left with his battalion, General Bodega followed. He was so moved by the battalion's discipline and resolution that he thought to go into battle with them. He even crossed the river, flitting above the water just at León's left, but when he came upon the still and bloodless body of a murdered sentry, his nerve broke, and he grew terrified, and he flew back across the river and up to the division bivouac and hid in León's sangar, quaking. As he fled, he passed the ghost of General Epifanio Mojón [75] who stood on the rocky bank, slimmed and youthful as he had been when he fought in Simón Bolívar's army at the Battle of Ayacucho. General Mojón sneered at him in contempt. Then he flew across the river and went in among the French companies and took his stance by León.

At the first light the massif of Colle Belvedere took shape before them, then half disappeared behind a veil of smoke and splintered rock. They heard the shellbursts on the mountain, and then the roar of all the guns on the French side echoing from emplacements far behind them, and then more shellbursts and the pop of Masers and the clattering of Spandaus and the louder, shorter rap-rap-rap of Brownings, and the rip (as of silk being torn) and crack of .88s, and the bark of Springfields and the frenzied whine of Schmeisers and the whiz and crunch of heavy shells, and the smack of bullets passing in the air, until all individual sound was swallowed in the pandemonic din of battle. [76] Then León's face grew taut, and then he grinned and put his palm on Private Boulala's shoulder, pressing him gently down, and lifted his own head there on the fringes of the bridgehead, and he saw men bunched over beneath their loads running in little groups up the incline, and one of them jumped weirdly in the air as his left leg flew sidewise, and he came down on his one leg and hopped and then fell on his face, and another man behind him jumped as well, raised on another mine blast, but the rest kept running. León saw tracers bend out toward these men from all the bunkers, and some fell down and others sat abruptly, but the rest kept running on across the open, bearing their charges in among the forts. He watched in fascination and excitement and impatience, as, years before, he'd watched the first plays of an inning while waiting his turn to hit.

Then he saw his colonel rise a good way forward, get to his feet and draw out his revolver and hold it aloft, so that the lanyard stretched back from the butt down to his epaulet, and then the men around the colonel rose and then the men behind and León too. He heard the shrilling of the colonel's whistle and heard Lieutenant Jordy cry, "*L'Onzième, en avant!*" and heard Bouakkaz howling in Arabic and himself yelling, "*Muchachos, adelante!*" and then he was sucked forward, running, by the men in front as both battalions charged up through the breach blown in the line of bunkers, broke up and out through the first ramparts of the Gustav Line, leaving the Germans there to be killed or captured by the men of 1st Battalion and the companies of armor which now were sweeping down toward the Rapido.

The wave of men poured through the breach and rushed ahead, then slapped on Colle Belvedere and broke, 2nd Battalion sliding on, 3rd carrying right, going to ground on the near bank of Riosecco. Germans were on the other bank, dug in and wide awake now, and there were Germans on the cliffs behind and Germans on the spur of Monte Cifalco, pouring an enfilading fire down the whole ravine. And so 9th Company moved right again, moved right by squads and slowly, to climb the flanking spur and clear it, and 10th Company found cover and engaged the enemy across the Secco, and 11th Company huddled back from the bank to breathe, for they were going to ford the river and go up the cliff.

León lay panting, hearing but not listening to the noise of battle from van and rear. He heard but didn't listen to Jabara tell Reveil that their attack had caught the Germans by surprise, that Monsabert was a fine general. León had been amazed that he'd called out in Spanish after so many years of thinking mainly in French, and as he lay with rough Abruzzi rock grating his side and the damp chill of European winter biting down through his clothes into his sweated body, his mind took leave back to Tinieblas and concerned itself with steamy heat and sugar-sweet ripe mangoes and the sun suspended like a ripening fruit over a placid sea. But then these images were smashed by an explosion, a loud crunch to his left and a hoarse cry and then three more loud crunches in succession, for a German mortar team up on the cliff was walking shells down in among them. So León roached himself into the rock and recalled his mind and beamed it back five miles into the gun pits of the French artillery. He imagined the gunners, helmet straps undone, field jackets open, stoking fat one-five-five shells into hot breeches, hunching, mouths gaped, hands pressed over their ears, as lanyards snapped and guns boomed and recoiled. He rammed his mind into the guns and flung it out along the barrels with the shells and arced it up over the French line, over the valley, down onto the crests of Belvedere, down onto the far bank of the Secco, down against the cliffs, and, finally, down onto the cliff top and the kneeling mortar team. León sent his mind out from his bug-cringed body, made it soar and plummet with the shells, and meanwhile the winter sun pushed down half-heartedly against the clouds and raised a wet fog up from Riosecco to blend with the smoke of shellbursts and the dust of blasted rock.

Then they were hustled forward, spidered up to the river, and someone called, "*Fusée!*" and León looked and saw a rocket arching wide above the out-spur of Cifalco, and Jordy rose and yelled, "*L'Onzième, en avant!*" and the whole company burst forward, and as 1st Section leaped down from the bank, a great salvo fell before them across the river and split the sky from Atina to Cassino.

León was in water to his hips. He held his rifle forward in both hands and leaned right against the current, dragging his legs forward. The water was icy and splashed crazily, as though dozens of hungry trout were all about him, leaping for flies. Something swung into him, bumping his right knee and calf as he thrashed his left leg ahead, and as he lost his footing, as he slid left into the river, as he went under and the current seized him, he had time to think: *Someone in 2nd Squad has gotten shot his body's knocked me down, I'm liable to be drowned now under this pack and all my soaking clothes.* Then something lifted on his knapsack, hauled him up, and when he'd got his feet beneath him, when he stood and turned, Sergeant Jabara was grinning at him, saying, "Come, Corporal León, this is no day for swimming," and as León shook the cold water from his face, Jabara turned him, saying, "Come, friend, the enemy is there."

Jabara went on ahead of him through the still wildly splashing water, and León cursed to himself in Spanish and shook his head again and marveled that he still had his rifle gripped in both his hands. Then he thrashed ahead through the now shallowing river, shouting, "*Gracias!*" to Sergeant Jabara, and Jabara turned back toward him as he reached the bank, grinning like a child under the wide frame of his helmet, and his grin flew back toward León, coming apart in air, bits of it splatting onto León's hands. Sergeant Jabara fell back into the river, his brown gazelle's eyes wide over red mush, and as León reached for him, the current bore him off, and his knapsack dragged him under.

León said, "*Gracias!*" again, but this time to himself, and this time he meant: Thanks that it wasn't me! He felt a warm rush of strength and a great superiority to Sergeant Jabara and some contempt for him. He felt superiority mixed with contempt for the soldier whose corpse had bumped him and for the men ahead of him whom he saw falling. Then he felt guilt at these feelings and sorrow for Jabara and self-hatred for being still alive now that his friend who'd saved his life was dead, and also retching nausea at the globs of splattered face between his fingers, and terror, and rage—rage at Jordy, rage at himself for following him, rage at the unknown men who sought to kill him. And then he caught his mind and pinched from it every thought and feeling save his rage against his enemies, and by that time he was out of the river and up the bank and skipping over rocks and fallen bodies, running in toward the cliff base, where the lead sections were still killing Germans in their holes and taking others captive and firing on still others who were fleeing left down the ravine.

There was a chimney in the bulking cliff, a cleft carved in the stone chin of the mountain by eons of melting snows. It mounted, sheer and narrow, to the cliff top. Here in the spring wild flowers might grow, and mosses, and tough shrubs knuckle roots into the rock, but it was dead now, only stone, cold dirt, and dry cascades of rock torn by the shellbursts. Still, on each side the cliff wall bulged protectively, shielding the cutoff from the view and deathreach of the enemy, and when they'd cleaned the bank of living Germans and brought their gravely wounded in under the cliff and sent their prisoners with their walking wounded back across the river and received two sections of 10th Company to hold the ground they'd taken, 11th Company entered this chimney and rose in it.

They went by sections, grimping their way up, ploying beneath their pack loads, hindered by slung rifles and soggy bedrolls, pattered by dirt kicked down by those above. They leaned in toward the cliff, scraped knees and elbows to the rock, snaked fingers out for handholds, groped with their slick-shod toes, tested their gripping points against their weight, pushed themselves up. Sometimes a foot would slip or a rock break out from the mountain, and a man would slide, tearing his hands and clothing, till he found a bold or was supported by a comrade. Arms ached and shoulders burned from pack straps, but here at least they weren't under fire, and León had time to grieve for Sergeant Jabara, to wish he might lift his head and see Jabara climbing above him, to miss his guidance and his cheerfulness and childish joy in battle, and to decide that were this world run correctly, Jabara would have lived and he be dead. He grew warm from exertion, felt the cleft snuggle him in safety, wished it might rise a thousand miles and they climb on until the war was over, But then came explosions in the cleft above and shouts and a shrill cry, and León held to the rock and craned his bead back, and he saw a man tumbling headlong downward, saw him sail down and strike the rock and bound out down and by him. And then another man came hurtling down and bounced and bowled butt-first into the chest of someone from 3rd Section who was hanging to the cliff and bashed him loose, and both came rolling, bouncing down, down through the flinching climbers, down past León, down on down the shaft, for as the lead section neared the funnel's mouth, the Germans on the cliff had begun pitching bombs down on them.

Then Bouakkaz shouted for the section to keep climbing, and León shouted to his squad to climb, and he looked down and saw Dax just below him, gaping white-faced, frozen in terror, moaning, "*Oh, les salauds, les salauds, oh, les salauds!*" León remembered Sergeant Jabara and tried to grin at Dax and called, "Come on, friend, climb," but Dax hung to the mountain, moaning. So León swung his foot out and knocked it hard on Dax's helmet and yelled, "*Monte, fils de pute! Monte, ou te jete moi-même!*" Then Dax glared up at him in hatred and began to climb, and León turned and kneed himself on up the rock, clinging as another man came howling, wheeling by, and then climbed on, ducking his head, not looking up because he knew quite well what he would see, knew it so well in fact that all his life he would be liable, dozing in first sleep, to see men tumbling toward him, flailing their arms in air, until they slammed into his eyes and he woke shouting. León climbed and caught his mind and beamed it up to where 1st Section struggled, rained in grenades, and he imagined soldiers clawing out of the cleft and up onto the cliff top to shoot the grenadiers and others clambering up, unslinging weapons, firing, and men behind them swarming up and placing automatic weapons, flinging fire up across the slopes, and men in field grey fleeing toward the crest, falling sprawled forward, and the whole section surging up, spreading across the cliff top right and left, shooting and scuttling forward. And by the time he had imagined all that clearly, he was up there himself.

He led his squad right at a crouched half-waddle, around the flank of 2nd Section, where Bouakkaz had waved him, and as they moved toward the first crest, the German guns off on Belmonte and the other higher hills ranged on the cliff top, scouring it with shells. Thunder fell in on León, and he dropped and let his rifle drop ahead of him and reached his arms out and embraced the heaving mountain. His body tried to turn itself to water and flow down into the crevices between the rocks, and his mind jumped insanely back and forth, out of his grasp. He pressed his face against the rock and whimpered. But then, almost at once, he heard a voice roar in his ear: "Be a man, for the love of God! *Sea hombre!*"

He twisted his head, cringing, and saw his great-grandfather General Epifanio Mojón standing above him with his booted legs spread wide, his tunic splashed in blood, scowling down at him from beneath his high cocked hat, waving a bloody saber.

"Be a man, bastard!" yelled General Mojón. "Get up and be a man!"

León got up then on one knee, and General Mojón nodded grimly and told him to get his weapon, and León picked his rifle up and cradled it, and just then a shell burst off to his left front, and he flinched and ducked and heard shrapnel tear by him and felt rock fragments scatter on his back.

"Steady!" said his great-grandfather. "Steady! You've men under you now; set an example!"

León raised up again and looked out over the mountain. It was all plumed in shellbursts, spangled in tracers. On his left he saw men gone to ground, some firing at the German crest, some with their heads ducked. Noncoms scuttled among them, crouched, hollered orders which were swallowed in the noise, got them to crawl ahead. Behind him his squad lay prone. Djemal was fumbling at his weapon, trying to clear it; El Haoui and Boulala looked at him; the others lay head down.

General Mojón stabbed forward with his saber. "There's cover on the crest," he said. "The German pits and sangars. Lead your men up there! No more cringing now! But there . . ." He pointed with his saber to a knoll some eighty meters off. "They have a gun there—can't you hear it? Take it and show your men some courage."

It was then—at two or so P.M. on 25th January, 1944—that León Fuertes was received into the secret mystery of war and learned in his own flesh why war is so beloved of men that it (along with language) is what sets the species off from all the other forms of earthly life. He had already felt and learned to savor how a war group binds men to each other. He had discovered how a welter of unpleasant thoughts and feelings may be cast out by rage against an enemy. Now, as he heard his ancestor's command, he found his terror alchemized into a grand exhilaration.

It was not that he enjoyed a loosening of tensions such as he'd felt on entering the cleft, such as one often feels on gaining a safe haven out of risk, a sinecure or an annuity or yet some other kind of surrogate placenta. He knew that all about him men were being killed and smashed and morseled and that he might be next, and yet this knowledge, rather than terrifying him, now made each instant tasty. He felt alive in every cell as during love—except this was more turbulent than love and deeper, pulsed by the blood of thousands. Yes, love was something like it, and sport also, and performing to a crowd. All that was *like* it, in a tame, childish way. This was the thing itself.

He rose onto his feet and called his squad, turned smiling to them like a father who calls his children out through breakers to the sun-warmed swells—a little peeved at their reluctance, impatient that they shed their fear and taste the sweet of life, yet kind, rolling his strength and confidence back to them. He led his people forward to a little ridge and placed them there and told them to put fire on the knoll. Then he went up and killed the German gunners.

He moved as he'd been trained, running four seconds, crawling, then running again. Time slowed deliciously for him so that he saw the bullets as they cracked toward and by him and the rough chunks of shrapnel sizzling by, and savored every meter of his progress right and forward. When he was opposite the knoll and right of it and saw the helmets of the crouching gunners, he thought first of grenading them and then decided to save his grenades and shoot the men instead. The choice took but an instant, yet he made it with the same calm and leisure as, years before, he had at times hefted a bat and then picked up another before going to the plate. He moved ahead till he could see the Germans' faces. He rose onto one knee and put his left arm through his rifle's sling. He palmed the butt with his right hand and wedged it to his shoulder. He thumbed the safety down and breathed and sighted on the nearer gunner, noting that the man had a strong profile, a straight nose, a firm chin, that he was about his own age or a little younger, that, from his fixed smile, he was caught also in the glow of battle, joyous and unafraid. He piked the German's head on his front sight, let half his breath out, squeezed. He felt his rifle buck and heard it blast. He followed the bullet whirling down the barrel, through the condom on the muzzle, through the air, and through the German's skin under his helmet, through the bone into his skull, where it churned a frenzied tunnel through millions of minutely ordered brain cells, bored on through brittle bone and then burst out, punching hot blood and tissues on before it. León saw the man crash over onto his startled comrade and sensed immense relief through all his body and a great joy and feeling of accomplishment, yet even while he savored these sensations, he worked his rifle bolt and swung the barrel down from where recoil had lifted it and recomposed his picture through the sights on the far gunner's head and fired. He jerked the trigger now instead of squeezing it and pulled the barrel right so that his bullet struck not where he'd aimed it, not on flesh but steel. Still, it drove through the German's helmet and his skull bone and on through the bulged and tender tissues of his brain and on through bone again. Blunted, it bit the inside of the German's helmet and skidded down over the steel and dropped inside his scarf and collar, still red hot, onto his winter-pale grimed neck, searing the flesh, but the German did not feel it.

Something had made León snap his second shot, and even as he felt his rifle buck, the same something made him fling himself down and forward so that he rolled on the rough rock, and at that moment a burst of fire from the crest cracked the air where he had just been kneeling. He came to his feet running and worked his rifle bolt and charged up to the gun post, ready to fire, but his two enemies lay as if dumped carelessly together over their gun, inert as sand-and-canvas dummies even when he poked them with his rifle. He raised his rifle and let out a singing cry and climbed up on the knoll and stood against the sky and called his people forward. General Epifanio Mojón stood beside him, waving his bloody saber, and the two of them stood there together until León's squad reached the knoll. Then General Mojón stalked off toward the crest, roaring, and León followed, leading his squad, and the whole company moved forward through the shellbursts and swept the Germans from the crest, killing some there and sending others fleeing back to the still higher crest beyond.

16. Illumination

WHEN 11TH COMPANY had seized Crest 718 and taken cover in the German fire pits, León's exhilaration left him. He lay against the rock all trembling, sweating cold, and watched Boulala and Reveil embrace as though the war were over, and watched Djemal prod a dead German with the muzzle of his BAR, and watched El Haoui and Barelli strip off another's watch and wedding ring and hoist him up and roll him from the pit. León felt himself about to urinate, and only with great effort was he able to rise and crouch—for on no account would he go out where shells were bursting—, and when he'd drained onto the rocks where he'd been lying, he fell back exhausted. He recalled his vision of General Mojón and instantly decided not to think of it. Then he recalled his joy in killing and pinched that from his mind as well. Then, more to guard against pernicious thought[77] than from a sense of duty, he heaved himself up and began to see about defending their position. All along the crest 11th Company breathed and drank and rolled dead Germans from their pits and reloaded weapons and set themselves to be counterattacked.

They were shelled first and then attacked, but they held firm. Two sections of the 10th had gotten up by then to reinforce them, and they killed the Germans in the trough between their crest and Crest 862. General Mojón stood in the air above them as they cut the Germans down, but León could not see him and he felt no glow. He aimed and squeezed and let his rifle punch his shoulder and felt as though he stood in the rank mire of an abattoir, braining mewling beasts with a rude club.

Night fell and with it freezing rain and an incessant peltering of mortar bombs, and Lieutenant Jordy said, "So much the better; while they're mortaring they won't attack." They lay all shrouded in their sopping bedrolls, shivering on cold humps of rock, and for a long time León could neither sleep nor catch his mind to aim it. His mind flew nervously about like a crazed insect, alighting sometimes on the face, of the first man he'd killed, sometimes on scenes of peace, but it would never stay at rest more than an instant, and its fluttered gyres were so enervating that León took relief when its whirled course was fixed by a close explosion. At last he slept, and when he did General Mojón came to him and scowled at him from under his cocked hat and said he was proud of him, that León was the worthiest of all his many descendants. Then the image faded, for though General Mojón had no flesh and bone to ache in the drilling cold, the bleakness of that vigil on the mountain weighed on his spirit, and he retired to his own world, planning to return when there was fighting. León dreamed on, though. His great-grandmother Raquel Fuertes wove him an animated tapestry of the atrocities wrought by General Mojón after he came to power and his courage went fester into cruelty: men and young women chained to crosses in the bay of Ciudad Tinieblas, their living bodies rent by savage sharks, while General Mojón watched from the palace terrace. León felt the anguish of his great-grandfather, who needed victims as a healthy man needs love, yet the most horrid sufferings now brought no ease, and the groans of a whole country left him unsatisfied. León knew then the fearful price one pays for pleasure seized in violence, but he chose to defer his own debt and let it grow. He turned from the dream Raquel had brought him and constructed a different one, a dream where the German gunner fell dead under his bullet and then was resurrected, only to fall again. The scene brought him relief, and thus he slept under the rain and mortars.

Before dawn two German companies filtered down from Crest 862, and at first light they charged out of a hail of shellfire. Their wave carried to the stone lips of the French fire pits, and when it ebbed it left a flotsam of smashed manhood strewn along the crest. One more attack would have won the positions, for 11th Company had no more hand grenades and little ammunition, but instead the Germans tried to blast them off the mountain. All day the top of

Belvedere was a great orchard of explosions. The German shells fell
in heavy salvos, raising sheafs of flame over the French crest, and
from the valley the French guns responded, till the whole summit
bloomed in splintered steel and rock, and one would have thought
nothing could live there, not a flea, not a microbe. Men huddled in
the pits like rodents, twitching, gibbering, soiling themselves, but
León Fuertes kept his mind gripped, as it were in both his fists, and
shouted to his people that the Germans felt it worse. He helped them
bear the pounding, but at length Dax could bear it no longer, and he
leaped to his feet and made to climb out of the pit and run away,
though there was nowhere to run to. A shell burst over him, and a
chunk of steel tore his throat out, and he died kicking, choked in his
own blood, and León watched him die and filled his mind with rage
and violence and imagined shells falling on the German crest, blasting men to pieces.

That afternoon, when the bombardment lightened, a draggled
group came in carrying a mortar and two .50-caliber machine guns
and some ammunition and a radio-pitiful, precious store, all borne
up on men's backs in a twelve-hour, inching progress under fire. Lieutenant Jordy spoke to Commandant Gandoët by radio and learned
they could not hope to be reinforced or further supplied that day,
and he decided that they could not hold against a German charge,
hence must attack themselves and take Crest 862 that night. But first
they would have to reduce a forward spur where the Germans had
heavy machine guns. Sublieutenant Bouakkaz had learned from the
bearers that his friend Lieutenant El Hadi had been killed with 9th
Company on Monte Cifalco, and he asked to lead the attack and
swore he would be first onto the spur, and so at dusk he led his section out of the pits and right, along an escarpment just below the
rim of Belvedere, and another section followed. When they were
grouped below the spur, they unslung rifles and fixed bayonets, and
when León drew out the long knife and fixed it to his rifle, he felt the
thrill of violence sweep him, and his weariness drained from him,
and his blood sang, and he caught sight of General Epifanio Mojón
standing above him in the air, looking down at him, licking his lips,
nodding and smiling grimly.

Bouakkaz rose and called out in a high-pitched cry, "*La Allah il
Allah!*" He bolted up and forward, and both platoons charged with

him, screaming the same cry. All the Arabs cried it, and all the French, and Barelli, who had made contrition in Latin on the night before the battle, and Djemal, who had prayed in Hebrew, and León, who had cried out before in Spanish. They cried above the din of German guns and dashed on wildly. Tracers swept toward them like a cloud of sparks, and fire flashed from the gun barrels above, and the sky opened above the mountain and all the stars glared at them. Time stopped for León then, and as he ran forward screaming he knew that never in this world would he see anything so beautiful.

Then Sublieutitenant Bouakkaz fell forward, and his cry was stilled, and both sections stopped in place, astonished, and their chant died in their throats. They hung against the wall of fire, silent, but Sergeant Mohammed ben Abdelkadar went to his officer and lifted him, and León followed, and the two of them lifted Bouakkaz on their crossed rifles and bore him forward, though his skull was shattered and his head lolled and his brains spilled on the ground. Both sections charged behind them, drunk beyond pain or terror on their rage and hate, crying their war chant, rolling up through grenades and bullets to take the German forts by bayonet. And when he and Abdelkadar had reached the summit of the spur and held Bouakkaz's corpse a moment standing and then laid it down, face to the enemy, while Abdelkadar retrieved the flare gun from Bouakkaz's body and sent the signal that the spur was theirs, León leaped down into the seething frenzy of a German gun pit and gave himself up to the hallucinating joy of thrust and stab, and when he came to himself, panting hoarsely, his rifle was no longer in his hand but stuck fast by the bayonet in a man's skull, jabbed through the face and wedged there, and León was kneeling on the back of a still thrashing enemy, sawing the man's gullet with his razor.

He rose, sated and weak, and let his razor drop. He smeared his reeking hands against his field pants. He saw his rifle and pulled it free, holding the dead man's chest down with his foot so that air was forced from him in a final sigh. He unfixed his bayonet and wiped it on his leg and sheathed it. He climbed out, stepping on corpses, and stood uneasily and then sat down. He felt a great lassitude and reverberating tremors of satiety, but then he thought of what he had just done and of the inexpressible pleasure it had brought him, and he jumped to his feet and called his squad[78] yelling their names quickly, and while he was collecting those who were still alive and thus keeping his mind empty of thought, Lieutenant Jordy led the other sections forward in general assault and drove the Germans from Crest 862.

Gandoët joined them there at dawn with the rest of 10th Company, and 2nd Battalion seized Crest 915, and 1st Battalion occupied the slopes, and Colonel Roux informed General Monsabert that all his regiment's objectives were now carried and the Gustav Line deeply breached, but Monsabert had no fresh troops to consolidate these victories, much less exploit them, and the Germans counterattacked with two regiments and surrounded 2nd Battalion and pounded it and overran it, so that 2nd Battalion ceased to exist, and forced Gandoët's battalion to withdraw from 862 back to the lower crest and retook the spur of Monte Cifalco, annihilating 9th Company, and regained both the banks of Riosecco and captured Colonel Roux in his command post, and ambushed convoys of supplies and wounded, and drew a circle of flame about the troops who clung on Belvedere. Then the days and nights fell together[79] for these men and were confused in noise and terror, and companies and squads and sections merged, and grey and khaki spilled into each other, and metal fused with bone and rock with flesh, and blood and sleet mixed roughly, and there was no more order anywhere on earth. Then neither was there food, nor warmth, nor medicines, nor bandages, nor shelter from the elements, nor cover from the enemy, nor sleep, nor ease save death. When it was light each individual movement was the object of a murderous salvo, and with the dark the Germans crept down in little groups and then assembled to assault in furious shocks. Each time the tirailleurs rose to meet them with bayonet, and each time they drove them back and then rummaged the bodies of dead enemies for weapons and munitions before regrouping in an ever-tighter circle. In this manner they held on the mountain, while below, the 3rd and 7th Algerian Regiments struggled to reopen contact with them.

During this time my father, León Fuertes, passed into a protohuman manner of existence, a trance outside the pale of thought and over the frontier of most emotion. His frontal lobes suspended operation save to emit a nagging whine of worry which remained constant whether shells fell near or farther off. Other centers of his brain shut down entirely. He saw men die, comrades and enemies, their bodies blown apart or pierced or riddled, as one who sits nodding at the window of a train sees telegraph posts step by and disappear. He heard screams and the crash of high explosives as a townsman hears street sounds. He was conscious of the random pass of death as a particular Tinieblan might on Sunday morning know the lottery was being drawn and sums both great and small disbursed at hazard, but the drawing has been held each week as long as he remembers and will be held next week and next and next, and in his weariness and headache he cannot recall his number or where he's put his ticket or even if he's bought one, and the whole thing is of little moment, win or lose. The regions of León's cortex that held the program of his infantry training remained in function. The survival centers of his lower brain were working well. By day crawling was his natural way of locomotion, and he adapted to terrain like bug or lizard. By night he sensed the approach of enemies and could without fearing he'd guessed wrong take men to brace a threatened point in the perimeter. At each attack he felt a strong fix of adrenaline bang through his body, and his fatigue would melt, and he would rise, soaked in clean fury, to meet the fury of the men who sought to kill him. Grunting and bellowing, he thrust his bayonet into men's chests and rammed his rifle butt up in men's faces, and each thrust or blow that hit brought animal satisfaction, but he neither thought of what he did nor reflected on it later nor could remember or look forward to another mode of life. This state continued with him after 3rd Battalion was reinforced and resupplied— twelve men out of a platoon of fifty who'd set off from the ravine to reach them, five, mules out of five dozen with ammunition but no rations—and 11th Company went over to the attack again. It continued through the wash and slide of combat on the slopes of 862, through the charge that took him and Boulala —the last men still alive out of their squad of eight-and perhaps twenty others to the summit of the crest. It continued into his fifth night on Belvedere, when half a German company flowed in around them and went up to wipe them out, when he and Boulala stood in a forward gun pit, firing their rifles at the shapes that scrambled toward them. Then their cartridges were gone, and Boulala crawled out to a dying German to take his weapon, and the German killed him, and with that León stepped from his trance into a great clarity.

León's clarity spread through his brain and out like an aurora for a space of several meters all about him. It was bright as an arc light and pulsed rhythmically, and my aunt Rosario saw it from above the lower crest and followed its light to León. She had been searching for him, stepping among the crouched soldiers of his battalion, peering desperately into their faces, and when she saw the light of his clarity, which no living person saw, she went to him and sat down beside his friend Boulala's body. León didn't see her, for in his clarity he was recalling every detail of his five days and nights of battle even those details he'd been unconscious of as they occurred. He recalled Jabara's death, and Dax frozen in terror on the cliff face, and how he'd fired on the Germans in the trough between the crests and how he'd stabbed and clubbed men in the dark. He recalled the face of the first man he'd killed exactly and the face of a man he'd bayoneted after Bouakkaz's charge and how he'd stabbed another through the face. His point had struck on bone near the man's nose and slid into his eye and driven through into his skull and wedged there. León recalled the human pleasure he had taken in this act of killing and the great surge of pleasure that swelled in him when he seized another man, a man who held his palms up, pleading, and threw him, twisting, down and held him down and found the razor, opened it, and cut—yes, cut through the man's throat so that blood spurted, thick and hot, on León's hands. When he recalled all this, León felt hideously guilty, more soiled with guilt than when he'd been a catamite.

He knew each living thing was doomed to die, and always by some agency. To be the agency of death, as well as life, was in the destiny of everything on earth. But man, who had the faculty of thought, ought not to kill unthinkingly, without considering what he killed or why, or to take pleasure as death's agent. Joy in battle was correct, as joy in any part of life, but one ought not to kill unthinkingly or out of selfish pleasure.

Then León realized that his whole life had been a constant self-indulgence.[80] As a child he had indulged himself in the power of being family breadwinner, and he had bathed in self-indulgence while he lived with Dr. Grillo. He had indulged himself in the hardships of desert journey, and his merging with the army was an acute form of self-indulgence. No doubt he was fated to live selfishly, indulging and asserting his own self, but he ought to acknowledge his nature and bear it consciously. All his life he had evaded and denied his human obligation to consider, to understand his life and bear it consciously. For eight years he had smothered this obligation, in degradation, in action, in the monastic fraternity of soldiering, and before that also he had lived thoughtlessly, without considering. He had, especially, loved thoughtlessly and thus become the agency of Rosario's death. It was time he considered that and acknowledged it and bore it consciously. As these thoughts came to him, he saw his sister-love Rosario sitting beside Boulala's body, smiling at him, and his clarity grew calm.

Then León pardoned whatever agency might cause his death, the man of the opposing army who might kill him in the next instant or the myriad army of bacilli that might invest and kill him years ahead. He pardoned the soldier who had killed his friend Jabara and the artillerymen who had killed his comrade Dax and the men who'd killed his other comrades and the dying man three meters off who'd killed Boulala. And when he'd given pardon, he asked it for himself. He first asked pardon of Rosario, and she gave it to him, smiling. Then he asked pardon of the men he'd killed, a special pardon of the men whose killing had been done in pleasure, then pardon of the men he'd killed in present self-defense. As he did so, the Germans charged again, and León's vision of Rosario was broken by a man who ran over and through her, firing a pistol, and as he reached the pit where León stood, he roared and aimed his pistol down at León, and, asking pardon, León reached up and slid his bayonet without difficulty into the man's belly.

The man fell forward and crashed down on León, and his pistol crashed on León's face, and León fell back senseless. He came to himself lying at the bottom of the pit with the man on top of him, screaming, trying to choke him, but his great clarity was with him still, and he pried the man's grip gently from is throat and gently pushed him up and raised himself, so that the German across his lap, which was drenched with the German's blood. Then León calmed him, cradling his head and caressing his check, which was filthy and stubbled, soiled by sweat and tears, and the man's screams softened into whimpers. Then León looked at the man's wound.

The bayonet had pulled free when the man fell, leaving a slit in his grey trousers from which blood pumped. Gently León opened the man's belt and then his trousers and drew them down. A sausage of intestine pocked from the wound, and León cradled the man gently and pushed the roll of gut back into him and, having nothing else, took off his woolen cap and pressed it over the wound—uselessly, for the man was surely dying. While León tended him, the man whimpered and wriggled weakly, but now he let his head lie against León's chest, breathing heavily, and with that León began to weep.

The Germans did not attack again. There were only a handful of them left around the crest, half of them wounded, but had they attacked, León would not have noticed. He sat at the bottom of a pit about the width and depth of a man's grave, cradling his enemy, weeping for all the living things on earth that have to die and mostly for the human beings of this world, who have to think about their death and bear it consciously.

At length the German moved his head and opened his eyes and looked at León, and León stopped weeping and looked down at him. *"Mutti?"* the German murmured. *"Mutti?"*

León cradled him, and the man smiled faintly. Then he died.

That midnight the soldiers of both armies crouched on the freezing top of Colle Belvedere heard singing from the summit of Crest 862. A voice sang a song called *"La Golandrina,"* sang it through once quite slowly, then was silent. None of the men who heard it understood the words, but the song spoke so piercingly to them of grief, the voice so swelled with joy and with lament, that they believed they'd dreamed both song and singer. In the morning, when 3rd Battalion, 4th Tunisian Tirailleurs stormed the crest and reached the little group who held the summit, their commanding officer found an exhausted corporal sleeping in a gun pit with the body of a dead German cradled in his arms.

On 4th February, 1944, the 4th Tunisian Tirailleurs were relieved from Colle Belvedere. In little groups, followed by German shells, they came down off the mountain, tattered, smeared with blood and filth, bearded, pale, eyes sunken. In two hundred forty hours of uninterrupted combat the regiment had taken fifteen hundred casualties, well more than half its strength, nearly three hundred killed, more than four hundred missing. In 3rd Battalion all three company commanders had been killed and every other officer killed or wounded, so when the regiment returned to action early in May, León Fuertes was a sublieutenant.

He was wounded leading his section in the assault on Monte Pico in the last chapter of the Battle of Cassino, receiving the Médaille Militaire for his conduct in this action. By the time he was returned to duty, Juin's Expeditionary Corps had been withdrawn from Italy and made a part of the newly formed French First Army under de Lattre de Tassigny. León took part in the landings on the Riviera and fought with his regiment through France and into Germany. When the war ended he held the rank of captain and was commanding a company on the headwaters of the Danube.

During his months of combat after Belvedere he showed consistent valor under fire and received several decorations, French and Allied, but he never killed again or used a weapon. It was not that he now thought war or killing wrong. While his regiment was resting and refitting after Belvedere, he took pains to inform himself on recent history and came to the obvious conclusion that Hitler and those who followed him in arms had best be extirpated, as quickly as possible, as violently as necessary. He directed men bravely and efficiently in combat, and the units that he led killed many Germans. León did not kill personally because he feared he might enjoy it. To be an agency of death was oftentimes an honorable and sacred occupation, but one ought not take selfish pleasure in it, and as he had found killing could bring exquisite pleasure, León, in self-defense, adopted the custom of British officers and went into battle with his revolver holstered, carrying a little cedar swagger stick, which was capped at one end with a highly polished .30-06 cartridge case and which he jokingly called "La Joyeuse," after Charlemagne's sword.

Thus equipped, León no longer enjoyed the company of his great-grandfather General Epifanio Mojón. My aunt Rosario was with him constantly, however, beside him in every battle, so that he felt her presence though he could not see her, and in his dreams each night. In these dreams they conversed chastely and hence guiltlessly, as neither lovers nor siblings but as friends. Thus, in Rosario's company and burdened with a consciousness which he strove always to bear firmly and yet lightly, my father, León Fuertes, came out of the wilderness regions of his life.

PART FOUR
HIS MATURITY, HIS MINISTRY, HIS MARTYDOM (1946-1964)

17. Money

MY FATHER, León Fuertes, returned to Tinieblas ten years to the day after his departure. He arrived on the *Minerve* from Cherbourg with a law degree and a new personality. My grandmother Rebeca was on the pier to meet him. They had not communicated in any way, but on the day he landed, at the moment when León glimpsed a shore bird from the foredeck of the ship, Rebeca poured the coffee she had just made for my uncle Pepe back into the pot.

"Go save me a seat on the bus to Bastidas. Your brother León's coming back from the dead."[81]

She did not recognize the balding fellow in the cheap tweed suit until she felt his hands on her shoulders. Her lips chewed earnestly, but no sound emerged.

"It's all right, Mamá," León said, embracing her. "I know you forgive me. I forgive you your curse."

Tinieblas too forgave him. Following his departure he had become the object of intense and general resentment. Those whom his singing had transfigured, whom his athletic feats had stuffed with tribal pride, felt abandoned, and there grew up a copious apocrypha of slander to explain his sudden slinking off. In one version he'd sold out to Tío Sam and Coca-Cola, had snatched a gaudy wad of greenbacks to change his nationality. Don Vitelio Mosca gave it spurious confirmation when, upon returning from the 1941 World Series, he claimed to have seen León with his hair dyed and a gringo nickname playing shortstop for Los Esquivadores de Brooklyn. Another text held that León had murdered Rosario in a jealous fit, that he had refuged in Stockholm of in Lisbon or in Bern and earned a dishonorable fortune forging Caruso records. Men of the left snorted that he was a spy for Mussolini, while rightists figured him a paid assassin of the Comintern. He was accused of every crime except the one he'd actually committed and written boldly in, the catalog of traitors that Tinieblans cherish in their hearts as an excuse for our republic's insignificance.

When he returned, though, he received a hero's welcome. This was not particularly surprising, for he engineered it. Through the new León's calculating intervention—he published a series of pseudonymous articles about his war deeds in the French press and had former commanders write letters to de Gaulle—the French Ambassador in Ciudad Tinieblas got a lengthy résumé of his war record, an early warning of his coming home, and an advice that French influence and commerce would be benefited by some official clucking over León's service under the tricolor. So scarcely had León got his bags unpacked when His Excellency convoked a glittering reception at which the citations of León's several decorations were read aloud in opulent translation and León was received into the *Légion d'honneur*. Great Britain and the United States refused to be upstaged and came through with entertainments, scrolls, and medals. The local press spared no expense of adjectives, retold his feats of arms, invented new ones for him, and contrived to have him fighting on several fronts at once. Then, two weeks after his return, on the four hundred thirty-first anniversary of the discovery of Tinieblas, President Luis Manuel Gusano presented him with a second Grand Cross of the Order of Palmiro Inchado, saluting him publicly on the palace balcony before a huge and roaring[82] throng.

In private Gusano urged León to accept a commission as lieutenant colonel in the Guardia Civil, pledging to promote him and name him Commandant as soon as Colonel Genaro Culata could be decently retired. León declined. He declined as well the plaintive invitations of three opposition parties and a number of independent mainchancers that he be a vice-presidential candidate in the next elections. He bad small interest in public office and none in letting others trade on his war-hero glamour. He meant to trade on it himself. He had come home to make a fortune, dishonorable if need be, as a counselor-at-law.

This may at first glance seem a strange design.[83] It is true that León's father, Dr. Azael Burlando, dealt his station in the next world for wealth in this one, but this very greed made him anomalous in León's ancestry. It is, besides, well known that lawyers have been the chief woe, bane, pest, and canker of our hemisphere from the day the first one put foot oil Hispaniola down to the recent scandals in the U.S.A., that (in the words of Dr. Eudemio Lobo) "if the New World sent the Old World syphilis, it was a meek and insufficient provocation for the plague of law-titled hypocrites and swindlers which the Old World sent the New, and which has cultured here unchecked and grown endemic." Since León was blessed (or cursed) with the potential to excel at any number of pursuits, one may well blink in wonder that he chose to enter a profession so hated and mistrusted by those whom it has not deluded or corrupted. But one night in Ulm, in the fell, freezing March of '45, with the great seats of culture smashed about him and humans necromanced by war to wolves or rats, León had dreamed that he slept dreamlessly in a wide, airy house beside our southern sea, that a calm, fragile woman slept beside him swathed in luxury and ease, that she had borne him sons who played with grace at gentlemanly games and a daughter who woke all breathed in jasmine and with heart aflutter[84] when well-bred youths came In the midnight to lift a serenata to her window. And dreaming there, deep in his dream yet conscious of the ruin and savagery around him, León thought his dream good. On waking, he put it by as one will, being called to a low, messy labor, put off a subtle garment, but when the war was over, he drew his dream out and he tried it on and liked the feel of it. My father was not a man to let a dream stay dream: the dreams he liked he fleshed. Nor was he a man of original, conceptions. Among the essentials of his dream were Tinieblas, money, and respectability, and law is the traditional, hoof-beaten track to money and position in this country. Law appealed to him, moreover, as a predatory game with stringent rules. He had researched himself and found a potent drive to self-assertion. The courts with their rites and ceremonies; the judges, counsel, bailiffs, clerks, and clients with their appointed parts and places; the legal system with its ordered staves and movements, proffered a fit stage, accompaniment, and orchestration for the performance of that drive.

When Germany fell, León left the army. He went to Paris and enrolled at the Sorbonne. There he lied blithely that he'd studied law at Caen before the war—this to assure that he might sit for his exams without needless delay. No one presumed to doubt the word of a gallant officer;[85] had anyone done so, he would have had a hard time proving his doubts, for Caen had been a battleground after the Normandy invasion, and the town was rubbled and many records lost. León went up into an attic on l'Île Saint-Louis and dumped the law texts in his brain by shovelfuls. A year later he flung them back to his examiners and got his strip of parchment. Then he organized himself a hero's welcome and went home.

He was not prepared to hang out his own shingle. His degree was excellent. He'd picked up copies of the Tinieblan Codes at our embassy in Paris and memorized them on shipboard. He'd been an expert liar since his childhood, and his study of jurisprudence had honed his native skill to a fine point. His celebrity assured him clients. But he hadn't an inkling of how justice was managed in Tinieblas: how much to bribe this or that judge for a continuance; whose palm to grease to get a case onto the docket or a corporation registered without interminable delay; what doctor to consult when one's client had need of an invisible infirmity; which ministers to approach through their wives and which through their mistresses; who among one's colleagues at the bar possessed the means to rig a trial beyond all hope of counter-rigging, hence when to settle out of court even if one's case was airtight; which magistrates were drunks and which were senile; which liked to have the issue heard forthwith and which demanded a good show of rhetoric, some histrionics, and a tear or two; what pleas might be accepted, what judgments handed down, what fees paid promptly. So León chose to enter partnership.

He did not lack for opportunities. Dr. Erasmo Sancudo Montes, former President of the Republic (1936-1940), future Justice of the Supreme Court, newspaper magnate, and chief power in the august and lucred firm of Anguila, Anguila y Sancudo, made León an ornate Byzantine approach in which he pledged nothing of substance but blew out a perfumed mist of possibilities, among them marriage to his daughter. Avispa y Abeja dangled a junior partnership. Comején-Oruga-Tábano offered to put his name alongside theirs. He might, in fact, have entered any law firm in the country, yet he threw in with a young fellow of apparently dim prospects, about whom there were whispered imputations of honesty.

Carlitos Gavilán (referred to by the diminutive to distinguish him from his father, also christened Carlos, also a lawyer) was León Fuertes' most intimate collaborator from December, 1946, till León's death in January, 1964: in law practice, in the *golpe* of 1952 which deposed President Alejandro Sancudo and preserved the Constitution, in the founding of the Partido Progresista, in the Chamber of Deputies, and in the government. He spoke for León at his wedding, stood namesake and godfather to León's first-born, managed León's campaign for the presidency, served in his cabinet, pronounced his eulogy, and executed his testament. He was León's partner and lieutenant, his beneficiary and his victim, his friend, his confidant, and, like Dr. Escolástico Grillo before him, his complaisant and self-sacrificing worshiper. Their association had, in a sense, long antedated León's lawyerhood, for Carlitos had played catcher on the national selection baseball team of 1934 and had, in this capacity, displayed a trait of character that León valued highly. Years later, when I was twelve or so and we were living in the palace, my father happened to come in my room and look over my shoulder as I was snapping a school exercise into my notebook.

"Aren't you going-to copy this?" my father asked, stabbing a finger at some blots and cross-outs on the paper.

"It doesn't matter. It's not for grade."

My father pursed his lips and nodded. "You know your brother's godfather." Gavilán was Minister of Justice at that time, but my father chose to identify him that way. "He wasn't nearly as good at playing ball as you are at your studies. He couldn't hit, and he caught more pitches on his chest than in his mitt. But when we were playing in Maracaibo on the last day of the Central American Games, when it was hot as hell and we were losing twelve to one and no one was in the stands, Carlitos still went down the line, full speed in all his gear, to back up infielders' throws to first. There's only two ways to look at the world, Camilo. Either everything matters, or nothing does."

Besides the first of these two views—which in Spanish is called being a "serious man"—Gavilán possessed the virtue of loyalty. In 1960, when León was speaker of the Chamber, Humberto Ladilla asked for a seat on the Rules Committee. Ladilla wasn't a Progresista. He had his own party, the Partido Oportunista Personal, of which he was the only officeholder, but he pledged to support León whenever he was right.

"That's not much of an offer," León told him. "What I need on that committee are men like Carlitos. He supports me when I'm wrong."

And Gavilán's stolidity, his utter lack of glamour and flamboyance, his iron refusal to be brilliant (though he had a first-rate brain), commended him to León as the perfect foil for León Fuertes, lawyer.

This figure incorporated diverse components of several other Leóns. The urchin's wiliness, the scholar's faculty for taking pains, the athlete's delight in competition, the artist's arrogance and longing for the center of the stage, the warrior's killer instinct—all found accommodation. But these "borrowed" traits were reimagined and reshaped, then recombined with attitudes not in the psychic baggage of the prior Leóns, so that León, lawyer, was in no kind an imitation or a repetition of known and familiar features. To confront new circumstances, León arrayed himself in a new form, a form which was, by virtue of its novelty, complete. Such transformations were his normal mode of living. My father was not natural; that is, he had no nature. He was not tombed in any static actuality; he swam freely in a sea of possibilities.

León Fuertes, lawyer, was a pushy man, a man in a hurry, a man who took himself seriously, which is not quite the same as being a "serious man." Observe, for example, his attitude toward his war service. A sedentary, contemplative son may well take pleasure that his father bore himself with courage on harsh battlefields. It is less pleasant to see him finagle honors for himself, but that is what León did, along with stage-managing his homecoming and, from that moment, never letting anyone forget he had exposed his life for freedom, for democracy, for Western culture, for the brotherhood of man, for an embarrassment of such abstractions, which, emptied by mention, give off a soothing sound when beaten. At no time or place that smacked at all of business was he ever seen without his *Légion d'honneur* rosette. He had a box of them, in fact, one for each suit. He wore only white suits, by the way. These were, admittedly, the fashion for men of means, but León wore his very much like consecrated armor, and on formal occasions he wore his decorations: three rows of miniature medals and the sash of the Order of Palmiro Inchado with both Grand Crosses slinging from it. He missed no chance to make the war work for him. On one famous occasion, for example—and this is but one instance out of many—while seeking to sustain a plea of self-defense on behalf of a homicide, León kept judge, jury, even prosecuting counsel gripped in terror for some forty minutes as he told how, during the fight for Strasbourg, he'd found himself in peril of his life, staring into the barrel of an SS trooper's Luger. This memoir, which linked the victim of the case to Hitler's hordes and cast both León and his client as the good guys, was in no wise less effective for being totally imaginary.

León the lawyer danced to rhythms altogether out of synchrony with the saurian *tempo largo* of tropical life. He was always either just come from the courtroom or on his way to a negotiation, and he carried with him an ambience of tension and energy such as one feels near an electric turbine or in the communications center of a state at war. He was a member of the Club Mercantil, but no one ever saw him lounging by the pool or chatting over cocktails with some cronies. He played tennis, but strictly for the exercise: two furious sets each dawn with the club pro. He played bridge, sometimes straight through the night, but he made money playing, as much as he made at law some weeks, and widened his contacts among businessmen and bankers. And if he sometimes stopped briefly by the bar or locker room to joke—he was a famous raconteur of vulgar stories—it was because the men whom he amused were clients or, more likely, might become clients if he amused them well.

There was no relaxation to the man; he was all business.

His mere presence often goaded others to surprising prodigies of effort. Juan Tábano, for instance, was born rich beyond all need of labor and, besides, shared amply in our climate's patrimony of sloth. More, he nurtured his laziness like a prize orchid and could quite fairly claim to have no sense of time or obligation whatsoever. Yet when he hired León to try an action for one of his clients, Tábano found himself, to his unspeakable amazement, showing up on time for meetings; producing all the necessary documents signed, sealed, stamped, franked, and witnessed; pledging on his own initiative to search out others that might come in handy—in short, acting with such terrifying vigor and efficiency that although his client won a generous judgment and paid a generous fee, he never dared to deal

with León after. Those who, on the other hand, resisted the pull of
León's field of energy or could not respond to it or, having responded
to their limits, still did not work up to his satisfaction, found him, according to which tactic be thought apt, a fearful bully or a cajoling
suitor or the both. Hardly a day passed when he did not by a frown
reduce his secretaries to uncontrolled weeping, yet he was just as
able, at the dispensing of a smile, to put them in orgasm. They and
the messengers and, later on, the young associate lawyers received
the going wage, no more, worked easily three times as hard as anyone else in the country, yet never dreamed of quitting, even when
tempted by more generous and less exigent employers.

Still more impressive was León's effect on our public functionaries,
who set a standard of incompetence and torpor that their counterparts in other lands may yearn toward but never reach. On entering
a public office in my country, one invariably finds a number of petitioners waiting in tomblike patience while, at the desks, bored, som-
nolent young women lacquer their nails. These girls are hired in
consideration of nocturnal services rendered the minister or the vice-
minister or the chief of some department; they are not expected to
work by day. Behind them and discreetly shielded by partitions,
minor officials pass the hours sleeping or in the contemplation of
indecent photos. These hold their posts through the ascendancy
of relatives, and to continue holding them they need but show their
patrons proper deference when the family gathers. Still farther back
are the sancta of the bureaucrats. They are not in, and it will do one's
case no good to query why. The sane man, the man who wishes to
preserve his sanity, does not exhort this system to activity. He imitates the yogi and trances till his bribe has taken bold. Licentiate
León Fuertes, for his part, romanced the girls, railed at the clerks,
and badgered the chiefs of section without pity, and though this was
not the Tinieblan way, though the premier advocates of Zurich and
New York had tried it only to have their papers irretrievably mis-
placed and themselves consigned to rest homes, León succeeded with
it. He managed to get more or less instant action whenever he sought
a document or a determination.

He managed, likewise, to conscript a legion of enemies, who
hindered León, statesman, later on, and no doubt silently rejoiced
at his assassination. If it was un-Tinieblan to expect hard work from

others, it was inhuman to demand it from oneself. León took an immense number of cases; in fact, he never turned a case away—unless he was bribed to do so. He prepared each case with painstaking diligence and gave each the full measure of his energy. He never gave up, no matter how desperate his client's situation; he never eased up, no matter how certain victory appeared. Furthermore, in seeming paradox, he found the easy cases the most difficult, for they denied him the full exercise of his aggression and tenacity. No item in a negotiation was too insignificant, no sum too picayune to escape León's hawk eye and bulldog obstinacy. It is said that he never yielded up a point without getting three in return, that he never ceased to threaten endless litigation until his adversary had submitted, that he never tossed a defeated opponent even the merest sop to let him save face or mollify his client. This may be exaggeration, but one cannot disregard a remark by that feared advocate Dr. Inocencio Listín, who after nine hours of behind-doors argument over Aquilino Piojo's divorce declared that he would rather be cystoscoped than bargain with León Fuertes.

Along with this drive and diligence, León, lawyer, had the temerity and guile to cut his corners. We have seen how he lied and thereby risked disgrace and failure to save himself a year or so of study. In his law practice he not only was at all times able to rise above scruple but took a pride and relish in his frauds, and much less than worry over risk, he reveled in it. In 1947, when he agreed to represent the journalist Lazarillo Agudo in an obscure suit for damages that went back seven years and involved a number of people since exiled from the country, Carlitos Gavilán asked him how he meant to get his evidence.

"I'm not going to get it," León answered. "I'm going to fake it."

"Fake it all!"

"Exactly. Agudo has some stuff. I could dig through the records and get more. I could go down to Paraguay and take depositions. No doubt I'd win that way, but faking's better. Saves time and money. Makes for a stronger case. The temptation is to take the good stuff that I have, find more, and fake only what I really need to fake, but I'm going to fake everything. Fake events, fake records, fake depositions, and fake witnesses. That way it'll hold together. The truth happens to be on my side in this case," he added earnestly, "but I'd sooner it weren't. A careful fake is better than the truth. The truth lacks realism."[86]

On another occasion he actually sought sympathy from his partner after one of his more outrageous bits of trumpery had sluiced through trial and appeal without a shrug from judge or justices.

"I had a brilliant counterargument all ready," he complained. "You know, Carlitos, an artist like me is wasted on the judicial system of this country. A great artist deserves sharp critics."

In public León, lawyer, presented himself as the soul of truth and breath of honesty, packaging his lies in a solemnity that impressed clients and infuriated adversaries. Years later, when he had constructed and assumed a different figure, he could look back in irony at his career before the bar. During his presidency, for example, he entertained the Costaguanan novelist Gameliel Garza and toasted him as "the most ingenious confector of fictions to work in Spanish since I retired from law practice." The lawyer was, however, incapable of such salutary humor. He took himself eternally in earnest.

The recipe was completed by a synthetically-sweetened yet highcaloric charm the main steps in whose fabrication were the collection and retention of a volume of seemingly useless data. León Fuertes, lawyer, could, while filing an incorporation document at the Registro Nacional, pick up and store a clerk's remark that Pito Latino, the subassistant chief, was in bad humor over having missed the lottery prize by one slim digit. He was, thus, able, on returning some days later, to give Pito touching condolence in the form of a full sheet of lottery for the next drawing, hence to pluck from Pito's ego the stings of countless browbeatings. He heard and noted that Captain Franco Punzón of the Tinieblan Civil Guard had acquired yet a third young concubine and founded yet a fourth family, and when he next went down to see a client awaiting trial in Bondadosa Prison, he complimented the captain on his virility, citing the distinguished aphorist G. S. Patton on the correlation between martial valor and hyperactive gonads. He had on file the distribution of a bridge hand, dealt in 1947, that Don Anselmo Chinche, who was always Minister of Something, no matter who was in power, had played brilliantly, and, to Don Anselmo's infinite joy and gratitude, he replayed the hand for all the card room of the Club Mercantil, laying out the cards and annotating subtleties, after Don Anselmo had just bungled three cold contracts. When Judge Armando Desgracia's obese, myopic daughter was at last proposed to, León learned first and was the first to offer his congratulations. When Doña Fecunda de Obario, who was always suing someone, dragged her decrepit frame into his office one day without notice, León remembered—the Lord knows how!—that she had been Carnival Queen in 1926 and professed (with the sincerity attained only by expert counterfeiting) that he had seen her ride in state along Bahia Avenue and been, then and forever, captivated. He knew when the receptionist had lost a cherished boyfriend and when the President of the Republic had found a girlfriend who could make him potent, and he was ready with fit comment, gesture, glance. And so the country was persuaded that although he fought his cases tooth and nail, trod heavily at times on people's feelings, and let nothing stand between himself and money, León Fuertes was at heart deeply concerned about his fellow man.

The full beam of León's charm fell on his partner, but he bounced it adroitly off Gavilán's twins, Bolivar and Dolores, so that Carlitos got the glow by reflection and, though disarmed by it, was spared all mawkishness. León treated Lilo and Loli like adults whose society he valued—and did so without affectation. When he played catch with Lilo, he gave no hint that he was babying his throws, and he and Lilo argued the relative merits of José DiMaggio and Teodoro Williams with the intensity of bleacher-seaters. He taught Loli canasta and gave himself as fully to their games as to thousand inchado rubbers at the club. If there was any side of León, lawyer's character that in another man might be called "natural," it was his affection for these and most other children. Both kids adored him, which would have been enough, but León was, besides, uncannily adept at showing up *chez* Gavilán when they were raising hell and at the point of pitching both their parents to hysterics. A twitch of his eyebrows would bring them hurtling gleefully into his arms and salvage his partner's weekend. For this—more, certainly, than for the money León earned their firm—Carlitos loved him and bore his bullyings, his demands, his presumption of Carlitos's total loyalty to his person, and his utter disregard for ethics. Carlitos Gavilán was as near as one finds in life to an honest lawyer, a creature which, like the winged bull and the plumed serpent, exists only in fancy. But he put up even with León's trickiness because of León's charm.

Armed in this figure, weaponed with these traits, my father, León Fuertes, became the most successful lawyer ever to practice on our continent. He performed feats of jury-rigging which were instant legends, as when, defending Pura del Busto for the murder of her husband, he inveigled into the box three of her cousins, her chief lover, and her favorite aunt. The juries that he didn't rig he hypnotized, and veniremen were wont, the morning following a trial, to smack their foreheads in amazement when they read of their participation in some crook's acquittal. His mere presence in the courtroom seemed to exert an occult influence over opposing counsel and hostile witnesses. His summings-up drew such crowds that it was reckoned that were the courts permitted to sell tickets for them, the whole budget of the Ministry of Justice might thereby be deferred. And in these perorations León could, as it suited him, draw limpid truths out of a swamp of error or so confuse a hitherto clear issue that all the rabbis of Jerusalem would be unable to unravel it. In court—in the old Cortes on Plaza Inchado, where four-bladed ceiling fans turned lazily and flies droned with the monotony of prosecutors, where judges yawned cavernously in the heat and the rococo moldings were sodden with falsehood—all eyes were constantly on León, no matter who was speaking. There was no telling when he might leap from his dignified repose and draw gasps of admiration even from his adversaries with a linked series of juristic handsprings. At his jaunty entrances and exits he was trailed by a retinue of journalists, petitioners, and fans such as are drawn by bullfighters or movie stars. Yet he was not all flash. Well could he rant and rave, pound witnesses to splinters with his shouting, seethe an opponent's soul in sarcasm, or by repeated volleys of objections and citations drive a stern judge back from a point of law, yet there were cases which he argued in apparent meekness, planting three or four timid questions which, like the "quiet" moves at chess that commentators later on discover and score with exclamation points, turned the whole contest.

In his entire career, a career of great activity, my father lost but six cases. These are among his masterpieces, for he took princely bribes to lose them yet appeared to fight with such determination and to lose with such bitterness that his duped clients begged him not to take the thing so hard. When he represented plaintiffs in suits for damages, he worked by contingency, agreeing to take in fee everything above a stipulated figure. He won unheard-of judgments, and often ended up with much more than his client. Real wealth for a Tinieblan lawyer comes, however, in representing the great U.S. corporations—Hirudo Oil, Galactic Fruit, Yankee and Celestial Energy—with interests here, and though at León's advent to the bar all the guzzling places at this trough had long been taken by established firms, he managed nonetheless to gorge from it. He began by taking cases against these corporations and flogged terrible awards from them. Soon it was enough for him merely to give out that he was thinking of proceeding on behalf of Tal-y-Tal, S.A., against So-and-So, Inc., and he would receive an embassy from Mosca, Luciérnaga or Avispa y Abeja and be offered a fat bribe to pass the case on to another lawyer. This variant of the protection racket earned him cash and saved him time. Each year he made money on ten or twenty cases that he never accepted, much less prepared and argued. To preserve the flow, he took to ferreting out abuses that had not yet been perceived and then advising the offended parties. Thus he battened on the gringo interests while making a valuable reputation as a patriot.

This reputation furnished him defense against the constant innuendo that he was only out for money, as did his few but spectacular appearances on behalf of injured indigents and his celebrated pilgrimage to Costaguana, where, in the shadow of his client's gallows and at risk of his own life, he pleaded successfully for the life and liberty of the opposition leader Apolonio Varón.[87] And these exhibitions of altruism garnered him more clients and more money.

In short, he made his fortune. After five years of full-time lawyering he was a wealthy man. When he went into politics in 1952, he reduced the scope and intensity of his practice, but since by then he had his pick of clients and could invest his money with the prescience of one who controls events, his wealth grew on. It never bulged obscenely like the Ladilla family's or the Tábano family's, but it financed his dream and funded his later honesty. It also fostered culture and advanced science, for it allowed his second son a first-rate education and is at present subsidizing the confection of this history.

In passing, León, lawyer, freed some innocents, righted some wrongs. The truth was on his side sometimes, however inconveniently. He took joy in his work and in the celebrity it brought him. Like all León's figures, the lawyer was adroitly tailored and worn comfortably. But León saw the lawyer clearly for what he was: a predatory trickster.

In 1950, when Dr. Inocencio Listín was elected President of the Tinieblan College of Attorneys and gave a speech full of grand periodic sentences about the right of every litigant to have his side of an issue staunchly argued and the obligation of every lawyer to forget his personal feelings and defend his client's interests to the limit of his eloquence and skill, León remarked to his partner that Listín was speaking mainly to himself.

"We all lie," León whispered. "That's what a lawyer's paid for. But since no one pays me to lie to myself, I don't do it."

As he had no delusions about the lawyer, León put him aside when he had time to and dressed himself privately in other figures. León, athlete, showed up on the tennis court each morning, modest as ever. León, scholar, appeared most midnights to search for a few hours into physics or philology or anything but law. Two entirely new Leóns were also fashioned: León Fuertes, husband, and León Fuertes, lecher. We may now with convenience turn to these.

18. Marriage

IN THE TWILIGHT of the Seventeenth Century, Don Alonso de Alcapara y Cebolla Picada, Viceroy of Tinieblas, abandoned a long struggle with the paranoia of command and fortified his capital against a rabble of phantom pirates who had for years been pillaging through his imagination. Such projects don't admit of skimping, and to this day the colonial quarter of Ciudad Tinieblas remains gartered on its seafront by broad and sturdy walls,[88] the top of which—rimmed with a salt-stained battlement and brooded from (at the elbow promontory opposite the Cortes) by three squat cannons—provides a promenade for citizens and Kodak-fodder for tourists. Somewhat before sunset, then, one day in January, 1947, when the dry season was upon the country and the heat split up a little by fresh breezes off the Humboldt Current, a young woman stood on Don

Alonso's wall, now reading, now looking out over the bay. The western wind held her about the waist with one hand and with the other
pressed the folds of her white linen dress against her thighs and
knees. The sun (who in our latitude is potent on his deathbed) had
sired triplet flecks of perspiration along her upper lip. She was mem-
orizing verses in a foreign language, gathering them from the page
three at a time and then mutely declaiming them to an audience of
sailing pelicans. This so absorbed her that though a man approached
and stood some time beside her, she was not conscious of his presence till he spoke.

"What's the book?"

"Shelley." She did not look up.

"Hmm."

"English poet of the Romantic epoch."

"Hmm."

"Born in Sussex, 1792. Drowned in the Gulf of Spezia, 1822."

"And meantime married to the *mamá* of Dr. Frankenstein."

She closed her book and looked at him. She blinked and smiled.
"Oh." She turned toward him. "If I had known I was going to make
your acquaintance, I would have brought someone more heroic.
Byron, I suppose."

"No matter." He smiled but looked at her steadily. "The important
thing is that the children will be encouraged to learn English. My
mother actually forbade me to learn English. Foolish, and something
of a handicap."

"What children?"

"Ours. No, please, don't be offended. Wait, let me tell you a dream
I had two years ago. You were in it."

"You don't even know who I am!"

"You were in my dream all the same. Wait, let me tell you."

Thus, anyway, the meeting was recounted to my brother, Carlos,
my sister, Clara, and me on various occasions in our childhood. Saving brief reference to the place, the hour, and the pelicans, my mother
did not set the scene. She would, however, cite the intensity of my father's gaze and the rakish tilt of his panama, then gruff her voice up
for his portions of the dialogue. He, if he happened to be home,
would harumph happily at his allusion to Mary Shelley, then break
in to claim that he had said "Your children" and that he'd made no

mention whatsoever of any dream until some evenings later. It was a tough jury for him; he got only Carlos's vote. But even if, on appeal, the reader chooses to grant him his two points, the essential facts of his conduct that afternoon are not in question: he left the office he was already sharing with Carlitos Gavilán; he took the sea wall, not the street, north toward the Club Mercantil; he saw my mother, whom he did not know but whom he recognized at once as the woman in his wartime dream; he approached her and pressed himself upon her. Had he instead searched round the globe as relentlessly as the Flying Dutchman, he could nowhere have found a woman at once so loving and so opposite to him.

León Fuertes snacked at a smorgasbord of worlds, tasting each separately as different men. For Soledad Piérida the world was one, a perfect oval, fissureless and whole, composed of love. It was not that she felt love to be the main thing or what truly counted. Only love existed. Love might display itself in different form, like gold in a charm bracelet. Love might be twisted clumsily into an Adolf or an A-bomb. But as prime matter it was ever one and pure. One morning in 1928, when at age three she sat alone on the balcony of her father's house in Calle Justo Canino, she heard a spider singing at its loom under the eaves, wooing the fat flies, and for the next few years such music whispered to her solitary games—the trek anthem of parasol ants as they safari'd out across the patio, the work chantey of black ants heave-hoing a moth's carcass nestward over *sala* tiles. Later, when she received religious instruction, her epiphanies of love took divine form. She was so visibly imbued with the holy spirit that contentious adults grew calm in her presence, and Monseñor Irribarri, the archbishop of Tinieblas and a worldly priest if there ever was one, went to her in a throng of first communicants and, to his own amazement, knelt and asked her blessing. She had frequent and protracted visions of the blessed virgin, who came to her as a girl of her own age and played with her. After the first of these visitations, which her parents, with worried looks between them, told her to think no more of, Soledad stopped speaking of them, but they remained regular occurrences, however wonderful. They ceased with her puberty and were replaced with the sound of verses in the air around her. Her first thought was to write these down and show them to her father, but he was so shocked and furious at their passionate character that she never more put poems down on paper but merely listened. They brought her no shame. Nor did she feel that godhead had abandoned her; love, which had shown itself to her in one form then another, had now assumed a different avatar.

Toward the end of Soledad's adolescence the verses she alone heard faded, but by then she had discovered the verses and tales others had heard and had been suffered to write down and publish, and she immersed herself in this love and decided to absorb it so she might pass it on to others. Love was made audible in words to certain people, and their part was to hear it clearly and transcribe it accurately. Others participated at a next remove, preserving and distributing. Daughters of the Tinieblan ruling class were not supposed to use their minds, much less to study, much, much less to enter a profession, and Soledad's father, my grandfather Don Adelberto Piérida, was more than normally preoccupied with the dignity of his name and the exalted level of his place in the society and the canons of *machismo,* but by a campaign of implacable sweetness Soledad persuaded him to send her abroad to prepare herself as a teacher. He chose a convent college in Virginia with the most stringent restrictions imaginable and, to enforce them, a complement of nuns that any tyrant would have grinned to have among his gaolers. None of this bothered Soledad, for the place had a good library. She studied for four years without interruption, while her father worried without interruption for her virtue, which could have been no safer had she been cased in a block of ice. (He would have done better to worry about his younger daughter, Alegra, who also believed in love but on a less spiritual plane than did my mother. Alegra married in great haste at seventeen and was delivered six months later of a son whose paternity remains a mystery. Alberto Avispa, who was unaware of the existence—not to say the abundance—of other suspects, copped a plea when indicted, but Alegra fingered him without the slightest certainty he was the guilty man.) Soledad had been back in Tinieblas half a year, teaching fifth and sixth form English at the Instituto de la Virgin Santísima, when love sought her newly in the person of my father.

It came to Soledad one day that León Fuertes was the embodiment of love precisely fashioned for her custody and worship, but this was by no means an immediate revelation. She had never perceived love in the form of human male, and for a good while her feelings toward

León were ambivalent. She knew of him before they met, had in fact been present with her parents at all the embassies where he was feted, yet while his courage appealed to her romantic nature, the things he'd done to prove it (as retold in his citations) repelled her. At their meeting she was at once charmed by his spontaneity and frightened by his head-on assault. After he began courting her, she went one day to see him at trial and, deep in the gallery, unnoticed by him, happened to catch one of his best early performances. It climaxed with him backed Flynn- or Fairbankslike against the reporters' table, engaging judge and opposing counsel in a flashing cut and thrust of argument until both yielded, yet while Soledad was impressed by his intelligence, his violent wielding of it put her off. Following each of his visits to her home, her father took pains to predict León would soon be rich and important—the clearest earnest Don Adelberto could give of favoring a match—but though Soledad wanted to please her father, she had never cared for riches or importance. León's attentions to her were both captivating and unsettling. She enjoyed his company, which as a manifestation of a León he was building expressly for their life together was tender, ardent, and attentive, yet could not reconcile it with his ferocity in court. She let him tell her his dream and found the house admirably sited, the children lovely, the wife fortunate, but she refused to find herself in it. She refused because, as she and her world were one and whole, she could not countenance things partial and disjointed. She saw no unity to León, and her instinct told her that his love for her was transitory. In this her instinct was both wrong and right: the love was constant but it was felt by an inconstant León, a part-time León who alternated in one body with some several others. Thus all his qualities, each one of which might facilely have won another girl, failed to win Soledad. Still he persisted, and with a light heart, for every hour of her society further convinced him he had seen her in his dream of peace and order.

Then one day it came to her. She had gone walking to the place where they first met and stood again beside the battlement above the bay, not reading now, thinking of León, and, of a sudden, she perceived him—as she had heard the spider's song and seen the Blessed Virgin—as an embodiment of love sent to and for her. He had, I guess, by then completed work on León, husband, and Soledad may have mistaken this new figure for a conversion in a whole man. She may perhaps have sensed his essential hunger, the only constant (save his body) to the several Leóns. Whatever the case—and one cannot give "reasons" for irrational epiphanies—from that moment she loved him with her entire being, not till death parted them but beyond death, which is an eye-blink of no consequence anyway. Five weeks later they were married.

Soledad and León were, then, each for the other, the incarnation of a vision—a charming circumstance for maid and man to be caught up in, except the visions were distinctly unalike. For León, Soledad was the consort of one of his many, separate lives; for Soledad, León was the projection of love's unity. Each was ill formed to wear the other's dream. My aunt Rosario, who was León's double with the sex reversed, who shared his soul and whose soul León shared, would (incest taboos aside) have been has perfect co-star in the six-reel epic of a marriage, adapting herself gracefully to as many Leóns as he cared to bring onto the screen. My mother, Soledad, would have played perfectly beside him in a lyric interlude, for while neither she nor León ever understood the other for so much as ten seconds in the sense of feeling what the other felt, both were forever reaching poignantly out toward each other across the gulf between them. Destiny, at times no more perceptive than a Hollywood caricature of a Hollywood producer, cast each lady in the other one's best role.

Reaching . . . My mother[89] formed her life around my father. Without regret or hesitation, she exchanged the teacher's calling for the helpmeet's, turned her intelligence and strength of heart to building León's dream, dissolved her will in his, and strove to mold herself into his image of her. By nature shy and sensitive, she nonetheless inured herself to prominence, to having her surname bandied in the vulgar mouth and her husband clamored for and at, to being (once he went into politics) an object of attention and of gossip, to living (as First Lady) in the fishbowl of public scrutiny under the wink and stare of cameras, and rather than bear all these intrusions with a grudged ill humor, she so pretended to take pleasure in my father's fame that he was spared all guilt in foisting it upon her, while many thought it was her hunger, not his, that goaded him along. At God knows what psychic cost, she masked her native sincerity behind a dulcet smile and helped León charm clients and politicians he himself despised but had to humor. She accepted, even helped choose, the luxuries he poured upon her, the profusion of French silk and Irish linen dresses, the Costaguanan emeralds, the Worcester china and the Baccarat crystal, the extra servants, the ornately swollen cars—all the accouterments of pillowed ease and costly glitter. She trained herself first to enjoy these, then to depend upon them, so that those who met her after she had been for some years married to my father assumed her an heiress pampered from infancy, to whom the most lavish opulence was bare necessity. She gave León the children he desired and reared them in concert with his dream. We were the mirror of young gentlefolk, Carlos, Clara, and I; accorded every mode of cultivation and admonished constantly to take the full advantage. In this the reason and the plea were ever one: "to please your father." Studying one's schoolwork, attending one's private tutors, practicing one's piano scales, perfecting one's tennis game—all such would "please your father." Carelessness, negligence, or sloth would "make your father sad." Our young ears hummed with a changeless litany about how hard that father worked, how kind he was, how much he loved us. In our bicameral universe of the house on Bahia Avenue and the villa at Medusa Beach there was one god, León Fuertes, and my mother was his prophet. She bent her heart and soul to bring his dream alive and to approximate the woman in it, and she succeeded save in one particular: she wasn't happy.

My mother did a fine job concealing her failure to supply this key feature of my father's dream. Few outsiders suspected that she suffered, much less that her suffering proceeded from her marriage. Women, my father's casual loves included, envied her. Men found their own wives restless by comparison. Still, she grieved, and it was not because she felt despoiled of her identity or shrunk to an appendage or otherwise impaled upon a feminist cliché. She wished for nothing but to lose herself in love, to be a mirror of some form of love that showed itself to her. No; if my mother wept in her vast bed, if she lay sighing all a rainy afternoon on her silk-covered Recamier, if she allowed her gaze to flutter weakly round the breakfast room and die by her bone teacup, it was because the man to whom she gave herself entirely returned her but a fraction of himself, was always leaving her a widow.

Reaching . . . Of all my father's figures, none was so nobly planned or finely crafted as León Fuertes, husband. He was the only León permitted in my mother's company and was, in all respects save one, ideal. To say that León, husband, loved his wife would be superfluous: he doted on her. A hundred thousand small attentions proved her ever in his thoughts. Each morning he called from court or office to inquire how she'd slept. Each afternoon he brought her flowers, or a book he'd seen and thought she might enjoy, or still some other loving trifle. He got *Le Figaro and Corriere della Sera* at his office, and when he'd come home, calling "Sóle!" and embraced her and pulled off his tie and coat and collapsed smiling in the Otán-weave hemp hammock that was slung for him across a corner of the *sala,* when he'd kicked off his shoes and drunk his *limonada* in two or three parched gulps, he would fish out a scissored piece by Mauriac or a review of the new Malaparte and translate it to my mother along with comments, questions, and expectant glances for approval. He brought her the news, and bits of gossip which he recounted with a luxury of detail, hanging on her responses. Never did León, artist, strive so eagerly to please an audience or León, scholar, give such weight to an authority's opinion. My father's manner in these afternoon three-quarter hours was less that of a husband or a lover than of a special kind of friend: the antique gentleman, lonely, near destitute, and yet most courtly, whose only welcome moments of existence come in his visits to a matron half his age. Perhaps he loved her mother long ago or stood beside her father in some fight. No doubt he held her at the font when she was christened and at her marriage stood deep in the church biting his lip to hold back tears of joy, and now he comes each day at the same hour to bring her gilded butterflies of wit, enameled singing birds of conversation, and so to warm his spirit in her smile.

When darkness washed in around them, though, León grew youthful, would swing his legs out of the hammock and rise and go to her and take her hand, bend to her, kiss a bride's blush onto her lifted cheek, whisper a low, shy laugh from her turned throat, lead her upstairs. His ardor for her was as strong on their last evening as on their wedding night.

The way he gloried in my mother's company was the despair of other husbands, who were forever having him held up a model for them by their own wives. When León and Soledad went out together, he did not flee to rumble business with the men or flirt with other

women, and if they were pulled apart by tides of conversation, he
kept in touch with her by smiles and glances. Even when he was President and she First Lady and they presided at state entertainments or
were themselves hosted in foreign capitals, he let no pomp or protocol divide them long but would seek her across the room to stand
holding her hand while he conversed. Their couplehood was so
charming and so obvious that during their official stay in France in
1962, M. Malraux remarked to my mother that the Elysée orchestra
ought to have marked their entrance with a waltz from *Les deux pi-
geons* rather than the Tinieblan anthem. One would have thought
my father had no other purpose in his life besides his marriage.

León Fuertes never raised his voice to his wife, even in the seclusion
of their bedroom. He deferred to her judgment in all points of taste,
from the décor of their apartments at the Palace (which was done
over out of his private means) to his own dress. Nor did he ever
countermand her dispositions where their children were concerned,
though he had very firm ideas on child rearing as a dry run for the
struggles of this life. My mother, for example, tended to spoil her
second son, cute little Camilito, future historian, whom I self-portray
from the glass of memory as a wily brat parlaying his huge eyes and
scrawny body into more than his fair share of Mama's love. I feared
and loathed the breakers at Medusa Beach, which at flow tide were
mountainous, snarl-lipped with greasy foam, and slimed with seaweed, while my father's dearest joy—shared idiotically by both Clara
and Carlos—was to romp in them. We would wade out, all holding
hands like figures in the *danse macabre,* until one of these monsters
loomed above us, and then dive through the base of it so that it broke
harmlessly past us, and this I valiantly endured, having my father's
hand and, more, the prospect, once we were past the waves, of riding
tadpoled to his back on the calm, limpid, sun-flecked swells beyond.
My father, though, would often leave us on the sand to swim far out
alone and then, returning to the far fringe of the breaker line, call us
out to him. Carlos and Clara would go happily, dolphining through
the waves, but when a big one rose above me, I, stonied by mixed
disgust and terror, would refuse the dive, would get the full weight
of the ocean on my fragile ribs, would be bowled up across the shin-
gles, foam in my nostrils, seaweed on my lips, sobbing for air and
safety. Then, when I'd floundered to my feet and wiped my tears, my

father, who understood my problem (though I didn't think so then), who suffered my anguish more than I did (though I sense this only in retrospect), but who felt obliged to urge me toward self-mastery (though at the time I put his motive down as tyrant's *Machtlust*), would call, "Come on, don't let it beat you," and I, of all things most afraid of his displeasure, would stumble shivering back to try again. My mother was wont, however, to cancel whole runs of this tragi-farce. She might, if the seas were breaking, put on a stern face and with pained gravity, as though it were a cruel blow to me, proclaim: "Camilo can't swim today. He has a fever." I would contrive to look both sick and shattered, a tough role since I could now anticipate delicious hours lounging near her under the striped umbrella or, still better, snuggled beside her in the porch hammock while she read to me. My father, scarcely deceived and visibly annoyed, would merely purse his lips and nod, would not so much as test my forehead with his palm, much less call us both sneaks and overrule her.

My father's presence brought at once excitement and security, a sea breath of freedom, a wide horizon of delight and possibility, a steadiness of firm and weathered decks. The spirits of my mother and us children thrived or withered with his entrances and exits, and since his pride of place was ever beyond question, he had no call to be a bully in his home, to govern arbitrarily or demand kowtows. At dinner, which we took together most nights as a family, he drew his children into conversation and heard us out with interest and respect. Further, he often let us stay when there was company, a provision that he likened to Plato's idea of taking future leaders to the battle-field as children to observe in safety and be blooded like young hounds, for to our home came the cleverest people in Tinieblas and distinguished foreigners as well-artists, journalists, politicians—and their debates moved wide- and wittily through every theater of the intellect. Here one might glimpse in León, husband, evidence of other Leóns; he was not always able to restrain the athlete's-lawyer's-warrior's thirst for strife and triumph. He never competed with my mother, though, or pushed her down. My parents ruled in harmony, Sultan and Grand Vizir, so that their only fault was to leave us chil-dren ignorant, hence cruelly unprepared, for the sex wars that rage by other hearths.

León, husband, was withal loving, attentive, and respectful to his wife; kindly, strong, and bountiful to his children. Besides, he suffered himself to be adored by her and them, to be the sun around which their world orbited. This was a burden, for as he was now bound to examine his life, he knew that León, husband, his virtues else aside, was stamped with one defect which corrupted him to failure: he had no staying power. Think of a star athlete who frustrates fans and teammates by missing half the season every year. Think of a writer whose lightest phrase is genius, who never sets a word down out of place, but who, seduced from art by love of life, strays from his desk and starves his public on a few slim volumes sparsed across the decades. Think then of León, husband, superspouse and author of his family's joy, who was forever vanishing, leaving the grin of his perfections in the air behind.

Each of León, husband's, vanishings was a departure[90] from existence. His body was in use to other Leóns, his spirit limbo'd for uncertain time. At dawn he vanished into León, athlete, for his two sets of tennis, and but for a telephonic moment at midmorning he remained vanished until five or six P.M. León, lawyer, or León, politician, had the workday. Any siesta time or otherwise spare minutes went to León, lecher (who makes his entrance in a page or two). When León, husband, had made late-afternoon devotions to his wife and dined with his family, he was liable to vanish once again, and even if he remained throughout the remnant portion of the evening, answered an invitation with his wife or hosted guests at home, he vanished for the midnight hours into León, scholar. None of these other Leóns had a family; none was even married. None cared for Soledad Piérida de Fuertes, and none could pass even at a scrape as an embodiment of love formed for her custody and worship.

Thus Soledad and León failed, each in his way, of being the true incarnation of the other's vision. León failed Soledad and knew it, was not wholly hers, left her in main a widow, but he was in no wise able to give up his separate lives and form himself into one person about León, husband. Soledad knew she failed León, but she could not love partially, could not forbear to grieve her husband's vanishings. Neither reproached the other for his failure; each bore his guilt and heaviness in silence. León and Soledad, Soledad and León, reaching, mostly in vain.

19. Lechery

SINCE SIGMUND THE GLAD proclaimed that the essence of the human species throbs between its thighs, it has become the mode among biographers to rummage in their subjects' sex lives with exceeding thoroughness and, upon pulling forth their plums, to say: "What a good boy am I!" I loathe, detest, abhor, condemn this fashion. Can catalogs of humps and spasms solve the human mystery? Must scholar vie with scribbler in contriving that the reader's groin be starched or gooied every fifteen pages? But though sex is not everything, while it is surely not the only thing, it is at times part of the bio that one graphs. This work has thus allowed itself a few grudged gropes below the belt and now must make another. No history of León Fuertes would be complete or balanced without considering that he reached for other ladies besides his wife.

León came young to venery and wenched with sufficient industry to clap himself before he was fourteen. He was an ardent if unknowing incesteer and the crown princess of Riviera homodom. For six years he practiced the weirdest of all sexual perversions: total chastity. Then, on his return to Tinieblas in November, 1946, he embarked upon a progress through the hearts and parts of women which continued unarrested till his death.

No respectable León could be this kind of tourist. The athlete was a man's man, the scholar a eunuch, the lawyer chastely trothed to frigid wealth. The husband was enveloped in monogamy; the leader craved no more from women than their votes. But with us Fuertes the taste for respectability reciprocates an equal, opposite fuck-youism. Hence León, artist—but he, apparently, had lost his voice on Colle Belvedere. So when my father created León, lawyer, León, lecher, sprang boldly dingus'd from his loins.

As my father was male, some females sought to entertain him. Some were excited by his grace of body, some by his mental brilliance, some by his wealth, some by his prominence, some by the tenderness he showed his family, some by his ruthlessness in court, some by some combination of these features. None knew he split himself in a plurality of Leóns. Subtly or blatantly, each in her way,

they made it known they were at home to León Fuertes. They spread
the welcome mat; they asked him to drop in. Sometimes a message
of this nature reached my father when he was in the visiting mood;
sometimes it actually provoked his transformation into León, lecher.
But had León, lecher, called only on those ladies who sent him invitations, he would not merit a full chapter in this history. What commands our interest is the number of doors he knocked on uninvited
and the invariable warmth of his reception.[91] He knocked when and
where he cared to, entirely without regard to the race, creed, ethnic
derivation, social standing, economic condition, or marital status of
his prospective hostesses. He called generally on women of from
eighteen to thirty-five but made enough exceptions at both ends of
this scale to prove his freedom from prejudice. He wasted no time in
courting, paid no mind to logistical inconvenience, had no sense of
decency, and met with no rebuffs, so as his health was strong, his
need persistent, and his whim eclectic, his wang was known to a
good portion of the females in the land.

León, lecher, exerted a hypnotic fascination over women of all
rank and temper. The chief source of this power was his concentration, a trait common to all the Leóns. As León, lawyer, was all business, León, lecher, was all lust. When the gonadine fit was on him,
all León's energy was focus'd in desire and beamed upon his target.
But he was by no means pushy or ostensibly intense. He lounged, he
drawled, he grinned in a perfect counter felt of relaxation, picturing
forth the overstroked indifference that women find bedeviling.
Meanwhile his gaze would grasp a woman by the hips, steal beneath
her clothing, palp her breasts and loins, so that she found herself first
paralyzed, then randy. His voice would nuzzle up between her thighs
and buttocks. His presence would flush her skin and melt her tendons. Consider, in illustration, the case of Luz Ahumada, whom he
enjoyed impromptu on the morning of 7th February, 1956:

Luz arrived at the Club Mercantil at about seven-thirty for an early
swim and was on the point of entering the ladies' locker room (which
gave on the tennis courts) when León, who had played two sets, finished screwing the press' down on his racket and looked up at her.
She was nineteen, tall and slender, with shapely legs, palm-sized buttocks, and smoky-soft grey eyes. She was, besides, scheduled (and
destined) to be married four days later to Jacinto Salmón, an associ-

ate at Gavilán y Fuertes, and it may have been her prenuptial glow that, heightening her normal loveliness, transformed León from athlete to lecher. At once in steaming rut, he called hello and, masking his bulged groin with his racket, gimped to her. When his smile touched her, she felt the openings of her body fill up with warm wax. During the next two minutes she heard the small-talk that her mouth kept making like radio noises from a distant room, now and then shivering uncontrollably as his laugh tongued languidly across her abdomen. When he guided her inside, she opened her mouth to protest but instead gave it to León, who lapped behind her upper teeth, causing her soul to pour out of her body and soak the bottom of the one-piece bathing suit she wore under her dress. She stood docilely while he peeled her naked, but when he drew her to a shower stall and closed the curtain, as he stripped his sweat-sopped shirt and shorts, she began to twist her hips and squeeze her thighs together. He steadied her haunches and pushed gently, collapsing her to the tiles. He dropped between her raised calves and pillowed his knees with his clothing. When he, entered her, she smiled in pain and bit her lip in pleasure, but it was only later, when he had helped her to her feet and opened the tap, when she saw her blood wash down the shower drain, that she began to realize what had happened.[92]

León, lecher, was at all times ready to assume command of my father's body and had besides a knack for exploiting an unpromising situation. Witness, for example, his seduction of Inelda de Comején, attempted on the provocation of a glance and accomplished in the presence of her husband. This was in the living room of the Comején apartment on a rainy evening in the early fifties. León had gone to discuss a case with his colleague and coeval Francisco Comején, had finished by settling it out of court to his own advantage, and had in the process so stung his host's ego that Comején, who was chess champion of Tinieblas and one of the strongest boards in Central America, insisted that they play a game or two and called his wife in to observe his triumphs. He crushed León twice, spotting him first a knight and then a castle, then proposed to play blindfolded—actually from a chair at the far end of the room facing away from the table.

"I'll give you pawn and move, Leoncito, and the beating of your life in the bargain!"

At that, Inelda de Comején, dumpling-plump matron of twenty-seven, glanced at León Fuertes. One might have wrung that glance like a dishrag and not squeezed out one drop of prurient invitation. It contained no more than an excuse for Comején's arrogance, a plea that León humor him and go through with the game, and a hint that she was rooting for the underdog. It was made, however, with a certain tenderness and complicity—a chaste tenderness, a mild complicity, yet sufficient to relieve León, lawyer, from duty and, call up León, lecher.

"You're on!"'

Comején swung the board so that the whites faced León. He plucked the black king pawn and set it on the table. Then he rose, stalked off, turned a rattan armchair toward the closed door, and slouched into it. "Your move!"

"If you turn your head, the game's forfeit. Agreed?"

"Agreed, agreed. Just move!"

León touched his queen pawn forward and called the move to Comején, at the same time leering shyly at Inelda and fondling the pawn's glistening nub with his thumb and forefinger. She crossed her legs and squirmed. Developing, he put light pressure on Comején's king bishop pawn and Inelda's downy forearm, then attacked boldly, extending his knight toward Comején's flank and his tongue in dumb-show lappings toward Inelda's center.

"What! What are you . . .?"

"Inelda! Please keep quiet! I'm concentrating!"

After some more advances León captured a pawn from Comején and Inelda's fluttering left bubby.

"Ohhhh!"

"Did you move?"

"*J'adoube,*" said León, twisting gently.

He followed with a succession of forward probes, then, in a daring suite, opened his center file, exposed his Bishop, and pointed it at the dame!—winning the piece but putting himself in a difficult position:

Inelda stood on tiptoe, her skirt up, her girdle down, her trunk draped forward over the back of her chair, while León addressed her shuddering stern, squelched her mooings with a firm left palm, watched the board, moved chessmen with his right hand, and called his moves. In this manner he held off Comején's counterattack until he had mated Inelda soundly.

A real trouper, León, lecher, appeared ad lib on any stage at all with every type of co-star. He made his debut on the Bastidas-Ciudad Tinieblas bus the night of his return from Europe with a *mulata* girl whose hips synched with the humps and swayings of the road as she knelt spraddled to him in the humid stifle, her bum jouncing in his hands like caramel custard. He did daytime walk-ons in the offices of private firms and government departments with the likes of Lisa Pestaña, lynx-eyed receptionist at Hirudo Oil, who billboarded her availability the instant he walked in, who approved his lingering to flirt with her once he had done his business, but who, expecting to be taken out, was instead taken on her desk as soon as the other staff had left for lunch; with Professor Pilar de Yglesias (M.A., Chicago, 1950), Vice-Minister of Social Welfare in the Government of Juan Ardilla (1960-1962), who gave León, politician, a cool welcome—he'd been thumping the administration pretty hard—and León, lecher, a torrid one, the change of heart and Leóns transpiring in a ten-minute pavane which began near her swivel chair and finale'd on the floor below a panting air conditioner; with Nuris Ciervo and Lelis Liebre and Dalys Cordero, file clerks at the Registro Nacional, who on one or more occasions found themselves splayed to León Fuertes up against the dusty storeroom shelves; with other castings in other locales. He played matinees on his office couch with secretaries or sometimes with clients, and kept after-dark engagements in motel rooms and in private homes and in his car. He even did a gig once in the Reservation, standing in for León, scholar, who went one evening to the Post Library at Fort Shafter to consult the *Atlas of American Wars* (Col. Vincent R. Esposito, ed.) in connection with a study he was making of Batallón Tinieblas in Korea. The scholar was completing a fourcolor tracing of the positions along Heartbreak Ridge when Ensign Amy Wrigley, USN, brushed by his table, leaving a mixed whiff of musk and soapsuds, which shooed him from the communal Fuertes frame and cued in León, lecher. He did his act with Amy in a corner of the stacks, then (since the place closed in the interval) followed with an encore in a nest of piled chair cushions. Some days León, lecher, gave two or three performances with different ladies, and when he was President he played the Palace.

Women often emerged from these embraces as from a trance, astounded by their actions, but my father was himself quite com-

monly surprised by León, lecher. One night a few weeks before his
marriage, while he was dining at the home of his partner and closest
friend, Carlitos Gavilán, some laugh or gesture by Gavilán's wife,
Marcia, sent León, lecher, surging to his body. My father was
amazed, somewhat annoyed, at length amused, but was in any case
able to keep the wanton down till he was needed. He turned to Carlitos and talked shop for a cool half-hour until the latter finished his
coffee and repaired to his study to work on a brief. He took the twins
up to their room and storied them to sleep. Then, and only then, did
he commit his body to the care of León, lecher, and in that character,
disposing of the powers proper to that special León, charm Marcia
into quivering consent and thoroughly pleasure both her and himself.

The pleasures León Fuertes found with women were three: the
physical pleasure of tension and release; the psychic pleasure of
conferring pleasure; the moral pleasure of tearing free from all
moral constraints. He formed León, lecher, unconsciously, but deliberately allowed him to procure these pleasures. Since my father
found intellectual pleasure in his work and studies, social pleasure
in his public life, and affective pleasure in his wife and family, he
did not require of a paramour that she have this or that mentality
or come from a particular background or feel compassionate about
his life. He reserved sentiment for his wife and approached other
women with good-humored hedonism. Judging by results, this was
an adroit procedure; his embraces were neither resisted nor resented.
Though he had many adventures, each produced in him an enthusiasm that recalls the Greek root of that word: "possessed by a
god." Few were, however, extended to a second episode, and in the
whole career of León, lecher, there were but two relationships that
might be called affairs.

Irene Manta de Hormiga was something of a female counterpart
to León, lecher. Her charms were irresistible and her desire boundless. But sensuality was not just a fragment of her nature: the whole
of her was given up to it. From the time she left convent school at
eighteen she lived in the act of Love or in repose from it or in its
preparations, and when, at forty-three, still at the summit of her
beauty, she learned she was developing sclerosis, she seduced a CIA
case officer and had him bring her one of those Bondish cyanide pills
(which she said was for her husband), and hiding the capsule in her

mouth and welcoming her lover with a special tenderness, died in climax.

Irene Hormiga breathed forth a promise of delight that moved the stoniest men to passion. Her skin was smoothed by the satiety of love, her dark hair perfumed with love's anticipation, And since she was bound over into love so firmly that she literally could not live without it, Irene studied love and mastered all its arts, especially the art of dreaming herself into her lover's mind and body and thereby pleasing him fully and perfectly. Men who became her lovers took such joy in her that they could scarcely credit their own senses. They were awed while she loved them and pierced with wild regret and longing when she released them and in neither case able to boast of having her. Hence she managed to maintain a spotless reputation though she deceived her husband with at least three hundred men, one each month for twenty-five years.

At first she was disturbed by her behavior. Each month she found herself drawn to a certain man. He might be an ambassador or a laborer, but she would find his attraction irresistible, and she would yield and receive him and enjoy him and consecrate herself to him and lavish on him all the pleasures of the Muslim heaven. Then he would shrink dim and wasted in her eyes and, wondering sadly at his faded power, she would abandon him and make a new selection.[93] Later she realized that she was vassaled in the regnance of the moon, who rules by revolution, and that her lovers took allure from her in moonly rhythm. From then on she chose her consorts without guilt or sadness.

One month she chose León Fuertes—or tried to choose him, for he did not choose to serve. This was in the fall of 1950, soon after President Alejandro Sancudo acquired several miles of empty beachfront at a place called Medusa and had the Ministry of Public Works put in an access road and streets and make a golf course and do landscaping. Most well-to-do Tinieblans were buying lots and building villas, and León went there for a weekend with his family to see if he should do the same. His one-time fellow rounder Nacho Hormiga was his host, and on Sunday morning, as León was treading water and calculating real estate values out beyond the breakers, Irene swam out to him and, cavorting between him and the beach, contrived to lose the top of her bikini and show him her glorious breasts. The signal was loud and clear yet went unanswered. My mother was in plain view, sunning herself on a beach towel with her handsome second son of just two months, and my father was entirely León, husband. For the first and last time in her life, Irene found herself rejected.

She was more puzzled than offended; her response was to study León Fuertes. Few women and fewer men attempt to understand their lovers, present or prospective, being in the main preoccupied with their own emotions. It is, of course, almost impossible not to learn something about a person with whom one associates closely for any length of time, and a certain random gathering of data often goes on during the first stages of a love affair, but few people have minds to begin with, few of these discipline their minds, while of this latter few only a minute fraction will flog their minds to swim against a tide of hormones. As a specialist in love, however—one would say as a professional if the term did not have pornic connotations—Irene studied her lovers with great interest and imagination, though, since it was easier that way (and more fun too), she normally did not begin until she was in bed with them. She approached each as a particular and fascinating mystery worthy of her total concentration, and it was this attitude, of course, that accounted for her success. Had she been ugly as Sycorax, she would have still had all the men she wanted.

It rarely took Irene long to "solve" a man, but she spent almost a year on León. He was a complicated subject and besides that uncooperative. The main enigma, after all, was that Irene had been unable at her first attempt to get him between the sheets of a good lab. She had only the unfamiliar tools of remote field observation and informant interview. She went to court to hear him argue cases. She watched him at parties. She led her lovers into talking of him and found discreet opportunities to chat with Soledad. She became the confidence of several likely matrons of her age and class and showed such envy at their escapades that three of them confessed they'd been to bed with León and gave details on his modus operandi. The picture gradually developed—or rather a gallery of irreconcilably different portraits, all purportedly of the same man—until she glimpsed the secret of his subdivided personality.

He would, clearly, never make a proper full-time consort, not even for a month. On the other hand, his prolificity excited her, and it was foolish, having gone to so much trouble, to deprive herself. Irene put herself in León's path and avenged his rejection of her, not actually repulsing his advance but making him wait. When he "ran into her" in the lobby of the Excelsior and offered (with an unequivocally lustful grin) to drive her "somewhere," she grinned right back and said:

"If you mean 'take me to bed,' I'd love to, Leoncito. But not now. I'll drop by your office one of these days."

"I hope I'll be in," he answered, meaning in the mood, but to his great surprise he found himself looking forward to her visit. He was even more surprised when, two weeks later, as he lay sated in her arms, he realized he would want more of her.

León, lecher, was not incapable of a recurring urge for the same woman, but one had never before come with premeditation. The fact was that his circumscribed accomplishments were inadequate to cope with Irene Hormiga, for as an *après-amour* diversion she had described the mensual rhythm of her love life, then given a witty and perceptive reading of León himself. In so doing she managed to engage my father's intellect as completely as his genitalia. Thus doubly pleased and stimulated, he was receptive to the proposal she next made him:

"I'm the most exciting woman in this country, Leoncito, and you're the most interesting man. We ought to get together whenever it's convenient for us both."

It was the only contract he ever acceded to without negotiation. They sealed it on the spot and honored it monthly on the slack day between the paling of her old love and the rising of her new, he installing a spacious new office couch and she giving him a watch that told the phases of the moon.

Irene Hormiga provided León, lecher, with one of his two human relationships. His connections with other women (one alone excepted) were rodential quickies, but with Irene he laughed and compared notes, philosophized on love and pleasure, regaled her with tales of his adventures, listened with delight to tales of hers. At the same time the addition of a human dimension stretched León, lecher, beyond the limits of a figure formed for casual lust. In the warmth of Irene's visits his predatory keenness laxed, and at length he suffered an unmasking which, but for her, might have got the whole crew of seg-regated Leóns hashed together. One day he simply forgot to lock the door and was surprised in ecstasy by his son and future biographer.

I happened to come in at a critical moment and stood dumb-struck, rooted in my tracks, entranced by the grunts and stunts of the strange multilimbed biceph on Papa's couch. When it at last grew calm, one head opened a sloe eye, spied me, and whispered to the other. The beast then split apart abruptly, and when the top half turned out to be my father, I realized what I'd witnessed. Ever my mother's partisan, I was outraged and vengeful. I instantly resolved to inform Nacho Hormiga and see both the culprits chastised. My fa-ther, totally nonplused, was occupied with a recalcitrant zipper, but Irene must have guessed my intent, for she sighed and shook her head at me in supplicating languor, rippling her hair, which lay like a dark lake across the ocher leather.

"Ay, Camilito, don't betray us! You'll understand soon enough." Then she gave me a marvelous smile of satisfaction, as though it had been I who'd made her pretty toes curl toward the ceiling, and prophesied, falsely but nonetheless charmingly, "You'll be a bigger bandit than your father."

At once her thrall, I withdrew blushing, having tasted the delicious guilt of infidelity at the apt age of eight.

León, lecher's other extended liaison was with Dolores Gavilán, his partner's daughter-honey-skinned, green-eyed Loli, who chrysalised to nymphhood in his arms.

I have in part describes how León Fuertes charmed his partner's children, nurturing their infant personalities, showing them unforced affection, receiving their adoration in return. His was no pro-forma honorary uncledom such as is often feoffed to bachelors by their con-nubed chums and later on resigned when they too marry and get children of their own. By the time he was three months back in Tinieblas he was as important a personage to Lilo and Loli as their own parents, and as the years passed his stature in their lives only in-creased. He liked children in general and Gavilán's in particular. He liked Lilo's seriousness, which he called a "Corsican temperament" and which cast life as a somber drama on the theme of honor, iron loyalties, and enmities. He liked the impish joy with which Loli cheated at games and teased her smoldering brother. He did not expel them from his affections to make room for his own kids; there was room for all. Carlos, Clara, and I called Lilo and Loli "cousin," but they were in fact more like elder siblings to us. To them León was a kind of superdad with whom their blood father could scarcely compete.

Lilo worshiped him openly. He imitated León's walk and diction, defended León's name against such base envidious slurs as might be foisted by the wise-ass sons of other politicians, and deferred to León's children as a king's valet to young princes of the blood. He took proprietary pride in León's achievements and when asked what he meant to be when he grew up, replied variously, "A soldier, like my uncle León," or, "A lawyer, like my uncle León," or, "A leader, like my uncle León."

Loli was less obvious about it. She never said she meant to marry someone like her uncle León. In the first place, whenever anyone mentioned marriage—her mother, mine, some other lady—Loli would grab her throat and make a retching noise. She was a beach hoyden, a water rat who scrambled in the sun, sand in her hair, se-rapes on her knees and elbows. Then, at some precise instant in 1959, perhaps at noontide on the summer solstice (which fell a month or so before her fifteenth birthday), her carriage altered to a feline amble and her throat forgot how to giggle and she withdrew from the swarm of children to a cocoon of love dreams. Her mind teemed with shrouded fantasies of unknown men, but when she closed her eyes, one image appeared instantly and clearly.

It happened then that on the night before her birthday Loli was standing by the water's edge about a kilometer south of her parents' villa. Some boys and girls of her own age had built a bonfire on the beach and sat about it singing, but when they began splitting up in pairs, Loli got up and wandered off to where the fire was only a faint glow behind a ridge of sand; she had no use for boys. It happened also that León Fuertes had got from the bed where he lay reading and put on swimming trunks and jogged down to the water. Only the day before President Enrique Abeja and two Lincolnfuls of politi-cians had come from the capital to urge him (unsuccessfully) to seek the presidency, and that night, moved by the nervousness that af-flicted him at ever-quickening intervals during the years when he felt his destiny closing in on him and yet sought to postpone it, he swam far out into the dark Pacific. Great sharks swim also in those waters, and León was of two minds whether he hoped or feared to meet one, but it was not his destiny to be eaten by sharks, and he turned and swam back in to shore. The tide had carried him about a kilometer south. And so it happened that at midnight, as Loli opened her eyes from a dream of León, León came out of the sea toward her, his head and shoulders wreathed in phosphorescent glimmerings of moonlight. She looked at him longingly, and the look morphed him to León, lecher.

Nevertheless, he hesitated for a moment with the waves slapping against the hollows of his knees. Not from apprehension over Loli. She would be had by one man or another sooner or later; soon, by the look of her, and what better man than he? Making love to her might, however, involve him in being more than one León at a time, might merge some worlds that better were kept separate. He could be many men and live in many worlds, but only if he kept them all apart. Then he laughed and stepped forward toward her. Loli was too adorable to miss. Besides, he'd taught her how to swim, and how to hit a top-spin backhand, and how to shoot the pistol he'd brought from the war. What was more logical than that he teach her how to love?

He tossed her jeans and sweater high up on the beach and took her on the strand with soft waves foaming up about their loins.

With Loli, León's affections were engaged, and so the liaison continued. They did not make love often, but it became a kind of rite for her to call for him at dawn when our two families were at the beach, and they would swim awhile and then rest on the sand, she sitting with her thighs tucked up against her chest and her sweat shirt pulled over her knees and calves, he reclining near her, chatting together (as it might appear) father to daughter. She was happy to possess a fragment of her dream and never intruded on his other lives. I doubt that Loli would have taken her next breath had she thought León might be vexed by it. He found a special joy in helping her grow into her new womanhood. But here, as with Irene, León, lecher, stumbled out of character. What was he doing dispensing tender wisdom to a girl? Why should he care about her life? Where did he get these cumbersome affections? It was as though he'd sloughed his most valuable traits and, in their place, grabbed some from León, husband-father. The figure was no longer firm and rounded, or uniformly costumed for its role

20. Polities

MY FATHER,[94] León Fuertes, entered public life in January, 1952. That he'd been disinclined to do so until then was looked on as a considerable bizarrity, for your Tinieblan takes to politics as alligators do to fragrant swamps, and will, at the least chance, plunge in and wallow for as long as possible. León had had chances. He had, in fact, been offered high public office, which to your true Tinieblan is paradise itself, where one sits at banquet, anointed with flattery and graft. When León declined the commandancy of the Guardia Civil, President Luis Gusano assumed the war had left him shell-shocked. Rebeca, for her part, was furious.

"It's God's curse on me for whoring myself to Burlando! I should have known his seed was putrid. Four generations broke their bowels to get you, and you turn out a ninny! You haven't testicles enough to pick up power when they hand it to you on a plate. Oof!"

"Ay, Mamá," said León, smiling. "How can you expect me to have any? In our family the women have them all."

"Don't mock me! I'm cursed, and that's the end of it. I opened my womb three times and got a Chinaman, a ninny, and a cripple. But no one escapes destiny." She stabbed León with a pudgy forefinger. "You'll be President of the Republic whether you want to or not!"

He didn't want to; it wasn't in his dream. He had several extremely pleasant lives and was already President of the Associated Avatars of León Fuertes, a loose confederation whose government allowed him ample exercise of parliamentary skills. Rebeca had, besides, struck the truth at least a glancing blow when she implied he was afraid of power. He had no fear of standing out from the herd, exposed to envy and the fangs of predators. He had a taste for that. And those who, later on, accused León of being starved for power also got a piece of the truth. Hunger was León's essence, after all. He was, however, wary of indulging his appetite for power. His study of history had revealed power to be a habit-forming hallucinogen which blasts the minds of all but the most disciplined of its users, conferring euphoric visions which encourage dependence, and engendering hideous waking nightmares which even massive doses can but momently dispel. His study of himself had meanwhile disclosed his vulnerability to all manner of addictions. He therefore curbed his taste for power as sternly as he'd curbed his taste for killing. For five years he avoided all contact with power, and first touched it only to remove a stash from an addict who'd become a public menace.

From the end of our civil wars (1883-1893) through sixty-odd years of this century, power in Tinieblas was in the main held and dispensed by a peculiar class, a group of families, mostly from the capital and mostly white, whom their detractors called *los bichos*. The term, which is best translated "the vermin," was coined by Dr. Amado del Busto during his brief tenure in the presidency in 1905. It conveys the demagogue's repugnance for those who move by stealth, not honest violence, and gives apt inference of busy mandibles and ceaselessly swaying feelers. The bichos infested most of what was tasty in the land. They were not, however, terribly noxious as ruling groups go. They killed no one, either in their own or in other countries. They were not cruel or brutal or stupid. Now that they have been superseded, it is hard for the dispassionate observer not to view them with mild nostalgia.

Plato observed that greed is the vice of oligarchs; the *bichos* confirm the observation. They pursued power as a means to money and money as a means to family survival. The original *bichos* had survived obscurely since the days of the Spanish colony. When the national id had raped itself limp in the train of General Feliciano Luna and the national superego had sermoned itself hoarse in Monseñor Jesús Llorente's pulpit, the *bichos* emerged in egoistic vigor. Hildebrando Ladilla crept to prominence from a dank office in the customs shed because he'd taken neither side in the bloody ten-year wrangles between Liberals and Conservative—or rather because he'd outwardly toadied to (and covertly fleeced) both sides so earnestly that each thought him their cohort. He enjoyed being President. It is said he wore the presidential sash to bed, pinned to his nightshirt. But he put duty to family before love of office and rather than lash himself to the helm of a nation foundering in bankruptcy, abandoned ship, taking what was left of the treasury with him. His son Heriberto Ladilla (1871-1937, President of Tinieblas 1920-1923, 1924-1927) plowed the money back into what was now the family business, twice purchasing the presidency during a period when several foreign oil firms were competing for concessions in our country. Heriberto, who spent part of his youth in exile, was the author of a very touching sonnet on the beauties of Tinieblas, but he did not let love of country blind him to his duty to his heirs. He dealt the national oil patrimony to the firm that offered him the largest kickback and hatched his father's nest egg to a proudly crowing fortune. Unencumbered by ideology, by patriotism, or by love of power for its own sake, the Ladillas responded with agility to the call of family interest. They were a model for their class.

Family loyalty was the mortar of *bicho* class cohesion. Bichos paired with *bichos* in marriage, and often in adultery as well, so that their genealogies present not trees but an entangled mangrove, with branches growing back into their roots and stalks engrafted one upon another. Aquilino Piojo, an altogether typical example, had Chinches and Ladillas on his father's side and on his mother's Tábanos, Gusanos, and Hormigas. He married Andrea Comején, whose mother was a Mosca and who had Grillo and Avispa grandmothers, and maintained a liaison (solemnized by marriage after his and her divorces) with his cousin Marina née Chinche, who was his cousin Hunfredo's first wife and who had Abejas, Grillos, and Arañas among her immediate antecedents and, further back, Luciérnagas, Piéridas, and Mariposas. Piojo's issue thus bore the blood of fourteen bicho breeds doubly and trebly blended, and as they have married back into their class, the twine of genes threatens to become inextricable. Marital unions reflected and provoked commercial ties. Politics took on the aspect of a parlor game, an endless round of Monopoly on a set owned by close cousins, who compete with guile, combine and recombine, make deals, go back on them, cheat now and then, exchange mild insults, but never come to blows; and who, a winner having grinned and losers grumbled, simply start in again with the same players. Outsiders might kibitz or even sit in if there was room, but if one of them lost his temper and began playing for blood, if he became violent or abusive, if he sought to ban a cousin from the game or tried to take it out into the street and play with his own buddies, he was pushed from the board, gently but firmly.

Sometime around the turn of the century, about a decade after the *bichos* scuttled from the economic molding of the country and crawled up from beneath the social flagstones which ten years of war had overturned, they were struck with a collective amnesia. One morning Modesto Gusano, who was Minister of Finance and would soon be President of the Republic, received a petitioner, a fellow who aspired to some minor post and who prefaced his request by remarking that Gusano had scarcely changed—physically, he meant—since the days when he sold sweet rolls door to door.

The minister blinked in perplexity and murmured, "Sweet rolls?" and the petitioner, thinking he was furthering his case, replied "The best in Tinieblas! No one bakes like your mother (may she rest in peace) these days."

"My mother?"

The petitioner's tongue swam in the remembered taste of sweet rolls, and his thumb itched with the remembered feel of the tiny silver two-and-a-halfcentavo pieces that were in circulation back in the days when President Gustavo Puig went crazy and was deposed by his vice-president, General Saturnino Aguila, and that would buy a plump, sugar-glistening sweet roll from the plump, sweat-glistening ten-year-old who came waddling down the middle of the street bawling, "Sweeeet rolls!" with a basket of them (shielded from sun and flies by a limp sheet of newspaper) wobbling on his head. The petitioner's nose twitched to the remembered fragrance of sweet rolls baked by Señora Gusano, whose husband had failed selling hardware and then failed selling dry goods and would fail again selling vegetables in the public market before civil war mercifully broke out and he made his fortune, starting with a one-wagon commissary roped to a Conservative battalion. But the Minister of Finance could not, try as he might, remember either the sweet rolls or the woman who had baked them or the boy who had sold them or the merchant who had failed. He remembered Don Prudence Gusano, Vice-Minister of War for Supply and Transport in the Government of Monseñor Jesús Llorente, and Doña Candelaria de Gusano, Vice-President of the United Conservative and Catholic Ladies of Tinieblas, and Licentiate Modesto Gusano, Assistant General Manager of the Gusano Patriotic Sales Corporation. He remembered them with great clarity riding together in a pearl-grey landau to the hanging of General Feliciano Luna. But that was in 1893, and he could remember nothing before that.

Gusano broached the problem to his wife that night and learned that she too had lost a good part of her memory. She could remember back as far as Palm Sunday morning in 1895, when her father, Ernesto Chinche, announced that President Rudolfo Tábano had offered him a ministry, but all before that was blank. All the *bichos* were suddenly afflicted with the same syndrome: none could recall a time when their families were not powerful, or at least important and well off. From then they put on the air of dynasts, assumed the arrogance of Moguls or of Manchus. They took to speaking English among themselves, as Tolstoy's counts and princesses spoke French. They fraternized only with the diplomatic corps, executives of foreign banks and companies, and senior Reservation officers. They came to feel that nothing native to Tinieblas could possibly be good, and their despite for the very term "domestic" grew so ingrained that when they went to Paris they automatically refused French wine and called for imported vintages.

Still, snobbery did not paralyze them totally. From time to time a *bicho* family would marry a daughter to a promising young outsider—to strengthen the breed, as it were, or to assimilate a potential enemy. León Fuertes became eligible for bichohood by this dispensation when he married into the Piérida family, who were *bichos* in morphology if not behavior, as peacocks are birds along with rooks and shitepokes. León never really exercised his option, however; nor was he really recruited. Don Adelberto Piérida favored the match between his daughter Soledad and León Fuertes, but he did not make León the kind of business proposition Erasmo Sancudo had offered.

Erasmo Sancudo was himself the great example of miraculous bichification. He was an orphan from Remedios with some unfashionable indian and negroid genes who came to the capital barefoot at age twelve and peddled newspapers, until Don Fernando Araña observed how cleverly he shortchanged customers and took him in and gave him an education. He was the ugliest man in Tinieblas, with all the poorest features of his several racial strains, but he was also the shrewdest man in America, and Don Fermín Anguila gave him his daughter Beatriz in marriage and made him a partner in his law firm—the sort of deal León rejected—confirming him a *bicho*. Sancudo became the power in the firm, and publisher of the same newspapers he'd peddled, and a director of companies, and a maker of Presidents, and President of the Republic (1936-1940), and Pres-

ident of the Chamber, and President of the Supreme Court. He was
at all times a true and perfect *bicho*, defending his class, its interests,
and its principles even against the machinations of his mad brother
Alejandro.

The *bichos* believed in strong currency and weak government, the
weaker the better so long as property and contracts were respected.
They disbelieved in despotism and democracy, and particularly dis-
trusted popular leaders, who, as history shows, often invoke the second and institute the first. Accordingly, they clamped the inchado to
the gringo greenback and scrutinized ambitious men for telltale signs
of charisma or social conscience. They considered national dignity
(along with great men, noble causes, glorious sacrifices, and utopian
programs) a luxury which a poor country like Tinieblas could simply
not afford. Their foreign policy was to grovel, mainly to the United
States. But if the United States made use of the *bichos* to exploit
Tinieblan resources, the *bichos* made even more effective use of the
United States. In 1905 the populace deposed President Modesto Gusano and installed its favorite, Dr. Amado del Busto, in the Palace.
He instantly issued a sheaf of egalitarian decrees and appointed an
army of unbribable officials to enforce them, but he and his abominations were soon swept away. *El Diario de la Bahia*—the Chinche
family owned it—published an interview with the new president, a
strident interview in which Dr. del Busto reached new peaks of patriotic eloquence, pledging in one paragraph to triple taxes for the
Galactic Fruit Company and in the next to expropriate its holdings
down to the last banana plant, no recompense allowed. It was a total
fabrication, every word thought up, weighed out, and then set down
by Maximo Chinche himself, but the mob so loved those pledges
that del Busto could not disavow them, and inside a week he was
deposed by Marine effectives from the Reservation. This theme was
replayed with appropriate variations in 1917 and 1942 for the dancing pleasure of such bichophobes as Eudemio Lobo and Alejandro
Sancudo. (In Lobo's case the *bichos* floated so many rumors about
his German sympathies that he eventually developed some and sent
a cable of congratulations to the commander of the U-boat that sank
the *Lusitania*. The gringos threw him out of office the next day.) At
critical moments during half a century the *bichos* disposed of the
military and diplomatic resources of the United States as fully as the

U.S. president. Nor were bones made about it. In 1919, when President Victoriano Mosca vetoed an appropriation for the Guardia Civil, he told the Chamber that Tinieblas didn't need armed forces. "In any emergency we can use the gringo army. It beat the Kaiser, and that's good enough for me."

The *bichos* governed by the client system of ancient Rome—not that they copied it; it came to them by nature. Each *bicho* patriarch sat on a scaffolding of agents, fixers, arm-twisters, rumor-pushers, vote-buyers, post-sellers, go-betweens, goon-masters, and hacks, which held him high above the muck in the pure air of power. From each depended a candelabrum of deputies, judges, councilmen, province *jefes*, *barrio* bosses, functionaries (grand and petty), and *guardias* (commissioned and non-), which spread his glow of influence over the land and beamed it down into the lowest hovel. These practical fixtures were sprayed with a cosmetic film of ideology, which, while transparent, gave them a modern sheen. The *bichos* owned and operated parties, some taken over from their past proprietors and some constructed new, whose names evoked the soarings of political philosophy. These names, however, had rather less symbolical significance than do the shapes of the tin figurettes that circle a Monopoly board. No one gaped in wonder when the Universal Socialists merged with the Patriotic Nationalists. That merely meant that the Avispa and Abeja families were in alliance, and since Arnulfo Avispa and Rufino Abeja were cousins three times over and the best of friends, since they agreed to the last particle on how Tinieblas should be governed, since Don Rufi was neither a patriot nor a nationalist while Don Fufi would have cut cane in Remedios before espousing socialism, there was little to wonder at.

The *bichos* were bankers and brokers, importers and exporters, speculators and peculators. A *bicho* patriarch was like as not a minister, when he was not taking his turn in the Presidential Palace. His son sat in the Chamber, when he was not farming a consulate abroad. The *bichos* wore white linen suits and everyone who could afford to wore them also. They sent their sons to prostitutes at puberty and later on to foreign universities, enjoining them in both instances to learn how the world worked but not to become burdened with any useless sentiment or knowledge. Their daughters went to convent schools for preservation, not for education. They married young and, with but few exceptions, led lives of physical torpor, mental blankness, and emotional turmoil, spawning swarms of clever, greedy *bichitos*.

The *bichos* thrived in undiminished vigor for about three generations, munching up the goodies of the country but keeping their greed nicely calibrated to what they could get away with as a class and, meanwhile, running the Tinieblan show with Hurokabilly verve and Barnumstorming confidence. Then missing memories began to straggle home. Memories that had disappeared like Speer's Jewish neighbors began showing up in the best residential quarters of Ciudad Tinieblas, and *bicho* men and women who had never known anything but luxury began to recall an epoch when their families were poor and powerless. Alberto Avispa found his brain stuffed with memories that had originally belonged to his grandfather, including some depressingly clear memories of that grandfather's father, one Pablo Avispa, who got up at dawn day to buy crustacea at a wharf near what is now the Yacht Club and then trudged till dusk, dragging a stinking cart about the city. Irma Araña had wincing smellovision memories of her grandmother's hide-factor uncle, who stank of pig dung and the tannery. No one mentioned these memories, but almost every bicho had a number of them slouching in the foyers of his mind, and their ragged, interloping presence moved the *bichos* to wonder if they were destined to be powerful forever. Silently, separately, the *bichos* began to question their capacity to stay in power, even their right to rule. There followed from this questioning a doubt, and from this doubt a fear, and from this fear an attitude which answered their questioning and confirmed their doubt and fear. The *bichos* began to take the attitude that their world was coming to an end.

From then on they gave their greed free rein, they gouged and grafted wildly, they grabbed for everything within their reach. Humberto Ladilla sold lottery chances on the government jobs in his patronage. Dagoberto Comején put his entire family on the payroll of the Ministry of Justice, including all his cousins to the fourth remove and children down to the age of seven. He had his dog, a Doberman called Ilse, commissioned with the rank of captain in the Guardia Civil, and when she was killed in the line of duty—hit by a neighbor's auto while patrolling the approaches to Comején's driveway—the state paid her pups a pension. Filiberto Alacrán took a huge bribe and opened Tinieblas to a U.S. gambling syndicate, and when school gyms and cafeterias filled up with slot machines, he justified them on the ground that they helped children learn game theory and the laws of probability. In their rapacity the *bichos* fought with one another over trifles. They betrayed their class to outsiders for short-term profit. They fostered enmity among themselves. They grew incapable of banding firm against a common enemy. Most seriously, they ceased to look and act like rulers, hence they forfeited their legitimacy.

The end came in 1970. That is, the events of 1970 made it clear the *bichos* had no power anymore. Few lamented, but an era of freedom ended with them, for the *bichos* believed in freedom, freedom of expression and freedom of assembly and freedom of thought, as well as freedom to give and receive bribes and freedom to charge what the market will bear and freedom to go out and rig the market. Graft, of course, continues, but now it goes to people who believe in slavery and terror.

The end might have come sooner. In 1951 Alejandro Sancudo, who had returned to the presidency in 1948 despite the last united effort the *bichos* ever mounted and who had then governed for three years with uncharacteristic lucidity and restraint, reverted to the madness that power and his craving for it had made chronic to him. He established a People's Congress and used it to promote class hatred. With his left hand he encouraged violent demonstrations, then crushed them with his right. He contrived chaos and screamed for order. His aim was to fumigate Tinieblas of its ruling class and seize total power, and he would surely have succeeded but for León Fuertes.

León was at his mother's house on the December day his public future sought him out. For three months Alejandro Sancudo had been furrowing the land with discord and fecundating it with evil humors of resentment, had sown unrest and cultivated violence. A miasma of bile and choler hung about the country and seeped into the recesses of every private life, and León Fuertes became poisoned. León, lawyer, found his workdays fouled with reveries in which he wrangled issues with himself. León, scholar, could not concentrate because his fancy teemed with images of fury. León, husband, snarled and shouted at his family; León, athlete, took to smashing balls in his opponents' faces and hurling his racket petulantly about the court; León, lecher, degraded is companions with enforced perversions. Vile passions curded all León's sweet lives, and at night his sleep was venomed by a dreamed dispute with President Sancudo.

In this dream, which was replayed each night in ever clearer detail, León would march into the Presidential Palace and collar President Sancudo and sit him down and speak him some plain sense. He would point out that he had seen New York during the Great Depression and Europe during Adolf Hitler's war and that experience had taught him something: though it was small and poor and backward, an object of patronizing ridicule (if not contempt) to those few who had heard of it beyond its borders, the Republic of Tinieblas enjoyed great good fortune.[95] Tinieblas had slept placidly through half of the worst century since Adam, disturbed by neither war nor revolution, innocent of massacre and torture. One could count on one's fingers the countries that had not known sword or famine in the last fifty years, yet Tinieblas was among them. Its President ought not tempt fate. Sancudo would merely sneer and answer that he wasn't tempting fate, he was fate's instrument. The people of Tinieblas were free and sovereign and entitled to equality among the nations, to a fair share in the marvels of the century, its refinements of strife and agony, its advancements in terror and despair.

León would wake enraged, then give himself a lecture in his shaving mirror: the bunglings of politicians were not his business; the country's mess was none of his affair; if he stayed out of it, it would not touch him. But of course, it had touched him already.

On the day in mention León felt particularly agitated. He had the unbanishable sensation of a rendezvous to keep somewhere, and yet his calendar was empty and his secretary assured him he had no appointments. He could not sit at his desk for the feeling that he was expected somewhere. At length he left his office and drove aimlessly about the city—or rather drove according to an unknown aim, letting his hands turn the steering wheel at their own impulse, as years before, lost in the desert, he had let his camel lead him to water. He stopped beside the Alameda.

General Feliciano Luna's statue was decked in crepe, and someone had hung a sign about his neck that read: "I DIED FOR THE FATHERLAND, SOLD TO THE GRINCOS BY THE BICHOS," but politics had not yet reached the south end of the park, where boys were playing baseball. León got out and wandered toward the backstop. The fielding team was short a player, and as he noticed this a thought hopped crazily across two decades into his mind: today he might get a game. With that, a great calm and confidence came over him, a relaxed alertness and anticipation, the exact complex of sentiments he'd had twenty years earlier when he first took his turn at bat on this same field. For the first time in three months he felt healthy. He turned in midstride, as though shouted at, and walked jauntily toward his mother's house, a young man of affairs in a white linen suit and whiter panama, on his way to an important meeting

Rebeca was in her rocker on the porch, fondling her grey cat, but she said nothing to León when he came up the steps. He merely nodded to her and took a chair beside her. They had had nothing to say to each other for three years, since the day he bought her the red-roofed bungalow.

"You can buy me the Taj Mahal if you feel like it," Rebeca had told him, taking the deed, "or Nebuchadnezzar's gardens, but I won't be clean of the Burlando stain till you stop acting like a ninny and do what you were born for."

From then on he sent her money through his brother Pepe but rarely visited.

They sat in silence for about five minutes. Then a boy came by selling the *Informe Trópico,* and León beckoned him onto the porch and bought a paper from him.

President Alejandro Sancudo sneered up from a decree he had been signing. The headlines howled about a People's Court of Economic, Political, and Social Justice. León opened to page three and learned that the new tribunal would try *bichos* for so-called class crimes, including those allegedly committed by their parents, grandparents, and great-grandparents. Then the sentences looped round his chest, binding his upper arms, constricting his breathing. The paper took on the weight of a cuneiform tablet. He bent it closed and let it press against his thighs, but when his glance fell on page one, he found it altered. León Fuertes was striding down the steps of the Presidential Palace, followed by Colonel Aiax Tolete of the Civil Guard and Carlos Gavilán. "SANCUDO FLEES PALACE—FUERTES REFUSES SASH." León had just time to glimpse part of the date—January, 1952—before his eyes closed in a catalepsy so brief Rebeca did not notice it. When he regained consciousness, the paper was as it had been when he took it from the newsboy.

It was the first of three prophecies León received about his public life, and he accepted it unquestioningly.

"From the look on your face," Rebeca said, "the news can't he all bad."

"I'm going to throw Alejo out of office."

"It's about time! When Alexander the Great was your age, he'd been dead over a year. What post will you give your brother Pepe?"

"None. I'm going to throw Alejo out and then go home."

"Oof!" Rebeca began rocking. "There's not a man born in this country who hasn't thought of throwing out the President. But never just to go back where he was before. But go ahead. You have my blessing. At least you sound like a man, for a change."

A new León had, in fact, been born: León, politician; León, leader.

Most humans suffer spells of terror and self-loathing. Some of the worst afflicted become politicians. When one lives in profound and constant terror, when one feels leprous in his very soul, he may seek out a tranquilizing fix of power and a cleansing douche of public deference. But since compulsive use of power brings on nightmare, since deference defiles recipient and giver, these medicines exacerbate the symptoms. The best specific against fear is danger; the cure for self-hatred is humility. My father, León Fuertes, had conquered these infirmities by correct treatment; he did not enter public life to ease his private ills. León, politician, or León, leader, was rather his spontaneous response to the distemper of the country, an antibody reaction to toxins spreading in Tinieblans. Though he appeared on short notice, he was not a makeshift figure; my father had been composing him unconsciously for twenty years, and all his qualities were present in his maiden effort, the coup against Alejandro Sancudo.

León, leader, was unique among my father's transformations in that he cared about the commonweal he lived in. This concern, projected with great energy, gave him a presence of authority. The morning following his visit to Rebeca, León informed his partner, Carlos Gavilán, that he was going to unseat Sancudo and then suggested that Gavilán, who got most of his clients from the middle class, might know some non-bichos who could head committees of public safety. Gavilán straightaway found himself involved in forming skeleton organizations and making discreet contact with picked men. It was some days before he thought to ask León why he was so certain of success, why he thought people would follow him.

"You tell me why," said León by way of answer. "You're a steady fellow with a family to look out for. You surely wouldn't jeopardize them merely out of friendship. Alejo hasn't harmed you personally. I've promised you nothing. I haven't even asked you anything, just told you what I'm going to do and shown how you can help. Yet you're following me. You've been committing what (if we got caught) would be called treason, You've made, yourself an 'enemy of the Tinieblan masses.' You've jumped up to your ass in a subversive conspiracy, all on my say-so. Why?"

"*Carajo,* León! Someone has to throw that lunatic out before he wrecks the country!"

León smiled and nodded. "Exactly."

And Gavilán found himself hard put to reconcile the man before him with the main-chance virtuoso and protector of number one who'd been his partner for five years. The man before him cared about his country. He knew what was best for it. He could do the job.

Men gifted with a presence of authority quite commonly abuse it, but León, leader, was hedged with firm restraints. His emergence represented an admission by the other Leóns that none of them could flourish without a sound environment of freedom. They were León, politician's prime constituency; his first responsibility was to keep Tinieblas healthy for them. They granted him part of their time and energy, they gave him their support, but they were by no means willing to cede him a despot's hegemony over the communal body, to commit suicide so that he might play politics all day and all night long. They suffered him existence only insofar as he was needed to secure their liberties. The other Leóns checked and balanced León, politician; thus though my father had a taste for power, he never got stoned or hooked. Thus though he was destined to lead, he accepted that destiny piecemeal, as it was forced on him by circumstance.

Since his ambitions were well fenced, León, leader, could permit himself a degree of honesty which few politicians feel they can afford. This quality was evident even to such skeptics as Don Luis Gusano,

General Manager of the Pelf Fiduciary Trust's Tinieblas branch and former President of the Republic.

"I think you're the best man to raise a fund, Don Lucho. Three hundred thousand ought to do. Cash, no pledges."

"Are you suggesting we retain you to defend us in Alejo's People's Court?"

"No. I'm going to throw Alejo out of office. To do it I'm going to take the Guardia away from him. The best way is to buy it."

Gusano rubbed his palms together. "Make my son-in-law Bertito Minister of Finance."

León shook his head. "I'm not making anybody anything, Don Lucho. Not myself or anybody else. I'm going to make Alejo an ex-president. That's all. I'll need the money by the first of the year."

Luis Gusano, like his father, Felipe, and his grandfather Modesto, had enriched his family and become President of Tinieblas by the simple expedient of never trusting anyone, but he raised three hundred thousand inchados and gave them to León Fuertes, no questions asked.

León, leader's first act was the overthrow of an elected president. Later, as Deputy and then as President of the Republic, he was identified with the profound social changes that took place in Tinieblas in the 1950s and early 1960s. He was, however, in essence a conservative.

"The original meaning of the word 'revolution' is 'turning back,'" he told Arsenio Poroto, Chief Engineer of the Compañía Tinieblina de Electricidad y Gas (a subsidiary of Yankee and Celestial Energy). He had approached Poroto to arrange for the palace telephones to be cut off once the coup was under way, and while Poroto didn't care much for Sancudo (who'd put Poroto's brother-in-law in jail for writing uncomplimentary verses), he wanted no part of any revolution.

"I'd like to turn things back to where they were four months ago," León went on. "Then, if things have to change, maybe they can change calmly. That's the only revolution you'll get from me. Alejo is the kind of revolutionary you're leery of. He wants to turn everything upside down so the country will be as confused as he is."

Although my father had no nature and steadfastly avoided forming one, the politician-leader was perhaps the most "natural" of all the Leóns. During the first week in January, 1952, while Sancudo was

indicting bichos in his People's Court and canceling their passports
and freezing their bank accounts, while Carlos Gavilán was urging
him to move before they were arrested, León displayed an easiness
that amazed my mother. She'd seen him lose weight during a big law-
suit, had watched him pace their bedroom trying to convince himself
he'd not forgotten some detail. She'd heard him grind his teeth in his
sleep the night before he went to Costaguana to defend Apolonio
Varón. Now he was going to overthrow the government, send people
to the streets, and risk his life and theirs, yet he was perfectly relaxed.

"I'm waiting for Alejo," he told her. "I'm in no rush. One of these
days he's going to make the blunder that antagonizes everybody.
Maybe tonight, maybe tomorrow, maybe next week. It's not for me
to hustle the events. That's his style, not mine."

At eleven A.M. on 8th January, 1952, President Alejandro Sancudo
sat down before the microphones of a national radio hookup. First
he abolished the Constitution, the Chamber of Deputies, and the
Supreme Court of Justice. Then, after pausing for breath, he out-
lawed all political parties, his own included, and canceled the national elections scheduled for 1st April. Then he poured himself a
goblet of Evian mineral water from a crystal carafe and, sipping it,
proclaimed himself Sole and Perpetual Guardian of the Tinieblan
State and People for the period of his natural existence on this planet.

The address, which lasted about three minutes, caused a certain
consternation in the country, particularly the points about parties
and elections, for politics is the Tinieblan national pastime. It did
not catch León Fuertes unprepared. Before Sancudo's voice was off
the air, León had got his partner started making phone calls and was
on his way to Civil Guard Headquarters with a Gladstone bag full
of cash. By noon the Guard was in its barracks getting paid, the
streets were full of demonstrators, and the palace was cut off from
all the world.

"Let's go in and get him!" cried a citizen when León spoke to the
crowd in Plaza Cervantes.

"Oh, no. Let's sing instead. Alejo will fall like a rotten papaya in
a few hours. Meanwhile we might as well enjoy ourselves."

Surely the fall of Alejandro Sancudo was in my fathers mind two
years and some months later when an American journalist who was
visiting our house—an august personage of immense influence whose

clipped speech and perpetually twisted lips gave the impression that he suffered from chronic constipation—decried the "carnival atmosphere" of the Army-McCarthy hearings in the U.S. Senate, for León replied that the most salutary function of politics was to provide public entertainment for the community. "Why must tragedy and melodrama be the only respectable forms? Comedy is more popular and no less beneficial, especially the kind of piece where the hero-villain turns out to have been a clown all along."

For two days and nights the populace of Ciudad Tinieblas gave itself up to unrestrained gaiety, while Alejandro Sancudo dangled impotently in the Palace. Offices closed; shops were boarded up. The committees of public safety kept gentle, good-humored order, and the rest of the citizens sang, and danced in the streets, and chanted anti-Alejo slogans. At seven A.M. on the 10th, a report came from Córdoba in Salinas Province that a car carrying Sancudo and four close collaborators had been seen driving north along the Pan-American Highway, and León Fuertes went to the palace, accompanied by Carlos Gavilán and Colonel Aiax Tolete and the twelve chairmen of the committees of public safety. They found the building deserted save for a few servants, and were about to leave, when a large number of people who had been reveling in the nearby streets and had heard rumors of Sancudo's flight streamed into the Plaza Inchado and began shouting for León. When he did not appear on the balcony from which our presidents, elected or otherwise, traditionally greet their supporters, a group of men and women went in after him, bearing a makeshift presidential sash-three strips of purple, green, and yellow nylon safety-pinned together.

Colonel Tolete took the sash from them and made to hang it over León's neck, Gavilán stepped up to help him, and the twelve committee chairmen smiled their approval, but León held up his hands. Now that Sancudo was gone and the country out of danger, León, husband, remembered that he hadn't seen his children for two days. León, lawyer, thought of his neglected practice; León, athlete, of his missed workouts. There were, besides, many books that León, scholar, wished to read, and the world was full of willing girls for León, lecher.

"Call Oruga," León said to Carlos Gavilán. (Belisario Oruga was the constitutional Vice-President, whom Sancudo had exiled to an ambassadorship in Asia.)

"Aiax, you're in charge until he gets here.

"Take your orders from Colonel Tolete," he told the twelve committee chairmen. "I'm going home."

Rebeca visited him that afternoon to congratulate him and to tell him her stain was cleansed. "I understand now, " she said. "You have a deal with Beli Oruga. He'll be President from now till the elections. You'll run and he'll help count the votes. Just like Heri Ladilla's deal with Feli Gusano in 1924."

"No, Mamá," said León wearily. "You don't understand at all."

21. Ministry

ALL THE SAME, León returned to public life so quickly that, like Rebeca, most Tinieblans believed his "Great Denial" had been a ploy. Scarcely a month after the coup against Sancudo, the twelve committee leaders came to him and begged him to lead another.

"It's going to be worse than ever," said Mizael Indulto. "We helped you eliminate the Fumigator, and now the *bichos* will eat us alive."

The election campaign was under way, and there were six candidates for President and six hundred for the Chamber, all bichos, surrogate bichos, or aspirant *bichos*.

"The price of a vote has gone to seven inchados in Otán Province," said Ramiel Azarín. "Do you realize how much the winners will have to steal just to recoup their investment?"

"They all claim to be patriots," Abdiel Agudo continued, "but not one of them cares a whistle about the country."

"The money you used to keep the Guardia in the barracks has already been stolen back with interest," said Raziel Lindo. "If things go on this way, we'll wish we had stayed with the dictator."

"Licentiate, you made a start," said Uriel Lámpara. "Now you have to go through to the end of it."

León told them he didn't presume himself a messiah, and that he had never intended to do more than remove Sancudo, and that he certainly wasn't going to be overturning the government every three weeks. Privately he decided that the excitement of the golpe had gone to the men's heads so that their normal lives seemed boring by comparison; his firmness would snap them out of it and send them back to their stores and businesses. Instead they showed a firmness of their own. When León left home at six the next morning, one of them was waiting in the street. He followed León to the Club Mercantil and brooded mutely through León's tennis match and then trailed León to his office, where a second was already staked out. When León left for court two hours later, a third went with him, and at midday there was a fourth. They shadowed León about the city, hovering a few yards from him day and night, and when León took his family to Medusa Beach for the weekend, they tracked behind in convoy and then took turns sitting fully dressed on the sand before his villa. Their white suits and mournful faces gave them the aspect of albino buzzards, and at night they flocked in León's dreams, flapping their sleeves and croaking in chorus: "Tinieblas is a fortunate country, but all the century's misfortunes are on their way here to take residence."

For once León had no idea what to do, and he asked his partner, Carlos Gavilán, whether he ought to sue the men and if so, whether Gavilán would represent him.

"I'll have to disqualify myself on this one, León. You see, I put them up to it."

"For God's love, Carlos! I thought you were my friend! The only reason I threw Alejo out was to get a good night's sleep. Now I'm haunted by moon-struck storekeepers. I can understand their nostalgia for their hour of importance, but I expected more sense from you."

"Well, León, you're a mysterious man. Whenever I think I've a grip on you, you turn into someone else. For all I know, you'll turn into the man who can fix this country."

And León wandered back to his private office, shaking his head.

But the implacable presence of his twelve erstwhile lieutenants had set him thinking about Tinieblas and its discontents. The country wasn't healthy. His twelve shadows made life unlivable for all the Leóns, but they were no more than birds of omen signaling dangers ahead. So one Sunday, when their vigil had been going on nearly a fortnight, he called down from the terrace of his beach house to Rafael Almohada, who was sitting cross-legged on the fiery sand: "Get your fellow maniacs and my crazy partner. I'll speak to you after my swim."

They were waiting for him on the terrace when he came up from the sea twenty minutes later. Soledad Fuertes had made them two pitchers of *chicha de mango* and was refilling glasses. She excused herself, but León called her back.

"This concerns you as much as anyone, and I'd like to have one other sane person present."

He toweled off his face and sat down in a canvas deck chair and drew his sandy feet up under him.

"All right," he said, "the *golpe* wasn't a solution. This life doesn't have solutions. You push trouble down in one place and it pops up somewhere else. You push down the dictator and up pops the corrupt ruling class. Push them down, and up will pop the mob, or another dictator, or the United States Marines. Anarchy and violence, or repression and violence, or intervention and violence. The first step is to forget about solutions. If you want me to politic with you, get that idea out of your minds. It's a dangerous hallucination."

He paused and looked about from one man to another, as though he expected some to rise and leave. None budged, not even to sip chicha.

"In politics," he went on, "one can try to palliate the discomfort of a problem, or one can trade the problem in. New problems are exhilarating. They have the charm of virginity. But they are rarely an improvement on the old ones. Often they are worse. The second step is to venerate Lord Falkland: 'When it is not necessary to change, it is necessary not to change.' I won't be leading any coups this month."

He paused again, smiling. In his bunched pose and near nakedness, he looked to Gabriel Masamorra Verde more like an Oriental holy man than a political leader.

"The political problem of Tinieblas is that the ruling class has lost its confidence and hence is losing its authority. The people used to admire the *bichos* for clever thieves who at least looked after their own interests. The people trusted them to leave a little for the rest of us and to prevent the rise of despots. Now the *bichos* feel their day is ending and are out to steal everything they can while they still can, and the people begin to hate them. Now they cannot even protect themselves, and the people look down on them. It is more dangerous for a ruling group to be looked down on than to be hated. But if the *bichos* fall, there is nothing to replace them. Only the mob, or a dictator, or the United States Marines. Since they can't help themselves, someone must help them. Someone must moderate the *bichos*' greed and prop them up. Someone must calm the people down and soothe their resentment."

"The someone is you, Licentiate," said Miguel Ángel Camposanto.

"I was coming to that," said León, with a grin that faded instantly. "It seems I am the someone. But if so, it's only because I'm not obsessed with politics.[96] If I am capable of doing anything, it is because I know that no one can do much. If I am to be at all effective, I must never take myself as seriously as you do now. That's the third step: don't delude yourself or anyone else into believing you can do much good; that way you may be able to avoid doing much harm.

"If you can't accept these principles, stop bothering me. Go get Alejo out of jail and put him back in office. He has solutions; he enjoys the confusion of change; he believes in politics. If you accept my view, I will work with you to try to make things a little better, to try to make this country's luck hold a little longer. I will make no more brusque or dramatic movements, but if you like we can form a party. If you like I will run for deputy. And as a punishment for causing all this trouble, Carlos will run too. Nothing is lost when two lawyers enter politics, but you other gentlemen have productive work to do, so for the moment two candidates are enough."

Israfel Bandeja suggested that they call theirs the Progressive party, and León winced. The name was soggy with optimism. Then he decided he had done enough lecturing for one morning. "Why not? If it will stop you gentlemen from hounding me, we shall already have made some progress."

Until recently, when politics became a Civil Guard cartel, Tinieblas was one of the world's leading producers of candidates for public office. León Fuertes was the strangest of them all. His campaigns were innocent of horn-blare motorcades and torchlight rallies, of patriotic fanfares and half-dressed prancing girls. He made no irrational appeals. He drew on no demonic fonts of passion. He shrouded up his glamour in the sackcloth of common sense. He stopped wearing decorations, and when, at a public meeting near the end of the 1952 campaign, Ituriel Frasada introduced him as "the bane of tyrants and defender of our freedoms," León began his speech by chiding Frasada for extravagance of language.

"The *golpe* of 8th-9th January was an exercise in garbage disposal," he said. "Those who took part in it deserve no more credit than do the employees of the Department of Sanitation for the performance of their daily chores."

From the first he was wary of the fervor his public presence generated. "In this business," he told his wife, "what look like assets are in fact liabilities. It's not just that I restored the Constitution. People insist on remembering a baseball game I played in years ago. They want a hero, and I'm the most vulnerable man in the country on that score. You watch: no matter how I act or what I say, they're going to convince themselves that I can solve their problems. They're going to get it in their heads that I can save them. That by some magic I can turn Tinieblas into a world power. Have the gringos cringing in their boots. Make everyone around here millionaires. Then, when I don't deliver, they'll tear me to pieces and go looking for another sucker."

So while he couldn't help being an object of enthusiasm, he did nothing to encourage it. .

"Don't cheer yet!" he told a crowd in the La Cuenca *barrio* in 1962, when he was running for President. They looked on him as a native son and howled support whenever he paused for breath. "Wait till I've retired," he told them. "Or better yet, wait till I'm dead. Wait till you're sure that I accomplished something and didn't leave the country worse off than it was before."

He was infuriated by the promises of certain other politicians, whose trick was to excite and exploit the people's aspirations. They pictured Tinieblas as a land of immense riches, of which the people were being cheated by their rivals and the United States.

"Fly now, pay later," he told Gavilán in disgust. "And it's people like you and me who'll get the bill."

His own speeches were painfully low-key. Tinieblas was not a rich country: a little oil; barely enough fertile land to feed its population; a lot of people who couldn't read or write, much less understand modern technology and use it. Perhaps the country might allocate its meager resources a little more efficiently. If elected, he would work in that direction. People were ingenious when it came to stealing money. But perhaps ways could be found to curb some of the more flagrant abuses of the public trust. Blaming one's problems on a remote and potent force brought only an illusion of relief. Perhaps the United States could be persuaded to change its policies, could be shown how such a change was in its interest. But no one should expect much. The people of the United States were no more intelligent when it came to their own interests than were the people of Tinieblas. Particularly, no one should expect too much of him.

"If elected," he told every group he spoke to, "I will belong to nobody." That invariably drew a cheer, and he would frown and calm his with raised hands. "Wait. Wait a moment. I won't belong to you either. I won't pawn my brain to you for votes. I'll listen to you, but I'm going to do what I think best, whether you like it or not. If you don't like that, vote for someone else. There are plenty of ventriloquist's dummies in the race already."

"Spoken like a perfect ninny!" Rebeca told him after one such pronouncement. "Of course you'll do what you feel like once you get elected, but why rub their faces in it now? I don't understand you. You used to be a first-rate liar. Don't you want to win?"

"I can't help winning, Mamá. The only thing I've never succeeded at is failure. But these campaigns always leave an awful hangover, and I don't want to make people any more depressed than necessary."

León, politician, could not, for example, help displaying a trait borrowed from León, lawyer, and then significantly reworked. He too banked all kinds of data on all kinds of people and could withdraw it effortlessly at opportune moments. He could, while shaking hands in the working-class barrio of Laguna Seca, recognize a stonemason who, years before, had been a witness in a tort case León had heard part of while waiting for one of his own suits to be called. He could, moreover, remember enough details of the man's testimony to ask whether his child had recovered from his injuries and if the driver who had knocked him down had paid a compensation. The difference was that León, politician, actually cared about the fellow's troubles, so that when he heard that the case had been thrown out of court and that the child was crippled, León arranged for him to get physiotherapy at San Bruno Hospital and got him a free pass on the bus line back and forth. While rival candidates strove to project an image of concern, León possessed the substance. Concern for people was standard equipment on León, politician, and he could not help benefiting by it.

An even more advantageous property was León's aura of legitimacy. His intelligence, his energy, his experience, his concern were all
good reasons for his being in a place of leadership, but while he stood
on these and did all he could to minimize irrational attractions, his
successive candidacies were touched with what in another century
would have been called divine right. The spirits of General Isidro
Bodega and General Epifanio Mojón and General Feliciano Luna
went campaigning with him and stood beside him when he addressed
the Chamber and sat at his right hand when he was in the Palace. It
made no difference that they had often abused power. They had all
been President of the Republic, and they were León's direct forebears. León never invoked them, yet their presence near him, perceived subliminally by Tinieblans of all classes, gave him an air of
rightfulness such as in other times surrounded persons of royal
blood. It was insight, not arrogance, that made him say he couldn't
help winning.

The magical authority the Tinieblan people discovered in León
Fuertes was felt even by other politicians. How else, if not by magic,
was he able to instill a sense of public spirit into men who in their
lifetimes had never cared for anything but personal or family interest? It was not merely that León was often able to persuade his colleagues that what he advocated was good for the country. When
León spoke to them, men who were depositing their hopes in numbered Swiss accounts began to have the nagging feeling that what
was best for Tinieblas was best for them as well.

"Business is business, León," Juanchi Tábano told him when León
urged scrapping the vast program of highways to nowhere that
Tábano meant to introduce as Minister of Public Works and batten
off as principal contractor. "My seat in the Cabinet cost me eighty
thousand."

"Do you have to double it during your first month in office?
You're not a businessman, Juanchi, you're a walking PR campaign
for the disciples of Karl Marx.[97] Do you think you'll be happy in
Miami? If you survive, that is. You'll haunt the airport yearning to
come home and eat your liver in nostalgia and sit around with other
exiles snarling at the communists. But if the communists had any
sense of gratitude, they'd be building you a monument. You'd better
start doing something for this country, Juanchi. That's not your best

move it's your only move."

Meanwhile he strove to disabuse others of the fantasy that Tinieblas might be transformed into Utopia by the necromancy of revolution. This delusion was particularly widespread among the students, who suffered the squalor of the lower-class *barrios* like a personal leprosy and felt the presence of the Reservation like a malignant tumor. Its main locus during the late fifties was in the Instituto Politécnico, and León monitored it through Lilo Gavilán.

North American educators will have no difficulty these days believing that prestige in Tinieblas's largest secondary school depended on social consciousness, not athletic prowess, and that the best and brightest of our country's students dreamed not of money and fast cars, or even of fornication, but rather of saving their country. The most attractive dream (because it was the simplest) was that if the existing social, political, and economic order was swept away by the most violent possible means, Tinieblas would be at once mystically enveloped in complete and eternal bliss. Lilo was not that deranged himself, but he had friends who were. He was, besides, stuffed to the ears with the highest ideals imaginable, and had these not been fused with his hero-worship for León Fuertes, he might have been as militant as anyone. It was as much for Lilo's sake as for the country's that León took to meeting with the young lunatics and listening to them rave about taking nirvana by storm.

"Yes, I take them seriously," he told President Enrique Abeja when the latter chided him for paying attention to the students and hinted an accusations that León was building a constituency among them. "That's the only way to ease their pain. No, I am not merely doing good works and storing up indulgences, but I'm not making a Fuertes Jugend either. Unfortunately, Señor Presidente, this country hasn't progressed to the point where you can get the Guardia to fire on their own children. We're not that advanced as yet. They went to the streets when Alejo called them and twice since then, and if it's all been mild so far, that's only our good fortune. So I take them seriously; I try to calm them down. I give them therapy, and sometimes little pieces of my mind."

He would go up to the former classroom that had been set aside as an office for the Tinieblan Students' Syndicate, a narrow room high up under the eaves whose glassless, rusty-screened window

looked out across the Avenida Jorge Washington onto Fort Shafter
and whose air stank acridly of extremist slogans and young men's
sweat. There he sat down with fanatics like Manfredo Canino and
Tonio Burrón and their slightly less rabid sycophants and let them
talk till they wearied. It was surely therapeutic for some of them,
being heard out by the President of the Chamber, who was also a
war hero and a successful government-toppler, and afterward he told
them little stories. One of his favorites was the story of Albania, a
country, he would say, that played its last trump in world affairs in
280 B.C. It was called Epirus then and had a king named Pyrrhus,
who unsuccessfully invaded Italy. After that it abandoned conquest
and took up experimenting with different forms of government. The
country now known as Albania had been ruled by Roman procon-
suls, Byzantine emperors, and Turkish sultans. It had been a Moslem
principality with a German Protestant prince. It had been a certifi-
able anarchy with no less than six governments all claiming legitimacy, a regentless regency under a council of elders, a democratic
republic, and then a constitutional monarchy. It had tried fascism
Italian-style, and then Russian-style communism. It was now a
"socialist state" on the Peking model. No one could fault the Alba-
nians' readiness to change their system. If changing the system was
the answer, Albania ought to be a happy land. Yet throughout all
these changes, many of them revolutionary, most of them as violent
as ever one might wish, Albania had remained the most wretched
country in Europe.

He told them the story of Russia, which concerned how a great
people managed at an immense expense in human suffering to relabel
their troubles while making them somewhat worse. The Tsar was relabeled Secretary General of the Communist party. The boyars were
relabeled commissars. The Okhrana was relabeled Cheka, then
OGPU, then NKVD, then KGB. He also told the story of Cuba, in
which a handful of brave and determined men led their country out
of foreign bondage by the master stroke of leading it into a different
foreign bondage. Preaching in parable, he tried to wean the students
from their faith in monster-breeding dreams. He taught that where
it came to improving life in this world, the possibilities of human
action were severely limited.

This attitude of León's was organic. The students were revolutionaries out of personal frustration; León could acknowledge the limits of polities because his personal lives afforded infinite possibilities for fulfillment. His constant theme was that revolution, like war, was an exciting activity which made the world seem simple for a while but which accomplished nothing of value save the relief of nervous tension.

"If you truly care about the people, you'll give it up," he told Canino. "The people always pay the bill for revolution, but they never get full value. They rarely get anything at all. If violence relaxes you, that's different. But why delude yourself or be a hypocrite?"

"You're the hypocrite! A conservative who founded the Progressive Party!"

León smiled. "No contradiction, Fredo. No hypocrisy. If they teach physics here, you must know that things tend to run down, that order falls apart. Anyone who reverses that trend, even in the slightest, even if it's just to keep things going, is making progress."

He tried, then, to keep things going. He was the nuclear figure of Tinieblas from his entry into public life until his exit from this world. His personality was a core of cohesive energy holding the commonwealth together against the centrifugal forces of his time, and his career, both in the Chamber and as President, constituted a ministry of preservation to his country.

Meanwhile he continued to live his other lives, but León, politician, poached more and more time from them. It was as ironical as any of his parables. The politician had come forth so that the other Leóns might go on finding their respective stimulations, but the more León, politician, achieved, the more he had to struggle. Each time he acted responsibly, other men were persuaded to cede some of their responsibilities to him. Each time he demonstrated concern for the people, the people grew more inclined to regard him as their savior and demand more. The students he convinced to abandon the dream of revolution did not stop dreaming altogether but rather installed León Fuertes above the altar previously consecrated to Marx or Lenin or Mao or Ho or Castro. And whenever he managed to inject a few cc's of civic sense into one member of the ruling class—and thus make the order of the country a bit more stable—two or three others would decide they needn't worry about the future and would begin competing for whatever scheme to loot the public trust the first one had renounced. It was bad enough that citizens of all classes were badgering him to run for President. León himself began to feel that if he was ever to be free again, he would have to make some permanent repairs in Tinieblas—and at the same time he knew perfectly well that there was no such thing as permanent repair, that the very idea was an illusion.

This was the period when his destiny began pursuing him night and day, while he flitted nervously from one avatar to another trying to hide from it. Leaving the Chamber after yet another exhausting session where each member tried to profit from his fairness and thus cheat the rest, León would find his destiny staring at him pitilessly from the eyes of a barefoot *campesino* or a mongoloid beggar child or a rebel student or fat Juanchi Tábano, and he would flee away to hide from it among his family or with his books or between some girl's raised thighs. Dreaming of the clean ascetic freedom of the Sahara, he would look over his shoulder and see his hyena destiny trailing him with lolled tongue and rolling eyes. Six hours after he told President Enrique Abeja that he would not run in 1960, as he lay wide awake in bed in his beach villa reading Gottfried von Strassburg's *Tristan* (which, he judged, was the least political book he owned), an embassy composed of the spirits of Generals Isidro Bodega and Epifanio Mojón and Feliciano Luna sailed in through the open window and informed him—each of his ancestors repeating in his turn the selfsame speech—that León would be President of the Republic sooner or later, like it or not, and León, who believed only in this world and who thought the generals a hallucination, grew so distraught he left his bed and got into a bathing suit and swam far out into the Pacific. He had rather meet a shark than his destiny, but his destiny was implacable, more ravenous than a meridian of sharks.

During 1961-1962, while a constituent assembly was restructuring the Constitution and Juan de la Cruz Ardilla served meekly in the Palace, León's destiny began to come at him from every quarter of the compass. The Tinieblan middle class was not large by the standards of North America or Europe, but it had gone entirely to the Progressive Party and made it the most dynamic political force in the country. The Progresistas had never run a candidate for President, for the simple reason that León would not suffer his name to be put in nomination, while no one else would put himself before him, but now the party demanded that he stand for election.

"Run yourself," he told Carlitos Gavilán. "I'll support you. We have a party, after all, not a León Fuertes fan club."

"That's what you think, León. People believe in the party's message because you articulate it."

"It ought to be the other way around."

"Agreed. But it isn't. Were as bad as the Tinieblistas with Alejo. Instead of his being the party's candidate, it was always the candidate's party. If you don't run, no one will believe what the party says. They'll think you've abandoned us. I wouldn't get fifty thousand votes in the whole country, and the country deserves to have a Progresista in the Palace."

Meanwhile all but the least responsible elements of the ruling class were begging León to run, and this plea was echoed by groups as disparate as the Students' Syndicate and the commandants of the Guardia Civil. Neither the Guardia nor the students had any confidence in any other politician, and both vowed that if León did not become President at the next constitutional opportunity, they would take the affairs of the country into their own hands. (Nor were they bluffing: eight months after León Fuertes' assassination, the students staged an uprising, which was followed immediately by a military coup d'état.) Given these pressures, León could scarcely declare that he would not be a candidate in 1962, and hardly a week went by when he was not scolded in the press or by his colleagues for trifling with the affections of the country.

"There's nothing lower than a cock-teaser," Dr. Erasmo Sancudo told him, putting the matter bluntly. "The Tinieblista Party has had hard times since you threw my crazy brother out of office, but we'll let bygones be bygones and give you our unqualified support if you will only stop flirting. I know it must be marvelously soothing to be told how much you're wanted, but this continued coyness is disgusting."

The fact was that León didn't want to be wanted and wished people would turn to someone else.

"The will to power is nothing but a symptom," he told Irene Hormiga at a noontide assignation late in 1961. "Stalin's father beat him, and Churchill's mother whored around, and rich as he was, Kennedy was looked down on by his schoolmates for being Catholic and never forgot it for a minute. We don't even have to talk about poor, miserable runts like Napoleon the Great or failed artists like

Nero and Hitler. Political ambition is like a sign around a fellow's neck that says 'Something missing.' But me, I have the best of everything. Here he patted Irene's muff. "I don't have anything to prove to anybody on this planet. Why should I run for President?"

And so he temporized and sought alternatives and concocted improbable scenarios wherein this or that obscure or discredited politician miraculously emerged as a consensus candidate for President, and all the while he grew more and more nervous and each and every separate León clamored for more time and energy, as though in protest against León, politician. Then, finally, he accepted his destiny and embraced it, as every living thing in this world must.

León was at Rebeca's house beside the Alameda on the day it was made manifest to him that he would be President of the Republic. This was in December, 1961, a few weeks before the political conventions. He had gone there seeking a kind of respite, for not only was he being pestered constantly by journalists and politicians, with the telephone ringing incessantly at his home and at his law office and in his office in the Legislative Palace, but even León, lecher's girls were asking in the midst of being plowed whether or not he'd run, while the print in León, scholar's books rearranged itself into press releases dealing with his candidacy. Rebeca had already made her mind up he was running, no matter what he said, so he could visit her without fear of being bored by questions. He was, moreover, rewarded by finding her away from home. She had gone out, her maid said, to buy some lottery, so he sat down on the rattan armchair in her living room and let the heat sponge up his nervousness. Then, just as he was starting to relax, he felt an agitation at the bottom of his forehead, a pulsing behind his eyebrows which made him want to press his thumbs against the roof of his eye sockets, but he could not move his arms or any other portion of his body. And as he sat, frozen in worry and anticipation, his mother's grey cat bounded across the tiles and stood with its forepaws resting on the panel of the television set opposite him and drew the switch out with its mouth.

The screen flickered to life, showing the interior of the Legislative Palace with its wide Orozco-style mural of Simón Mocoso opening the Constituent Assembly of 1821 and its raised dais, on the left of which sat the justices of he Supreme Court, headed by Dr. Erasmo Sancudo, and on the right Vice-President Aristóteles Avispa and the

Ministers of the Cabinet, and behind hem in the great chair of the
President of the Chamber, Carlos Gavilán. Below sat the Deputies, all
in white linen suits like the men on the dais, some lounging back in
their rich leather chairs and some hunched forward with their elbows
on their mahogany desks, and León saw that the entire center wedge
of desks and chairs was filled with men of his own party. Then the
camera panned about the gallery, and the sound came on, and an
announcer pointed out those present: the diplomats accredited in the
country and, in the first row, special representatives of certain heads
of state; the correspondents of the foreign press; the distinguished
leaders of the banking and business communities; the guests present
by special invitation of the most excellent President-elect. The camera
stared at these for a long moment, and León recognized twelve storekeepers who had directed committees of public safety during the
golpe of 8th-9th January, 1952: Mizael Indulto and Ramiel Azarín
and Abdiel Agudo and Raziel Lindo and Uriel Lámpara and Rafael
Almohada and Gabriel Masamorra Verde and Miguel Ángel Camposanto and Israfel Bandeja and Ituriel Frasada and Zofiel Viento
and Azrael Ataúd. And finally the camera swung to the extreme right
comer of the gallery onto a placidly smiling lady in a tailored suit of
what was probably dark blue Italian silk, whom the announcer presented (some two or three minutes before the fact) as "La excelen-
tisima Primera Dama de la República, Doña Soledad Piérida de
Fuertes!" She was accompanied by a little girl and two boys, the
smaller of whom, a sensitive-looking chap of ten or so, held his
mother's arm protectively. Beside this last sat Rebeca Fuertes,
sconced in a pachydermic dignity of years and flesh, while above her
hung the spirits of Rosalba Fuertes and Raquel Fuertes and Rosenda
Fuertes, who had traveled from the next world to be present at the
flaming of the dream kindled in their ovaries.

León might have wondered at their presence, but at once a band
located somewhere at the rear of the gallery struck up the National
Hymn, and the scene flashed back to the left comer of the dais, where
President Juan de la Cruz Ardilla entered, dressed all in white and
wearing the tricolor presidential sash. All the men on the dais rose
and looked to their right, not at President Ardilla but behind him,
and then León saw himself enter and heard the packed hall and
gallery break into spontaneous applause.

León was surprised to see that he was wearing a dark suit; he was
the only Tinieblan in the room so dressed, and in seventy years no
one had ever worn anything but white to an important public ceremony. His expression was calm. As he came abreast of where the
justices were sitting, he turned his face a little to the right and nodded at the Deputies, gravely but not curtly, in acknowledgement of
their applause—then as he took his place opposite Ardilla in front of
the platform where Carlos Gavilán was standing, he raised his head
and sent a brief but warm smile floating up an invisible kite string to
his wife and children.

Then Dr. Erasmo Sancudo, his face worn smooth as a doorknob by
a lifetime of professional hypocrisy, rose and went to the center of the
dais so that he stood between the President and the President-elect
and took a Bible from a red plush cushion held by a white-suited
clerk and administered the oath of office, and León, sitting in a rattan chair in his mother's red-roofed bungalow beside the Alameda,
looked six months and two weeks into the future and saw himself
raise his right hand and lay his left hand on the book, and heard himself swear in a clear, firm voice to guard, honor, and revere the Constitution of the Republic, and to enforce its laws without fear or
favor, to defend its sovereignty and preserve its independence, and to
keep vigil over the liberties of its citizens and protect their welfare for
as long as Divine Providence and the laws of the state maintained
him in his magistrature. Then the clerk unpinned the presidential
sash from Juan Ardilla's chest, and Ardilla stepped forward and
pinned it across the chest of León Fuertes and then embraced him,
and with that León, sitting in his mother's house, fell into a trance.

"I thought you didn't like soap operas," Rebeca said to him as she
waddled in from the porch with her knit change purse held before
her in both hands.

León opened his eyes and saw that the television screen was
scabbed with the characters of a serial drama of such incredible triteness that he had fired a housemaid for letting his daughter, Clara,
watch it.

"I'm going to be President," he said.

"Oof! I've known that for forty-four years. It's about time it
dawned on you."

22. Some View of León, President

TINIEBLANS REMEMBER the one year, seven months, and ten days of León Fuertes' presidency as a period of innovation, and León himself as something of a radical. In fact, however, his veneration for Lord Falkland remained as firm as ever, He merely judged—and this was the chief reason why he embraced his destiny cheerfully—that if the substance of life was to remain stable for himself and for the country, some outward forms would have to change. These formal alterations were what Tinieblans noticed—as they were meant to—when León translated the seat of his ministry to the Presidential Palace. León Fuertes brought to the Tinieblan Presidency intelligence, energy, personal authority, and the magnetism that nowadays is called charisma, but the trait that most marked his term in office was his knack for forming and performing integrated figures. He undertook to express in his own person how the government and the society ought to behave. I can, therefore, make a few sketches for an iconographic history of his administration such as might be sculpted in relief on door panels or fresco'd across a stretch of wall.

The first (already done in Chapter 21 above) shows his inauguration and function s through the symbolism of dress. When León put off his white linen suit, he announced to his countrymen that the *bichos* were no longer models of comportment.

He did not turn on them. He included them in his government, making Aquilino Piojo Minister of Finance, for example. He protected that portion of their prosperity which did not depend on graft. But he also gave public expression to a particular reality: the *bichos'* system of values no longer constituted a cogent response to the circumstances of the country.

"A fellow like Castro would shoot some of them and ship the rest to Miami," he told Soledad. "My way is less exciting but less costly."

León wasn't interested in eliminating specific classes or even specific people, an activity he deemed both futile and dangerous, since it fostered the false hope that things would improve magically. He meant to provide an interim of stability during which the value of personal (or family) greed might be replaced by loyalty to the commonwealth. A few *bichos* had already managed this conversion; if more could achieve it, so much the better. But his lesson was directed to all Tinieblans. It failed. His interim was brief, and it is likely no amount of time would have sufficed. But on 1st June, 1962, white linen suits went out of style for good, while much of what they stood for—graft, for example, and elitist contempt for the people—went out of style for one year, seven months, and ten days.

Our next view is of León Fuertes dismissing his Presidential guard. The unit, a special company of Guardia outfitted in chrome casques and marine blue uniforms and armed with Uzi machine pistols, is drawn up under the nine A.M. June sun in the little park opposite the porte-cochere of the Presidential Palace. León has trooped their line, followed by their commanding officer, Captain Dmitri Látigo, his military aide-de-camp, Major Dorindo Azote (who wears his right sleeve doubled in souvenir of his Korean service with Batallón Tinieblas), and the Guardia Commandant, Colonel Aiax Tolete. He has taken a position in front of Tolete and Azote near the statue of Simón Mocoso, has asked Captain "Látigo to give his men parade rest, and has assumed that attitude himself. He has told the company in his best drill field bellow that they are as soldierly a unit as he has ever been privileged to see and that he would be honored to lead them in battle. His expression is stern, but a twinkle in his eyes suggests that he is enjoying the event immensely and yet can view it with ironical perspective. (Ten minutes later he will remark to César Enrique Sancudo, who is about to take leave for his embassy in Madrid and who watches the scene from a Palace window, that with garrison troops, as with female jurors, it's best to lay it on with a trowel, but that hyperbole comes easily at military reviews since few men—and León is no exception—ever mature to the point where they lose their taste for playing with toy soldiers.) Now, however, he takes his right hand from behind his back and sweeps it, fingers spread, across the line of troops: he is telling them he is dispensing with their services.

"This act involves no lack of respect for you as men and soldiers. My concept of government simply does not provide for leaders to be shielded with the instruments of violence; or set off from other citizens by the flattery of uniformed salutes; or insulated from the people in any fashion. I assure you, however, that I have too high a regard for the profession of arms, which once was my own calling, to break up so excellent a unit. Your commandant, Colonel Tolete, with whom I have consulted in this decision, will find an honorable place for you where you can put your discipline and valor to the protection of the people, whose servants we all are. For the duration of my period in office, the Presidential Guard will stand dismissed!"

He like wise dismissed the plain-clothes bodyguards who had been automatically assigned to him the morning of his inauguration and the leash of motorcycle cops whose job was to escort presidential limousines. The limousines themselves he ordered sold at auction. He retained a driver on the payroll to chauffeur my mother about in the family Cranston, a current-model four-door sedan, sea green In color and perfectly presentable, but without so much as an official license plate, much less fender flags or a presidential seal, to distinguish it from the cars of other well-to-do Tinieblans. For personal use he kept has blue Wildebeest hardtop, which he drove himself, unless he was traveling to the interior. More, since the Club Mercantil was only a few blocks from the Palace, citizens became accustomed to seeing the President of the Republic strolling unattended along the street below the sea wall, dressed in shorts and tennis shoes, carrying his racket. People took to greeting him informally as he passed, while some walked along with him to pass the time of day and offer comments on the business of the country, and León would answer in an easygoing, fraternal tone.

Thus León expressed his theory of government in his own person to three distinct audiences. The people were informed that while the President might be the first citizen of the country, the stress was on "citizen," not "first." Public servants were set a good example. Most cabinet ministers gave up their own limousines, and other members of León's Administration dispensed with similar amenities, but the point was not that state funds were thereby saved. León's example tended to restrain officials from grandiose feelings of their own importance. Finally, León himself was furnished some protection against the toxic effects of power.

"Power is both the drug and the hallucination," he told my mother the night before he accepted the sash of office. "People in what are called positions of power often develop the illusion that they control events and human beings. The people who reach such positions are usually hooked on power to begin with and put their faith in it. But the sanest man can have his perceptions terribly distorted by being whisked around in a limousine, with armed men sweeping ordinary mortals from his path. The worst part is he mightn't even realize he's stopped seeing things straight. When I was on morphine, I at least knew when I'd had a fix and when I hadn't, but power's a lot sneakier than morphine. I'm going to take what steps I can against addiction. If they don't seem to be working, for God's sake let me know."

Next we see the rotunda vestibule of the Ministry of Finance. Here citizens pay their taxes and obtain the square blue forms that certify they are at peace with the treasury and without which no one can leave the country or do any business with the state. Long queues of patient folk twist back from the windows in the frosted-glass partition, behind which clerks enjoy the air conditioning and now and then deign to give a little surly service. The fellow standing halfway between the street and the Property Tax window, the one in sports slacks, *guayabera* shirt, and shades, who keeps has face stuck in his copy of *Informe Trópico,* is León Fuertes, President of the Republic, Head of State and Government. He has been waiting twenty minutes and will wait another twenty-five before he reaches the window, stands glaring over his newspaper while the clerk debates the sex appeal of certain film stars with a colleague, at length gains her indolent attention, drops his paper, removes his dark glasses, and, in passing her a few expressions of controlled fury along with a cashier's check and the assessments on his home and beach house, performs what he will always consider his most significant act of public service.

By the time León was back in the Palace—and he delayed only a few moments, apologizing to other long-sufferers for the inefficiency of the service and promising to improve it even if he had to put His Excellency the Minister behind one of the windows—every state employee in the land knew how the president had spent the past hour and expected him to show up any minute at his own place of work. Nor did the fear and trembling cease until León Fuertes was assassinated, so that for the duration of his time in office the members of his administration, from ministers of state to charwomen, not only got to work on time and stayed through their appointed hours and made some attempt at coherent effort, but actually treated the public with respect and decency.

Despite its air of placidity, the fourth frame or panel is a *Cleansing the Temple* scene. We have a view of the Salón Amarillo, the most sumptuous room of the Presidential Palace, whose walls and furniture are covered in daffodil-hue silk with tiny fleurs-de-lis, the room where General Isidro Bodega (who appreciated *ancien régime* elegance) received Rosalba Fuertes.

A table, spread in damask and set with the best Palace service, stands near the window. President León Fuertes is lunching special guests, executives of a branch company of a subsidiary corporation of the most powerful commercial conglomerate in the United States ("Bigger than U.S. Steel," in the words of its Board Chairman, Mr. Meyer Lansky): the General Manager, Security Chief, and Sales Officer of Felicidad, S.A., a locally incorporated firm which for some years has operated gambling casinos, slot machines, and other recreative facilities and implements in Tinieblas. The slight, grey-haired gentleman in tinted glasses who shares the center of our scene with León is Mr. Albert Malocchio. The gentleman whose bald dome, bulged neck, and hippo shoulders fill half the lower foreground is Mr. Carmine ("Dum-Dum Charlie") Fessobabbuino. And on León's left, preening pearl teeth and cinematic profile and keeping one hand on the attaché case beside his chair, is Mr. Joseph Sporcati. (I am tempted here to let my sketch traduce historical accuracy, to change the material of Mr. Sporcati's case from leather to translucent plastic, and thus to display some of the large-denomination U.S, banknotes banded and stacked therein, but any knowledgeable Tinieblan would, on recognizing the President's guests, realize that the occasion was the day in August, 1962, when the Chamber considered renewal of Felicidad's contract with the Ministry of Tourism and, further, be aware that, by tradition, whenever a foreign businessman brought luggage into the Palace it was likely to contain currency, if not gold bars.) Dessert plates and coffee cups are on the table. Mr. Malocchio has extracted a large Havana from its aluminum tube and cedar swaddling and is about to load it into lips that have not yet quite ceased smiling. But León Fuertes has taken from his Legislative Aide Bernardo Zancado (who stands half bowing at Malocchio's left shoulder, holding an open manila folder), not the renewed contract (which the Chamber has just voted down on the President's recommendation and despite the impassioned oratory of Filiberto Alacrán, former Minister of

Tourism), but a packet of airline tickets (First-Class, one-way, Tinieblas-Miami), which he offers to Malocchio, smiling gravely.

In short, it was not my father's style to rage around overturning tables and ranting melodramatic pronouncements, though Mr. Malocchio and associates were more malign than moneychangers or parrot-sellers. He acted legally and with utmost civility. He gave Mr. Malocchio an excellent lunch and free transportation home for himself and his employees, croupiers and shills included. He ordered generous compensation to Malocchio's firm for the real property it had acquired in Tinieblas, and had all its movables, from the huge roulette wheel at El Opulento down to the last pair of trained dice, packed and sent north by air freight at the government's expense. He acted neither in prudishness nor xenophobia: he made it clear by presiding at the next drawing of the National Lottery that he had no wish to deny his countrymen exercise of their passion for risk, and his administration encouraged foreign investment of a healthy kind. The point was not that Mr. Malocchio and his principals in Miami were gamblers; it was not that they were foreigners. The point was that they were leeches, and León's actions in their regard were an example to the Tinieblan people, to its government, and to firms like Hirudo Oil, which spend more on public relations than the Mafia but whose motives and methods are often much the same. Tinieblans ought not to put up with leeches. In dealing with leeches the Tinieblan Government ought to proceed calmly, to avoid noisy manifestoes, to show courtesy, to adhere scrupulously to the law, to make due compensation, but to pluck them from the country with dispatch. Present or potential leeches ought take note.

"You shouldn't do this," Mr. Malocchio protested when President Fuertes professed unconcern with the contents of Mr. Sporcati's attaché case and suggested that the gentlemen make use of their tickets as soon as possible, "It isn't right. We paid an honest bribe to come in here, and we'll pay to stay."

"I understand." Since the conversation was proceeding in Italian, León pushed his palm against the invisible wall between him and Malocchio. "I understand and I sympathize. I've given and accepted honest bribes myself. But now I'm dealing for my country, and my country's going to do things differently. I'd appreciate it if you'd spread that word around."

A final picture might show the living room of the United States Embassy residence at San José, Costa Rica—a long view in from the dining room toward a couch flanked by two armchairs and above it a large, gilt-framed reproduction of M. M. Sanford's *Washington at Princeton*. Sitting about a yard apart on the couch, their shoulders hunched, their forearms on their knees, are Carlos Gavilán and Richard N. Schwartztrauber, Jr. The former looks to his right. The latter stares fixedly at the loafer-shod feet of John Fitzgerald Kennedy, plunked up on the coffee table as their owner lounges back in the right-hand armchair, one set of knuckles pressed to his lips, his eyes crinkled in an uneasy smile-scowl. In the left-band chair, his trunk erect, his right hand poked forward in a Kennedyesque jab, is León Fuertes. He is quoting, verbatim and in Boston-baa'd English, from a speech made by Kennedy the day before.

No tick can bite nor stray dog hunch to scratch it in the independent, sovereign Republic of Tinieblas without being somehow affected by the state of our relations with the U.S.A. This homey fact is dramatized by the presence, tumored against our capital, of an entire Gringoland in Miniature. It had, of course, been voguish back in 1898 for world powers to plant excrescences like the Reservation upon their weaker neighbors. Time had, however, passed and fashions altered. Thus León Fuertes judged that no matter what success he might have with other matters, he would not be able to preserve the tranquility of Tinieblas without putting our relations with the U.S.A. in modern dress: to wit, without replacing the Day-Cornudo Treaty with a contemporary instrument.

The problem was that his aim was peace and quiet, while—as he put it to his Cabinet at one of their first meetings—"in foreign affairs as in domestic matters, the U.S. Government works on the principle that unless you howl you never get a hearing; you never get attention till you kick them in the nuts." Had León put himself out in front of the student radicals; had he made himself a merchant of abuse and insult; had he bred hatred and incited violence; had he bared the foamed canines of such afflicted beasts as these days pass for leaders almost everywhere and sent a good searing squeal toward Washington, he would have got a hearing for Tinieblas straightaway. But such action, though it would surely have made him look a hero to the home fans, would have defeated the very purpose of his existence as a leader. It would have stung the resentments of the people into fury. It would have flogged their expectations to the point where nothing would content them. It would have racked the country to such torment as to make it unlivable for the generality of citizens and the other Leóns in particular.

He took a course, then, that was more difficult and dangerous for him personally. He used his popularity to sponge up the evil humors that the Reservation generated in Tinieblans. Then he put himself face to face with the head of the United States government and, unsupported by any gallery of cheering countrymen, without the least security that his countrymen would ever know of, much less reward his effort, found the wit and courage to land a swift one in the tenderest parts of his adversary's ego.

Both during his campaign and while in office, León took the refreshingly original line of saying publicly, over and again, that the United States was a great power and Tinieblas poor and weak, that both were located in the same hemisphere, that realities of this order were denied only at grave peril, that under his administration Tinieblan relations with the United States would be correct and friendly, and that while he would seek relief from certain injustices, no one should expect very much. He insisted on observing the provisions of the Day-Cornudo Treaty down to the last comma, and in his contacts with the students, which continued while he was President, though in diminished frequency due to their disillusionment with him, he retold the parable of Cuba until both he and his listeners were heartily sick of it. Meanwhile, he spent his spirit lavishly preparing for a trial by single combat in which he hoped to secure a general restructuring of our relations with the United States. Yet since the success of any effort in this direction depended on keeping Tinieblan expectations low, he kept these preparations secret and comported himself outwardly as if he were resigned to things as they were. Accordingly, those who had hoped for miracles from the baseball hero of New Year's, 1934, were cruelly disappointed. And as for León's popularity with the students and the urban masses of the capital, it dwindled to the point where large elements of both these sectors took to calling him "*Superbicho*" and, more cuttingly, "Meestair Forts."

On the day after his election, León began studying English with

Soledad. He took a ninety-minute class with her each evening and, as soon as he was able, spoke only English with her when they were alone together. He devoted his midnight reading exclusively to English, immersing himself in grammar books and dictionaries and giving special attention to U.S. history and literature. With the best part of León, husband, and all of León, scholar, thus engaged, he soon became perfectly fluent and attuned to most nuances in the language. So secret did he keep this activity, however, that his own children—who were themselves wrestling with the irrationalities of English and would have given Papa sympathy—were unaware of it.

He also studied John F. Kennedy. Every Tinieblan President since 1948 had, upon taking office, informed the Government of the United States that Tinieblas wished the Day-Cornudo Treaty abrogated and a new agreement negotiated to replace it. The sum of these efforts remained zero. León resolved to take an indirect approach. He did not mention Day-Cornudo to the U.S. Ambassador in Tinieblas or have his ambassador in Washington contact the State Department. He did not request a meeting with the President of the United States. Rather he trusted that the flow of events would bring a more or less impromptu encounter between John Kennedy and him, and he prepared himself to exploit that opportunity. He read Kennedy's own published works and all the articles about him. He studied Kennedy's state messages and public speeches, and memorized the declarations on Latin America so that he could quote the text and give the date and place of each specific statement. Most particularly, he tried, as an actor might, to work out the pattern of Kennedy's personal values, throwing his imagination into Kennedy's mind and body. The aim of these preparations is subsumed in the military principle of superiority of force at the point of contact. León hoped to meet Kennedy a certain distance from their official identities, on personal ground.

It would take a riot, an armed attack upon the Reservation, and a respectably high body count to make a President of the United States give serious attention to anything said by a President of what is probably referred to in Washington as the Banana Republic of What's-its-name. On the other hand, John Kennedy might listen to León Fuertes. Now, León realized that Kennedy would not forget that he was President of the United States, yet there was cause to hope that if a meeting came Kennedy would not keep himself entirely bandaged up in protocol and presidential seals. He was supposed to enjoy mental stimulation, and would not expect to find much in a formal meeting with the head of an insignificant state. Given the chance, he would surely prefer to be Jack Kennedy, and chat with León Fuertes. The two had come into the world in the same year. They bad fought on the same side in the same war, and had come out of it with more or less the same distinction. Both bad a preference for the active life, yet had intellectual attainments. Both practiced politics with zest and yet with skepticism. Yes, Kennedy had enough self-confidence to meet León man to man. If so, León knew how to capture his attention.

León would ask for nothing. Asking for things would merely transform two equals back into the President of the world's first power and the President of a little fly-speck pinch of mud and jungle. That would be boring: everyone approached the U.S. President for handouts. León meant to offer his coeval and brother politician Jack Kennedy something of value. The man had, or at least thought he had, certain principles. He aspired to a certain moral leadership. He considered himself to be a serious man and thought that was the kind of man to be. Now, León, in his readings in American fiction, had come upon one word that had a kind of French precision to it. He decided with some reluctance that he would not be able to try the word on Kennedy, but he hoped to evoke its connotations. He meant to offer Jack Kennedy a chance to prove—first of all to himself and in passing to others concerned—that he and his Latin American policy weren't full of bullshit.

Let us now proceed without further digression to the scene sketched above. I shall not set forth León's state of mind when it was announced that Kennedy would attend the meeting of Central American Presidents called at San José in spring, 1963, save to say that León was ready. I shall not describe the visit he received shortly following the announcement from the U.S. Ambassador to Tinieblas, except to record that León used an interpreter and the ambassador his Berlitz stutter; that the ambassador advised León that the President of the United States hoped to meet privately with his several Central American colleagues during the conference and asked León to furnish the embassy with his views on an agenda; that León

replied that he had had enough head-of-state ritual from Charles de
Gaulle to last a lifetime and that he hoped to meet John Kennedy informally; and that it was at length worked out that the two Presidents would breakfast together, each bringing one adviser. I shall give
no details of the table talk but simply note that Kennedy did not
stand on ceremony; that he was pleasantly surprised to find León at
his ease in English and took advantage of the unexpected nature of
this circumstance to crimson the cars of Dr. Schwartztrauber (a two-
time Pulitzer laureate) with a remark about the brilliant, well-in-
formed advice he was getting on Latin America from a man who,
until he joined the White House staff, was a simple professor of sociology at an obscure college in New Haven; that the conversation
ranged freely without touching hemispheric questions onto a discussion of the military mind—a tough subject to treat clearly, León said,
since the phrase itself was a contradiction in terms; that Kennedy
then recalled that his Secretary of Labor had once warned him
against assuming a man's knowledge bounded by his current place in
life, and said he'd been informed (God knew how accurately) that
Señor Fuertes had served in the French Army, and asked—since the
subject might be of more than academia interest, and since he'd had
opinion on it from men who didn't think much of the French Army,
but since it was his experience that men usually thought well of organizations in which they'd served with conspicuous distinction—
León's view of why the French Army had been whipped by the
Vietminh; that León spoke to this question for several minutes, saying that difficult terrain took most of the technology from war and
prevented Western soldiers from fighting according to their culture,
citing the French Command's temptation to underestimate an enemy
led by generals who had never seen Saint Cyr, arguing that no Western army would have done much better, and being in this fashion so
prophetic that were I to reproduce his discourse here it would seem
gilded by hindsight; and that Kennedy listened with great interest
and when León had finished, deadpanned to Schwartztrauber about
requesting a memo from Señor Fuertes on another thorny guerrilla
problem: how to handle the reform faction of the Democratic Party
in New York. I need scarcely say that it was Kennedy, not León
Fuertes, who at length turned the conversation toward Latin America, remarking when the four men had removed to the living room

that it was time he started earning his day's pay, asking what steps Señor Fuertes thought might be taken to improve relations between the United States and its neighbors, and adding that this was the first chance he'd had to put that question to a Latin American leader: he'd met with many of them in the past few years, but all had given their opinions long before they were requested.

León laughed and said he might well have done the same under different circumstances, but that while he could not speak for other countries, relations between the United States and the Republic of Tinieblas could not possibly be better—now that Mr. Kennedy had decided to abrogate the Day-Cornudo Treaty.

Kennedy looked to Schwartztrauber in puzzlement; Schwartztrauber shrugged back. "Excuse me, Señor Fuertes, but I have decided nothing of the sort."

"Excuse me, Mr. Kennedy, but you announced that decision only yesterday."

And without further preamble, León began reciting, in Kennedy's own tones and with his gestures, from an address Kennedy had delivered the day before at the University of Costa Rica, a portion of which affirmed a continent-wide "right to social justice" and called for "an end to ancient institutions which perpetuate privilege." León's crammed data bank of Kennedy speeches thus remained untapped. Kennedy had given him fresher and more potent ammunition there in San José.

"That's not a bad imitation," said Kennedy with some impatience, "but I don't see what it has to do with the treaty between our two countries."

"No? The Day-Cornudo Treaty is the very thing you spoke of: 'an ancient institution which perpetuates privilege.'" Here again, and whenever he repeated the phrase, León imitated Kennedy's distinctive accent. "It reflects an epoch of history remote from our own," León continued. "It grants a foreigner the privilege to quarter soldiers in our house. It perpetuates that privilege well into the future. You have called stridently and in the clearest terms for an end to such institutions. You have it in your power to end this one, since we Tinieblans are more than willing to bid it a farewell. The only possible conclusion is that you have decided to abrogate the treaty."

Kennedy pressed the index and middle fingers of his right hand

together and poked them softly at León. He had begun to show the
kind of annoyance that might come to a tennis player when his opponent, who has been playing a straightforward game of clean, flat
strokes all morning, suddenly begins to slice, to cut, to chop, to hit
his first service underhand so that the ball staggers over the net and
then falls limply, to interrupt crisp baseline rallies with interminable
successions of great, blooping lobs, and meanwhile to dance about
grinning, making wise remarks, as though to mock him and the
sport itself. "That treaty was signed by your President, and ratified
by your Assembly, Mr. Fuertes."

"Ah, Mr. Kennedy, some people say—even some North American
scholars—that the treaty was signed by your dupe, or your captive,
or your bribed agent; and ratified by your fleet. But why go into that?
That is old history. Part of a remote, an ancient epoch. Yesterday,
right here in San José, John Kennedy called for 'an end to ancient
institutions which perpetuate privilege.' That speech made history!
That call rang in a new epoch!" León beamed admiration at his host,
then twisted his face in question. "You weren't joking, were you?"

Although he did not change his relaxed posture, Kennedy was
clearly nearing the end of what Mr. Dave Powers has called his
"short fuse." He poked a bit more strongly with his fingers: "Mr.
Fuertes, you had best take any statement by the President of the
United States just as seriously as you can."

"Excellent!" León met Kennedy's gaze without the slightest un-
easiness. "Then the Day-Cornudo Treaty stands abrogated."

Kennedy swung his feet down from the coffee table. "All right,
Mr. President. Let's cut out the crap. Day-Cornudo is a *bona fide*
treaty. I haven't abrogated one word of it, and you know goddamn
well I haven't. That kind of crap may go where you come from, but
don't play games with me."

"Very well. Then let me return to the question you were kind
enough to pose me earlier. About improving relations. I am sure you
will agree that an important element of good relations is clear communication. You have made statements that bear on relations in this
hemisphere. You have made them in your own country, and around
Latin America, and here in San José. They are inspiring statements,
but I suggest that they need clarification. My 'game' was an illustration of that need. I suggest that the Day-Cornudo Treaty offers you

an opportunity to clarify your personal views and the Latin American policy of your government. I suggest that a military-base treaty done in 1898 and not scheduled to expire for nine hundred thirty-four more years stands in some dissonance to your stated views and policy. I suggest we abrogate that treaty and negotiate a new one to replace it. I suggest that to do so is in your interest. Otherwise those who listen to your speeches, and you yourself, unless you have great powers of self-deception, may very well conclude that John Kennedy pretends to principles he doesn't have, and makes statements he doesn't believe in."

Let us draw a veil over the next few minutes, a semi-opaque veil which transmits a general outline yet filters out the grosser gestures. And let us mute the volume. Neither man did himself much credit, and neither is around to defend or excuse his comportment. Kennedy, on the whole, came off a little better. He merely showed his Irish, whereas León needled without mercy, trading on the basic decency and good will of a man he admired. Let us simply catch a phrase here and there: Kennedy announcing in cold rage that when a man told him to put up or shut up, he expected the man to tell him how he planned to *back* up the demand; León replying in apparent calm that since the conflict was not between him and Kennedy but between some inspiring statements and a degrading treaty, he made no demand but simply suggested means to resolve the conflict; Kennedy saying in disgust that everyone he'd met with in San José wanted something to take home and show the folks, but at least the rest had been straightforward about it; León saying that it was true he'd been a beggar in New York during the Depression, but that he hadn't been successful in the profession and had given it up, permanently—he would get by one way or another, but he couldn't see how Kennedy could make a speech like the one he'd made yesterday and go on perpetuating privilege. Let us hear the advisers getting in the act: Schwartztrauber suggesting that President Kennedy had been referring in his university speech to "institutions like the Club Mercantil clique and the thirteen families who run Tinieblas"; Carlitos returning him some warm remarks about how President Fuertes and the Progressive Party had broken the ruling-class monopolies. Kennedy admonished Schwartztrauber for equivocating, for making him sound like Nixon. León admonished Carlitos for defending when they needed no defense, and for making him sound like Castro. In the end, Castro and Nixon were the peacemakers.

"I'm not Fidel Castro," León said to Kennedy. "I will not turn my country over to the Russians. It's bad enough that others turned it over to you. I will try to hold out, enduring Day-Cornudo, until you, or some other President of your country, decide to put your speeches into practice. They are good speeches, really. So good that I refuse to accept that you don't believe them."

Kennedy sighed. "Well, Mr. Fuertes, I know what I believe. But as I understand your argument—and it's a forceful case—the only way I can avoid sounding as hypocritical as my late opponent is to negotiate a new treaty with your country. Tell me, how would you have proceeded if Nixon had won in 1960?"

"I'd have sought counsel from some of my country's more traditional politicians, Mr. Kennedy. They would probably have advised me to wait till he was running for a second term, and then get in touch with his campaign finance chairman."

"Yes, Mr. Fuertes." A smile flickered on Kennedy's face. "You have an instinct for a man's Achilles heel."

Then Kennedy said he saw no bar to considering the abrogation of the Day-Cornudo treaty, and assured León that he was personally committed to modernizing a great many relationships. He mentioned the nuclear test ban treaty with the Soviets, which he was shortly to announce, and spoke of the difficulties he anticipated in securing passage for it in the Senate. He couldn't throw too many treaties at the Senate all at once, and abrogating Day-Cornudo might have implications for the United States with regard to third countries. Those would have to be examined before he could make a commitment. He could say this, though, and he hoped León took him seriously: he would give the matter of negotiating a new treaty his personal attention. If León liked, if he would find it helpful, they could announce that they had discussed modernizing the treaty relationship between their two countries and had agreed in principle that efforts in that direction should be pursued.

León preferred, however, not to put anyone's hopes up.

"Let's just say," he answered, "that we swapped war stories. That way, should you find abrogation impossible, only Carlos and I will be disappointed. On the other hand, if you decide, as I think you will, to go forward, I can suggest an interesting scenario. It has you speaking at our university sometime next year, declaring that in line with your desire to put an end to those 'ancient institutions,' you, on your own initiative, would like to abrogate Day-Cornudo and negotiate a new treaty."

And so the official communiqué said merely that the two Presidents had discussed matters of mutual interest.

León Fuertes and John Kennedy were in each other's company on several occasions thereafter during the conference, but never privately, and neither mentioned Day-Cornudo. Late in the fall, however, Kennedy wrote León, saying that it was "time to put an end, or at least the beginning of an end, to a certain 'ancient institution'" and inviting León to come to Palm Beach, Florida, early in December to discuss the matter with him. By December, 1963, of course, Kennedy's body was in Arlington, Virginia, and his spirit in the next world.

It remains for me now to describe the circumstances under which León Fuertes made a similar migration.

23. Discord and Disfavor

PRESIDENT LEÓN FUERTES returned from San José to find his honeymoon with the Republic of Tinieblas over. The communiqué regarding his meeting with John Kennedy preceded him, and he was met at Monteseguro Airport by a sizable mob of strife-peddlers who accused him by voice and placard of having betrayed his country.

The specifications were at once a tribute to the paranoid imagination and a proof of that segment of information theory which holds zero can be a cause. From the absence in the communiqué of any reference to the Day-Cornudo Treaty, Canino and claque charged that León and Kennedy had concluded a secret pact which confirmed Day-Cornudo in perpetuity and granted the United States missile bases in Otán and Tuquetá; that León had accepted a check for five million dollars drawn by Joseph P. Kennedy and countersigned by Richard Cardinal Cushing; that León had applied for U.S. citizenship.

After a glance at the placards and an earful of shouts, León refused the microphone that had been set up at the foot of the ramp, asked his wife and the other members of his party to excuse him for a moment, and walked jauntily toward the mob, which a line of sweating *guardias* was restraining in the shadow of the terminal. The demonstrators pushed toward him angrily, buckling the soldiers' line, but without slowing his pace León spread his arms, palms forward, in front of him, and the crowd opened as though divided by a wedge. He went in among them.

"What would I do with gringo citizenship?" he asked a signbearer, grinning at him, clapping him on the neck with the kind of rough affection coaches give their athletes. "My mamá would disown me."

"One gringo base is more than enough," he told another. "Do you really think I offered them others?"

"I told you when I was running not to expect much," he said to a group of the loudest shouters, who now stood congealed in silence, wincing as he stabbed a finger at them. "I'm telling you now I didn't sell the country out. I'm not going to mention that again. If you want to believe in fairy tales, go right ahead, but this country doesn't need to be sold out. I'm not ashamed of this country, so I can face the facts about it. Tinieblas isn't a world power. We don't have much to bargain with against the U.S.A. I know how you feel. I sympathize. I'm doing what I can. But I have to think of all the people's welfare, not just your obsessions."

He turned then and walked away, and the demonstration crumbled behind him, but his difficulties were only beginning. A few weeks later he brought the anger of both landowners and peasants on himself by vetoing a land reform bill prepared by his own Ministry of Agriculture but passed by the Chamber in grossly diluted form.

"No one can call me an extremist," he told the Deputies, taking his veto message to them personally, "but this bill is too moderate for me to sign. Some people, people who don't own land, like land reform because it allows them to feel saintly at the expense of others. Others like it because our friends to the north have made it the condition of some tasty grants and loans. For my part, I dislike it. I understand that the only way to make a go of agriculture is with decently large tracts. But the *campesinos* will give us no peace until we give them land, so on top of all my other sins I directed the Ministry of Agriculture to prepare a bill of land reform. But reform cannot be done in dribbles. The bill you passed may satisfy those who practice charity by proxy. It may satisfy the U.S. Ambassador. It may satisfy the landowners, who were afraid of mine. Unfortunately, it will not satisfy the *campesinos*. It will only whet their appetites. Were I to sign it, I would have to request another one next year, which you would no doubt geld in committee. Dribble would follow dribble. Appetites would grow. We would finish by giving the *campesinos* more land than they need, or know what to do with, or really want, and even that wouldn't be enough. This bill is veto'd. I urge you to go back and pass the bill my government prepared on careful study. Since land reform cannot be avoided, it must be done correctly straightaway. Then we shall perhaps have time next year to deal with the problems of reduced yield which this inevitable reform will inevitably generate."

The large holders, who had lobbied ceaselessly to water the bill down, were furious. The peasants listened sullenly to León's explanation of his veto, which he made over and again by radio and on a painful swing through the interior, and then found it simpler to believe certain agitators, who charged that León was duping them, that he was in cahoots with the landlords, that he would never permit any land reform. There followed a wave of crop burnings on the cane plantations of La Merced, which León was obliged to put down firmly. Aware that the immediate application of overwhelming force is less cruel and costly than half-hearted measures, he declared martial law in La Merced, named Major Dorindo Azote Military Governor of the province, and gave him three companies of *guardias* to reinforce the regular garrisons. The disturbances were quashed in short order without loss of life, and when courts-martial gave the ringleaders long terms in the penal colony on Fangosa Island, León first arranged for them to remain in local jails and then, at Christmas, commuted their sentences. The events turned the peasants strongly against him, however, and since the Chamber chose to dawdle futilely with land reform for the remainder of the session, he never won them back—or rather not until he'd gained an honest martyrdom with his body meatballed across Via Venezuela.

Meanwhile, the landowners found a more craven outlet for their spite: inspired by two gentlemen whom this history will not dignify by naming and who discovered a forgotten clause in the Club Mercantil charter denying membership to men of illegitimate birth, they called for León's expulsion in a series of private letters to the club president. He, though properly apologetic, felt compelled to bring the matter to León's attention. My father resigned at once, saying that he was glad to be a naturally born and not a self-made bastard, but the incident rankled him cruelly, having pierced the tenderest zone of his character, his urge for respectability.

"I'm surprised a thing like this can hurt," he told Soledad, "considering all I've been through in my life and all the ways I've found to stuff my ego. But I dreamed Clarita might be club Carnival Queen someday."

"She doesn't mind."

"I know. She's not as childish as I am. The worst part is I have to hold it in. It's been suggested—as if I hadn't thought of it myself— that I make the thing political and win some favor with the lower classes. Half this country was born out of wedlock. But I can't do it. I can't even knock anyone's teeth out till my term is up. People would think I've declared a revolution."

León's political opponents, whom his great popularity had cowed to an unnatural and agonizing silence, took heart from these events and filled the press and every public forum with their yelpings. At the same time, a number of his followers deserted him. During the troubles in La Merced the Chamber had overwhelmingly endorsed León's vigorous action. Once order was restored, in the very instant of the danger's passing a motion of censure was introduced, charging that President Fuertes and his government had overreacted. A number of Progressive Party Deputies—though not enough to make up a majority—supported it, invariably asking time to explain their votes and then driveling out grave empty phrases about the painfulness of the decision and the telling weight of moral imperatives over personal friendship and party royalty.

"It's part cowardice and part ambition," Rosendo Salmón told León. A Tinieblista member from Salinas, he had nonetheless voted against censure. "But the main thing is they've never forgiven you for helping them get where they are. I don't owe you anything, and besides, every once in a while I give myself the luxury of voting like a man."

Student protest continued. Canino's faction won control of the Students' Syndicate, and scarcely a week passed without a campus demonstration or a rally in Plaza Cervantes. Canino dealt entirely in

abusive falsehood but was inventive at it and had the peasant troubles to embroider on as well as Day-Cornudo. His rantings drew
large audiences from the lower-class barrios, and by fall the atmosphere of the capital was nearly as polluted with resentment and frustration as in the last days of 1951. Now, however, the target of
invective was not a class but an individual: "*Superbicho, the
campesino* killer"; "Meestair Forts, the first gringo President of
Tinieblas." The scenario that León had outlined during his first campaign was developing as he foresaw: Without any encouragement
from him, the country had installed him as its hero. Tinieblas
nonetheless remained Tinieblas; no magical transformation had ensued. León must now be punished for failing to incarnate the fantasies he had tried consistently to dispel.

The woes of León, politician, were aggravated by the rebellion of
the other Leóns. They had ceded portions of their time and energy to
León, politician, so that he might, acting as their agent, maintain a
favorable environment for their stimulations and fulfillments. Upon
becoming President, however, and with the growing instability of the
Tinieblan system during the summer and fall of 1963, León, politician, absorbed an ever-increasing share of the common patrimony, so
that the other Leóns, finding themselves ever less free to act, judged
him a tyrant and declared their independence.

After suffering himself to be denied for several weeks following
my father's resignation from the Club Mercantil, León, athlete,
picked the day after a blustery speech by the Commander of the
American Legion in the Reservation—"We've got the right to stay
here nine hundred thirty-four more years, and we'll stay another
thousand after that if we feel like it!"—to seize command of the communal body and sneak to the tennis courts at Fort Shafter. There he
remained for seven hours, enjoying himself hugely and fraternizing
in the greatest good humor with the gringos whom he found there
and with the many others who, as news of his presence spread, came
to look on. Inevitably, word of his whereabouts reached the news
desks of the Tinieblan papers, and by midafternoon four carloads of
journalists had arrived to witness him partner the commandant's
daughter (a properly photogenic blonde of twenty-two) at mixed
doubles and, by way of keying up her game, drench her with gal-
lantries in fluent English. The motion to censure was at that time

being debated in the Chamber, and the headlines, pictures, leaders, editorials, and feature stories that began appearing the next morning and that continued till the last dram of scandal was wrung from the incident "disclosure" that León was divorcing Soledad to marry Miss O'Moore—contributed materially to the closeness of the vote. And as if this were not sufficient proof of his existence and autonomy, León, athlete, continued to play tennis at Fort Shafter now and then—to the great aid and comfort of Manfredo Canino and associated fanatics—and to make León, politician's life otherwise more difficult by flitting over to the grass court behind the British Embassy Residence whenever he took the notion, even if there was a crisis on or a cabinet meeting scheduled.

León, lecher, whom interest of state and the all-seeing eye of the news media had denied his normal complement of romps, took to leaping palace maids and secretaries at the most inappropriate times and places. Important visitors huffed in anterooms while the presidential office served as a humpodrome, and the discretion of presidential aides was sorely strained by glimpses of El Jefe tearing one off in the pantry or on the service stairs. Beyond asserting his independence, León, lecher, seemed bent on destroying León, politician, altogether. The Tinieblan Constitution stipulates that the President of the Republic may not leave national territory without the formal consent of the Chamber of Deputies, and yet only the last-minute intervention of Carlos Gavilán (who used his authority as Minister of Justice to order all flights leaving Monteseguro Airport temporarily grounded) prevented León, lecher, wearing a false beard and bearing an even falser passport in the name of Panurgo Burlando, from decamping to New Orleans in the company of an atypically well-nourished and perfectly adorable young gringa fashion model who had been appearing in an international display of *couture sportive* at the Hotel Excelsior. Like all the members of my father's repertory company of personalities, León, lecher, passed these months in a wild drive for primacy—no, for exclusivity. He resented all bounds, even his own commitment to careless futtering, and on top of his pitiless assaults on targets of opportunity persuaded Loli Gavilán not to return to her studies in Lausanne when summer ended, so that he might continue unimpeded a liaison that engaged his heart as fully as his gonads.

Nor were León, scholar, and León, husband, any less rebellious.

The former, who was the meekest of all my father's figures, recalled the long hours he had spent poring over English grammars, decided he had been vilely manipulated for the purposes of polities, and reacted with amazing boldness. Previously content with an abbreviated and nocturnal existence' he now appeared during the day and seized control of my father's mind and body at his pleasure. Ministers and other conferees grew accustomed to seeing León's face go blank even as they posed him important questions, to hearing him mutter phrases of no currency at all in the argument at hand, to witnessing him snatch up a pencil and fill his notepad with the incomprehensible hieroglyphics of topology or physics. He was wont, during cabinet meetings, to pull from his jacket pocket a folio anthology of the poems of Blake and engross himself therein, sometimes quoting from it in the original, sometimes translating passages whose opacity to the men of affairs present was in no way pierced by being put in Spanish, and invariably remarking, slapping the book on the glossed table before tucking it away, that Blake was the only justification for his having learned English, one verse of his being worth fifty interviews with Kennedy. Don Felix Grillo del Campo gave the most acute appreciation of the problem. Invited along with other leaders of the banking community to inform the President on certain economic questions and then treated to a performance by León, scholar, Grillo went from the meeting to the private apartments of the Palace and urged Soledad Fuertes to make her husband take a rest.

"I don't want to alarm you, Sóle, and I have the greatest confidence in León, but just now I had to pinch myself to make sure I wasn't dreaming of my crazy uncle Escolástico."

My mother was not alarmed by Grillo's comment for the simple reason that she had been alarmed before he made it. But overwork did not seem to be the problem. Soledad could not recall a period when my father had been more willing to give time to his family. He would loll in bed of mornings chatting playfully, would drop in on her at odd times in the day, would neglect his work to linger in her company in a, manner altogether unprecedented in their sixteen years of wedlock. More, on the impulse of the moment he would whisk her arid the children to the beach, scoffing alike at their school obligations and his official duties. In short, León, husband, too was asserting himself freely.

Yet however much Soledad enjoyed my father's company and appreciated spontaneous attentions, León, husband's behavior was too uneven not to be disturbing, His goings were as unpredictable as his comings. He was liable now to disappear during a family dinner, to give way to León, scholar, for example, in the midst of a conversation—though neither Soledad nor the children understood the process whereby Papá's gaze would glide off into nowhere and his penless hand start scribbling on the tablecloth. Or he might suddenly be replaced by León, lecher—who, heretofore, had always kept his distance whenever Soledad was anywhere around—as when, during a poolside party at the home of Aquilino Piojo, my father (with the unconcern of a cocktail tippler dipping in the peanut dish) slipped his fingers and at least half his palm under the dorsal fold of Pastora Avispa's bikini bottom. Soledad's world was love, and love and jealousy are mutually exclusive,[98] but she had to be alarmed at this: her husband was acting weirdly, and she bad no notion why.

Had Soledad understood León and possessed a rudimentary grasp of cybernetics, she would have realized (1) that the complex open system known as León Fuertes achieved stability (homeostasis) by means of a built-in, selfcorrective feedback mechanism which regulated the flow of energy to several component systems (León, husband—León, scholar; etc.); (2) that the stability of the overall system depended on continual small alterations in the allotments to components; (3) that while the introduction (in response to external pressure) of a new component (León, politician) had been accomplished without excessive disturbance to the system's balance, the application of new external pressures, beginning in June, 1962, and intensifying during summer and fall, 1963, resulted in a massive increase in the energy allotment to this particular component (4) that the system's self-corrective feedback mechanism responded to this change in one variable by effecting similarly dramatic changes in the other variables, so that the normal pattern of continual small changes in the flow of energy to the component systems was warped into a blunder of abrupt, wild fluctuations, ragged zigzags, zingy swings; and therefore (5) that under external pressure the system's internal stabilizing mechanism had pushed the system into instability. In other, more familiar words, my father's psychical ecology was gravely out of whack.

That fall, as the interior festered in resentment and the capital suppurated radical dissent, León Fuertes appeared to withdraw from events, so that many Tinieblans felt he'd lost his nerve. It was, rather, that the other Leóns restricted León, politician's freedom of action and attention. Not that they found much profit in it: they restricted each other's freedom also. None could thrive unless all did. And as if that were not enough, León's ancestors combined against him—or rather took action far more noxious than intrigue or attack. Concerned for his welfare and with the best intentions, they began hustling him in very wrong directions.

It is something the custom of my country for important men to repair in times of crisis to the Palace, there to give counsel to the President of the Republic and to themselves reaffirmation of their own importance. All through the latter half of 1963, President León Fuertes received visitations, both in dreams and during waking moments, from Generals Isidro Bodega, Feliciano Luna, and Epifanio Mojón. They all had done the state some service. They all possessed executive experience. They all could cite not only patriotism but ties of blood in motive for their urge to counsel the incumbent. And so, in the Tinieblan fashion, they went to León Fuertes uninvited and served him generous slices of their minds.

When León told Soledad it had been suggested that he milk political advantage from his bastardy, he did not tell her the suggestor was his grandfather General Feliciano Luna, who had cantered into León's dreams on a black mare the very night León resigned from the Club Mercantil and who, rising in his stirrups and brandishing his Martini-Henry rifle, had volleyed blasphemies against solemnized procreation that shook the sky above him. Nothing could come of it, he bellowed, but "fags and cowards and thinshanked whining girls with cunts as dry as chalk! There's never been a man with balls born yet, or a good hot-bottomed woman either, who wasn't got by simple honest fucking, with the priests and magistrates left out of it! That's how I made my children, fifty sons and Christ knows how many daughters! You just be proud you were made the same way!"

General Luna went on to advise León to get all the "bastards, drab-dropped foundlings, and other sons of whores" on his side and wipe out the Club Mercantil and all its members. These were, after all, the descendants of the very men who had connived with Mon-

señor Jesús Llorente and the gringos to have General Luna hanged.
This was perfectly in line with the program General Luna had been
proposing and continued to propose in León's dreams and in what
León thought hallucinations. Revolution and guerrilla war were,
General Luna argued, the best policy for León and Tinieblas, and he
went into considerable detail on how vulnerable the Reservation was
to surprise attack, on how León might, in a lightning blow, rub out
the entire garrison, or at least a large portion of it, along with oodles
of civilians, and, more important, seize all the arms and ammunition
he would need. As for U.S. retaliation, León should take his people
down to Selva Trópica and let the gringos come looking for him in
the jungle.

"They won't enjoy it much, you can believe me. Your trouble is
that when you hear the word 'war' you think of armies squaring off
in open battle. Guerrilla war is different, boy, and a lot more fun besides. You can hold out for decades, doing as you please. They'll
never land a solid punch on you, and between you and the jungle
they'll lose thousands and get sick of the whole business."

"But what of the people?" León would ask. "Our towns would all
be occupied by foreign troops. You've seen how soldiers act when
they occupy a country during war."

"To shit with the people! The ones who want to fight will be with
you in the jungle, killing their enemies like free men. The ones who
don't want to fight deserve what happens to them!"

León had no argument for this. He simply had to steel himself
against his grandfather's seductive simplifications, to bear General
Luna's harangues and sneers in silence, to remember the gentle people in Tinieblas—there were many of them, after all—and cling to his
own values.

General Bodega's advice was the opposite of General Luna's, no
less seductive, but in the end no more acceptable. Bodega had a way
of flitting in (light as a butterfly despite his ample paunch) through
the window of the presidential office while León was at paper work
or in conference with one or two close aides, of taking a position of
repose in midair near the bronze bust of him that filled a niche above
the sofa, of waiting placidly till León could attend him. He counseled
peace, above all peace with the gringos.

"'Hyena of the Pentagon. Lackey of the Wall Street plutocrats,'" he would say, parroting Canino's jargon. "Why not? Those aren't insults, they're encomiums. Do you know why the hyena laughs, my boy? Because the lion does the work and takes the risks. And who is a better model of rational behavior than Figaro? Lackey to them, by all means! They are strong and rich; we are poor and weak. They can afford to be stupid, so we must try to be clever. Hyena them and be happy, until a stronger lion comes along."

General Bodega chided León for expelling the Miami syndicate and bothering Kennedy about Day-Cornudo. What Tinieblas needed was more foreign intervention, more foreign economic and military presence, enough foreigner involvement to ensure that should unrest worsen, the foreigners would handle it with their own troops and funds.

"Foreigners ran this country while I was President," Bodega remarked with pride, "and I lived in this Palace for eighteen years without an hour of distress in the whole time. With a little cleverness and luck you can turn Tinieblas into the fifty-first state of the North American Union. De facto, of course, not de jure! You don't want to have to pay them taxes! If you won't think of your own peace of mind, think of the people. Aren't they better off laughing? Then imitate the action of the hyena."

And León would have to summon memories of his hyena season on the Bowery and remind himself of the foul taste of offal.

This world was giving León Fuertes enough trouble. He needed no fresh shipments from the next. Entertaining Generals Luna and Bodega, listening to their criticisms and resisting their bad advice, put a measurable drain upon his strength and his good temper. Yet while he would have cheerfully dispensed with their visits, he greatly preferred them to those of General Mojón. That gentleman was not merely an ex-President of the Republic and a concerned forebear; he was a professional advance man for the Four Horsemen of the Apocalypse, with half a century's experience disseminating terror and despair. When Epifanio Mojón staged a nightmare, he didn't fart about. He meant to make his great-grandson León Fuertes into a proper despot in the high standard and tradition of our time, and he went flat out at turning León on to power.

From July into November León could never lay his head down, not even for the briefest of siestas, without fear of having hideous dreams of weakness, the most pleasant of which involved his being torn apart by mobs, and which crescendoed gradually in horror through piecemeal mutilation and impalement to a scene where León, unbound but paralyzed by cowardice, watched his children chopped to messes, stewed, and served to him. Each episode concluded with a warning from General Mojón that this was what the future held for León if he didn't change his ways. In counterpoint accompaniment there went a program of demonstration lectures on the uses of cruelty. One morning, for example, the morning after a particularly vociferous and disrespectful protest rally, General Mojón sat down beside León as he was breakfasting on the Palace terrace and invited him to glance out to his left. There, beyond the sea wall, León saw a pair of crosses, each hung with a sharkstripped skeleton.

"That's how I handled dissent," General Mojón said softly. "When I was President, you didn't hear a peep out of this country. And aside from their effect on public order and respect for authority—a telling effect, you can be sure—my policies were personally satisfying. Look."

General Mojón waved his hand across the bayscape, and instead of two crosses there were ten or twenty, each bearing a naked youth or girl, Manfredo Canino and other students whom León had listened to so patiently and tried to reach but who had turned against him. General Mojón lifted his palm, and the tide rose, and the sharks came slicing in around the crosses.

"Or perhaps something more contemporary," General Mojón suggested, and the sun-shot, glistening vista of the bay faded, and León saw instead a room much like an operating theater, lit cleanly from a bank of blue-green fluorescent lamps. In place of a table, though, there was a kind of dental chair in which, strapped down and wired with electrodes, a young man squirmed and grunted as a technician played the knobs of an enameled console.

"Now, isn't that an improvement on your current situation? Isn't that more enjoyable than being slandered and insulted? Better still, you surely can recall the awful helplessness you felt during your dream last night. You're still hung over with it, aren't you? Well, have that fellow there turn the juice up. Just give a mental order, he'll obey. There!" The "patient" shrieked. His body arced, then jerked convulsively against the straps. "Now tell me you don't feel stronger right away. Just watch that kid jump! Tell me it doesn't bring relief. You never got results like that by chatting with them, did you? There's one brat who's picking up your message. You're getting through to him, no doubt of that."

León endured these abominable hallucinations in mixed disgust and fascination. General Mojón's advice on how to run a country had a palpable attraction. It would work.

"A firm hand, and you'll have no trouble. There's nothing so dependable as suffering. No human motive can compete with fear. Just give some of them a dose of calculated agony, and the rest will foul their pants at the mere mention of your name."

León's sole defense was to remind himself of some things General Epifanio Mojón had never learned, despite the fact that by the time his soldiers deposed him and hung him up on one of his own crosses in the bay, he was so rotten that the sharks refused to feed on him and buzzards turned away from him in nausea: No one can dominate and yet stay separate. Everyone is affected by what he affects. Brutality brutalizes. Terrorizing makes one terrified. The trouble with General Mojón's methods was that they worked too well, so that even if León cared for no one but himself, he would be foolish to apply them. He would be his own first victim. He would have no other life but León, despot, and that figure would be as enslaved, dehumanized, and racked with suffering as any prisoner in his torture chamber.

In these months my father, León Fuertes, bore torment from all quarters. His opponents clamored against him and his followers deserted him. His personalities rose up in anarchy, and his ancestors tempted him with false counsel. By day he was pelted with an endless hail of problems and shaken by strange visions which, since he did not believe in spirits or another world, caused him to doubt his sanity. At night he writhed and sweated in frightful and debilitating dreams. By November, when the rains broke hourly upon city and countryside and men walked bent and stifled under a press of clouds, every satisfaction had been peeled from his poor life. No one of his figures could maintain himself for more than a few minutes at a time. They came and went in dizzying succession, incapable of sustained action. León, athlete's movements were spastic; León, lecher's loins were flaccid; León, scholar's mind was a jumble of disoriented thoughts. For the first time in his life León Fuertes was, in effect, no one at all, and beyond him, as though reacting to his troubles in macrocosmic sympathy, the country too was losing its identity as class and faction surged back and forth across the landscape of events, all striving futilely for dominance.

By this time, besides his family, only Carlos Gavilán and Gavilán's children retained much faith in León. Carlitos urged him to go out and win the people back, but León never left the Palace now except to slink out after dark. Lilo was perhaps his most effective ally. In his idealism Lilo had refused to go abroad to study. He wanted no advantage over anybody else and enrolled at the National University. There he organized a democratic students' group, and in 1963 his was the clearest voice rebutting Canino's slanders and supporting León Fuertes. As for Loli, who had taken a job teaching at a private girls' school and moved into a flat on the Via Venezuela, she gathered a few boyfriends as camouflage and gave León some warrior's repose. She was nineteen, lovely, and in love with him, yet—since in these days he was as limp as any capon—more like a daughter to him than a mistress, comforting him in the manner of Cordelia with gaga Lear while he lay meekly in her arms and told her stories from his past, recounting them without the slightest arrogance, as though they were episodes from some heroic fantasy which had no truth except in metaphor.

A good gauge of how little León was himself is his reaction to John Kennedy's letter. He flung away his skepticism of "solutions" and invested the letter with the aura of a celestial sign. Although he had been saying for years that half the trouble in our continent came from regarding the United States as a *deus ex machina*, León viewed the letter as his salvation, and to make his faith manifest and thus magically insure results, he burned all mental bridges from Palm Beach. He stopped tending to the troubles of the country, When aides brought him problems—most of which had nothing to do with the Reservation or Tinieblan relations with the United States—he grinned moronically and said it didn't matter, in a few weeks the whole country would be in love with him again. Or he might frown and say it didn't matter, in a few weeks everything would be decided, one way or another.

"If Kennedy betrays me," he told Gavilán one day, seizing his friend's elbow and glaring into his eyes, "I'll resign! I'll take the path of Quadros," he went on fiercely, as though his threat might tremble all the world, "and resign! But Kennedy won't betray me. He's a decent man, after all. That's the difference between a sailor and an infantryman." León was now beaming shrewdly and had released his grip to pat Gavilán on the neck. "Kennedy's never stuck a bayonet in anybody."

And he shrugged off Gavilán's remark that someone had certainly stuck something into Adlai Stevenson after the Bay of Pigs debacle.

Finally, despite the unrest that racked Tinieblas, León decided to precede his visit to Palm Beach by ten days' vacation and booked passage on a flight to Nassau all for the evening of 22nd November.

Vice-President Bonifacio Aguado and Dr. Erasmo Sancudo, President of the Supreme Court of Justice, were with León in his state office at the Palace at 12:40 P.M. that day. In accord with the Constitution, Aguado would have to take the oath of office and assume temporary possession of the presidency, and the three men were about to move to the Salón Amarillo for the ceremony when León was informed of an urgent phone call from the United States Ambassador. He went to take it in his adjacent private study. When he reappeared, some seconds passed before Aguado and Sancudo recognized him: his shoulders drooped; his hands shook spasmodically; his features wriggled in an anarchy of tics.

"They've shot Kennedy," he said finally. "Head wound, or wounds; they're giving him last rites. Get yourself sworn in," he told Aguado. "You try making sense out of this shitheap world."

Now, neither Aguado nor Dr. Sancudo realized it, but León meant his statement as a resignation. When he shambled from his office, his left hand cupped over his forehead, he fully believed that he would never see the room again. He left the Palace by a side door and took his car, aiming for the airport and the first plane out, wherever it was headed, but when he'd followed Via Venezuela as far as the Alameda, the steering wheel pulled left under his hands like a dowsing rod. Thirty seconds later Dr. José Fuertes, the Minister of Health, clumped clubfooted out onto the porch of his mother's bungalow, where he had been lunching, and saw his half brother León's car careened opposite, two wheels on the curb, and León himself crawling toward him across the sidewalk. As he helped León up the steps, my

uncle Pepe had to remember the sweat-rank evenings of his childhood in La Cuenca, when León would come in shepherding Florencio Merluza.

Thus it happened that my father, León Fuertes, was at Rebeca's
house when the third prophecy was given to him. For twenty-four
hours León lay belly down with his nose hung over the edge of Rebeca's couch, staring at the floor. Then he turned over and for a second twenty-four hours lay belly up, staring at the ceiling. Then he sat
up and stared at the far wall for a third twenty-four hours. During
this time he was watched over by Soledad (who wanted him moved
to San Bruno Hospital, or at least seen by a physician) and Rebeca
(who held he would make it on his own and was best off where he
was, since bad publicity now might finish him), and visited intermit-
tently by Pepe (who cast the deciding vote with Rebeca, not because
he shared her faith in León's recuperative powers but because he
knew his country's history and remembered how Dr. Ildefonso Cornudo had become President of the Republic and was intriguing fran-
tically in hope of setting off the same chain reaction of resignations
in my father's cabinet as had occurred in Hildebrando Ladilla's). My
father was unable to influence the debate because the dispersed brain
circuits that made sense of his perceptions—a factory-installed analog computer superior in capacity (though similar in design) to earlier
and cheaper models standard on mammals, birds, and many other
creatures, even earthworms, apparently, since they can learn by trial
and error—had been overloaded till the breakers popped. León was
tombed in a hallucination far too slovenly to blame on next-world
meddling: a dark swirl of mud and a great noise of static. Just after
midday, however, on Monday, 25th November, 1963, he began de-
coding signals: the roughly triangular pattern ("Night on Mount
Pubis" would have been a good Rorschach response) produced by
sunlight refracted past Rebeca's porchside rosebush onto the wall
opposite him; the deep breathing of Soledad, who had dozed off in
an armchair; the steady rush of Rebeca's bath water. He had just
managed to orient himself when the large, glossy-black Japanese
radio, which Pepe had been carrying about with him since he first got
word of Kennedy's assassination and which he had neglected take
up from the coffee table after his morning visit, switched itself on. It
was a marvelous instrument, all studded with keen knobs and levers

such as one associates with the control panels of experimental aircraft and equipped with five bands (three of them shortwave), a pop-
up antenna, and a spring timing device that could send or cut off
juice to the transistors after whatever interval (up to three hours) the
proud owner wished. This last device switched the set on, and a station out of New York began replaying coverage of Kennedy's
progress through Dallas three days earlier. A moment passed before
León realized where the voice in English came from and what it was
describing. Then he listened, rapt and expectant, recalling a dictum
of Dr. Grillo's that in authentic tragedy suspense is heightened, not
diminished, if the audience has prior knowledge of the denouement.
But as the announcer brought Kennedy's motorcade into Dealey
Plaza, the broadcast modulated into Spanish.

León recognized the voice of his friend and early collaborator
Zofiel Viento (who sponsored his record store with a post-midnight
program of classical music on Radio Bahia), making explicatory
comments on the work just played: "Siegfried's Rhine journey" from
Götterddämmerung. Before León had time to wonder at this strange
confusion of hours, bands, and frequencies, Viento stopped in midsentence. There was a pause, a gasped *"Dios mio!"* and another
pause. Then, in the sterile monotone that sometimes comes to men
in shock, Viento announced:

"Senoras y senores, I have just received the following announcement from Civil Guard Headquarters: the President of the Republic
has been assassinated. Fellow Tinieblans, León Fuertes is dead."

Viento's voice broke then, and he sobbed an apology and promised
information later and, with a propriety he could scarcely have bet-
tered had he known the events beforehand and spent all day preparing for them in his music library, put on the next-programmed work:
Wagner's great funeral march for his murdered hero. León's limbs
cooled and stiffened. He tried to rise but could not move a millimeter.
Then, as the music swelled in the grave leitmotif of destiny accepted,
his tension melted and he fell into a gentle sleep which lasted but a
few instants but which pared all trouble from his heart.

Soledad's kiss woke him. She had been roused by the radio, which
was describing preparations for John Kennedy's funeral, and seeing
León with his eyes closed, breathing peacefully, she knew he had recovered. León embraced her, then held her back from him. How long

had he been there? What was happening in the country?

"It's Monday, and there's nothing new. The students are demon-strating at the campus. Tonight you'll be denounced publicly again in Cervantes."

"Something to do with . . .?" León gestured toward the radio.

"With you and him. They know about Palm Beach."

Then, without the slightest hesitation, León Fuertes accepted his destiny and, pausing only to call in to his mother that he was all right, rose and returned to the Palace and resumed the presidency of Tinieblas.

24. The Death of León Fuertes

FROM SHORTLY after midday on 25th November, 1963, when he chose his destiny, until shortly before midnight on 10th January, 1964, when he was plastic-bombed into the next world, my father León Fuertes lived in a manner altogether different from the other portion of his years. He seemed restored to his old self. He was, in fact, transfigured.

In the first place, the diverse personages he had fashioned and kept rigorously separate melted together. Each had passed easily for a whole man, though each was crafted for but a single aspect of our human situation. Now they combined into a unity. Each was fully present at every moment during my father's last six weeks and four days in this world. His last transformation integrated all those that went before.

León unveiled this new and final figure in the Plaza Cervantes on the night of his return to office. Professor Schwartztrauber had let slip during an interview that, among other matters of December busi-ness, John Kennedy had planned to entertain the President of Tinieblas, and when the phraselet reached our country, it incubated to a headline. This was swilled up in the collective mental maw of the United Young Paranoids at our national university and shot like a green mango through their collective mental bowel, getting an en-zyme bath of hate and anger, and suffering a tripe-change into some-thing foul and strange: Secret meeting! Sellout! Treachery! By nine P.M. Plaza Cervantes brimmed with such excreta.

By day Plaza Cervantes (Which lies along the north side of Avenida Bolívar some three hundred meters east of Plaza Inchado and the Presidential Palace) is an unprepossessing little square flanked by the Hotel Colón (occupied for one night in 1878 by Sarah Bernhardt and since then in decline) and the squat Church of San Geronimo (muraled in bird droppings after the style of Jackson Pollack), and containing a few stone benches, a covered bandstand, and an empty pedestal designed (but never destined) to bear a statue of Quixote. By night it *is* a place of magic. It is the open place in the midst of our city where people go to speak against those in power. Here Amado del Busto harangued the mob that overthrew Modesto Gusano. Here León Fuertes led a crowd in singing before the fall of Alejandro Sancudo. Here agitators, power freaks, and merchants of unrest have conscripted all the highest human aspirations in the service of the basest human lusts, and here authentic patriots have shackled ogre id in the dream of freedom. Even on tranquil nights, even now when—as during the dictatorship of General Epifanio Mojón—one doesn't hear a peep out of this country, the shadows of the bandstand teem with spirits. The shades of former orators visit here and congregate, along with those of men, Tinieblans and foreigners as well, whose names have been invoked here in the cause of liberty or license. On the night of 25th November, 1963, half the spirits of Resentment and Revenge were in attendance. They issued in a steady stream from the mouth of Manfredo Canino and rose tumbling in the air, lifted on the shouting of the crowd. Then a rippled whisper spread down from the steps of San Geronimo and slapped against Canino's peroration. The President of the Republic was standing all alone in the doorway of the church.

Canino stilled in midsentence and, with the others who were with him on the bandstand, stared at León in amazement.

"Don't stop for me, Manny," León called to him. "But when you've finished, I'd like to say a word or two."

Canino knew the crowd was his. Besides, the sight of León had flushed the remnant of his speech out of his mind. "Go ahead now!" he shouted. "I give you my permission! There he is, comrades! The traitor, Meestair Forts, in person!"

The crowd turned toward León, jeering and whistling. León smiled and nodded, as though acknowledging applause. Then he walked down toward them, but stopped at the rim of the square and got up on one of the stone benches. It was the first time a man holding public office had ever come to peak in Plaza Cervantes, and the last time too, at least as of this writing. Much better fora are available to men in power, and Cervantes is, by tradition, the rostrum of outsiders. In essence, though, that tradition remained unbroken, for when he began speaking León was not merely an outsider but an outcast.

His first words were stifled in catcalls, but he continued without shouting or losing his composure, and after a time those closest to him turned and shushed those farther off, and little by little the crowd stilled. Then he began again, thanking Canino for permitting him to speak and begging the crowd's pardon in advance, "since what I have to say may rob you of the delicious feelings of self-pity Manny gives you. I know how warm and wonderful it is to feel sorry for oneself. There was a time in my life when I made a career of it."

This brought shouts of insult and derision, but León smiled and held up his hand and said they needn't worry. He would only rob them temporarily. "In a short time you can go back to feeling yourselves betrayed, and calling me a traitor, and blaming me for all your discontents. Meantime I'll tell you of my dealings with John Kennedy. In preface, let me admit that as the thing turned out, I achieved nothing, not even the betrayal of our country, which, by the way, was never in my mind."

It was the first of many stories that he told that night, and he did not tell it exactly as I have in Chapter 22 above. As León, lawyer, had once pointed out, the truth lacks realism. My father retailed essential truth by packaging it in fiction. He scholared in the stacks of memory, gathering details; then lawyered them into a web that trapped the fancy of his listeners. He refused, for example, to sling Kennedy's feet up on a coffee table but posed him standing with one elbow on a marble mantelpiece chiseled from the Élysée Palace and masoned carefully into the tale. He gave Kennedy fine rolling cadences and florid metaphors, such as his listeners were accustomed to hear from politicians. He made the voice of León Fuertes quaver just a bit in trepidation, so that his listeners might identify with it and dream themselves face to face with the leader of a great power. He didn't have his President of Tinieblas bait his President of the United States, rubbing Kennedy's face in his own speech. Who would believe that?

What decent man would care to link himself with such conduct now that John Kennedy had been assassinated? No, León set his story one day earlier in time and made Kennedy's speech an outgrowth of his meeting with León Fuertes. Not that the León of the story could take much credit for it. The León of León's story did no more than bring the nature of the Day-Cornudo Treaty to Kennedy's attention, and Kennedy, out of his own nobility, perceived a wrong and said he'd try to right it. He pledged as much in his speech, but could make no specific reference to Day-Cornudo then, or in the communiqué, because he was not a dictator who ruled by fiat, but had to consult with others and work out ways and means. Thus León wove an illusion of reality and wrapped essential truth inside it, and he gave it to the people through the voice of León, artist.

The artist returned to León Fuertes that night after an exile of twenty-seven years, but now he was part of a new unity, and his instrument had timbres unknown to it in León's early life: the hypnotic mastery of León the Don Juan; the yielding anima of León, Riviera *femme fatale;* the protective tenderness of León, husband and father; the violence of León, warrior. All those tones glowed in my father's voice that night and, under its charm, the crowd forgot the pleasures of resentment and went over to him, while Canino and the others on the bandstand winced and shriveled, until they were no more than dwarfs, glaring at him over the railing. He finished the story with Kennedy's letter.

"You may be tempted now, as I was tempted, to feel sorry for yourselves, to feel betrayed by the universe. But the universe owes us nothing.[99] No one can say that had the meeting in Florida taken place, it would have produced all or even part of what you and I want. It's best to face the facts like grown-ups. The man is dead, and the whole effort came to nothing.

"It might have worked. It seemed the best approach to go directly to President Kennedy. I erred in not foreseeing that he might die. I should have. Who of us here can say for sure he'll be alive tomorrow?

"So, then, with that last thought in mind, and since you knew part of it already, I have come here and, with Manny Canino's kind permission, have told you the full story. Clearly, I made no error in keeping it to myself until tonight. It would have put your hopes up, and, as you see, it came to nothing, as things so often do."

He stepped down from the bench then and turned away, but the crowd called him and begged him not to leave.

"But this is Manny Canino's meeting," he protested, smiling. "You'll want to hear him and the other bright young men go on denouncing me as a traitor."

But Canino and his disciples had shrunk to the size of roaches and slipped through the cracks between the floorboards of the bandstand and disappeared.

Then León walked through the crowd to the center of the plaza and got up on the empty pedestal and sat down cross-legged on it and drew the people in toward him with his hands. And when those nearest him had sat down about him on the ground and the others gathered in, he began telling stories. They were stories out of the history of our country, stories of the discovery and conquest, the founding of cities and the cultivation of the land, the days of the Spanish colony and the gestures of independence and the birth of the republic. He told stories also of the days of his forebears Generals Bodega and Mojón and Luna, and stories of the civil wars, and of the time of the *bichos*. All were stories of wild dreams and ceaseless disappointments, of incredible achievements whose substance at once faded, of splendid porticoes of hope which opened on despair. Each was the story of some effort that had come to nothing, yet the people listening in the square in no way grew despondent, for as my father told these stories, the joy of struggle overweighed the grief of ultimate defeat. It was as though those gathered round him in the shadows were the last remnant of the nation, exiled and shipwrecked on an alien shore, and León Fuertes sat all night among them, passing them the memory of their community and, coded in it, the memory of all human community on this planet, past, present, and future, along the continuum of time. His face, bathed palely in the yellow glow of the bug-swarmed lamps around the bandstand, took on a parchment semblance of immense antiquity. His gestures grew ever less pronounced, till he sat motionless as an idol save for the almost imperceptible movements of his mouth. His voice, though, remained clear and youthful to the last.

Lastly, he told them the story of his ministry, why he had sought office in the first place and what he conceived to be the function of a leader and how he had tried and was still trying to preserve our tiny patrimony of good fortune. The story was, he said, as yet unfinished, yet there was little question of its ending. His effort too would no doubt come to nothing. It too would crumble, and leave nothing behind.

Here he was interrupted by shouts of "No!" He listened, motionless, then smiled and raised his hands.

"All right," he said, as to small children. "It may endure, and be something to build on."

With that, he got down stiffly and began to walk away, but the people nearest to him caught his sleeves and held him.

"No!" He shook his arms free. "Enough! You'd best start learning to get on without me!"

The people drew back, frightened, and stood staring at him.

Then he said he was sorry but he had no more stories for them.

"I'm sorry, but I have nothing left."

He took a step toward Avenida Bolívar, but then turned suddenly and held up both his hands. "Wait. I have a song left.

"Crazy country!" He laughed. "What can be said of a country where the President sits all night in a public park, telling stories? — Crazy President and crazy people! Even crazier if he should sing!

"There was a time, though, when I did not sing badly, and I feel like singing, crazy or not."

And so León lifted his face to the sky, which was paling now beyond the low church belfry, and holding his hands clenched by his sides sang the joyous, grieving song *"La Golandrina."* He sang it through in the *piano* tones that gifted tenors can lift to the last recesses of an opera house or stadium. Then he sang the last lines once again, in his full voice:

> *También yo estoy*
> *En la región perdido—*
> *Ay cielo santo!—*
> *Y sin poder volar.*

He turned then and walked through the people to Avenida Bolívar, and down it toward the Palace, and no one in the plaza moved or spoke till he was far away.

It were a pleasant task to say now that León was then miraculously restored to favor, but such was not the case. That took more than his performance in Plaza Cervantes. That took a bomb. Protest continued. Even those touched by his presence on that night entertained resentment for him during the next weeks. Canino still drew crowds. His immediate disciples were as closely bound to him as ever, and to these he added a new convert, of whom more in a few pages. But León's visit to Plaza Cervantes had not been in the nature of a campaign stop, and he made no special effort to curry favor with the country.

With the melding of his transformations in one human unity, my father found his life altered in another aspect: the hunger that had been the only common trait to all his personalities faded entirely. Although he knew his days were numbered—no doubt *because* he knew, because he had, in accepting his fate and returning to his ministry, chosen that they be brief—he did not seek phrase is Yeats's) to "ram them with the sun." He went about business and pleasure with as much energy and enthusiasm as ever, yet felt no tug of urgency. He was apt even to linger fondly on some trifle and find the universe in it.

There was for instance, the afternoon—18th or 19th December, as far as I can ascertain—when, as he and members of the Cabinet were lunching with the Costaguanan Foreign Minister (in town for discussions on the Central American Common Market), his daughter, Clara (then just ten years old), entered the dining room carrying her little inlaid wood jewel chest and seeking executive relief: she was invited to her cousin Alma's birthday; she wished to wear the medallion her uncle Pandolfo had brought her from Lourdes, but its gold chain was tangled up with every knickknack in the box. Nodding an excuse to his guests, President Fuertes pushed back his plate and dumped the jumble of baubles, beads, and bracelets onto the tablecloth before him. Then, smiling gravely to Clarita, he spread it gently with his fingers and, with the air of a surgeon, took up his clean dessert fork and began probing delicately.

"Here," he remarked without looking up, "is a concrete metaphor of good politics in action: unraveling a mess provoked by neglect and carelessness. Or"—he raised a strand of chain on a fork tine, then took it between his left thumb and forefinger and worked it through a twist of beads—"of science and creative art: bringing meaning, that is, order, out of an apparent chaos of occurrences."

"Why not follow Alexander?" suggested the Costaguanan, proffering his steak knife. "Surely a new chain can be found to hang the medal on."

My father looked up briefly and shook his head. "The military approach. Solve the problem by destroying it. Simplification via violence." He extracted an earring from the scrum and laid it beside his butter plate. "Brute force substituted for imagination. Crude and costly. justifiable only in the last resort." Jiggling gently, he freed the chain from a bracelet charm. "The aim the optimum"—he flicked the bracelet aside and began plucking at a rope of indian beads—"is to achieve order while preserving each diverse element. For example"—here he permitted himself to glance up for a moment—"we prefer the slow work of setting up a customs union to having one of our countries invade and conquer all the others."

Discoursing thus, he patiently undid the snares and tangles, and only when he had dropped the medal and its chain into Clarita's hand and accepted her kiss in payment did he turn back to state affairs.

Much less than pressing him, time slowed as it had done two decades earlier on Colle Belvedere. He felt the same awareness and vitality, but not the violence that had later left foul lees. He drew his breath in passionate detachment: his life had never seemed so sweet and precious, and yet he accepted its coming loss without anxiety. He was involved in the world, concerned for the welfare of his family and country, and yet he could face calmly the fact that they would have to get on without him. His one regret was that he ha not been able to achieve this mode of living earlier. His temptation was not to seek a postponement of his fate (e.g., by ringing himself with guards or by restricting his movements) but to teach his children something of his present attitude. He refused to puzzle or worry them with grave, solemn testaments—he felt neither grave nor solemn anyway—but he yielded to the extent of having his sons memorize two passages from Homer (*Iliad*, XVIII: 115-21; *Odyssey*, V: 221-24).

He was amazed at his state of mind. He had flashes of anger—some son of a whore was going to murder him!—and then recalled that long ago he had pardoned the agency of his death. He had moments of sadness, and then took stock as he had done on the night before he first went into battle. He had no ties now to any company of warriors, nor was he faced by an opposing company for which he might feel enmity, but he held the chief office in his commonwealth and struggled against forces of disorder. He was no longer free of obligations to people who depended on him and for whom he cared, but his responsibilities were the measure of his full use of life. More valuable men had died before and would die after him. He had no call to raise a fuss. And apart from these flashes and these moments—which, in any case, were few and brief—he felt inexplicably light-hearted. This might have made him feel indecorous had anyone else known what was in store for him. Condemned men were supposed to mope about with a long face or, if they had to smile, smile bitterly, and show proper respect for the Grim Reaper.

It was not until 6th January, 1964, that León understood the cause and nature of this gaiety. Tinieblas celebrates the Feast of the Epiphany, and since it fell on Monday that year, making a long weekend, León spent it at Medusa Beach with his family, as did his friend and beach house neighbor Carlos Gavilán. At about 3:00 P.M., then, on that most holy day, León Fuertes woke smiling from a dreamless siesta and spoke the word "Love."

Puzzled at this spontaneous utterance, he got up and pulled on a pair of shorts and stepped out on the empty terrace. As he felt the tropic sun embrace his shoulders, as his eyes "heard" the contrapuntal harmony of heat waves bowing saltato across glaring sand, and ocean blowing long, cool horn notes, he spoke the word "Love" again.

He was about to sit down and think about this when the puzzle fell in place of itself: he was filled with love. His life was suffused in love even as the beach and ocean were suffused in sunlight. It had been that way six weeks now.

He had known only one similar period: four weeks, twenty-seven years before. Since then he had felt love only for brief moments so rare he could recall them easily, as, for example, on Colle Belvedere when an unknown enemy died in his arms. He had taken joy in life. He had gone out passionately to a few people and to many actions. But he had scarcely felt selfless love. The activity or person had never been an end to him. Learning, art, sport, war, law, lechery had all been means to fill his hunger. Politics, the presidency of his country, had been a means to other means. And he had cherished his wife and family as means to his dream of order. His hunger for "more" had driven him to treat the world as a means, and that mode of life had sharpened his hunger.

León laughed, more in amusement than self-mockery, and strolled down the steps and out across the burning sand, concentrating on a measured pace against the pain in his soles. What an amazing way to live! Not that it was the worst. It had brought him a great deal of what was valuable, that is of joy and grief, proof that he was alive. It had not involved much selfless loving—four weeks and certain moments—but he'd got by well enough on that. If he'd cared to live differently, he would have. You couldn't accuse a man who'd walked across the Sahara Desert of lacking will to live the way he wished. His way of life had been one of the best! And yet his present way was much superior.

How, then, had he seized upon it? He hadn't; it had come to him. It had come to him when he stopped wanting "more." No, it had come to him *and* he'd stopped wanting "more" when he turned his will to flow with the world's current.

León stopped, nodding slowly. He'd reached moist sand, and his soles echoed his mind's relief in having solved the problem. Then he began to think of some of the things and people he loved now for themselves: a country, a tiny backwater country whose existence citizens of other lands approved because it gave them something to look down on; a people, all caprice, no staying power, who made him now their totem, now their sacrifice, who would have themselves a magic beast at all cost, rather than simply a man who tried his best; a ministry, twelve years of toil hung on an eyelash, ready to fall the moment he was gone, and the moment was approaching—, a wife who had never understood him for an instant; children who would never know him as a human being because they would never watch him grow old as they grew to man- and womanhood. León loved each and all without censure, as, without guilt, he loved the country he had done so little for, and the people whom he hadn't saved from themselves, and the ministry he hadn't built strongly enough, and the wife he'd never understood (unless just now he had begun to understand her), and the children he was going to abandon, and the friend he had betrayed, and the surrogate son he had made use of, and the surrogate daughter he had seduced. León loved each and all passionately.

Don Anselmo Chinche walrused from the surf and saw the President of the Republic standing some ten meters off, but as the President's chin was dipped into his chest hair—borne down, no doubt, by some burden of state—gave no greeting. León spotted him, however, out of the corner of his eye and looked up and called, "*Olá, Don 'Selmo! Buen día pa' la playa, no es cierto?*" Don Anselmo grinned like a child and tramped up to pass the time of day, and as he stood there babbling, salt water streaming down his flaccid chest onto his paunch, León felt love for him. When Don Anselmo Chinche went to meet his Maker—and it wouldn't be long now, León judged —when the Lord asked him what of any worth he'd done in life, all Don Anselmo would have to say for himself was that one night in 1947 he'd played a bridge hand decently. Yet León Fuertes loved him.

It was amazing, León thought as he disengaged himself politely and strolled on across the firm sand near the water's edge, his gaze aimed just before his toes, his hands clasped at his back. There was no end to it! If he loved old 'Selmo Chinche, he loved everything. His murderer? Christ! He would probably end up loving him too! And why not? The stupid whoreson turd was a key figure, vital to the whole process, and as important to the particle of it called León Fuertes as Dr. Azael Burlando. The latter's urge had flung him in the world; the former's would fling him out. As well an angry moron as an earthquake or a culture of flu bugs. León loved the world itself, which in its perversity had dragged him into it unasked and mocked him with possibilities and soon would push him out.

Twenty minutes later Bolívar Gavilán, the faithful Lilo, was granted an epiphany of León's love—though it brought him none of León's gaiety. 6th January, 1964, was, altogether, a trying day for Lilo. He spent the morning in dialectic combat on two fronts with the Ardilla brothers, Augustín and Tomás Aquino, who were home on vacation from studies in Spain and France respectively. Tomás, who later went to Chile as a consultant to Salvador Allende and disappeared after the latter's fall, was a communist. Augustín (now a monsignor somewhere in the Vatican) was preparing to enter the Society of Jesus. Although the brothers were completely opposed in ideology, they were identical in personality, displaying the most profound fanaticism imaginable. Lilo tried, after the

fashion of his idol, León Fuertes, to advance moderate positions
against them, but as their minds, like those of all true believers, were
sealed tight as a pharaonic tomb, he could make no headway whatsoever and succeeded only in appearing foolish to their younger sister
Pía, whom he loved to distraction. The struggle raged through lunch,
with Lilo assailed unmercifully from both left and right, smirked at
by Pía, and consoled mutely and unwelcomely by Juan de la Cruz
Ardilla, the former President of the Republic and a moderate's moderate, who was every day more convinced that his wife (God rest her
soul) had born him bastards. At length Lilo tossed in the sponge and
escaped with Pía, leaving the two brothers roaring at each other, and
their putative father downing his fourth brandy. But escape did not
bring case.

At seventeen, Pía Ardilla was the most accomplished little tease in
all Tinieblas and might, had she adopted the custom of fighter pilots,
have painted rows of broken hearts and swollen gonads on her
apple-smooth cheeks, her supple, delicately-downed midriff, and her
firm, pale-golden thighs. At nineteen, Lilo Gavilán was the oldest
virgin in the country, male or female, with the possible exception of
a few members of religious orders. This was due to no physical dis-
figurement or disability. Lilo was as handsome as his twin sister Loli
was beautiful, and as well furnished with testosterone as any other
fellow of his age. He nurtured an obsessive respect for what used to
be called "nice girls," however—having somehow got it in his head
that his idol, León Fuertes, took the same neochivalric attitude—and
was incapable of making lewd advances to them, or even of accepting those that they might make to him. That would seem to leave a
considerable portion of the female population fair game, but there
were further complications. First, in accord with our culture, Lilo
divided womankind into two camps: "nice girls" and whores. Second, he thought it unmanly to consort with the latter, for he had
somehow got it in his head that León Fuertes held this view. Actually,
both Lilo's misconceptions of León's attitude toward women were
understandable enough: Lilo had never met León, lecher. For these
misconceptions, Lilo was virginal. And for these misconceptions—
being otherwise in health and, hence, attracted sexually to Pía
Ardilla-Lilo was compelled to love her and, loving her, to think of
matrimony. At the same time Lilo knew that León Fuertes would

never think of matrimony if he were, like Lilo, still a student and unable to provide for a wife and family. Thus as Lilo and Pía walked hand in hand along the asphalt road behind the Ardilla beach house (she flirting gaily, he in a Keatsian dejection), as they turned onto the pitted gravel road that led to the deserted villa of the exiled ex-President A. Sancudo (she pausing to brush his forelock back with counterfeit tenderness, he smiling shyly in a dream of husbandhood), as they penetrated deeper into the tunnel of foliage which, after years of neglect, now enclosed the road (she slipping a pale-golden arm about his waist, he reciprocating with an arm somewhat lobstered by an uncustomary weekend in the sun), Lilo had, with the unwitting and yet crucial help of his hero, León Fuertes, worked himself into a textbook example of what theorists of schizophrenogenia have called a "double bind."

Pía, for her part, suffered no conflicts. She was swooping toward another kill. When she and Lilo had proceeded about fifty meters—this was, I judge, about the time when León Fuertes waded into the surf, dove through a breaking wave, emerged in the trough of a soft swell, and began pulling in a powerful crawl out around the jungled point separating the settled portion of Medusa Beach from the Sancudo villa—Pía stopped, turned, ran her fingers up under Lilo's T-shirt along the hollow of his back, and, smiling up at him, putting her glistening jube-jube tongue-point out through pouting lips, provoked him to what he honestly thought would be a chaste kiss. But Pía kissed with a lascivious expertise that the harlots of old Babylon may have aspired to yet probably never achieved. And Pía crushed her breasts against his breast, and touched her shorts against his tented trousers. For nearly a minute—long enough for León Fuertes to swim fifty meters—Lilo's principles were swamped in a flood of hormones. For the best part of that time he remained absolutely still, paralyzed by passion. For a few seconds more only his arms and hands moved, clutching at Pía's shoulders. Then, after what seemed an age, his hips and loins began to make a commonplace mammalian movement. But at the first suggestion of a thrust—no! at the mere intimation of a hump—Pía (whose timing was superb) leaped backward out of his arms and seared his naked face with blowtorch eyes.

"Disgusting animal!"

It's a near question which punished Lilo more severely, Pía's shriveling look and epithet or his own reviving principles. He had but one manner of reprieve from either: he proposed marriage.

In sympathy for Lilo, I shall not go into detail on what followed. It is enough to state baldly that Pía refused him, that she did not show him the courtesy of making her refusal angry (much less kind), that she laughed at him with the sort of total contempt for his impertinent presumption which (if one may be allowed a spot of anthropomorphism) females show to males among the mantids, and that she then stalked off, leaving him wandering in the gloomy wood, his groin engorged and his spirit utterly deflated.

He wandered then, and nearing the sea (whose breaking roar muffled his footfalls and his passage through the undergrowth), blundered upon a scene such as might have been put to canvas had Douanier Rousseau accepted a commission from the Baron de Charlus to paint a *Déjeuner sur l'herbe*. There was a clearing, no larger than a bed, all wreathed in luridly green fronds and walled about so densely by wild palms entwined with creepers that Lilo was almost in it when he saw it. Within, spotlit in sunlight, her flanks porcelain white against the deep tan of her limbs and the lush greenery about her, Lilo's twin sister, Loli, knelt above the reclining body and unreclining joint of León Fuertes. Gently she bent to lunch. Just as gently León took her head between his hands and, after a long moment, raised her, kissed her lovingly, turned her, and, still gently, mounted her—and with that Lilo Gavilán experienced what Dr. I. P. Pavlov called the "ultra-paradoxical phase" and Saint Paul called "conversion." In the space of seconds, without benefit of conscious thought, all his beliefs concerning León Fuertes were revised, all his attitudes reversed. Working at electronic speed, the analog computing instrument in Lilo's head rewired its own circuits, accepted the new data, processed them, and composed a print-out: León Fuertes was a traitor to his country and the human species; he had to be destroyed.

León and Loli then began to make some commonplace mammalian movements. Let them proceed in privacy; Lilo was no longer watching. Lilo was thrashing toward the gravel road. When he reached it, he ran along it till it met the asphalt. Then he ran the seven miles to the Pan American Highway, dropping to a dog trot when his wind flagged, but never stopping. When he reached the highway, he ran south along it until he was overtaken by a car with

four of his school chums in it. He accepted the lift but not their conversation. By nightfall he was beating on the door of a room (above
the Cantina Ronda) belonging to a barmaid whom Manfredo
Canino lived with and off.

When the door opened, Lilo pushed his way past the girl and told
Canino in an even voice he wished to join the movement. Canino
said he thought Lilo a spy. Lilo said he wasn't. Canino asked how he
meant to prove it. Lilo asked if murdering León Fuertes would be
sufficient proof.

Canino looked at Lilo carefully and nodded. He knew a true be-
liever when he saw one. "You'll never get away with it."

"Getting away doesn't really interest me."

León Fuertes was, of course, Canino's greatest enemy: ideologically
because he was the chief obstacle to revolution in Tinieblas; personally because he had shown Canino kindness and respect. Canino
wished Lilo the best of luck. Lilo said he preferred material support.
He didn't think a gun or knife safe weapons. Men had survived them.
He needed a bomb. (Lilo did not say that it was insufficient simply
to kill traitors like León, that they had to be obliterated, along with
those stupid enough to have been betrayed by them.) Canino allowed
himself to be persuaded. (He did not mention that bombs were ideologically sound as well as materially effective, that a bomb, being a
true socialist among weapons, might not discriminate between victim
and assassin, the last of whom would be an embarrassment to the
movement if taken live.)

It took three days for Canino to meet his connection in the Reservation and get some plastic explosive and a detonator. It took part
of another day for Tonio Burrón, who'd trained in Cuba, to make the
bomb. Burrón wanted to save part of the plastic for future need, but
Lilo insisted that he use every gram, and Canino supported him.

"Coño! There's enough here to blow up the whole country."

Lilo eyed the stuff and shook his head. "I doubt it. But if so, that's
all right too."

When León Fuertes left Loli Gavilán's apartment shortly before
midnight on Friday, 10th January, 1964, Lilo Gavilán was waiting
for him.

My father, León Fuertes, passed that day as follows: He rose from
dreamless sleep at 6:30 A.M., showered, shaved, dressed, and took

his coffee on the Palace terrace, undisturbed by any spirit, certainly not that of General Mojón. He then went to his private study and worked for two hours on an epic history of the Republic of Tinieblas which he had begun on New Year's Day. It pleased him that he would not live to finish the work, that he would perhaps not even finish the first chapter (the last turned out to be the case), for in such circumstances he could work purely, for the sole sake of research and composition, without fear of his motives' being fouled by thoughts of fame or profit. At 9:00 he put aside his pages (with the discoverer of Tinieblas still a lad in Cádiz), stepped to his state office, and took up the toil of government, which that day included a meeting with the Minister of Agriculture concerning a new Land Reform Bill scheduled for introduction when the Chamber reconvened the following week; a meeting with Carlitos Gavilán in which they drafted a letter to Lyndon Johnson about the Day-Cornudo Treaty; a meeting with a delegation of banana workers and their union's legal counsel, Dr. Garibaldi Saenz; and, from 11:15 A.M. till well past noon, the first Cabinet meeting of 1964 and the last of León Fuertes' Administration. He lunched and then siesta'd with his wife. I would give no details of the latter if I had them, but I can say that I left school early that afternoon to endure orthodontia, that I stopped "home" to leave my books, and that on entering my mother's room to get a kiss for courage, I found her snuggled up in very rumpled bedclothes, humming to herself. León then met for over two hours with the Progressive Party Members of the Chamber, explaining his legislative program to them in laborious detail, attempting to persuade them of its urgency, pleading humbly for their support, pledging to reward their loyalty, and promising to make life as difficult as he was able for any renegades. He spent the next ninety minutes in the library with M. Armand Bonsoir, the Cultural Attaché of the French Embassy and a most competent accompanist, preparing for a recital of Schumann *lieder* that he planned to give later that month on the anniversary of the day he met Soledad Piérida. He then had a light dinner *en famille* and took his children to a baseball game between the Cerveza Cortes Teutones and the Café Sancudo Zorros of the Tinieblan Winter League.

By the seventh inning he had become so disgusted with the meekness of the Teutones hitters, and so vocal in his disgust, that the author of this history (who at thirteen was, sadly, something of a wise guy) asked him rhetorically if he thought he could do better. He replied that, by God, he could—the gringo pitching for the Zorros was fast but had no curve and rarely threw his change-up; a hitter (one who wasn't seared, that was) could dig in on him and wait for the right pitch. The author remained unconvinced by this analysis (though it was accurate: according to the Saint Louis *Sporting News,* the pitcher in question, Clyde Hyde, did not develop a curve ball [and thus realize his potential excellence] until 1965). He said as much, but his attention was distracted by a fine shoe-string catch behind second base, and when he looked about, León had left the box. León was next seen conferring with the league president, Guillermo Gorgojo Lindo, in a box behind the Teutones' dugout. The Teutones' manager participated briefly in this meeting. Then León disappeared again. Ten minutes later, during the bottom of the eighth and after the Teutones had managed, at the cost of one out and with some aid and comfort from the Zorro infield, to put men on first and second, a player whose number was not on the scorecard and whose deeply-tilted cap brim concealed his face came up to pinch-hit. He spiked his feet up to his shoe tops in the batter's box, took a ball high and very tight, took a strike low on the outside corner, and then (as I may have mentioned an agony of chapters back) slapped a single wide of first into right field, bringing the tying run around and sending what proved to be the winning run to third. Only when a man was sent in to run for him was it announced over the PA system that he was León Fuertes. (The resulting roar moved pitcher Hyde to ask his Tfinieblan shortstop who the geezer was that got the hit; on learning that the geezer was President of the Republic, Hyde wiped his forehead and said, "Sheet! Way he dug in, if my duster'd gone where I aimed it, he'd be the ex-President by now!") Following the game, León drove his children back to the Palace, then went to Loli Cavilán's apartment.

The world has known no more (though it's been buffalo'd much less) about the assassination of León Fuertes than about the assassination of his coeval John Fitzgerald Kennedy. In the latter case the wrong man was framed, then murdered. In the former case the right man was taken for an innocent by-product victim and then mourned. No counterfeit assassin was ever officially passed to the Tinieblan people, but a wealth of candidates were privately advanced and a wealth of motives argued. The only point on which everyone agreed was that a time bomb was placed in León's car. Here, as elsewhere, everyone was wrong. The reader of this history now knows who and why. It remains only to tell how.

When León Fuertes, at peace with all the world and in the deepest state of body-soul well-being, exited the building in which Loli had her flat and, singing (sotto voce) an air by Schumann, entered has blue Wildebeest coupe, he discovered Lilo sitting rigid in the right-hand bucket. Lilo was holding on his lap a brown paper bag containing a kilogram of plastic explosive with an electric detonator embedded in it, a dry-cell battery, a simple switch, and the necessary wires. León greeted Lilo with surprise and pleasure; Lilo mumbled a reply. León asked if Lilo would like a lift home; Lilo nodded. León then started his car and began proceeding northwest at moderate speed along Via Venezuela.

"Traitors must die," announced Lilo.

"What?"

"You are a traitor." Lilo put his right hand into the paper bag.

"What's the matter, Lilo?" He stopped the car in the middle of the street opposite the Alameda.

"You have betrayed the toiling masses of our country and the workers of the world. You are the agent of the plutocrat oppressors and the warmongers." Lilo was weeping.

"You know about Loli and me?"

"You are a running dog of the warlords."

León grinned, as he always did at such jargon, then stopped at once: his son Lilo was suffering. He reached out his right hand and touched Lilo's neck affectionately. He smiled at Lilo in compassion.

"It is my duty and privilege to destroy you."

As the bomb went off the analog computing instrument in León's head printed out the following discrete nonverbal messages with the functional simultaneity of electronic speed: love for his son Lilo; compassion for his suffering and admiration for his courage; satisfaction for the way he, León, had spent his day; the warmth of Soledad's smile, of Schumann's music, of his children's laughter, of Loli's kiss; the sensation of moving easily with a great current; intense and cleansing pain.

By the time the few unvaporized chunks of his and Lilo's bodies—
the largest of which might have made an Ollie-Burger-fell back[100] to
the pavement, my father, León Fuertes, had told Lilo Gavilán (whose
spirit was as yet mingled with his) that he had pardoned him long
ago and that he loved him, and was asking Lilo for his pardon.

NOTES

1. *Our current simianisimo*
   General Genghis Manduco Torcido (b. 1930), Commander-in-Chief of the Tinieblan Civil Guard, self-chosen leader of the so-called Tinieblan Revolution (see note 10 below), and dictator of Tinieblas since 1970.

   Our neighbors in the United States, who through their taxes subsidize the Civil Guard and General Manduco, are wont to extol the virtues of barrackroorn despotism, a form of government they have never chosen to embrace themselves but which they think is just the thing for us. Like most of life's joys, however, it must be experienced to be appreciated. I am happy to devote a footnote to such an occurrence:

   One recent evening the American novelist Sig Heilanstalt, whom the U.S. Government has Fulbrighted to our National University, was driving in Ciudad Tinieblas. While lolling in the right-hand lane of Avenida Balboa, he chanced to flash his bearded grin into an official car occupied by two uniformed *guardias* and a mysterious shadow in mufti. Ten seconds and twenty yards later he was rammed to the curb, boarded by a sergeant, and ordered to Guard Headquarters. There he was hauled from his crumpled Puma and pistol-prodded up the steps into the guardroom, where with sweeping salute and crunch of boot heels the sergeant accused him to the duty officer of having laughed at members of the Tinieblan armed forces. The gravity of the charge was evident. According to Sig, he defended himself eloquently if ungrammatically, in the noble tradition of Nicola Sacco. I rather think he was stuttering with terror, but in any case he admits concluding with an abject apology to all present. This plea was but vaguely successful. He was not taken downstairs and beaten, but his silky conquistador's fringe was scissored to frightful asymmetry, and he was thrust roughly back into the street with a boot-punctuated warning to show more respect.

2. *His hell is a bureaucracy*
   This is not quite the place to present a general plan of the next world. My investigations have, however, proved the plans of others (e.g., Virgil's, Dante's) grossly inaccurate. In the first place, the "good" are not conspicu-

ously rewarded, the "bad" nowhere punished as such. A vast number of activities are offered, and the arriving spirit applies according to his preference. Vacancies are not always available, however; lengthy waits often occur. General Epifanio Mojón applied for Orgies and Abominations; it was, then as now, heavily oversubscribed. He languished for nearly a century, then applied for Politics, and was appointed to a committee that concocts schemes for projection into the minds of earthly tyrants. He is a good deal happier than he expected to be but complains of overwork.

3. General Mojón's procurer

Theopompos Anaxagoras Canelopulos (1819-1867), an Alexandrine Greek was for some years engaged in the Afro-Arabian slave trade. He emigrated to the Western Hemisphere in I 851, after running afoul of the British consul at Zanzibar. Learning that General Mojón was seeking an experienced procurer, he accepted the post before learning that it was contingent upon his being gelded. I met him first in May, 1971, when he paid me an unsolicited visit featuring a color-slide lecture on his investiture (performed in the basement of the Tinieblan Presidential Palace by General Mojón's Mexican aidede-camp). I did not enjoy the interview, but one must not let terror retard the advancement of knowledge. When I began doing research for this dissertation, I consulted Canelopulos in hope of fleshing out the meager record on Raquel Fuertes. I found him an enthusiastic though somewhat hysterical informant.

4. Procedure

This is the place for me to say a few words about my research procedure, which consists mainly in communication with the so-called "dead."

True science refuses to dismiss those phenomena it cannot yet explain, but with the rise of scientism this perfectly natural form of communication has been cruelly discredited, so that serious thinkers have, for the most part, neglected it, abandoning the field to charlatans. (In this regard, I am reminded of an incident in the home of Doña Reina de Abeja, an amateuse of the occult, who some years ago brought a medium from Duluth, Minnesota, for the delectation of her cronies. The séance was held in Don Lorenzo Abeja's thick-curtained cardroom. Lights were doused and candles lit. Dr. Rickenhouse withdrew to the bathroom, whence the spirits then emerged. Doña Rosario Lergo de Cristal requested an interview with her brother Inocencio, who in this life scarcely spoke Spanish, much less any foreign tongue, yet when his supposed spirit clomped from the John, he spoke nothing but English, and that with a ringing Midwest twang. Doña Rosario was entirely taken in, sobbed hysterically, and attempted to embrace her "brother," who faded canward in great haste, but given the frequency of this sort of crude bamboozlement, it is understandable that minds less festered by the will to believe doubt Dr. Rickenhouse and ilk, and the very possibility of conversing with the departed.)

Now, the truth is that the "dead"—and in these notes I put the word in quote marks to cleanse it of taints of finality—can talk to us and we to them, though as with everything else, some people are better at it than others. I have a gift for such communication. When I was but five, my uncle Nicolas Fuertes, who was shot by U.S. Marines in Nicaragua in 1932, used to visit me while I was supposed to be napping and entertain me with tales of Augusto Sandino and his *guerrilleros*. My love of history was born then, in an airless alcove swaddled from the sunlight by drapes the color of dried blood and strewn with odd pieces from my brother, Carlos's, Erector Set, but my uncle's visits ceased abruptly after I recounted to my parents the description he had given me of a particularly bloody raid on Jinotega and my mother, with some butterflying glances at my father, decreed that from then on I would siesta with my baby sister, Clara, and her nurse. There followed a period during which my parents chuckled about "Camilo's vivid imagination" and insipidly compared my conversations with my uncle Nicolas to the invisible playmates Carlos had invented at age four. Under this pressure even I began to think I'd been imagining things. Thus parents, in their eagerness to ground a child in one reality, can blind and deafen him to others.

My gift reasserted itself in adolescence. Uncle Nicolas resumed his visits. Other spirits came. Later, after her "death," my mother would drop by, sometimes in sleep but often when I sat among my books. I would feel her presence and look up to her soft, sad smile. No one need ever be lost to us.

"I'm glad you're studying, Camilo," she'd say to me. "Your father puts great store in learning and is proud of you."

"And you, Mamá? Are you happy now?"

"I'm happy when I can be with him. He gives recitals for us now and then, and they allow me a few minutes with him in his dressing room. And I'm happy when I visit you and Carlos and Clarita, though they look right through me and never hear my voice."

"It's not their fault, Mamá."

"I know. But it's so lonely waiting. I've applied for Love, you know, and vacancies come up so rarely. It's lonely waiting, but Love's really the only thing I want."

Other "dead" would visit me as well, men and women out of the times I studied. Like every other form of communication, one has to be prepared to receive it. One has to listen. One can't allow oneself to be distracted by noise. Most people's receiving apparatus is so clotted with the noise of here and now no other message can get through. And, obviously, one has to know the language of one's visitor.

While I was an undergraduate, after I had resolved to devote my life to history, I began honing my gift into a research tool. The general advantages are self-evident: the vast majority of witnesses to a historical event do not put their experiences in writing, and even if one finds documents to work with, one cannot cross-question them. Such a tool seemed, besides, particularly valuable, for I planned to specialize in the history of my country. There are no proper archives in Tinieblas. Few Tinieblans write memoirs; none publish their letters. Tinieblas has no tradition of independent journalism. All newspapers are now run by the state, while before the advent of our current tyranny, each was the creature of some interested faction and its reports no more reliable than the yelping of wild dogs. More, since General Manduco took over, Tinieblans have become reluctant to talk about anything more controversial than the weather. The conventional techniques of scholarly investigation simply will not work here.

At first, like many of my contemporaries who have gifts or believe they have them, I experimented with drugs. The most effective turned out to be a plant called *flor de sueño,* which, as far as I know, grows only on the Island of Mituco in Tinieblas and which may be taken in infusion, but drugs ultimately proved disappointing. Spirits came, but I was unable to choose them, or to control them once they showed up. As in the case of Canelopulos's first visit, they would, as it were, take the bit in their teeth and tell and show me things I didn't care to know. I learned the hard way that life admits no shortcuts to any worthwhile goal. I gave drugs up and, in time, perfected the following technique:

I abstain for at least one week from sexual activity. I fast for at least twelve hours. At dusk I isolate myself, assume an attitude of poised repose (the lotus position, for example), and come to complete immobility. As my heartbeat and respiration slow, I concentrate on the spirit I wish to interview. If he does not respond I am almost always able to reach someone close to him. Unsought spirits remain aloof while I am actively seeking others, but this procedure does not dissuade them from visiting me on their own at other times. Much the reverse: my contact with the next world grows ever closer.

At seven P.M. on 7th March, 1973, then, I returned to our apartment on Barracuda Street in Sunburst, Florida, and shut myself in the spare bedroom, which, since my wife and I were not as yet sleeping in separate rooms, I used as a study. I turned out the light, lit a candle, placed it on the floor, sat down before it, twined my legs, and began concentrating on the gross Greek whose emasculation had so terrified me two years earlier. After what seemed a very short period—it is impossible to judge the passage of time when summoning spirits—Canelopulos's fat jowls and fleshy dugs appeared before me. I admonished him not to bother me anymore about his eunuchizing but to answer my questions, and in the course of that night he gave me the facts concerning Raquel Fuertes related in text above.

5. She went after him

The zeal with which our young women pursue political figures is proverbial in Tinieblas. It is no more irrational, however, and perhaps a wee bit more decorous, than your gringa's propensity to throw herself at rock musicians, pop novelists, and other purveyors of pseudo-artistic blare.

With regard to the indecorous irrationality of North American females, I submit the following incident, which took place during the research for this chapter:

I conversed with Rosenda Fuertes at Sunburst during the night of 11th—12th March, 1973, an interview in which she gave details of her connection with General Luna and also furnished in formation valuable in the composition of Chapter 2 of this essay. But General Luna declined to answer my astralograms. I TWX'd him strongly and repeatedly from dusk till nearly dawn on 14th-15th March, but raised only the perforated ghost of Nicademo Lágrimas, who, since he had applied successfully for Resentment and Revenge, retained his bullet holes. Then, at 5:17 A.M., when I was on the point of reaching General Luna, my wife, Elizabeth, appeared in his stead, slippered and dressing-gowned, holding our Westclox Baby Ben.

Had I any idea what time it was?

I had not, and was incapable of speech in any case, with every kilowatt of my brainpower beamed into the next world.

Didn't I hear her?

I did, unfortunately, but was striving not to let that distract me.

If I didn't answer, she would scream.

I didn't, and her scream woke everyone in the building.

Did I hear her now? Did I know she was here now? Should she scream again?

I was trying to mouth an answer when she decided she should.

Well? Well? Well? Was I satisfied? Would I come to bed now? Would I show her some attention now?

"Of course, darling." I smiled sarcastically through the shattered fragments of my trance. "How very foolish of me to waste my time in scholarly research when I might be tending a madwoman."

"Research!" She threw the clock at me. I ducked it adroitly, rather a feat of agility from the lotus position. It hit the wall behind me and rebounded past my knee, wailing with alarm and establishing the time of the event for future investigators.

"You are insane, Camilo!" The throw had popped her right breast out of her nightgown so that she resembled Liberty leading the people. "You're out of your mind. Talking to spirits! Why don't you screw them? That's what I think you do! I think you stay up all night playing with yourself and pretend you're screwing spirits. Your research! Your dissertation! Your goddamn dissertation and your goddamn father! The great man! The martyred hero! I bet he was a queer just like you!"

I am ashamed to admit that at this point I lost my self-control. In extenuation I can plead that I had been engaged all night in a difficult and frustrating investigation and that the concentration demanded by communion with spirits stretches the nerves to great tension. I cannot recall exactly what I said or did during the next few moments, but when I was brought to myself by an intense pummeling at our front door (occasioned, I soon learned, by a policeman's night stick), I was clutching Liz's throat and howling: "I AM A SCHOLAR, YOU IGNORANT GRINGA BITCH! MY WORK IS THE DIFFERENCE BETWEEN MEN AND MONKEYS! YOU WILL LEARN TO RESPECT IT OR DIE!"

6. *A balding gentleman in black velvet*

One Wednesday evening in October, 1970, while I was still an undergraduate and at a time when the seeds of this essay had scarcely begun incubating in my brain, I decided to seek ease of flesh in the company of my cousin (mother's sister's daughter) Adana Avispa, who was attending Thornchasm College in Leaping Manor, New York. I bribed a lift from a classmate and casual acquaintance, Noel Whitbread II (or perhaps III), by arranging for Adana to get him a date, and en route developed the following simple plan of operation: I would install our foursome in the cocktail lounge of the Playtime Spa Hotel off the thruway; when we were two-thirds through our first round of drinks, I would disengage from the table, feint toward the men's room, countermarch swiftly to the reception desk, secure a base upstairs, and be back before the conversation faltered; once I had advised Adana that there was a bed waiting, one that, for a quarter, could be induced to vibrate along with us, hormones would do the rest.

But the best schemed lays gang aft a-gley. In the very dorm waiting room where we collected them—a barren veldt of frayed carpet vultured with an oil portrait of the foundress, the girls made their own dispositions. Whitbread, an overmuscled lacrosse player with a US prime sirloin brain, possessed charms soothing to the female breast. (He was, in fact, the model for the *jeune premier* of a film script and novel seagulled by his faculty adviser from themes dumped off the stern of *Cosmopolitan*. The author drained his whole thimbleful of imagination finding his hero a new name, sport, and university, but his soul congrued in triteness with the public's, to the immense enrichment of his producer, his publisher, and himself. Money is when you never have to say you're sorry.) Adana, who, unlike me, had never seen Whitbread in the shower, drew a false analogy from his thick and ruddy neck and resolved to have him. Meantime, the tall, tawny blonde booked for him was (more perceptively) drawn to me. They worked it all out in a quick whisper, and when we reached his Exterminator R/T, even Whitbread realized the switch was on. Adana lynxed into the right-hand bucket and began fondling the glans of the gearshift; her friend dragged me into the back. That scrapped my predictable pounce with Adana, but I was not annoyed. Your true Tnieblan would rather buy lottery than bonds—not, as one might imagine, because the return can be so much grander, but just for the suspense of the draw.

Ritual reconnaissance was then conducted at a roadhouse cocktail bar, across its dance floor, and in the car. I discovered that my companion's name was Elizabeth Cleaver, that she was majoring in English literature, that she eschewed brassieres (this is all germane, Professor Lilywhite) and had healthy Bartholins. Our pairings—determined, let the record show, without my participation—were deemed acceptable. Liz and Adana marched chastely into their dorm precisely at midnight. Twelve minutes thereafter Whitbread and I sneaked in through a fire door opened by the girls. (Romantic Sig would, doubtless, have us scrambling up the ivy and through a moon-drenched casement, but I am constrained to historical accuracy.) A moment later Liz bolted the door to her cubicle behind the two of us.

And straightaway grew nervous, turned her mouth away, asked me if I had anything to smoke. I hadn't, but there happened to be a tea bag of dried *flor de sueño* blossoms in my watch pocket. It acts slowly and, unlike cannabis, does not particularly banish inhibitions, vestigial Puritanism, fear of poor performance, etc., but wanting somehow to dispel her tension and counting on a placebo effect, I used her electric hot plate to brew us an infusion. We sipped this quickly from a Princeton beer mug which we passed back and forth, I perched on the straight chair beside her book-strewn desk, she cross-legged on her narrow bed beneath her *art nouveau* peace poster. Since I had been well primed since morning, since she imagined a relaxing glow the drug does not confer, since we were both young and sound, attracted to each other, and fresh from an hour's fumbling in the back of Whitbread's car, we were soon tearing at each other's lips and clothing. When I entered her, she had just time to assure me she was on the pill before commencing a grand clasping come that gurgled on through the some ninety seconds it took me to catch up. As in the Elizabethan theater, we proceeded through acts two, three, four, and five without intermission. Then (I approach the point, good Dr. Grimes), as we lay tumbled in the wake of love, side by side, her head on my left shoulder, her right leg over my left thigh, both gazing at the ceiling (spotlit by the yellow circle from her study lamp), the drug kicked in.

Liz, I learned later, had a Shakespeare quiz scheduled for the morning; she was no doubt unconsciously preoccupied by it. I have never been far from Tinieblas in my inmost thoughts. Our souls were still dueting in the receding echoes of shared pleasure. We were never closer, though we have been love and torment to each other for almost four years, wife and husband for almost three. This is how I explain our blended vision of the past. The circle on the ceiling fuzzed like a TV screen, then focused on the London tavern scene described in text above. I recognized the poet from his portraits but (I am ashamed to admit) had to ask Liz later who Prosper was. Liz knew the boatswain for one of Drake's men but was bewildered as to what part of the world he was storying.

Together, then, we glimpsed the incident that links Shakespeare to Tinieblas, binds Mituco up with Prospero's strange island, stitches the fabric of my father's life onto the stuff of dreams, and melds my history with art's insubstantial pageant. I could never have accomplished that piece of research on my own, and I shall love Liz always for her help with it. This I vow firmly, though it is past two in the morning and the bitch is still not home.

7. Teachers hired in Europe

Among them the symbolist poet Jacinthe Malhaleine, who spent three years on Mituco and remembered it in three lines (518-520) of his self-portrait in verse, "Orages":

> Ensuite, je fit un bel exil
> Tout mariné de rêves subtils
> Au paradis des crocodiles.

It is the round-nosed caiman, of course (not the rhyming Egyptian crocodile), that abounds in Mituco and many other regions of Tinieblas and is our heraldic national animal. This slimed and indolent beast lacks the majesty of Britain's lion and the alert intelligence of France's cock, but (poaching gringos be warned) has a heavy tail, and most sharp teeth, and snapping jaws which crush and maim and kill.

8. Rebeca

The principal source for this and the following three chapters is Rebeca Fuertes herself. I heard expurgated versions of her autobiography when, as a child, I would sit with her in her red-roofed bungalow beside the Alameda park while my brother, Carlos, romped on the ball field. My grandmother would receive me like any other gentleman caller, nodding me to the wicker chair beside her hide-backed rocker, having her maid serve me a glass of *chicha de tamarindo,* inquiring after my family, and then interrupting my reply with research of lost time. I knew her as a blobbish ancient dame with sagging jowls who sprawled kimono'd in a rocker scuffling her sandals on the floor tiles, but her eyes, like jewels found in a ruin, made credible her claim to vanished splendor, while her stories, like those of Scheherazade, were entrancing, even in a children's edition. She lived well into her eighty-eighth year, long enough to see two sons elected president, one assassinated, the other impeached, and recaptured the past in the final hour of the uremia that killed her. The delirium of her illness repealed six decades and transformed her hospital bed with its debris of tubes and needles into a divan in a brothel of Tsinan. She took me for some rich lover, and sighed with such sweet languor, "*Amène-moi en Europe; je te ferai heureux,*" that I learned once and for all that the main substance of our life is memory. In that moment I conceived this history.

Since her "death" my grandmother has visited me some twelve or fifteen times, clarifying many details of her own life and my father's. Like him, she has been accepted for Performing Arts and advanced to stellar roles. They are, in fact, now trying to arrange a performance of Gounod's *Faust* in which he will sing the lead and she dance the adagio in the fifth act ballet.

I have resolved to compose two chapters of this dissertation every month, and I have begun those dealing with my grandmother's life on schedule. Not without difficulties, however, thanks to my dear wife. Oh, no, prying examiners! You will get no details. This is not one of Siggy's novels, all sloshed with overflowing ordure from the author's private life. I mention difficulties merely to document my scholarly dedication. But I should ask the skeptic—and there are always skeptics, clods who grunt smugly as if to say, "He was probably to blame anyway"—whether it is unreasonable for a man to question a wife who returns from the movies a full four hours after the film has ended; whether it is abnormal for such a man to wax a bit annoyed, not to say furious, when such a wife, far from responding to polite inquiry, flounces by without a glance and, humming gaily, bolts herself in her bedroom; whether it is truly reprehensible for that man to kick the door in, splintering the panel and tearing the bolt screws from the molding; and whether it is fair for the wife, upon observing that, in the process, he has gashed his ankle cruelly, to cackle in glee instead of showing sympathy. Does Toynbee have to bear this? Was Gibbon thus tormented? Did Tacitus have his repose mangled in brawling? Was Thucydides forced to work with an aching heart and a throbbing ankle? I doubt it. But I too have been chosen for a bringer of order. I too accept that fate. And I shall make my history despite all interference and all obstacles.

9. *Gauguin and L'Isle-Adam*

The gentlemen with whom Don Patricio Garza associated in *Belle Époque* Paris need no introduction. The ladies shared the fate of the boatswain mentioned in Chapter 1 in that they served as raw material for a verbal universe-maker, in their case Marcel Proust. I have this on the authority of my wife, Elizabeth Cleaver Fuertes, B.A., whose Thornchasm College senior seminar (Comp. Lit. 414) provided a kind of scorecard with the "real life" equivalents of Proust's personages. Such information is, of course, about as valuable for an understanding of *Á la recherche du temps perdu* as, say, the balance sheet of the firm that milled the paper for the Pléiade edition, but at least it comes in handy here. A more polluting effusion from the seminar is a questionnaire supposedly elaborated by Proust as an aid to constructing characters. Reborn as a parlor game, it contributed to the difficulties that I am presently enduring, that I have hinted at already in note 8, and that my examiners must know more of if they are to arrive at a sentient evaluation of this dissertation.

I completed my course work at Sunburst at the end of quarter I, 1973-1974, in other words during the second week in December, 1973. It remained for me to write this dissertation, and as the cost of living is lower and the surroundings more favorable for research in Tinieblas than in Florida, my wife and I came here at once. Barely were we settled in when she informed me that she was having some friends over. Where she had got friends from I could not imagine. I have no friends. It turned out that she referred to people she had met at the Instituto Tinieblino-Norteamericano, a cultural center supported by the United States Information Service, where she had found work teaching English. She managed to fill out rattan set, six aluminum chairs kidnapped from the dinette, and a good portion of out living room floor with them. Most of the names, faces, and affectations have, happily, faded from my memory, but I recall a Mr. Pismire, who had something to do with the administration of the Instituto, his companion, a stridently undeodorized young Frenchwoman, and a hairdresser student of Liz's who turned out to be catamite to one of General Manduco's bodyguards. The star attraction was the novelist Sig Heilanstalt, who was about to take up his Fulbright duties at the National University. I don't know if Liz invited him personally or if Pismire brought him, but he sprawled on the chaise like the entrails the old Teutons hung on fir trees, stroking his beard and soaking up attention. At about eleven he made as if to rise; I smiled for the first time in the evening, and dear Liz announced that she knew a "fun game." She dashed to her bedroom and returned with a pair of mimeographed sheets.

"It's Proust's questionnaire. Do you know it, Sig?"

"No. What is it? A test for latent heterosexuality?"

Ha ha's all around, and a giggle from the hairdresser.

"It might do that. It reveals character. We used to play it at college." She flung her best smile into his ego's gaping maw. "Would you like to play?"

"Why not? There are no reporters present."

The sycophant chorus howled, "Yes!"

"Okay. Number one: 'What for you is the depth of misery?'"

"Not being recognized by a headwaiter."

"'Where would you like to live?'"

"In Ringsend, with a red-headed whore."

"Where is zat?" asked the French girl.

"Joyce," said Liz.

"No. His pal Gogarty." Sig brogued to declaim:

> "I will live in Ringsend
> With a red-headed whore,
> And the fan-light gone in
> Where it lights the hall-door;
> And listen each night
> For her querulous shout,
> As at last she streels in
> And the pubs empty out."

"Bravo!" cried Mr. Pismire.

"I ration myself to one use of the verb 'streel' in each novel."

"Number three," said Liz: "'For which fault have you the greatest indulgence?'"

"Unchastity." He looked steadily at her. "If that's still considered a fault."

Liz looked quickly back to her paper. "'Who is your favorite fictional character?'"

"Carlo Snyde, news photographer and master of sang-froid. I last left him in the Sinai, excising the chastity of an Israeli girl corporal during an Egyptian counterattack. I may call the book *Blood and Sand.*"

Here, as after most of Sig's answers, there was copious congratulatory laughter.

"'Your favorite historical personage?'"

"Rasputin."

"'Which women are your heroines in real life?'"

"Christine Keeler and Mandy Rice-Davies. Are you old enough to remember them?"

"Who they are?" asked the hairdresser.

"*Un par de putas británicas,*" answered I.

"Oh, no!" moaned Sig. "Much more than just whores. They put the English-speaking world back into the grand tradition of *Fotzepolitik.*"

"The Profumo case, right?" Liz was sitting up like a spaniel.

"Right. Caught in *fragrante!*" Sig guffawed his puny pun; Liz yelped ecstatically.

"Number seven: 'Which women do you prefer in works of fiction?'"

"Isolde, Medea, Circe; witches and bitches all."

"Do you believe in witchcraft?" I asked.

"Is that on the questionnaire?"

"No," said Liz.

"I'll answer anyway: I've met a few women who could cast a spell and was married to one who could raise the devil."

"I'd like to hear her side of the story," said Liz.

"She threatens to tell it to *Ms.* whenever I delay with a maintenance check."

"Do you have any children?"

"I will answer only what Proust put down."

"All right. 'What quality do you prefer in a man, in a woman?'"

"Energy in a man, affection in a woman, absence in a fairy, and conversion in a dyke."

"'What is your favorite virtue?'"

"Impatience. Impatience is a good south wind that winnoweth the bullshit out of life."

"'Your favorite occupation?'"

"Careless love."

"'Who would you have liked to be?'"

"Errol Flynn. I had the privilege to know him slightly on Mallorca nineteen years ago, when he was already over the hill and I about to start climbing. He was a man entirely without frontal lobes and hence inordinately happy."

"'What is the principal trait of your character?'"

"Impatience."

"'What do you most appreciate in your friends?'"

"Patience."

"'What is your principal defect?'"

"The compulsion to put words on paper, which robs me of much time for careless love."

"'What is the dream which you would most like to realize?'"

"Continued popular acclaim, followed closely by immortality."

"You believe in immortality, then?" I asked. The man, after all, might not be completely worthless.

"In the sense of being remembered, in Stendhal's sense of being read in a hundred years. I don't want to sound more presumptuous than necessary. We were speaking of dreams."

"You don't believe in another life, then?"

"No. Do you?"

"With me, Mr. Heilanstalt, it's not a matter of belief. It's a matter of concrete—"

"Camilo! We're playing a game."

"Play on, Liz. Play on, then, by all means."

"I just don't think we should go off on that tangent."

"I perfectly agree. Play on."

"All right. Where was I?" She ruffled the sheets nervously. "All right. Here. 'What for you would be the greatest unhappiness?'"

"To be out of print."

"'If you weren't a person, what would you like to be?'"

"Ridiculous question! Did Proust write that? A bidet, then. Or a girl's bicycle seat."

"*Qué crudo!*" squealed the hairdresser.

"At least I didn't say a boy's seat."

"'What is your favorite color?'"

"Have none."

"Do you want to stop playing?"

He smiled and shook his head. "No, dear. I love to play."

"'What is your favorite flower?'"

"Rose of Washington Square."

"'Bird?'"

"The cuckoo." He managed not to look my way.

"Which are your favorite prose authors?'"

"Scheherazade and Rabelais."

"'Poets?'"

"Homer and Homer. There are two, you know."

"'Who are your present-day real-life heroes?'"

"General Genghis Manduco. When in Rome . . ." (Sig changed his mind soon afterward. See note l.)

"'Who are your heroines in history?'"

"Joan of Arc and Dido. Each a terrific piece of ash." The last phrase was partially crushed in Siggy's giggle.

"'What names do you prefer?'"

"Siegfried and Sieglinde."

"'What do you most detest?'"

"An unresponsive woman." He glowed Lizward; Liz glowed back. Nothing to detest there.

"'What military deed do you most admire?'"

"The Battle of the Little Bighorn."

"'Which natural gift would you most like to possess?'"

"Personal magnetism."

"'What is the present state of your personality and spirit?'"

"Magnetic."

"'How would you like to die?'"

"Ha ha! In the saddle, like John Garfield."

"How is zat?"

"*En baisant, ma chére. En baisant.*"

"'If you had to choose a personal motto, what would it be?'"

"Every man for himself."

"That's all."

"And my character, or lack of it, has been revealed."

"I guess so."

He leaned back and clasped his hands behind his head. "Well, dear. If you've any other games to play, just let me know."

10. So-called revolution

Alejandro Sancudo (born 1900, President of Tinieblas 1930, 1940-1942, 1948-1952, 1970) took office as constitutional President of the Republic on 1st June, 1970, after a campaign in which his supporters assured the nation that the lunacy that had led to his being deposed three times was now entirely mellowed from his mind. His first official act was to install his barber as Commander of the Presidential Guard, an appointment based more on loyalty—the fellow held a razor to Sancudo's throat each morning, after all—than on ability or experience. He then began to purge the civil service down to the last charwoman and, more importantly, to geld the Civil Guard. Plans were made, and cackled over with excessive glee by cronies of the President's, to dispatch key officers to unsalaried attachéships in obscure and distant lands. A commission was formed to draft blueprints for converting the Officers' Club into a music-drama conservatory—not a bad idea so far as national priorities went but one unpopular with the Guard. Then, on 8th June, 1970, General Narses Puñete, who had been promised reappointment as Guard Commandant, was summoned to the Presidential Palace and presented with a retirement order and a ticket to Miami. Puñete accepted both, but that evening, while President Sancudo was at the movies (the film was Pasolini's *Oedipus*), troops led by a group of junior officers occupied the ministries, the radio and television stations, the offices of the Compañía Interplanetaria de Telecommunications, and, of course, the Palace (which Sancudo's barber surrendered without a fight), imprisoned a great number of Sancudo's supporters (including his daughter-in-law, the film star Elena Delfi), and threw the President out of office for the fourth time in his long and lively career.

Among the officers who directed this coup the least distinguished was a forty-year-old major named Genghis Manduco. I do not know how he managed in the succeeding weeks to make himself master of his colleagues and, hence, the country, but it is more than clear that the takeover was not attempted for any of the vaguely noble purposes with which the term "revolution" is sometimes coupled. Manduco and company acted to save their salaries, their status, and their club. Having thieved the state from a freely elected, constitutionally anointed (if mentally unbalanced) President, they chose to justify their theft—and this may have been Manduco's contribution—by adopting the modish title of "revolutionaries." Had they stopped there, had they contented themselves with normal rations of graft and power, they would have been no worse than Sancudo. Unfortunately, they began to justify their justification. Of the changes General Manduco has wrought in our country, his new traffic plan for the capital has proved successful. Against this benefit one must, however, weigh the abolishment of party politics (our national pastime—see note 97), the suppression of the rights of assembly, expression, and habeas corpus, and the establishment of torture, exile, and official murder as means of persuading people that the general has their interests at heart. Despite all his efforts, General Manduco has not yet made Tinieblas over to a paradise, though we have been told so on numerous windy occasions, the one in question being 8th June, 1973, the third anniversary of Manduco's sneak to power.

By "party given by General Manduco" I do not mean the huge, public genuflection arranged in Bolívar Plaza for the morning of the 8th. For this the country was shut down; public employees were mobilized (those who did not attend were fired); schoolchildren were taught a song called "Genghis Will Save Us" and paraded, chanting, by their teachers; peasants were dragooned from the fields of the interior and bussed in for the show; gigantic portraits of the "Leader" were prepared and draped about the city; and an immense reviewing stand was constructed from which Manduco, his worries calmed by whiskey and his body swaddled in a bulletproof vest, harangued the multitude and sponged its forced and orchestrated adulation: in short, an elaborate fabrication of popular support, suitable for export. By "party" I mean the bacchanal that night at every Guardia barracks in the country, at which each officer and man is supposed to have received two whores for his private delectation. According to General Manduco's accountants, Sancudo's inaugural party cost the state one hundred thousand dollars. We will have no idea how much Manduco's party cost until he, in turn, is overthrown. Both may have cost more than Rebeca's party, even when seventy years of inflation is figured in, but grandeur depends at least as much on imagination as on expense, and here Rebeca's party wins with case.

(Apropos of imaginative parties, it is worth mentioning Juan Tábano's 1962 Kitzbühell party, when a jetload of Alpine snow was piled across the lawn and guests schussed down it on water skis and Don Alberto Avispa passed out in a drift beside the mango tree and became the only case of death by frostbite in Tinieblan history. Certain novelists, whose imagination extends no further than lewd innuendo, could quite well to crib their fictions from our rich past.)

11. Eerie music

It may be heard in its original spot in Tcbaikovsky's score on side five of the Soviet Melodiya recording (Angel, SRC-4106), Moscow Radio Symphony Orchestra, Gennady Rozhdestvensky conducting. It is more familiar to Western audiences as the variation danced by the great Fonteyn during the "Black Swan" pas de deux in the Unitel movie choreographed by Nureyev. The film played at the Artis on Fifty-fifth Street that weekend, several millennia ago, when Liz and I first rendezvous'd in New York City, but we did not see it then. We glanced at the display of stills beside the box office, then hurried to our room, having our own adagios to dance and our own betrayals to prepare and our own romantic myth to orchestrate.

12. Worthy and worthless people

The universe, like all closed systems, may be at least partially explained by the second law of thermodynamics (I work both Lord Snow's cultures, Professor Lilywhite; do you?), to wit: order tends to decrease, chaos tends to increase. The universe runs down, stutters toward uniformity and death, encourages the random weed and blights the rose of pattern. Thus order is at a premium, and a human being's value is determined by the volume of order he transfuses into the cosmos.

As we have scales for hurricanes and earthquakes, I hope soon, in another place, to offer a detailed Fuertes Scale of Human Worth. My computations are still inexact, but I conceive a scale ranging from plus to minus ten. At the top (since order isn't ordinary) are merchants of the rich and strange, artists, scientists, and historians, those centaur figures with the scientist's honed mind and artist's horsy gonads. Off on the minus side are those who drain order away: fritterers of worthy people's time, dream smashers who, wanting everything the same (sameness isn't order, it's the reverse), will tell you why your scheme won't work, hence oughtn't to be tried—purveyors of the probable (e.g., deans who enforce syllabi, professors who test by multiple choice, all dictators, most generals, and some hippies: people who demand one kind of uniformity or another); and, among too many others, false scientists and artists, those for whom science is the pack-ratting of loose data, art the Xeroxing of what is called "real life."

So, to connect, Rebeca, as an interpretive artist, an expert in transmuting hugely improbable, highly patterned, wholly human fantasies (e.g., Tchaikovsky-Petipa ballets) into concrete experience, rates high, though not, perhaps, so high as the creators. Sukasin, who was himself an artist but a lazy one, who was, besides, a trainer, nurturing Rebeca's art with sugar lumps of insight and bracing doses of abuse, but who also weighed on it like ice upon a sapling, who bent it and snapped it at the last, rates (at the most indulgent) empty zero.

It often chances for nines or tens to pair with ones or zeroes. (Shakespeare and his prettyboy, for example, or Shakespeare and his dark lady. The vain and vapid silly, cheating fop gave poor Will fits, cost him good sleep, turned him against himself; the sulfurpot scorched his brain and poxed his body; he managed to make poetry of both.) Zeroes appreciate their zerodom and seek out tens in compensation. Tens, being generous, optimistic, naïve, open, trusting, and indulgent to a fault of faults in others, are easily deceived. "Muse" is a romantic term used to describe such zeroes; "irritant" is much the better word. Irritation, suffering, can be of value to creators; it goads them, keeps them striving, links them to the world of ordinary people. But a grain of dirt is a grain of dirt, even if an oyster makes a pearl around it, and a zero (Are all you zeroes listening?) is a zero.

(If, by the way, one cares to fit the scale to the contemporary Republic of Tinieblas, General Genghis Manduco, archmediocrity and coprocrat, squats at the bottom while I, Camilo Fuertes, arranger of the past and guide into the future, stand at the top.)

13. Hack

"Sig Heilanstalt was born on Long Island, New York, in 1934—His daddy was rich and his ma was good-looking. He attended school in Andover, Mass., and college in Princeton, New Jersey. As a deck officer with the Sixth Fleet he saw action in the fleshpots of Beirut and Barcelona, picking up (among others) the germ of his first novel, *Across the Twilight Wave,* which won the Poynter, Ponce Award for 1962. He is the author of two other major works of fiction, A *Sudden Flaring Blaze* (1968) and, now, *In a Haunted Wood,* and two satirical entertainments, *Fashionable Madmen* (1964) and *Ogres and Pygmies* (1970), all of which are published by Poynter, Ponce.

"Mr. Heilanstalt plays a blistering game of tennis and holds master rank at chessboard and bridge table. A frequent visitor on network talk shows, he currently teaches creative writing at Maidenhair College in Vermont."

This squib, no doubt flacked up by Sig himself, is from the back flap of *In a Haunted Wood,* which is, alas, not a ghost story but "a major work of fiction," "a searching tableau [I quote here from the front flap; I wouldn't try to make a tableau search] of today's rebellious students." A copy, beloved of Liz more for its flyleaf (inscribes "To Elizabeth, in another country") and back cover (a glossy of shirtless, hairy-shouldered Sig correcting galleys in a courtside deck chair) than for anything in between—four years with me have given her some taste—has crept into my study. I surprised it here this morning (26th June, 1974), sprawled like a prematurely ejaculated rapist on the chaste pages of my Rebeca chapters, and have it now to hand.

It is six inches by nine inches by three hundred fifteen pages. It retails for $7.95 American, but the author apparently possesses a stock of copies for inscribed distribution to female admirers. It has a three-color, mod-art front cover, a Library of Congress Catalog Card Number, and an epigraph fished up from Auden by means of a lump of well-chewed juicy Fruit stuck on a cane:

> Lost in a haunted wood,
> Children afraid of the night
> Who have never been happy or good.

Sexual activity is described with what is called "realism" on pp. 27-34 (manipulation of a college freshman by her art instructor and, after some dialogue, a return of the favor), pp. 63-72 (devirgination of the freshman by an undergraduate of a neighboring university), pp. 101-109 (fellation of the instructor by a female professor of linguistics), pp. 132-138 (gunpoint buggery of the undergraduate by an officer of the state highway patrol), and, one feels certain even without reading further, at predictable intervals thereafter. There is a protest demonstration which flowers into riot and a bomb plot (against the university registrar's office) which I can only hope succeeds, but there is neither wit nor wonder. Byron Braden (should I recognize the name?) calls the book "Explosive!" referring, perhaps, to the relentless cannonade of cliché, which leaves the reader dazed and dispirited like a combatant at some unimaginative battle of attrition. It was just this kind of thing Rebeca had to live through in Vienna.

To continue (and dispense) with Sig himself, he is tall (an inch or so under six feet) and handsome in the manner of his idol Errol, though (now that his beard is shaved) somewhat weak-chinned. Like all too many gringos of his ilk—the rootless refugees from Pepsi-Cola ads—he has discovered the secret of eternal adolescence and neither looks nor acts his forty years. Long ago, no doubt while still unpublished, he spun a cocoon of brash wiseguyness about his tender ego; this mask has since become engrafted to his face. His culture is rich but shallow: marigolds grow well there, but not the oak or elm. He speaks fluent and inaccurate Spanish, of which, characteristically, he is more confident than his command would warrant.

I know nothing of Sig's "satirical entertainments," but I suspect they are more play- and artful than his "major works." I am quite willing to believe that he does well on TV talk shows, where heat and breadth count more than light and depth. I do not consider him a fraud for pretending to teach creative writing; the blame is with those deans who hold that such a trick is teachable. I imagine he chatted about books on Monday mornings, then met his charges individually for twenty-minute sessions later in the week. There he scored the faulty grammar in the stories of the plain and stimulated the talents of the pretty with hot beef injections. In any case, he earned his pay and pleasure reading all that treacle.

At sport as at the typewriter, Sig is competitive, takes the direct approach, relies on force, scorns subtlety, and lacks imagination. I speak here re his tennis, which I had ample chance to gauge yesterday morning. Liz began trying to promote a match on Sig's first evening at our home and continued tirelessly thereafter. Tennis was jammed into the conversation when Sig dropped by to tell us of his scrape with the Guardia, when we dined out together at his invitation, when he phoned, inviting us to share his cabana at El Opulento. Tennis was served to me with coffee at my breakfast, lobbed past me when I headed toward my study after lunch, stroked at me on the sofa after dinner. Why didn't I play some tennis with Sig? I was too tense; I needed a break. I had forgone all custom of exercises, grown fat and scant of breath. How trim I'd been that first fall in California when I played every morning before class, and it wasn't until I stopped playing that I got so nervous. I'd feel better if I played, and we'd make love again. We'd made love every day, sometimes three times a day, when I was in good shape and playing tennis.

What she wanted, I suppose, was Sig's company, for at first he made no attempt to see her without me present. He seemed (and seems still, to a point) more eager for my society than hers. His disappointment rang genuine whenever I declines an invitation, and on the evenings that the three of us did spend together he spoke mainly to me, asking me endless questions about Tinieblas, giving me the entire benefit of his uninformed views, seeking to involve me in literary discussions, arid inquiring without surcease whether I'd had time to read his book. Or, since she'd never seen me play, perhaps Liz looked forward to my blistered humiliation at Sig's hand. Or, more simply, she saw in tennis a means of weaning me— from my work, of which (see note 5) she is insanely jealous. Whatever her motive, I wasn't going to lose a morning's work playing with Sig, any more than I cared to waste an afternoon sitting with him by the pool or an evening movieing with him.

Then, the day after the night mentioned in note 8, she came to me, all tearful, while I worked, and claimed she'd spent the missing hours driving round the city—to make me jealous, to make me show her some attention, but she was sorry now. I was so well at work there I forgave her. I even pretended to believe her, and then she begged me, please, leave off my work a bit, please be more normal, give her some time, please, take some, please, for myself. Poor Liz has no vocation. How could I blame her for not comprehending what my craft's to me? How can she know that I have histories to make that twenty lifetimes would flash by with, or voices from the past bursting my brain? I admit succumbing to an uncharacteristic but perhaps pardonable tenderness, provoked quite possibly by the pain in my ankle. In any case, I promised her a day.

She wanted it at once, of course. I couldn't break until I had Rebeca's travels told. Within a day or so her sweet repentance had curdled to krait venom, but I am not a liar. Two days ago I completed the text of "Rebeca's Odyssey" and announced that I would not only give Liz a day but meet her friend at tennis in the bargain.

I began the morning by revising the last paragraphs of my chapter but was soon interrupted by Liz, who reminded me (superfluously) of our appointment, accused me (falsely) of being scared of facing Sig, urged me (pompously) to change my stained khakis for a clean pair of shorts, and left me (finally) in peace, to buff a few splintery sentences. I had then but to exhume my warped Davis from beneath the winter clothes in our trunk and descend to our Yasuda Firefly, which Liz had maneuvered from the lot behind our building and in which she sat, drumming the wheel with her fingernails. We arrived at El Opulento precisely at ten, as specified.

Sig was waiting for us at his cabana, dressed for the nonce in white leather tennis shoes by Adidas, fluffy white wool socks, and pressed, snowy shorts and jersey by Fred Perry with blue laurel crown embossed at thigh and breast. A large white canvas racket case reposed by his right foot. He grinned, leaped to his feet, pumped my hand, pecked Liz's proffered check.

"The courts are this way," he said, gesturing grandly, so much more at home than poor Camilo, though poor Camilo's uncle Pandolfo Piérida had designed El Opulento, though poor Camilo himself was not exactly unfamiliar with those very courts. I followed him and Liz dutifully through the break in the line of cabanas and past the pro shop, in whose window the huge cup donated by Don Luis Gusano for the national championship sat gleaming. Had Sig or Liz looked, they might have read my name opposite the year 1969.

At courtside Sig opened his case and removed terry-cloth sweatbands-for his wrist and forehead, Ray-Ban sunglasses fitted with an elastic strap that gripped them to his head, a large towel with "BEVERLY HILLS HOTEL" scrolled down the middle, a gut-strung championship-model Head racket, and a can of creamy-white, green-panthered Slazenger tennis balls which he held to his ear while opening ("I like to hear the cherry pop"). He hung his towel on a corner of the net and jogged to the baseline. I took the other court and knocked his first ball weakly in the net. The second came to my back-hand, and I sliced it against the judge's stand. I blooped the third back to him; he hit it firmly; I blooped again. We rallied thus for some eight or ten shots until I flailed the ball high against the wind-screened fence behind him.

"I'm ready. Your serve."

Both Sig and Liz protested that I take more warm-ups, but I declared gamely that I was as ready as I'd ever be. Of course, if Sig wanted more . . . No, no, but didn't I want to spin for serve? I shook my head. He shrugged at Liz. She shrugged back. We took positions.

Learned examiners, I give you Mr. Sig Heilanstalt, the emblem of bronzed and hairy confidence, poised just off the center of the baseline, grasping two balls in his palm, cuffing a third onto the cement with his racket and catching it between thumb and forefinger. Observe him carefully. He is about to self-destruct.

"I'll take two practice."

"Take all you want. I'll play the first that's in."

"Okay. Service!"

He wound, tossed, reached, and laced the ball into my service court, charg-ing after it toward the net. I passed him down the line on his backhand side.

"Good shot!" He was clearly hopeful that the match might not be too one-sided.

I waved graciously and took the other court.

"Okay," he said, regaining the baseline. "Love-fifteen."

He leaned back, whacked a hummer to my backhand corner, and charged again. I whirled, turning my back to the net, flicked a lob, and strolled away toward the baseline. I heard Sig's racket swish. I heard him grunt. I heard the ball plop fuzzily. I heard him cry, "Good shot!"

"Good, you say?" turning to receive service.

"Three inches in."

I waved again.

"Love-thirty. Service!"

Sig missed his first serve, cut his second, and did not charge. I chopped a cruel little cross-court drop shot. He got to it but wound up draped on the net as I tapped his return beyond him.

"Are you all right?" Liz asked with alarm.

"Yes, God damn it! But I think I've been conned."

He tramped back, howled, "Love-forty," and double-faulted loudly to the tape. "Your game."

Why be verbose? I took the match at love. Not a dull match, however. The news that I was playing—and I had not played in Tinieblas since 1970, when

my brother, Carlos, and I pushed the Costaguanan Davis Cuppers to five sets
—must have spread quickly through the cabana club (which was reasonably
well attended for a weekday morning), for by Sig's second service a little
gallery had convened: the hotel pro, Enrique Cuerdas, my teacher after my
father "died"; Alfonso Sancudo, the deposed President's greying son, newly
reprieved from exile and with a matched pair of gringa stewardesses at halter;
a slight, white, pigeon-breasted gentleman in a blue beach robe who later on
revealed himself as Her Britannic Majesty's Ambassador and offered me the
use of the Embassy Residence court "any time at all"; a mixed doubles foursome who had been playing on the lower court, the men with towels scarfed
round their necks, the ladies flushed and glistening as by a bout of love; a
comely, trim, and gifted graphic artist of about my age, vacationing, she said
later, from California, who sketched me volleying a forehand and Sig lunging
manfully though vainly to retrieve it; and a well-tanned cigar chomper in canary slacks, also a hotel guest, who plunked himself down by Liz, introduced
himself as Arnie Something, and, without further foreplay, proposed a weekend for two in Acapulco. They sat on wooden folding chairs under the
spearmint-striped awning that Cuerdas cranked out when the sun burned
through the haze. They riffled us applause after good rallies and oohed with
pleasure at exciting shots. We entertained them well, Siggy and I, gave them
a sort of bullfight with him as the bull. He learned not to charge wildly and
yet stayed *bravo,* running for every ball, and I would move him smoothly, left
and right, up and back, then nail him with a volley stabbed behind him. And
now and then he'd catch me: when I grew careless, say, assuming that he
couldn't reach a ball, and failed to take position. Then, like as not, he'd pluck
it from the air and smash it past me and, grinning grimly, trot back to the line.
After a point like that I'd take some care to put him in his place. I'd send him
galloping from line to line till he was blown and lathered, till he was scraped
and bloody from collisions with the fence. I'd volley balls I knew were going
out to keep him running. I'd bring him stumbling to the net and then dispatch
him into the narrow shadow of the backstop. He was dangerous enough to
make the show exciting, game enough to make it work, gringo enough to
justify its cruelty. Our gallery got its clapping's worth and Liz a new perspective on us both, but the true beneficiaries were Sig and myself. It would be
mendacious for me to claim I didn't deeply enjoy giving him a thrashing, yet
beyond that animal pleasure—the rush Tuan Mongoose gets when he
crunches intruding Cobra-san's slick head—I felt the wholly human joy of
the game itself, of ordered violence and polite aggression. It made me forget
for a solid hour that I am not in this world to live, but rather to make sense
out of the lives of others. As for Sig, he got a most valuable lesson. His game
improved vastly, but that's not what I mean. I mean I let sufficient gas out of
his ego to bring him back near earth, and I believe that if I played a set or two
with him each morning before some spectators, at least with Liz around, I

might make an artist of him after all. His loss is that I've neither the time nor the vocation to give therapy.

I trust, sweet Dr. Crimes and gentle Professor Lilywhite, that this generous note has fully illumined my text's reference to hacks.

14. *Penis envy*

The passage quoted in text is from "Analisis Terminable e Interminable," in Sigmund Freud, *Obras Completas,* Ramon Rey Ardid, translator and editor (Madrid, 1968), p. 570. The Spanish-English translation is my own. All Professor Rey Ardid can say about the paper, unpublished during Freud's lifetime, is that it was composed between 1905 and 1937. The thrilling coincidence that the notion of penis envy came to Freud on the very morning of Rebeca Fuertes' metamorphosis is my own discovery.

In January, 1972, while a patient at the Fasholt Clinic outside Los Angeles, I received nocturnal visits from the spirit of a Parisian Jewess (a cousin, so she claimed, of Mme Proust's) whom Freud had treated for hysteria during the winter of 1903-1904. This gentlewoman (who bore, quite by the way, a strong resemblance to Mrs. Helene Leibowitz, a fellow patient with whom I bashed tin sheets into ashtrays every afternoon) maintained that she had planted the lotion of penis envy in the Master's mind, citing in evidence the scratch sheet mentioned in text above, which she glimpsed on Freud's desk when he was called briefly from the consulting room and which, she claimed, were notes about her case. According to this spirit, Freud's sheet was dated 7th February, 1904, the date, she said, of one of her most penetrating analytic hours. Much, much more interestingly, it was the date, suspected at once by me and later confirmed by Rebeca, of my grandmother's first transsexual migration.

I made the mistake of divulging this suspicion to my astral visitor. She took it as a disputation of her claim to have been a decisive influence on Freud's thought. In fact, I had no intention of denying her this honor. I do not doubt that pipe dreams like penis envy were the inevitable result in Freud of prolonged contact with neurotics like my visitor. What fascinated me was that the healthy refutation went unnoticed just a few blocks away. In any case, my visitor furnished me a full field display of pyrotechnic hysterics and departed, never to return; which was a pity, for she was a cultivated woman and remarkably well preserved, a charming companion for otherwise distressing evenings (I was locked in), and, potentially, a valuable source for my investigations. She had applied for Sex Change and Return and while awaiting a vacancy had twice attended concerts of my father's. She compared his voice favorably to that of the young Caruso, whom she had heard in life. I hope one day she will forget her pique and drop, by again.

15. *A private school for girls*

The school on whose top floor nine men (nine muses?) met secretly at the end of July, 1921, to found the Chinese Communist Party. A Hunan peasant's son named Mao Tse-tung was chosen secretary. The nine argued policy for four days before being interrupted by a suspicious person in a long coat. Ten minutes later the police arrived to find the meeting place deserted.

16. Dr. Azael Burlando

For reasons detailed in note 18 below, I am unable to communicate with my paternal grandfather, Dr. Azael Burlando. My source for information concerning his comportment and reputation in Mituco Maritimo 1912-1917 is Don Pedro Caoba, a dividended gentleman of total leisure who spent most of his waking time in the Café Progreso. Don Pedro visited me several times at the Fasholt Clinic, Las Ansias, California, in early 1972, and was willing, after a game or two of chess on my magnetic pocket set, to chat about my grandfather, whose flair for the royal game and delight in complex situations I have inherited. (Don Pedro, who has chosen idleness in the other world just as he did in this one, has continued to drop in on me in Florida and here, but I have no time for chess these days and he is, in any case, not much competition.)

For Dr. Burlando's relationship with my grandmother Rebeca Fuertes I have had to rely on her. I am well aware, however, that bedfellows are not objective informants about each other, and have taken pains to guess at and include some of his side of the story.

Concerning Dr. Burlando's activities 1882-1912, particularly his obtaining of a considerable fortune, I have been privileged to have a truly illustrious informant, François Villon (b. 1431), the Parisian balladeer and jailbird, Having in this world lived in great disorder, Villon, on reaching the next, opted to be an organization man and joined the Astral Service. His present post is Deputy Assistant Chief of Terrestrial Recruitment in the Directorate of Astral Activities. In October, 1973, after I had spent several painful nights in fruitless efforts to reach Dr. Burlando, Villon visited me, saying that he could not leave so persistent a call unanswered and that, besides, he was somewhat homesick for his "days in the field." He is about my height (five feet, eight inches) and wiry, with a large, oft-broken beak and twisted smile. Conservatively dressed and crisply manicured, he looks like an ex-sergeant of the Legion who now owns a fleet of taxis or a successful restaurant.

Villon refused to discuss his verse and merely smiled when I asked him if in fact he'd "died" on the gallows, as he'd always feared he would. When I tried to draw him out on imprisonment (or, parallelly, confinement in a mental institution) as a stimulus to intellectual activity, he said only, "There's no treasure like living at one's ease" (*"Il n'est trésor que de vívre à son aise"*). He did, however, tell me a great deal about the organization of the other world and about Dr. Burlando, whom he knew personally and whose dossier he had rechecked before calling on me. For more on this, see note 18 below.

17. Inchados

The national money of the Republic of Tinieblas. The term is the kidnapped surname of Palmiro Inchado de los Huevos (1465?-1515), Castilian courtier and main-chance artist, who, sailing northwest from Panama with letters patent from Carlos V, discovered and named Tinieblas on 28th November, 1515. The name was adopted and the first coins struck in 1821 after Tinieblas declared its independence from the Spanish Crown. Since 1899 the inchado has been pegged to (or, in the phrase of Dr. Eudemio Lobo [1865-1923, President of Tinieblas 1916-1917], "nailed to the cross of") the U.S. dollar, Dr. Burlando's nugget bags weighed fifty pounds apiece and the value of his fortune was one hundred twelve thousand dollars, a handy sum today, a dandy one back then.

18. The transaction

That there is commerce between this world and the other has been well known for at least thirty centuries and probably for much longer. References to this economic intercourse have been, however, made in works of art, not science, in terms and forms where accuracy is sacrificed to entertainment. (A few examples are the Midas story, Greek tales and vase paintings of Hermes gifting gold-fleeced rams to such heroes as Phrixus and Atreus, and the Faust legend, plays, and poem.) Superstitious people (the people of Mituco, for example) take these poetic references literally; devotees of scientism pass them off as myth. It is high time the truth about this commerce was dispassionately presented.

In the first place, there is no malice in it. The management of the next world enters into contracts with residents of this one for perfectly sound and simple business reasons. Both sides, of course, seek the best deal possible; the representatives of the next world have been around for a good while and are experienced negotiators; residents of this world are often forced by circumstance to bargain from positions of weakness. But the astral management does not indulge in gloating, while attempts at trickery invariably originate from the terrestrial party.

As I have said (see note 2), the next world offers a wide gamut of activities. The only limits to indulgence of individuality are, in fact, those imposed by administrative necessity or by lack of individual talent. Performing Arts, for example, will not accept the tongue-tied or tone deaf or paralytic. As fashions change, certain activities become oversubscribed—a problem exacerbated by the recent dramatic growth in population—and the applying spirit must either choose a field that's open or wait till the activity is expanded or someone transfers out. Freedom of choice is the principle, a laudable one, I think, though whether one applauds or not is quite beside the point; the next world is arranged that way, like it or not. But if you are going to have activities like Murder—always a popular activity and packed to the seams right now; like

Torture—applications up seventy-one percent since 1945; like Persecution and Prejudice, like Insult and Abuse (and if you canceled these activities you'd be restricting choice), you can't very well get along without Victim. And Victim is not a popular activity.

Two programs feed spirits into Victim to supplement those masochists who volunteer—the popular activity Risk assigns spirits for service in Victim according to the terms of wagers they have made and lost, and the Directorate of Astral Activities recruits residents of this world for posthumous duty in Victim. Recruiters offer bonuses in worldly goods (and sometimes services, e.g., the deal made by Paris of Troy with a recruiter whom the bards call Aphrodite). Amounts depend on length of enlistment. Through these two programs Victim has been maintained at authorized strength despite the expansion demanded by the fashions of the times and the population explosion.

Victim is run like central casting at a film studio. Requests come in from other activities; spirits are selected and dispatched. In a normal week a spirit attached to Victim might be lynched by a mob from Persecution and Prejudice; sneered at and denigrated in the clubrooms of Insult and Abuse; ganged by freaks from Rape; poisoned, choked, or chopped to messes by someone from Murder; tormented in the elaborately equipped dungeons and interrogation rooms of Torture; and gassed, stoned, trampled, and terrified as an innocent bystander in Riot. Victims are confined (but not ill treated) when off duty, and are strictly forbidden to communicate with residents of this world, not so much lest their stories hurt the recruiting program as because they might give a distorted view of the next world and thus increase the fear of so-called "death." Reports concerning Victim have reached this world mainly from newly paroled inmates who have managed to make dream contact with terrestrial poets or preachers while their sufferings are still fresh. Passages from Homer, Virgil, Dante, and others are based on these reports. (Milton, however, who was attentive only to the sound of his own voice, had no gift for hearing spirits—hence the lack of detail in his vision of the next world, which is wholly inaccurate and fanciful.)

My grandfather Azael Burlando was approached for Victim in Montreal, Canada, May, 1912. "The circumstances were bizarre," Villon told me, "and he handled them in a manner characteristic of his life and reminiscent of my own. He is a great prankster, your grandpapa, a greater one than I; and more of a thief as well, I'm sad to say."

Villon, then Field Recruiter for French Canada, had an extensive network of informants—bartenders, prostitutes, physicians, several lawyers, and a priest or two. "I heard of a good prospect—let's call him Dubois—who was desperate for money and who, my spies said, soaked his cares in absinthe each evening at a certain restaurant. I dropped by and, sure enough, there was a type who fitted the description drinking absinthe at a corner table, so I went over and asked if he was by any chance M. Dubois. He replied that he most assuredly was, and what could he do for me? So I introduced myself—I used my father's name, Montcorbier, in those days as a *nom d'affaires*—and mentioned mutual acquaintances. He said, Oh, yes, Maitre Dupont, Docteur Dupuy, and asked me to sit down. Now, the truth was Dubois had hanged himself that morning, while the man I took for him was your grandfather, Burlando, who just happened to be drinking absinthe there that evening. But he played along perfectly straight-faced, nodding gravely when I referred to his recent and unfortunate financial setbacks and pulling resolutely at his moustache when I said that old Dupuy had classed him as a man disposed to wager all for all. He took me in completely and, I assure you, I'm not easily taken in.

"When I look back I can recall some things that might have tipped me off His accent wasn't quite right, for example; but it wasn't foreign, just more Parisian than Canadian. And he bargained a bit too cagily for a desperate man. But of course, if he hadn't bargained hard I'd have suspected right away, and his resistance spurred me on, made me want to close the deal, prevented me from adjourning our negotiations till the next day—by which time I would have heard of Dubois's demise.

"I bought us a round of drinks and after some chitchat about wheat futures (in which Dubois had taken a bad drubbing), asked your grandfather if he believed in the next world.

" '*Bien sûr*,' he answered. 'It's this one I don't believe in.'

"I started to tell him about our organization, the way things are set up on the other side—always the tricky part of a recruitment. People are willing enough to accept the existence of a next world, but they like to think that what you do there depends on what you've done here. Old Alighieri, for example, still clings to that, and he's been 'dead' six hundred years. He signed up for five centuries in Victim, which he insisted upon calling Purgatory. Now he's in Contemplation, which he insists on calling Paradise. Your grandfather smiled at me benignly, like one humoring a madman—the overwhelmingly common reaction a recruiter gets at first. In fact, he knew a great deal about the next world, even about Victim. He had a gift for communicating with spirits—a gift that, evidently, you've inherited—and one of his great-uncles had spent ten years in Victim following an unwise bet in Risk.

"Well, finally he pretended to be won over to my view. I revealed myself as an agent of Terrestrial Recruitment and we got down to business. I gave him the straight word on Victim. I suffered too much myself in this world to mislead a man or woman about the next, and anyway, our policy strictly forbids any glossing over. But I did make clear that enlistments are for finite periods and that eternity lasts a long time. When he accepted that—and he resisted quite a while—we turned to price. God, how we haggled! It lasted well past midnight, and the more he drank, the sharper he became. I swear I'd rather spend a year in Victim myself than bargain with a man like that again! Finally we settled on seven fifty-pound bags of river-pure gold nuggets for a seven-decade enlistment, the easiest terms I'd ever had to give and only just within what I was authorized to grant without approval of superiors. I might have wondered at that also, but frankly, I was somewhat drunk. It was I who insisted we close the deal that night—I still marvel how he led me into that. My base was Montreal, and I had a large safe in my rooms. When we got there, Burlando opened every bag and fingered every nugget. Then I filled in the enlistment contract, and he signed it—André Marie Dubois. I had a sample of Dubois's signature, of course, to check with, but Burlando must have got a glimpse at it while I was opening the safe, for his forgery fooled not only me but several experts at the home office. Poor Dubois had the devil's time proving he'd been 'dead' and already checked in at Reception when that signature went on the contract. I helped Burlando lug the gold downstairs to a cab. I shook his hand. I think I clapped him on the back. And that's the last I saw of him for five years and a half.

"When it came out how I'd let him trick me, they kicked me upstairs to a desk job. I had time—more free time than I wanted, in point of fact—to run a full check on that grandfather of yours. At least I learned I wasn't his first patsy. [Here Villon sketched my grandfather's career. Some escapades are touched upon in text above] We tried to get him when he 'died.' There was a requisition order for his spirit waiting at Reception when he checked in. He appealed, of course, and got Elihu the Buzite to represent him. Elihu argued that the alleged fraud, if it occurred at all—you can't match a Jewish lawyer for bald-faced gall; if I'd had one I'd have never spent a day in prison—took place outside astral jurisdiction, and cited the principle of caveat emptor and the precedent of Anton Fugger, who duped us for a bundle back in the sixteenth century with a contract signed in disappearing ink. In the end it was no contest. All we had was Dubois's forged signature on the contract and my word against Burlando's. And the truth, of course, but what does the truth count for in a court of law? Burlando's appeal was sustained, and all we could manage was a little unofficial harassment. Burlando's application for Performing Arts—your family seems to go for that activity—has been held up on one technicality after another. And Electronics has arranged a static halo that keeps him from communicating with anyone here. But I have to admit it: he got away scot free, the clever dog, and on a purely improvised swindle too!"

19. The trenches of marriage

To which Liz and I dug annexes in the suburbs of Los Angeles and through the placid streets of Sunburst, Florida, and which we've now extended to the tropics, burrowing out bunkers and masoning revetments here in the Miraflores section of Ciudad Tinieblas—or rather which we've stretched from the Ostend of our minds to the Swiss border of our loins with impregnable fortifications around the Verdun of our hearts.

20. *Another patient*

A slim young foreigner of middle height, a graduate assistant at a nearby university, whose nerves snapped like an E string at Christmastide in I 971. He was committed to the Fasholt Clinic by his wife, a U S. citizen; an uncle who resided in Miami undertook to pay all fees. Dr. Elias Fafnir diagnosed schizophrenia: the chap heard voices, after all, saw visions, and claimed he could make contact with the "dead."

This exile from his country and himself molested no one. He sat most calmly in the garden, his handsome though somewhat prematurely furrowed face turned to the winter sun, or pounded dutifully away at metal plates in occupational therapy. Sometimes he took a turn pushing a paraplegic fellow-countryman of his about the grounds. He even spoke to this man—not much, it's true, but what he said seemed quite articulate. He was not rude or vulgar to the staff. He certainly was not obscene. But when he saw his gifts dismissed as lunacy, he simply kept his silence and, not caring to lie down, would sit the session long smiling politely at his psychiatrist. His only violence was directed to himself: sometimes he beat his head against his wall. Not out of any urge for self-destruction, however. He merely wished to translate into physical pain—which, after all, is bearable—the mental agony produced by superhuman feats of concentration. And for this—they said it was for this, but possibly they were enraged because he wouldn't speak to them—they strapped him down and fixed electrodes to his feet and forehead and jazzed a current through him till he screamed and shat, till he twitched and shuddered like a gaffed dolphin and passed into unconsciousness.

After they'd done this to him twice, he prudently resolved to play their game. He wasn't stupid, after all, and reasoned he could bear the indignity of discussing his childhood and sex life with strangers more easily than the indignity of being tortured. He told his doctor that the voices and visions were gone. This was true, but he refrained from saying he was sure that he could get them back as soon as he was in more congenial surroundings. He privately admitted to himself that he had pushed himself too hard, becoming in fact unable to exist in two realities at once and then opting, foolishly, it turned out, for one most people can't perceive and won't believe in. He had been quite insane—though not the way the doctors diagnosed—to mention his revolutionary research techniques to an incompetent dean with a vested interest in traditional scholarship. He had been unfair (and unwise) in taking the loss of his fellowship out on his wife. This he admitted to himself, to his doctor he declared that he was now back in touch with reality—as if there were only one reality, the way the doctors all insisted. He vowed to give up using drugs, partly to pacify the doctor, mainly because they had proved counterproductive to his purposes. Allowed at last to leave the grounds for a few hours, he wooed his wife to a motel and there made love to her with sufficient tenderness (he didn't know yet that she'd authorized his "treatments"), skill (he knew that old dance well), and vigorous resilience (he'd been a celibate four months) to convince her of anything, even his fundamental sanity. She helped him, then, to convince the doctors, who, in any case, were yearning to congratulate themselves on his "cure." Early in May he bade his paraplegic countryman *adiós;* shook hands with the old queer whose advances he'd resisted but whom he'd not denounced for trying to kiss him behind the ear; see-you-later-but-not-here'd the several drying-out drunks and methadoning junkies whose society he'd frequented after his "treatments" as a means of showing Dr. Fafnir and colleagues how much he loved "reality"; kissed the well-preserved cheek of a Jewish matron he'd banged ashtrays with; took down the name and home address of a certain attendant whose balls he meant to kick in if he ever got the chance (see how sane he was?); and decamped the clinic and the state. By summer quarter he was enrolled in another (if less prestigious) university, without a fellowship but with his gifts intact, and with a special knowledge, a wariness, about this world— it's not a fair place; neither is the next—which stood to serve him well among the snoops and sneaks, the autobrainwashed knowers of the Way, the self-proclaimed inheritors of the earth, who, being at the very best one-eyed, seek to blind everyone who truly sees.

21. León Fuertes

With the birth of my father and chief subject, Part One of this dissertation is complete. It is now 5:15 A.M., Wednesday, 27th February, 1974. My wife is sleeping sweetly in her bedroom; in the big oak beneath my window swallows are waking up. Within a quarter of an hour the sun will bob up (as though punted) from behind the cordillera, and I will lie down to rest an hour before Sig picks me up for his tennis lesson. We have hit on this compromise: a lesson at six-thirty every morning on the secluded courts at Fort Shafter in the Reservation. He won't—and I can't blame him—play public matches with me, but I have found that exercise and human contact, taken in small doses, help me work. And getting Sig official status in our life—her friend and some-time escort; my friend and tennis protégé—has greatly tranquilized dear Liz. I am too busy, luckily enough, to wonder much about his unofficial status and have enjoyed some healthy and productive weeks.

But it has been all simple composition from notes taken long ago, I haven't had to beam my mind out to the Astral Plane, nor, happily, have any uninvited spirits bothered me. My research is complete on León Fuertes' infancy, but soon I shall have to seek out new informants and try again to reach my father's spirit. He has never deigned to answer me, though I have called and called. Perhaps "deigned" is unfair. Perhaps the press of work, the exigencies of a heavy concert schedule, keep him too busy, but I am nagged by worry that he may feel me still unworthy of his confidence. I must try harder, and it frightens me, the strains that I shall face.

I could, of course, stop here. I have a decent monograph right now, one that would satisfy requirements. (I mean you no offense, Drs. Lilywhite and Crimes, but we all know that yours is but a second-rate department in a third-rate university.) I could polish it and alter my prospectus, arrange to take the orals at the end of spring quarter, and have my doctorate forthwith. I'd have time then to compose my private life before taking the post that's waiting for me at the National University. Then other decent little papers. There's the whole history of this country to discover and get down, and I could pick my subjects. No painful delving into family griefs, no agonizing calls to unresponsive spirits, no overly ambitious expeditions, no endless treks into the core of meaning where felines from the id snarl out to maul you and your hands pull weakly at the dank lianas of madness: nothing to tax my strength or risk my sanity. My classes, my little monographs, my happy home, my balanced life.

But I'll not take that road. For me the epic vision, the grand triptych, the deathdrop down to monsterdom for truth, the darkest chaos ordered—or else madness. Nor is there any courage in the choice; I cannot otherwise. So I shall weave this history until it's finished or my mind unravels. And then the next one and the next. There won't be time for all of them, and so I can't afford a balanced life. Sorry, Liz. You'll have to save yourself as best you can. No one can save me, not even on this lovely morning with the sun come up rubbed clean by our rough mountains.

PART TWO

22. Duality

Concerning Rebeca's attitude toward her Tsinan clientela, I have written (Chapter 3): "the artist's blend of solicitude and scorn, interpenetrating feelings which imply an eagerness to please and a refusal to be influenced." Similarly, I, Camilo Fuertes, Rebeca's grandson, León's son, yearn to have my mind stamped "KOSHER" by the academia rabbinate and yet refuse (as Dr. Emil Vertilanz well knows and you, Professors Crimes and Lilywhite, are learning) to adhere slavishly to academic ritual. The duality may, thus, reside in the Fuertes chromosomes.

How much more interesting is this complexity than the simplicities to either side, Sig's lobeless Errol or ant men whose antennae twitch only to the swarming of the heap! Moreover, what I shall call the "Fuertes Split" seems to be characteristic of certain forms of excellence:

BOLD BANDIT BONY HUMPS HOMELY HAPSBURG!

WILD WORDSMITH WILL COVETS COAT OF ARMS!

The urge for respectability, as manifested in the soldier-statesman, the poetplay-wright, and the Fuertes family, does not imply retreat from the fuck-youism of genius. The two drives coexist. They meld and alternate. They strain the soul like teams at tug o' war.

This was not the only interesting complexity of my father's character; nor is it the only one of his son's. I assure you, patient examiners, that many other fascinating items will, like the snow-furred, opal-eyed bunny that quivers in El Magnífico's silk sombrero, be elegantly produced at appropriate moments in my text and notes.

23. Virginity

Dr. Elias Fafnir, of the Fasholt Clinic, once (in late March, I think, of 1972) had the effrontery to suggest that I was morbidly obsessed with female virginity—this after a conversation in which dear, simplicistic Liz assured him that the trouble with our marriage, hence with me, sprang from my brooding over her lack of virginity at our first embrace. Considerations of self-preservation (see note 20) constrained me at the time to bear this charge in silence. I shall here permit myself to set the record straight.

In the first place, virginity is at once a concept of abiding human interest and a commodity of increasing scarcity. As an abstraction, virginity is a natural object for the contemplation of inquiring and active minds, e.g., my own, while, as a specific and tangible membrane attached at birth to the body of my wife, Elizabeth, it can be numbered among my legitimate husbandly concerns. Intellectual curiosity and such no doubt unscientific but entirely normal and laudable considerations as love, marital responsibility, and friendly interest led me, therefore, once our relation had been solemnized at law and in the sight of God, to request an account of how, where, when, why, and by whom Liz was divested of this abstract attribute and concrete strip of flesh. Had she returned me a frank and loving answer, the matter would have ended there and then. Instead she hedged: "You're the first man I ever *loved*, Camilo, that's all that matters"; or grudged: "I'm entitled to a past, Camilo"; or whined: "Oh, please, Camilo, please just let me love you!" or bitched: "Is that what you need now to get turned on—the juicy, the *bloody* details of me screwing someone else?" Sometimes she managed genuine salt tears. I recall a November afternoon at the St. Moritz in New York when, while sleet lashed roughly on the windowpane and twenty-two slimed mastodons savaged across the mute, unwatched TV screen, we nested naked in each other's arms, stretching the liquid filament of joy with anguished kisses, then pausing, breath trapped, lest the cable part and let us go ballooning off into oblivion, until, hard after one of her Oh-God-I-love-yous, I asked, "How was it then?"

"How was what, darling?" sighing.

"Your first time. Tell me how it was. Was it as good as this?"

And she shrieked, "No, not now, oh, God, not now, oh, Jesus Christ, not now!" and then cascaded into sobs.

Shortly thereafter (early December, 1971) she took to answering with concocted lies. That is, she gave a number of conflicting versions of the same event. In one she rendered up her cherry to the drummer of a rock group, under the bandstand during an outdoor concert held near Tarrytown in May of '69 (her sophomore year). The concert was real enough—I checked it with cousin Adana—but the coupling was, I think, invented. Either that, or she was already deflowered at the time, for within a day or two she came up with a marvelously detailed account of her seduction (at age fifteen!) by her second cousin Willis Tweed, a descendant of the Manhattan politician and a Regular Air Force Captain (DFC with cluster), who was reported missing in action over Haiphong in April, 1967, and who is now presumed dead. According to Liz, this Tweed, then a green lieutenant on leave following his graduation from the Air Force Academy, romanced her for the best part of two weeks in Northampton, Long Island, New York (where her parents have a summer home), and availing himself of the hawkish mood generated by the so-called Tonkin Gulf Incident (5th August, I 964), his orders to Southeast Asia, a harvest moon, the rhythmic beat of breakers on the beach, and an undetermined quantity of Scotch whisky from his pewter hip flask, managed to perforate her effectively but rather too sandily for either's pleasure in a secluded hollow in the dunes. Yet scarcely had I accepted this—Tweed, officer and somewhat gentleman, airman and dead war hero, was at once more and less acceptable than the unnamed noisemaker—when, in response to certain discreet probes for background information, she told me Tweed was not the man at all. She had, she now said, been still virginal at age eighteen when, gassed on grass at a Williams College house party, she was "more or less raped" by a Theta Delta Chi pledge and—she wasn't sure—one or two of his sponsors. She let these monsters marinate in my mind for a day or so, then replaced them with a Negro film and nightclub entertainer whom legal considerations forbid my naming here. In this tale she was picked up one Friday in a Fifth Avenue bookshop, invited to a recording session somewhere on the West Side ("He sang each cut to me"), wined at Orsini's, taken to bed on black silk sheets ("I was the only white thing in the room") in a suite at the Hotel Gotham, initiated to the more common variants of coitus, and then regaled with African delights for the remainder of the weekend.

It is, I think, unnecessary for me to recount any of her succeeding stories. My point will have by now been made. Either I never got the truth, or I got it so smeared with falsehood that I cannot even yet distinguish it. I will not, out of simple charity, use these pages to accuse my wife of trying to drive me mad (though that is what I thought both at the time and in the weeks after my breakdown). I am content, in the second place, to submit that there was a lot more wrong with our marriage than my "brooding over her lack of virginity at our first meeting."

Thirdly, my marriage was, unfortunately, the least of my troubles. There was, just for example, the intransigent stupidity of Dr. Emil Vertilanz (a man with no more business in a deaconate of graduate study than I have in a moon capsule), the loss of my fellowship, the fear (the kind shared and described by Aleksandr Solzhenitsyn [Russian novelist, born 1918, Nobel laureate 1970]) that I would never be allowed to exercise my gifts, the headaches that tormented me each day, the spirits who molested me each night. Oh, no; the Cleaver diagnosis is too simple.

Fourthly and finally, it strikes me (Are you listening, fat Faf?) that an Iberian concern for the honor of womanhood, strange as it may appear in Gringoland, is a far sight less morbid than a Frenchman's obsession with the chastity of books, Sig's thrill at exercising droit de seigneur over a can of tennis balls (see note 13), or the strange state of mind that leads motel managers in the Good Old USA to equip guest toilet seats with paper hymens.

24. *The intrusions of a priest*

Since last Sunday (17th March, 1974) I have received daily, unsolicited, predawn visits from a young man of the cloth—or rather from his spirit. At first I took him for a member of Performing Arts made tip for a production of *Jesus Christ Superstar* (a so-called rock opera to which Liz dragged me when we were in New York at Thanksgivingtide in 1971). Besides shoulder-length hair and auburn beard, he has stigmata on both palms and the wistful, infinite-compassion gaze associated in pop religion with the Prince of Peace, but his white shirt with gold lapel cross (the uniform of foot soldiers of the progressive, socially conscious Church in Latin America) and his fluent prayer Latin have convinced me he is a *bona fide* divine.

I noticed him grieving at me from beside the closet door at about 4 A.M. last Sunday morning while I was summarizing the record of Rebeca's trial for witchcraft (see note 25 below). He seemed about to speak when I asked him point-blank whether he had any information concerning León Fuertes, his ancestry, etc. My visitor shook his head, and I told him, courteously but firmly, that I was fully occupied with a lengthy and complicated investigation and that I could not and would not allow myself to be distracted.

Lest the reader condemn this attitude as uncivil or inhospitable, let me note that there are a great, great many spirits, that most of them are hungry for contact with this world, and that there are only a very few of us here able to communicate with them. For reasons of personal health, as well as of good scholarship, I cannot afford a reoccurrence of the situation that obtained in California in December, 1971, when my home, my workroom, and my mind were infested with uninvited spirits, all clamoring for my attention. I am willing (see note 21) to risk madness in the interest of historical science, but not simply for the entertainment of a pack of lazy ghosts. And of course, this dissertation must have my full attention if it is to be up to my standards, and well beyond those of the Department of History, Sunburst University.

My visitor began to cry—not unseemly sobbing, I'll say that much for him, but a single tear pearling from the outer corner of his left eye to soak into his beard. I told him to come back in a few months, say after Christmas. He nodded sadly, gave me an *"Ego te absolvo"* with cross, and faded. A well-bred fellow, I said to myself; then I got back to work. But my great weakness is a tendency to overestimate the decency of other people. Father Whoever-he-is has been back every night since then. He kneels in a corner mumbling Latin prayers until I nag him off, and that means up to five or more minutes, for I cannot raise my voice with Liz asleep next door. I have no doubt but that he will appear again this morning, and there is not a thing that I can do to stop him. Sooner or later he will give up on me and go bother someone else, but he has a lot more time on his hands than I do.

As I have said (see note 4), our life permits no shortcuts to achievement. Interviewing spirits has its difficulties, and I mention this one as a caveat to those scholars who may be gifted and interested enough to care to try my methods.

25. The charges against Rebeca Fuertes

I do not disprize conventional techniques. My perfection of spirit interview, my application of it to the goals of scholarship, are invaluable contributions, more than sufficient to win me an early Nobel were the Swedes only bright enough to offer one for history, but there is nothing like a document for certain kinds of research. Rebeca was unable to tell me much about her trial— she had not (as I've noted) paid attention—but Don Pedro Caoba informed me fully on the tenor of proceedings, the décor of the courtroom, the mood of the spectators, etc. Nevertheless, I did not for an instant consider treating a matter so vitally important for an understanding of León Fuertes' life and character without consulting the court record. Accordingly, on 7th-8th March, 1974, I visited Mituco Marítimo.

I do not drive. I know how, of course, but just don't do it. There is no longer any regular boat service between Ciudad Tinieblas and Mituco, and I lack the romantic temperament which recommends the danger and discomfort of Tinieblan bus rides to hippie wanderers. Hence I asked my wife to drive me. She felt compelled to mention our projected journey to Mr. Heilanstalt. He expressed an irrepressible urge to see something of the Tinieblan interior and proffered his services as chauffeur. I reminded him of his lectures. He reminded me that at our National University professors have no more compunction about cutting class than students do. The three of us departed Ciudad Tinieblas at 7:00 A.M. on the 7th in Sig's air-conditioned Puma.

The arrangement turned out to be a good deal more agreeable than I had expected. I was able to sleep while Sig and Liz amused themselves with conversation, which penetrated my slumber soothingly like the chirpings of a bluejay answered by the cooings of a dove. We were almost to Belém when Sig swerved me off the back seat and Liz well over toward his corner of the front to avoid a crew-cut, crucifix-bearing priest and straggle of brown peasants who had preempted our lane of the highway, and by then it was lunchtime anyway. A generous ration of chicken rice and fried plantain and three bottles of icy Cortes Beer—taken in an open-air but trellised restaurant opposite the town hall and its "BELÉM IS WITH YOU GENGHIS" banner—put me in such good humor that I bent my rule on not discussing my work enough to tell the story of Great-great-grandmother Raquel's recruitment for the bed of General Epifanio Mojón. The event took place more than a century ago but no more than a hundred meters from where we were sitting. Sig responded with the news that he had shelved his Carlo Snyde satire to take notes for a "big book, a 'nonfiction novel' about Tinieblas and General Manduco." He meant, he said, to elbow himself a place at the trough between Mailer and Capote. (Good manners forbade my glossing that since he lacked the patience for scholarship and the imagination for art, he was well suited to a hybrid form that, like the Mule, is sturdy, gross, insensitive to punishment, and sterile.) Did I know, he went on brightly, that the General's brother was carving himself a considerable. fief out of the peasant squatting of this very (Belém) region? Or that a Costaguanan priest—imagine a Catholic country importing priests!—was making the first peeps of protest against Manduco by organizing the peasants? I explained how we Tinieblans, being the most civilized and skeptical of nations, imported priests from fanatical Costaguana and credulous Spain, while exporting con men throughout the hemisphere and world, and we continued this pleasant and mildly stimulating chitchat for the remainder of our journey, with Liz contributing a titbit now and then but mainly beaming on like the proud mother of two clever, well-behaved young sons.

We slept that night at the Mituco Guest House, Liz and I in the same room and bed for the first time in years, and here the languor of the trip, the justified surcease from trying labor, the aromatic breathings of the island, and the salt freshness of Pacific breezes contributed first to a restful sleep, then to a mutual awakening and some hesitant caresses, and finally, incredibly, to a mute and infinitely tender episode of love in which months of conflict and resentment were (for the moment anyway) swept off like wisps of smoke. Later Sig and Liz saw sights while I, gorged with well-being, pored through the Registry to find and Minox-photograph the record of the trial.

The point, honored examiners, to this charming preamble to the documentation of a piece of text is that conventional research is a thousand—no, a million times easier and more pleasant than my revolutionary method. If I rely mainly on spirit interview, it is not (as Dr. Vertilanz's slimy charge asserted) because I am too lazy to check documents. No; much the reverse, it is because I spare myself no labor and no risk in my commitment to the advancement of science. If you have got that through your heads, I shall now present the charges against Rebeca:

That the defendant, Rebeca Fuertes, did, on 6th June, 1894, criminally and with evil intent bewitch, charm, and enchant out of all sentient concern for his own best interest Señor Don Patricio Garza Cortada, and, further, that, during the period of 6th June, 1894, to 6th June, 1899, the defendant made use of powers and accomplishments vouchsafed her by the Prince of Darkness to extract from the aforementioned Señor Garza bed, board, material goods, and affection, to the grave detriment of the aforementioned Señor Garza's spiritual, physical, and financial well-being and in heinous contravention of the laws of God and the Republic of Tinieblas;

That the defendant, Rebeca Fuertes, did, during the period of August, 1914, to February, 1917, visit upon the mind and body of Señor Dr. Azael Burlando spells, enchantments, and bewitchments, thereby compelling the aforementioned Dr. Burlando to furnish her bed, board, material goods, and affection, and further causing him to contrive, sign, and certify instruments ceding to her and her issue material goods of high value, to wit, a large dwelling formerly the property of Señor Don Patricio Garza Cortada and twenty shares of common stock of the Mituco Company of Infinite Progress, and that the defendant performed these actions knowingly and with evil intent to the detriment of the aforementioned Dr. Burlando's spiritual, physical, and financial well-being, to the prejudice of the financial well-being of the aforementioned Dr. Burlando's legitimate spouse and heir, in deep and open threat to the peace and public order of the Independent District of Mituco, and in profound contravention of the laws of God and the Republic of Tinieblas;

That the defendant, Rebeca Fuertes, did, on or about 12th February, 1917, knowingly, willingly, and criminally consort, copulate, and have sexual congress with His Satanic Majesty, Lucifer, Prince of Darkness, and/or one or other of his deputies, ministers, affiliated demons, etc., for the hideous purpose and with the resultant effect of conceiving issue, thereby to defraud the aforementioned Dr. Azael Burlando, the Mituco Company of Infinite Progress, and the citizens and government of the Independent District of Mituco, and in flagrant contravention of the laws of God and the Republic of Tinieblas;

That the defendant, Rebeca Fuertes, did, on the evening of 12th November, 1917, knowingly, willingly, and with criminal intent make use of powers and enchantments vouchsafed her by infernal forces to murder, assassinate, and deprive of earthly existence the aforementioned Dr. Azael Burlando, to the disruption of the peace and public order of the Independent District of Mituco and in revolting contravention of the laws of God and the Republic of Tinieblas;

And that the defendant, Rebeca Fuertes, did, during the period of 13th-14th November, 1917, knowingly, willingly, and criminally perform service as the agent of His Satanic Majesty, Lucifer, Prince of Darkness, causing storms, hurricanoes, and tempests to blast and buffet the Island of Mituco, aiding diabolic officers in the collection of the immortal soul of the aforementioned Dr. Azael Burlando and the abstracting of his body, to the grave prejudice of the life, health, and property of the citizens of the Independent District of Mituco and in fearsome contravention of the laws of God and the Republic of Tinieblas.

26. *Her other children and her maid*

Following Rebeca's flight with Leon, the imaginative *mituqueños* decided that she was not just a witch but a German spy as well, and that she had escaped from the island on board the German surface raider *Wolf*. This famous predator had a large wardrobe of sheep's clothing—phony funnels, movable masts, collapsible cargo crates—and hinged steel lips to hide her six-inch fangs. She had denned from time to time in Tinieblan waters, and the rumor went that Rebeca had somehow managed to get a message to Kapitän Nerger (then nipping nitrate carriers off the approaches to the Panama Canal), and that he had brought his vessel to Mituco and taken Rebeca northwest into Mexico. Acting on this misinformation, the Chinese maid decamped Mituco de Tierra Firme in the wrong direction, taking León's brother and twin sister with her.

They got as far as Puerto Guineo in the Republic of Ticamala, where they remained until 1924, when the Chinese woman was killed accidentally. The little girl was taken in by strangers. Young Nicolas set out to find his mother, but every step took him farther away. By age fifteen he had wandered into the backlands of Nicaragua and joined Augusto Sandino's *guetrilleros*.

My uncle Nicolas participated with Fuertes vigor in raids on Jinotega, Chinandega, Matagalpa, Guanacastillo, and San Francisco de Carnicero. The conjunction in him of Manchu and Mojón genes made him a polished executioner, a Harvey Cushing of the machete with all the *cortes* (this useful and hard-working word means "court" as well as "cuts") in his repertoire: the *chaleco* or vest cut, which lopped arms at the shoulders; the *cumbo* or gourd, where the top of the skull was sliced off to expose the brain, so that the victim died in horrible convulsions; the "bloomers"—legs chopped at middle thigh; *the corbata* or necktie-throat slashed and tongue pulled through; the *cigarro*, where the victim got his penis for a stogy. In these rigorous and heady sports he forgot his loveless infancy and the mother who abandoned him, the onus of mixed blood, the homeless scavenging in hostile lands, the loneliness and terror. Unless he lied to me, he was the happiest of all the Fuertes—for a few years at least, until the morning when he blundered whistling on a gringo ambush and three swift tongues of flame translated him into a notch on the pistol butt of Lieutenant (later General) Victor Steel, USMC.

27. *A particularly blatant extortion caper*

The so-called Tinieblan Dispute of 1898, which culminated in the Day-Cornudo Treaty and the founding of the Reservation, is treated cursorily in the standard U.S. texts. Ezra Banner Swart *(American Diplomacy* [New

Haven, 1939]), for example, devotes two paragraphs to showing a gringo Saint George, acting in utter piety and altruism, rescuing a Tinieblan maiden from a Teutonic dragon. More recently, Stephen Lamont *(The Foreign Policy of the American Nation* [New York, 1955]) allows that in the Tinieblan Dispute and other, similar incidents between 1895 and 1904, the Monroe Doctrine, originally enunciated to deter European intervention, became perverted into an instrument of United States intervention, but he is, nonetheless, persuaded that the benefits to Tinieblas greatly outweighed the injuries. A less sanguine view is held by the few Tinieblans who have written on the matter (e.g., Eugenio Lobo, *Infamias del imperialismo yanqui* [Ciudad Tinieblas, 1951]), but their pretensions are more polemical than scholarly. The bare facts are available to anyone who cares to consult the newspapers of the day, and I give them in my text. As far as the long-term implications of the incident for Tinieblas and the U.S. are concerned, the subject awaits the attentions of a disciplined monographer.

The building of the Reservation is heroically retold in "Bastion in the Tropics," a pamphlet put out in 1959 by the Public Information Office, United States Hemispheric Interdiction Team, Fort Shafter. The same document gives copious information concerning the base's facilities, most of which I have seen with my own eyes. Since 1947 Tinieblans have been allowed to visit the Reservation Club as accompanied guests and to ease their bowels and bladders in receptacles formerly reserved for U.S. citizens, but the double wage scale remains in effect.

Rebeca Fuertes refuses, for reasons that the text makes clear, to comment on her sojourn in the Reservation. I have not yet been able to contact León Fuertes; in any case, he would surely not remember much. I have relied, therefore, on the testimony of Ned C. Cod, whom I interviewed at Sunburst during the first week of November, 1973.

Sergeant Cod served out his thirty years' enlistment in the U.S. Army, retired in 1928, and "died" four years later during the Bonus March on Washington). He then applied for War and was accepted. War is organized in the other world much like professional sport in this one. (Astral Sport, on the other hand, has a distinctly amateur flavor.) There are an Eastern and a Western League, each of which fields six armies. (Plans are now being considered to expand the leagues to eight armies each.) Armies fight scheduled campaigns on home and away battlefields, and league leaders meet regularly for the Championship. Participants are traded back and forth; soldiers are advanced and demoted; commanders are appointed and relieved. No spectators are permitted, however, and the battlefields are kept rigorously free of noncombatants. Since war, like love, is a basic human pursuit, War is an original Astral Activity, but all combat is conducted with pre-gunpowder weapons, the Director of Astral Activities agreeing with Colonel T. E. Lawrence that the humanity went out of war after the Battle of Crécy.

On being accepted for War, Cod went to the Azure Invincibles of the Western League (John Churchill, Duke of Marlborough, Commanding) and was assigned to his old arm, the cavalry. He has fought with distinction in two Championships and at present serves in a troop commanded by George S. Patton, an officer who, on recruitment, demanded general rank but whom the army commander has judged incompetent to direct large formations. Cod remembered Rebeca and León perfectly and spoke of them with great affection.

28. *This bit of parody*

Issues from the union of two of Mr. S. Heilanstalt's current interests: a survey course in English poetry that he is offering at the National University, and a study of Tinieblan history that he has undertaken in connection with his new book. The verses were born in my living room at eleven or so on the evening of Wednesday, 20th March, 1974, after a gestation of about three minutes. Sig and my wife, Elizabeth (whom he has taken as an assistant for his courses), came in after his class at about 10:30. Liz had forgot her key; I bad to open for them—Sig instantly began pumping me about the DayCornudo Treaty. He had, it came out later, been discussing Coleridge that same evening, and when I began describing the making of the Reservation, he smacked his forehead with his palm, plucked a ballpoint from his pocket, and started scribbling beside the headline ("PRIEST BOLTS WITH CO-OP CASH") on a copy of the tabloid *Informe Trópico* that had been lying near him on the couch and that I have before me.

Sig read us his brainchild with great pride and glee, receiving immediate appreciation from Liz. I didn't get the joke, I must confess, until he quoted me the first eleven lines of Coleridge's masterpiece. I am still not competent to judge his execution, but his conception seems most apt, and I include the jingle in my text with his permission for the following good reasons:

1. In connecting and contrasting Kubla and McKinley, an artful pleasure dome and a gross military complex, Sig comments meaningfully on the nature of US imperial civilization;

2. Tinieblas compares well with Xanadu as an exotic if not mythical domain;

3. Parody and bathos are among the very few sane responses to U.S.-Tinieblan relations and to this world in general.

This note will, I trust, acquit me of any charge of malice against Mr. Heilanstalt and demonstrate the serenity with which I am able to give the devil is due.

29. *She cooked . . .*

But not Liz Cleaver Fuertes. Liz toiled not, neither did she spin. She slept until midmorning, then. lay abed past noon. She made vigorous love each afternoon and tender love each evening. Between, she read, or sunned herself, or strolled along the beach. On Sundays she did the *Times* (N.Y., not L.A.) crossword, consulting *Roget's Thesaurus* and the microprinted O.E.D., drafting with a number 4 pencil, fair-copying with a felt-tipped pen, calling in to her husband's study for help with Spanish, French, and Latin words. On odd occasions she might open up a can and heat its contents. Mostly she nibbled cold cuts from the Frigidaire or, late at night, munched on the honeyed toast her husband brought her. When she undressed, she tossed her clothes into a bedroom chair. When the pile attained a certain volume, she wrapped it in a bed sheet for her husband to take to the laundromat. She lived thus some three months (June-August, 1971), sugared in ease and pampered like a princess, until the afternoon when, on the occasion of her husband's experiencing some difficulty in achieving erection—the perfectly normal and predictable result of stewing ninety days in hothouse lust—she remarked that since he couldn't get it up, he might as well take out the laundry. He threw her out of bed and the laundry out the window, and things were never quite the same again.

30. Conjugal rights

The word "conjugal," as even you, Professors Crimes and Lilywhite, must know derives from the Latin *iugum*, a yoke, the symbol of submission for defeated enemies, the substance of bondage for beasts of the field. It is cognate with both "yogi" and "yokel" and carries complementary connotations of patience and stupidity. The term "conjugal rights" denotes one of the more disgusting human conventions: authority to molest another person sexually. As for claiming such rights, civilized voices have been loud to cry out against the husband, be he enraged, inebriated, or simply gorged with letch, who takes the rites of marriage for the right to rape, but how much more cruel is this situation when reversed! Moral violence can be worse than physical. Brute force acquires a certain dignity when compared with pitiless nagging, with insult, with threats of scandalous adultery. Husbands deserve respect as much as wives, especially if they are engaged in intense and valuable mental activity, especially if, given a spate of rest and congenial surroundings, they are willing and able to provide not a mere bestial prodding but an act of love (see note 25). But increase of appetite grows by what it feeds on, and the bitch is up to her old complaints again.

31. Hung by the door

My priest (see note 24) takes this stance now. I have never known a spirit at once so persistent and so polite. He has not missed a visit for fifteen days, and yet (with one exception) he has been a perfect gentleman. My experience of spirits has been that they like to play by their own rules, as if existence in the other world gave them the right to patronize or bully those of us here who can perceive them, but while this fellow clearly wants to get something off his chest and has picked me out for his confessor, he has the decency to be as unobtrusive as he can. His good manners have, in fact, so impressed me that the other night, at the risk of overly encouraging him, I offered to take his name and call him when I'd time. He merely shook his head and let me go back to my work. In this regard his single outburst, if one can call it that, is strange indeed. Last Friday, as I was copying Sig's verses for my text (see note 28 above), he gave out a most piteous groan and, when I looked around, asked how could I, an educated man, pay attention to such abomination? Perhaps he was offended by the phrase "short-arm inspections," though he doesn't seem one of your priggish clerics. He may be an amateur of romantic poetry, or even a distant relative of S. T. Coleridge's. But while I have, lately, been willing to let him watch me for as long as he cares to, I cannot tolerate interruption. I shoo'd him off directly. He returned the next midnight, and the next, with the wounds on his hands freshly opened like summer roses and blood (as from a crown of thorns) dripping profusely down his forehead. He was there tonight, beside the door, when I began the last passage of Chapter 6, and were I to turn my head right now I might well see his martyred eyes still smiling sweetly at me. It is all I can do—perhaps because he reminds me of my mother—to steel myself against him, to keep from giving up a night or more to hear his story.

32. *León Fuertes*

"Señor Fuertes will give no interviews till further notice." So says a twit from the PR Department of Performing Arts, as if I were a scandalmongering hack and not a scholar, not León Fuertes' son. Nor can I be certain that the blame rests with Performing Arts; my father may be purposely avoiding me.

Having by the end of Chapter 6 reached a point in this history where the data I compiled last year gets very thin and where my father could give vital information, I began serious efforts to contact his spirit. I used the procedure traced in note 4 and have besides canceled my tennis dates with Sig and contrived to isolate myself from all distractions. Results have been at once encouraging and bleak: I have been able to tune in clearly to the Astral Plane; I've raised a host of spirits who know my father there or knew him here; I have caused to materialize in this room, speedily and at no great cost in mental energy, some very obscure spirits who had information germane to this dissertation; but I have not had a whisper from León Fuertes himself. Spirits who know or know of my father in the next world have told me, variously, that he plans to transfer from Performing Arts to Sport; that he has gone AWOL from Performing Arts to Idyll in the company of his sometime leading lady Geraldine Farrar; that he is in Victim, (a) because Lev Bronstein (L. Trotsky), who stages spectacles, not uprisings, these days and who'll direct three operas later on this year, wants him to use the Method approach for his role as Mario in *Tosca*, or (b) as a result of a bad wager made during a weekend spent in Risk. My mother says he must be resting after the long season and that the PR people are terrible about forwarding messages, even those from close relatives, but this last is no excuse or comfort. I need no Astral functionaries to pass my messages. I beam them loud and clear, and unless my father is, in fact, in Victim, he's heard me calling. Can it be that he disapproves of me? No statesman can afford to disprize the work of a serious historian, but does he, like Dr. Vertilanz, consider me an unbalanced dilettante? Can he be so myopic? Was Dr. Vertilanz correct? Or is it that my father so enjoys his new career that he cares no more for this world, for his children, for his country, for his place in history? The melding of his soul to noble music, communion with the masters, "Bravo!"s ringing to the gilded ceilings of great halls, the thrills of Risk ("That's Fuertes, the tenor, over there. God, what a plunger!"), time dripping sweetly through the boughs of Idyll with a proud and lovely diva by his side—what can he care for us?

For reasons that the text makes clear, Rebeca Fuertes could throw little light on the events describes in Chapter 7. León's stepfather, Florencio Merluza, whom I interviewed on 12th and 13th August, was of some help, though not so much as I had hoped before I learned that upon "dying," he chose Drink. Of the many spirits who broke in while I was calling León Fuertes, three had data pertinent to what I've called my father's urchinhood. These I recalled and interviewed on I 6th August. I have also used information from one living source, José R. Fuertes, my uncle Pepe (see note 35 below). A vein on the right side of my nose is throbbing fiercely.

33. She'd horn him

A favorite threat of my own wife's when she feels bored or restless. Today, for example, I was asleep—I now go to bed around seven A.M., get up for lunch, then take a short siesta—when Liz came in, lay down beside me, fumbled about until she noticed my erection, and, having nothing else to do, woke me to claim it. Now, it is scientific fact (see Gay Gaer Luce and Julius Segal, *Sleep* [New York, 1966], p. 203) that sleeping men experience periodic erections, which have nothing to do with sexual excitement. I tried to explain this to Liz, but she persisted in her advances. The *sine qua* non of controlled astral communication is sexual continence (see note 4), and as I had no intention of missing a week's calls—my father might respond later tonight, for all I know—I had to be quite firm in my refusal. She cried a bit, then, in a flash, went over to defiance, screamed she'd be damned before she'd beg for love, said she would get it in the street if not at home. The main thing is I managed to keep calm, but none of this makes my work any easier.

34. Mystery

The mysterious disappearance of Father Celso Labrador, a Costaguanan priest assigned to a rural parish near Belém, has become the chief topic of concern in the country. Labrador, who may have been the priest Sig almost flattened on our way to Mituco (see note 25), was last seen on the evening of Thursday, 7th March, when someone as yet unidentified called him from the board hut he shared with a peasant family. Two days later, on my return from Mituco, our maid (cook, family retainer—she brought my mother up), Arnulfa, who goes to mass each morning, told me that "a priest has vanished," but I paid no mind to it. On 20th March the government gave out—all newspapers are under state control—that Labrador had fled to Costaguana with the cash fund of a cooperative farm he organized, but the Tinieblan Church denied this charge from every pulpit in the country, citing a letter from the Costaguanan Ambassador that Labrador's passport is at the embassy, having been in the process of being renewed when he disappeared, and another from the General Manager of the Pelf Fiduciary Trust branch in La Merced that no large withdrawals have been made from the co-op's account. The Church demanded an inquiry; the government saw no cause to hold one. The Church resolved to hold an inquiry of its own and hired a Ticamalan detective; the government declared this an insult to the nation, denied the Ticamalan entry, and announced the opening of an official probe. This now proceeds with great deliberation while gales of rumor sweep the country from end to end. Some supporters of the government hold that Labrador died of a heart attack while copulating with his host's daughter and was discreetly buried by the Church. Others say he was abducted by the CIA just to embarrass Genghis. Most people believe that he was murdered either by landlords, on whose holdings he had encouraged peasants to squat, or by the Civil Guard. Publicly the lists are drawn with the radio, television, and newspapers denouncing Father Labrador and the "foreigner-controlled" Church, while the Church keeps asking "Where is Padre Celso?" and offering masses for his soul, and asking anyone with knowledge of the matter to come forward and confess on pain of excommunication. You, my learned examiners, are no doubt thinking that the solution of this mystery may lie within my grasp, and you no doubt are right. I'd bet my seventy-two hours of graduate course credit that the principal figure of the controversy is right this moment staring meekly at my back from his habitual corner near the door. But if you think that I will let matters of momentary import, mere "current events," distract me from the work of making history, you are wrong. Wrong, Dr. Grimes. Wrong, Professor Lilywhite. Wrong, wrong, wrong.

35. José

José Rosendo Fuertes (born 1921, President of Tinieblas 1966-1970), my uncle Pepe. My father and uncle are an excellent example of how two brothers may develop different personalities. León was direct and prodigal; Pepe is devious and mean. León led by example; Pepe never commits himself until he has a firm grip on the other fellow's privates. And so on. One of the first dentists graduated from our National University, Pepe, who is ambidextrous and who, in compensation for his crippled leg, built up his arms and shoulders by working out with spring devices, was able to pluck molars agilely with either hand, but, by his own gleeful admission, his success came from his uncanny ability to divine within an inchado or two how much a patient could afford to pay. When treating my brother Carlos and myself, he eschewed the use of Novocaine on the grounds that pain builds character and that children will brush their teeth more conscientiously when they fear the dentist's drill. I am convinced that thrift was his sole motive. He abandoned dentistry in 1962, when he persuaded my father to appoint him Minister of Public Health. He continued in the cabinet after my father's assassination, had a lean year when my father's successor, Bonifacio Aguado, was deposed by the Guardia Civil, but snatched the brass ring in 1966, conning the leaders of the Progressive Party into nominating him for President and winning the election after the front runner, César Sancudo, was gunned down and disabled. He must—since no amount of dental fees could pay his present splendor—have made a fortune in four years as President of the Republic. In March, 1970, he was impeached but not convicted. In April he was soundly thrashed at the polls by Alejandro Sancudo. He left Tinieblas for Miami on Intercontinental flight 487 at 11:59 P.M. on 31st May, 1970, his last day in office, and now resides in Coral Gables.

36. Diverse sources

Slides 1 and 2 are by Italo Bambolini (1888-1956), bartender at the Happy Time from 1925 to 1950. Bambolini was born in the Abruzzi, served briefly as an infantryman in World War I, worked as a waiter at the Royal Danieli, and emigrated to Tinieblas after Mussolini's rise to power. He was among the most vociferous of the spirits who broke in while I was calling León Fuertes. He claimed possession of most vital information, and the glimpse he gives us of young León has a certain value, but has main wish was just to pass some time. He has applied for Earthly Delights, which has a frightfully long waiting list, and like most waiting spirits will do anything for a few moments of diversion.

(Spirits not yet accepted in activities may visit this world, and Performing Arts entertains them with concerts, plays, etc. They are, however, in the main quite bored and restless, and their condition has given rise to terrestrial superstitions—e.g., the Greek view that one cannot enter Hades unless and until his body receives proper burial. Virgil takes this up [in *Aeneid,* VI: 305-330] and comes fairly close to the truth when he says that the unburied must wait a hundred years before they cross the Acheron. A spirit rarely has to wait more than a century. Dogmatic Dante, convinced that what happens to you in the next world depends on what you've done in this one and committed to a system of final solutions, gives us [in *Inferno,* III: 22-69] a great throng of souls who were in this life but lukewarm, who did neither good nor evil, who since they never really lived "have no hope of death," and who must roam the hither bank of Acheron, goaded by wasps and filthed with pus and vermin, throughout eternity. This wonderfully imagined scene perhaps informs a valid view of this world but tells us little more than nothing of the next. As usual, Dante allowed his lust for order to distort his insight.)

Slide 3 is by my uncle Pepe, who remembered León's dive from Lola's mainmast for Liz and me in June of 1972 when we visited him and my aunt Clara briefly in Coral Cables. Florencio Merluza did slide 4.

The author of slide 5, Sarita Paz, "died" of amoebic dysentery in 1940 and now is in Good Works, an activity whose complement includes a high percentage of former prostitutes. Along with other things, spirits attached to Good Works try to project charitable impulses to people in this world. Like many others moved by good intentions, they can be annoying. Señorita Paz, for example, squandered an hour of my time and a great volume of my patience in meek and yet persistent sermonizing on my conduct toward my wife. Where she got her information I don't know, but it was badly garbled, almost as though dear Liz possessed the gift of astral conversation. I did not stoop, of course, to tell "my side of the story," and I resisted the nearly irresistible impulse to suggest to Señorita Paz that my private life is none of her sainted business. In charity to her, I assume that if she had the facts and Liz could hear her, she'd aim her good intentions at the proper target. When I could bring her to the point, she told me that she knew my father well, for he visited her place of employment most every evening for six years, sometimes alone and sometimes with Merluza, selling smokes. After giving me the picture shown in text above, she went on to say that León crept out while his prey was orgasming, that she did not see what happened when the bully put his sneaker on but that she heard his scream, and that when she, a colleague, and the madam reached the room, his foot had swollen to the size and consistency of a soccer ball. As you gringos say, witty examiners, it couldn't have happened to a nicer guy.

I was introduced to Maribel Canoa, author and cosubject of slide 6, by my mother. Both are on the waiting list for Love; both loved my father, each in her own way; they have become fast friends. Maribel and León continued to see each other on and off until 1936, when he left Tinieblas. Later she followed his career from afar. She "died" by fire during the United States intervention of November, 1966, applied for Love, went into Prorogation, recognized my mother, who had preceded her by but two months and whose name and picture she had oftentimes seen in the papers, and, unable to restrain her curiosity, approached her. Each had a tinge of jealousy to overcome, but each was hungry for the other-'s view of León Fuertes, the one man in my mother's life and the most illustrious one in Maribel's. I am sure that Maribel did not give my mother so candid a glimpse of young León as she gave me.

It is said that I resemble my father in his sterner moods—my brother, Carlos, has his smile—while some women have found me attractive in my own right. In any case, I think that Maribel, who is a very loving woman, was drawn to me and might have, were such contacts possible for spirits still in Prorogation, sought to press our intercourse beyond the verbal. In lieu of more substantial titillations, she gave the snapshot of my father's first and her most innocent amour. If Liz possessed her playful, generous nature, I might find it more difficult to meet the physical requirements I set myself for astral communication.

37. *Learning*

Following his "death" in 1939, Dr. Escolástico Grillo, who is the chief source for this chapter, entered Learning, a very ancient (though not original) astral activity established some ten thousand years ago by a group of former shamans. Since Learning neither grants degrees nor offers an athletic program, it has not been oversubscribed during this century.

On expression of desire to enter Learning, a spirit goes before a board of scholars. If found acceptable, he is assigned a cell, issued a library/laboratory card, and left to himself. Members may write theses, give lectures, conduct tutorials, which other members may read, attend, take. Some members form societies where papers are read and discussed; others remain aloof. Contact with this world and other activities of the next is maintained through the Information Circle and the Inspiration Club. The former brings distinguished spirits, many of them newly "dead," to address the Circle and its guests; the latter projects discoveries and insights to people in this world and prepares an annual report for the Director of Astral Activities. Like everything else in Learning, these groups are run by their participants. Learning supports no faculty, retains no rector, employs no deans.

On joining Learning, Dr. Grillo returned to his first love, philology, to study the "lost" plays of Sophocles. (The Library, which grew from the Papyrus Club founded by Pythagoras of Samos, preserves everything of importance from this world and the next, with editing done on the premises and the task of duplication contracted to Work through the good offices of the Director of Astral Activities.) Some thirty years ago he decided to learn Chinese and assimilate the corpus of that culture. He now considers himself on the way to becoming a competent Sinologist and looks forward to several centuries of study in that discipline.

I had no difficulty contacting Dr. Grillo or persuading him to visit me here in Ciudad Tinieblas. He was enchanted to be in touch with a son of León Fuertes' and to discover that a son of León's is a scholar. He gave me four consecutive nights of interview, 22nd-25th April, 1974, responding freely and in detail to my inquiries concerning León's sojourn in his tutelage and informing me on Learning. He consented kindly to look over some chapters of this dissertation and, even more kindly, praised them. He could not, unfortunately, give me any information on my father's current whereabouts, or on his reluctance (or inability) to return my calls.

38. *The decisive moment*

When I had scavenged Dr. Grillo's brain for the last scrap of datum touching on my father and found out all I cared to for the moment about Learning, I thanked him and bade him farewell and, exhausted by our interviews, fell in a sleep so deep that I failed to hear Liz calling me for lunch, and came to only with the evening. It was raining, and as I lay drugged in lethargy, thoughts falling randomly onto my consciousness like the unpatterned slapping of fat drops onto the tin roofs of the carports past my window, Dr. Grillo materialized before me in his inky gown and asked me if I cared to go to Learning.

I sat up, kneading my temples. "Can that be done?"

"The next world is as easy to reach as the next room. You have but to 'die.'"

"That's what I thought."

"It's nothing to be glum about. 'Death's had a lot of undeserved bad press." He tucked up the skirts of his gown and sat down in my pink-plastic-webbed aluminum lawn chair. "It's been tarred with the brush of pain, which, if present at all, is merely incidental. It's been associated with oblivion, which isn't involved, unless, of course, one opts for Spirit Recycling and voluntarily surrenders self. It's been very stupidly confused with permanent assignment to Victim. I'm appalled at the volume of libelous error this world puts out concerning 'death.'"

"This world isn't very well organized, is it?"

"An utter bungle! I'd hardly say it's organized at all! Now, ours, on the other hand—" He pursed his lips in satisfaction. "Ours has a first-rate plan and first-rate execution."

Oddly, I felt a stab of doubt. I guess my mind was misted still with sleep, but what if, as my doctors had contended (see note 20), I was making it all up, my spirit visitors included?

"Death," I said softly. I switched on the lamp.

"A simple and natural process." Dr. Grillo waved the words in like the first bars of a waltz. "The cord that moors you to your body slips. You drift away. That's all there is to it."

I nodded, feeling steadier. Doubt was insane against the witness of my eyes and ears. They might as well say I was inventing this world too.

"There's a nostalgia for the body. It passes. There's fear of the unknown for most, for there are very few true scholars or adventurers who welcome the unknown. It passes too; Reception has had eons of experience putting new arrivals at their case. The only problem is making a good activity, and in your case the problem doesn't exist."

Dr. Grillo went on to tell me that some people enter Astral Activities while still in this world, attaining a kind of candidate membership. The process resembles recruitment for Victim (see note 18) in that the individual has a place reserved for him in the next world before he departs this one. It differs in that the compact may be made unconsciously and that the compensation is neither wealth nor favor but direction for one's life on earth. In theory the pledge may back out at any time; in practice he is nearly always hooked, for sense of purpose operates like an addictive drug, bringing delicious "highs" and hideous withdrawal effects.

"You pledged for Learning years ago, Camilo. There's a place for you with us, and we want you."

" 'Where is thy sting?' "

"Exactly! Adjustment's difficult for many. The point of our world is that each activity is designed as an end in itself, whereas most people here consider what they're doing merely a means to something else. When they arrive *chez nous*, they find nothing they care to spend centuries on, or at the best one or two appealing activities, which are like as not oversubscribed. But for you there's no sting at all. You are dedicated to learning now, and one might say that Learning was devised with you in mind: no distractions whatsoever, and the companionship of cultivated minds when and if one craves it. I tell you, my boy, I was happier in this world than you are, yet if I'd known Learning existed, I'd have suicided before I turned twenty."

I sighed and waved toward my desk with its typewriter and boxes full of cards. "My work."

"Ridiculous! Your work is of great value. It's amazingly impressive, in fact, when one considers the difficulties you have to overcome. But if you really want to work, you'll come to us. I've checked the card file on your area of interest. We have eight times more material on the discovery and conquest of Spanish America than the Archivo de las Indias at Seville. Our holdings on the colonial period and on the period since independence are even more impressive. An abundance of first sources! State memoranda, bills of lading, private papers. Documents like Carlos Gavilán's draft charter for the Progressive Party with your father's notes. We've everything you need to make a comprehensive history of Tinieblas—something which, by the way, exists no more in our world than in yours. Well, Camilo?" He grinned pimpishly. "What have you to say to that?"

"What can I say? With those documents . . . I'd supplement them with interviews. I assume one can locate spirits in their various activities?"

"A great deal more easily than you can from here. The Directorate has everyone on file and is quite good about facilitating research."

"I could turn time around and bring the past back whole. I could make sense of it."

Dr. Grillo smiled and nodded. "Why wait, then?"

Erudite examiners, I did not ponder long. It is just possible that you once possessed a shred of scholarly ideals. If so, cast your thoughts back to the days when you were slaving as a graduate assistant. Imagine that a distinguished scholar from Camford or Hale presented himself to you and offered you a lifetime—no, an eternal fellowship at his institution. Would you have turned him down, even if it meant leaving a spouse you got along with a great deal better than I do with mine? Your body? Well, whether having a body brings one more joy than pain is a matter of nice discrimination. I couldn't work that out with any scientific accuracy. But I judged that if I came to crave a physical existence, I could always apply for Transmigration and recycle back as goat or monkey. Why wait indeed!

"May I suggest opening a vein," said Dr. Grillo. "They say it's painless after the first slash. I've noticed you keep a razor blade in your desk."

"For sharpening pencils."

"I don't doubt it, my boy, but it seemed keen enough, and you scarcely have to worry about infection. Come. You can chat with me like Petronius until the end. Or rather till the beginning."

The blade was where I'd left it, one edge wrapped in adhesive plaster. I took it and sat down at my desk—in the saddle, as it were. I pulled the wastebasket out and held my left hand over it. No need to leave a mess for poor Arnulfa.

"Ssu-ma Ch'ien has agreed to admit you to his seminar," said Dr. Grillo cheerily.

"The Han historian?" I touched the blade to my left wrist.

"Yes. He was my tutor for a while, and we've remained quite friendly."

The rain continued its unpatterned slapping. I pressed—and then the door of the apartment slammed and Liz's voice called out, "Camilo?"

39. Success . . . superior to failure

Of all life's endeavors, none demonstrates so clearly as does suicide the superiority of success to failure. The successful suicide achieves a freedom few others know. The failure, on the other hand, must expect an indeterminate period of imprisonment featuring the kind of abuse otherwise reserved for the captured enemies of despots. One need not even actually attempt suicide to reap the fruits of failure. It is enough, revered examiners, merely to be suspected of suicidal tendencies on the flimsiest of evidence (e.g., having hit one's head against the wall to clear one's thoughts) for one to be all but electrocuted. There is no future at all in an unsuccessful outright attempt.

Admittedly, suicide is not a particularly difficult act to perform successfully. No special talent is required. Anyone with a sincere desire and a bit of guts can manage it—given some luck, for with the less painful methods there comes a moment between the departure of strength and/or consciousness and the arrival of "death" when the aspiring suicide is vulnerable to what is misdirectedly called rescue. There, and nowhere else, is the rub.

On the evening mentioned in note 38, I had the will but lacked the luck. And since no one, repeat, no one, is ever, repeat, ever, going to strap me down and shock the feces out of me again, I chose to abandon hope of success for the moment rather than risk failure. I dropped the blade into the wastebasket and with my shirttail stanched the single drop of blood I'd drawn.

"*Hasta muy pronto*," said Dr. Grillo, fading.

Liz was knocking at the door, calling, "Camilo?"

40. A sexual urge

I have not been able to find a physiological explanation of why hanged men get erections, and personal experience prompts me to offer here the suggestion that the characteristic "hang wang" or "goner-boner" may be a "Here I stand!" affirmation of the flesh made in the face of impending fleshly dissolution. When I aborted a takeoff for the next world, I found myself possessed by a sexual urge.

I admit that my wife, Elizabeth, is an attractive woman and that when I opened my study door to her on the evening in question she looked particularly desirable. Her face and throat were flushed (from running up the stairs, I suppose). Her eyes sparkled. Her lips were moist and puffed. Her hair, unbound and somewhat disarrayed, was softly touched by raindrops. But I was well aroused when I got up from my chair—in other words, *before* I saw her. And my desire persisted despite her vigorous if brief resistance.

She blinked nervously and, seeing my question in my eyes, said she'd had the strange presentiment I was in trouble, had rushed home . . . I took her in my arms, touched by this proof of affection and pleased that she might be developing, by contagion as it were, some of my powers.

She pulled back and asked if anyone had called. Between kisses I reminded her our phone was out of order. She relaxed a bit, but when I started to remove her blouse—which was half unbuttoned to begin with—she protested: Sig was downstairs in the car; they would be late for his lecture.

Normally this would have made me angry. In fact, I am amazed I didn't answer her, for I've listened to enough complaints from her about my "coldness" (which is, of course, nothing of the sort but rather dedication to my work) not to suffer rejection kindly. I put my refusal to be distracted into argument down to the strength of my desire. My body, redeemed from extinction, was getting even. My mouth had better things to do than tell her I didn't care who was waiting, nor did my hands let hers prevent getting her slacks unzipped. I think her reluctance was all mental anyway, for her flesh was warm, and when I fingered down inside her panties I found her body quite prepared for love. She began giggling somewhat hysterically, squirmed, cursed me, then repented, and murmuring, "It never rains. . ." consented.

Some twenty minutes after Liz had shivered, sighed, smiled, snuggled, then squibbed me out, squirted from under me, snatched up her clothes, and sashayed to the bathroom; after she had reappeared clothed, combed, and, I suppose, abluted, to eye me slyly from the doorway, smirk, and blow a kiss; after the apartment door had slammed again and Siggy's Puma snarled among the rainslaps, I found myself considering the opening sentences of Chapter 8; noticed my ideas flowing easily and clearly; decided that the experience and satisfaction of fleshly appetite (e.g., a sexual urge) might be of value, brutish kicks aside, as an aid to intellectual effort; and since I was not sure that the excellence of Learning's facilities for scholarship constituted adequate compensation for the loss of such contributions as the flesh offers, resolved on purely professional ground—my work remaining my chief if not sole value— to postpone my departure from this world for an indefinite period.

41. *The solution*

The solution to the Case of the Crestfallen Cleric was revealed to me the same night. I suffered more than sought it, but included at no extra charge was news of my father—proof, I suppose, that a scholar should stay alert to tangent possibilities.

Having decided not to shuffle off quite yet, I got to work and rattled away at Chapter 8 with a great fluency. Liz came home sometime after ten, and I saw her to her bed in friendly fashion. When she said she was hungry, I remembered that I hadn't eaten in more than twenty-four hours and went to fix hot milk and sandwiches—melted cheddar for her, cold ham and Dijon mustard for myself—which I carried to her room. We munched in tandem, she propped on pillows, I perched at the foot of her bed, she mock-chiding me for having "raped" her, I mock-chiding her for having taken the conventionally wise tactic: relax and enjoy it. We might almost have staged a reconstruction of the crime, but she yawned between bites and sips, and I had work to do. I kissed her, took the crockery back to the kitchen, and then went to my study. My priest was waiting.

He looked as woebegone as ever, while I, *post coitum tristis* to the contrary notwithstanding, was in the sort of excellent good humor that inspires acts of charity. So despite my eagerness to get on with my crisply-begun new chapter, I did not chase him off as I had done each night for near six weeks but, in the best psychoanalytic style, offered him the couchlike lawn chair, pulled my work chair round behind it, and suggested that he get his problem off his chest.

He began melodramatically ("I am a father's spirit . . .") and, uncertain that he'd captured my attention, fell to ranting ("List, list, O list!"), and then demanded, if I did ever my dear country love, that I revenge his foul and most unnatural murder. I heard this out—at some psychic cost, for he might have woken Liz—and at length he calmed enough to identify himself as Father Celso Labrador, the missing Costaguanan priest (see note 34), and to relate substantially as follows:

While still a teen and still, of course, "alive," Padre Celso joined Justice, a militant outfit designed to right wrongs of this world. His enlistment was largely subliminal, but he can, in retrospect, date it to 21st January, 1961, when he heard (via the Voice of America) a floridly translated and impassionedly intoned version of the inaugural address of John Fitzgerald Kennedy (1917-1963, President of the United States I 961-1963). When the announcer urged, *"Mejor Pregunten '¿Que es lo que podemos hacer juntos para la humanidad?'"* young Celso grew so obsessed and furious with something the majority of us scarcely remark, viz., the wildly unequal distribution in this world of human dignity and freedom, that he pledged for Justice.

Five years later he joined the priesthood. His prior enlistment in Justice had little to do with this decision, which he took mainly to please his mother. It did, however, determine the kind of priest he was:

Item—When confronted, in the confessional or out, with situations where human dignity conflicted with Church dogma, he invariably put himself on the human side.

Item—When offered a promising spot in the Vatican, he asked to remain in Costaguana or, failing that, to be sent to some other poor country.

Item—When assigned as secretary to the Archbishop of Tinieblas, he requested a parish in the interior.

Item—When posted to Belém, he moved in with a peasant family, organized a peasant cooperative, and spent most of his time at labor in the fields.

Item—When his parishioners were served eviction orders, he did not counsel them to render unto Genghis and seek reward in heaven but mobilized them to struggle for the land they worked.

In short, while others fondled altar boys or schnozzled down the sacramental wine, Padre Celso was ruled by a morbid craving for justice which he sought constantly to appease.

Shortly before 9:00 P.M. on 7th March, 1974, while Liz and I were bedding down in the Mituco Guest House (see note 25), an olive Veldtmaster (with a winch at the front and "GUARDIA CIVIL/ACCIÓN CÍVICA" stencilled in yellow on the doors above flaked *Alianza* handclasps) four-wheeled to the top of the dirt track below the orange-crate and flattened-tin-can hovel—property of one Nepo Delgado, campesino—where Padre Celso lived. On board were Major Lisandro Empulgueras, chief of the Fourth Military District; Sergeant Evaristo Tranca; Sergeants Martillo and Tenazas from the barracks at Otán; Private Punzón, driver. Martillo and Tenazas, who wore civilian clothes and weren't known around Belém, got out and climbed up with a story: Someone (they didn't bother to make up, a name) was hurt, yes, kicked by a mule and stepped on, and needed—what you call it?—unction. They brought Padre Celso down, grabbed him a few steps from the vehicle, told him if he yelled they'd take his hosts, shoved him in with Major Empulgueras, slammed the door, hopped the tailgate, and squatted in the back.

Padre Celso asked where they were taking him. Major Lisandro Empulgueras said that depended: would he be a good boy and stop causing trouble? Padre Celso pretended not to understand: they'd said a man was injured. Major Lisandro Empulgueras hawed and asked if Padre Celso thought that he, the military district chief, would traipse out to the bush for crap like that.

Padre Celso allowed that Major Empulgueras wasn't known for the amount of time and energy he spent on errands of compassion. Major Lisandro Empulgueras warned Padre Celso not to show disrespect, boy. Padre Celso reminded Major Empulgueras to call him "Father." Major Lisandro Empulgueras took Padre Celso's ear and twisted so that Padre Celso's head bent back toward the tailgate and said that Padre Celso was not his father. The major knew who his father was. Did Padre Celso think the major didn't know his father? Given that syntax, Padre Celso couldn't answer yes or no. Major Lisandro Empulgueras twisted; Padre Celso's head bent back until he smelled the peppermint on Sergeant Tenazas's breath. He told the major no, he didn't think that; yes, the major knew his father. Major Lisandro Empulgueras released the ear and patted Padre Celso's close-cropped head. That was good; he was a good boy.

All this time the Veldtmaster rocked down the dirt track like a trawler in deep swells. Now it stopped, and Private Punzón got out to switch the front wheels back for two-wheel drive. Padre Celso put his hand on the door handle. Sergeant Tenazas put his hand on Padre Celso's neck. Padre Celso put his hand back in his lap.

When the Veldtmaster pulled out onto the high-crowned asphalt road, Padre Celso asked Major Empulgueras why they didn't let him go. Major Lisandro Empulgueras poked Padre Celso in the ribs and said he'd been a bad boy, hadn't he?—butting in and stirring people up and causing trouble. Tinieblas was a happy, well-run country where people ought to mind their own affairs, foreigners especially. If Padre Celso promised to behave, he could go home.

When Padre Celso did not reply but kept his eyes trained over Sergeant Evaristo Tranca's shoulder out along the bug-clogged cones of light poked forward by the headlamps, Major Lisandro Empulgueras reminded him that the Fourth Military District comprised the province of La Merced, and Mituco, and the Pacific Ocean for two hundred miles out from the coast, and all the sky above that land and water, and that its chief had many things to do and all the power necessary to do them. He, Lisandro Empulgueras, could have had Padre Celso picked up anytime and taught harsh lessons in comportment and, if need be, deported from the province and the country—from this world, in fact. But he, Lisandro Empulgueras, was a reasonable man who understood that people make mistakes, a man who tried to do his duty, which was to run a tranquil district, without resorting to extreme solutions or showing disrespect to anyone, foreigners included. So he had gone out of his way to be both courteous and discreet, coming in person to ask the padre to be-have, taking great care to keep their meeting secret, and bringing with him trusted men who didn't see or hear, and hence would not remember, anything their major didn't want them to.

Padre Celso looked on ahead over Sergeant Tranca's shoulder and said, fi-nally, that the major didn't want a scandal, that he didn't want him, Padre Celso, to lose his credit with the peasants, that he wanted to use him with the peasants.

Major Lisandro Empulgueras sighed and remarked to no one in particular that the trouble with most Costaguanans was that they were devious and, hence, attributed deceit to other people. Then he said it was no matter and asked Padre Celso if he'd be a good boy now, if he'd behave himself, if he'd cooperate with the authorities of the state, a state in which he was a guest, correct? and respect the principle of private ownership, a principle supported by the Church, wasn't that so? and help avoid violence and disorder, which no one wanted, right? least of all Major Empulgueras and the Tinieblan Civil Guard—though both were well prepared to deal with violence if it came and to keep order—and get his pack of filthy, stinking peasant squatters off Don Kublai Manduco's land.

Now, when Padre Celso left his home that night with strangers, he was ap-prehensive; and when they laid hands on him and told him not to yell, he was alarmed, and when he saw the Guardia vehicle, he was quite worried; and when he recognized Major Lisandro Empulgueras, with his neat brown-and-green camouflage uniform and his high-polished boots and his gold stars, he was afraid; and when the Veldtmaster rolled off along the high-crowned asphalt road toward Belém, where Major Empulgueras had his headquarters, his prison, and his basement interrogation chamber, he was terrified; and when the major mentioned casually—it was a matter of small novelty and consequence to him, after all—that he could have him killed, he was pos-sessed by a deep, sphincter-loosening dread; but when he heard the major refer crudely to his peasants, he felt such an intense craving for justice that he forgot his fear and vulnerability and turned to look the major in the eye. Didn't he see? It wasn't Kublai Manduco's land, it was theirs! They'd lived on it for years! They'd worked it! Their title was their sweat! And now they were organized in a cooperative and could farm properly. There was no rea-son for them to leave.

Major Lisandro Empulgueras raised both hands, tensed like a pair of claws, and held them under Padre Celso's chin. Then he turned and clamped his hands onto the top of the front seat back on either side of Private Punzón's neck and leaned forward, grinding his teeth and twisting his body like a man undergoing prostatic massage. At length he spread his hands and raised them an inch or so and, as though pressing on the inch or so of air between the seat-back and his palms, forced his shoulders back. Then, in the hoarse and halting voice of one showing heroic self-control, he told Padre Celso that he was not discussing anything. He was informing him that the peasants would depart, one way or another. Agitation and disrespect for law would cease, one way or another. He was asking him to behave, to be a good boy, to help out. He asked this for the good of all. The men with him were witnesses: he, Lisandro Empulgueras, was being reasonable.

But Padre Celso was stoned on justice and beyond the reach of human reason. He reminded Major Empulgueras that the Tinieblan Revolution had, supposedly, been organized to halt the exploitation of the people, that the Revolutionary Government had promised land reform and land titles to *campesinos,* that in his New Year's speech General Genghis Manduco—

Major Lisandro Empulgueras seized Padre Celso's shirt and yanked him down and forward so that the padre's face pressed in the major's lap. He advised Padre Celso not to talk to him about his general. He got his orders from his general. His general wanted Padre Celso to behave, to be a good boy, to stop making trouble, to clean up the mess he'd made. Now, was the padre going to behave? If he didn't know how, the major would instruct him. What did the padre say?

Padre Celso twisted his face up from Major Empulgueras's lap and told the major to take his hands off his cloth.

The major's fists began to shake uncontrollably, bouncing Padre Celso's face into the major's lap. But then the Veldtmaster, which all this while had been rolling at moderate speed along the high-crowned asphalt road, slowed and pulled onto the shoulder and stopped, and when it stopped, so did the major's fists. Then the major asked once more if Padre Celso was going to be good, and the padre, after some twisting of his face, replied that he didn't get his orders from the major's general.

Major Lisandro Empulgueras jerked his fists up and flung Padre Celso over to the right side of the Veldtmaster. He wiped his hands on his brown and green camouflage tunic as if there were something sticky on them, and opened his door and got out and shut the door softly behind him. He turned and stuck his head in through the window and, very softly, told the men inside to teach Padre Celso to behave. He stood and reached into a trouser pocket and pulled out a little brown-and-green camouflage beret and set it on his head at a brave and military angle. Then he strode off along the bug-clogged cone of light poked forward by the Veldtmaster's left headlamp toward a sedan parked up ahead. As be did so, Sergeant Tenazas took a burlap sack from behind the rear seat and bagged it over Padre Celso's head. Then he and Sergeant Martillo swarmed over the rear seat, pushing Padre Celso down onto the floor with his hands crumpled under him against the muddy rubber mat and his gut mashed by the hump of the drive shaft, and, not sparing him some prods and stomps, held him down with their feet.

At this point I got up and advised Padre Celso that his hour was over. Actually, what with the wealth of detail he'd included and the way he hopped about from his experience in this world to what he'd found out in the next, he'd already had some seven minutes extra, but I'd withheld my interruption until what seemed a natural break—more than the shrinks back at the Fasholt quackery would ever do. He gasped in astonishment: what did I mean? I meant, I said, that I had work to do. But didn't I want to hear the rest? I told him, sincerely, that of course I did: it was a gripping tale, enlivened by topicality and the coincidence that I had glimpsed him on the very afternoon of his misadventure. But I ruled myself with a stern discipline. Compelling as it was, I could not let his story keep me longer from my work. I was pledged to Learning even as he had been to Justice, a situation that he, of all people, ought easily to comprehend. In any case, I pointed out, he'd said at the outset that he'd been murdered, so I supposed that was the denouement.

He sighed and shook his head, which was all gouted with blood from the scratches round his brow. "But your father said—"

"What about my father? Have you seen him? Where is he?"

"Let me go on."

"Oh, no. Tell me right now. Speak, or I'll exorcise you from this house! There's not another person in this country who can even see you, much less hear your twaddle! Spit it out, damn you! What about my father?"

He smiled his sad smile and wrung his stigmata'd bands and said he pitied me. Then he told me that when he "died" there'd been a mix-up. He showed up at Reception in such awful shape that he was taken for an escapee from Victim and dispatched there forthwith. Before they got his papers straightened out, he met my father.

"In Victim?"

"On a long stretch, I'm afraid."

"But why? What for?"

"I'm sorry, I don't know. He was more interested in hearing me than in telling me his troubles. Oh, I don't know if it was me so much, but he cares a lot about this country. He told me to find you and tell you what they'd done to me and how they're grabbing up the land. He said you'd do something about it."

"Me?"

"Yes. He said to see his son, Carlos Fuertes."

I smiled and sat down on my bed. "Well, that explains it. You've got the wrong son. My name's Camilo. You want my elder brother. He's the man of action in the family."

"I see. How stupid of me. Six weeks wasted." He sighed again and stood. "I'm sorry to have taken up your time; you've been most kind. Perhaps you will tell me where to find your brother."

"I don't know. No one has heard from him in years. But even if I knew, it wouldn't help you much. You couldn't possibly communicate with him. My mother's tried a thousand times."

"He doesn't believe in spirits?"

"Worse. He won't believe. At the least mention of anything beyond the material universe—religion, spiritism, what you will—he mobilizes all his intelligence and will to disbelieve."

"And you? Can you do nothing for me, for your country?"

"Yes . . . I think I can. I can put your story in my notes. I think the information that you've given me about my father justifies that. Yes, I'll give it a footnote."

He smiled and nodded sadly. "Poor brothers. One can't believe, the other cannot act."

"Look, sir, Father, I'm trying to get the past arranged. I can't afford to care about the present or the future."

"I should say you can't afford not to. But I understand. Thank you, in any case," He made to go.

"Wait." Seeping compassion wore away my will. "Come back again, say in a day or two. I'm not an activist, please understand, but we can have another session. Perhaps you will feel better."

"Would you try to locate your brother for me? One never knows, I might be able . . ."

"All right. I'll call my uncle. I'll ask around. And you might ask after my father. "

"Agreed. Till later, then." And he backed slowly through the wall.

I pulled the paper out of my machine and sat down at once to draft this note. I trust that it constitutes adequate proof of my good faith toward Padre Celso.

42. *Scandalmongering*

Remains a popular diversion in this disgusting little country. At least that is the conclusion I must draw from the phone call I received earlier tonight (Thursday, 2nd May, 1974) in which the string-activated voice of one of Mr. S. Heilanstalt's discarded dolls tried to persuade me that Sig and my wife, Liz, have an adulterous connection. I've had such thoughts myself in moments of depression, and I confess I was on the way to being persuaded until my anonymous scandalmonger (who said she has a key to Sig's apartment and received my congratulations thereon) claimed to have surprised Liz and Sig "fucking each other" (the phrase is Scandalmonger's, not mine) on his couch last Friday evening. That proved the tale a fabrication, dreamed up, no doubt, in hope of procuring its authoress some revenge against a man who'd dropped her, for on that particular evening Liz had no need of adultery but was in fact the most satisfied woman in Christendom (see note 40), thanks to her own husband. Furthermore, a moment's reflection (accomplished after I had set the phone receiver softly in its cradle) convinced me that Liz would scarcely betray me for Sig. Oh, no, my examiners! The tenth particle of an authentic genius, who can call spirits from the vasty deep (including that of Sofonias de Bisagra, main source for Chapter 9, who is waiting patiently while I complete this note), is worth a whole network of talk-show-blabbing scribblers, and Liz knows it.

It is distressing, nonetheless, to consider the anguish scandalmongering sows among the ungifted and fraily-ego'd.

43. Feet

As soon as the Veldtmaster began moving, Padre Celso began struggling. He almost made it to his knees and, during the attempt, experienced the fantasy that he would gain the door, fling himself out, survive the impact, elude his captors, reach the capital, and, with the blessing of the Archbishop and the support of the Church, so rouse the populace to righteous indignation that the dictatorship would fall and a regime of justice replace it. Then a boot-shod foot clubbed into the base of his spine, and a second boot-shod foot stomped on his shoulder, and a third boot-shod foot clamped on the back of his right knee, and a fourth boot-shod foot exploded down onto his neck, mashing it against the floor mat. The feet were followed by a weary voice advising him to "Calm down, cocksucker," and, after a bit, Padre Celso grew calm.

It was not that he gave up. The feet had given him a new fix of justice. They might have been stomping other people, after all; instead they were occupied with him. In absorbing this admittedly minute portion of the world's pain and degradation, and thus insuring that it was not distributed to others, Padre Celso felt be was advancing the cause of justice, and he was aware, as never before, of the purpose of his life. He was in fact so crazed with his sense of purpose that he would have felt deprived had he been turned loose. At first he adopted toward Sergeants Martillo and Tenazas more or less the attitude of the Caracas diplomatic corps toward General Genghis Manduco's brother Mangu when the latter, who was then serving as Tinieblan Ambassador to Venezuela, got drunk at a reception and urinated into the Foreign Minister's swimming pool: he decided to ignore the louts as beneath attention, much less his contempt. Then he took pity on them, for clearly they led pointless lives compared to his.

It would not, on the face of it, appear that to be crammed down on the floor of a vehicle under two pairs of boot-shod feet, with a burlap sack over one's head and one's neck pinned against the floor mat and one's guts squashed by the hump of the driveshaft, is a situation particularly conducive to human dignity and freedom, but according to Padre Celso Labrador (who may be granted some authority on the matter), it's not one's situation that counts but rather one's perception of it. In his case, he felt that he was where he ought to be, doing what he ought to do. In this manner he rode to Belém.

44. Lord Balfour

Arthur James Balfour, 1st Earl of Balfour (1848-1930). This scion of the famous Cecil family and former Prime Minister of Great Britain, whose dedication to public service has endured beyond the grave and who is presently a Special Assistant to the Director of Astral Activities, visited me tonight (8th May, 1974) in connection with inquiries Padre Celso Labrador has been making on my behalf concerning León Fuertes, During an hour's conversation Balfour showed great charm, wit, and (alas) discretion, for despite all my pumping he released only a drop of information: Earlier this year León Fuertes stopped by Risk, wagered a century in Victim against an hour of True Love, and lost.

Now, my father gambled a bit in this world, but it is most unlike him to offer odds like that. I protested. I pleaded for more news. Balfour merely smiled his blue eyes at me, shook his moustache languidly, and turned away my pleas and protests with brilliantly phrased, inconsequential chit-chat. At length I grew somewhat hysterical, and he put me in my place—but even then he remained civil.

"My dear boy," he said, climbing from the chair where he'd been lounging to stand loosely before me, his hands hung on his jacket lapels, "we don't give out information concerning spirits assigned in Victim, The policy's quite clear. It's been in force for more than a millennium. The Director has shown you a good deal of consideration as it is. He might very well have ignored your queries. Or sent someone like Otto Bismarck to shout you down. Quite a competent fellow, Otto—we share a suite of offices, you know—but rather more iron hand than velvet glove. So you see, you've no call to throw a tantrum. I should have thought you'd show better breeding in any case."

"But it's a question of my work! I must talk with my father!"

"You'll simply have to get along without that. Unless you care to wait a hundred years. In any event, we shall entertain no further inquiries about your father's present status."

For my part, I have been unable to inform Padre Celso on my brother Carlos's whereabouts. I have, however (as the reader will have noticed), heard him out through another installment of his martyrdom.

45. Cruelty

The Civil Guard installation at Belém is on the edge of town, about two hundred meters from the restaurant where Liz and Sig and I lunched the afternoon of our trip to Mituco (see note 25). A high wall topped with electrified barbed wire encloses the District Headquarters, a jail, a barrack, and a motor pool. The Veldtmaster (with Padre Celso tamped down out of sight) drove in calmly, Sergeant Evaristo Tranca exchanging wisecracks with the guard at the gate, and pulled round to the rear of the district headquarters. Tranca jumped out and opened a door leading to the cellar. Sergeants Martillo and Tenazas hauled Padre Celso from the vehicle floor, dragged him to the door, but (since Tranca warned "Don't mark him!") did not throw him down the stairs but dragged-pushed-carried him instead. Meantime Tranca told Private Punzón to check the Veldtmaster back into the motor pool and disappear.

The main room of the District Headquarters cellar contained, among others, the following training aids: a wooden chair, a roll of telephone cord, some three-quarter-inch Manila rope, a selection of radiator hoses. Sergeants Martillo and Tenazas sat Padre Celso in the chair, and Sergeant Evaristo Tranca cut a piece of telephone cord and joined Padre Celso's elbows behind the chair back. He tied another piece of cord around Padre Celso's head so that a fold of burlap was held firmly in his mouth. Finally he looped a length of cord three times around Padre Celso's thighs, binding him securely to the seat. He smiled at Sergeants Martillo and Tenazas and said thanks for their trouble, they could take off now. They said they'd stay and help, and Sergeant Evaristo Tranca said they didn't have to, it wouldn't be a long or tedious lesson, but they said it was still early and they didn't know anyone in Belém and hadn't much of anything to do, so Sergeant Tranca said all right, stick around. All this time Padre Celso sat with his thighs bound to the chair seat and his elbows joined behind the chair back and the burlap sack tied over his head.

Then Sergeant Evaristo Tranca picked out a three-inch truck radiator hose about two and one-half feet long from the pile in the corner and gripped it just above one end and swung it softly against his calf a couple times and walked over to the chair and stood at a diagonal to it, so that his crotch was over Padre Celso's right knee, and started beating Padre Celso on the side of his left breast. Sergeant Tranca swung the hose crisply, with a good follow through though not particularly hard, at about the tempo used by circus bands to toot "The Skaters' Waltz" for trapeze artists. He gave the padre thirty or forty swats, hitting without anger or enjoyment, like a housewife beating a rug. Then he stopped and massaged his right forearm and bicep. All this time Padre Celso made no sound, not even the crushed grunts and gasps one might have expected to leak out through the burlap.

Sergeant Martillo offered to spell him for a while, but Tranca said the lesson was probably over. He dropped his hose and untied the cord from Padre Celso's head and plucked the soggy fold of burlap from his mouth and asked him (very much in the style of Major Lisandro Empulgueras) if he'd decided to be good. Padre Celso said nothing.

Martillo repeated his offer. Sergeant Tenazas suggested they use a thinner hose. Tranca said to wait and pulled the sack off Padre Celso's head.

Now, when Sergeant Evaristo Tranca pulled the burlap sack off Padre Celso's head, he jumped back as though smacked with a radiator hose, and Sergeants Martillo and Tenazas jumped back also, Martillo slapping his forehead with the heel of his right hand and Tenazas gasping, *"Chucha madre! Coño! Carajo! La puta!"* for Padre Celso, whom they had all seen get in the Veldtmaster clean-shaven and close-shorn, now had an auburn beard and hair that flowed onto his shoulders. Worse, much worse, the padre neither wept nor whined nor whimpered. The three sergeants had seen hard cases bleat and blubber after the kind of beating Tranca had administered, yet Padre Celso, who hadn't seemed tough at all, merely regarded them with a wistful, infinitecompassion gaze. That gaze drilled into the three sergeants with fearful cruelty.

46. *Twisted and hateful*

This, sympathetic examiners—and if you have a scrap of human feeling you can scarcely fail to sympathize with me—is the most recent characterization of me offered by my loving helpmeet. The occasion was a comment so inoffensive that it does not merit reproduction here. Even if we credit her protests of good faith, even if we grant her claim that she thought I was awake already —a claim that is by no means proved—do I deserve to be called twisted at a time like this? Suicide, mass murder, the destruction of the world itself would have been perfectly justified responses to the Balfour Declaration (see note 44). My father is in Victim! My gift and all the agonies I've suffered perfecting it now count for nothing!

Momentum carried me forward, reeling, through notes 44 and 45, through a good portion of Chapter 9. Iron discipline enabled me to prevent my despair's leaking onto the page. Two Seconals blessed me with dreamless sleep. . . . And then the inconsiderate drab comes in and wakes me, drags me back to my blind alley. She flits in humming, and boots me back to reality. She coos about its being a lovely afternoon, when it is surely the most hideous afternoon in human history, with the possible exception of the afternoon I lost my fellowship. She swoops at me—purportedly to kiss me, but if so, so what? And when I make a minor, inoffensive grumble, touching, it so happens, on her and her darling Siggy, but in any case too innocent to merit reproduction here, she dips into her bottomless well of unfairness and calls me hateful.

It was mainly habit that sent me back to work after she huffed out. That and the need for some distraction. The thought of my father's sufferings, the news that I shall not have him as a source for this history, are too terrible to bear for longer than brief instants. Accordingly, I finished Chapter 9. I then spent a quarter of an hour considering emigration to the next world and a long enough enlistment in Victim to interview my father, León Fuertes. I was on the point—or rather on the edge—of doing exactly that when it occurred to me that certain people must be taught a lesson. Dr. Emil Vertilanz must be taught a lesson. Mrs. Elizabeth Cleaver Fuertes must be taught a lesson. Arthur James Balfour, Lord Balfour, must be taught a lesson, Smug morons must be taught that there are more things in this world and the next than are dreamt of in their philistiny, and that there exist a certain few human beings who simply will not abandon the work of civilization, no matter how many obstacles smug morons strew into their path.

47. Baseball

As soon as the three sergeants had recovered from their shock, they reacted to the cruelty of Padre Celso's gaze. They began shouting at the padre and abusing him with curses. Sergeant Martillo smacked his forehead with the heel of his right hand and yelled, "He's making fun of us, the freak! He's mocking us! He knows he shouldn't have his hair like that! You freak, you know we don't allow that in this country, no hair like that, no filthy stinking beards!" He made as if to smash Padre Celso in the face, but Sergeant Tranca grabbed his arm and yelled, "Don't mark him!" so Sergeant Martillo fell to cursing Padre Celso for a filthy stinking weirdo faggot freak. Sergeant Tenazas began to curse as well. He hopped about as though someone had put a blowtorch to his bottom, screaming about what they did to freaks if they caught them in Otán, until he and Martillo were so worked up they made a rush for Padre Celso, and Sergeant Evaristo Tranca, who was furious himself but not so furious that he forgot his duty, threw himself between Padre Celso and the two Otán sergeants, shouting, "Don't mark him, *carajo!* Don't mark the fucker up!"

All this while Padre Celso sat quietly, tormenting the three sergeants with his gaze. His composure cost him no effort. It was true he wasn't tough. He had felt every one of Sergeant Tranca's blows most keenly. But the pain of each blow confirmed that he was serving justice and reinforced the purpose of his life, so that he was now totally tripped out. Had he realized that his gaze was torturing the three sergeants, he would have looked away. He bore them no ill will. Insofar as he was conscious of their presence, he bore them gratitude, gratitude mingled with pity, since they would clearly never know his peace and sense of purpose.

At length the three sergeants calmed down. Martillo was right, said Sergeant Evaristo Tranca. The padre was making fun of them. He was making fun of the Guardia Civil and the Revolutionary Government and General Genghis Manduco. He hadn't learned his lesson—far from it! Several things night be done in a case like this, and Sergeant Tranca felt the best would be to play some baseball.

48. The ball

While Sergeant Evaristo Tranca went to the barracks to recruit players, Sergeants Martillo and Tenazas took the following steps to provide a ball:

1. Martillo kicked the chair over with the padre in it and cut the cord that bound him to the seat and pulled off his trousers and underpants and bound his ankles firmly.

2. Tenazas selected a length of rope and put one end between the padre's knees and pulled it through and drew the rope against the cord that bound the padre's ankles.

3. Tenazas set the chair up and, standing on it, reeved both ends of the rope through a steel ring bolted to the ceiling beam near the big bulb that lit the room.

4. Martillo and Tenazas hauled the padre up so that he hung with his long hair just brushing the square drain in the center of the cement floor.

5. Martillo held the padre aloft while Tenazas made the rope fast to a steel ring set in the cement wall.

6. Martillo gathered the padre's shirt and furled it so that it hung bunched about his neck and armpits.

Scarcely had step 6 been completed, when Sergeant Tranca emerged onto the field with half a dozen players.

49. The line-up

Leading off, batting right-banded, Sergeant Carlos Martillo, a twelve-year Guardia veteran from Aguascalientes in Salinas Province, who now makes his home in Otán. Though short and stumpy, Martillo gets a lot of power out of those thick wrists and heavy shoulders.

On deck, another Otán favorite, Sergeant Emilio Tenazas, in his tenth year with the Guard. Tenazas likes the whip-action of a two-and-one-half-inch Mopar baby, and there he is, limbering up, riffling a few practice swings.

Hitting third is Private Juan Calimba, out of Sombras in Selva Trópica. The big southpaw is only in his second year, but he gets a lot of respect at the plate.

Batting cleanup, from Bastidas in Tuquetá, Private Longino Horca. Before coming to Belém, Horca spent four years with the Guard detachment at Fangosa Island Penal Colony. He has power to all fields.

In fifth position, Private Alfonso Estilete, a farm boy from Remedios. This is Estilete's first season with the Guardia, but you can't call him a rookie, not with his four years sledging steers in the Angostura slaughterhouse.

Batting sixth, the nine-year veteran Corporal Elvio Bastón. Elvio's a local boy from nearby San Carlos, and you can bet he's not going to let his home province down tonight.

In the seventh spot, Private Alvaro Manopla, from the nation's capital, Ciudad Tinieblas. The reason why Alvaro's wearing clogs and skivvies is that be was in the shower when he learned there was a game tonight. He's never missed a game in five years with the Guardia, and being out of uniform shouldn't affect his hitting.

And rounding out the order, also from Ciudad Tinieblas, the seventeen-year-old rookie Private Casto Porra, in his very first Guardia game.

The old swamp fox himself, Sergeant Evaristo Tranca, will be doing the pitching. Catcher, of course, is anyone who isn't up at bat.

50. The game

Sergeant Evaristo Tranca bent and grabbed two fistfuls of Padre Celso
Labrador's long auburn hair and walked back toward the wall, pulling the
padre up and back so that he hung at about a forty-five-degree angle to the
floor, and Sergeant Martillo stood in, crowding the plate (which was the
square drain in the center of the floor), swishing the fat radiator hose back
and forth in his big blue-veined hands. Then Sergeant Tranca let the padre
swing down toward the drain, and Sergeant Martillo dipped his left shoulder
and stepped forward with his left foot and whipped the hose around, clean
and level, into Padre Celso's stomach.

Thwap!

"Attaway!"

"Good hit!"

Corporal Bastón caught Padre Celso around the waist where be was swinging and took hold of the telephone cord that bound his elbows together behind his back and walked him to Sergeant Tranca. Tranca took him by the
hair again and pulled him up and back as far as he would go, and meanwhile
Sergeant Tenazas stepped in with his thin, switch-action hose. Then the padre
went whizzing down again, and Sergeant Tenazas stepped out with his left
foot, bailing out from the inside fast ball, and golfed the hose up across Padre
Celso's chest.

Thwunk!

"Good hit! Good bit!"

Sergeant Martillo caught Padre Celso where he swung and walked him
back toward Sergeant Tranca, and Tranca came halfway down and grabbed
the padre's hair, and while he hauled the padre back, Private Calimba stepped
up to the drain, with the others calling, "Come on, Juanchi! Get a piece of
'im, Juan baby!" Tranca let fly again, pushing the padre so that his hair
brushed right across the drain, and Calimba squared around and swung like
an axman splitting cordwood on a stump and flailed the hose end down on
Padre Celso's testicles, which, since his legs were bound tightly together, were
bunched forward by his thighs.

Thwop!

"'At's it, Juanchi! Knock 'em up 'is ass!"

"Way to go, Juan baby! He doesn't use 'em anyway!"

Then Padre Celso began screaming. His left hip had knocked against Private Calimba's shoulder so that he began spinning on the rope by which he
hung, and as he spun he screamed. And as he swung, spinning and screaming,
just as Private Estilete went to catch him and walk him back to Sergeant
Tranca, he began to vomit. Private Estilete jumped back so as not to be vom-
ited on, and the rest of the hitters, some of whom had been congratulating
Private Calimba on what had to be scored a homer, groaned and shook their
heads, like real baseball players surprised during a big inning by sudden rain.

Padre Celso swung back and forth, vomiting the yucca and fried beans and rice with lentils of his supper. Vomit gushed from his mouth and flowed into his nose and eyes and splattered from the floor into his hair. Private Porra got sick and ran upstairs to vomit out of doors, and Private Horca grew so disgusted by the spectacle and stink he snatched the hose from Private Calimba and walked over to the padre and, taking care not to get 'his boots splashed with vomit, drubbed the padre in the back and kidneys, yelling for him to be a man. Meanwhile the other hitters stood about, bored and annoyed.

What was Padre Celso thinking as he hung upside down and naked in the cellar of the Fourth Military District Headquarters, vomiting and retching, gasping for breath, his chest battered and his testicles bashed up into his abdomen and his head bursting from a weight of blood and his eyes stinging from the acid of his vomit? Well, he wasn't thinking at all. One doesn't think during that kind of nightmare. He could feel, however, and for one thing, his justice high was over. Private Juan Calimba bad fed him a real downer, and his high was gone. Padre Celso felt pain and dread and anguish, and beyond that he felt ashamed. Padre Celso felt disgusted—not with the men who beat him; with himself. It was his own fault, after all, that he was trussed up like a quail, choked and aching, fouled with his own filth, helpless and degraded among savages. He ought to have known he'd get a bill someday for having a sense of purpose, for hooking himself on justice. He no longer felt pity for Sergeant Tranca and the others. He felt envy. They seemed to get as big a rush, as much direction for their lives, passing out pain and degradation as he had got trying to distribute freedom and dignity, and no one knocked their nuts in for it either. He tried to say he'd learned his lesson, that he would be a good boy and behave, but his mouth was full of vomit, and then he couldn't get his breath. He made his mind up, however, and at that instant his enlistment in justice was dissolved.

51. Play was suspended . . . The game resumed

Sergeant Evaristo Tranca had played a lot of baseball in his day, there in Belém, and in Guardia Headquarters in Ciudad Tinieblas, and in half the barracks in the country. He'd seen just about every situation that could come up, including a game's having to be called because the ball had choked to death in its vomit. And so he told Private Horca to take it easy and went to the next room and got the pail of water that, in accord with fire regulations, had to be kept, one on each floor, in every Guardia building, and brought it in and splashed some water into Padre Celso's face. If Padre Celso had kept on vomiting and gasping, Sergeant Tranca would have let him down awhile, but after a few splashes he quieted, and Sergeant Tranca used the remaining water to wash some of the vomit toward the drain. Then, just for the record—for he didn't want to call the game so soon, not after having brought men from the barracks, not when only three had come to bat—be asked

Padre Celso if he'd decided to be good. But in asking, he looked down into Padre Celso's face and saw, across his forehead, just above his eyebrows (or rather just below, since Padre Celso was hanging upside down), a row of bloody scratches. Without waiting for an answer, he turned and started chewing out the men, calling them pubic hairs and sons of whores, demanding to know which of them had marked the prisoner while his back was turned. They all professed innocence, and then Private Horca, who was standing half behind the Padre, broke in saying that his hands—were cut as well, and sure enough, when Sergeant Tranca looked, he saw bloody boles in both the padre's palms. Sergeant Tranca shouted that they'd play baseball with the man who'd made those marks, and he went over to Private Alvaro Manopla, whom he'd never cared for anyway, and accused him of having marked the prisoner, and if he didn't make a free confession, they would beat one out of him soon enough. But then Sergeant Tenazas started shouting, pointing his hose up at Padre Celso's feet, and when the others looked they saw a bloody hole in each of Padre Celso's ankles. Private Manopla yelled that not he or anyone else or the bunch of them together could have made all those marks in the few seconds Sergeant Tranca had been absent from the room, and Sergeant Tenazas yelled yes, it was the prisoner's fault, he was still mocking them, trying to split them up and get them all in trouble. Sergeant Evaristo Tranca scratched his head and said that must be it, that must be it. Then he grabbed the padre by the hair and shouted, "Batter up!"

Now, during the commotion Padre Celso made no effort to be heard, to say that he'd decided to be good, and even while Sergeant Evaristo Tranca dragged him up and back by his long hair he remained silent. It wasn't that his pain had disappeared, nor that, once he'd stopped vomiting and caught his breath, he'd lost his shame. No, he hurt as much as ever and felt as helpless and degraded. But when his pact with justice was dissolved, he had felt something else, something far worse. The moment he renounced his pledge to justice, the following withdrawal symptoms struck: Padre Celso Labrador realized that this world is utterly without a purpose or a point, that there's no program to it and no plan, that what we sometimes take for order was not built in by any architect, does not, in fact, exist but is a dream piped up by wishful man the way a man may gaze up at a blob of cloud and see the outline of a dromedary. And with this knowledge came an awful solitude. It was worse than pain. It was worse than the shame of being strung up by the feet and *played* with. Padre Celso was on his way to becoming an instant expert in suffering, but so far he had found nothing worse than the solitude of a pointless world. It was such a change from the comradeship of a world whose purpose was the liberation of mankind that Padre Celso simply couldn't bear it. And so he scrambled for the only thing he knew might ward it off: another fix of justice. It was the only thing he had. There he was, an intelligent and cultured fellow with his whole life before him, so trapped by his addiction that he had no choice but to go on bearing pain and dread and degradation for the dubious land claims of a pack of ragged *campesinos* in an unimportant corner of an obscure and misruled sick joke of a country. When Sergeant Evaristo Tranca asked him if he'd decided to behave, he said nothing. When, as the game got under way again, the hitters' voices calmed, he still said nothing. And in the Directorate of Astral Activities his enlistment in justice was reinstituted.

52. The final out

When the hitters had batted around four or five times, Sergeant Tranca called time out and examined the ball. Padre Celso had been groaning with each hit and moaning each time he was dragged back to the mound and screaming energetically whenever a batter—and they all tried—connected after the fashion of Private Calimba. Now Sergeant Tranca asked him if he'd learned his lesson. But even as he voiced the question, Sergeant Tranca saw wound open in Padre Celso's side. The flesh of Padre Celso's right side opened like a tulip at dawn and let a thin stream of blood trickle to his armpit. With that, Sergeant Evaristo Tranca lost control of himself.

(Three days later, when Sergeant Evaristo Tranca was summoned to Civil Guard Headquarters in Ciudad Tinieblas and taken to task for his loss of self-control and for the events that proceeded from it, Major Lisandro Empulgueras, Chief of the Military District, spoke in his defense. Major Empulgueras pointed out that a soldier cannot be expected to act like a permissive social worker. Discipline and self-restraint are one thing, cowardly tolerance of insults to one's honor quite another. The enemy had subjected Sergeant Tranca to intolerable provocation. Sergeant Tranca had made exemplary efforts to accomplish his mission without excessive force. The enemy had persisted in frustrating these efforts. The enemy had persisted in marking himself so as to cast a spurious stain on Sergeant Tranca's honor and the honor of the Tinieblan Civil Guard. It was true that Sergeant Tranca's actions had resulted in the partial failure of his mission. But it was just as true that different action on the Sergeant's part might clearly have resulted in grave damage to the morale of the troops under his command and, with that, irreparable impairment of their capacity to show courage in the face of the enemy. The enemy had placed Sergeant Tranca in a situation where any action on his part would probably have been counter-productive. Perhaps a productive course of action might have been worked out, but it must be remembered that Sergeant Tranca was not sitting at his ease in a calm office. He was facing the enemy in a situation fraught with pressure. He acted instinctively and, given the circumstances, in a soldierly manner.)

Sergeant Evaristo Tranca's soldierly action was, specifically, a terrific kick into Padre Celso's head. Sergeant Tranca's boot hit just below (or, if you like, above—since Padre Celso was hanging upside down) the padre's ear, breaking his jawbone, but the real damage done by this instinctive action was to cause the others present to believe that the ball was being taken out of play. The bench emptied, as it were. Everyone surged up to get his kicks while there was time—everyone, that is, except Private Manopla, who was wearing rubber shower clogs and who contented himself with reaching over the other's heads to drub at Padre Celso's groin with his radiator hose. Some minutes passed before passions cooled. Then it was discovered that during the rhubarb, someone had landed a swift kick on Padre Celso's nose, driving the bone into his brain for the final out.

53. *Lépido Perron*

Señor Perron is without question the most disgusting spirit with whom the research for this dissertation has so far put me in touch. His name was suggested by Dr. Gusano Bosquez. He answered my call at once. Then, instead of being helpful, he blustered about being very "big" in Resentment and Revenge, cursed my family copiously, and barfed up a venomous account of the torments he has been inflicting on my father. These evidently overstepped the ample bounds of Victim, for by Perron's gloating admission, Victim now refuses to send my father to him any more frequently than once a month.

Besides torturing my father, Perron has been sending me some troubling hallucinations. He is noxious. He is persistent. He is as difficult to comb out of one's life as a crab louse. But he is not and never will be "big" anywhere. I hope my treatment of him in text conveys something of his repulsiveness.

54. *Love*

"I just came in to say I love you."

"I wasn't asleep yet."

"Lucky for me."

"I'm sorry about the other day. I wasn't in good shape. I've had a had setback, and I suppose I didn't want to wake up to it."

"You seem all right now. It's good to see you smiling, even ruefully."

"I worked all night. I got a good bit done. I always feel better after work"

"Almost human."

"That's right. Almost."

"It's good to hear you laugh. So you got through the trouble?"

"No. No chance of that. Not through it or over it. I'm working around it. Where I am now I can still do that. But if I had any brains, I'd quit the whole thing. I haven't really faced up to the problem yet. I go on out of habit, and out of spite. But the thing's going to be flawed, Liz, like everything else in this stupid world. It's not going to be what I wanted. I ought to give it up."

"I'm sure it will be wonderful."

"What the fuck do you know about it? No! Walt! I'm sorry."

"I just wanted to . . ."

"I know, I know. I'm sorry. I am. It's not your fault, and I . . . Look, Liz, you believe in my gift, don't you? You believe I'm in touch with the spirits. You believe in the spirits themselves."

"Yes, Camilo. I've never seen them, but—"

"Shit! You saw Shakespeare, didn't you? Who do you want to see—Jesus, Mary, and Joseph? The Three Kings? Lot's Wife? And it wasn't the drug either. The drug may make it easier sometimes, but the drug doesn't invent."

"I said 'Yes,' Camilo. If I didn't believe I couldn't live with you."

"Why'd you have me committed, then?"

"I had to do something, Camilo."

"Like have me electrocuted, right?"

"Camilo, the doctors said—"

"The fucking doctors!"

"Yon tried to kill yourself, Camilo. And me too."

"I didn't try anything. I hit my head a couple times, and when you tried to stop me I pushed you, for which I'm sorry. If I'd *tried* to kill anyone I'd have succeeded. But all right. You authorized the shocks out of revenge."

"No, Camilo. And not because you see spirits either. I just had to do something. Why do we have to go over this now?"

"All right, all right, I'm sorry. It started because I was going to tell you about my setback. I'm not going to be able to get through to my father. That was the whole point, and I'm not going to be able to do it."

"I'm sorry, Camilo."

"Not as much as me. I could do Napoleon, do you realize that? I could do Tamerlane the Great, All that would take is ten years or so to learn Mongolian, or whatever the hell he spoke. I could do just about anyone except who I want to do. My goddamn pop had to get himself put away in Victim."

"Where, Camilo?"

"It doesn't matter. The thing is I can't reach him."

"I'm sorry, Camilo. I love you."

"Do you really, Liz?"

"Why do you think I stay with you?"

"Christ, I don't know. Sometimes I think I'm a genius, but sometimes I'm not sure."

"Love hasn't anything to do with that."

"I suppose not. Well, maybe you do. Sometimes I think you're my enemy. In the last few days I've been thinking you're in love with the Great Sigmundo. There's this spirit . . . He has it in for the old man. The old man made it with this creep's wife, and he's been taking it out on me in part, sending me visions and audio hallucinations of you and Sig. You know, now and then I've thought that you and Sig . . . But it's another thing to see you going at it."

"You see?"

"See. Hear. The whole bit. So I've been thinking."

"You ought to take a rest, Camilo."

"What do you mean? If a person has the gift, or curse, to communicate with spirits, there isn't any way to take a rest from them. They come and that's it. The decent ones will go away if you ask them to. The only thing to do with this creep is to wait him out and not let him get to me. As for my work, if anything it's a defense. And the dissertation isn't going to get done by me resting."

"Camilo. Even if there was something between Sig and me, it wouldn't mean I don't love you."

"It would to me."

"That's jealousy, not love. Jealousy hasn't anything to do with love, Camilo."

"That's your theory. My view is that if you could get your rocks off with Siguito Piguito, there's no way you could love me. No way, Liz."

"Do you love me, Camilo?"

"Why do you think I stay with you?"

"I think you stay with me because you need me. You need me to keep you in contact with reality."

"Which one?"

"Which what?"

"Which reality? There are all kinds, you know."

"What you call 'this world.' I think that's why you stay with me."

"What if I don't need this world? What if I'd just as soon live in the next world, or the past?"

"I hope you don't decide to do that, Camilo. Then you wouldn't need me anymore, and whatever you think, I love you."

"Maybe you do, Liz. Maybe you do."

55. Distractions

The Fugathon came on again at sunset. Emcee'd by Lépido Perron and starring Liz and Sig. Or rather, since the format is closer to soap opera, Resentment and Revenge presented another episode of "Furtive Firking." My bathroom mirror became a screen, the sink drain a speaker. Perron came on first. He thanked me for tuning in (as if I had a choice), made a quick pitch for the product, then introduced the adulterers, who committed gleeful abominations until the next commercial.

I didn't watch. Like the network productions on which it's modeled, the show is unspeakably banal, repetitive, and boring, and yet, for some reason, difficult to turn away from if you watch a frame or two. The first time it went on I stayed through to the finish, wasting an entire hour and no doubt encouraging Perron's sponsor to pick up his option. This though I knew the show for a hoax to begin with. I've lived with Liz for over four years now and know her tastes. Perron had his phantom of her doing stunts Liz simply doesn't go for. I admit an initial shock, but I soon realized what his game was and refused to give him the satisfaction of reacting angrily.

This afternoon I shut the bathroom door and went on with my work. I could hear the sound track, of course: gasped avowals, passionate moans, tender whispers; Perron coming back on with Castilian-lisped indignation, urging me to get even with the faithless slut and the shameless poacher; then more grunts and squishes. I kept my concentration more or less and got the Jacaranda scene, where León and Rosario meet, down on paper. By that time Perron had signed off till tomorrow, and it was fully dark outside. I got myself an apple and some cheese and waited for Rosario. Padre Celso showed up instead, and I lost my temper.

"Look here! I can't have this! This is too much! I'm trying to get some work done! I'm expecting an important source! Don't you have any consideration? You know the difficulties I'm facing. I can't bear any more distractions. First that degenerate, now you. It's too much! You'll have to go at once!"

He had his infinite-compassion gaze on, and all stigmata were "go."

"Who do you think you are, God damn you? I've done your 'Passion'! I've put it in my notes! What do you want now, a 'Descent'? A 'Pietà'? Maybe you'd like me to do a 'Resurrection'!"

"They put me in a cardboard carton and buried me under the headquarters. They broke the cement floor of the storeroom with pickaxes and dug a pit and buried me and poured new cement on top. Then three days later the order came for them to take my body in a helicopter and drop it in the Pacific, but when they dug the carton up, it was full of rocks."

"Marvelous! A 'Resurrection,' by all means, and then a 'Harrowing of Hell'!"

"When my spirit reached the next world, it was sent to Victim, but when the Director learned of this mistake, He asked me what I wished in compensation, and I asked Him to reprieve whom he could from Victim. He commuted the terms of many and reassigned them, and He brought me out and put me at His right hand in Justice."

"Terrific! Now why don't you go back?"

"I have much to do here in this country, Camilo."

"Good luck! So far all you've done is get yourself kicked to 'death' over the illegal land claims of some peasants and your own ambitions for a slot in the next world."

"What I did I did even for you, Camilo. Now I need your help."

"What you need is a few shock treatments. They probably won't remove your grandiose ideas, but they might teach you to keep them to yourself. As for me, I need a little peace. I'm not some blocked novelist or burnt-out poet with nothing else to do but be 'engaged'! I have work to do! Out you go now! Bugger off!"

He gave a little shrug and shook his head. He bled a tear onto his cheek and wept a drop of blood across his temple. Then he backed slowly through the wall into the evening, and to the last bended his gaze on me.

56. The show

I have never been to Sig's rooms at the Apartamentos Amueblados San Felipe, but I am convinced Perron has had them copied scrupulously for his sets. Since the building caters to gringo expense-accounters, I am quite prepared to believe that its fiats are furnished in Marriott Garish. It is, furthermore, like Sig to have made himself a bookcase out of cement construction blocks and one-inch planks, and to use the plastic dining table for a desk. Also, at the beginning of the show this afternoon (something-or-other June, 1974), phantom Sig was discovered studying a well-thumbed copy of Dr. Eugenio Lobo's *Infamias del imperialismo yanqui,* a copy indistinguishable at camera glance from the one I loaned the real Sig in March and have still not gotten back. It is that kind of piling up of detail which suspends the viewer's disbelief. Perron must have the services of an experienced producer from Performing Arts.

The director is a pro as well. The real Liz left home this afternoon wearing a Grecian robe-style dress gathered at her waist with a silk cord; the director had his phantom so attired. The real Liz wears no bra, and he brought phantom Liz to today's tryst braless. More, he had her slip her panties off before she pressed the bell and (at phantom Sig's call of "Coming, coming in my pants") undo the cord and draw her dress wide open, so that when phantom Sig let her in she was shown virtually naked, smiling impishly and bumping her tawny bush at the camera. That is just the sort of vulgar gesture which the real Liz delighted in practicing on me during our early days and which it took more than a year to break her of.

Perron must do the scripts, however, for they are the weak link. As I have said, the show is banal, but then an affair between Liz and Sig would be banal as well. The show might tempt me sorely to invest emotionally in the existence of such an affair, but that, at crucial moments, Perron allows his tasteless thirst for the sensational to split his phantom from its model. After today's commercial, for example, there was a fade-in to phantom Sig sprawled sleeping with his dong at half-staff in a vortex of churned sheets. Phantom Liz entered from the bath, surveilled him lovingly, then dropped her head to graze. Phantom Sig groaned, fluttered his eyelids, closed them, smiled excrementivorously, and drew a pillow over his face. Phantom Liz knelt slowly to the floor, gripping the bed with her right hand, resting her left high on his inner thigh. Her long hair fell across her face onto his abdomen; her cheeks plumped and concaved in slow rhythm, like the bellows of an oxygen mask. After about two minutes of this, the camera slid away artfully along phantom Sig's quivering legs. A weak thrashing of his feet against the bedclothes; a curling of toes; the sound track moaned for Jesus. At length there was a shot of him pushing back the pillow, smiling. "You make a bell of an alarm clock."

Close-up of phantom Liz, head raised now. Brushes her hair aside. Swallows. "I love going down. I just love it."

Brilliant! Masterful! Finely calibrated to drive me mad with pain! Except that the real Liz, my Liz, loves nothing of the sort. She can, at rare intervals, be prevailed upon, but it is never worth the bribe or the diplomacy, for since she does not love it—does not, in fact, enjoy it in the slightest—she does not do it well. The whole scene was, thus, out of character, the statement false, the swallow ludicrous. In straining for sensation for its own sake, Perron rendered today's program and the entire series unconvincing.

Luckily for my peace of mind, Perron is a bungler. I shall not waste another minute on his disgusting fabrications.

57 Who has not known?

I have known from the first. I have been called insane, but never stupid. In my own home, on the first night they met, within instants after headache drove me to my bedroom, they were at it like a pair of goats or monkeys. In the center of our living room, no doubt. With all the others cheering their encouragement, I well imagine. Dog style, most probably: Liz with her rump raised; Sig slavering onto her nape. I smelled fucking on her when she came in later. I have known all along. Insane perhaps, stupid never.

There was no point in saying anything. When one is married to a demented nymphomaniac, when one has given one's good name to a she-otter, when one has pledged oneself in God's sight to a scumbag, one keeps one's mouth shut. The trull believed she'd fooled me. Having no sniff of honor anywhere about her, she cannot perceive it in another. She is, in any case, entirely too self-centered ever to thank me for bearing her cuntishness in silence, but you, my examiners, will appreciate my native urge to spare even so slimed a reputation as hers and will, thus, excuse certain equivocations in these notes. I have, I say again, known all along.

My actions this evening were, then, simply a diversion, a momentary lapse in my heroic decency, a very mildly malicious experiment in discomfiting a pair who have done me frightful and repeated injury. They were not an effort to discover if the Perron Show was shot live and, hence, if my wife was faithless.

How could they be? I have known for months. In fact, on our wedding night, more than four years ago, I had a detailed presentiment of this whole tawdry episode, for besides being an accomplished medium and a telepathist of genius, I have the gift of precognition. I was forewarned and thus forearmed. How else was I able to endure betrayal with such exemplary stoicism? Yes, I have known for years!

I caught the show again this evening (afternoon—whatever time it was). I confess no weakness of will, no crumbling of resolution. Like other mortals, I have to urinate now and again. I avoided my own bathroom and went to Liz's. The show was on in there too. I could scarcely help watching while I pissed.

Sig, who is rather a lazy lover, lay back with his head and shoulders braced on pillows. Liz perched above him like a jockey. She posted down slowly, and came to rest.

"Don't move. Just let me milk you."

"Christ! Where did you learn that?"

"In college." Her lips drew tight, then relaxed. "My daddy told me to learn all I could." Squeeeeeze. "My seminar prof taught me." Squeeze. "It's in Burton's notes to *The Arabian Nights*. Stop moving!"

He shut his eyes and flung his left hand out limply, brushing his fingers against the dial of the phone on his night table. Possessed at once by a mild maliciousness, I zipped, adjusted the mirror-backed bathroom door, and hurried to the phone beside Liz's bed. Seconds later, Sig's phone began ringing on the sound track.

The cheese I'd eaten earlier must have been rancid, for I was seized with intense nausea. I slammed the receiver down and dashed, retching, to the bowl. I felt a little better after a moment, but I could scarcely help watching as I rinsed my mouth.

"God! I'm going crazy!" Sig writhed his hips. "Oh, Siggy. Just be cool."

I set the door, went back, and dialed again. "Don't answer."

"Of course I'll answer. Telephone conversation is a great aid to coolness."

Sig's image, reflected in the door mirror' picked up the phone. His "Hello" rang on the sound track and in the receiver at my ear.

"Hello, Sig. How about some tennis? The lights are on tonight at the hotel."

"Sorry, Camilo." He drew a finger across his lips for Liz. She squeezed, then gave him a Giaconda smile. "I have to be in class in half an hour."

"Too bad. Well, let me speak to Liz."

"Liz isn't here, Camilo." They grinned at each other. "She's probably over at the university."

"Stop lying, pig face! You've got your cock stuck in her halfway to her eyeteeth! Don't tell me she isn't there!"

He went white and (if the look on Liz's face is a fair witness) limp as well.

"What are you talking about?"

"I don't know what it's known as in the whorehouse where your mother worked, but I believe Masters and Johnson call it the 'female-superior' position."

He tipped Liz off him and stuffed the phone under his pillow. "He's watching us from somewhere!" Horrified stare toward the window, which was heavily curtained, then around the room. "He must have a camera hidden in here somewhere!"

"Oh, my God!"

I experienced unquestionable pleasure in seeing the revolting pair wrenched from lust to terror, but I soon realized that Señor Perron's product is grossly overrated. Resentment is for people with no talent. Revenge is for those with nothing else to do. I was just as glad when Liz groped up the phone receiver and I could get the matter finished.

"Camilo?" By this time she was weeping.

"Don't speak. Don't expect results from crocodile tears. Above all, don't come here. There will be blood if, you do. I'll have Arnulfa pack your things and set them in the hall. Pick them up tomorrow while I'm sleeping. Noon will be good. Make as little noise as possible. Don't come inside. You may keep the car."

I put the phone down softly. I watched Liz kneeling naked on Sig's bed with the phone clutched to her face. Then the picture faded. I do not think the program will be aired tomorrow.

58. *My aunt Rosario*

My aunt Rosario Fuertes was the chief source for Chapter II. Also of help were Dr. Alonso Gusano Bosquez, Natalia de Triana, Dora Corpiño (formerly the check girl at the Jacaranda), and José Puñal and Pablo Patada (formerly members of the Tinieblan Civil Guard), al] of whom I contacted by spirit interview, and Señor Gustavo Oruga, whom I spoke with by telephone—a baby-blue Princess model telephone, to be exact, which some time later sailed through the air, cord tearing from its umbilicus, and crashed into the door mirror, smashing same to shards.

Rosario visited me without my calling. Her name—not her maiden name, you may be sure—came up during my interview with Dr. Gusano, and an instant later, just as I realized how much I craved to speak with this marvelous woman who'd been my father's lover, she appeared. Her reunion with Dr. Gusano was most touching: when she greeted him as her dear friend, he knelt weeping, as before a queen or saint.

Later that night and in many successive interviews, Rosario spoke with complete candor of her childhood, her travels with Perron's company, and her idyll with León. I had, of course, heard stories about a beautiful cabaret entertainer with whom my father had a tragic amour before he left Tinieblas, but I was entirely ignorant of Rosario's existence as a member of my family. It seems that neither my father nor my grandmother Rebeca ever mentioned her after that night of frightful revelations. Certainly neither ever mentioned her to me while they were in this world, and during all my conversations with Rebeca's spirit she offered nothing about her daughter. After I had spoken with the Spanish surgeon who delivered León and Rosario, I asked my grandmother about León's twin sister. Rebeca answered, "Lost," and said no more.

Rosario told me all with such disarming frankness that I felt not the least revulsion at her and León's breaking of humanity's most terrible taboo. Sadness surely, but not revulsion. I have tried to compose my text so that the reader will feel none either.

I was ecstatic to discover yet another magnificent female among my close relations and overjoyed to have her help. Without it I should surely have been unable to discover two vital aspects of my father's history: the entrance of love into his life and the secret of his exile from Tinieblas. Like everything else of value in this world, however, it had to be paid for. My aunt was as free with opinions as with recollections. She deplored my attitude toward women. She persisted in averring that I used my wife ill. She did not stick at likening me to her own husband, with whom (she said) I share certain unpleasant characteristics. She called me self-centered, for instance, and in example cited my conduct with Padre Celso Labrador, whom, as far as I am concerned, I have treated with a patience and consideration that borders on the saintly. Like all the Fuertes women, Rosario can at times show a barbed tongue, but I took no real hurt or anger because, despite some misguided views, she clearly had my welfare to heart. When, for example, she accused me of being unwilling to love and I, rather than oppose her, replied that my business in this world isn't loving but bringing meaning, she smiled, much like my mother, with sweet sadness, and said she loved me all the same and always would.

I must say she was marvelous tonight. She was at my side, all consolation, before the last mirror splinters had bit the tiles, and only for a moment was she anything but understanding. That was some time later, about nine o'clock, I should suppose, when she had got me to lie down in my room and had sat down beside me.

"You must forgive her," she said, speaking of my wife. I shook my head.

"What did you expect?"

"Loyalty."

"Amazing. Why on earth, Camilo, should you have expected her to be loyal?"

"I married her."

"And she married you. All right, I won't press that now, but she wasn't so terribly disloyal, you know. Taking pleasure with someone else is the least of all possible disloyalties. She believes in you."

"And therefore had me imprisoned and tortured!"

"All right, dear. All right. I understand. No more for tonight, I promise."

Then my lovely aunt Rosario—surely the loveliest woman in either this world or the next—proposed a wondrous thing in my behalf. Upon her "death," racked with guilt at her unknowing sin of incest, Rosario had applied for Good Works and had been accepted. Some years later she had enrolled in a subdivision of that activity called Guardian Spirits, for it was her desire to watch over her brother León and guide him if she could. In the interval she had followed his life in this world, and once she entered Guardian

Spirits she was never far from his side. She could, therefore, report on the trajectory of his life, tell me the great part of his thoughts and feelings, and, of course, point me toward other sources who might fill in lacunae in her knowledge and balance her admittedly subjective views. In short, learned examiners, my aunt Rosario proposed to help me with this dissertation.

"Not because I feel sorry for you," she added. "Or in compensation for supposed 'wrongs' done to you by a member of my sex. Your father was a man, Camilo, and studying his life may help you to become one also."

"That's not really my ambition. I want to be a scholar."

"Well, to be anything, you have to be a human being first, man or woman as the case may be."

She did not promise to make my research easy. She cannot do that anyway. It is enough that she may make it possible. There will be new trials. I accept them.

Rosario left me around midnight at my urging. I wanted to tie up the loose ends of Part Two of this dissertation, concerning my father's early life, before pressing my investigations further, and my aunt agreed, saying that work was probably the best thing for me, if not the only thing, at least for a time. She will return tomorrow.

Accordingly, I sat down among the decomposing remains of my private life, blew their fetid stench from my mind's nose, and finished Chapter 11. Then I composed these last two notes. It is now false dawn on something-or-other June, 1974. The apartment is quiet; it will remain so. The composition of note 57 brought back certain unpleasant images and smells; Seconal will quash them. I look forward to an uninterrupted life of the mind, entirely free of the great inconvenience of this world: other human beings.

PART THREE

59. *He ceased to bathe, to shave or groom himself*

I have followed suit.

No, my conclusion-jumping examiners, not from neglect inspired by a personal despair. I have never been happier. I admit that when I awoke from the pill-produced sleep looked forward to in note 58 above, I was in no wise concerned with vanity or hygiene, that I did not bother to change the clothing I'd collapsed in or so much as touch my toothbrush, but got on to my aunt Rosario Fuertes and begged her to come at once, so that I might cleanse my brain of certain foul thoughts and images in the clear stream of historical research; but after hearing her description of my father's state and her gratuitous comment that I too appeared somewhat unkempt, I resolved to imitate his action purposefully, as a Stanislavskian aid to understanding and relating his condition. Fellow scholars will, I am sure, find a report on this experiment of interest.

I no longer pay attention to what day it is, but five days or so have, I believe, gone by. This afternoon when I sat down to begin composing Chapter 12, I found my fingernails a little long for typing and, therefore, clipped them, but I have made no other concessions. I perform no physical exertion, but the temperature in Tinieblas varies this time of year between seventy-six and eighty-nine degrees Fahrenheit, with the humidity above ninety percent, and while my personal odor is no longer discernible to me, a wrinkling of Arnulfa's nose this morning suggests that it grows ripe. My beard is thick, or feels thick at any rate (I no longer consult mirrors). Although I note no important sores or ulcers, a ubiquitous and constant itch envelops all my person, and certain sectors have been scratched quite raw. These are the chief physical consequences. Mentally, I have developed an intense sympathy for the subject of this dissertation, my father, León Fuertes. Not only have I clearly imagines my father's essays in self-degradation; I have relived them, both while interviewing sources and in dreams. The reader is better placed than I to judge the quality of Chapter 12, but I anticipate success with it, an anticipation that seems to me borne out already in my work tonight. I have produced a quantity of pages. Quality control appears good. If I can manage to maintain this standard to the completion of the chapter, I may then permit myself a rinse and change of clothes.

My aunt Rosario Fuertes was not so much the source for Chapter 12 as a source of sources, the more important of whom will be duly credited in future notes, but I must continue to acknowledge her assistance, which is both material and moral. I should have had a frightful time scrounging up data without her, and she has been an unchecked fount of comfort and encouragement, particularly at those times—and there were many—when I suffered my father's debased state acutely. She has not (and I thank her for it) made any reference to my personal life.

My personal life has, in fact, withered away most reassuringly now that other humans no longer infest my environs. I burned without opening the letter that my wife left when she collected her effects. I dismantled the doorbell; the telephone remains ripped from its cord. I have authorized Arnulfa to sleep home in La Cuenca, have given her a check for five hundred inchados, which ought to last for months, and have told her she need come only in the mornings to bring me food and make a thermos of coffee. She is the only living person whom I see, and that (I calculate) for no more than a few minutes per month. I suffer no interruptions, nor any obligation to maintain an artificial schedule. I work until exhausted, then collapse and dream about my father. Since the dreams are, I believe, as valuable as formal interviews of spirits, I waste no time at all. I have become a machine for researching and recording history, The facilities of Learning may be more elaborate but I doubt that they are more congenial than the ones I now enjoy, and my one complaint about my current situation is that it prevents my letting a certain whore know how agreeable it is.

60. Patrons

Good Works maintains a record of residents of this world who give assistance to their fellow human beings—not (as is sometimes superstitiously believed) in order to reward philanthropists with time off from such sentences in Victim as they may someday have to serve, but as an aid to recruitment.

Works is chronically under strength, and it is believed that those who have done good works in this world may be likely prospects; hence the file. Guardian Spirits, who spend much of their time in this world, are expected to contribute data to this file, and although my aunt Rosario was not assigned as León Fuertes' Guardian Spirit until after he had emerged from vagabondage, she nonetheless managed to identify half a dozen of his patrons. Four of these—Mrs. Tunafish and Messrs Finnegan, Abrhams-Hoof, and Ross—are now resident in the next world. They were kind enough to visit me and furnish information concerning León Fuertes' bumhood. Their help is herewith gratefully acknowledged, along with that of Miss Dosby, who is still in this world but who is able to communicate with spirits and who recalled her contact with León Fuertes for my aunt Rosario, who then related it to me.

A certain sluttish former English major would no doubt cancer herself with envy should she learn I spent an hour in the company of Winfield S. Finnegan. The jade in question idolizes him, but for the wrong reasons, romanticizing his utterly bungled life and paying slight attention to his art. "Death" has not withered his handsome features, nor boozing staled his boyish charm. He was touchingly touched that I both knew and enjoyed his work, insisted on reading a portion of my own, and praised it. (Or so, in any case, I took his comments. He took this dissertation for a novel and referred to spirit scholarship as "marvelous imagination," but I put that down to his being tight.) Upon arriving in the next world, Mr. Finnegan entered Drink, which he describes to me as a virtually infinite region of taverns, bars, cantinas, bistros, beer halls, alehouses, wineshops, cocktail lounges, gin mills, and saloons, where bartenders are always in good humor and every round is on the house, where one never gets hangovers, or d.t.'s, or the shakes, and one's liver's warranted against cirrhosis. I am thus happy to report that this gentleman, who despite the self-inflicted torments of his life brought pleasure to so many, has found his paradise.

Group Captain Richard Abrhams-Hoof, D.S.O., O.B.E., credits his brief encounter with León Fuertes not only for the consummation of his amour for Miss Withers but also for part of his success as a pursuit pilot. The fatalism engendered in him when he saw my father stood him in good stead in that profession. Abrhams-Hoof returned to England with an advanced degree in aeronautical engineering shortly before the outbreak of World War II. He joined the Royal Air Force immediately thereafter, completed pilot training in time to fly sorties over Dunkirk, and distinguished himself in the Battle of

Britain, the defense of Malta, and many other campaigns. He gained twenty-six confirmed victories and was himself shot down four times, each time parachuting safely. At war's end, having earned the rank and decorations noted above, he went to work for De Quincey Flight Machines, Ltd., as a designer and test pilot. He was cindered from this world in September, 1947, while trying (against government restrictions) to break the sound barrier in a De Quincey Apparition. On reaching the next world, Captain Abrhams-Hoof spent most of his time in Risk and, as a consequence, served several short terms in Victim. Upon his latest release ten months ago, he applied for Transmigration and has been advised that he will shortly return to this world as a seagull.

Barney Ross, who is now a coach in Sport, added to my knowledge of that activity. Sport, like its sister activity, Games, involves a good amount of rivalry but (as prior researches had led me to expect) stresses amateurism in its pristine and highest sense, participation out of love. In illustration, Ross cited the case of Mr. Vincent Lombardi, whose application for Sport was rejected with the following notation: "In Astral Sport, winning isn't very much at all. Suggest applicant consider War." Sport offers elaborate facilities for every type of athletic endeavor and provides instruction for those interested. Participants are graded to insure fair competition. Umpires are provided and spectators allowed. But there is very little formal structure. Hall of Fame Baseball, for example, is played in a magnificent stadium before huge crowds, yet proceeds as on a sandlot, with stars like Ruth and Robinson choosing up sides in an impromptu fashion from among such luminaries of the diamond as have happened to show up that day. According to Ross, my father, León Fuertes, dropped by Sport regularly between his concerts to work out, and is rumored to have considered applying for a transfer into that activity. Would he had done so, instead of seeking empty thrills in Risk!

61. Dr. Felix Heilanstalt

Sig's dad, of course, who else?

"What a marvelous coincidence!" Dr. Heilanstalt is the kind of gringo who sixty years ago would have said, "Bully!" He entered my room rather as Stanley must have entered Livingstone's mud hut.

"I was in these parts only two weeks ago," he went on enthusiastically, "looking in on my son Sigmund. He can't see or hear me, won't even let himself recall the dreams I visit him in, but I like to keep an eye on him. Needs watching too, I'm afraid. Seems to have got himself mixed up with someone's wife. At least she refers to a husband. What he'd call poetic license, I guess, but a fellow could get shot doing that in one of these Latin countries. Well, anyway, I noticed the name Camilo Fuertes on a list of phone numbers taped to his wall, and I wondered whether it might be any relation to a patient I had many years ago, a very memorable patient, but thought no, that would be too coincidental. Now I learn that you're León Fuertes' son. Simply marvelous!"

You, perspicacious examiners, will appreciate that while I knew the doctor had saved my father's life (and thus made possible my own), I found it something less than marvelous to owe so large a debt of gratitude to anyone named Heilanstalt. It was, besides, even less marvelous to consider that my esteemed visitor had glimpsed his spawn at roguer with my spouse, that he had no doubt watched close up and licked his chops. But a scholar must not let personal considerations divert his search for knowledge. Dr. Heilanstalt had information germane to my inquiry. I therefore suppressed my emotions; that is, I bit my lip and let him tell his story, which I have now refigured in my text above. Take note then, if you will, of my exemplary devotion to historical investigation, of my heroic preservation of a scholarly demeanor, observe as well the even-handed treatment I have accorded one who, although my father's savior, is nonetheless my injurer's father. (And if it seem immodest in me that I draw express attention to these my little excellences, remember that there are morons loose in every walk of life, perhaps even in the history department of a third-rate university, and that morons cannot be counted on to see things for themselves. It is a hard thing for an original mind to hang pendant on the judgment of mediocrities, if not of morons. He cannot help but fear from time to time that his discoveries may, for their originality, be condemned as lunatic ravings. He may, hence, be permitted to point out some of his accomplishments.)

Dr. Heilanstalt remembered León Fuertes with great clarity and not only informed me fully about his accident and his recovery, but also gave me a glimpse of his posthumous career.

"I saw his debut," the doctor told me, "his first appearance in a leading role. His name rang no bell, and I'd never have recognized him as the dilapidated bum I almost lost except that he was singing Rodolfo in *La Bohème,* the very opera my wife and I were on our way home from the night he stepped in front of our car. I had that uneasy déjà vu feeling from the moment the curtain went up, and during the last act it clicked. I went backstage after the performance —which, by the way, was terrific! A voice as lyrical as Bjoerling's and as robust as Gigli's! Well, anyway, I went backstage and introduced myself. His dressing room was packed. I mean I had to fight my way through people backed up to the stage door, and not just anybody either. The composer was there himself, refusing to let your father call him 'maestro' and saying it was as though he'd heard his music for the first time! That from Puccini! Imagine it! There was a new star in the firmament that night, no doubt about it. That has been clear from the fourth phrase of his first-act aria, and don't think your father didn't know it. He sat there on a corner of his dressing table with a silk robe draped over his shoulders—I'm sure he'd taken time to get his shirt ruffles to poke out just right—with his makeup smeared by kisses from the like s of Duse and Galli-Curci, sipping tea out of a glass and making falsely modest chitchat in all the languages of Western Europe. It was every bit as much of a performance as the one he'd just given out on stage. Well, when I'd finally pushed close enough to be received, when at last I'd got his attention and introduced myself, he made a great show of not recalling who I was-which was the tip-off that he knew at once—and then laid his head to one side and nodded, smiling.

" 'Ah, yes, the good doctor,' he said in English, a language he hadn't spoken a word of when I knew him in New York. 'Do you still go about knocking people down to fill your hospital?'

"I didn't hold it against him. I've been a star myself. One year, when the A.M.A. had its convention in New York, about a hundred doctors came over to see me work. I performed thirty-two major operations without a break, including one that had never been done successfully before, and when I finished that one, I looked up at the theater and pulled off my mask and invited any skeptics to come back for breakfast with the patient the next morning. Oh, yes, I know how it is to be in the limelight. I have no hard feelings against your father, and I hadn't any then. But I must say I had the most terrific urge to remind him that he hadn't always been so goddamn cocky."

Dr. Heilanstalt also told me something of his own astral existence and, in so doing, furnished me knowledge of the next world that, I think, merits inclusion in this note:

The Astral Plane is not a particularly happy place for a great surgeon. It lacks even the grossly overrated "death" we know of here, while such bodies as are issued to the participants in activities that require them are replaced whole in the advent of malfunction. Medicine is not even offered as separate activity. There is a medical adjunct to Learning, to be sure, but it is directed entirely toward research, with the participants advancing the results of their experiments for possible projection into the minds of earthly physicians. Reception offers a psychoanalytic counseling service to help new arrivals accustom themselves to their surroundings; Selection gives similar help toward choosing activities. Prorogation maintains a psychiatric clinic for dejected rejects and others who after having been accepted in an activity cannot adapt and have to be released. Part of Torture is set up as a hospital, and one finds a few former sawbones there. But the only place in the next world where a surgeon can come close to practicing his art is in War. In War each army fights a nine-campaign "season," each campaign lasting for from three months to a year. Since no new bodies are issued until after the Championship each decade, surgeons are in demand to ease the torments of the fallen and to patch them up for the next battle or the next campaign. Each army has its medical service.

It is understandable, however, that despite Dr. Heilanstalt's devotion to his calling, he did not choose to practice it in War. He arrived in the next world directly from a field hospital in the Ardennes where he'd been operating under fire for more than sixteen hours when an .88 shell came through the tent roof and, as he put it, "that was that." "That" was the termination of three years of military service, and he'd had his fill of battle. Etching had been one of his earthly hobbies, and so he spent ten years in Graphic Arts, He had talent, but not enough for greatness. Then he did neurological research in Learning, working on the links between psychiatry and physiology, but an aseptically pure life of the mind bored him. He is now on leave from his laboratory and engaged in private philosophical investigations to prepare himself for a project in the New Activities branch of Astral Administration.

"The great deficiency in the other world," says Dr. Heilanstalt, "is that it nowhere provides the most acute experience of this one: holding precious, perishable life—your own or someone else's, it doesn't matter—in your hands. Risk, War, Flirtation, Learning all have their excitements, but they don't give that life-or-death sensation. I'm going to set up an activity which provides that. I don't know yet what it will be. I've only certain vague ideas at present. But I'm going to establish that activity or transmigrate back here— as a rat or a sand flea if that's all that's open. And when I've set it up, I'll enroll as a charter participant!"

62. *One may imagine*

I, on the other hand, need not. I am informed by spirits. My Guardian Spirit, moved always by love, scans the far reaches of the Astral Plane to find me sources, and at my call they come at light-speed to me, and empty up the past into my ears. About me a city of deaf and blind idiots sleeps crushed under the sodden tropic night, while to this room are come the great and small of the vast world beyond, for all must heed the summons of my gift; and should they prove coy or stubborn, reticent to speak me what they know, I have the power to unlock their hearts and spill the truth before me.

Purblind and spirit-deaf examiners, you may imagine. If you possess imagination, use it. Raise the words from my page and flesh them with imagination. Imagining's the best that you can hope for, lacking second sight. You may imagine, therefore. I need not.

When Edna Scallop blushed hypocritically and set her equine teeth and would not tell me what there was between her and my father, I feared for a brief moment I might have to fall back on imagination; but then I moved as though drawn by an iron hand to my night table, and looked down in the mess of objects there, and in the crystal of my unwound watch I saw it all. When Braquemard Fauconnier tried to wrap his swinishness in euphemisms, I looked at the bare wall above his head and saw a film of his "romance" with León. He lounged limply in my lawn chair, flapping his spongy lip—garrulous, evasive, breaking off every second phrase with a "Dear boy, I scarcely have to give the gory details"—and no, he scarcely had to: they were all there before me. His putrid memories spilled up across the wall. No, my examiners, I need not imagine. I can see.

I have to look, though. I put down what I see in words, and you may, if you choose, imagine it to life, but first I have to look. To see, one has to look, Professor Lilywhite. One must not look away, dear Dr. Grimes. And I have looked on horrors.

Hypocrite examiners, the human heart is not a pretty thing when looked in very deeply, I have looked on the abominations of degenerates, and seen myself and you in every frame.

You too might see if you could dare to look.

63. *Great Faggots of Art and Letters*
There are none.

Your faggot is a full-time invert. He lives for his narcissistic gropes, for the flirtations that precede them, for the self-pity and defilement they provoke.

Art involves the whole human being. Letters too levies demands. The world does not suffer people to become great artists or great writers while living for a rival occupation.

Some faggots tiptoe in the vestibules of art and letters; they do not penetrate the inner sancta. Certain great artists and great writers have copulated with their own sex, but none were faggots.

Proust was a great poet who went to bed with other men. He was not a faggot.

Wilde was a wit of genius with a flair for dramatic structure. He might have been a great writer, but he chose faggothood instead. Overweening faggotry drove him to prison, where he renounced faggotdom and all its works and wrote a nearly great poem.

V. is a flaming faggot and a polemicist for faggotism and other unwholesome causes. Because V.'s literary dabblings are blended faggotly out of sophistication and vulgarity, they have sold well. Because reviewers fear the faggotine cruelty of his ripostes, some of his work has been unjustly lauded. Because his faggatoid presence has slimed the TV screen on numerous occasions, his name is a familiar (if not household) word, like "vomit." His work is, nonetheless, entirely mediocre. Mediocrity is about the highest point a faggot can attain in art or letters.

Life is compounded out of yang and yin, animus and anima, masculine and feminine. No human can work greatness anywhere, except these opposites be balanced in his spirit. But that has nothing at all to do with how one employs the orifices and projections of one's body. Shakespeare and Sappho wrote great poems, but not by buggery or tribadism—any more than Wagner wrote great music by swiving other people's wives. The argument used everywhere by faggots to justly faggotism and recruit converts—to wit, that great artists and great writers have been faggots and, hence, that faggotry's the path to beauty —is false. Faggotry leads nowhere. Faggothood is (pardon me) a cul-de-sac.

64. Bottom

This world is not especially well-organized, but neither is it entirely random. Patterns and correspondences exist (e.g., the yang-yin correspondence mentioned in note 63 above). There is a general correspondence of order and disorder, one of whose particular manifestations involves human joy and suffering. I do not mean there is a perfect balance. Disorder is more common than order (as thermodynamic lawyers will understand); suffering is more probable than joy. A clear relationship obtains, however. It may be expressed in various metaphors, of which one from tourism pleases me at present.

No one can travel to the heights whose psychic passport is not visa'd for the bottom. It is not strictly true (although it is the usual procedure) that one must travel to the bottom either before or after visiting the heights; swift, painless "death" may cancel one's booking. It is certainly not true that those who tour the bottom automatically receive permission to visit the heights; many more descend than ever climb. What is true is that the mental-spiritual equipment one needs to scale the heights serves very well (or better) for speleologizing to the bottom; that when one accepts or fashions climbing gear, he is outfitting himself for a descent; and that if he so much as asks to glance at a brochure of the heights, he is booking himself a voyage to the bottom.

Most of humanity prefer—like you, pusillanimous examiners—to live suspended in between, in mediocrity.

The bottom is a region of the heart-mind-spirit. You are not there if you don't know you're there. Or you've not been if, upon subsequent reflection, you do not realize that you've been. To live out of the sun in a muggy room strewn with roached cheese rinds—to go unbathed, unshaved, ungroomed; to spend long hours in the company of loathsome ghosts like Dédé-le-julot—that is faintly unpleasant but not nearly bottom. To contemplate a loved parent's degradation; to watch him (and, by sympathy, yourself) star in an interminable pornographic film of which each scene is more disgusting than the one before it—that's a bit worse but is still leagues above bottom. To live each filthy incident yourself, first in your dreams, then when it's time to put the matter down on paper—that is still worse but is not bottom either. All that is mere occupational inconvenience: the grime on a mechanic's fingers, the spike wounds on a second baseman's shins.

Bottom is, for example, when your richly furnished and well-cared-for mind becomes a recreation hall for rowdy spirits; when any ill-mannered ghost with nothing else to do can tramp in and yell his head off; when it is not only impossible to keep them out or keep them quiet, but when you cannot even prevent them from rough-housing, from staging free-for-alls and dionysiac dances, from leaping about exposing their private parts, from scrawling obscene slogans on the walls, from pissing on the rug, from taking a quick dump in a neat corner. Bottom is when your carefully nurtured gifts betray you—not just for the odd hour or a day or two, but on and on and on.

Bottom is when professional tormentors mew about helping you and then send goons to ram you in a strait jacket, so that you cannot even hit your head against the wall to knock the spirits out. Bottom is a bit different for each different person, but that, innocent examiners, is a very fair example.

Travelers to the bottom who return therefrom possess a certain toughness. (I have heard that some pick up humility as well but I cannot comment personally on that rumor.) Handle them with care, O my examiners. You will know them when you see them. And do not think you have much knowledge of this world until you have seen bottom.

65. Ancestors

I have now had the pleasure of meeting all my known ancestors, saving only my grandfather Dr. Azael Burlando. Rosalba, Raquel, and Rosenda Fuertes visited me here a week or so ago in the company of my aunt Rosario and informed me on the incidents recounted in the last four paragraphs of Chapter 12. They also gave me a full account of my father's state of soul when he hit bottom, for spirits have no trouble discerning the thoughts of those residents of this world to whom they are bound by ties of blood or love. Then, when I began doing research on León Fuertes' efforts toward self-reclamation, I contacted Generals Isidro Bodega, Epifanio Mojón, and Feliciano Luna and, with my aunt Rosario's help, brought them here also. They told me of their dream appearance to León and claimed credit for setting him on the right path.

It is not true that ancestors are universally preoccupied with their descendants' progress in this world. Many spirits have no family feeling at all. Others are busy with their own affairs. It is, however, not uncommon for an ancestor to take an interest in the earthly life of a particular descendant, and this phenomenon has given rise to superstitions and (in some sectors of the Orient especially) even religions. My father, León Fuertes, was a special case. For Rosalba, Raquel, and Rosenda he represented the potential fulfillment of a dream, an obsession, a destiny. Generals Bodega, Mojón, and Luna recognized him as the most promising of all their progeny and hoped he might do them honor. León was, therefore, the beneficiary of more than ordinary ancestral concern, attention, and guidance.

General Luna, for instance, accompanied my father during portions of his journey across the Sahara Desert, encouraging him and reminding him of the example he, General Luna, had set during the cruel marches of our civil wars. Luna was an important source for Chapter 13, returning here alone on three subsequent occasions to tell me of León's desert ordeal and to give me in passing much gratuitous commentary on his careers in this world and the next.

After his "death" by hanging, Luna applied for War but was turned down. Five of the six Western League armies were at the time under strength and actively recruiting, but none would take Feliciano Luna. His courage, his horse-manship, and his martial skills were undisputed, but his contempt for authority and his unconventional approach to warfare disqualified him for service with a regular formation. None of the commanders felt he could be trusted with a squadron or a troop: he seemed unlikely to stay where he was placed but liable, rather, to go swanning off on his own at any moment. He was willing to serve in the ranks, yet it was feared that one with such an independent attitude would be an evil influence on other soldiers. Disgusted at being turned away from the only activity that meant anything to him, Luna entered Drink—only to be expelled almost at once for demolishing a couple of cantinas and terrorizing fellow participants. For fifty years he blundered from activity to activity—Murder, Torture, Risk, Victim (where he fell into the hands of former victims whom he'd murdered and tortured). Then, while visiting this world in connection with his concern for his grandson León Fuertes, he had a chance to watch combat in Libya. This experience so provoked him to nostalgia that he applied for War again.

General Luna was drafted into the ranks of the Golden Horde of the Eastern League (Tamerlane the Great Commanding), an outfit which, according to Western League warriors (e.g., Sergeant Ned Cod), resembles more a rabble than an army but which is nonetheless respected. Luna so distinguished himself during his first "season" that at the start of his second the commander gave him about a thousand of the most unruly soldiers in the army, men no one else could handle, and simply turned him loose. It would be an understatement to say that General Feliciano Luna is a contented spirit. He told me personally that he would let himself be hanged a thousand times to achieve his present happiness.

Generals Bodega and Mojón likewise traveled frequently to this world in order to guide León Fuertes. Their attentions did not come, however, until sometime after his desert journey, so I shall recall them at convenient moments later on.

As scholars will perforce be interested in (not to say gape-mouthed with fascination over) my research method and its efficacy, I here permit myself to point out the ease with which I now summon and debrief spirit informants. A glance at note 5 above will remind the reader of certain difficulties I experienced earlier this year in contacting General Luna. Now I get through at once without the slightest interference and, unless he happens to be in the thick of fighting, can have him at my side at once, gabbing away in the most cooperative manner imaginable. So goes it with the others I have need of. Nor do I have much trouble with spirits barging in uncalled. Padre Celso was an uninvited visitor, but there was never any question as to which of us was in command. He did not speak till he was spoken to, and when he began to be a nuisance, I whistled him off. Perron came at my bidding but then hung around, yet I was able to get rid of him through a psychological application of jujitsu strategy. When ignoring him did no good, I simply went the way he pulled me. He's not bothered me since. Surely I have come a long way from the terrible days (see note 64) when spirits *used* me. For all practical purposes, am now in complete control.

I must admit I am a little less successful with living human beings, not that dominating other people is my ambition. A certain strumpet was by earlier. I had supposed she'd left Tinieblas, but perhaps a certain hack has taken her in. Or she may dream of worming back in here. That, at least, seemed the purpose of her trans-portal whinings, for she claimed to be concerned over my welfare, She rapped at the door like Poe's raven for a good five minutes, and when at length I could bear the sound no longer and went to shoo the intruder off, she heard my footfalls and squeaked, "Camilo?" I of course said nothing, but she whined for a few moments nonetheless. In fact, she was still whining when I retreated to my bathroom and wadded toilet paper in my ears.

My aunt Rosario, who came by a bit later, chid me for my conduct, called it cowardly, in fact, and in defense I said that if I'd let the whore in or even spoken to her, I might have become violent.

"That would have been healthier," answered Rosario. Like all the Fuertes women, she is riddled with romanticism.

In any case, I do not care to control my fellow humans. It is enough that I be isolated from them. And since in that I have succeeded perfectly, the above-mentioned incident alone excepted, my work goes swimmingly.

A final word on my ancestors. I think I shall have them all together for a reunion one of these days—the generals, the genetrixes, Rebeca, and my mother. Perhaps my father and Dr. Burlando will be given dispensation to attend. My doctoring would be a fit occasion. I doubt that Sunburst University has ever had such a distinguished group of visitors at its commencement exercises, but I promise you, Professor Lilywhite, dear Dr. Crimes, that I shall bring them to campus for the ceremony when my Ph.D. is awarded.

66. A bus

Buses are the main means of public transport in the Republic of Tinieblas. Until recently the capital and its environs were serviced by three private bus companies and a good number of free-lance drivers with their own heavily mortgaged vehicles. The Revolutionary Government has driven two of the companies out of business and has established in their place a state-owned Surface Transport Authority. One private company (which happens to have retained General Manduco's brother Mangu as a public relations consultant) remains in operation. There are, besides, the free lances.

These last have been in the habit for as long as I can recall of decorating their conveyances with art- and/or sloganwork. The stern of such a bus may display a sylvan scene or a beachscape or, more usually, a portrait. Dr. Ernesto

Guevara, Dr. Martin Luther King, Jr., General Feliciano Luna, President León Fuertes, Señor César E. Sancudo, and Jesus of Nazareth are among the personages thus honored. A representative sample of slogans (translated from the Spanish) follows:

"LOVE IS KEEPING YOUR DISTANCE."

"YOU LEFT ME—I'LL GET EVEN."

"OUR FLAG IN THE RESERVATION" (above Señor Sancudo's portrait).

"HE ASKED FOR LIBERTY—THEY GAVE HIM DEATH" (scrolled beside Dr. King).

Such embellishments contribute to the generally colorful character of Tinieblan life but rarely attract much notice. Now they have become a cause célèbre. Nothing has appeared in the state-controlled mass media of communication but, according to Arnulfa, who recounted it to me, the following incident is known to all the capital:

Two days ago a bus was seen on Via Venezuela bearing a likeness of Padre Celso Labrador. It was observed by many people; it occasioned great amazement and not a little comment on the courage or insanity of the owner-driver on whose bus it was displayed, for the whole subject of Padre Celso and his disappearance is now strongly taboo'd. In due course it attracted the attention of two members of the Civil Guard in a patrol truck. They waved the offending bus to the curb and arrested its driver. When he asked what was the matter, they dragged him to the rear of his vehicle and, each seizing a handful of his hair, shoved his face into the portrait. When he professed total surprise at the existence of the portrait and protested hysterically that he had not caused it to be painted on his bus, the arresting officers first took the precaution of placing handcuffs on him, then beat him unconscious with their truncheons. During this pageant of law in action, the debarked passengers and a small crowd which had formed observed the following phenomena: (1) The slogan "FORGIVE THEM FATHER FOR THEY KNOW NOT WHAT THEY DO" appeared ballooned as in a comic strip above the portrait; (2) The portrait wept palpable, wet tears, which flowed down the paneling, dripped to the ground, and collected in small puddles. The driver was carted off, but the portrait kept on weeping. A few minutes later a truckload of *guardias* arrived to disperse the crowd and arrest three or four of them. A sergeant boarded the bus and drove it to Guard Headquarters, presumably as evidence. The portrait wept all the way.

It would appear a certain spirit has chosen a bus as the instrument to make his presence felt here. Since the reader of this dissertation cannot fail to have developed an ardent interest in spirits, I include this example of their strange powers and bizarre acts.

67. He walked

It was never a question of reenacting León Fuertes' fearful journey. The author of this history does not claim to be a man of action. He is not so presumptuous as to believe he could survive an entire trans-Sahara passage. He merely wished as a scholar to make the gap between him and his subject a bit narrower. The grant-pampered darlings of the academia establishment can afford jet accommodations to Brussels and rental cars from there to Waterloo. They can fit out grand expeditions, and hire planes to retrace the route of a Xenophon or a Perry. The author of this work is not thus funded. Therefore, he walked.

When my researches into my father's life had reached the point where he decided to join General Leclerc, I made the following preparations: I had Arnulfa buy me some soda biscuits, some tinned beef, and a few packages of dates, then gave her two weeks off; I dug from my trunk the Boy Scout knapsack that my freshman-year roommate, Preston Twill, abandoned when he dropped out of college and packed it with the above-mentioned provisions, a wine bottle full of water, and a blanket; I went about this apartment pulling the furniture out to the center of each room but this one; I advised my spirit informants that I would be on a diurnal schedule until further notice and rearranged my appointments with them accordingly. At first light the next morning I set out.

My route ran east along the hall from my bedroom-study doorway to the room slept in until recently by a trollop of my acquaintance. It circumnavigated that room, reentered the hall, and proceeded eastward again into the living room, whose perimeter it followed north, then east, then south, in a great half circle. It then describes a tight one-hundred-eighty-degree left turn and continued through the doorway of the kitchen and around it, north, then east, then south, then west, back to the doorway. Here it swung left again one hundred eighty degrees into the dinette and ran east along the dinette-kitchen wall, south along the east wall of the apartment, and then west, a direction that it followed, hugging the south wall of the apartment, past the front door, across the wide entrance of the living room, into the hall again, and back to my bedroom doorway. It was one hundred twenty-seven paces long. Marching at an easy yet purposeful gait, I covered it in one minute fifteen seconds.

Figuring my pace at seventy centimeters, the total length of this circuit is eighty-eight point nine meters, eighty-nine for roundness. Considering I maintained a steady pace—and I strove to do so—I completed forty-eight circuits each hour, but let us for safety's sake reduce this to forty-five. My average speed was, then, four and five one-thousandths kilometers per hour, for roundness simply four. I marched from daybreak till full dark, so that, allowing for infrequent and brief rests and a reasonably long noon break, I covered at least forty kilometers (twenty-five miles) per day. I remained on March until my sources had informed me fully about my father's entire journey from Touggourt to Fort-Lamy, and since this took the best part of a fortnight, I traveled something over four hundred kilometers—about the distance, Floridian examiners, from Miami Beach to Disney World.

I slept on the floor. I refilled my water bottle only in the evening. My food ran out before the reports of my informants had brought León Fuertes to his destination, and I marched for two days on an empty stomach. Privations of thirst and hunger, while nowhere near what my father suffered, contributed signally, I think, to the success of my journey.

My informants were, besides General Feliciano Luna, my aunt Rosario Fuertes, who by fall, 1940, had become my father's Guardian Spirit, Dr. Escolástico Grillo, who, as the reader of my text will see, accompanied my father in the desert from time to time, and a German-born former noncommissioned officer of the French Foreign Legion who refused to reveal his name (and, hence, can receive only this maimed acknowledgment) but who was with the Legion party that found my father wandering on the Grand Erg Oriental and saved his life. They responded to my queries with long monologues, which I gathered up en route and noted down during rest periods. In this way I learned the details of my father's journey, and of his state of mind and spirit during it.

I was also interested in learning what I could about the character of the Sahara. Thus, on my second day of travel, after the ex-legionary had told me of my father's brush with "death," I asked him to stay on awhile and tell me about the desert. He talked straight through my noon break while I lay resting on the floor, munching a few dates and sipping at my water bottle, and then, perhaps an hour later, as I tramped round and round, listening to him relive his years under that pitiless sun, a phenomenon occurred whose mechanism I don't understand but whose effect was clear enough. This apartment brightened as if a hundred banks of klieg lights in its ceiling were being slowly dimmed up to full power. An immense weight of dry heat fell onto my shoulders, and the air around me became a furnace breath. I staggered, then pushed on, but scarcely had I completed my circuit when the furniture melted away, and the tiling of the floor crumbled to sand, and the walls and ceiling dissolved onto an endless vista of scorched sand and sky.

I marched on, my head down, my eyes narrowed to slits against the glare. I marched, and the voice of my ghostly legionnaire droned on. Soon I could no longer grasp what he was saying. It took all my concentration just to put one foot before the other. Then it seemed he'd left me there alone, but at length, hours later, when I collapsed gasping to the sand and lay crushed on that fiery plain, I saw him standing over me in his blue uniform and white kepi. He smiled down at me bitterly and nodded.

"*Tu as compris maintenant, mon gars? Tu commences peut-être à comprendre maintenant?*"

It may be that he hypnotized me, or that I hypnotized myself. It may be— and I tend toward this view—that my spirit moved onto the Astral Plane and telepathed sensations to my body. I leave the how and why to any specialists who are interested; the what is all I need for my history. For eight or so days more I traveled under similar conditions, and though a week has passed since I stopped walking, the skin of my face is still blistered and peeling.

At night my apartment recomposed itself around me. The tap was there for me to drink at and fill my water bottle. I could hear cars passing in the street below, and rain slapping in the courtyard. But by day, after I'd made a dozen or so circuits, the Afric sun would explode above me like a million flash bulbs, and the walls would disappear, etc. I was soon well enough acclimated to question and listen to informants, but like my father I struggled over sand and rock. Like him I reeled now and then with heatstroke. Like his my lips parched and cracked. For a few days only—I claim no great feat of endurance—but long enough to understand.

No one can understand what he has not lived in one way or another. No one can recount to others what he does not understand. Those who presume on other people's patience to relate them histories must make their little journeys of exploration. Those who would rather sit at ease at home should choose another occupation.

Patient examiners, I hope you find Chapter 13 illuminating. I walked a portion of the Sahara Desert to gather data for it. In any case, regardless of your evaluation, I am happy to have had means to make the trip.

68. His solitude grew oppressive

Although he had great powers of concentration and took consequent pride in mastering his mind, in keeping it at all times at close rein and aimed in the direction of his choice' he discovered himself one midnight slumped forward with his forehead pressed against his typewriter while his mind ambled loosely in a field it chose itself. His mind chose to imagine (or perhaps recall) nights which thickened like sheltering walls about him and a loved woman while he drank the nectar and the poison of her breath. Often they said imperishable things on nights which opened back onto infinite spaces while he breathed the perfume of her blood. The woman turned out to be a harlot, and yet his mind persisted in recalling (or perhaps imagining) such nights.

Then his solitude grew oppressive. He tried to call some spirit, any spirit, to converse with him, but his mind pranced and reared and refused to turn in that direction. He tried to think of going out. For months now he hadn't cared to think of going out, but now his solitude grew fearfully oppressive, and he tried to think of rising from his desk, of walking to the door and opening it, of hurrying along dark, silent streets to someplace where there were other people. His mind refused to turn that way, however. His mind moved on through nights sultry with vows, with perfumes, with infinite kisses.

Therefore he raised his head and brought his forehead smartly down on the corner of the key guard of his typewriter. He repeated this procedure several times, first with the spasmodic urgency of despair, later deliberately, to make sure his mind learned its lesson. When, at length, he sat back in his chair, he found the plastic key guard cracked and a flange of it pushed down so that it impeded typing, but after he removed this piece and chucked it into a corner, the machine functioned serviceably. More important, his mind was now perfectly obedient and his solitude no longer in any way oppressive.

69. His face

Lo, where it comes again!

While en route here this morning, Arnulfa herself beheld the face of Padre Celso Labrador blazoned in living color below the rear window of a bus abandoned in Avenida Bolívar.

She at once got down from the bus *she* was riding in and went to inspect. The face was long-locked, auburn-bearded, sad-smiled, and delicately dripped with blood from forehead scratches—in short, exactly as I saw it in this room and have described it in these notes. The slogan "GET THEE BEHIND ME GENGHIS" floated beside it in a balloon arrowed to its mouth.

A member of the crowd that was collecting, a self-confessed former passenger on the iconized bus, announced with great unease to everyone in hearing that as the bus flowed slowly with the morning traffic, a newsboy had bicycled by the driver's window and shouted in that he was "wearing the padre!"—whereupon the driver yanked the hand brake, switched the motor off, leaped to the street, dashed round, gaped at the face, and then, pausing only to unscrew the license plate with a coin, fled into an alley.

This tale was punctuated by a howl of sirens, and Arnulfa too made herself scarce, but one may assume the Civil Guard removed the offending and subversive vehicle, and probably a few citizens as well.

70. The French African Army

For a history of this formation during World War II, see Pierre Darcourt, *Armée d'Afrique: La revanche des drapeaux* (Éditions de la Table Ronde, Paris, 1972). The author is entirely sympathetic to his subject. He scrounges excuses for the deafness of most commanders to de Gaulle's "call to honor." As his subtitle suggests, he is not much interested in those units whose flags needed no revenge: e.g., the 13th Half Brigade of the Foreign Legion, which never paid a rnoment's fealty to the Vichy regime and which won France her first laurels of the war at Bir Hakeim. And he waves the *tricouleur* in great swaths throughout, but all these are minor carpings. M. Darcourt provides detailed and reliable information on the campaigns germane to this history, and I gratefully acknowledge his assistance.

I acquired a copy of *Armée d'Afrique* in 1973. I was particularly pleased to find that it includes a preface by General Aimé de Goislard de Monsabert, León Fuertes' divisional commander at Cassino, and enough references by name to soldiers, noncoms, and company-grade officers killed in action for me to develop many knowledgeable sources from it. I read it with great interest, making extensive notes of instruction to myself inside it. I valued it so highly that when I returned here at the end of last year I did not trust it to the freight company that shipped my trunk and crates of other books or the handlers who stowed my suitcase on the airplane, but carried it on my person. Imagine, then, my rage and anguish when, on having completed the text and notes of Chapter 13 and begun in-depth research for the period of León Fuertes' military service, I discovered that my precious book had been carried off—inadvertently, no doubt, but what solace was that?—by a baggage to whom I furnished bed, board, and affection until recently!

There was no question of my ordering another copy out from Paris: that would take months. I might either proceed as best I could without the book, or approach the tramp and sue for its return.

I admit that I was tempted toward the latter course of action. You, my examiners, know well what sacrifices I am prepared to make for scholarship and for this history. I have proved myself ready to give my sanity; I would give my life itself if that were called for. If there be a more dedicated investigator on earth or in the next world, point him out to me, and I shall study his example. Till you do that, though, I rest content with the strength of my commitment to the advancement of knowledge. Yes, I was tempted; but I did not yield. Not even science is so valuable that one ought pawn his honor for it. I cursed the bitch at length, and then pressed on without the benefit of published sources.

Four years' cohabitation with me must have put the shadow of an edge on her dull telepathic sense. At midmorning the next day, while I was sleeping, she stopped by and gave the book to Arnulfa, saying she had just discovered it among the belongings she removed from here some weeks ago. On opening it that night, I was unable to avoid noticing the following note of hers to me scrawled on the flyleaf:

> Please let me see you. I'm sorry I hurt you, I love you and you need me.

I ripped the page from tile book and burned it, but her screed was already grafted to my memory. I reproduce it here on the odd chance that the reader may be interested in the presumptuousness of sluts. How can she conceive herself capable of having hurt me? With which foul words does she define the notion love so as to lower it enough for her to claim feeling it? And what delusion moves her to think I need her, her of all the millions on this earth and in the other world?

Surely the presumptuousness of sluts is an infinite commodity, whose stock exceeds all inventory.

71. *General Isidro Bodega*

Isidro Bodega was born in San Juan de Puerto Rico in 1780, the son of a Spanish officer and a Creole woman. He was commissioned an ensign in the Spanish Army in 1797. During twenty-four years of garrison service in New

Spain he was at all times the perfect martinet, impeccably uniformed, preter-naturally grave, steeped in the arcana of moribund traditions, and attentive to the last punctilio of military form. Woe to the soldier who found himself a centimeter out of dress with his formation when Isidro Bodega was inspecting! God's mercy on the junior officer who traduced the least significant of regu-lations while serving under Bodega's command. In all the history of standing armies there was never an officer who went more closely by the book.

In 1819 Bodega was posted to the colony of Tinieblas, breveted to colonel, and put in charge of the plaza at Otán. Two years later, when Tinieblans rose for independence and the Otán barracks were approached by a few dozen ill-armed ranchers and field hands, Isidro Bodega discovered he was a complete physical coward and experienced what Saint Paul called "conversion" and Dr. I. P. Pavlov the "ultra-paradoxical phase." He surrendered at once, went over to the rebels, and henceforth until his "death" nearly three decades later adhered invariably to the path of least resistance.

Bodega epilogued his capitulation with some florid discourse on the rights of man; it was in the insurgents' interest to exaggerate their strength. The news was therefore broadcast through the land that the royal colors had been struck in the face of overwhelming material and moral force. Thus presented, Bodega's act set an example for the commanders of other garrisons, and he claimed and got credit for the painless character of our nation's birth. Simón Mocoso made him Captain General of the Tinieblan Army (the ancestor of our present Civil Guard), a post he held until his "death." Under Bodega's command, this force maintained a level of indiscipline and slovenliness remarkable even in Central America.

In Chapter 1 I have classed Bodega with the "uniformed gorillocrats" who from time to time have occupied our Presidential Palace. I shall not revise this characterization, but now that I have met the man in person and heard his story from his own lips, I must qualify it. It is true that in 1830 Bodega deposed President Julio Canino in a bloodless coup and became President himself—but only because Canino had so bungled the state's finances as to put in jeopardy the value of some considerable land holdings Bodega had ac-cumulated. It is true Bodega continued to wear uniforms, but he did not make violence the basic principle of his administration. It is, further, true that dur-ing Bodega's eighteen years in the Palace no legislature was called to session and no opposition tolerated, but Bodega was himself neither cruel nor crazed for power. He recruited a cabinet of energetic, avaricious foreigners and put the country in their hands, allowing them to steal freely so long as they ran their ministries efficiently. Among them was an East Prussian Junker, the Min-ister of justice, a man whose mere presence radiated such severity and terror that he was able to keep order and suppress dissent without killing hardly anyone. Bodega rarely intervened in the administration of government and comported himself more like a hereditary monarch than a usurping dictator.

After his "death" Bodega entered Gastronomy, an activity grossly defamed in the *Divine Comedy (Inferno,* Canto VI). The slimy filth with which the poet lines the third circle of his imaginary hell comes from his own mind, not from Gastronomy, which has always maintained the highest sanitary standards, while his harping on gluttony is exaggerated (though not entirely out of place), for Gastronomy caters more to the gourmet than to the gourmand. I gather from Bodega's account that Gastronomy is organized along the lines of Drink: an infinity of restaurants offers every conceivable kind of fare and national dish, as well as astral specialities unknown in this world, save in superstitions such as Homer's blather about nectar and ambrosia. Whereas no food is served in Drink, however, Gastronomes enjoy fine wines of this and other-worldly vintage, as well as a wide variety of digestive liqueurs.

When León Fuertes was assigned from L Force to the 3rd Algerian Infantry Division, General Bodega took leave of absence from Gastronomy and wangled a temporary appointment in Guardian Spirits, the better to watch over his now partially-reclaimed descendant. He was with León constantly from July, 1943, until January, 1944. No one knows more about this period of my father's life, and no one could possibly be a more cooperative informant General Bodega was the chief source for Chapter 14.

As occultists have long known the spirit often takes French leave from the body during sleep. Actual visits to the Astral Plane by the spirits of those still resident in this world are rare, but not at all impossible to bring off with the active aid of Guardian Spirits. (Cf. Dante, who made dream visits to the next world in the company of Virgil and Beatrice Portinari. His mind was so warped by religious prejudice and overrigid toilet training that he saw nothing as it was, but for a poet's vision to be thus distorted is no great calamity, as the beauty of his *Comedy* attests. As a scholar, I have no pretensions to "*bel stilo,*" much less to reverberating themal consonances, or architectonic symmetries, or cunningly interset Chinese boxes of metaphor, but I do achieve a little accuracy.) Nightly, General Bodega whisked León Fuertes to the Astral Plane, specifically to the drill grounds of War, which he had obtained permission to use; though since no military man ever tells a subordinate more than he needs to know for his immediate mission, my father never realized where he was and thought the whole business merely a series of dreams.

In midwifing the birth of León Fuertes, soldier, General Bodega reverted to his pre-Otán personality and drew effectively on his quarter century of experience as a regular officer in the army of a world power. The training facilities of War are, as the reader may imagine, extensive and excellent. War's refusal to countenance firearms (see note 27) posed no insurmountable problems. For marksmanship practice General Bodega put León on the longbow range with a rifle borrowed from The Hunt, and a dagger was lashed to this for bayonet training.

72. *The Battle of Cassino*

There are dozens of books, dozens and dozens, that treat or touch upon the Battle of Cassino, and I, incredulous examiners, have read them all. I have consumed the self-serving memoirs of the opposing commanders, Kesselring and Clark, and shuddered at their tastelessness. (The one claims moral superiority over the Allies—imagine a German general capable of that!—because the latter bombed the monastery; the other attempts to justify his turn toward Rome, a maneuver which enabled him to get his picture in the newspapers as the "liberator" of the Holy City but which allowed his enemy to escape intact and thus vitiated the sacrifices of his soldiers.) I have choked down immense dry chunks of the official histories of this and that nation's war participation (e.g., *The Official History of New Zealand in the Second World War*, Volume I) and gobbled up saucy unofficial paeans to national valor (e.g., *L'épopée française en Italie*). And I have devoured works on the Battle itself, munching with relish—on two of them: Dominick Graham, *Cassino* (New York, 1971) and Fred Majdalany, *Cassino: Portrait of a Battle* (London). The first has marvelous maps—the second (by a former company commander) gives the feel of the Battle. For the part played by French forces at Cassino, see Darcourt, op. cit. (pp. 117-191), on whom I have relied to supplement spirit sources. Merci *mille fois, cher M. Darcourt!*

73. *Sangar*

I built one in the living room ten days ago to specifications given me by General Bodega. I used books, of course, not rocks, and roofed it with a blanket, not a poncho, but it served excellently well to summon up the ambience of campaigning in the Abruzzi. I conducted my informant interviews inside it; inside it I consulted published works. I slept inside it also, fully clothed except for footwear. When I had retraced my father's life up to the eve of his baptism of fire, I carried my typewriter in from my desk and, setting it on the floor, sat down before it, half inside and half outside my sangar. In this manner, evocative perhaps of Ernie Pyle, I composed Chapter 14.

Nothing untoward occurred until after I had brought León into Italy with his division. Then, as I was describing the physical aspect of the positions round Cassino, I looked up from the keyboard and saw not the wall of my apartment and the Judas-windowed door but the rubbled slopes of the Rapido Valley and the enemy-held massifs beyond. I have stayed here to do these notes and can regard the same vista when I care to. Now that I have begun my battle and am ready to commit León Fuertes' unit, I think I shall keep my base here for the duration of the fight for Belvedere.

74. *A force*

"Some sinister force" erased eighteen minutes of signal from a magnetic recording of a conversation held on 20th June, 1972, in the office of the Honorable Richard M. Nixon, President of the United States. Such is the view put forward by General Alexander Haig (any relation, one wonders, to dunderhead Sir Douglas?), White House Chief of Staff, but despite the relatively high esteem in which General Haig is held, his theory had not gained a wide acceptance.

"No mystic force but a pack of counterrevolutionary jackals" is responsible for the appearance of images of Padre Celso Labrador on a number of Ciudad Tinieblas buses. That is the dogma delivered *ex cathedra crudelitatis* by Colonel Atila Guadaña, Security Chief of the Tinieblan Civil Guard and Minister of Justice, and despite the fear and loathing Guadaña's name inspires, I am sure that his opinion is accepted by most educated people.

Yet General Haig is right, and Colonel Guadaña wrong.

Because the whole matter of relations between this world and the other is of the highest order of significance; because it nonetheless receives the shabbiest possible treatment by the academic community; because it is a crucial factor in the preparation of this dissertation; and because the author is one of the very few trained investigators to consider it, I shall now speak briefly to the question of astral forces that impinge upon this world. My points of departure are the events that prompted General Haig's and Colonel Guadaña's statements. My immediate authority is General Epifanio Mojón, participant in the Astral Activity of Polities and member of the Committee for the Dissemination of Terror and Despair. General Mojón, who will be the major source for Chapter 15, was with me earlier this evening. We fell to a discussion of the Case of the Beautified Buses, moved from there to the general question of spirit intervention into this world, caromed thence to what General Mojón called the "Nixon Imbroglio" (which has evidently dumped as foul if not as big a mess on his side of the grave as on ours), and so touched on the force referred to by General Haig, whose nature and aim I shall consider first.

As students of his career may readily imagine, Richard Nixon pledged unconsciously for Resentment and Revenge while still an adolescent. This pledge was closely analogous to Padre Celso's pledge for Justice and mine for Learning: it furnished Mr. Nixon a reason for existence on this planet and animated all his days henceforward. Most mysteries surrounding Mr. Nixon's actions and positions are at once cleared up when one considers that his spirit has been pledged to Resentment and Revenge almost constantly for the last fifty years.

I say "almost" because on 31st March, 1968, Mr. Nixon broke his pledge.

Let me make it clear that Mr. Nixon did not lightly repudiate the principles of Resentment and Revenge, which had inspired his whole adult life and which are the only principles he has ever known. He broke his pledge only under psychic torment as intense as the physical torment under which Padre Celso broke his pledge (see note 50). When President Lyndon Johnson announced he would not seek another term, Mr. Nixon saw his hope of being President of the United States within his reach again. He felt compelled to make sure he would grasp it. As this compulsion was unbearable, he yielded to it. He made a deal with the Office of Terrestrial Recruitment (see note 18). As soon as he did so, his pledge was dissolved, for the deal Mr. Nixon made committed him to service in another activity.

A negotiation between a fellow as ingenious as E. A. Poe (for he was the recruiter; the job seems to appeal to former poets) and one as devious as Mr. Nixon deserves a monograph of its own, but I've no time at present for that sort of research. All I could learn from General Mojón, who remembered it from his committee's dossier on Mr. Nixon, was that the haggling was fierce and that the final agreement provided as follows: Astral Activities would insure that the Democratic presidential nomination went to Hubert Humphrey (the only man in the United States whom Mr. Nixon felt he had a decent chance of beating) and would throw in a riot at the National Convention; Mr. Nixon would serve thirty-seven years and seven months in Victim following his "death." The agreement led directly to Mr. Nixon's electoral victory. The breaking of his pledge to Resentment and Revenge accounted for the so-called new Nixon that bloomed briefly during the campaign.

Even before he took office, in fact within an hour of his certification by the Electoral College, Mr. Nixon began trying to sneak out of his commitment. I cannot describe his machinations, which I gather were as dreary as any he ever pulled on residents of this world; I can say only that they failed. The time for plea bargaining had passed, and the Director of Astral Activities does not grant executive clemency to enlistees who cash their bonuses. Then, on the night of his first inauguration, Mr. Nixon received a visit from another representative of the dark side of North American polities, his former Senate colleague Joe McCarthy, a very junior assistant to the Chairman of the Committee for the Dissemination of Terror and Despair. The committee, McCarthy said, and its chairman, Josef Vissarionovich Dzugashvili, had long had an eye on Mr. Nixon. Interest was yet greater now that he was President of the United States. If Mr. Nixon would work with the committee, its counsel would show him a perfectly legal way to avoid serving time in Victim. For once Mr. Nixon did not haggle.

Committee counsel had discovered an old regulation which permits spirits assigned to Victim to be surrogated for by their spouses. (Cf. the Alcestis-Admetus myth, which is based on this provision.) Mr. Nixon wormed through this loophole. General Mojón could not tell me if Mrs. Nixon knew what she was signing, but she signed. Free now of posthumous obligations, Mr. Nixon reaffirmed his pledge to Resentment and Revenge and was welcomed back as swiftly as Padre Celso was to justice (see note 51). His dedication to this bifurcated activity has been evident since his first days in the White House, while certain melancholy episodes of his presidency were inspired by the committee.

No one can accuse me of gringophilia, but I always give credit where it's due. The United States has fostered and maintained certain institutions that support the principle of human freedom. These are great barriers to the spread of terror and despair, and the committee, quite understandably, would like them crushed. You may judge for yourselves, *Time*-saving Professor Lilywhite and tube-fed Dr. Grimes, whether Mr. Nixon has been helpful in this regard. It is enough for me to say that the committee thinks so. It went to some trouble to acquire Mr. Nixon's cooperation; it has gone to a great deal more to prolong it—or rather to prolong its usefulness, since there is clearly little value in the cooperation of a demagistratured pol.

General Mojón was emphatic that the committee had nothing at all to do with dispatching burglars to the Watergate, but at its first session after their arrest the committee voted unanimously to help Mr. Nixon wriggle off the hook again, and authorized the chairman to bear news of this decision to Mr. Nixon personally, as earnest of the committee's firm support. A meeting between the President of the United States and the Chairman of the Committee for the Dissemination of Terror and Despair thus took place in the Oval Office on 20th June, 1972. The Chairman arrived while the President was in conference with Mr. H. R. Haldeman, who was dismissed until the meeting ended, about a quarter of an hour later. General Mojón does not know what was discussed—the expression of the committee's support aside— but thinks a purge of dissidents may have been mentioned since the Chairman has great fondness for and experience with this tactic, but he has firsthand knowledge of the rage with which the Chairman greeted news (divulged nearly a year later) that his and his interpreter's voices had been bugged. More was involved than the personal slight—though the Chairman is acutely sensitive to slights and does not suffer them kindly. Were it to become public knowledge that he was in jovial alliance with a President of the United States, even such a President as Richard Nixon, the cult of his personality, already gravely damaged since his "death," might be destroyed entirely, while the position of his followers in this world, all of them enthusiastic spreaders of despair and terror, would be severely weakened. The most infuriating part was that the Chairman had to go on supporting Mr. Nixon anyway, Mr. Nixon could be counted on to go public with a distorted version of the meeting if the committee withdrew its aid and comfort.

The Chairman's entire wrath fell on poor Joe McCarthy—though, characteristically, he gave McCarthy no inkling of his fall from favor till too late. He praised McCarthy before the whole committee, beamed on McCarthy like a proud uncle, declared that McCarthy had suspected Richard Nixon from the first and had given confidential warning not to trust him. This wasn't so, but the Chairman had McCarthy himself believing it within a minute. Who was McCarthy to dispute the Chairman's views? Who was McCarthy to turn down promotion or refuse the holiday in Drink the Chairman offered? There, of course, two of the Chairman's secret agents made themselves his buddies, sang smutty songs with him, laughed at his gross jokes, and, finally, waltzed him, reeling, over to Risk and conned him into a disastrous wager. He is now serving a thousand-year sentence in Victim.

Besides this, the only action the Chairman felt he could take was to destroy the evidence of his visit to the White House. That way, if Mr. Nixon tried to publicize the meeting, it would be his word against the Chairman's-a pretty fair contest in credibility. The "sinister force," then, to which General Alexander Haig referred was a beam of thought waves from the Chairman of the Committee for the Dissemination of Terror and Despair, which demagnetized that portion of the tape whereon his chat with Richard Nixon was recorded. I doubt that General Haig acknowledges the existence of another world, much less comprehends its workings. I take his reference to the "force" as an accidental hit smack in the bull's eye such as a blind man might make once in a million shots.

Let us proceed now to our second illustration:

Not all extraterrestrial forces are sinister. All spirits—saving those in Victim and those who, like my grandfather Dr. Azael Burlando, have been singled out for isolation (see note 18)—can visit this world and communicate with receptive people here, thus sometimes gaining influence with them. Spirits may as well exert subliminal persuasion on residents of this world who cannot consciously perceive them: e.g., on the Mayor of Chicago, Illinois, and on members of his police force. Besides this, since thought waves are a form of electromagnetic energy, they can be focused in a beam, thereby to exert physical force upon material. A very, very few residents of this world possess is power. I, alas, do not. The Directorate of Astral Activities encourages the cultivation of this power, pampers spirits who have it, and dissuades them from cycling back here. Such spirits can pick up the thought waves of others, amplify them, focus them, etc. Politics is not the only Astral Activity to which such spirits seek assignment. Justice has some as well.

As I at once suspected (see note 66), Padre Celso Labrador is responsible (through the good offices of a gifted Justice colleague) for the images of him that continue to appear on buses in this capital. More, he is going about it in a very energetic fashion. There were several sightings during the past week, all on private buses as before, and now he is branching out. Yesterday afternoon he embellished a bus belonging to the Surface Transport Authority.

According to Arnulfa, who heard of it by rumorphone, and veiledly confirmed by today's *Diario de la Bahia*, a large, state-owned, and spankingnew bus was transfigured with an emblem of the padre as it passed along Calle Saturnino Aguila between Civil Guard Headquarters and Bondadosa Prison. Padre Celso displayed himself full length, resplendent in a white cassock and brandishing a bloody sword. The legend "RENDER UNTO GENGHIS THAT WHICH IS GENGHIS'S" appeared in the customary dialogue balloon.

In the first official mention of this sort of occurrence, the newspaper (a

government slave like all the others) carried the statement by Colonel
Guadaña paraphrased earlier in this note, and went on to say that the driver
of the bus had been arrested and was being questioned *(question extraordi-
naire,* I fear). Neither the colonel nor the reporter told what happened; they
merely alluded to a display of subversive propaganda by counterrevolutionary conspirators. The article held, however, that "the conspiracy is probably
of foreign inspiration, considering the advanced technology employed to
make the treacherous and blasphemous exhibit appear at a precise moment," and closed in the expectation that Colonel Guadaña would soon
"have all the traitors under lock and key, and at the disposal of the people's
revolutionary justice."

According to General Mojón, Padre Celso's intent is to discredit the Manduco regime. This has caused no slight concern among the members of General Mojón's committee. A subcommittee on which General Mojón serves is
seeking means to make Padre Celso cease and desist.

The point, in any case, is that forces from the next world intervene in this
one, in a variety of ways, for a variety of motives. Unfortunately, hardly anyone is studying this intervention, despite its critical effect upon events. No
support is offered for such study. Such study is actively opposed by the academic establishment and often punished cruelly by those responsible for what
is called "mental health." The depressing result is that our civilization knows
less about spirit intervention than did the ancients, who saw it for the natural
process that it is. No one put Plutarch in a strait jacket for describing the apparition Marcus Brutus saw at Abydos and at Philippi, but I know the risks
I run just hinting at Stalin's role in the Watergate cover-up and mentioning his
spirit's presence in the White House.

75. *General Epifanio Mojón*

The most repugnant of all my ancestors, a man who enlisted his one potentially redeeming quality, determination, in the service of human suffering.

Existence filled my great-great-grandfather—and no doubt fills him still—
with a great terror. He has managed to conceal it, even from himself, by immersing himself in violence and cruelty. This cost him his humanity, which he
paid out in installments over a period of years. Let it be noted that he never
wavered when a payment came due, but what else can be said for one who
traded his capacity to connect with other human beings for the knack of finding strength and safety in creating victims?

Perhaps I might discover something else if General Mojón would present
himself to me in a less disgusting aspect. I don't demand the trim youthfulness
he put on when he accompanied my father in the assault on Belvedere, but I
do wish he'd choose a mean between that and what he wears when he comes
here. To me General Mojón shows himself as he looked near the end of his
earthly life: bloated; decayed; a jaw slack and slavering like an old hyena's;

a complexion like a half-cooked flapjack that in the act of being turned has slithered from the pan onto the grease-splashed stove and lies bunched there, displaying its yellow-white, pocked, oozy face—so perfectly repulsive, all in all, that when he was hung up in the bay on a cross designed for one of his own victims, neither the sharks nor the buzzards would touch a morsel of him. He seems content with his appearance. No doubt it harmonizes with that of his fellow committeemen. But it is all I can do to keep from glancing away, or gagging.

He is a valuable informant, though, and as such worth the nausea. And the weight of his contempt, for he regards me as one might a shoe sole that has blundered into fresh dog droppings. He does not hold with the life of contemplation, and as for the word, thinks its only fit employment is in false witness. He was, besides, most disappointed in my father, whom he hoped to mold into a despot after his own model, and detests León's being memorialized in this dissertation. He can't avoid testifying—a resident of this world with my strength of mind and my connections can subpoena just about any spirit—but his volubility is, I suspect, motivated by an urge to scare me. In this he succeeded, both in his discourse and in some "special effects" through which he gave me a personal taste of battle (for this, see my next note).

General Mojón took such relish in transmitting me the horrors of combat that I asked him why he did not choose War as his Astral Activity. He dismissed it as "a game for babies." Astral warriors suffer no permanent mutilations and know no fear of "death." Astral battles produce no civilian casualties, disfigure and debase no women and children, destroy no painfully constructed institutions of civilized life. And astral armies have no artillery.

"War without cannon is for babies!" General Mojón declared, and then glowingly described the effect of chain shot on massed infantry when fired at a range of fifty meters. He is happy to note that terrestrial artillerymen can now achieve an improved grapeshot result with the so-called beehive round, which General Mojón observed while accompanying my brother, Carlos, in Vietnam, and he finds napalm marvelous—except that, as with high explosive, the men who actually deliver it don't get to watch what it does to human flesh. He'd come too far by the time he "died," he said, to play around with swords and arrows. His present position affords him the chance to provoke modern wars, whose weapons produce truly spectacular abominations and whose participants feel mortal, trouser-fouling terror most of the time.

76. *The pandemonic din of battle*

I have heard it in this room, amazed examiners! I have smelled cordite. I have felt the reverberations of shellbursts. I have seen tracers arching through the air. I have tasted the fear and exhilaration of battle.

I have watched comrades shot to pieces, and enemies fall at my hand. I have been to war.

Let me say at once that I claim no credit for this experience. I built my sangar and lived in it and in this way put myself a little in the mood of mountain warfare, but when it came to flesh-and-bone knowledge of combat, I was a passive subject in an experiment by General Epifanio Mojón. I judge the experience to have been of inestimable value in the preparation of Chapter 15, and yet I wish I had never had it— not because it was painful—though painful it surely was—but because it entailed some suffering on my father's part, which I knew nothing of at the time but which I fain would have spared him.

After General Mojón had described the fording of the Rapido River and the pre-dawn vigil of the tirailleur battalions, he began relating the first stages of the action: the opening bombardment, the German s' off-balance response, the commitment of assault companies. But when he reached the point where Colonel Roux ordered a general attack, he broke off: Had I the guts to go to war myself?

I asked him what he meant, and he replied he meant just what he said: Was I man enough to get my knowledge at first hand, to take part myself instead of merely listening in case and safety to a story?

How could I manage that? I wondered, and he said how didn't matter, yes or no was enough. If I said yes, he'd try to take me to Cassino. If he could do it, and if I survived, he'd explain later. If I said no . . . He snorted in disgust.

Honored examiners, I accepted at once. I had no need to prove my courage to the likes of Epifanio Mojón. Nor did I feel the kind of solipsistic yen to find out how I'd do that drives so many peace-loving young fellows into combat. But I will run any risk and explore any avenue to gather information germane to my investigations.

General Mojón told me he'd be back the following evening and disappeared. I busied myself studying Darcourt's account of the engagement (op. cit., pp. 130-149). The next night I went into battle.

But I had best describe what General Mojón had in mind:

Human beings (like all animals) possess organs sensitive to such external events as light, sound, heat, pressure, etc. The responses of these organs are coded electro-chemically and transmitted to an analog computing instrument which organizes and records them. The organizing/analyzing process may provoke such internal events as the secretion of hormones and their flow into the bloodstream, which in turn provoke further internal events (e.g., changes in the rate of pulse, breathing, and metabolism. Messages relating to these secondary internal events are fed back into the computer, which organizes and records them. Poets call these messages emotions. The record of perceptions may be played back.

It is now helpful to consider certain metallic devices that correspond roughly to the protoplasmic organs I have referred to. A combination TV-sound recorder, for example, may he equipped with a camera and an impedance microphone. As such, this machine senses light and sound waves, codes perceptions of them electronically, records these perceptions on magnetic tape, and (when hooked up to a suitable receiver) plays them back. Two recorders may also be linked together, so that a recording made by one may be transmitted to and recorded by the other. For such an operation no sensing devices, no camera eye or microphone car, are necessary. Such an operation may, moreover, be performed, say, thirty years and eight thousand kilometers from the time and place of the original recording. Barring deterioration of the tape, the second recording is as sharp as the original.

What General Mojón had in mind was to retrieve from my father's memory the complete record of his experiences and emotions during the first twelve hours of the fight for Colle Belvedere, and to feed this record directly into my brain, so that I should see, hear, taste, smell, feel, think, suffer, and exult exactly as my father had. The technique of such retrieval and transmission was developed by a team of medical researchers formerly citizens of Germany, now participants in Torture. At the time it was performed with me, the operation had been tried successfully (if that is in fact the correct word) with a number of spirits from Victim, but never with a resident of this world.

During experiments conducted in Torture, the supposed witchmaster Urbain Grandier, the attempted regicide Robert Damiens, and the sodomite lover of King Edward II, Hugh Despenser, were put in deep hypnosis and caused to relive their executions, which experiences were simultaneously transmitted to a representative sample of subjects. So effective is the process in reproducing in one individual sensations and emotions felt by another that when Despenser relived the moment when his generative organ was seized in pincers and sliced off, a female subject who was the beneficiary of this experience displayed a most convincing agony, although she had never possessed an organ of that sort herself.

There is, of course, no reason why this process need be used only for tormentive purposes. It might give paralytics the thrills of Olympic competition, allow the blind to study history of art, and let the deaf hear Mozart. It might put stay-at-homes in moon capsules, or "Silent, upon a peak in Darien." And it might close the gulf between the sexes, permitting men to know childbirth and women to know fatherbood, as well, of course, as to participate in sexual congress from each other's points of view (as, in fact, León and Rosario were able to do without the help of Nazi doctors—see Chapter 11). General Mojón's experiment with me is a case in point. Whatever his motive in arranging it and despite its being somewhat unpleasant—especially with regard to side effects (of which more later)—the experience not only enlarged my own consciousness but contributed to the advancement of human knowledge. I can only hope my father, who after all was neither consulted nor rewarded, did not mind too much reliving his first day of combat.

But I learned all these particulars only after my pilgrimage to Belvedere,

When General Mojón ordered me to stop my cars with cotton, blindfold myself, and lie down on my bed, I had to overcome considerable trepidations. I
lay there in great unease for about half an hour while he wrangled with tech-
nicians on the Astral Plane. I could get only his side of the communication,
and it scarcely calmed me to hear him bark, "Come in, Torture; Torture,
come in!" every few minutes when whoever he was on to left him, no doubt
to supervise some detail of the preparations. Nor did I receive any warning
whatsoever, unless one might count Mojón's satisfied grunt just before my father's mind juiced into mine. All at once I lay soaked and shivering on rough
stones, peering into icy darkness, charged with adrenaline, thinking in French.

But let me be accurate: I was not Camilo Fuertes, candidate for the Ph.D.
degree in history. I was León Fuertes, corporal, 3rd Squad, 4th Section, 11th
Company, 3rd Battalion, 4th Tunisian Tirailleurs. I did not ask myself: What's
going on? Where am I? I knew exactly what was going on and where I was.
A regimental attack was going on, and I was on the west bank of the Rapido
River waiting for dawn and the assault. And though I knew that, I did not say
to myself: Keep your eyes open; note everything you can and remember it so
you can write it down accurately later. I had no thought at all of writing history. I didn't even think that the battle I was about to take part in might be
mentioned in history books someday, though I suppose this is not an uncommon thought among soldiers. I make this point because there is no such thing
as a Camilo Fuertes who is not concerned with history. Camilo Fuertes had,
therefore, ceased to exist. The analog computing organ containing the program of Camilo Fuertes' identity was temporarily filled to the last neuron
with impulses from León Fuertes' memory.

What I experienced during the next twelve hours is described in text above.
Mental and physical stress, fear of "death," joy in murder, rage at the enemy,
and grief for slaughtered comrades: it is all there. Because I experienced it
personally, because I *was* León Fuertes for that period, I found some difficulty
in using the third person. I marvel, in fact, at the pomposity of folks like Cae-
sar and de Gaulle, who can relate their experiences as though they had occurred to someone else. I had no trouble at all, on the other hand, recalling
what had happened. My problem, rather, was weeding out details that, however interesting in themselves, did not really demand inclusion in this dissertation. Chapter 15 would, otherwise, have grown monstrously long.

Worse than the actual experience of battle—which, as the reader will take
note, had its rewards for León—was its aftermath. General Mojón's experiment continued beyond the occupation of the German positions on Crest 718
(which I have judged the natural point to end Chapter 15) and included the
lull thereafter and the German counterattack (which I shall tell in the first
pages of Chapter 16). It ended at dusk with the repulse of that attack, so I did
not have to spend the night on the mountain under rain and fire, but I hardly
think that would have been a greater ordeal than what I actually went

through and must describe here as a caveat to others. The process of direct brain-to-brain transfer of experience may, after all, be taken up by other activities besides Torture and someday offered to the public of this world to provide people the kind of consciousness-expanding benefits I have touched on earlier in this note. Potential consumers must be aware of its side effects.

At the conclusion of the experiment I had no knowledge who or where I was. General Mojón did not stay on to ease me out of it. I woke up, as it were, blindfolded, with my ears stopped. On removing these sense mufflers, I found myself in an unfamiliar room dressed in unfamiliar clothing. I went to a mirror (for the first time, by the way, since the evening described in note 57) and saw an unfamiliar face. In short, I suffered total amnesia, a frightful state, concerned examiners, quite frightful.

I do not know how long it lasted. It might have gone on much longer than it did, but that Arnulfa's arrival brought me out of it. I had the presence of mind not to go flailing about wildly, not to turn everything upside down hunting for some identity document or rush out in the street for help. I lay down on the living room couch in the pool of warm sunlight from the courtyard, waiting for my heart to stop pounding and my breathing to calm. This had more or less occurred when Arnulfa, who had forgot her key, rang the doorbell and called out, "Don Camilo!" That brought me to myself, and I got up and let her in.

But my first thought, one that took me an unconscionably long time to overcome and pummel from my brain, was that I was mad. The battle experiences I'd got from my father rushed back to me along with my identity, and I believed them and the events that preceded them—my conversation with General Mojón, for example—hallucinations. I thought I was insane and desperately in need of help. This delusion has possessed me from time to time in the past. While in its grip I see nothing clearly and consider the whole world of spirits merely the figment of my diseased imagination. Compassionate examiners, this is a hideous condition. Hideous, hideous, hideous.

Next, I decided I'd been dreaming, or nightmaring rather. Luckily enough, I was able to reach this decision fairly quickly, perhaps in as short a time as twenty minutes, though it seemed longer, for I was at the point of suicide, and to one who believes the next world only a figment, suicide is a serious affair. I put the matter of spirits aside for the moment and decided I had grown myself a great, rearing nightmare by thinking too precisely on my father and the Battle of Cassino. This too was unpleasant, though nothing like what I'd just been through, since I felt I might be tempted to draw on what I now considered dream visions for this dissertation, and that would be a most unscholarly predicament to fall into.

Only after a long while was I able to put my universe back together crumb by crumb, to bring myself back to a belief in the reality of General Mojón's spirit and its responsibility for my voyage into the maelstrom of war. Only then did I sleep, and for some days afterward I remained shaken. I need scarcely say that when General Mojón showed up that evening for our scheduled interview, I demanded and received a full explanation, and gave him a stern tongue-lashing for tricking me into causing my father inconvenience.

I caution others to consider these side effects before participating in brain-to-brain transfer of perceptions. Perhaps the process will be improved to eliminate them. Perhaps they would not have occurred had the experiment been conducted out of some other activity than Torture, which is, unfortunately, the only activity that has the process as yet. Certainly the process is a valuable investigative aid. Certainly it has contributed to the preparation of this dissertation, both with regard to Chapter 15 and in furnishing me firsthand background information on my father's war that will no doubt be helpful in Chapter 16. Certainly it is the best means of researching my particular subject, given the lamentable reality that my father is presently held incommunicado in Victim. And certainly it might be of benefit to others. But one must take note of the side effects.

For my part, I can bear them. I'm no romantic seeking thrills and chills, but I can endure what others have endured, if it be in the advancement of knowledge. Where others have gone I too must journey, to bring the story back for those too busy or too weak to make the trip. As for side effects and other mental risks, I accept them. I did not fight at Ayacucho, or in our civil wars, or with Sandino in Nicaragua, or in Europe with the French, or in Vietnam, but no one can say I have less courage than the others of my line.

I will not harm others, though. I have told General Mojón to have his brilliant troupe of Dachau grads consult my father if they hope to run another brain-to-brain between their world and mine. Or find another subject; I won't take part in any more of them unless my father knows what's going on and freely consents. I am not quite so dedicated to "science" as the "physicians" of Auschwitz and Treblinka. I will suffer a bit myself, but not torment others. For all I know, the process may be worse for my father than it was for me, and he's suffering enough without my causing him pain.

Peace and mercy on him. I pray he may forgive me.

77. *To guard against pernicious thought*

The Government has begun assigning members of the Policía Urbana de Seguridad (PUS) to ride the buses.

These are not real cops but rather an auxiliary goonhood recruited earlier this year to supplement the more formal organs of repression. PUS agents are picked from the pool of minor criminals secreted by the slum quarters of the capital, the sort who mug old ladies in the narrow streets around the public market. They receive no training, wear no uniforms, and possess no qualifications beyond their bullies' readiness to brutalize the peaceful and defenseless and their thieves' loyalty to the regime. Their mission, as stated officially, is "to protect the state against counter-revolution and subversion." In practice this translates to such prodigies of national defense as apprehending (and in the process roughing up) a fishmonger who chanced to wrap a sea bass he'd just sold in a piece of newspaper bearing the photo of General Genghis Manduco, Chief of the Tinieblan State and Maximum Leader of the Tinieblan Revolution. The poor sap got two years, one for *lèse-autorité* and one for counter-revolution; his housewife customer, charged as an accessory before the fact, was absolved in reward for giving evidence.

These heroes, as I say, are being randomly assigned to ride the buses, in imitation, it would seem, of the anti-hijack guards put on board aircraft in the United States a few years back. No one is worried about buses' being hijacked, of course, but rumor has it—and rumor is the only reliable means of mass communication in this country—that the Government is at its wit's end to stop the displays arranged by Padre Celso Labrador, or at least neutralize their effect.

These displays have become more frequent and more variegated. Arnulfa saw one that, from her description, seems to have resembled the seven-headed beast of Revelation. Each head was in the likeness of an officer of Manduco's junta, and the design was topped with the scrolled legend: "HE THAT LEADETH INTO CAPTIVITY SHALL GO INTO CAPTIVITY—HE THAT KILLETH WITH THE SWORD MUST BE KILLED WITH THE SWORD." Another, which she heard of at second or third hand, depicted a number of high government officials. They had loathsome insect bodies and flew across the whole side of one of the huge new buses, and the phrase "FOR THEY COVERED THE FACE OF THE WHOLE LAND SO THAT THE LAND WAS DARKENED" was written beneath them in Day-Glo colors.

All the painters and graphic artists in the country have supposedly been put under arrest. The Civil Guard is on alert. The members of the Junta are said to be diarrhetic with worry. But relief may be at hand. According to General Mojón, the Committee for the Dissemination of Terror and Despair has entered negotiations with representatives from Justice, and has proposed (as of yesterday, 7th August, 1974) to cut off aid to Richard Nixon in return for a moritorium on the anti-Manduco campaign. Justice wants Mr. Nixon out of office very badly and will probably go along, though they are dragging the palaver out to let the padre get a few more licks in.

He makes a point of hitting buses with PUS agents on board. The agents console themselves by trying to guard against pernicious thought. They wonder out loud whether the bus they're in is destined for decoration and arrest anyone who seems to look forward to such an event. They spout wisecracks about the situation and arrest people who smile. And should the padre strike, they arrest those who fail to make a convincing show of righteous indignation. The result has been that few bus riders have trouble finding seats these days and that they proceed to their destinations in mute solemnity.

78. *His squad*

I was able to interview only one member of the squad my father, León Fuertes, led at Belvedere.

Dax, Djemal, Boulala, and El Haoui have all recycled to this world, Dax doing so at once, a not uncommon course of action with those who "die" in young adulthood. His memory was cleansed and his spirit sent back to this world before the end of 1944. (Memory erasure is, by the way, standard operating procedure' with all recycling spirits, but it is sometimes partially botched; hence the intimations of immortality and vague remembrance of past states experienced by some residents of this world.)

Djemal chose Getting and Spending and was there for three-plus years. Upon the establishment of Israel (May, 1948), he applied to be recycled there, and his spirit was put into one of the first embryos conceived in that country.

Boulala and El Haoui entered Warrior's Repose (also called Houri and so referred to on the application forms of female spirits). It is this activity that was described to Mahomet by a spirit named Gabriel and that forms the basis of that "Paradise" mentioned profusely throughout the Koran (see particularly Chapters XLIV, LV, and LVI).

Because he maintained prolonged contact with a single spirit source, Mahomet picked up a great deal of detailed information about a narrow spectrum of the next world. Besides Warrior's Repose/Houri, he knew only certain aspects of Victim, which he calls the Pit in his suras. What he knew, however, he knew well. The gardens, fountains, fruit trees; the tasty viands and the wine which leaves no hangover; the shady oases and soft carpets; the rich silks and fine brocades, are all depicted with great accuracy by the Prophet, while the houris are as "smooth and lovely" as he says they are. He erred only in holding that the activity is restricted to pious Muslims, and that the houris exist merely for male delectation.

Warrior's Repose/Houri is designed to accommodate not only hedonistic male spirits but also those *female* spirits whose idea of how to spend eternity is to be around hardy, possessive males—a rather widespread female dream, Steinem, Millett, Friedan, et al. to the contrary notwithstanding. (The mirror-image activity, Courtly Love, is offered for male spirits who enjoy paying elaborate and more or less chaste homage to females, and female spirits who enjoy collecting same.) The entrance requirements are: for males, valor; for females, virtue. The experience of millennia has shown a four-to-one ratio of fair to brave satisfying to all parties. No one becomes a houri save by choice; no one need remain a houri an hour longer than she desires—though, of course, an abrupt exit may entail a period of inactivity in Prorogation. In confecting his "Paradise" out of the information he received from Gabriel, Mahomet may have been influenced by his own fantasies. Or he may have distorted purposely to play on the male chauvinism of his neighbors; he was trying to establish a religion, after all. He knew nothing, moreover, of Courtly

Love, where the ratio of knight-troubadour to lady is likewise four to one. He certainly knew nothing of Amazonia, whose participants are exclusively female (as those in War are male), though not particularly violent. Viewed clearly and in panorama, the next world is neither male-supremacist nor female-supremacist.

As followers of Islam, Boulala and El Haoui expected to be received in Mahomet's "Paradise." Warrior's Repose/Houri did not disappoint them. At length, though, they tired of ease and pleasure and asked to be recycled. It is an interesting irony that El Haoui's spirit happened to be put back into an Arab body and that his new avatar fought in the late Mideast hostilities against a unit commanded by the reincarnation of his old messmate Djemal, an accountant from Tel Aviv named Kalish, who holds a reserve captaincy in the Israeli tank corps.

Barelli is in Contemplation. He does not care to recall his war experience, and I did not press to bring him here.

Joseph-Marie Reveil, the soldier who presciently gave León Fuertes his telephone *jeton* memento for safekeeping, "died" of wounds during the sixth day of 3rd Battalion's ordeal on Belvedere. He was accepted in Learning and spent ten years there reading sociology, a branch of knowledge he had been studying at the Sorbonne when Hitler marched on France. He then entered Astral Administration and is now an official in Reception. Reveil was able to supplement General Mojón's account of the bayonet charge led by Sublieutenant Bouakkaz and the chaotic fighting between Crests 718 and 862. He was instrumental in obtaining information on his former squadmates who have returned to this world, and background information on Warrior's Repose/ Houri.

Reveil was on duty when León Fuertes arrived in the next world. My father recognized him at once and told him that he had preserved his telephone *jeton* religiously, that he had taken it back to France with him on his state visit and shown it to General de Gaulle, and that he had had it on his person when he was assassinated. I have no way of authenticating this story. I cannot recall ever having seen a *jeton* among the effects—gold penknife, keys, loose change—my father would empty from his pockets to his night table before taking siesta, but then I didn't know *jetons* existed until I visited France in summer, 1968. I might have seen it a hundred times and thought it an odd coin. I am not about to bother the ghost of Charles de Gaulle over it.

I suspect my father made the whole tale up. He had no idea what the next world held in store, and lo! he came upon a former subordinate in a post of some authority. It would have been most like him to concoct an ingratiating fable, and get on Reveil's good side straightaway.

79. *Then the days and nights fell together*
During the composition of Chapter 15 I began to have extremely vivid war dreams—not replays of perceptions picked up from my father's memory but

original variations on themes from films and books. I would kill or be killed time and again, and these dreams were interspersed with visits from men who perished round Cassino. None of them knew my father; none was even from a French unit. They had got wind of someone interested in the battle, and they flocked to my sleeping ear and poured it full of strife. A Scots sergeant major told me how his outfit was annihilated during a night attack across the crests, whole platoons careering over precipices in the dark. A trooper of the Liebstandarten Adolf Hitler Division (Waffen S.S.) described the aerial bombardinents he went through and then turned green with terror when I mentioned the French forces, for a Moroccan goumier had taken both his ears for keepsakes as he lay dying. There were Gurkhas and Poles, who knew no language I could understand and who tried to explain their "deaths" in gesture, and a gigantic Texan who returned regularly to complain of being blown in two by a short round from his own artillery. One cannot banish spirits from one's dreams, and I was usually too fatigued to wake myself. My sleep was stewed in violence.

When awake I recalled my father's experiences and listened to General Mojón, arid when ever I looked up from my typewriter, whenever I turned my face from my informant's, I saw the massif of Belvedere looming before me and would huddle back instinctively into my sangar. I had no surcease from combat day or night.

Then the days and nights fell together and were confused in stress and anguish, and memories and dreams and visions merged, and thought and fancy spilled into each other, and present fused with past and here with there, and this world and the next mixed roughly, arid there was no more conscious order in my mind.

The demon war possessed me, pious examiners, and wrote most of these last two chapters.

80. Self-indulgence

My aunt Rosario, who is the source for the final portions of Chapter 16, described León Fuertes' reflections during his mountaintop clarity in such a manner as to imply that I am a selfish person, thus prompting the following dialogue, which I reproduce for the sidelight it sheds on the problems of researching this dissertation:

"Is it self-indulgence to do what I am in this world to do, despite all obstacles?"

"No, Camilo. Everyone owes loyalty to his destiny, though if the obstacles are human, it's nice to use some care when getting round them."

"Is it self-indulgence to refuse to tell the high and mighty they are right when I know they're wrong?"

"No. There's room between self-indulgence and self-privation, and everyone owes himself his truth, though it isn't always necessary to tell someone who's wrong that he's a moron."

"Well, then; I stand acquitted."

"Really. Isn't it selfish to refuge in your mission and your truth, to use them as means to evade responsibility?"

"I am an order-bringer! I help make this world make sense! That's what I do here, day and night, week in, week out! Do I take holidays? Do I cut corners on my research? Do I fake my data? Evade responsibility? Me? You must be joking!"

"I'm not talking about your work, Camilo. I'm talking about other people."

"I have nothing to do with other people."

My aunt Rosario smiled softly. "That's what I mean, dear."

"Mean what? I no longer conduct relations with living human beings. I have given that up—except for Arnulfa, of course, whom I pay well and treat decently. As I receive none of the benefits of contact with living humans, I incur no responsibilities toward them. Ergo, I evade none."

"It doesn't work like that, Camilo. Even someone who's totally alone is responsible to others. He is obliged to give and ask pardon. Your father learned that alone on Belvedere."

"Well. Give pardon. That I can do. Once and for all, since I have taken steps and will receive no more offenses. All right. Those who have offended me already, all but two, I pardon! I shall give pardon to Dr. Emil Vertilanz as soon as he begs me for it with suitable groveling to my scholarship in any recognized learned journal. As for the other, she I would gladly pardon here and now, except her offense is unpardonable. As for asking pardon, I have not offended anyone enough for that, and since I no longer am involved with living humans, cannot offend any in the future."

"It doesn't work like that, Camilo."

"In my relationships with spirits I give rather more liberally of myself than wisdom would recommend. I heard the padre out, for example, though I was extremely busy. I gave him several footnotes in my dissertation, though it was by no means clear at the time that his material would be germane. Any fair accounting of my dealings with residents of this world and yours will show a credit balance on my side."

"Accounting! Footnotes! Do you think your father would have given footnotes?"

"My father, dear Aunt Rosario, would have been unable to see the fellow in the first place. Or having by chance seen him, would have been unable to believe him real. This world is so organized—or ill organized—that the gift of action is distinct from the gift of insight, on all the deep important levels anyway. Besides, my father—whom I nonetheless respect and love— was himself self-indulgent, as he realized, as you report, and as I have learned independently."

"You don't know his whole story yet."

"No. I do not. So suppose we get on with it."

"I'm not going to go on, Camilo, if you refuse to learn. And I don't mean learn what happened at such a place on such and such a date. Your father's life means something! Oh, you're probably capable of getting the meaning down on paper without its registering in your mind or making any impact on your life, but I won't be a party to that kind of futility! Gift of insight, oof! You can't see anything that counts!"

And so I had to beg her to forgive my defects, to bear with my deficiencies. I had to cajole. I had to promise I would try to see. I had to mean it too, because there's no fooling spirits. At length she consented to continue—more out of family feeling, she said, than any hope that I'd "develop morally."

Tenured crotalids—are you there, Emil?—and other serpents in the groves of academe will observe that my research method is no "easy way," that I should scarcely use it were my motive comfort, that it can be a thousand times more trying than the conventional techniques of scholarly investigation. Documents do not bother people with personal criticisms. Published works do not threaten to disappear unless placated. Archives do not enjoin those who consult them to "moral development." And records do not utter ominous predictions.

"It's the hard way for you, I fear, Camilo." My aunt Rosario's sad smile put lead into her words. "Your father had to learn by pain. It's clear you'll have to also. Or worse, you may never learn at all."

PART FOUR

81. Back from the "dead"

I have been over to the next world and come back.

I have come back to this dissertation after an unexpected, bitter interruption. But since it and the journey it provoked both came to good, and since they touch upon the matter of this essay, I shall tell of them.

I have not come back to Tinieblas. As my text brings my father home to his country, my luck finds me in exile.

Good luck and salutary exile, let me say at once. My body, which was within a hair of going out of business, is recuperating in agreeable surroundings. My spirit is doing famously.

Dr. Esclepio Varón, President of the Republic of Costaguana, has villa'd me in the provincial capital of Cricamaña. Its site is high, its air is pure, its sun is brilliant. Its skies are cloudless, its days pleasant, its nights cool. And since its suburbs have spread back onto the hillside, the terrace where I sit now, with my typewriter set before me on a wrought-iron, glass-topped table, affords me an admirable vista of the pink-roofed town and the romantically chasm'd peaks beyond.

Costaguanans and their guests are, furthermore, presently enjoying one of the intervals of peace that come now and again to human societies like the entr'actes in *Titus Androicus*. That alone would be enough to soothe my spirit, but the circumstances that separated me from this dissertation enabled me to gather all the data I shall need to finish it, and brought other precious benefits besides. I am, then, in the most high and palmy state of spiritual well-being, a well-being whose overtones, I trust, will reverberate symphonically through this essay from here on.

I spent somewhat over three months in the next world, most of that time in the close company of my father, León Fuertes. The subject of this history is the main source for its concluding chapters.

82. Roaring

It began with a roaring at my door, roaring and pounding. These were necessary to attract my notice. I was in trance. I had decided that I was growing too dependent on my aunt Rosario for contacting spirit informants, and I was trying on my own to reach someone who knew my father during his postwar days in Paris. The roaring of my name, punctuated by heavy thumps, pierced my concentration and brought me to the door. I opened it and found Sig Heilanstalt.

"Liz is in jail!"

I shall not picture his disheveled aspect or his distracted stare. I shall not gloss on his anxiety, seven parts fear, I judge, and three embarrassment. Nor shall I try to reproduce his words, which tumbled forth in a most disordered and ill-dressed array for one who earns his bread by use of language. The gist of what he told me after I motioned him inside is as follows:

My wife, Elizabeth, had undertaken to retype an outline and draft portions of the book that Sig was writing. She was supposed to lunch with him that noon and bring the work along. She did not show up. After having waited for over an hour, Sig went to the pension where she had been living since ceasing to reside with me. Her car was there; she wasn't. Her landlady, a full-time snoop like most of the profession, told Sig Liz had gone out a little after midday, had tried without success to start her car, and had then boarded a bus headed downtown. Sig at once feared the worst, for while he was waiting in the restaurant, a fellow had rushed in, ordered a double gin, swigged it at gulp, and then announced that round the corner, on the main thoroughfare, in front of the Pelf Bank and opposite El Opulento, a bus had bloomed with an exceedingly uncomplimentary caricature of General Manduco, and that the PUS had taken everyone on board.

It took Sig the rest of the afternoon to prove his fears well grounded. The Officer of the Day at Civil Guard Headquarters advised him that if he really wanted to know who was behind bars, he could quite easily be put there himself for an extended stay. The United States Ambassador to Tinieblas declined to see him. The First Secretary of the Embassy kept him waiting half an hour, then couldn't fit him in. The Second Secretary kept him waiting, then referred him to the Political Officer; who kept him waiting, then re-

ferred him to the Consul General; who kept, him waiting, then referred him
to the Deputy Sub-Assistant Junior Vice-Consul. This seersuckered pippin
maintained all the traditions of sloth, pusillanimity, and unconcern for private citizens that the State Department has formed over the years: it did not
appear that Mrs. Fuertes was on register with the Consulate; it could not be
clearly established that she was a US citizen; it had not been proved that she
was under arrest; it would not do to pester the Tinieblans without firm information; it was not certain there was cause for action at this time; it would
get Mr. Heilanstalt nowhere to raise his voice or become violent. Sig had
been calling Liz's boardinghouse at fifteen-minute intervals, had been recalling his own treatment at Guard hands (see note l), had been imagining what
might happen to her if she was in their power and if someone who knew
English looked at the material she was carrying. His mind was not working
clearly. Only after he was hustled to the street by two Marines did he think
of the British Ambassador.

Forewarned examiners, if ever you are in trouble whilst abroad and unless
you are employed by the United Rapine Company or International Piracy
and Pillage, waste not your precious time appealing to your own foreign service: go to the British. Sir Henry received Sig cordially, remembered him and
Liz from the tennis morning describes in note 13, got him a whisky, heard him
out, picked up the telephone, called the Foreign Ministry, and asked in the polite yet iron voice we wogs know and respect if Mrs. Elizabeth Cleaver Fuertes
was under arrest. The reply came in about ten minutes: a woman who called
herself Miss Elizabeth Cleaver was being held strictly incommunicado on suspicion of counterrevolutionary terrorism and subversion. Sir Henry promised
to do what he could. Sig decided I had best be told.

I listened without expression. It wasn't up to me to put in little comments,
to give out soothing smiles and understanding nods, or otherwise to make
things easy for him. If he found it painful to face me, so much the better. He
could send the bill to his greedy gonads, and maybe pass up someone else's
wife. On the other hand, I didn't abuse him either. When he had finished, I
asked him if he had his car downstairs. He said yes, and began asking what
I had in mind. I motioned him to wait, went inside, undressed, bathed,
shaved, and put en clean clothes. Then I wrapped the manuscript of this dissertation in the dust cover of my typewriter, stuffed it in my briefcase, and carried it out into the living room.

"What are you going to do?"

"Get her out, of course. Come on"

83. This may at first glance seem a strange design

Attentive examiners, you will have detected a certain bitterness en my part
toward my wife, Elizabeth. You will have decided that this bitterness was not
entirely unjustified. You will have determined that in Tinieblas, as it is ruled

at present, concern for human rights is hazardous to health. You will have divined that I am not a man of action. And you will have deduced that no one could have blamed me—a solitary, private individual—had I left it to the embassies to get Liz—a faithless wife—out of jail. Why, then, you may demand, did I act?

I confess that when I came to ask myself that question, I was as baffled as you are. And observe that I acted first, considered only later, that I resolved to act when I heard Sig's first phrase and that from then on I thought only of tactics, with the result that by the time he finished speaking I had formed my plan. Well, then, when I did come to consider—and I shall soon describe the cleverly wrought contemplatorium furnished me by the Tinieblan Revolutionary Government through its Ministry of Justice —I was baffled, and could do no more than ascribe myself a number of possible motives. One was pride: Liz bore the name Fuertes, after all, worthily or not, and while I could put up with General Manduco's regime so long as it confined itself to theft and murder, locking a Fuertes up was going too far. Another was envy: there went Padre Celso and his colleagues from Justice producing open-air spectaculars, getting all kinds of attention, while I rotted away in isolation, without the merest notice for my labors. Or I may have acted out of anger. Not anger at the tyrants: anger at Liz and Sig for having compounded the offense of cuckoldry with the more heinous crime of interrupting me at work; anger at my father for having made a stupid bet and thus exacerbated all my problems; anger at my aunt Rosario for having helped me and, thereby, made me so dependent on her that I had to hear (if not to heed) her good advice; and great anger at myself for being Camilo Fuertes in the first place: Sig's phrase may have worked as an escape valve, opening a low-resistance path on which my anger could flow out. Laziness was yet another possibility. I've nothing against action, and action in the cause of justice cannot be disparaged, but there's no getting round the fact that action is a thousand times easier than the mind-wrenching toil of making this world mean something. Cervantes was more diligent than Don Quixote. Shakespeare worked harder than all his English monarchs rolled in one. I might have been too lazy to go on wrestling with the forces of disorder when circumstance brought an alternative my conscience could accept.

Liz believes I acted out of love, and she is welcome to that theory, but I hardly think love was involved. It seems to me I was entirely innocent of that impulse at the time, and even now know it but slenderly.

Pride, envy, wrath, sloth, or some combination of these were, then, as far as I could ascertain, my motives.

I think it, though, a great mistake to delve too deeply into human motivation. Things get more and more unpleasant as one descends. My action was correct and timely. Leave it at that.

84. With heart aflutter

Don't think, however, simplistic examiners, that I'd become a hero—in other words, that I'd lost the faculty of imagination. I wouldn't have wrapped my manuscript up, would I? and taken it along if I hadn't imagined some potential trouble. At that point I imagined the Civil Guard might search my place and seize my papers, but the closer Sig and I got to Civil Guard Headquarters, the more uneasy my imaginings became. I began to imagine defects in my plan, which (I blush to confess) had seemed quite sound at first devising. I began to imagine consequences of those defects which went beyond mere search and seizure. As we rolled briskly along Avenida de la Bahia, I began imagining myself as passive participant in a Civil Guard World Series, and I imagined my body—which had served me well for nearly a quarter of a century and for which during that time I had developed some affection—bashed and broken, tumbling from the side port of a helicopter down to the same dark and silent bay across which I could now glimpse the running lights of distant vessels. These imaginings brought me a great unease, and with it the novel urge to leap from Sig's car at the first stoplight and mingle with other humans—the young toughs in undershirts who lounged against parked cars in the street that led up to Plaza Bolívar, the laborers who sat swigging beer in the glow of storefronts. I might even have yielded to this urge, the urge to be with other people and be safe, but that as we entered the plaza, Sig began attempting to apologize for having horned me.

"Some women fuck dogs," I interrupted. "Others, they say, fuck donkeys. *The Arabian Nights,* with which, as you know, my wife is familiar, has several stories about women who fuck apes or chimpanzees. Kinsey and Pomeroy devote a portion of their report on *Sexual Behavior in the Human Female to* what they call 'animal contacts.' I find the subject tiresome."

"Camilo . . ."

"When you have let me out, go to the main gate of Fort Shafter. Wait there till someone comes. If no one comes by morning, try to get some action out of your embassy. I'm leaving this manuscript with you. Give it to Liz if she comes and I don't."

"Camilo . . ."

"Please shut up."

I herewith acknowledge a debt of gratitude to Mr. Sigmund Heilanstalt for providing me sufficient fresh rage to dispel my fearful imaginings temporarily. Thank you, Sig. You may now exit this dissertation and my life.

I soon began imagining again, however. When I got out onto the pavement in front of Guard Headquarters, opposite La Bondadosa Prison, my imagination was steaming at flank speed into murky waters. It was, then, with heart aflutter that I climbed the steps, entered the building, identified myself to the Officer of the Day as León Fuertes' son, and told him in tones of authority that I knew who was behind the bus pictures and would be happy to relate that information to Colonel Atila Guadaña.

85. *A gallant officer*

Stick a title before a fellow's name and you cannot avoid prejudicing people toward him, one way or another. When an English-speaking person hears the phrase "The Honorable," for example, he is immediately, invariably, and virtually convinced that the name which follows it belongs to a swindling poltroon. The title "Licenciado " (taken by lawyers) works about the same on Spanish-speakers. On the other hand, in most areas of the world a man before whose name the title "Colonel" marches has a lot going for him.

The word itself has a good forthright pedigree: by *colonnello* out of *colonna,* the strong and steady column, the unwavering pillar, to which weighty matters may be trusted, on which one can depend. When the word entered military service, it was assigned to the officer who led the first company of an infantry column, and it retains the notion of front-line responsibility: a colonel is the highest-ranking officer who may be expected to go into battle with his troops.

And what a wealth of noble associations the word evokes! Colonel T. E. Lawrence, a scholar and a *historian,* as well as a consummate guerrilla leader, a man gifted with both pen and sword, and one of the few authentic heroes of this century of anonymous mass slaughter. Faulkner's Colonel Bayard Sartoris, an epitome of aristocratic valor. García Marquez's Colonel Aureliano Buendía, a paragon of integrity in peace and war. The "Colonel Bogey March," the most stirring of all military airs. The Battle of Colonel, one of the most brilliant of modern naval actions. Such associations exalt the title "Colonel" above most others, and if Colonels Blimp and Sanders appear to drag it down—well, the first conveys bluff heartiness as well as stupidity, the second good cheer as well as commercialism. People tend, therefore, to be favorably prejudiced toward colonels.

Most everywhere, that is, except Tinieblas. Our colonels are so base and venal; so utterly without the merest shred of martial virtue; so completely given over to arrogance, that all the honor men of other countries have conferred upon the title "Colonel" is, for Tinieblans, totally befouled, to the point where Major Dorindo Azote, a brave and decent officer, refused repeatedly to take promotion even to *lieutenant* colonel. In Atila Guadaña all the qualities of a Tinieblan colonel achieved their full development.

He is about forty years old, short, stocky, but not fat. His eyes resemble the stagnant pools that form in shell holes on a bombarded no man's land. He had evidently been at some party or another when the Officer of the Day contacted him and had not bothered to change into uniform, and in his electric blue mod-style suit, his garish necktie, and his elevator shoes he looked the gangster he is—not an important gangster; an auxiliary goon destined to be rubbed out early in reel two when the boss goes semilegit and disposes of his now superfluous muscle. He greeted me with a reptilian attempt at affability, professing admiration for my father and complimenting me on my civic spirit for volunteering information vital to the state, but when I advised him that my declaration was contingent on the release of my estranged wife, unjustly arrested and more unjustly held, he straightaway displayed his bully's nature.

"We can beat it out of you! We can squeeze it out of your nuts!"

With this last, Colonel Guadaña crushed an imaginary pair of testicles in each fist and flung them in my face, but I was not particularly intimidated. In the first place, he had dashed directly to headquarters, indicating extreme eagerness to hear what I had to say and confirming the strength of my hand. Then, too, during the twenty minutes I had been waiting for him in the Deputy Commandant's office, "protected" by an armed sergeant but in no way abused, I had composed myself. I had, I told myself, already survived imprisonment and torture at the Fasholt Clinic, imprisonment on an openended term and torture by people who were restrained by no morality at all, since they thought they were helping me. I had walked four hundred kilometers across the Sahara Desert. I had been under artillery, mortar, and small arms fire at the Battle of Cassino. I was a veteran of the Bottom (see note 64). A certain tingle of fear was, perhaps, proper under the circumstances, but it was ridiculous for a man who had been through what I had to lose his self-control. In this manner I brainwashed myself into an aplomb worthy of the most unimaginative dolt conceivable, but the main ingredient of my marvelous sang-froid was supplied by Guadaña himself. He was so contemptibly clownish that I could not truly believe he actually held power among men and thus was-able to translate his threats to action. I knew it intellectually, but not in my flesh.

Sheltered examiners, intellect is not to be disprized, but it is a poor guide indeed to the dark places of the human spirit. You can read or hear all you want about the oafs who direct most nations, but you will be hard put to believe in them until they have their fingers round your throat, or other parts. Even then you are liable to think them only figments from a nightmare, and that is how they make it to the top. Few take them seriously until they've mashed the nuts off of entire populations, and then, as soon as they've left this world and the shrieking subsides, people start giggling at them and their kind again. The sergeant had saluted him and clomped his heels and barked, "*Mi Colonel!*" The Officer of the Day had addressed him as "*Ministro.*" But it was beyond me to believe an excretion like Guadaña might actually possess authority, even in the military establishment of a Tinieblas, even in an encampment of baboons. That is the chief reason why I was able to confront him calmly and, once he'd stopped shouting, to instruct him (via the Socratic method) in the deficiencies of torture as an information-gathering technique.

Didn't torture make some victims angry and thus retard responses?

Didn't torture inadvertently silence others permanently before they had contributed everything they might?

Didn't torture move most people to an altogether unreliable volubility? Wouldn't people say anything if tortured long enough? Wasn't it common practice for the torturer to continue, just to be on the safe side or simply out of zeal, after the victim had screamed "That's all I know!"—with the resulting production of a mass of fantasy that actually obscured the truth?

Didn't his duty as a minister of state require him to pass up personal pleasure once in a while? Wasn't this just such an occasion—an overriding problem and an informant who was willing to solve it for a very minor consideration?

Wouldn't it be irresponsible of him to waste time torturing me—for I would make every effort to resist—when the state could have my information in ten minutes?

Wouldn't he probably decide to let my estranged wife go anyway, when the U.S. Consul showed up tomorrow morning?

Mightn't it be inconvenient for the government to torture the son of a popular ex-president, who had told several hundred people where he was going and why?

It was, I think, much less the substance of these rhetorical questions than the tone in which I delivered them that impressed Guadaña. He was accustomed to having people quake before him, and I, for the reasons given above, did not. I spoke as one might to a clever twelve-year-old who one is sure will get the point sooner or later. And, then, I gave him some very tasty bait at the end.

"If you are bluffing . . ."

"Of course, of course. If I'm bluffing, I'll still be here, and you can torture me to your heart's content. You can play baseball with me the way you did with Padre Celso."

He snapped it up greedily. What did I know about Padre Celso? How did I know it? Who had told me? Where was the leak?

"I know everything. The pitcher was Sergeant Evaristo Tranca. The batting order was ... But why don't you give the order for my wife's release? Have her driven to the gate at Fort Shafter. Give her the number of this office so she can let me know when she's arrived. While we're waiting for her to get there, I'll tell you all about Padre Celso. Then when she's safe in the Reservation, I'll tell you about the buses. The two go together, as you have probably suspected."

It took quite a bit longer than ten minutes. Close to an hour passed between the time Guadaña wrote out an order and sent it over to the prison and the time Liz's call came, but for Guadaña it passed quickly. I gave him the whole story of Padre Celso's abduction and murder, in greater detail, I believe, than he'd had from Major Empulgueras's report, and he was astonished with the

scope of my knowledge. He was also entertained. He clapped his hands when
I describes Private Calimba's circuit swat (see note 50) and shook his head
mournfully at the final out (note 52). And he was on pins and needles to discover who my source was. I had come to the matter of the carton filled with
rocks when the phone rang. Guadaña took it, then, after a moment, passed
it to me.

"Camilo?"

"Are you in the Reservation?"

"Yes, but what about you?"

"Put Sig on so I can be certain." She might, of course, be just across the
street with a pistol at her head.

As soon as I heard Sig's voice, I passed the phone back to Guadaña.
"Thank you, Colonel. Now let me tell you about the buses."

86. *The truth lacks realism*

I was not to meet my father for another two weeks or so, but when I did
meet him and when, in the course of our conversations, he related me the incident of the Agudo suit and repeated the phrase he had originally made to
Carlos Gavilán, I was prepared to accept it without question, The plain, un-
varnished truth rarely convinces. Quite often it sounds preposterous.

I ought to have known as much without having to observe the truth's effect
on Colonel Atila Guadaña. I ought to have composed a careful fake. But I am
by nature honest, and I had lived too long out of the company of living people
to know that while honesty is surely the best policy for preserving the spirit,
it is often disastrous when it comes to saving one's poor skin.

I need not reproduce my declaration to Colonel Guadaña. The pertinent information regarding psychokinetic astral intervention in this world is set forth
at length in note 75. My statement was a paraphrase of that. Guadaña interrupted me early on in the mistaken inference that both Justice and the Committee for the Dissemination of Terror and Despair are terrestrial
organizations. I set him straight, and he kept silent from then on, regarding
me steadily, his mouth open, his tongue lolling on his lower lip, his head nodding slowly. I finished by assuring him that the Revolutionary Government
had little cause for concern over the bus incidents, as they would cease shortly
as a result of an agreement between Justice and the Committee. Those being
held in relation to the incidents might be released. The incidents were of entirely astral origin.

"You heard all this from General Epifanio Mojón?"

"Exactly."

"President Mojón? The one who died a hundred years ago?"

"One hundred fourteen years, to be precise."

"And the business about the priest?"

"From Padre Celso himself."

"And he's dead too?"

"He is no longer a resident of this world."

"And this is what you came down here to tell me? This is what I traded a prisoner for?"

"It is exactly what I promised. You and the government now know who is behind the bus pictures. You also know, and can take heart from it, that they will cease quite soon."

Colonel Atila Guadaña nodded his head slowly. Then he leaned forward, seized the telephone receiver, which was the nearest blunt instrument to hand, and brought it down with great force on the thin casing of my invaluable brain.

87. Apolonio Varón

My patron's father and, like him, one of the rare specimens of decency in the Costaguanan political zoo.

Varón senior distinguished himself in opposition. As a professor at the University of Chuchaganga, he offered philosophical opposition to the idea of Latin American unity, arguing that so long as there were twenty-odd presidents, the oil and mining companies would be unable to buy them all and exploitation might remain bearable. As head of the Liberal Democratic Party, he gave political opposition to the dictator General Dionisio Huevas Pandilla, by whom he was imprisoned, tortured into signing a false confession, and arraigned at a show trial. When no Costaguanan lawyer dared defend him, León Fuertes took his case and won him an acquittal, saving his life. His son Esclepio has now returned the favor by saving mine.

After Huevas fell from power, Apolonio Varón was elected President of Costaguana. He was assassinated by nitro bomb some twelve or fourteen minutes after taking the oath of office. Then rioting broke out, and General Huevas seized power and reimposed his tyranny, and the Costaguanans suffered through ten years of violence and repression.

I know, I know, weary examiners. This part of the world is a mess. But are things really that much better in Gringoland? Don't your good guys get bumped off pretty regularly? Aren't your bad guys pretty repulsive too? Turn up your noses at Greaseballia if you feel like it, but have you had a whiff of your own politics lately?

88. Walls

Two floors below ground in La Bondadosa Prison, the corridor between the stairs and the interrogation chamber is set with six iron doors. Behind each door is a cavity two feet wide and fifteen inches high that reaches back six feet into the foundation of the prison. Tiny louvered slits allow a little dank air to seep into the cavities while keeping out the light, which is too feeble and browbeaten down there anyway to make much of a try at getting

R. M. KOSTER

in. The cavities abound with insect life of both the scuttling-scavenging and creeping-bloodsucking varieties.

These cavities are the most exclusive lodgings provided by the Ministry of Justice anywhere in Tinieblas. Special guests are stuffed into them head-first, face-up, and naked. The operation resembles the loading of a heavy artillery piece. Guards swing the guest into the breach and ram him home, the floor of the cavity being more or less lubricated by fungoid slime and by material left on it either by the previous occupant or by the guest himself if he has already spent some time inside and is returning from an interrogation session. The door is then slammed—on the guest's ankles if he hasn't yet learned to squidge himself in quickly or if interrogation has left him incapable of speedy movement. The door is slammed and slammed until it shuts. When it does, the guest is so snuggly cased around with walls that he is, in effect, part of the masonry of the building.

I was not prepared for this experience. The cavities are nowhere described in the civics texts assigned in our secondary schools, nor are they so much as mentioned in the brochures put out by the Ministry of Tourism. Like most law-abiding citizens, I had never bothered to inform myself about our institutions of social control, which I assumed were reserved for that mysterious, quasi-human species Other People. Then, too, I was dazed from the clocking Colonel Guadaña had given me and from the shock of being "naked to mine enemies." I was thrust into that cavity in a state of utter, screaming panic—the same state, I imagine, as when I was first thrust into this world.

There I was, stripped to the skin, being prodded by yelling guards down a dimly-lit corridor two storeys below ground, and all at once the lead guard flung open a door in the wall, and the others seized me and lifted me and stuffed me in.

"Aaaaaaaaaaaah!"

"In you go, asshole!"

Head and shoulders. Torso. Then they hold your knees straight, one on each leg, and push against your heels. Pure terror. Not even the most fragmentary, disconnected thoughts. You scarcely feel your head hit the far wall or hear the door slam shut. You hardly notice that a roach has dropped from the ceiling into your open, screaming mouth. You are kicking your legs just as wildly, mindlessly, and uselessly as he is.

People are accustomed, not without some cause, to consider the so-called underdeveloped countries inefficient, yet at the risk of sounding chauvinistic I here take the liberty of pointing out the speed and economy with which the Tinieblan Ministry of Justice is able to transform a human being—e.g., a gifted, disciplined, superbly educated, and inordinately proud young man—into a bug.

Not permanently, at least not in my case. I descended to bughood, then rose, and then descended once again. I attained an animal awareness that my holemates were swarming all over me—pardonably, it seems to me at present since I had slid in on them without a by-your-leave, but nonetheless hideously. Later on I learned to clasp my genitals with one hand and brush my face with the other and to bear being infested and bitten in the remaining regions of my body, but my original reaction was to rub myself spastically wherever I could reach. Then I realized that the door was shut, that it would never again open, that I was never coming out, and that the entire prison was resting on my chest, pressing down so that I couldn't breath, and I began to scream again and thrash against the walls in a total absence of mental and physical control.

But pardon me, long-suffering examiners. You're not enjoying this. I can see you now, sitting in your clean and spacious offices, or in your no less comfy and spotless homes, pursing your lips in displeasure. Why, you surely wonder, should you have to read this sort of thing? What use is it to you? *You* will never break the law, and there will never be a tyranny in your marvelous country, so no one will ever bury you in a putrid prison hole. That's for the Other People. And besides, you know those Other People are accustomed to abuse, that they don't really mind it all that badly; although certain weaklings among them, Camilo Fuertes, for example, will squeal and squirm and soil themselves in a most disgusting fashion and then, long after the event, insist on nauseating decent folk with exaggerated accounts of their sufferings. All such stories must, you say, be exaggerated since their authors survived to tell them.

Well, perspicacious examiners, I shall grant a smidgen of your point. Perhaps I have painted the scene in tints a bit too somber. The place I was in— they call them "coffins" in La Bondadosa Prison—was a hideous, black, filthy place scarcely fit for the vermin that lived there by election. It certainly maximized a number of human antipathies, some built-in, some acquired through acculturation, such as fear of the dark, revulsion at slimy creeping things, hatred of filth, and horror of being constricted. It was, thus, frightfully unsuited for the retention of human dignity. But it had its silver lining. In my panicky thrashings I chanced to strike my forehead crisply on the stone, and having done so once, as it were fortuitously, I swung it up into the stone again, and then again, drawing down cleansing pain, and I repeated this maneuver deliberately until at length I grew calm. I was not, you see, completely helpless. My "coffin" left me free to knock some of the anguish out of me.

(You don't get that kind of freedom in a strait jacket, by the way. In a strait jacket, you can't move at all. You can't rake your cheeks with your fingernails or pound your temples with your fists, and the walls are far away and, in any case, padded. On the other hand, a strait jacket protects your nakedness while it constricts you. In every terrestrial endeavor, even stripping folks of their humanity, each expedient, however worthy in and of itself, drags a defect along with it.)

I lay, then, naked on dank stone, entombed by walls and crept over by vermin, yet calmed by a restorative dose of pain.

Indulgent examiners, please bear with me. I know your tastes, but this is the closest I can come to an up-beat ending for this note.

89. *My mother*

My mother visited me last night while I was sleeping. She is greatly relieved that I have found such comfortable refuge and that my health is sufficiently restored for me to work, She is also pleased with Chapter 18 as I outlined it to her. Much of the material I had from her own lips either while she was in this world or after her "death" by heart cancer in 1966. Much I observed myself during my childhood. The rest comes from my father.

My mother was by my side during most of my stay in prison, but I couldn't hear her voice. This was my fault, not hers, Her delicate spirit descended into the bowels of Bondadosa Prison to find and comfort me. She grieved beside me in my "coffin," but I had denied her.

As soon as I calmed myself, I tried to beam my mind out to the Astral Plane, but I couldn't concentrate. My mind fluttered weakly against the walls. If only I had been able to fling it up out of the pit! Other captives less practiced than I have done so and saved themselves, but shock had disabled me. I waited expectantly for the arrival of my Guardian Spirit. Then I despaired. My mother and my aunt Rosario and my grandmother Rebeca were all searching for me. My mind would have regained strength after a time. But I despaired. I gave myself up to self-pity. I judged myself abandoned by my gift and by my Guardian Spirit. I wept as though this and my imprisonment were universal calamities.

That was my diminished state when they took me for interrogation. I sat naked on a stool in a large, bare room, surrounded by guards and officers. Colonel Guadaña presided. The others regarded him with admiration, deference, and respect—similar, I suppose, to the treatment accorded Dr. Felix Heilanstalt by the personnel of his operating theater and visiting physicians (see note 61). My position was that of an object on which the master would now exercise his skill.

Colonel Guadaña said that while the extent of my criminality was not yet known, two counts were already clear: I had betrayed the Tinieblan state by obtaining the release of detained person on false pretense; I had personally insulted a minister. If there was one thing he had learned during his career, it was that corpses do not talk. Did I still maintain that I had received information from the corpse of Padre Celso Labrador?

I said I had received it from his spirit, not his corpse. I sat with my hands over my privates, shivering, though the room wasn't cold. My statement sounded far-fetched even to my own ears. Such was my depression and despair that I no longer believed anything with much conviction.

Colonel Guadaña nodded and said, "Go ahead!"

I was seized at my legs and shoulders. A guard rushed forward holding a long-handled ball-peen hammer. He knelt down, grabbed my left ankle, and, snapping his wrist, brought the hammer down on my little toe, mashing it flat against the cement floor.

It was so fast I didn't even scream. I was so shocked I hardly felt it. They released me. I looked down at my foot. It didn't seem to belong to me, certainly not that red mush there at the corner. Then I grimaced, and moaned a little.

"Good," said Colonel Guadaña. "Now I'll ask you again. If you give the wrong answer, he'll do exactly the same thing to your prick."

Fear net, alarmed examiners. I didn't wait for that. I didn't even wait for him to put the question. I answered, and I did not answer wrong. I denied the human spirit. I denied the next world. I denied my gift. I denied all mystical experience, all nonmaterialist philosophy, and all the gods from Adonai to Zoroaster. I denied transmigration, metempsychosis, and every concept of immortality that had come to my attention over years of study. I denied ESP, PSI, psychokinesis, clairvoyance, precognition, and the entire science of parapsychology. I kept on babbling denials until Colonel Guadaña told me I could stop, and I did so not from any commitment to physical love or the life of this world as symbolized in reproduction or my own manhood—which might have been redeeming reasons—but from simple fear of pain and mutilation.

How's that for efficiency, jingoist examiners? It had taken your supershrinks weeks to drag me to "reality," and even then I came with tongue in cheek, yet the Tinieblan Minister of Justice snapped me out of my delusions in a matter of minutes, without using expensive apparatus either, and my cure was complete. I knew Colonel Guadaña meant what he said, and I answered with equal sincerity. Every syllable of my answer came from the bottom of my heart.

Then he wanted to know where I had learned the details of Padre Celso's "death," and I was stumped. Where had I learned them? All I knew for sure was where I hadn't learned them. I hadn't learned them from any spirit. There were no such things as spirits. Corpses don't talk. When you're dead, you're dead, and no quote marks either. Fortunately, he gave me a hint. I had heard about it from a member of the Civil Guard, hadn't I?

Oh, yes! Oh, yes! That was it!

From one of the men who'd been in the district headquarters cellar that night, correct?

Yes! Yes!

Well, then, who was it?

I wanted another hint, just to be sure I didn't answer wrong, but I thought I saw him begin to glance in the direction of the fellow with the hammer, so I said the first name that came to mind: Calimba, Juan Calimba.

Then he wanted to know where and when and why, so I made up a trip to Belém and a stop-off at a cantina and a drunken Juan Calimba and some paragraphs of realistic dialogue. There was no end to the efficiency of the Tinieblan Ministry of justice and its chief officer: now they had transformed a historian into a hack novelist.

Next he asked me what I knew about the buses.

I told him I knew nothing, that I had pretended to know to get Liz out of jail, but I saw from his face that this was the wrong answer, so I said it was a counterrevolutionary conspiracy. I was the leader. No! The real leaders were foreigners. No! The leader was Alejandro Sancudo, the constitutional president whom Manduco had thrown out. He was in league with the Galactic Fruit Company, and I was in their pay. The counter-revolutionary propaganda was flashed onto the buses by laser beam from an orbiting satellite. It was worked by remote control from an underground bunker near Miami. Yes, yes, I would write it all down! If they would just give me a pencil and some paper!

When they put me back into my "coffin," my sentiments were those expressed in the lines:

> Home is the sailor, home from the sea,
> And the hunter home from the hill.

Home at last, where no one could get at me with a hammer! It was fitting that I lie in my own excrement and be companied by vermin, my next of kin. It is proper that the dead be buried.

Access to Learning is contingent on commitment to the truth, so my enlistment had been revoked—and my life emptied of purpose. I no longer believed in anything, so I could not hear my mother's voice when she came to me. all I could hear, in fact, was my own whimpering.

I thought I had touched bottom before. Ha!

90. Departure

I can't say how long I stayed there. The door was opened three or four times, but I don't know at what intervals. I would scrunch back as far as I could get and shield my face from the light and lie quivering as someone pushed in a piece of bread and a plastic cup of water. When the door had closed and I had calmed again, I would drink the water. I didn't eat.

I didn't think either. Electroencephalography tells us that the fetal mind is active, and my mind may have been active in that way. Freud and others claim to recall intrauterine experiences—and such claims argue a form of fetal thought—but they are probably kidding themselves, if not us, Before my interrogation I spent some time considering the motives that had led me from the refuge of my work into action, then prison. Immediately afterward I considered both the shame of having thrown away everything that gave my life some meaning and the satisfaction of being in my hole, but quite soon my thought processes shut down. So long as the door was shut, I was at peace.

They had to drag me out by main strength. I pressed my palms against the ceiling and dug my fingernails into the stone, and, weak as I was, it took two of them, one pulling on each foot, to drag me out. On reflection, I don't think my resistance was based solely on fear. The light was odious. That hole was as much my home as if I had burrowed it myself. I belonged there, not in the sight of people. A moldered corpse might, if it could, resist in the same fashion when dug up.

They dragged me to the small room beside the interrogation chamber where I had written my confession. I wouldn't walk but didn't struggle, and they each grabbed me by a bicep and a wrist and dragged me along the floor, grunting with the exertion. They put me on a stool beside the table. I sat there with my head bowed and my hands dangling between my knees.

After a while Colonel Guadaña came in alone. He was in uniform and carried a fiber attaché case, which he put down on the table and opened. When he looked at me, my head drooped again.

"Your confession has been typed. Also corrected. Look at me when I speak to you! It now includes your accomplices. Many members of ex-President Sancudo's family and party were also involved, isn't that so? Initial each page and sign it in the indicated place. You may also read it if you care to, but that isn't necessary."

He took a folder from his case and doubled the cover back. There was a sheaf of papers clipped inside. He held the whole thing forward toward me.

"The injury to your foot will be attended. You will be transferred to a regular cell and given the regular prison diet. Look at me when I'm speaking!" I raised my head a little and held out my hand for the folder. He took a pen out of his case and held it forth.

"Initial each page and sign at the place indicated." He smiled as I took the pen.

Cherished examiners, he ought to have denied himself that smile. He ought, in fact, to have left me in my burrow. I was at peace there and would have caused no trouble. He might have had the papers handed in; I would have signed them. If, later on, he needed testimony from me at a trial, he might have run a phone down to my hole; I would have said whatever was required. Instead the fool had me dragged out. Instead the fool allowed himself to smile in confidence and satisfaction. I had seen an identical expression on the face of Dr. Elias Fafnir four years before. When I made the connection, I experienced what Saint Paul called "conversion" and Dr. I. P. Pavlov the "ultra-paradoxical phase."

I had always resented the slightest annoyance on the fringes of my life. I would not suffer even those closest to me to bother me. I would not put up with the society of people who did not make a positive contribution to my private purpose. I tried—most usually with perfect success—to ignore the sufferings of others. I turned a blind eye to the tyrant in my country and the poacher in my home so that the delicious happiness I found in study might not be disturbed. Then, when that happiness was stripped from me, I made no murmur. I threw away the purpose of my life and was content in a foul hole. Now, though, all those responses were reversed. I no longer cared about protecting what I had. True enough, I had quite little. I lacked even a rag to cover me. I still had my life and youth, however, but I no longer cared about protecting them. I now cared about other things. I didn't want others to end up where I was. I didn't like Colonel Guadaña 's face. And—this was the main thing—my "confession" simply wasn't true. I pulled it from the folder and tore it first in halves and then in quarters. As soon as I had done so, I saw my mother and my aunt Rosario and my grandmother Rebeca standing at my right hand, weeping.

"You are a moron," I said to Colonel Guadaña.

"Take him inside!" he screamed, but as the guards laid hands on me, he screamed, "No! I'll send him there myself!"

He stepped from behind the table, drew back against the wall, and then ran toward me, howling, "Penalty!" and aimed a kick at my face. His boot caught me just under the chin. I flew backward off the stool. My butt hit. My head snapped back and smashed on the stone floor with a sound like a melon dropped from a good height. My spirit left my body.

91. *Reception*

It requires but little thought to comprehend the problems faced by Astral Reception. Spirits arrive ceaselessly and in great numbers from every corner of this world. The immense majority are at once bewildered and scared out of their wits. The first step, therefore, is to put them somewhat at their ease.

When this world was but sparsely populated and the "death" roll relatively small, each new arrival was met personally, often by someone from his own tribe or village. Later, participants in Creative Arts were asked to design an area whose very ambience might tranquilize arriving spirits and dispose them favorably to the next world. Motifs from terrestrial nature were drawn on; a sylvan-pastoral set was conceived and fashioned. It served quite handsomely until about two thousand years ago, when a group of artists, architects, and artisans, all of them reared in cities, sold the Director on a renovation along urban lines: gold-paved boulevards, alabaster palaces, pearly gates, the whole schmeer. In this design Reception was the subject of numerous visions by residents of this world and became the basis for a popular notion of the Christian heaven, *Urbs Syon Aurea,* Jerusalem the Golden—just as its earlier décor had given men the notion of Elysian Fields. Like everything of any note done anywhere, this renovation was criticized, particularly during the last two centuries by spirits associated while in this life with the Romantic Movement, More importantly, the Director of Astral Activities and his staff noted growing nostalgia on the part of residents of this world for the disappearing natural environment. In consequence it was determined that an urban setting no longer provided Reception the most tranquilizing surroundings possible and a second renovation was ordered under the general direction of Michelangelo Buonarroti, Richard Wagner, and Walt Disney. The new facilities had been in operation for about five months when I arrived in the Beyond.

Spirits emerge from the swirling darkness between this world and the next onto a vast cloud prairie pavilioned at wide intervals in pastel-tinted silks which float in place, weightless and unbuoyed. A perpetually dawn sky domes over head; a calm sea shimmers in the distance. Faint breezes bear the strains of the Performing Arts First Philharmonic Orchestra and Chorus rendering such works as Handel's *Messiah* and Beethoven's Ninth Symphony, as well as works unheard in this world, new works composed expressly for Reception by Bach Verdi, Wagner himself, and others. I have never known and cannot imagine a more inspiring audio-visual experience.

I arrived, of course, in the company of my mother, my grandmother, and my aunt. At first I felt a deep reluctance to leave the vicinity of my body, which lay in the subcellar of La Bondadosa Prison, bleeding desultorily from its ears and gaped at in annoyance by Colonel Atila Guadaña, but my three female companions were in a great rush to be gone from that place of groom, and so, after a moment, I fled with them up through the stone floors of the prison, into the night sky, and out across the gulf between the worlds of flesh and spirit. I had cause for relief at leaving this world behind. I knew a great deal, most of it good, about where I was headed. And how could I be worried or distraught, wrapped as I was in the love of those three ladies? But even the most wretched ghost—alone, untimely torn out of an easy life, all ignorant, and gibbering in terror—must surely feel calmed and uplifted emerging on that bright, harmonious scene. I stared about, wide-eyed. My three companions smiled at me and at each other, taking joy in my childlike wonder. And all about us streamed a multitude of spirits at once newly "dead" and newly "born."

A breeze bore us to the nearest pavilion, which was staffed, my aunt Rosario told me, with guides trained in Good Works. Their function is to discover the language of each arriving spirit, to see each on the breeze conveyor to the appropriate pavilion, and generally to dispense care and loving kindness. They wear flag emblems or native costume and are unfailingly tender to new arrivals, many of whom importune them in panicky shouts and wailings, despite the soothing light that flows through the translucent silks above. Special guides collect the spirits of unaccompanied infants and children, who go on to an extension pavilion of Childhood staffed with senior participants from Parent. Debilitated spirits, those too worn out or maimed by their life here to face the future for a time, are sent to a rest pavilion run by personnel of Sleep.

The several hundred orientation pavilions, each of which functions in a separate language, differ in size but not in form—this according to an acquaintance of my grandmother Rebeca's whom we met in the Spanish-speaking pavilion, which is about ten hectares in area. The cloud floor is dotted all over with low circular platforms on which musicians and other artists perform, inducing new arrivals to collect about them. Every so often the entertainment at one or another platform ceases, and an official of Reception delivers a little lecture on the organization of the next world. The reader of these notes will already possess more information than is contained in this orientation, which merely covers basics: One's life in the next world is not determined by one's life in this one. The cardinal principle of astral existence is individual freedom. A fresh start is available for all who wish one, or continuity for those who prefer that. Every human activity is offered. One or another may be fully occupied and fulfillment hence deferred, but time is plentiful. Recyclement into terrestrial existence is a possible option. One may look in on loved ones still on earth. The individual is limited only by his or her talents, directed only by his or her interests. Facilities for self-improvement are abundant. Personal counseling is provided. Above all, there is nothing to fear. Spirits may move on to their first interview as they desire. The lecturer steps down; entertainment resumes.

My alert examiners will have remarked the contrast between the haphazard fashion in which one enters this world and the orderliness of Reception. Despite the constant influx of spirits, there is no confusion, no sense of urgency. Accordingly, I lingered to chat, via Rebeca's interpretation, with her acquaintance, a Chinese acrobat whom she had met the year before in a Performing Arts mime class and who had been entertaining new arrivals since the opening of Reception's present facilities. He had worked in many of the pavilions, the largest of which, he said, was devoted to the English language since Chinese speakers were handled according to dialect. The best audiences were in the children's pavilion. He and his troupe had done so well there that they had been picked to play an extended gig in Childhood beginning shortly. It was not until I saw the respect he paid my grandmother that I realized what a very great star she has already become. I commented on this to her as we moved toward the interviewing area, and she shrugged with the charming false modesty common to primas.

"I've had some good roles, and Ling is a sweet boy. But you should have seen how they all fawned over your father. He was the real star of the family, and he threw it all away!"

There were, it seemed, about a thousand interviewers on duty, each at a teleprinter console. We found one, an Argentine by his accent, who had no queue of spirits waiting for him but only a single interviewee, to whom he was explaining the procedure for applying to activities, all of which is handled in Selection. As we waited, my mother pointed out a device resembling a napkin ring mounted on a rod and wondered what it was for: there had been nothing like it in the old Reception halls when she passed through eight years before.

My aunt Rosario, who as a Guardian Spirit had been briefed on the new facilities before they opened, explained it as an identifier.

Every spirit, she said, is separate and distinct. The Directorate maintains a file on each, entering each incarnation. Formerly, Reception officials took the arriving spirit's current name and birth data, but there were always mix ups, most of them created by spirits who refused to trust the basic orientation and who, fearing dispatch into some sort of hell, gave false information.

"Now you pass through the ring, and the central computer picks up identifying data and prints out a record of your avatars and any other pertinent information."

I had no trouble passing through when my turn came. I merely aimed at the ring and whooshed through without a trace of constriction. The teleprinter began to thump at once and went on for above a minute. When it had stopped, the Argentine turned up the paper and tore it off.

I learned I had had four incarnations prior to this one, three of them male and two of these scholars of sorts. Then he came to current data.

"Fuertes, Camilo. Tinieblan. Student. Born 1950."

I nodded.

"You hold a confirmed admission to Learning . . . revoked . . . hmm . . . reconfirmed today." He looked up and smiled. "Congratulations, Señor Fuertes! Learning is a marvelous activity. I hope to go there myself someday. It's, uh, rather an honor to have a confirmed admission waiting for one. You may report there immediately if you wish, though you may care to pass by Selection to get an idea of what Learning's like."

"I have an idea. But I don't think I'll go straight on. There's another activity I'd like to spend some time in first."

He blinked. "Really? That's odd. It says here you made an unconscious application to Learning more than a decade back. I don't—"

At that point a red light began flashing on his console. The teleprinter thumped again. "Hold on," he said. "There's something . . ."

He read the new print-out without removing it from the machine and pressed a button on his console. "Señor Fuertes. I'm afraid you're going to have to see my supervisor."

92. What had happened

What had happened, disconcerted examiners, was that my body had continued functioning. Did you perhaps assume that when my head meloned onto the stone floor of Bondadosa Prison, when my spirit jumped out, my body had quit functioning? I confess I had assumed as much myself, though you would have made no such assumption had you read Note 81 with care. Did you then, having made one false assumption, further assume that since I have returned to this world and resumed work on this dissertation—which, by the way, I shall soon come to Sunburst to defend—I am presently a reincarnation of myself? If so, you are more foolish than I thought. No one is ever incarnated twice in the same avatar. That goes for Jesus of Nazareth along with everyone else. His spirit has been reincarnated twice since the Crucifixion, once as the Dominican lay brother Martín de Porres (1579-1639, canonized 1962), presently as a nurse in Bangladesh. His spirit continues to serve Good Works in both worlds. But none of his avatars, not even the most famous of them, will ever be replayed. I journeyed to the next world and returned, still as Camilo Fuertes, but that was because my body stayed in business.

I've said a lot about the spirit, all of it worth saying in this materialistic age, but I intend no denigration of the body, certainly not of the particular body my spirit lodges in at present. If any of my statements in these notes imply such disrespect, I herewith disavow them! The body is a marvelous contraption—not built to last, unfortunately, but that's the great part of its charm. The whole excitement of this life is in the tensions generated when your immortal spirit has to ride about in your flower-fragile, disposable flesh frame. Those people with a talent for this life—and I don't claim to be among them—manage to keep the tensions nicely balanced. The spirit mustn't truckle to the flesh, but mustn't be a despot either. Therefore, among the several reforms I have resolved to institute since tripping to the Beyond—most of which, nosy examiners, are none of your concern—is to allow my body greater participation in my life.

How forlorn my body looked sprawled on the prison floor! How arrogant of my spirit to lead it into bondage and abuse, and then bail out as soon as things looked bleak! True enough, I did feel a great reluctance to abandon the poor forked thing entirely, and herein I was reacting normally, for while the spirit is often jarred from the body when the latter is badly injured, it will rarely range very far away until the body quits. And my body is no quitter. It lay ostensibly inert. It seemed shrunken, as lifeless bodies do. I was specially struck by the tininess of my private parts—which are of perfectly acceptable dimensions, snickering examiners; perfectly acceptable, let me assure you (and your wife, Dr. Grimes, and your daughter, Professor Lilywhite, if they are reading!), but which appeared at that moment to have shriveled almost to nothingness. Despite appearances, however, my body hadn't quit. My heart was pumping, my lungs bellowsing, my brain sending electro-chemical dispatches—all very weakly, it is true, but nonetheless courageously, since it was getting no aid or comfort from my spirit. I can only say in partial exculpation that I should never have left its vicinity but that my mother, grandmother, and aunt wished to be off.

And how bravely it hung in through all those months! How handsomely it is recuperating now! It will be sound as a barrel in a week or two, nothing the worse for the whole miserable experience (saving, of course, the absence of a toe, which had to be snipped off). I shall have it playing tennis inside the month. I have already had it up on my good wife for a prance—doctor's advice he damned!—whereat it performed most nobly, taking all the jumps without a wheeze. At this instant it is generously repaying me in pleasure for being allowed to soak the sunshine of this terrace. Denigrate the body? Never again! Certainly not this one. This is a very fine body. I shall not see its like in a dozen incarnations.

My body, then, remained in business, as the central computer of Astral Records had divined and verified. I learned later, after my return to earth, that at about the time I entered the first pavilion of Reception, my body was being bustled toward San Bruno Hospital, for while I might be a boon to the Tinieblan Revolutionary Government as a confessed subversive, I would be a headache to it as a corpse. This was because my wife, Elizabeth (whose own excellent body reclines, basted in Coppertone, a few feet from me now), raised a heady stink over her arrest and my imprisonment through her congressman uncle (Justin C. Cleaver, Rep., N.Y.); because the wire services transposed the story into Spanish and flashed it back to Central America; because President Esclepio Varón read it, remarked my name, and ordered his ambassador in Ciudad Tinieblas to make inquiries—all of which had been going on while I was in La Bondadosa, though of course I had no inkling of it. So the Tinieblan Revolutionary Government couldn't afford to garbage me. So my body was getting help to stay in business. So the Argentine interviewer's supervisor was put out.

"You shouldn't have come here in the first place," she told me. "You should go back at once!"

She was a large, strongly-lung'd woman, imposing at first sight in her dawn-pink double-breasted Chief Receptionist's uniform, but quite evidently a product of the seniority (as opposed to the merit) system of promotion. This problem didn't come up in the old days, she declared. She'd been with Reception for seven centuries; and for most of that time one had known when a spirit arrived that its avatar was done with and the work of processing it wouldn't go to waste. In the old days if a spirit was knocked out of its body, it either jumped right back inside or lost its avatar, but nowadays terrestrial doctors had the gall to keep spiritless bodies functioning for years. Spirits, of course, wouldn't reenter grossly damaged bodies and would in the end tire of hanging round them, would take off for Reception, would demand their right to select activities, always reserving their right to zoom back into their earthly bodies should these improve in status. Records got botched. A pernicious mood of disorder and uncertainty was engendered. And the morale of hard. working personnel in Reception and Selection inevitably suffered, since for all they knew, the effort put in on processing might be entirely wasted. She went on as if the whole science of medicine had been concocted as a personal affront to her. "As for you, your case is outrageous! You haven't been moping round a hospital for months, watching them drip plasma or whatever into your body! You ran off like a coward! You must go back at once and stay near your body till life is gone from it for good!"

She might have bulldozed a more diffident person. Or one less resolute. I felt a strong nostalgia for my body, and when I learned it was still functioning, the feeling deepened. Furthermore, though for all I knew my body was still in Bondadosa Prison, the course of action I'd resolved on was hardly less scary than returning there. But I am neither diffident nor irresolute. You have gleaned that much by now, dear examiners, if you have any wit at all, and that overbearing Chief Receptionist was not denied a demonstration of my character. I thanked her for advising me of my rights, I bowed to her with exaggerated gallantry and plucked the print-out from her trembling hand. I took my mother's and my grandmother's arms, beamed at Rosario, and said, "Lead on to Selection, won't you, Auntie." And with that the four of us breezed off.

93. Selection

The numberless pavilions of Selection range by the shore of that same placid sea which I saw glimmering far off when I first entered the next world. The adjective "numberless" is accurate enough. They extend left and right from the exits of Reception in a convincing illusion of infinity, and I met no one who could tell me exactly how many of them there are.

Each activity, Victim alone excepted, maintains a pavilion, the largest of the ones I saw being that of Astral Service. It floats immediately opposite the entranceway and is about a kilometer in diameter. Each pavilion contains exhibition areas with displays representing what the particular activity involves. According to my mother, these are exceedingly well done, and many new arrivals spend months visiting them, much more like tourists at a world's fair than prospective applicants. I could readily believe this last, for the crowds were fantastic. At least ten thousand spirits packed the open mall before the War pavilion watching a company of ceremonial guards from one of the Eastern League armies relieve a company from the Western League, while the queue at the Orgies and Abominations pavilion coiled entirely around it. The conveyors were similarly congested. We took the upper one, which branches left from the entrance, putting the pavilions on our right, and were at once sardined in a press of spirits, most of whom were jabbering excitedly in a babel of tongues. Recognizing English, I struck up a conversation with a Negro family of five from Alabama, who had been whisked into the next world together by a tornado nearly a year earlier and who had spent the whole time since wandering about Selection, "just seeing the sights," as the mother put it. The father advised me not to miss the Childhood pavilion, "where they let you try on a kid's body," at which his children of course sneered.

"I may take that as an activity," he went on. "Before, when I was working,

I used to say I'd like to sleep for a thousand years, and you can do that if you want. I might end up taking a job with the government. They're all white-collar jobs, and they train you, The hardest part is making up your mind."

His son, a lad of about fourteen, took loud issue with him here: "I know what I'm going to do. I'm going to join up with Hannibal and fight the honkies! "

He dragged them off to the War pavilion, which his mother said they'd already seen five times. I would have liked to browse in the pavilions also, but my resolution drew me on.

Each pavilion has inscription areas where spirits who are considering applying can have their inquiries answered in depth and their qualifications assessed. The Performing Arts pavilion, for example, has several small theaters, Rebeca said, and she has visited it two or three times to help audition dancers. But no spirit may enter an inscription area until he has had at least one general counseling session, and every twelfth pavilion is staffed with Selection personnel for this purpose. We got down at the first one we came to.

All through Reception and so far into Selection I had been making inquiries of my three lovely companions and listening to their answers and explanations, but now, as we were waiting for one of the Spanish-speaking counselors to be free to see me, my mother asked me a question: "Why don't you want to go to Learning, Camilito? What activity is it you want to enroll in first?"

I smiled at her. I could see by her strained expression that she was already divining my thoughts. Rebeca and Rosario also looked at me in anticipation, and I put my arms out to include all three, surely the three most charming ladies who ever showered their affection and concern on one poor fellow.

"I have to see my father," I said softly. "I have to go to Victim for a while."

They set up a wall of protest. I would be lost. Was I as foolish as my father? Hadn't I suffered enough already?

I replied, smiling. I told my mother that I hoped to find, not lose myself, and Rebeca that while I didn't understand my father's wager, I knew he was no fool. To Rosario I said I had decided to take her advice, which I thanked her for giving, and that in my case, if not in all cases, suffering seemed to be an incidental charge to the business of becoming human.

"I must see him. I made the decision the instant we left earth. It may be, also, that he needs me, or would at least be cheered by seeing me."

My mother nodded, weeping, and my aunt Rosario said I was a man, and though my grandmother Rebeca snorted and said men were all fools, ninnies, or worse, she looked at me with respect.

"Well," she said, "you've enough Burlando blood in you to trick them, I suppose. But you ought to think it over carefully all the same."

That was the interviewer's caution, He would neither ask nor question my motives for choosing Victim. Most newly-arrived spirits assumed the Astral Plane included some place of suffering. Few had any urge to go there. None whom he had interviewed in his near century of service possessed such definite information about it as did I. If I wanted Victim, so be it. He did wish, however, to point out that the minimum voluntary commitment was seven years. I might, of course, return to my earthly body at any time so long as it remained in operation, but he felt morally bound to give me a few caveats. My body might cease to function at any time. Even if I returned to it, it would surely cease to function someday, at which time I would have to serve out the remaining portion of my sentence. I had no hope whatsoever of confounding astral regulations on that score, and should not take my grandfather's experience as a precedent. (At this he flapped the elaborate print-out concerning me that his computer had thumped out and stared at me gravely.) Above all, he wished to warn me that Victim was not a place of recreation. Its inclusion among the Astral Activities was justified only because the general plan demanded that all human activities be offered. In the course of his training as a counselor he had visited Victim's confinement facility and had seen victims in use at several activities. He personally would do anything in reason to avoid sharing the victim's lot. I ought to think it over with great care.

I asked him if I would be able to spend time with my father, and he replied that which activities victims were dispatched to was a matter of hazard but that they were free to move about the confinement facility during recuperation periods. I told him my mind was made up, and he produced commitment forms, advising me that for a voluntary commitment, three witnesses were required.

Human life, my examiners, takes meaning only through the acts of human beings. I wished to give my life this meaning: that seven years of suffering count lightly beside the hope of true illumination. I craved to receive the past from my father's lips so that I might return self-reliant to the present. The world to come showed me the way. The witnesses were at hand. I had the will, I signed.

94. My father

Human examiners, perhaps your spirit has at one time or another been weighted down with care or sorrow, or with weariness of life. Most humans know such heaviness now and then, and when it is truly grave, the human spirit can in no wise soar or range about as normally it's able. Burdened and crushed, the spirit can but drag on. Such heaviness is infused into every spirit when he arrives in Victim, and that is why he may be taken out for use in this or that activity with slight concern lest he escape. Poured full of sorrow, care, and weariness, he wants but to sprawl immobile, and when he has to move his inclination is to creep. It's best, though, to summon strength and go erect. There's less risk of self-pity in that posture, and self-pity can corrode a spirit utterly. Those were my first pointers on victimhood, given me in the outer lock by a mad Russian on his second stretch.

From Selection I was teleported at light-speed across the vast expanses of the Astral Plane into the processing rooms of Victim. There my identity was checked and my spirit leadened. Then I was dropped into the outer lock, a horizontal cylinder some thirty meters long and about the diameter of a railway car. The great central confinement pen of Victim is ringed by three magnetic fields, and victims are locked in and out of it in lots of one hundred.

There was one other inside, sitting at the far end from me near the door to the first inner lock, and when I had crawled over to him, he addressed me first in Russian, then in German, then in French. I answered to the latter, and he asked how and why I'd come.

He had a broad, flat face with Tartar cheekbones and narrow eyes—a hard case indeed, I thought—but when I'd finished my brief story, he grinned fraternally, showing a wide glitter of white teeth, and welcomed me. Victim, he said, got deal-makers, gamblers, and madmen volunteers, the latter being either freaks or dreamers. The dreamers were the most valuable of all. I was clearly one, and so was he.

"I came in through Risk," he went on, "but don't let that confuse you. There are personal dreamers such as you and universal dreamers. I have a universal dream."

His dream was nothing less than the permanent abolishment of cruelty, which, along with love, is the basic quality of the human spirit. That dream had driven him back to Victim for his second hundred-year term.

He was Prince Alexei Borisovich Sukasin, an ancestor, I think, of Rebeca's seducer (see Chapter 2). He had been to bed with the Czaritza Catherine II, though that was no special distinction, considering the number of other Guards officers who could claim as much. Between his inheritance and her gifts he had owned over five thousand serfs, whom he abused in a manner extraordinary even in those despotic times. He had served with Suvorov against Pugachev's rebellion, slaughtering innumerable Cossacks—women and children, prisoners and wounded, as well as armed combatants. He had lived without remorse and "died" without repentance, and had continued in the same fashion after reaching the next world.

He joined War, the only activity, he judged, fitting for a man of his class, but found it tame and, whenever he got leave, gambled his spirit for sojourns in crueler activities. Risk, he explained, is open to all and offers the chance to visit activities or to switch permanently without going through the time-consuming and uncertain transfer process. One receives credit up to a century in Victim and plays against the house at roulette or chemin de fer or craps.

"At first I won. I spent my leaves in Rape or Murder." He paused, letting this sink in, before abandoning himself again to the slavic passion for breast-baring. "Then I lost my stake and was sent here."

In Victim he became converted and developed his dream.

"After you've been raped or murdered once or twice, you invariably develop one of two attitudes. Either you resolve to pass the favor on to someone else—and there are many former victims in the activities of cruelty—or you resolve never to be cruel again yourself. I have gone a step further. I have resolved to see cruelty eradicated from both chambers of the universe."

The people in justice, he said, spent all their energy trying to reform life on earth and thus wasted their efforts. The problem resided in the Astral Plane's devotion to human freedom. People were allowed to become torturers and victims.

"Freedom must be abolished," Prince Alexei declared, "if cruelty is to disappear."

The victims were as much to blame as anyone else. Victims inspired cruelty in others, and everyone who entered Victim did so by choice. The gamblers in Risk secretly longed for victimhood, though few realized it. Victim and Risk would have to be abolished, along with Murder, Rape, Resentment and Revenge, Insult and Abuse, Orgies and Abominations, etc. And since cruelty was learned on earth, as he knew from experience, recyclement would have to be abolished and life on earth allowed to cease.

"The practice of sending spirits back there must be abolished. They must not be put back, even into plants. Plants evolved into animals and animals into humans, and every human has some cruelty in him. No form of life on earth must be permitted."

I suggested that love also might be learned on earth as well as cruelty. If so, he answered, we would have to learn to do with out it.

"We must have no more cruelty!"

After serving his sentence, Prince Alexei made no effort to select another activity but remained in Prorogation, agitating the spirits there to make a revolution and move the next world from the principle of free choice. The authorities in no way interfered with him, for he received no support. Everyone was perfectly content with how the next world is arranged. In the end his obsession drove him to Risk with the idea of wagering another hundred years and running it up to a large enough sum to buy every last spirit out of Victim.

"Let the torturers torture themselves. Let the murderers murder each other."

He lost everything on the first spin of the wheel.

I pointed out to him that without free choice and its consequences he would never have experienced conversion or conceived his dream, much less had hope of realizing it, but he said that didn't matter any longer. Now that one spirit had glimpsed the solution to the problem, freedom might very well be abolished.

"I know you personal dreamers. You hope to improve, or even save yourselves. You think of a million tiny increments. One person. Another person. With me, it's everything or nothing. When these hundred years are up, I'll go back and try again. Sooner or later I'll get lucky."

He went on about a roulette system he was attempting to perfect, and had managed to get me thoroughly confused over it when the door at the far end of the lock opened and a triple file of victims began trudging in. They wore the bodies issued to them for their tours of torment and moved very slowly, some helping each other along. Prince Alexei explained to me in a whisper that it was a point of honor among victims to bring one's body in oneself, and he went on to give me the advice mentioned in the first paragraph of this note.

We rose as the first rank approached, led on by two guards, and as we did to the fellow on the right, who was all streamed in blood with twenty trenched gashes on his head, groaned and fell forward. I jumped to catch him, but one of the guards pushed me roughly back.

"Hands off him, pig!" Sukasin shouted. "You can't abuse us here! Learn your rights, Fuertes," he said to me. "Ill treatment's not allowed in the confinement."

At this the one who'd fallen looked up at me, amazed. Then the spirit stepped from the wounded body, and it was my turn for amazement.

"Yes," he said softly. "I am the father whom your boyhood lacked and suffered pain for lack of."

And I answered: "It was your spirit, Father, that compelled me here."

Well-read examiners, Homer and Virgil are misinformed. Ghosts can embrace each other. Shades can make that *abrazo* which the hispanic culture offers as the most profound form of greeting. We stood in each other's arms until those near us jostled us. Then my father pushed me gently back.

"Welcome to the pit, Camilo. I'm glad and sad to see you. But we'll talk later." He bent and took the wrists of the body he'd been wearing. "Here. Help me lug these guts inside."

The guards had swung the door open. I took the body's ankles and trudged behind my father into the next lock and toward the central pen of Victim.

95. Good fortune

I spent three months in Victim. During that time I held the dirty end of the stick in most of the activities of cruelty. These notes are not the place to give the details, but I will say (by way of furnishing a rough idea) that my least disagreeable assignment was to Insult and Abuse, where I wore a deformed dwarfsbody and did degrading things all day while people laughed and pointed. The worst was a "water cure" in Torture, from which I was unable to bring my body back. In short, I got a ninety-day dip into a concentrate of misery, and I can look forward to another six years and nine months of the same at some time in the future. Nevertheless, I do not regret my enlistment. On the contrary, I regard it as a piece of great good fortune.

Careful readers of these notes will have remarked that I am endowed with a normal human capacity for cruelty. A little victimhood and the expectation of a good deal more to come has made me most reluctant to exercise this capacity. Some victims envy their tormentors and crave to replace them. My reaction was a limitless contempt. Cruelty, moreover, taps the same source of energy as love, so that curtailing your capacity for one augments your capacity for the other. This is, of course, no secret. Some people seem to know it from birth. Others find it out more or less naturally. I had to go to Victim to learn it, but it is a good lesson to come by, late or soon, no matter in how stern a school.

The same reader will, likewise, have noticed that I have certain pretensions to knowledge. Yet suffering of one kind or another makes up a great portion of what goes on in the universe, and I knew little of it hitherto. My pretensions are a little less outlandish for the experience of victimhood.

But my enlistment in Victim was fortunate mainly in that it put me in my father's company.

Few terms are batted about so remorselessly these days as "generation gap." Because this world changes ceaselessly, fathers and sons are fated to be somewhat separated by their experience. Because this world is changing swiftly now, the "gap" is now wider than usual. But I was separated from my father physically. He was blown into the next world before I had much chance to grow apart from him emotionally. So while my coevals moaned of the defects in their all-too-palpable pops, my complaint—never voiced aloud—was that my perfect father had been vaporized. I didn't envy those coevals: their fathers, as I met them in flesh or in description, weren't worth having around. I suspect they envied me, but I also suspect it is relatively easy to feel filial piety for an honorable absent father, a shipwrecked hero like Telemachus's father, for example, or a murdered hero like Hamlet's and mine. In any case I was, am, and will stay a loving son. Adoring dependence gave way to an inchoate sense of loss, which has now given way to understanding. The object of unquestioning adulation has become the object of compassionate respect. Those interested in father-son conflict must seek elsewhere. Perhaps a certain novelist might treat the theme were he to biograph his medical old man, but I lack experience of it and use no imagination.

A thousand times during the years between his "death" and our meeting in Victim I longed to see my father. As I grew, so did that longing. With what pleasure and profit, for example, I might have discussed my studies with him! I made his life and times the subject of -my first important researches. And the reader knows how distressing it was for me that his spirit remained unreachable. On his side, success and fame had insulated him against my calls, but having come to Victim, he regretted that. Our three months together were no disappointment. A "gap" may separate you and your kids, unfortunate examiners, but not me and my father. It is the vanity and self-indulgence of both generations, I think, that keeps the famous "gap" unbridged, and there is nothing like victimhood to make one scrap petty considerations.

We stood together in adversity. I heard the story of his mature years (re-told in text above) and his speculations on the universe (see note 99). I told him of my own triumphs and disasters. Our spirits looked on each other in all their human strength and frailty. What else befell me was a small price for such good fortune.

96. *Not obsessed with politics*

The experience of centuries has revealed certain truths about the value of political influence. Those who lack it are generally bound to obey the law, work for a living, and pay taxes. For those who have it, on the other hand, these bonds relax. For some they dissolve entirely. To the extent that one possesses political influence, furthermore, one is able without sacrifice to help one's friends and without risk to hurt one's enemies. One is, therefore, gratified in proportion to one's political influence with the baboonish presentment of one's countrymen's and women's buttocks, metaphorically or physically, as the case and taste may be. Political influence is, hence, a valuable commodity.

The value varies, though, in different times and climes. Some societies allocate countervailing value to artistic talent, commercial acumen, martial courage, intellectual brilliance, scholarly erudition, technological expertise, or religious piety. In the Republic of Tinieblas, however, the market for these commodities is chronically depressed, so that those few Tinieblans who cultivate them to any degree of quality commonly export them elsewhere. The market for political influence is correspondingly firm and bullish. The manufacture and sale of political influence is the chief national industry. The acquisition of political influence is the favorite occupation. Speculation in political influence is the most common vice.

Considering the paucity of its population and the brevity of its history, Tinieblas has produced a surprising number of hypnotic demagogues, wily intriguers, and other masters of the manipulative skills. But ability aside, rare is the Tinieblan so poor in spirit as to doubt himself supremely gifted for a political career—as rare as the Italian who admits to being tone-deaf, or the Semite who confesses that he has no head for trade. Be he never so brutish, never so innocent alike of mother wit and formal education, your Tinieblan can envision himself President of the Republic, directing the nation to wealth and global puissance and meanwhile disposing of joyous support from an immense majority. Politics is the national art.

Tinieblan housewives do not gossip about who goes to bed with whom; they gossip about who goes to bed with which members of the government. When young Tinieblans couple up at parties, their ardent whispering is likely choked with ideology, not endearments. And while Tinieblas still enjoyed freedom of speech, one might on almost any evening hear Tinieblan schoolboys deliver up in public squares orations worthy in sonority and emptiness, in sophistry and outright bleeding falsehood, of a national convention in the United States. Political discourse is the national literature.

Like food in France, drink in Sweden, suffering in Russia, and fratricide in Ireland, politics is the Tinieblan national obsession. For politics doctors neglect their patients, merchants their businesses, students their studies, wives their husbands, and husbands their concubines. Our land now seethes with discontent, not so much because jails are full and larders empty, but because, under the fecearchy imposed upon it, politics is the private amusement of Genghis Manduco and a few smaller lumps.

My father did not share the national obsession, He was able to find gratification in the other possibilities of life. He had the energy and talent to flesh his private dreams; he needed no public stage to act them out on. That is why he was able to use power without abusing it.

"The problem with power," he told me, "is that the people most likely to get it are the people most likely to abuse it."

We lay in the central pen of Victim, which you may get an idea of, inquisitive examiners, by imagining a tire tube about a kilometer thick and thirty kilometers in circumference, with twelve valves (the sets of locks) projecting from the outer wall. A little ways off Adolf Hitler (Who is in Victim as a result of a deal made with a recruiter after the Munich *Putsch*) stood ranting about what he meant to do when his term was up and he transferred to Politics and the Committee for the Dissemination of Terror and Despair.

"Take a poor devil like that," my father continued, gesturing at Adolf. "Impotent. jumble-headed. Talentless. Utterly incapable of any private joy, be it physical or intellectual or emotional. Hideously deprived and hideously frightened. Too loathsome to give anybody pleasure. Too cowardly to inflict pain on his own. Too empty to find fulfillment in a solitary thing like art. His existence is constant pain and isolation. For a fellow like that, politics is the only hope. He can get a faint impression of being alive by manipulating others into doing great, dramatic things, things he can't do himself or paint pictures of. And because politics is his only hope, he is never distracted from it, not even for an instant. He can't even perceive the things that distract others from the pursuit of power, things like love or pleasure or intellectual curiosity. With that kind of single-minded concentration, he's more likely than most to reach power. And the monomania that is his chief advantage over others in obtaining power makes him incapable of using power moderately once he gets it.

"Hitler's an extreme case, but you can guide by him. Private joys are best. People who miss out on them need public platforms. The people who want power most are the most likely to get it, and the most liable to misuse it once they do. Perhaps a society might be created where happy, balanced men were sentenced to short terms in public office. That would be something new."

97. *Karl Marx*

German-Jewish fantast (1818-1883).

An heir to the Romantic Movement and a forebear of science fiction, Marx was (along with Sigmund Freud) the greatest German novelist of the nineteenth century. Like Freud and many other geniuses, however, Marx misunderstood his gift. He believed himself to be a political economist. An equally deluded world has taken him at his own word.

Marx's work has the appealing dignity of such huge and useless constructs as the pyramids. Read properly, it emerges as an immense prose epic. The heroine is called History, the hero Proletariat, They endure a long and tormented separation, but finally marry and live happily ever after.

Marx's chief contribution to philosophy is found in the following phrase (the reference for which I've lost): "The only antidote to mental suffering is physical pain." (See notes 20, 68, and 88.)

After his "death," Marx managed to unite his conscious drive to manipulate men with his unconscious drive to amuse them. After wandering from activity to activity for some six decades, he applied for Sex Change and Return. His spirit now inhabits the body of an employee of a massage parlor on Eighth Avenue near Forty-fourth Street in New York City.

98. *Love and jealousy are mutually exclusive*

This will be vigorously contested by those who shop their attitudes from such flea markets of the emotions as pop fiction, TV serial drama, and the periodicals subscribed to by beauty parlors, and who consequently hold love to be the cause of jealousy. The best criticism and statement of this view is found in Shakespeare, who creates a great booby, makes jealousy flog love from his large but cheaply-furnished heart, and then has him claim to have "lov'd not wisely, but too well." Othello speaks with the sincerity of boobyhood and loves himself excellently well throughout, but his love for Desdemona is on the run early in Act III.

Similarly, garbage brains believe that jealousy can be a cause of love: viz., the many real-life and staged dramas whose plots turn on an attempt by A to engender or revive love in B by flirting with C; that jealousy constitutes proof of love; and, conversely, that absence of jealousy argues absence of love. I have of late tried to wean my wife from this rancid dogma—strange in her, since she had glimpsed the true relationship between love and jealousy earlier (see note 54).

"You were really jealous, weren't you?" she purred to me happily last night. Since the light was out, I couldn't see the canary feathers on her chops, but I could hear them plainly enough.

I grunted assent.

She snuggled. "You must really love me."

"Right and wrong. I love you now. I didn't love you in the slightest then. My jealousy proves that."

I went on to point out that jealousy depends on the territorial instinct common in man and other animals and that it involves classing a fellow human as a piece of property, a chattel, which one does not wish alienated or used by others. Jealousy is an inflammation of the possessive, not the affective urge. It assumes rights of ownership and thereby debases its object from a person to a thing. It concerns itself with the enforcement of those assumed rights, frequently by violent means. But although rights of ownership are written into the marriage contract—"to have and to hold"—they have nothing to do with loving or cherishing. Love is concern for another, not for oneself and one's rights. Therefore, insofar as one loves, one cannot feel jealous, while insofar as one feels jealous, one does not love.

My wife fell asleep somewhere during the course of this exposition, as she often does when I attempt serious conversation after dark, but that does not in any way reduce the force of my argument. My current freedom from jealousy is not due to my wife's current fidelity—or, to be prudent, to the appearance thereof. That jealousy can invent a "cause" is shown in note 23. My capacity for love has recently been augmented (see note 95); hence I am no longer particularly given to jealousy.

My mother, Soledad Fuertes, was and is wholly committed to love; hence she was and is unable to feel the slightest twinge of jealousy, hence her reaction to the incident described in text above.

99. The universe owes us nothing

The statement implies a view of the universe, but since my father, León Fuertes, did not work that view out in detail until after his "death," I cannot properly present it in my text. However, since it bears on his earthly life, which is the subject of this dissertation, it merits mention in these notes.

My father's position may be called ecological stoicism: ecological because he saw the universe as a single, integrated system (which is, of course, what the etymology of the word "universe" implies); stoicism because he accepted it. His attitude toward Victim, for example, was an expression of this view.

"Don't wallow, but accept," he told me once soon after my arrival. We had been sent to Oppressor with a hundred or so others, as black slaves on a replica of a Louisiana cane plantation. Participants rode in among us, flogging us as we toiled. "Don't try to enjoy being a victim. But accept it. Bear it. Learn from it."

This attitude contrasted on the one hand with the oh-yes-please-flog-me mewlings of some, and on the other with Herr Hitler's alternating threats and pleas for mercy. Similarly, the philosophical position from which it grew contrasted with positions of partial or total rejection. Hitler, for example, endorsed flogging but objected to being on the sharp end of the whip. Prince Alexei, in the manner of true revolutionaries, was ready to scrap everything to eliminate cruelty, which he perceived as a defect. Each, in his way, lacked a sense of unity.

My father spoke to me during one of our recuperation periods about the difficulty of reaching and keeping this sense. Victims lay staring at the vaulted ceiling, or crept about whining, or yammered of escape and vengeance, or tried in one way or another to absent their thoughts. A few meters off, a little Jew named Levitski stood with his eyes closed, his chin tucked to his chest, his left arm crooked, his right arm sawing. up and down. He had been concertmaster of an orchestra in Poland and had entered the next world via the chimney of one of Herr Hitler's camps. He'd had a place in a Performing Arts chamber ensemble but had tried to gamble his way into Idyll and had lost. Now he spent his recuperation periods playing Mozart on an imaginary Stradivarius.

"What else?" he said to us once. "A real Strad I never touched, but why not dream first class?"

Farther off, Herr Kafka entertained a group of German -speakers with a story. They sat around him belching out gasps of laughter, though some of the women dabbed their eyes too now and then. He had volunteered for Victim—to be near his characters, he said—and seemed so perfectly at home I was unable to imagine he had ever known a different manner of existence.

"Consciousness," my father said, "is a bamboozling mechanism. It fosters the delusion that we are in the universe, not of it. I spent almost my entire life on earth considering myself a separate, independent entity. But we and everything else are woven into the whole. During my last weeks on earth I began to sense this. When I came over into this world, I lost that sense of unity. Applause crushed it from me. Now, here in Victim, I have regained it.

"Consciousness," he went on, "operates by organizing perceptions into separate categories. It invents conceptual tools like 'you' and 'me' and 'now' and 'then,' which work like dividers in a notebook. These divisions are imaginary and arbitrary. They have the same kind of reality as Levitski's fiddle. It helps him get along, so he imagines it. It might as well be a Guarneri as a Strad; matter of taste. Levitski couldn't endure Victim without his fiddle. People couldn't think consciously without their dividers. The trouble is it's hard to realize that they're arbitrary figments. Most people believe the universe is set up in neat divisions according to the way they organize their perceptions. I bathed in that error for most of my life on earth, and dove back into it as soon as I came to this world. I lived by the principle of separation, mainly the principle of the separate self. I'm over it now, hopefully for good."

On another occasion he went further, this time in the vestibule of Insult and Abuse while we were waiting to be called, for we lost no chance to converse. "There is a universal mind," he declared. "I don't mean it resides in one person or personage, such as the Director—who, by the way, doesn't direct as much as He thinks he does. It is everywhere.

426   R. M. KOSTER

"I'm not being mystical. I've no talent for mysticism. If I ever had one, I wrecked it by exclusive cultivation of intellect, which is the trick of separating. Consider half a hectare of our Tinieblan jungle. Hundreds of thousands of species, millions for all I know—I'm no biologist—interact in balance with each other and with things like dirt and sunlight, which may or may not be living depending on how you define life. That half-hectare system regulates itself maintains all kinds of balances. An oxygen-CO_2 balance in the air, a balance of nitrogen and other chemicals in the soil, a population balance among the species. And when we split the half hectare away for consideration, we were being arbitrary. The system encompasses the entire earth, and the sun too, of course, and all the stars, and this world of spirit, which is apparently distinct from the world of matter, but only apparently. Everything is connected. The segments we may choose to discern as separate—you, me, this kind of animal, that kind of flower—are interwoven. The universe is an integral, self-regulating system, and where one finds control, the concept 'mind' is perfectly applicable."

And again, at yet another time: "The universe regulates itself through what—from an individual point of view—appears to be gross waste. One female of a certain kind of beetle pumps out enough eggs during her short life to reproduce herself a hundred thousand times. Her fecundity is balanced by the equally profuse appetite of a certain kind of wasp, who likes to eat beetle larvae. This sort of thing offends our sense of separateness. Why do it that way? What about all those individual beetles potentially present in the gobbled larvae? Continuity and balance are achieved through profusion—profuse generation and profuse destruction—or so the individual point of view judges. Seen close up in nature, this way of doing things provokes disgust. Recognized in human life (which we like to separate from nature), it provokes horror. How many eggs produced in a human ovary, or sperm cells in a human testis? Each a potential human. Each human a potential victim. Each human inevitably a victim—of a germ culture, or an animal, or another human, or himself. Millions turned out, millions knocked off. What a waste! Horror!

"The horror has given rise to some charming dreams of economy, such as two people happy in a garden for ever and ever, if only they obey the rules. More recently it has given rise to vigorous action. Stamp out disease! Stamp out this kind of insect! Stamp out that category of people! Which upsets balances but scarcely reduces 'waste.' But there is no waste. The individual viewpoint is wrong because the sense of separateness is a delusion. The universe is an inseparable whole. It has no obligations to those segments of it which imagine themselves separate, nor owes them any explanations. It doesn't care if we accept it or not, but I think acceptance is the wisest attitude."

My father's view included an ecology of the spirit. As the body maintained balance or homeostasis by fluctuating between hunger and satiety, the spirit, he held, fluctuated between assertion and acceptance. In some spirits the swings were small, in others quite pronounced. These last went through a cycle which has been describes as follows: pride to error to suffering to humility to wisdom to mastery to pride, etc. The most common descriptions of this cycle were poetical. They usually focused only on a portion of it: pride to suffering, for example *(Oedipus Tyrannus)*, or humility to mastery *(Oedipus at Colonus)*. In practice, though, the cycle was continual.

"I made two complete circuits during my life on earth," my father told me. "And since I left earth I've made two-thirds of another. Well-balanced spirits like your mother scarcely vary at all.

"What interests me," he continued, "is that the swings are self-corrective. Near the end of my life I went through a period of suffering. Then, when I learned I was going to 'die'—and I thought that was the end of everything— I came to an acceptance and, with it, to the full use of my powers. When I passed over into this world, I exercised that mastery in art and won such acclaim that I came to consider myself the center of the universe. Which is ridiculous but not uncommon. The separate self is, as I've said, an illusion, and the center of the universe is everywhere. Anyway, I felt that way about myself and spent my time adorning my magnificence, to the neglect of those who cared for me, including—please pardon me, Camilo—you. But applause can be as boring as anything else. Fame too grows tiresome. So I went to Risk. And every time I played, I won. And every time I won, I grew more bored, and then went back again and upped the stakes. Until one day I made a truly crazy bet, and lost it, and came here to Victim.

"We see this all the time and wonder why. Some conjure up an 'urge for self-destruction' to explain it, but that's too limited a view. What you have here is a self-corrective mechanism at work, a built-in balancing device, a homeostatic governor on the spirit. Its function might be stated in the form of a law: When you gain, you lose; when you lose, you gain."

I said that this coincided with discoveries I had made in the basement of La Bondadosa Prison, and he laughed and nodded.

"What great 'discoveries' we make! The law I've just 'discovered' was published two millennia ago: 'First shall be last; and the last shall be first.' And there are earlier though slightly different formulations: 'Pride goeth before destruction, and an haughty spirit before a fall.' Also: 'Wisdom comes only through suffering.' The mechanism of spiritual balance was discovered long ago. The problem is almost everyone has to rediscover it for himself and then try to remember it."

He looked at me soberly. "Your mother was born wise, Camilo. Oh, I had a merry time, on earth and in this world too, but I only got glimpses of the secret. She knew it from the first and lives by it. And you know what I'm hoping?" Here he grinned. "I'm hoping that a hundred years in Victim may teach me something. I'm hoping I can halt these crazy swings. Maybe after a hundred years here I'll be ready for Love."

100. Back

After I had been in Victim for about two and a half months, my father urged me to return to earth and my body.

"It's not that I want my biography written," he said. "And we both know you'll have to come back here in a few years anyway. But I think you ought to finish your earthly avatar. You've learned things here and in La Bondadosa that can be put to good use on earth. And if you can manage to remember that you've got six-plus years of victimhood ahead of you, you might have a very profitable life. Awareness of suffering ahead sharpens the lessons of suffering past."

I might have added that I had left an important relationship in a very poor state of disarray and ought to do something to recompose it, but I was in no need of convincing. I hadn't progressed nearly so far as my father in accepting Victim, and there had never been any danger of my enjoying it. All I had been waiting for was his leave to go and the completion of my researches. As these were nearly done, I advised a guard the next time we were taken out that I had a body functioning on earth and wished to exercise my right to return to it .

Spirits who choose assignment as guards in Victim have, I should say, about the same level of intelligence as their counterparts in earthly confinement facilities, and not one whit more compassion. "No one gets out of here till his time is up," was the reply. "Move it on!"

Sensitive examiners, you will appreciate my apprehension. I hadn't truly missed earth and my body until I had cause to believe I might never return to them. I hadn't truly felt the weight of victimhood till then. But I had my father beside me and made a show of self-control for him.

"You're not the Director, are you?" I said coldly. "He makes the rules, not you. Check with your superiors."

"Don't tell me my job, victim. I'll check if I feel like it. Move it on!"

But if guards are sullen, stupid creatures in both houses of this bicameral universe, they are also slaves of rule. It took two weeks for my release to come through, but my release came.

I took leave of my father in an outer lock. He was bound for Resentment and Revenge with a lot of fifty, all wearing tall, sturdy blond bodies, all dressed in jackboots and black uniforms-ersatz Nazis to be thrown in among a horde of vengeful Jews.

"About an average tour," he said. "I'll bring this hulk back under my own power. Remember me, and this place, Camilo."

We embraced then, and it was I who wept, though my suffering was over for a time.

Above, in the processing room, my spirit was lightened. Then I sped to the twin exit portals of the Astral Plane.

I stopped first in Prorogation to see my mother, but an official there told me she had passed through to Love.

"There was never any doubt of her acceptance," he said. "A case of waiting for a vacancy, someone recycling back."

I pray my father may join her there someday.

It was nightfall when I reached Tinieblas. The streets were already nearly deserted. Sirens wailed hysterically along the Via Venezuela. Lit by floodlights, the six-storey portrait of General Genghis Manduco loomed against the façade of the university Law Faculty like the effigy of a pagan deity.

The prison wing of San Bruno Hospital was packed with smashed bodies, but none of them was mine. I flew about the hospital searching, but could find my body nowhere. I feared I'd come too late, that my body had failed and been buried, that I would have to return to Victim with my avatar unfinished. Then I heard two nurses talking about a patient in a coma whom the President of Costaguana was taking out by plane.

The light-blue Costaguanan Air Force transport was already airborne from Monteseguro when I reached it, banking high into the west, where a faint glow of sunset glimmered. Inside I found my body right enough, strapped down and plugged with tubes and needles, tended by a doctor and two nurses, watched over by lovely, sad-eyed Liz. The briefcase in which I'd stuffed the manuscript of this dissertation lay on the floor beside her. There are all kinds of loyalty, and some kinds mean more than others.

I confess to a sentimental urge to stay and watch that scene, but my earthly life looked to be potentially too pleasant to take any more chances with. I slipped inside, felt at once deathly cold, and then may have lost consciousness. I heard one of the nurses say, "His eyelids fluttered." I tried to open them but couldn't. I lay absolutely still, awake but with my eyes closed, unable to remember anything. Then memory returned, though everything that touched upon the next world seemed only a dream, a vision, a fantasy.

At length I managed to open my eyes and saw Liz looking down at me. She straightaway called for the doctor and then began to weep and laugh at once, and there occurred such a general bustling about that I felt powerfully like closing my eyes again and sleeping for a while. I held onto my strength, however, though being back in my injured body had brought me a great feebleness, and when things had calmed and Liz was bending over me again, I decided to see if I could speak. After a few tries I was able to ask her pardon.

The End of the *Dissertation*
January, 1971—September, 1974

The Prince
R.M. KOSTER
PAPERBACK · 978-1-4863-0117-5

PRAISE FOR *THE PRINCE*

"The Prince got to me . . . I liked its swaggering adventuresomeness,
its magnificent vanity, its almost comic sense of cruelty."
—Christopher Lehmann-Haupt, *The New York Times*

"The most extraordinary first novel by an American in years . . .
R.M. Koster offers something for everyone: adventure, sex, politics,
poetry, violence, fantasy, jokes, realism, tragedy, horror, calm, sadness,
beauty, wisdom—and characters who live and language that soars."
—*Life*

"Koster is that rare thing: a writer from the heart,
passionate and uncompromising." —John le Carré

THE OVERLOOK PRESS · NEW YORK, NY · WWW.OVERLOOKPRESS.COM